SMALL WONDERS

SMALL WONDERS

Marilyn Pappano

A DELL BOOK

SMALL WONDERS

Published by
Bantam Dell
A Division of Random House, Inc.
New York, New York

This is a work of fiction. Names, characters, places, and incidents either
are the product of the author's imagination or are used fictitiously. Any
resemblance to actual persons, living or dead, events, or locales is
entirely coincidental.

ISBN 0-7394-3680-5

Manufactured in the United States of America
Published simultaneously in Canada

A List of Characters

Leanne Wilson,
*owner of children's shop Small Wonders and
four-time loser at love*
Danny, *son*

Cole Jackson,
liar, con man, and charmer
Ryan, *son*

Nathan and Emilie Dalton Bishop,
*New York City detective turned small-town cop
and assistant manager at the local inn*
Michael, *son*
Alanna, Josie, and Brendan Dalton,
Emilie's nieces and nephew

Berry Dalton,
the Dalton children's drug-addicted mother

Corinna Winchester Humphries and Agatha Winchester
Grayson, *Bethlehem's grand dames and matchmakers
extraordinaire*

Ross and Maggie McKinney,
CEO of McKinney Industries and wife/mother
Rachel, *daughter*

J.D. and Kelsey Grayson,
psychiatrist and social worker
Trey, *J.D.'s son*
Faith, *J.D. and Kelsey's daughter*
Caleb, Jacob, Noah, and Gracie Brown–Grayson,
adopted children

Bud, *J.D.'s father and newly wed to Agatha Winchester Grayson*

Gabe and Noelle Rawlins,
engineer at McKinney Industries and angel-turned human
Sophy, Gloria, and Norma,
guardian angels; Noelle's replacements

Tom and Holly McBride Flynn,
second in charge at McKinney Industries and owner of McBride Inn

Ben and Lynda Barone Foster,
carpenter and top executive at McKinney Industries
Alanna Dalton,
Ben's daughter

Sebastian and Melina Dimitris-Knight,
carpenter and private investigator
Chrissy and Alyssa, *daughters*

Julie Bujold,
Alanna's homeless friend and caretaker

Bree Aiken,
Holly McBride Flynn's half sister

Alex and Melissa Thomas,
lawyer and plant nursery owner

Mitch and Shelley Walker,
chief of police and wife/mother

Harry Winslow and Maeve Carter,
owner and waitress at Harry's Diner

Chase and Nolie Wilson,
lawyer and feed store owner
Micahlyn, *daughter*

Chapter One

WHEN HE REACHED THE RESTAURANT, JACK Coleman's first stop was the men's room, where he checked his reflection in the mirror. The elderly attendant who watched him seemed to think it was vanity, or so his barely suppressed grin indicated, but it wasn't. In Jack's business, appearances were important. The people he was meeting for lunch put a lot of stock on the cut of a man's suit and the names on the labels. They would take him far more seriously in his Hugo Boss suit, with his diamond tie clasp and cuff links, than they would if they saw him in his usual scruffy jeans and T-shirt.

He wanted them to take him seriously.

He adjusted the knot in his silk tie and combed his fingers through his hair, then gave his reflection a critical once-over. Satisfied that he looked the part he was playing today, he drew a deep breath, then left the men's room. In the broad entrance to the dining room, he skimmed his gaze over the crowd until he located his marks—uh, prospective clients.

Sissy and Marvin Ravenel were among Savannah's historically and socially prominent residents. Marvin's however-many-times-great-grandfather had owned the biggest and most profitable plantation in pre-Civil War Georgia, along with the biggest and most lavish plantation house. Over the generations, the family had produced senators, governors, doctors, lawyers, professors, and a whole regiment of military leaders. Then there was Marvin. Not the brightest bulb in the box.

He was a lawyer by education, a gentleman of leisure by occupation. One thing every generation of Ravenels had excelled at was making money, which left Marvin in the enviable position of never wanting for anything. Why spend time in a stuffy office, taxing his brain, when he could play golf, sail, or travel with Sissy instead?

"Jack." Sissy presented her cheek for a kiss, which he pretended to give. *She* was part of Savannah's socially prominent, only through Marvin. Until their marriage, she'd been just another pretty girl who didn't want to live the rest of her life on the wrong side of the tracks. Having come from the wrong side of the tracks himself, Jack understood her ambition.

He shook hands with Marvin, ordered a martini from the waiter who hovered nearby, then traded small talk until the drink arrived. Truth was, he hated martinis and would be happier with a bottle of beer or, better yet, a Coke, but the Ravenels liked to drink, and liked company while they did it.

The waiter asked if they were ready to order and Sissy waved him away. "Tell us again about this investment opportunity," she said in her husky Georgia drawl. Her gaze seemed sharper than usual, her smile more satisfied.

Movement near the entrance distracted Jack for a moment. Two men in suits were talking to the maitre d', and all three were glancing in the general direction of the table Jack shared with the Ravenels. Granted, men in suits weren't out of place in this restaurant—every male diner wore them—but the two men were. They didn't look as if they made a habit of dropping seventy-five bucks for a meal and a drink or two.

Sissy reached across the table and laid her pampered, manicured hand on his. "Come now, Cole. We're about to hand over a very large check to you. Don't you think that entitles us to your attention?" she gently chided as she gave his fingers a squeeze.

The two men moved away from the door—and toward them. Every muscle tensed as he debated whether to stay where he was or make a hasty excuse and get the hell out. There were only two ways out of the dining room—through the main entrance, pretty much cut off by the men, and out the kitchen door. A glance that way showed a third man leaning against the wall, waiting.

He decided to stay put. If the bad feeling making his skin crawl was right and these men were looking for him, they'd caught him. If he was just being paranoid, taking flight would cost him the Ravenels' investment, which was apparently a sure thing. What had Sissy said? *Come now, Cole. We're about to hand over . . .*

Come now, Cole. Not Jack.

Oh, hell.

The two men reached their table and stood one on either side of him. One pulled a credentials case from an inside pocket, giving Jack a glimpse of the weapon hidden by his jacket. He showed the badge inside the case, then said, "Cole Jackson?"

Jack forced his most charming smile. "Close, but no cigar. Jack Coleman." He rose from his chair, offered his hand, and the silent cop snapped one-half of a set of handcuffs around his wrist.

"Mr. Jackson, you're under arrest."

Jack's smile slipped. "Gentlemen, there appears to be

some confusion. Obviously, my name is similar to this man you're looking for, but I assure you, I'm not him. I'd be happy to show you some identification if you'll just—"

The cop pulled his arms behind his back and secured the dangling bracelet around his left wrist. "We'll clear up the confusion at the station," he said in a seen-everything-heard-everything-didn't-believe-any-of-it voice.

Everyone in the dining room was staring. Most faces showed surprise, a few disinterest. Only one person was smiling. She eased to her feet, came a few steps closer, and raised onto her toes, to murmur, "I've worked way too hard to get Marvin's money to let some two-bit hustler walk away with even a dime of it."

He took offense at the *two-bit hustler* crack. He was a con artist, not a hustler, and he was damn good at it . . . most of the time. This time it appeared he'd made a fatal error. He'd underestimated the competition.

But they'd made a mistake, too. They'd arrested him *before* he took the Ravenels' money. The DA wouldn't have an easy time convicting him of theft, fraud, or anything else, when every Ravenel penny was safe in the Ravenel bank.

He grinned at Sissy as the detectives started him toward the door. "Oh, well . . . better luck next time, huh?"

She smiled smugly, picked up his martini, and polished it off.

Jack—or Cole; he was comfortable answering to any number of names—was still grinning when they walked out of the restaurant into the muggy Savannah afternoon. So he was being arrested. It had happened before and would probably happen again. He would bond out, then disappear and never set foot in the city again. That had happened before, too.

Then he saw the vehicles parked at the curb in front of

the restaurant. The first two, sedans marked as police cars only by the Kojak light on the dash, belonged to the Savannah cops. The third was a black-and-white SUV with a seven-pointed star on the door, and leaning against the front bumper was a uniformed cop.

Sergeant Nathan Bishop. Of the Bethlehem, New York, Police Department.

Cole's grin disappeared and icy dread spread through him, making him shiver in spite of the heat. For one crazy moment he considered making a break for it. At best, he would get away. His hands would be cuffed, but finding someone to remove that little problem wouldn't be difficult. At worst, the cops would shoot him for fleeing.

No, at worst, they would turn him over to Bishop and send him back to Bethlehem.

He was gauging the distance between them and the cars, judging the route most likely to lead to freedom, when the cops beside him took hold of his arms. They both outweighed him by thirty pounds or more, and they both had a grip that could stop a stronger man than he in his tracks.

They stuffed him in the backseat of their car. Just before the door closed, he heard one of them tell Bishop to follow them to the station. They would turn him over there.

As the car pulled away from the curb, he tilted his head back and closed his eyes. He'd made a fatal error, all right. Now, if he could just die before he had to face the consequences of it. . . .

TIME HEALED ALL WOUNDS, OR SO PEOPLE LIKED TO say—particularly people who weren't suffering—and Leanne Wilson considered herself living proof of it. Just once, though, she would like to prove true some other adage. Second time lucky, maybe, or third time's the charm. Even three strikes and you're out. If her third broken heart had taken her out of the game, she wouldn't have been around to go through number four.

But she was better now. Really. So what if she still didn't have a social life? If she spent every minute of her free time with the kids or her brother and sister-in-law? If she had zero desire to ever go on a date, share a kiss, or have sex again? She'd just turned thirty-three. She was older and wiser. She knew better than to get involved with a man again.

The bell over the door rang, signaling a customer's arrival. Dredging up a smile that she doubted would fool anyone, she rose from the wicker sofa, stepped into her shoes, and walked to the centrally located checkout counter. The smile faded a bit when she saw Mitch Walker. There wasn't much chance he was there to buy—Small Wonders was a kids' store, and Mitch's wife, Shelley, did all the shopping for their kids. Maybe it was just a friendly visit, but she'd discouraged friendly visits from everyone but family over the past few months.

The only option left was a professional visit. Considering that Mitch was the chief of police in Bethlehem, she would really prefer a friendly hello instead.

"Leanne."

"Mitch."

He removed his hat and glanced around the shop. Big, broad-shouldered, gun on his hip, he should have looked out of place in the pastel surroundings, with all the tiny clothes, toys, and child-sized furniture. Being every inch the family man, he didn't.

"How's the family?" she asked.

He smiled briefly. "They're fine. The kids are doing well

in school and are already looking forward to Halloween at the end of the month. How're your boys?"

"They're fine, too." For more than four years, her own little family had consisted only of her son, Danny, and herself. They'd added Ryan Jackson at the end of May. Twelve years old, abandoned—again—and angry as hell, he'd needed a home, and she'd needed to give it. There had been other choices, probably better choices, but she'd been the only one in town who really knew him, and since they'd both been abandoned by the same man, it had seemed fitting they should deal with it together. "Ryan's wondering why he has to go to school again this year when he just went last year, and Danny's whining because he *can't* go yet."

"Yeah. Give him a couple days in kindergarten, and he'll get over that." Mitch glanced around again, then, clearly uncomfortable, met her gaze. "I just got a call from Nathan. He's on his way back."

And that was significant because? . . . "I didn't know he'd gone anywhere."

"To Georgia. To pick up a prisoner. Cole Jackson."

Leanne stiffened. She'd thought they would never see Cole again. He was a con artist, a liar, and a thief. He'd run an investment scam in Bethlehem, then disappeared with more than $250,000 of their money, while leaving his son behind. The fact that he'd returned all of the money a few weeks later didn't even begin to undo the damage he'd done. He'd befriended them, gained their trust, even their affection, and he'd betrayed every one of them. That wasn't easily forgiven.

She didn't intend to ever forgive him, and neither did Ryan.

"So . . ." Her voice was breathy. "He'll go to trial."

"Yes."

"And to prison."

"Probably."

Cole in prison. He'd been so good-natured, so charming and outgoing. It was hard to imagine him behind bars. . . . Not that it would be a new experience for him. After he'd taken off with their money, Mitch had uncovered an extensive arrest record under various names. He'd spent his entire life ripping off people who trusted him. If he'd worked half as diligently at a legitimate job, he could have succeeded at anything.

"When will they be back?"

"Tomorrow night, maybe the next morning."

"I'll have to tell Ryan."

Looking as if he didn't envy her the task, Mitch nodded.

"Will this affect my having custody of him?"

"Nah. In fact, Family Services will probably look into terminating Jackson's parental rights. If he goes to prison, he can't take care of the kid, and if he doesn't go . . . well, he's proven he's not fit to be a father by abandoning the boy."

To say nothing of lying, cheating, and stealing his way through life, Leanne added silently. But he was still Ryan's father, and Ryan loved him. If he didn't, he wouldn't be so angry and bitter right now. He wouldn't feel so betrayed. She knew from her own experience.

"Anyway . . ." Mitch ran his fingers through his hair, then put his hat on. "I wanted to tell you before you heard it on the street. I figured you and the boy need the time to get ready."

"Yeah. Thanks, Mitch."

As he left, she sat down on the counter where she bagged purchases, rattled a hanger, then shifted away from it. So Cole had gotten caught. Ryan had been convinced it would never happen. Cole was too good, too smart, according to the boy. He was a con artist, not a hustler . . . not that Leanne understood the distinction. To her they were just different ways of saying the same thing—criminal. Crook. Bad guy. Besides, he'd had all those previous arrests. Not in a long time, granted, but still . . .

Oh, man, she really didn't want to tell Ryan his father was coming back to stand trial. Life was already tough enough for the kid, and having the entire town know what scum his father was, would only make it worse.

The bell rang again, this time announcing the arrival of her part-time help. Sophy Jones came to the counter, heaved her backpack underneath it, then flashed a grin. "Afternoon."

"Hm."

"Is something wrong?"

"Hm? Oh, no. I was just . . ." Leanne glanced at the clock. "You're early."

"I knew you were planning to decorate for Halloween today, and since I didn't have anything else to do, I came on in." Sophy grinned again. "I can leave again, and spend the next fifteen minutes sitting in the park across the street, if you'd like."

"No. Oh, no. In fact, I need to run upstairs for a few minutes." Without waiting for a response, Leanne got her keys from her purse, left the store, let herself in the door at the west end of the building, and climbed the long stairs to her apartment.

Today was the first holiday of the new school year, a warm Friday off for a teachers' meeting, so the television was tuned to a children's show, which she knew from experience only Danny would be watching. Ryan would be stretched out on the couch, reading one of the dozen books a week he checked out of the library. Books were his refuge, the places he went to forget that neither of his parents wanted him.

Sure enough, Danny was giggling at the antics of a cartoon dog, and Ryan had his nose in a book. She stood unnoticed in the doorway and watched them, feeling the protectiveness only a parent could know—though, apparently, not all parents.

There was enough similarity between the two boys that a stranger could mistake them for brothers. While Cole was a blond-haired, blue-eyed surfer type, Ryan was dark-haired, dark-eyed, dark-skinned. So was Danny, and so was she.

Ryan noticed her first, closed the book, and sat up. The kid must have read something in her face, because suddenly he looked years older. "Hey, Danny, why don't you go in the bedroom and get the video game set up? I'll be in in a minute, to play you."

If Leanne had made the same suggestion, Danny probably would have balked before obeying. Because it came from his big brother/idol, he said okay and jumped right up. He gave her a hug on the way past, then disappeared down the hall.

She crossed the room and sat at the opposite end of the sofa. The antique wicker gave a soft, comforting creak.

"You heard something about Cole." Ryan said it as fact, without emotion, as if he couldn't possibly care.

"Yeah. He . . . was arrested in Georgia. They're bringing him back here to stand trial."

Ryan's expression remained impassive. "Is he going to jail?"

"Most likely."

"Good." He opened the book again.

"He'll be back in town in a day or two. If you'd like, we can make arrangements for you to see him."

"I don't want to. I don't care if I never see him again as long as I live."

"Ryan . . ." What could she say? *He's your father?* What kind of father sneaked off in the middle of the night and left his son behind? *He didn't mean to hurt you?* Yeah, sure, like waking up in the morning to find he'd been tossed away like yesterday's garbage, wasn't guaranteed to hurt. *He loves you?* She wasn't sure Cole Jackson gave a damn about anyone but himself. He used people. He preyed on the trusting, then destroyed their trust.

And she had loved him, had thought he was the man she'd been looking for all her life. God, what a fool she was!

"You don't have to see him," she said at last. "I assume the trial will be fairly short, since he can't possibly defend what he did, and then he'll be transferred to prison. Chief Walker thinks it's likely his parental rights will be terminated this time, so you'll never have to see him again."

Ryan flinched, then his gaze shifted her way, filled with uncertainty and bravado. "Good. I hope he rots there."

Leanne knew she should respond to that, to gently chastise him or say something wise and insightful, but she remained silent because there was only one thing she wanted to say.

So do I.

COLE SAT, STIFF AND SILENT, IN THE BACKSEAT OF the SUV. His hands were cuffed in front of him, then attached to a chain around his waist, restricting any movement of more than a few inches. He wore leg irons, too, attached to a chain that passed through a steel loop bolted to the truck's floorboard, then to the waist chain.

His muscles ached from holding the same position all day, but he had no one to blame but himself. He'd been more comfortable the day before—handcuffed, but otherwise free to move. He'd been so comfortable, in fact, that when they'd stopped that evening to gas up and hit the bathrooms, he'd tried to move right on out of Bishop's custody. The chains and leg irons were the thanks he got for his effort.

He stared out the side window, barely noticing the woods and the occasional house. They'd passed through Howland sometime back. Soon they would start the descent into the valley where Bethlehem was located. Soon they would be there, and there wasn't a damn thing he could do about it.

From the moment the Savannah cops had turned him over to Bishop, Cole had wanted to ask about Ryan—Where was he? Was he all right? Who was taking care of him?—but had stubbornly refused to do so. The kid was better off without him. He needed a mother, a stable home, someone to teach him right from wrong. It hadn't escaped his notice or Cole's how hypocritical it was for Cole to try to do the teaching when he hadn't done an honest day's work in his life.

But he wanted Ryan to be a better man than him. That was why he'd left him behind. It didn't matter that it had been a lousy thing to do, or that Ryan would hate him for it. It had been best, and that was all that mattered.

Realizing that the road was curving steeply downward, he spoke for the first time all day. "How much longer?"

"Five, ten minutes."

Cole's gut knotted. It was a short walk from the parking lot outside the Bethlehem courthouse to the police department on the first floor and the jail in the basement. Was it too much to hope that he could make it without running into anyone he knew? Probably. But as long as he didn't see Ryan—or Leanne, a sly voice inside him whispered—he would be all right.

He'd had a whole lifetime of learning to be all right.

The church steeples came into view first, followed by rooftops. Long before he was ready, they were passing Hiram's Feed Store, owned by Nolie Harper. One Saturday night last spring he'd gone there with Leanne to take Nolie, suffering from a bad case of food poisoning, to the hospital. She'd been seeing Leanne's brother—probably still was—and had welcomed Cole into her home and trusted him with thirty grand and change, that was earmarked for her daughter's education.

The next business, just barely within the town limits, was a gas station and garage. Leon, the owner, had contributed five grand to Cole's scheme. Melvin Fitzgerald at the hardware store on the right had chipped in another five grand. Elena who owned the bookstore, Betty who worked there, Harry and Maeve at the diner, the Knights, the Graysons, the Winchester sisters, the pastors of most of the churches belonging to those steeples . . . He'd been an equal opportunity cheat.

Bishop turned on the far side of the square, drove to the end of the block, and parked outside the courthouse. Cole did his best not to look in the direction of Small Wonders, Leanne's shop across the street, or the Miller mansion, the house he'd shared with Ryan for his short residence in town. As usual when it came to good intentions, his best wasn't good enough.

The shop was closed and dark except for a few lights shining on the window displays and another over the cash register. There were also lights showing through the apartment windows upstairs, though neither Leanne nor Danny came near the windows for the few moments he could see.

Bishop opened the rear door and unlocked the chains,

then the leg irons, but he left the handcuffs in place. Cole slid to the ground, his joints creaking, a rush of pain shooting through his muscles at the sudden movement. He did his best to stretch, then with a nudge from Bishop, he started toward the courthouse. Jillian Freeman—in to him for seventy-five hundred—was standing outside the house across the street that was home to both her and her law office, her expression less than friendly. An officer leaving the courthouse—in for two grand—held the door for them and called Cole a thieving bastard when he passed.

He'd ripped off two of the three judges in town, both lawyers, and a fair number of cops. This was *not* a good place to stand trial.

After Cole was booked, Bishop escorted him downstairs and past the first and second cells, both empty, before locking him in the last cell. It was the only one with a window, set high in the wall and too small for even Ryan to wiggle through, and when Cole lay on his back on the cot and gazed out, all he could see was Leanne's apartment.

His punishment had already begun.

W HAT'S ON YOUR SCHEDULE TODAY?"
Alex Thomas slid his arm around his wife's waist as she topped off his coffee, then drew her into his lap, grunting for effect when he held her fully. "The usual stuff. Appointments, wills, dealing with companies who don't want to be dealt with, and"—he lowered his voice and mumbled the rest—"an arraignment."

Of course, Melissa heard him. "Really? For whom?"

"Cole Jackson."

"You sure know how to make a Monday even worse than usual." She wrinkled her nose in delicate disapproval. "I can't believe he had the gall to ask you to represent him when we're one"—she laid her hand protectively over her stomach—"two and a half of his victims. Isn't that a conflict of interest?"

"He didn't ask me. Judge Monroe left the choice to Jillian and me, and since Jillian's feeling less forgiving than me, I volunteered. Besides, we got our money back."

"That doesn't make him any less a thief."

No, Alex agreed, but it did show remorse on Jackson's part. About two weeks after he'd disappeared, Alex had received a check at the office for the full amount, down to the penny, along with a list of the people it belonged to. No one had understood why Jackson had returned the cash—regret, guilt, conscience?—and the only person who truly knew him, his son, hadn't been able to shed any light on the matter. Truthfully, though, few besides Alex cared about the why.

"You're not going to try to get him off, are you?" Melissa asked.

"I'm going to provide him with the best defense I can. It's the jury or the judge who will let him off, or not. Not me."

"But—" With an accepting sigh, she got to her feet again. "I know you don't have any choice. You're a lawyer. It's what you do. But you'll have to forgive me if I hope you lose."

"You've hoped I would lose every criminal case I've ever taken. It's a good thing that's a very small part of my practice, or we'd be in trouble."

"Wrong. I didn't hope you would lose Emilie's case. In fact, I prayed very hard you would win."

Winning Emilie Dalton Bishop's case had been more a matter of good fortune than legal skill. When she came to Bethlehem, she'd been running from kidnapping charges for taking her two nieces and nephew on the road, to prevent the state of Massachusetts from separating them in the foster-care system. Of course, the charges had caught up with her, but by then she'd found the support she needed to care for the kids herself.

Besides, it had been Christmas. Prime time for miracles in Bethlehem.

Whereas now it was October, and rather than trying to save his son, Cole Jackson had abandoned him, so he wasn't likely to find much support. Even the good citizens of Bethlehem had their limits, and helping a career criminal avoid prison most likely exceeded them.

Truth was, it exceeded some limit of Alex's, too, but that wouldn't stop him from ensuring that Jackson received a fair trial.

Across the kitchen, Melissa was rinsing their breakfast dishes. She still wore her nightgown, a thin clingy thing that molded to her seven-months-pregnant belly. Every time he looked at her these days, he wanted to get on his knees and thank God again for this baby. They'd married twelve years ago with the intention of starting a family right away, but they hadn't been so blessed. She'd had trouble getting pregnant, and every time they'd managed, she'd miscarried before five months. They'd both been through endless exams and tests, had consulted fertility experts, and after the fourth miscarriage, they'd accepted that having a child of their own wasn't going to happen.

Then, when they'd given up trying, she'd gotten pregnant. It hadn't been the happy celebration all the other pregnancies had been. Alex had been afraid to hope, afraid of those hopes being crushed again. But once she'd passed the four-month mark, then the fifth and the sixth, and both she and the baby had remained healthy and strong, the hope and dreams had overwhelmed him.

Now that she'd made it to seven months, he felt almost

like any normal father-to-be. He caught himself at odd times, thinking about swing sets for the backyard, about tricycles and baseball gloves, video games and soccer and driving lessons and dating rules. He wanted a son, but would love a daughter just as much, and wondered if whatever miracle had allowed this pregnancy to be normal could work a second time and maybe a third.

He'd become a greedy man.

Melissa turned, caught him staring at her, and smiled sweetly. "You'd better get going."

"Huh?" He looked at the clock, gulped the last of his coffee, and took the cup to the sink. Sliding his arms around her, he kissed her soundly. "I love you."

"I love you, too."

He bent and kissed her stomach. "Love you, too. Take it easy today."

His office was a five-minute drive from their house, located on the second floor of a circa-1840 building on Main Street. Next to him was an accountant, and next to her was a part-time tax preparer. On the other side of the hall was Earl Wilson's insurance office, and a title and abstract company. The space directly across from Alex was empty now, but had been home to Jackson Investments last spring.

Alex checked in with his secretary, returned a few phone calls, then walked the short distance to the courthouse. While he waited in an interrogation room, the jailer escorted Cole Jackson up from the basement.

Surprised, Jackson stopped just inside the door. "I didn't ask for a lawyer."

"The judge asked for you. Sit down."

After a distrusting look at the jailer, Jackson reluctantly pulled out the wooden chair across from Alex, sat down, and rested his cuffed hands on the tabletop. "I don't need a lawyer."

"You're charged with fraud, embezzling a quarter of a million dollars, and abandoning your son. You sure look like you need a lawyer to me . . . unless you're planning to plead guilty. Are you?"

"I haven't given it much thought," Jackson said, but from the evasive way he dropped his gaze and jerkily shrugged, Alex suspected he was lying. He'd been locked alone in his basement cell since Saturday evening, with nothing to do but think. Pleading guilty would be the honorable thing, if there really was any honor among thieves, and avoiding a trial was the kindest thing he could do for his son.

"You're scheduled to appear in front of Judge Monroe after lunch. You'd better think about it." Alex opened his briefcase and removed a legal pad and ink pen. "I need your full name, date and place of birth, and social security number."

"Why?"

"So I can start preparing your defense."

"And what would that be?"

Alex leaned back and studied him. Getting a hostile witness on the stand, who wasn't interested in helping convict or clear a defendant, wasn't unusual. Getting a hostile client, who wasn't interested in helping to clear himself, was. "I don't know yet. Our best bet would probably be to gain the jury's sympathy. Show them you had a lousy childhood, that you were neglected, misguided." He paused. "How was your childhood?"

"Perfect. Two parents, five brothers, and a dog. We lived in a great house, sat down to dinner together every night, and went to church every Sunday. Couldn't have been better."

Once again Alex was pretty sure he was lying, though there was nothing concrete he could point his finger at. Jackson's expression was cool, his gaze level, his eyes empty. Wait, that was it—they were *too* empty. As if he'd slipped behind a mask that showed nothing and protected everything.

Alex returned the pad and pen to his briefcase and closed it. He could get the necessary biographical data from the arrest report—assuming Cole Jackson was his real name, and the social security number he was using this time actually was his. He stood up, slid the chair close to the table, then faced Jackson again. "Why did you do it? Why did you steal from people who offered you trust and friendship?"

Jackson shrugged callously. If his hands were free, he probably would have raised them in a who-gives-a-damn gesture. "Because that's what I do. It's what I am."

Judging by his previous arrests, that was true. He'd been living off other people's hard work all his life. Once more Alex started to leave. Once more he stopped. "What about Ryan? Why did you abandon your own son?"

That question pierced the mask. For one very brief moment, Alex saw a range of emotions in his eyes—regret, shame, hurt, defeat. Then the cool blankness returned, and Jackson said nothing. It was as good an answer as any and better than most, because *nothing* could excuse what he'd done.

For that reason alone, like Melissa, Alex also hoped he would lose this case.

Chapter Two

THE FIRST FLOOR OF THE BETHLEHEM COURT-house was taken up with the police department and the sheriff's office. On the second floor were administrative offices and the courtrooms, and on the third were more offices. There were only two court-rooms, and the one Cole was escorted into shortly before one P.M. was small. Three tall windows let in light, but the dimpled frosted glass blocked the view outside. The panel-ing, woodwork, and plaster were probably original to the room—such quality work would cost a fortune these days. A mural depicting blind justice covered most of one wall, and wooden benches, worn to a sheen by years of use, filled the back half of the room.

He kept his head up, his shoulders back, and his gaze on the floor. He caught vague images of people sitting in the gallery, but didn't look to see if he knew them. He would rather not see any more familiar faces. They made him feel guilty, which, of course, he was. He just wasn't used to *feeling* it.

The jailer, accompanied by a deputy, nudged him into a seat at the defense table. This time the older man hadn't handcuffed Cole, and he'd been allowed to wear his own clothes. It was an improvement over the times in the past when he'd been forced to appear handcuffed and shackled and wearing a butt-ugly orange jumpsuit.

Alex Thomas already sat at the long oak table, looking none too friendly or hopeful. That was okay. The only thing Cole hoped for was to get out of Bethlehem as quickly as possible, and he didn't care where he had to go to do it—prison, hell . . .

At precisely one o'clock, the judge came out of her chambers and took a seat on the bench. Cole tuned out the proceedings, fixing his gaze on the glossy wood floor where it met the wall, willing his mind to go blank. It was a state he usually achieved without much effort, but this afternoon it wouldn't happen. Words from the prosecutor's speech kept slithering in—*defrauded, stole, abandoned.* Unfamiliar emotions kept seeping to the surface—regret, guilt, shame.

Every profession had its downside. Lawyers lost cases. Doctors lost patients. Teachers couldn't teach everyone. This—arrest, a trial, jail—was the downside of his business. Avoiding it was the challenge that made his work fun. Accepting when it couldn't be avoided, was the cost of doing business. It was a common setback, and it shouldn't make him feel so damn lousy. It never had before.

For the fact that this time it did, he blamed Bethlehem. Ryan. Leanne.

Thomas's chair scraped as he stood up, then he touched Cole's arm, gesturing for him to rise. Cole refocused his attention on the proceedings and his gaze on the judge, who was looking annoyed at obviously having to repeat herself.

"How do you plead, Mr. Jackson?"

You'd better think about your plea, Thomas had told him that morning, but when Cole had returned to his cell, he'd lain on the cot, stared at the windows of Leanne's apartment, and considered how completely he'd wasted his life. He was thirty years old, and he'd contributed *nothing* to society. He'd never made anyone happy, never helped anyone in need, had never done a damn thing that justified his continued existence. The world would be a better place without him in it.

That was one sorry epitaph.

The judge watched him, her mouth pursed in a thin line. If he tried to speak, he wasn't sure he could find his voice. The words he wanted to say, needed to say, didn't come easily to a man like him. From the time he was five years old, his father had taught him to always proclaim his innocence. To never admit guilt, even if he was caught red-handed.

Owen Jackson would box his ears for even thinking what he was thinking.

"Mr. Jackson," the judge prodded impatiently. "How do you plead?"

Thomas was looking at him. So was the prosecutor, the court reporter, the bailiff, and everyone in the gallery. He drew a breath, but his chest was tight and refused to accommodate more than a gasp. His voice was strong in spite of it, though his jaw was clenched so tightly that his mouth barely moved. A lifetime of learning could be difficult to overcome . . . but it *could* be overcome.

"Guilty."

The relief rushing through him was almost equal to the panic. No son of Owen Jackson's *ever* pled guilty. A jury might judge them so, but they always put up a fight. What the hell was he doing, rolling over without even trying?

He was accepting responsibility for what he'd done. No son of Owen Jackson's ever did that, either, and it felt damned scary, but good. Now he would go to prison. He would leave Bethlehem for the last time, and this time it really would be the last time.

He would never see Ryan again, or Leanne.

That was also one of the downsides of his line of work.

The judge set a sentencing date for the following Thursday, which brought more relief. He knew from experience that sentencing dates four weeks or more after a conviction or entering a plea weren't uncommon. If he was incredibly lucky, he could be out of town by Friday. He could stand four more days. As long as he didn't have to see anyone but the jailer or the officers who delivered his meals, he could stand anything.

The judge dismissed the court, and the deputy signaled Cole to leave the courtroom. He circled the table and walked behind the jailer and in front of the deputy, and was halfway to the door before some indefinable something jerked his gaze to the left. Standing just inside the door was Leanne, and she was giving him a look of pure loathing.

The deputy gave him a push, and Cole realized he'd stopped in his tracks. He started walking again, came abreast of her, gave her a cocky grin and a wink, and said, "Hey, sugar."

As if he hadn't stolen her money, or broken her heart, or done some damage to his own heart in the process.

Her expression didn't change—not a flicker of surprise, not a hint of temper. She just watched him as if he were scum scraped from the bottom of somebody's shoe.

In that moment, that was exactly how he felt.

As if he didn't have a care in the world, he walked through the doorway, then followed the jailer to the stairwell. A few minutes and three flights of stairs later, he was back in his cell with no place to go, no one to talk to, and nothing to do. He stretched out on the cot, with his head at the end where he couldn't see out the window, used his clasped hands for a pillow, and tried to concentrate on his future. Not the years he would spend in prison, but after that. Where he would go. What he would do. How he would live.

But it was hard to think about all that when other images kept intruding. Dark hair and dark eyes, filled with condemnation, contempt, confusion. Hell, he couldn't even say exactly whose image he was seeing. Ryan, Leanne, and even her son Danny, whom Cole had fallen so easily into the habit of calling *son,* all had identical dark hair, eyes, and skin.

And they all had good reason to hate him.

He closed his eyes, hoping that would chase away the vision. For a moment it worked, and the tension slowly started seeping from his muscles. Then he heard a sound— the soft scuff of a shoe on the concrete floor—and it came rushing back.

He opened his eyes, turned his head, and saw Leanne standing on the other side of the cell bars. He wished he could ignore her, pretend she wasn't there, make himself disappear. Of course, he couldn't, so he sat up, grinned, and leaned back against the stone wall. "I'd invite you in, but I seem to have misplaced the key."

For a long stiff moment she stared at him, looking as if any expression at all would cause her face to crack. Then she stepped forward, slid a plastic bag through the bars, and let it drop. It landed with a particularly loud *thump.*

He looked from her to the bag, then back. "What's that?"

"Books. Ryan thought you might be bored."

"Then why didn't Ryan bring them?"

"Because he's hoping he'll never have to see you again."

Pain slashed through Cole, tightening his chest, forcing him to swallow hard. It had been too much to hope that Ryan would understand why Cole had left him behind. He was a kid, after all—just twelve years old. When he got a little older, though, he would see that Cole had owed him better, and had done his best to see that he got it. A kid couldn't ask for a better place to grow up than Bethlehem, or better people to grow up with.

Cole shrugged callously, as if he didn't give a damn about Ryan's hopes. "If that's all you wanted, you can leave now."

She didn't. Instead, she came closer to the bars, resting one hand on the crossbar. "I talked to the jailer, and to Alex, and to Nathan. You haven't even asked about Ryan."

He shrugged again. "He's not my problem anymore."

Her mouth worked, but no sound came out, and her fingers tightened around the steel bar until they turned white. After a moment, she found her voice. "You worthless, lying, coldhearted *bastard,* I hope you burn in hell!"

Spinning away, she stormed off toward the opposite end of the corridor, and he watched her go. Once the heavy steel door closed after her, his shoulders slumped and he bowed his head. Burning in hell sounded preferable to the mess his life had become. All he'd wanted was to do the right thing for Ryan, for Leanne, even for Danny—to get out of their lives and make room for someone who deserved them—but as usual, he'd screwed up. It was proof that he wasn't cut out for being decent, and he damn sure didn't deserve to care about anyone.

THE STARLITE LOUNGE DIDN'T OFFICIALLY OPEN until five, but Leanne knew the owner was there most afternoons. This one was no exception, she found, when she tugged the heavy door and it swung open. The bar was more brightly lit than usual, no music blared from the jukebox or the corner where live bands performed on weekends, and the air, though smelling of smoke and beer, was clear enough to actually see through.

Christian Rourke, owner and chief bartender, was sitting at a table, papers spread in front of him. For obvious reasons, he went by his last name only—what tough-guy bartender wanted to answer to a sissy name like Christian? She would bet half the people who considered him a friend had forgotten or never known his first name.

He looked up as she approached. "Is business so good at the store you can take off in the middle of the afternoon, or so bad?"

"It's good enough that I can afford a part-time clerk, but not so good that we both need to be there every minute." She slid into the chair opposite him and glanced at the papers spread out. Timecards and work schedules. Her business would never be so good that she would have to bother with those things, and she wouldn't want it to be. She harbored no dreams of great success. She simply wanted to provide a comfortable living for herself and the kids, while still having time for a life.

"Want a drink?" Rourke was already on his feet, moving toward the bar.

"Or two or three," she muttered. She wasn't the sort to drink herself into oblivion. In fact, she couldn't remember the last time she'd been even a bit tipsy. Certainly not since Danny was born. But her brief visit to the jail had left a bitter taste in her mouth and a fire in her gut that anything less strong wouldn't touch.

He returned with a bottle of scotch and one glass, sat down, poured, and served her. She took a sip, felt it burn all the way down to her stomach, took another, then set the glass down and watched Rourke watch her. Leanne drinking in the middle of the afternoon was a rare enough occurrence that anyone else she knew in town would be on their fifth question by now, trying to ferret out the problem, but not him. If she wanted to talk, he would listen, but he wouldn't ask questions. She wasn't sure whether he respected her right to privacy, or just didn't care, or what. Whatever the reason, she was grateful.

She gestured toward the schedule. "Go on with what you were doing. I don't mind."

He took her at her word—another thing she liked about him—and turned his attention back to his work. She sat quietly, sipping her drink, gauging her tension level, sipping again. The bad taste was gone from her mouth, but all the scotch in the world wouldn't diminish the fury inside her. She wanted to hurt Cole. She wanted to make him sorry he'd ever set foot in Bethlehem.

Just as she was damned sorry she'd ever met him. If she could go back to the spring and undo meeting him, dancing with him, kissing him, loving him, she would. Even with a string of broken hearts behind her, wanting to totally erase one bad affair from her life and her memory was a first. But she would do it if she could.

By the time she neared the bottom of the glass, Rourke was stacking his paperwork and setting it aside, then fixing his gaze on her again. His hair was brown with a hint of auburn that gleamed in the sun, and his eyes were hazel. At the moment, he was wearing contact lenses, but when he tended bar at night, he switched to glasses because the smoke irritated his eyes. At a few inches under six feet, he was shorter than Leanne generally liked, but physically he could hold his own against any man in town. He jogged, lifted weights, and had, at some point in his past, been a pretty good amateur boxer, which explained why his nose sat just a hair off-center in his face.

He was handsome, intelligent, and nicer than a lot of guys, and they'd both been single in the same town for years, but they had never considered being single together. She wondered why, thought of Cole, and answered her own curiosity. She attracted losers the way bug lights attracted insects. Rourke was way too respectable for her.

"How's the kid?"

"Danny's fine."

"And the other kid?"

She shrugged. Ryan had pretty much brooded all weekend, then had tried to get out of going to school that morning. She'd been tempted to pack him and Danny into her SUV and steal away for a day or three or five, so they could pretend nothing was happening back home. But since she wasn't *that* good at pretending, and Ryan was having a tough enough time in school without missing an entire week, she'd resisted the temptation.

She wished she had resisted the temptation to go to Cole's arraignment or to take the books to him. She'd certainly had no intention of setting foot in the courthouse, but that morning, while staring out the window at the jail, Ryan had commented how boring it would be to have nothing to read for days at a time. He'd been clutching one of his own books at the time, as if losing them would be a fate worse than death, and like an idiot, she'd asked if he would like to take some books to his father.

No, he'd answered immediately, sharply, then hesitantly added, *But you could.* So she had. And to repay his son's concern, Cole had carelessly shrugged and said, *He's not my problem anymore.*

Bastard. Low-down, unfeeling snake. Forget the money he'd stolen, the trust he'd betrayed, the people he'd used. Forget that he'd broken her heart. He deserved a lifetime in prison for nothing more than what he'd done to his son.

"I went by your store last night. It's all decorated for Halloween."

She steered her attention back to Rourke and the cynical note in his voice. "Hey, Halloween is a profitable holiday for a place that sells costumes along with everything else. I've got the most adorable bunny-rabbit baby outfits this year and some princess costumes to die for." She grinned when he responded with a very un-holiday-friendly grunt. "You know, you could have a hell of a party here. Put up some spiderwebs and crepe paper and glow-in-the-dark stuff, have everyone dress up in costumes, have plenty of beer on hand, and *voilà!* Lots of customers, lots of profit."

"Have a costume party," he said skeptically. "Here, at the Starlite."

"Your customers would love it."

"Halloween is already a busy night for us. Everyone who wants to get away from all those little buggers ringing the doorbell nonstop comes here."

"Coming here to have a burger or a drink or a dance is fine. Coming for a party would be even finer."

He grunted again, as if he might consider it, then nodded toward her glass. "Want a refill?"

She studied the empty glass for a moment. She didn't feel great, but she wasn't quite as sick as when she'd walked in the door, or quite as angry. "No, thanks," she said at last. "I'm okay."

"Are you really?" It sounded as meaningless as the *How are you?* everyone greeted everyone else with, but the look in Rourke's eyes made it quite possibly the most personal question he'd ever asked her.

"I am," she replied softly. "At least, I will be." In time. A few months, a few years—who knew how long it would take her to get over Cole? But she would. Life and love had made her a survivor. Maybe she was slow to learn, but she did learn. She wouldn't make the same mistake again.

She pulled a few bills from her purse to pay for the drink, but Rourke waved them away. "We're not open for business yet, so you're a guest, not a customer."

"Thank you, sir. Drop by the shop sometime and I'll return the favor—at least, if you have a taste for raspberry tea."

"Me—drinking prissy tea in a store where kids go?"

"Oh, yeah, I forgot. You went into the saloon business because it was the only one you could legally keep kids out of."

"It was either that, a liquor store, or an adult bookstore. Bethlehem already has a liquor store, and I don't think they'd stand for an adult bookstore."

"I don't think they would." She stood up and slid her purse strap over one shoulder. "I appreciate the drink and the conversation."

"We didn't talk about anything."

"I know. And that's exactly what I needed."

WHEN THE JAILER CAME WITH BREAKFAST AT SIX-thirty Thursday morning, Cole sat up, looked at the food, knew the knot in his gut wouldn't let him eat, and lay back down to snooze again. The next time he awoke, several hours had passed and a man was sitting outside his cell, his wooden chair rocked back on two legs and a newspaper open in front of him. Instead of a cop's or deputy's uniform, he wore jeans and a button-down shirt, but looked way too young to be a detective. He looked way too young to be much of anything.

When Cole sat up, the cot squeaked and the kid put down the paper, let the front chair legs hit the floor, and stood up. "Good morning."

Cole offered no response. In an hour or so he was going upstairs to face Judge Monroe while she sentenced him probably to the maximum prison term possible. It wasn't a good morning for him.

"I'm Eli." He gestured to the breakfast tray sitting on the

floor. "You should have eaten. The food comes from Harry's, and it's just about the best you can get in Bethlehem . . . unless you get an invitation from the Winchester sisters. You remember them—Miss Corinna and Miss Agatha? They delivered homemade cinnamon rolls when you first moved in, and they invited you and your son to Sunday dinner, and you stole about six thousand dollars from them."

A scowl settled over Cole's face. Of course he remembered the two old ladies. They always had a crowd for Sunday dinner, and both sisters and every guest had made him and Ryan feel as if they belonged right smack dab in their middle. *That* had made him feel as low as a snake in a ditch.

But he'd taken their money anyway.

"What do you want?" Cole asked harshly.

"What makes you think I want anything? Because that's the way *you* operate?"

Cole decided to ignore the kid, but that was easier said than done. He was a captive audience, and Eli knew it.

"You always have an ulterior motive for everything you do, don't you?" Eli asked. "You haven't made a selfless or sincere gesture in longer than you can remember."

"I took in Ryan three and a half years ago." *And left him four months ago.*

"What choice did you have? He's your son . . . isn't he?"

His scowl sharpening, Cole looked at the kid. Eli looked back, his gaze level and unwavering. Unable to maintain his bravado, Cole dropped his gaze away first and stared at the floor instead.

"Besides, taking him in wasn't selfless. You were just recruiting another sucker for the family business, weren't you?"

That brought him to his feet. "That's not true! I've kept him out of it completely!"

"So it was just coincidence that he got caught stealing back in Cleveland."

Cole paced the length of the cell, then tilted his head back to gaze out the window. At such a sharp angle, all he could see was the top edge of Leanne's building, a few tree branches, and clear blue sky. He hadn't realized how much Ryan loved books until the kid had gotten nabbed by store security in Cleveland and a search of his room had turned up a full box of them in his closet and another under the bed, not a single one obtained honestly.

Books. As a kid, Cole had stolen a lot of things—food when he and his brothers were hungry, medicine when one was sick, money to pay the rent or keep the utilities from being shut off. But he'd never risked getting caught over something as trivial as a book.

He'd paid for all the books Ryan had taken, then made the kid work to pay him back, and he'd wondered how they had lived together for nearly three years without his learning something so basic about the boy. It was just one more example of his failures as a father . . . which he *didn't* need pointed out to him by some stranger barely two-thirds his age.

"Who the hell are you, and what the hell do you want?"

"I told you—my name is Eli." He conveniently ignored the second half of the question. "You're going to be seeing a lot of me."

"I doubt it," Cole said dryly. "If you were going where I am, you'd be on this side of those bars." His gaze narrowed suspiciously. "Are you from social services?"

Eli considered it a moment, then shrugged. "In a manner of speaking."

The response made Cole feel about as cold as Leanne had accused him of being. There was only one thing social services could want from him—Ryan. To ensure that he never got within a million miles of the kid again. Hell, he had no problem with that. Wasn't that why he'd left the kid in the first place?

But judging himself an unfit father was one thing. Having the state do the same, was worse.

The opening of the steel door at the end of the corridor made Eli look that way. So did Cole. This time the jailer was accompanied by two deputies, as if the officials feared Cole would run at the first opportunity. They were probably right.

"See you," Eli said, then walked away, nodding politely to the three men as he passed them.

"You ready, Jackson?" the jailer asked as he unlocked the door.

"Aw, you mean it's check-out time already?" Cole stood in the center of the cell, arms at his sides, wondering if they were counting on the deputies' sizes and presumably quick reaction times to intimidate him, or if he'd wind up in handcuffs and leg irons. If he were them, he would truss himself up. After all, what did he have to lose by making a break for freedom?

The question lingered in his mind as they took the stairs to the first floor. The sun shone through the glass double doors of the main courthouse entrance, drawing his gaze that way. What *did* he have to lose? His pride? Dignity? Self-respect? All long gone. Ryan's respect, or Leanne's? Gone, too. His life? In prison or out, it really wasn't worth much.

But when his escort started up the next flight of stairs, he turned away from the doors and followed.

They walked into the second-floor courtroom, then stopped abruptly due to a tie-up in the aisle up ahead. He risked a quick look around and saw Eli, grinning from his seat in the last row and, a few rows up, Leanne. He would recognize her dark hair and slender shoulders anywhere.

The redhead beside her was Nolie Harper, and next to her was Leanne's brother, Chase.

Maybe he *should* have tried for an escape downstairs. Whatever the results, it would have been better than knowing Leanne had come to see him sentenced to prison.

At least Ryan wasn't there. Thank God for small miracles.

Finally they reached the defense table at the front, where Alex Thomas was waiting. Cole sprawled in his chair, shooting for a casual effect. The jailer left, and the two deputies took up position a few yards away, leaning against the nearest wall.

Conversation in the gallery was muted but ongoing. Thomas made a few polite attempts at small talk, then gave up. Cole watched the second hand on the clock high above the judge's bench sweep around and around and tried not to fidget, but by nine-ten, he was antsy. "Let's get this show on the road," he muttered.

Thomas looked at him. "Are you so eager to spend the next few years in prison?"

"There are all kinds of prisons," Cole replied. Restlessly, he drummed his fingers on the table, then gave in to the impulse to look around. There were more people in the courtroom than he'd drawn Monday, but still not many. Jillian Freeman scowled at him from the opposite side of the peanut gallery. The Winchester sisters sat beside her, both prim and pursed-mouthed. Kelsey Grayson, another social worker, sat next to Thomas's pregnant wife. The chief of police and the sheriff shared a bench with Judge McKechnie.

Except for Eli and a handful of old men who looked like regular benchwarmers, that was all . . . well, except for the Wilson-Harper contingent. Knowing it was a bad idea, Cole turned the few degrees necessary to see them. Chase was scowling. Nolie's sweet gaze was full of sympathy—

surely for Leanne and Ryan, not him. And Leanne . . . she still wore that look of loathing.

Just as he'd done Monday, he grinned and winked at her, making her jaw tighten, but she didn't look away.

The bailiff announced the judge's arrival with the command to rise, and Cole slowly turned and eased to his feet. The woman taking the bench wore a judge's black robes, but that was where the resemblance between her and Judge Monroe ended. Monroe was maybe forty, tall and slim, with carefully styled hair and carefully schooled expressions, and she took herself very seriously. This new judge was probably ten years older, give or take, none too tall, and chunky. The robe reached to her ankles, where a pair of sturdy old-lady shoes peeked out. Her hair was about equal amounts brown and gray, and though it was cut in a simple enough style—short, parted down the middle—it looked as if she'd combed it with an eggbeater.

The biggest difference, though, was her smile. It stretched from ear to ear as she settled onto the bench and surveyed the courtroom. Judge Monroe was stern and straitlaced, while this woman looked as if she didn't know the meaning of the words. "Good morning," she greeted after the bailiff commanded them to sit. "I'm sorry for the delay, but I didn't find out until this morning that I'd be filling in for Judge Monroe. Let's see . . ."

She perched a pair of glasses on the tip of her nose, opened a file, and looked through it. "Hmm . . . oh, dear . . . really . . ." Peering over the top of the glasses, she focused on Cole. "It appears you've been a busy boy, Mr. Johnson."

"Jackson," he corrected her.

"All right—Jackson. You can call me Gloria." She beamed a motherly smile in his direction.

Judge Gloria? Sounded like some crappy TV courtroom show. He glanced at Thomas, who didn't seem to find anything the least bit odd about the woman. No one did, apparently, except him.

"Let's see . . . you've pleaded guilty. Oh, good. It's always best to tell the truth, you know. And you gave the money back, every penny of it. That's good, too. Shows you have at least a passing acquaintance with the notion of honesty. So we're here today to . . . hmm, to sentence you for your crimes." Her forehead wrinkled in a frown, and she rested her elbows on the desk, then her chin in her hands. "You know, some people believe the consequences of a crime should be punishment, nothing more, nothing less. Personally, Jack, I think you should learn a few lessons in the process and emerge from the experience a better man for it. Therefore, I sentence you—" At a gesture from the bailiff, she rolled her eyes. "Oh, I forgot. Please stand up. You, too, Alec."

Bewildered, Cole got to his feet, as did Alex Thomas.

"Now, where was I? Oh, yes, Jack Johnson, I sentence you to five thousand hours of community service, to be served right here in Bethlehem under the supervision of Eli. Hi, Eli." She waved, and from the back of the courthouse came a familiar voice.

"Hi, Gloria."

"Any questions?" she asked, but didn't wait for an answer before she banged the gavel. "Court is adjourned." Then she grinned at the gavel. "I always wanted to do that."

"But—Wait—You can't—I don't want—" Cole's protests were cut off as the deputies began moving him toward the door. In front of Thomas, he stood his ground. "What the hell is this? I don't want to do community service!"

Thomas shrugged as he picked up his briefcase. "It's only for a couple of years, two and a half at the most."

"I'd rather be in prison!"

"It's an unconventional sentence, I admit—"

"It's crazy as hell! I don't want to stay here! I *won't* stay here!"

Thomas went on as if he hadn't spoken. "—but Bethlehem's an unconventional town. The judge is giving you another chance, Jackson. You don't get that often, so don't blow it."

"But—"

Apparently tired of waiting, the deputies herded him away. As they approached the last row, Eli grinned. "Told you so."

"Go to hell," Cole muttered.

"No can do," Eli said cheerfully.

That was what Cole was facing if he stuck around to serve out his sentence—two years or more of pure hell. The key word there, of course, was *if*. Now he had the best reason in the world to make an escape attempt. If he succeeded, he could leave town. If he didn't . . . well, surely that would convince loopy Judge Gloria that he couldn't be trusted, and force her to send him off to the nearest penitentiary with high walls and armed guards.

"Don't try to run," Eli advised. "You won't get away, and it won't change Gloria's mind. Nothing will. Besides, I'd find you. No matter where you go, no matter where you hide."

As the deputies nudged him out the door, Cole looked over his shoulder at the kid. He couldn't be much more than twenty-two, and he didn't look even that old. His expression was open and friendly and innocent.

So how did he manage to make his last words sound so damn threatening?

Chapter Three

I T WAS A SOMBER GROUP GATHERED AT NOLIE AND Chase's house Friday evening for their weekly hot-dog night. Only the two younger kids—Danny and Nolie's five-year-old daughter, Micahlyn—were their usual cheerful selves. Huddled in a sweater against the chilly night air, Leanne stood near the grill on the small patio, her back to the fire, and watched her brother watch the hot dogs. "It's a stupid sentence."

She'd said that a dozen times before, though repeating it only annoyed her . . . which didn't change her utter belief in the truth of the statement.

"Sometimes sentences are."

"He should be in prison." She'd said that a dozen times, too, and she believed it almost wholeheartedly, though there was still a silly part of her that flinched away from the idea of Cole in prison.

"A lot of people should be who aren't, and some who shouldn't be are," Chase said without emotion, but his gaze had taken on a distant tinge. He was a prime example. After being convicted of a crime he didn't commit, he'd spent twenty-two months in a Massachusetts prison. She shuddered at the thought of her brother, bewildered, frustrated, and estranged from his family, *knowing* he was innocent, but helpless to prove it.

She didn't need any proof beyond knowing him, and neither did Nolie. He'd been wise to marry her as quickly as they could throw a wedding together. A woman like Nolie was a rare find.

Besides, Leanne added with a rueful grin for her own selfishness, it had been the only bright spot in her recent life, and she'd really needed that brightness.

"Maybe he won't stick around," she said with a shiver as a brisk wind gusted through the trees. "How closely will he be supervised?"

"I don't know. I never represented anyone who got that kind of sentence. Besides, this is Bethlehem. They have their own way of doing things." Picking up the tongs, he transferred the plump hot dogs from the grill to a pan, handed it to her, then shut off the gas. She warmed her fingers on the bottom of the pan as she hustled inside, then deposited them on the counter next to the stove, where chili and sauerkraut heated in saucepans.

Her sister-in-law glanced up as she finished shredding a chunk of cheddar. "Your cheeks are red. Standing too close to the grill?"

"Freezing my butt off," Leanne retorted. "It's a little nippy out there."

"Hmm. Weenie-roast weather. Maybe we'll do that next Friday night."

Leanne shivered at her words, but it was only for effect. She loved weenie roasts on cold fall nights—the velvety dark sky, the popping and crackling of the fire, the fragrance of wood smoke mingling with fresh, crisp autumn scents . . . oh, and the ooey-gooey sweetness of a perfectly roasted marshmallow dripping off a stick and into her mouth. Mmm.

And someone to share it with. Not just kids or family or friends, but someone special. Someone to snuggle close to and keep her warm, to steal smoky kisses from, to stargaze with.

Even as the image formed in her mind, she sharply rebuked herself. *No, not someone like Cole.* If she got near him with a blazing fire and a sharp pointed stick, marshmallows weren't likely to be the only thing she would roast.

"You want to call the kids?" Nolie asked as she lined up the various bowls and pans of their dinner on the counter, along with all the usual condiments.

"Aw, do we have to?" Leanne went through the living room to the bottom of the stairs. "Danny, Micahlyn, dinner's ready!" Upon hearing the resulting thunder of small feet, she headed for the recliner, where Ryan was pretending to read a book. Instead, he was staring out the window, a lost, wounded look on his face. When he realized he wasn't alone, he quickly jerked his gaze to the book. She didn't mention his distraction as she sat on the arm of the chair. "Good story?"

"Uh-huh."

"You hungry?"

"A little."

"Give your eyes a break and come fix your hot dogs— but save some room for dessert. Nolie made banana-split cake—your favorite."

With a grudging smile, he slid a bookmark into place, laid the book aside, and followed the younger kids into the kitchen. Leanne remained where she was. He'd been listless and blue for a week, and she didn't have a clue how to shake him out of it. She'd tried to talk to him about his father several times, but each time he'd bluntly changed the subject. So she'd tried *not* talking about his father, but that didn't seem to help, either.

That afternoon she'd decided to get professional advice. After school Monday, the two of them had an appointment with J.D. Grayson, a psychiatrist at the local hospital whose specialty was the treatment of children. His years of practice were complemented by real-life experience, with six kids of his own at home. Faith in his abilities gave her a sense of hopefulness for the future, but damned if she was looking forward to getting there.

Squaring her shoulders, she returned to the kitchen where Nolie and Chase were fixing plates for Danny and Micahlyn, and Ryan was leaning against the opposite counter, waiting his turn. She leaned next to him, folded her arms over her chest, and loudly said, "Man, some people are *slow.* I bet I could have already fixed and eaten one whole hot dog in the time I've been standing here, waiting."

"That's because you've got a big mouth," Chase retorted.

"A big mouth? *Moi?*" She feigned offense. "I resemble that remark."

Micahlyn peered up at her through her thick glasses. "I don't think your mouth is big, Aunt Leanne."

"That's 'cause she never yells at *you,*" Danny said with a giggle.

"Oh, and we can tell she yells at you all the time." Holding a plate in one hand, Nolie placed her other hand on Danny's head and shepherded him toward the living room. "She looks like such a mean mama, and you look so scaaared."

"I'm not scared of nothin'," Danny boasted. "Except vampires. And mummies. And monsters."

Chase gave Leanne a dry look. "Letting him watch old horror movies with you, huh?"

"Just getting him in the Halloween spirit." As he delivered Micahlyn and her dinner into the living room, she gently elbowed Ryan. "Want me to fix your plate for you?"

He didn't answer, but took a plate. On good days, he ate like the growing boy he was. On moody days, he just picked, even at his favorite foods. She could have guessed how down he was by nothing more than his dinner—one wiener, one bun, a squirt of mustard. As she loaded the extras on her two hot dogs until they overflowed onto the plate, she cursed the man responsible for the hundredth time.

It didn't make her feel better, but at the moment, she didn't have a clue what would. She could blame Cole for that, too.

But things were bound to improve. Look at Chase. When he'd gone to prison over two years ago, he'd thought everything was over—his legal career, his marriage, life as he knew it. He had probably never guessed that, soon after his release, he would meet the love of his life and get a daughter and an even more wonderful life in the process. And Nolie . . . after losing her parents when she was seventeen and her husband when she was twenty-two, she hadn't expected to be this much in love again three short years later. And Alex and Melissa Thomas, about to have the baby they'd worked so hard to get . . .

Bethlehem was filled with miracles. Surely two of them—*please, God*—had her and Ryan's names on them.

S ATURDAY MORNING FOUND COLE LYING ON HIS COT, eyes closed, his mind wandering to Pennsylvania, where his father lived, and to Tennessee, where his mother stayed sometimes. He hadn't bothered to notify them or his brothers that he was out of commission for a while. Owen wouldn't offer much sympathy, not after a guilty plea, and Eloise . . . hell, sympathy wasn't one of her strong suits. Neither was concern or consideration or any of the gentler emotions a mother was supposed to feel.

As for his brothers . . . they all looked alike, they were all in the same business, and they all had their own lives to worry about. They wouldn't even notice that he and Ryan had dropped out of sight until one of them needed Cole's help executing a con. That would be soon enough for them to find out.

The heavy steel door opened, then footsteps echoed along the corridor. When they stopped in front of his cell, he forced himself to keep his breaths slow and steady, and he didn't move a muscle until the person spoke.

"Are you ready to go?" It was Eli, the baby-faced kid who was supposed to tell him what to do and when and how to do it for the next two and a half years.

Cole didn't open his eyes or sit up. Instead he folded his hands under his head and settled more comfortably. "I'm not going."

"Sure, you are."

"I'd rather go to prison."

"That's not gonna happen, if I have anything to say about it."

Finally Cole turned his head and looked at him. "You don't."

Eli smiled. "My word counts for a lot more with Gloria than yours does."

"You take me out of here, I'm skippin' town."

"No, you're not."

Cole sat up, drew his feet onto the edge of the cot, and let his arms rest on his knees. "What are you gonna do?

Keep me in handcuffs and leg irons twenty-four and seven?"

"No. I'm going to finish the job your being in Bethlehem has already started."

"And what job is that?"

"Reforming you." Eli said the words with a smile.

Cole greeted them with a snort. "Don't waste your time trying. I've been a crook all my life and I like it. I choose my own jobs, set my own hours, and never have to struggle with issues like honesty, morals, ethics, or a conscience."

"You have a conscience."

Cole shook his head. He came from a long line of lawbreakers with a different view of right and wrong, good and bad. He knew what he did was wrong. He just didn't let that stop him.

"Then why did you give the money back?"

A shudder of something uncomfortable swept through Cole, and he disguised it with a careless shrug. "I figured it would keep the police from looking for me."

Eli didn't look convinced. "Everytime you leave a place, the police are looking for you, but this was the first time you returned what you'd stolen."

Another shrug. "I didn't need the money."

"You haven't *needed* the money since the time you were eighteen and your brother David was about to get his right hand cut off for borrowing from the wrong guys."

Cole let his arms drop to his sides, his feet slide to the floor, and stood up. He crossed the cell in three strides. "How do you know about that?"

"You're my responsibility for the next five thousand hours. It's my job to know. So . . ." Eli opened the cell door, then stood back. "You ready to go?"

Hell, no. But Cole picked up his only belongings—the books Leanne had delivered from Ryan—and walked out the door. He was going along for one reason only—because escape from outside might be tough, but from inside it was damn near impossible.

Ten minutes later he stepped outside for the first time in a week, officially released into Eli's custody. The sun was shining brightly, though the air was cool. It was a busy morning downtown, with all the weekday workers taking advantage of the day off to run errands and shop. The grocery store parking lot was crowded, and more parking spaces around the square were occupied than not.

He wondered how business was at Small Wonders this morning, and was glad the massive stone courthouse blocked his view.

Eli gestured toward the parking lot, and Cole turned in that direction. The kid didn't head for any vehicles parked there, though, but cut across to the sidewalk on the opposite side, then turned left. They were headed straight for the intersection where Leanne's store sat.

He didn't want to look, but couldn't help it. The display windows across the front and one side of the building were decorated for Halloween, with scarecrows and witches and ghosts. A crescent moon swayed from side to side, and so did the eyes and tail of the black cat perched on it. A cauldron sat on a fire of red cellophane illuminated by a light inside, while gray crepe-paper smoke streamed to the ceiling.

When he was a kid, Halloween was an occasion for mischief. What better time to snatch a purse or wallet than when every kid around was wearing a costume and mask? He'd been able to stand face-to-face with his victims, and the best description they could give was, "He was a goblin."

He followed Eli across the street, then they immediately crossed again. There on the corner was the Miller mansion, the house he had "bought" for his stay in Bethlehem. The family had wanted to unload the old place, so they'd readily agreed to let him live there while waiting for the loan to go through. Of course, by the time they'd found it would never go through, he was already a half-dozen states to the west.

When Eli turned in at the gate of the old house, Cole stopped short, still on the sidewalk. "You've got to be kidding."

Eli stopped, looking from the house to him. "About what?"

"Why are we here?"

"Rather than have it stand empty, the Miller family has offered it as a home for our program, at least until it sells. This is where we'll be staying."

Cole shook his head. "No freakin' way."

"You say that as if you have a choice in the matter."

"I'm not staying—" In the house he'd stolen the use of. The house he'd shared with Ryan. The house directly across the street from Leanne's. The house where he'd had great sex with her for the better part of a few incredible nights.

Eli came back to the gate. "Maybe I didn't make myself clear. You don't have a choice."

"I can go back to jail."

"They don't want you."

That wasn't news. He'd spent his entire life not being wanted by someone or other. His mother had regularly gone seeking greener pastures, leaving all six kids behind, and his father had raised them as accomplices rather than sons. Most towns where he'd run his scams had been happy to see the last of him, particularly if there was a little jail time involved, and God knew, most of his victims hadn't wanted him around after they'd discovered the truth about him. Unfortunately for them, they'd always discovered it too late to protect themselves.

Except for Sissy Ravenel. Even if she was directly responsible for his being back in Bethlehem, he had to admire her ability to look out for herself and her husband's fortune.

Eli was waiting without the least bit of impatience. The kid had no doubt Cole was going to do exactly what he wanted, and it pissed off Cole that in this, at least, he was right. Reluctantly, he walked through the gate, forcing one foot in front of the other. When he reached the steps, he hesitated again, clenched his jaw, and climbed to the porch.

Eli unlocked the door, then stepped back for Cole to enter first. He did, stopping a few feet inside the foyer. On the left was the living room where Ryan had watched too much TV and read too many books. Straight ahead was the kitchen where Cole had cooked their meals, usually just for Ryan and him, but a couple of times for Leanne and Danny, too. The stairs on the right led to the second floor and four bedrooms. Ryan's had been at the back of the house, near the back stairs, and Cole had chosen the room at the front—the one that faced Leanne's bedroom.

This time he'd just as soon sleep in the basement.

Eli tossed his keys on the hall table. "I had the hotel where you were staying in Savannah pack up your belongings and ship them here. They're in your room upstairs. I took the liberty of returning a few things to their rightful owners—a Mont Blanc pen, a Rolex, an antique money clip, and the diamond cuff links."

Cole didn't ask how he'd found out who their rightful owners were. He wouldn't get a straight answer, and it didn't matter anyway.

"Go on up, unpack, then meet me in the kitchen. We'll discuss the rules of the program."

Grudgingly, Cole started up the stairs, resisting the urge to point out that he'd never been big on obeying other people's rules. Every rule was meant to be broken, his father used to say, and Cole had spent his entire life doing just that. It was too late to change.

He was halfway to the top when Eli spoke again. "It's never too late to change, not until the last breath has left your body."

His fingers curled tightly around the bannister, Cole slowly turned to look at the kid, but all he saw was Eli's back as he disappeared down the hall. Coincidence, he told himself, starting his climb again one slow step at a time. Just as it was coincidence that Eli's do-gooder program was housed in the same place Cole had called home during his short time in town.

Just as it was coincidence that the idiot had given him that same front bedroom where he'd slept before.

Cole discovered that after futilely checking the other three bedrooms for his stuff. Two were unoccupied; the third had a stack of books—social work mumbo jumbo—on the nightstand and a jacket tossed across the foot of the bed.

Two large boxes stood at the foot of the bed in the front room. Both bore the return address of the hotel in Savannah, and both had been opened. He didn't bother unpacking them, but walked past and to the window. His gaze went straight to Leanne's window, its blinds closed, then dropped to the shop window below before shifting to a group of boys on the sidewalk. It slid past the four strangers and zeroed in on Ryan.

He was leaning against the stone wall of Leanne's building, and the other kids were apparently trying to talk him into something. He shook his head several times, and finally the other boys left, heading toward Main Street. Ryan stayed where he was, staring off into the distance, until Leanne came around the corner. They talked a moment, then she slid her arm around him and together they disappeared back around the corner.

Long after they had gone, Cole expelled the breath that had caught in his lungs. Some people believed the consequences of a crime should be punishment, the judge had said—nothing more, nothing less. *This* went beyond punishment. This was torment, plain and simple.

And damned if he was going to stick around for it.

WITH THE EXCEPTION OF THE EARLY MONTHS OF her marriage, Melissa Thomas couldn't recall a time when life had been more perfect. It was her favorite season—autumn, with the leaves turned rich shades of crimson, bronze, and gold, and the air smelling clean and sharp with a hint of the winter to come. Physically, she'd never felt better, even though she was carrying an extra twenty-six pounds around and her back ached with the burden. Spiritually, she was more satisfied and hopeful than ever. And in December, the month of miracles, their baby would join them, just in time for Christmas.

Life couldn't get any better.

She'd gone downtown to pick up a few things for dinner, but found herself parked in front of Small Wonders instead of the grocery store. Fearing yet another miscarriage, she'd stayed away from the shop through the first five months of her pregnancy. Even after that, she hadn't allowed herself to buy much for the baby. Alex had painted one of the guest rooms green, and she'd picked out a crib and dressing table, sheets and curtains, and a few whimsical pictures for the wall. But she hadn't bought any *real* baby things—no sleepers or tiny shoes or outfits, no diapers or pacifiers, receiving blankets or bibs.

She'd waited long enough.

Easing out of the car, she shivered as a chilly wind rustled around her, then hurried across the sidewalk and inside. The bell announcing her arrival was soft, its melodic chimes designed not to disturb sleeping babies. It was *so* soft and melodic that it didn't penetrate the mental fog Leanne was drifting in.

Melissa walked to the window Leanne was staring out, glanced at the courthouse and the square, saw nothing worthy of such concentration, and gently nudged her friend. Eyes widening, breath catching, Leanne jerked her gaze to Melissa's. "Oh. Hi. I'm sorry. I didn't hear . . ."

"You were a million miles away."

"Actually, less than a mile. Ryan should have been home from school fifteen minutes ago."

"I'm sure he's all right."

"No, he's not." Leanne looked at her again, then smiled weakly. "Of course nothing's happened. It's just . . . he's been having some problems since his father was brought back."

Melissa nodded sympathetically. She couldn't understand how a person could possibly abandon his own child. She and Alex had tried for so long, had grieved for every baby they'd lost, had prayed and pleaded and hoped, and Cole Jackson, who'd been blessed with such a gift, had simply turned and walked away. If the police hadn't caught him, he probably never would have looked back. She wasn't a vindictive woman, but she wanted him to suffer for that.

"How are *you* dealing with his father being back?" she asked gently.

Abruptly, Leanne began straightening shelves that didn't

need it. "There's nothing to deal with. I'm so far over him that he doesn't matter anymore, except for how it affects Ryan. I couldn't care less. I think he belongs in prison and the judge's ruling showed astonishingly poor judgment, but it doesn't affect me in the least."

Melissa wanted to hug her close and remind her that they'd been friends ever since Melissa had married Alex and moved to Bethlehem. She knew Leanne threw herself into love wholeheartedly, and that every broken heart hurt as bad as the one before, and mere months weren't enough to render Cole Jackson insignificant in her life. But they *had* been friends forever, and if Leanne wanted to pretend Cole meant nothing, who was she to argue?

"What can I help you with today?"

Looking around the shop, Melissa smiled. "I don't suppose you could pack up all your baby stuff and deliver it to my house."

"It might take a while, but, yeah, I could do that. Then I could take the boys off to some distant beach for a vacation."

"A beach is exactly where I feel like I belong, along with the other whales."

Leanne looked her up and down. "Oh, honey, you're doing just fine. When I was pregnant with Danny, I gained nearly sixty pounds. Of course, I spent about five months of that time trying to eat away my misery."

Melissa remembered. Danny's father had been handsome, charming, and totally unwilling to face fatherhood. The day he'd found out they had a baby on the way, he'd bowed out of Leanne's life so fast her head had spun. Just in case she hadn't hated him enough for it, Melissa had despised him, too.

After another look at her watch, Leanne forced a smile. "So . . . are you looking for anything in particular today?"

"Just some hopes and dreams."

"You're in luck. We just got in a new order of hopes and double that of dreams. Why don't you look around and see what you can find? I'm going to try to track down Ryan."

As she headed for the counter near the back, Melissa turned to the Halloween costumes. Some were mass-produced, but the ones she liked best were made by Hailey Montgomery, a local seamstress and cousin of Leanne's. It was too easy to imagine her own little boy in the faux-fur rabbit suit with floppy pink ears and a matching pompom tail, or a sweet little girl in the green-and-brown turtle cos-tume—so easy, in fact, she considered buying one of each for next year, just to be prepared. She resisted the tempta-tion, though she did pick out two of Hailey's crib quilts, one an appliqued sampler, the other a three-dimensional landscape that bore a resemblance to Bethlehem and the valley that sheltered it.

Next she debated the merits of one-piece footed sleep-ers versus gowns with drawstrings at the bottom, then opted for three of each . . . for starters. She'd waited so long for this child that he would no doubt be the best-provided-for child in town.

She was browsing through hooded bath towels on her way to tiny shoes of satin, cotton, and the softest leathers when the doorbell rang and Ryan Jackson came in. His book bag was slung over one shoulder, his head was down, and his lower lip stuck out. He looked the very picture of a sullen teenager as he slouched his way to the counter.

Melissa couldn't resist smiling. She couldn't wait for the terrible twos and the terrible teens and everything in-between. She was looking forward to separation anxiety, temper tantrums, first-day-of-school jitters, and first-date jitters. She couldn't wait to get up-to-date on the latest in video games or computer technology, to learn the name of every significant cartoon character, to add new slang to her vocabulary and new concerns to her worry list.

She couldn't wait to be a mother in fact, as she already was in her heart.

Y OU'RE LATE," LEANNE ANNOUNCED.
Ryan ducked his head and mumbled something unintelligible.

"We have an appointment with Dr. Grayson in ten minutes."

That made him look up. "I don't need no shrink."

"Don't call him that. He's a psychiatrist and, sweetie, I think we *all* could benefit from some time with him." Especially Ryan's father, though of course she didn't say so out loud.

"There's nothin' wrong with me." His tone was defensive, as if he wanted very much to believe that, but harbored a few doubts. Being abandoned by one parent was easy enough to blame on the parent, but when *both* parents chose to walk away, a kid couldn't help but wonder if he was to blame.

"You're right," she said with a cheerfulness she didn't feel. "There's nothing wrong with you—or with me, either, for that matter. But there's something about our . . . situation, that Dr. Grayson might be able to help us with."

His gaze narrowed. "You mean, you havin' to take me in 'cause Cole ran off."

"I didn't *have* to take you in. There were plenty of families who wanted you." She ignored his snort at that. "I just happened to want you more. Come on."

He folded his arms over his chest and scowled at her. "I don't wanna go."

She reached under the counter for her purse, then went

to the storeroom door, opening it a few inches. "Sophy, I'm leaving now. If you need anything, call my cell. Melissa, when you're ready to check out, give a holler for Sophy in the back room."

When she came even with the counter again, she looped her arm through Ryan's as if he wasn't being difficult and turned him unwillingly toward the door. "It won't hurt at all," she teased in the same cheery voice she used to reassure Danny, "and if you're really good, I'll treat you to ice cream when we're done."

Ryan shot her a chiding look, but quit dragging his feet as they reached the door.

It was such a pretty day that they could have walked to J.D.'s office at the hospital if Ryan had come straight home. Since he hadn't, she pulled him around the corner, to where her SUV was parked. She settled into the driver's seat, glanced at Ryan, slumped against the passenger door, then backed out and headed for Bethlehem Memorial.

Truthfully, she wasn't looking forward to this meeting with J.D. any more than Ryan was. She didn't want to talk about Cole, didn't want to even think about him. The first was pretty easy to avoid, except for the occasional well-intentioned questions like the one from Melissa earlier. But not thinking about him was one of the toughest things she'd ever tried. Anytime she relaxed her guard, he weaseled his way into her thoughts like the slippery crook he was. She didn't have to see him—she hadn't done that since Thursday—or even hear his name. If she just closed her eyes and let her mind wander, it wandered straight to him.

J.D.'s office was on the first floor of the hospital, a compact space with battered furniture, two narrow windows, and a small library's worth of books. The family photographs on the walls overshadowed the Harvard medical degree, and the man waiting there overshadowed it all. He was tall, broad-shouldered, and looked as if he would be more at home on a construction site than behind a desk. He was the only doctor she knew who liked filling his spare time with hard labor, and he had the muscles to show for it.

"Leanne. Ryan." He brushed a kiss to her forehead, then extended his hand to Ryan.

The boy grudgingly shook hands, then dropped into one of the two chairs that fronted J.D.'s desk. Leanne chose the other, and J.D. shoved a stack of papers back to sit on the edge of the desk. "How's school this year, Ryan?"

He shrugged. "Okay, I guess."

"My son, Caleb, is in your grade. He says you're quite a runner." When Ryan's eyes widened, J.D. hastened to reassure him. "Nothing we talk about leaves this office. I don't discuss work with my kids, my wife, or anyone else. No one will know you've come to see me unless you choose to tell."

A bit of the tension that held Ryan stiff seeped away, but not enough, Leanne thought regretfully.

"Have you seen your father since he came back to Bethlehem?"

Ryan gave another of those derisive snorts she was beginning to hate. "No, and I don't want to. They should'a put him in jail."

He spoke as if seeing his father behind bars wasn't an unusual thing. She tried to imagine her own father locked up, but it was too unlikely an image to form. It would be a horrible thing . . . but then, her father wasn't a career criminal. Cole was.

A career criminal with a *son*. The day he'd helped give

life to Ryan, Cole should have given up his crooked ways and taken the first honest job to come along. He'd had an obligation to his child, to not get himself thrown in jail, to not do anything to threaten that child's safety and well-being, to never hurt or shame him.

But she knew better than most how many fathers failed to live up to their obligations. Danny's father was a perfect example. The man had never paid a penny to take care of his son. He'd never even laid eyes on him.

And Danny was wonderfully happy and well-adjusted anyway. Someday Ryan would be, too.

J.D. moved to sit behind his desk. "Tell me about your mother, Ryan."

The change of subject caught Ryan off-guard. His gaze narrowed and he sank lower in the seat. "What about her?"

"Whatever you want to tell me."

The question piqued Leanne's curiosity. She knew nothing about Ryan's mother except that she had abandoned him three years ago and he still had nightmares about his time with her. She didn't know if Cole had married the woman, or if he'd loved her, or if she'd been just one more victim in one more of his scams. She didn't know if the woman hated Cole as much as *she* did, but she was pretty sure the answer was yes.

Ryan seemed at a loss for anything to say. He hunched his shoulders and let his chin sink to his chest. The posture made him look small and vulnerable, an impression emphasized by the shadows in his eyes.

"When did you last see her?" J.D. asked, his tone soothing, nonconfrontational.

"A while ago."

"How long?"

Ryan shrugged, as if he didn't have a clue. Leanne would bet he knew, right down to the day.

"Where is she now?"

Another shrug.

"Are she and your father divorced?"

Ryan let a put-upon sigh escape. "They weren't ever married. Cole's not real big on doing things the way other people do."

Like working for a living, Leanne thought. Setting a good example for his son. Obeying the law.

J.D. gave him a chance to go on. When he didn't, the doctor leaned back in his chair. "Okay. Let's talk about your father."

"You mean Cole."

"Isn't he your father?"

Scowling, Ryan got up and walked to the window. There wasn't much out there—yellowed grass, a few of the hospital's outbuildings, a wooded area—but he concentrated on it even as he shrugged yet again. "I guess."

"How do you feel about him leaving the way he did?"

The question brought the boy's head jerking around. "How do you think it feels? It sucks."

"Why do you think he left?"

"Because that's what he does. He uses people, and then he leaves 'em." His voice quavered there at the end, and as if to make up for it, he adopted a belligerent stance and a cold stare. More than anything Leanne wanted to wrap her arms around him and promise with all her heart that he would never be left again. Only her faith in J.D. kept her in her seat.

Ryan turned his back on them again, and his voice took on a low, careless tone. "It's no big deal. I knew it was gonna happen sooner or later. I don't need him anyway."

After another brief silence, J.D. asked his next question. "What was your first reaction when you heard he'd been arrested and was coming back to town?"

Her first reaction had been shock, joined quickly by dismay, anger, grim satisfaction, regret. She would like to think she'd hidden it from Mitch Walker, but there was no way she'd hidden it as well as Ryan had. When she'd told him, his expression had been utterly unemotional, as if she'd said nothing more important than *Your shoelace is untied.*

Ryan leaned against the windowsill and folded his arms over his chest. "I was surprised. I didn't think he'd get caught. He's a con artist, not a hustler."

"What does that mean?" J.D. asked.

"A con artist plans his cons and chooses his marks. A hustler just hustles anyone who's ripe for the pickin'. A con artist leaves town when he's ready, but a hustler leaves when someone else, like the cops, decides it's time." He flashed a mockery of a smile. "Owen taught me that. He's a con artist, too."

"Who's Owen?"

"Cole's dad."

"Your grandfather," J.D. clarified.

For an instant, Ryan went still, as if he'd never considered the relationship before, and for the thousandth time, Leanne wanted to hurt Cole. Mitch had been right that day in her store. Cole wasn't fit to be a father, and apparently, his own father wasn't fit to be a grandfather.

Which suggested he probably hadn't been much of a father to Cole, some sly little demon whispered. After all, he was a crook who'd raised his son to follow in his own footsteps.

"Sounds like you spend a lot of time with your grandfather," J.D. remarked.

"I stay with him sometimes when Cole's workin', and we always go there—" Ryan caught himself and his expression tightened. "We always went there for Christmas and in the summer sometimes."

"How do you get along with your grandfather?"

Dragging the toe of his sneaker back and forth, Ryan watched the scuff marks appear in the carpet, then disappear, before finally lifting one shoulder. "He's okay. He doesn't treat me like a kid and get all bossy. He doesn't have a bunch of rules, or get upset about things like other people do."

Oh, Owen Jackson had rules, Leanne thought scornfully. Just not the sort any self-respecting parent would pass on to his child or grandchild.

"Do you like staying with him?"

"It's okay." Ryan made another careless gesture, but all the shrugs and casual responses in the world couldn't hide his hurt and vulnerability. "It doesn't matter much to me where I stay, and I like Owen. He's cool."

J.D. made a note in the file open in front of him, then changed the subject. "What do you think of the sentence the judge gave your father?"

It wasn't *fair*, Leanne silently insisted, and expected Ryan to echo her thought. He didn't.

"It's kinda cool. He'll hate it, 'cause he never sticks around after he takes people's money. He'd rather be locked up." Then the pleasure that had appeared briefly in his expression disappeared. "But he won't stick around. Unless they watch him real close, he'll be outta here first chance he gets."

But maybe he would think twice before he tried to con an entire little town like Bethlehem again.

"Maybe he won't stick around, or maybe they are watching him closely," J.D. said. "But as long as he's here, you're liable to run into him sometime. What will you say to him?"

"It ain't gonna happen."

"Bethlehem's a small town, and he's living right across the street from you. It will—"

"He's what?" Leanne's face flushed hot, and too late she realized she shouldn't have interrupted, but J.D. couldn't drop a bombshell like that and expect her to take it in quietly.

The doctor shifted his gaze to her. "He's living across the street. I figured you'd heard. The Millers have donated temporary use of the mansion to the program he's in."

"Why didn't I know that? There should have been gossip, talk—"

"Complaint?" J.D. paused. "You're familiar with the not-in-my-backyard syndrome, aren't you? Prisons, garbage dumps, nuclear facilities, and halfway houses are all well and good, as long as they're not in our own backyards. I imagine the news has been kept relatively quiet in case folks decided they didn't like the idea of a convict serving his sentence in their neighborhood." He smiled dryly. "Not that you would be so narrow-minded."

She forced her own smile. "I have nothing against convicts." But she held one hell of a grudge against Cole.

Ryan reclaimed the conversation, repeating, "It ain't gonna happen. I don't wanna see him, and no one can make me."

And if he did see Cole, he could ignore him. That was certainly a skill *she* was going to cultivate.

"Just play along with me, will you?" J.D. asked reasonably. "If, by some really rotten luck, you should run into him, how will you handle it?"

Tight-lipped, Ryan shook his head.

They waited, the silence growing heavier with each moment. When it became too much for Ryan to bear, he shoved himself away from the window ledge and headed for the door. "This is stupid. Talking never fixes anything. I'm outta here."

The slamming door punctuated his words.

Leanne slowly got to her feet. "Well . . . I'm sorry. . . ."

J.D. grinned. "You didn't think this would all get straightened out in one visit, did you?"

"A woman can hope, can't she?"

"He's a kid without a whole lot of stability in his life. His mother abandoned him, then his father. Now Jackson's back, but not because he wanted to come back, not because he regretted leaving Ryan. The kid's got a lot of anger, resentment, hurt, and fear inside him, and he doesn't know what to do with it. That's our job—to help him cope. I'll do what I do best, and you'll do what you do best, and we hope."

She nodded in agreement, then blankly asked, "What is it I do best?"

"Love him. Make him feel safe. Be there for him."

"Sounds like I've got the easier job."

"It bodes well for the kid that you think so." Coming around his desk, he walked into the corridor with her. Where the hallway ended in the hospital lobby, Ryan stood, staring out the window. He looked so alone that her heart ached.

"Thanks, J.D."

"My secretary will call to set up a schedule with you."

She said good-bye, then walked a half-dozen yards before he spoke again. "Leanne? You need to be thinking about your own answer to that last question I asked Ryan. When you run into Jackson—and you *will*—how will you handle it?"

She held his gaze for a long time before walking away. She had only one answer to give, and she didn't think it would satisfy him any more than it did her.

Damned if I know.

Chapter Four

COLE AWOKE BEFORE DAWN TUESDAY MORNING, eased from the bed, and went to the window that looked out on the courthouse, the square, and Leanne's shop and apartment. He wasn't looking to see if she was up. Really, it was the courthouse that drew him—his daily reminder that, lack of bars and guards notwithstanding, he was in prison.

Though he guessed Eli was a guard of sorts. Not that he couldn't take the kid in a fight. Eli was a few inches shorter and twenty pounds lighter, and his old man probably hadn't taught him to fight dirty practically from the cradle, like Owen had.

What Eli mostly was, was annoying. The only peace Cole had found in the house since he'd moved in was in this room or the bathroom. Outside those two places, he was apparently fair game for Eli's company, nosy questions, psychological mumbo jumbo, and constant scrutiny.

Prison—the uniform, the eight-by-ten cell, the bad company, the restrictions—couldn't possibly be worse.

He was about to turn away, take a shower, and grab some breakfast when lights came on across the street. He stopped and watched, even though the blinds were closed, even though Leanne was one of the last people he wanted to see, and he waited, hardly breathing, moment after long moment. Finally, disgusted, he forced himself to walk away. He hadn't engaged in such juvenile behavior even when he was a juvenile. He was too damn old to start now.

By the time he'd finished his shower and dressed, Eli was in the kitchen, flipping pancakes and frying sausage. Not so long ago, Cole had fixed that same breakfast, and had eaten his at the sink while Leanne's little boy made a mess at the table. Afterward, he'd cleaned up Danny, then delivered him to his mother across the street, fully intending to start backing off from their affair. Then she'd come to the door, so pretty and sweet, and had given him one of those smiles that drove all rational thought from his mind, and backing off had zoomed to the top of his list of things he wanted least.

Well, he wouldn't have to worry about getting any more of those smiles. She was more likely to snarl.

Eli set two loaded plates on the table, added two glasses of milk—Cole couldn't comprehend how anyone could prefer milk over coffee first thing in the morning—then sat down. "What kind of work have you done? Besides the scams, I mean."

Cole slid into his chair and spread butter and syrup over his pancakes before he shrugged. "Nothing."

"Nothing? You've never held a legitimate job?"

"Nope." Though he'd been tempted a time or two— had wondered what it would be like to make an honest living, to not feel that vague little anxiety every time he saw a cop, wondering if the guy was looking for *him*.

I once considered going straight, his father used to say. *But I laid down and soon the temptation went away.*

"So what can you do? Besides scamming people."

"You put unreasonable limits on your questions, you don't leave me many answers."

Eli grinned, knocking about ten years off his appearance—probably not the effect he was going for, since he had such a baby face anyway. "Okay, forget the limits. What can you do?"

"I can lie, cheat, and steal with the best of 'em. I can pick a pocket so smooth the mark never knows what's happened. I can pick locks, hustle the best pool players in town, palm cards, sell things that don't exist, and charm a woman out of her money while making her think it was her idea to give it to me. Give me a laptop computer"—one thing that hadn't been returned to him with his clothes—"and I can steal a name, a social security number, a credit card number, or the contents of some sucker's bank accounts. I don't do that often, though. It lacks the challenge of the face-to-face con."

"And you can cook."

Cole blinked. He'd expected more of a reaction to his boasting, but Eli acted as if he'd recited a perfectly normal resume instead. "Yeah, I've done some cooking." It had been his responsibility all those times his mother had gone off looking for greener pastures, and most of the times when she came back. Eloise had lacked all maternal instincts, as well as those of a housewifely nature. No cooking or cleaning or laundry for her, but maternal or not, she'd still managed to turn out six sons. *Someone* had to take up the slack, and Owen had been too busy providing for them, to do all that homemaking stuff.

"And you've taken care of Ryan."

He snorted, to hide the ache the mere mention of the boy stirred. "Ryan never needed taking care of. He probably changed his own diapers and fixed his own bottles."

"You weren't around to know?"

Cole's jaw tightened. "No. He was nine when he came to live with me."

"But you saw him before that."

"Nope."

"Oh. I see."

See what? he wanted to demand. That he was as sorry an excuse for a father as ever lived? There was a reason he hadn't known Ryan when he was young, and a good one—he didn't know the kid existed. But telling Eli that would only lead to other questions, other assumptions . . . unless he told the truth.

He could probably count on one hand the number of times he'd done that in his thirty years, so why start now?

Eli carried their dishes to the sink and rinsed them. "We're going to be working in City Park today. Ever want to be Paul Bunyan when you were a kid?"

"Those weren't the kind of bedtime stories my old man told." No, he'd gotten primers on hiding the larcenous soul of a devil behind the smile of an angel, on when to talk and when to shut up, on the arts of distraction, flattery, and subterfuge.

"Grab a jacket and meet me out front," Eli said as he headed down the hall.

Cole climbed the back stairs to his room, took a leather bomber jacket from its hanger, then put it back and reached for a sweatshirt instead. He wasn't up on kiddie lore, but as far as he could recall, Paul Bunyan had been some kind of outdoors guy. No need to risk a four-hundred-dollar jacket on whatever dirty work Eli had dreamed up.

It was a good decision. Their work in City Park in-volved cutting down dead trees. More than a dozen of them had been flagged with yellow strips tied around their trunks. Eli pulled his beat-up old truck onto the grass, got out, and lowered the tailgate. In the truck bed were chain saws, a couple cans of gasoline, work gloves, plastic safety glasses, and an axe.

"Aren't you concerned about putting a potential weapon in my hands?" Cole asked dryly.

Eli didn't look the least bit concerned. "Just about anything has the potential to be a weapon. Besides, you've never resorted to violence, except for the time you broke that guy's nose, arm, and jaw, when he'd tried to kill Frank."

God, that had been a lifetime ago. He'd been nineteen, and Frank, the youngest and wildest of the Jackson boys, had just turned fourteen. No one had believed he was going to make it to fifteen, but he'd surprised them. Hell, he'd really surprised them when he'd turned twenty-five, especially having suffered nothing more serious than a few broken bones.

Eli gave him a how-to on the chain saw and the finer points of cutting down trees, and they set to work. It was dirty, hot, and frustrating. The saw blade kept getting hung up, no matter how precisely he followed the kid's instructions. When the first tree fell—and in the direction he'd wanted it to, no less—he was surprised. By the time the sixth one went down, he was dirtier, hotter, not so frustrated, and tired of the effort. About the only good thing he could find about the whole job was that the chain saws were so loud, conversation was kept to a minimum. He hadn't known Eli could say so little for so long.

After what surely must have been hours, Eli signaled him to stop. When he cut off the saw, the kid said, "Let's get some lunch."

Cole automatically glanced at his left wrist, but the Rolex he'd worn for the past five years was gone. "Why don't you go ahead and bring it back?"

Eli's look was as dry as the desert. "Like you'd be here waiting? Come on."

Still Cole didn't move. "Where?"

"Where everyone goes for lunch. Harry's."

"Nope." Cole started the saw again, revved the engine, and prepared to remove a limb from the tree he'd just downed. Before the blade touched the wood, though, the saw died. He started it, it sputtered for a moment, then went dead again.

"Come on," Eli repeated, pulling the saw from his hands. "Let's go."

Against his will, Cole climbed into the truck. In his weeks in Bethlehem, he'd become a regular at Harry's. He'd known all the other regulars, had his own usual table. He'd made so many contacts in there, that he'd joked with Harry about splitting the commissions with him. Of course, there'd been no commissions because there'd been no investments.

And Eli wanted him to walk in there and face everyone now that they knew the truth.

He wasn't sure he could do it.

He had only a few minutes to find the courage to pull it off. Then Eli was pulling into a parking space, shutting off the engine, and waiting pointedly for him to get out.

According to the sign outside the bank down the street, it was twelve-thirty-five. That alone was enough to tell him that Harry's would be busy. Looking at the sidewalk, he walked beside Eli to the diner entrance, took a deep breath, lifted his gaze, and walked in the door.

The reaction inside wasn't anything so dramatic as a sudden silence. No one yelled obscenities at him, pointed their fingers in censure, or snickered at his predicament, and neither Harry nor Maeve, the longtime waitress who seemed to think the joint was as much hers as Harry's, threw him out. But there were looks—some quick and furtive, others long and judgmental, some disdainful, some expressionless.

There was Fred Miller, who'd invested five grand in addition to letting Cole live rent-free in his mother's house while waiting for a nonexistent loan to go through. And Dean Elliott, an artist who lived outside town, where he created strange but valuable pieces, some of the profits of which he'd sunk into Cole's scheme. And Mrs. Larrabee, widow of the former mayor and as grandmotherly as anyone he'd ever known—as trusting, too, as her buy-in had shown. And Leanne—

He stiffened. She was sitting in a booth next to the plate-glass window, looking outside while the woman across from her chattered. Her dark hair was pulled back and tied at her neck with a fat red bow that matched her sweater, and she looked beautiful. Untouchable.

"Afternoon, boys," Maeve greeted. Her smile dimmed as she looked from Eli to Cole, then brightened once more when she spoke to the kid. "If you can find a place to sit, I can serve you."

"You're having a busy day," Eli remarked.

"Every day's a busy day. Thank the Lord for that."

Cole scanned the room, careful not to make eye contact with anyone, and saw no empty seats. He was about to suggest they eat at the house when Eli gestured. "There . . . she'll share her table with us."

Never bring attention to yourself, Owen had taught, *but once you have it, don't cower from it.* Keeping that in mind, Cole kept his head up and shoulders back as he followed Eli between tables. He was so busy wishing he was elsewhere, that when the kid stopped, he almost plowed into him.

"Imagine meeting you here," Eli said, his tone too friendly, too phonily surprised. "Mind if we join you?"

Cole shifted to the side so he could see this *friend,* and recognized the pretty blonde with Leanne. "No," he said flatly. "Huh-uh."

He turned to walk out, but Eli caught his arm, his grasp unexpectedly strong. Cole could break it, and maybe even a few of his fingers in the process, but that would draw even more attention his way, when he was smothering with what he already had.

"Ladies?" Eli prompted.

"You can have my place," Leanne said, grabbing her purse and sliding toward the end of the bench. "I've lost my appetite."

Eli blocked her way. "You've hardly touched your food. No one walks away from Harry's lunch special. It's the best food in town. Slide over, Sophy. Let Cole sit beside you."

With a narrow-eyed scowl for Eli, the blonde obeyed, leaving more than half the bench for Cole. Unwillingly, Leanne did the same, so Eli could sit next to her.

"This is *not* a good idea," Sophy announced, still scowling at Eli.

Her annoyance had no effect on him. "It's lunchtime. You're hungry. We're hungry. The place is packed. It's an efficient use of time and space. What could possibly not be good about it?"

"Spoken like a man," she muttered.

Maeve appeared with an order pad and pen, and a smile for Eli. "What can I get you?"

While he ordered, Cole stared at the tabletop, acutely aware of Leanne doing the same. A moment later he felt the weight of Maeve's disapproving stare. "What about you?"

"I'll have the same," he murmured, not knowing what he'd just asked for, and not caring. As soon as the waitress left, he stood up, but managed only one step before Eli was on his feet, too.

"Where are you going?"

"To the bathroom, to wash up."

Eli studied him, as if debating whether to trust him. Leanne helped him along with a sarcastically sweet smile. "It's safe. That hall goes to the bathrooms and nowhere else. There are no windows, no way to escape."

Relaxing, Eli sat down again. "Go ahead. We'll be right here when you get back."

Not if she could help it, Leanne thought belligerently. It was bad enough she had to live with Cole in town—had to lie in bed at night, unable to sleep, knowing he was only a few yards away in his own bed. She damn well wouldn't have lunch with him.

As soon as he disappeared through the door marked REST ROOMS, she offered Sophy a tight smile. "I'm going to head back to the shop. I've been gone too long."

"Fifteen minutes," Sophy scoffed.

"I don't close during the day."

"It doesn't hurt once in a while. Anyone who wants to shop and finds it closed, will come back later. After all"— she smiled wheedlingly—"where else can they buy all the wonderful stuff you carry?"

Feeling her temper rising, Leanne took a calming breath. It didn't ease the tension in her voice. "Okay, no subterfuge. I couldn't care less about the shop being closed in the middle of the day. But you were right when you said this is a bad idea. I'm not sitting here with him."

"Why? What did I do?"

Leanne glared at the young man beside her. She'd seen him in court last week, had heard the judge call him Eli, but that was all she knew about him. He was new to Bethlehem, new to her, and at the rate he was going, they *weren't* going to become friendly enough to learn more.

She didn't bother to answer his questions, but turned her attention back to Sophy. "Tell your friend to get out of my way."

"He's no friend of mine," the girl replied with a toss of her blonde curls. "He wouldn't listen to me anyway. He never does."

"I'd listen if you had something important to contribute," Eli said, his voice smug and condescending.

As Leanne had ignored him, so did Sophy. "You have to eat, Leanne. Besides, Cole's going to be around a long time. You can't run away every time you see him. You can't let him make you afraid to go out. What kind of lesson would that teach Ryan?"

The same lesson Cole had already taught him the hard way—when things got tough, the tough got going. But she wasn't ready to be in the same building with him, much less at the same table. Besides, he had run out on her. Wasn't it only fair that she should be allowed to run out on him?

But who guaranteed that life would be fair? God knows, *hers* certainly hadn't been. Or Ryan's. Or Cole's—

No. No sympathy. He didn't deserve it.

The question became moot when the REST ROOMS door swung open and Cole returned to the table. He'd washed his face, arms, and hands, combed his fingers through his hair, and dusted away the layer of sawdust that had coated his clothes. He looked amazingly handsome.

He sat down beside Sophy—two blonds, both blue-eyed and tanned, looking more like brother and sister than virtual strangers—and fixed his gaze on the table. Where were the cocky grin and wink and the *Hey, sugar* that she'd wanted to smack him for last week in the courthouse?

Where was all that arrogance, that don't-give-a-damn-about-anything attitude? Surely a lousy one and a half day's work hadn't beaten it out of him.

Almost as if he sensed her thoughts, he took a breath, raised his head, grinned, and transformed into the Cole who'd first come to town last April. The difference was as obvious as night and day, and it made her stare, wondering which was real and which was an act. Or was it all an act? Was there anything at all about him that was real?

"Did you miss me while I was gone?" he asked, a drawl more apparent in his voice than when he'd first come to town. Of course, he'd been masquerading as an L.A. native then, and they all knew now he'd been born and raised in the heart of Texas.

"Yeah, I did," she replied carelessly. "But my aim's getting better every day."

"How's Danny?"

"He's fine. He's forgotten all about you." She didn't look at him as she spoke—didn't want to see if her jibe had any effect. Instead she focused on cutting a piece of tender pork chop, dipping it in gravy, and lifting it to her mouth.

"Nolie still seeing your brother?"

"They're married now. You know, that thing two people do when they're in love and want to be together and have a family." Then she faked a big regretful frown. "Oh, that's right. You wouldn't know anything about that, because you don't care about anyone but yourself."

His voice was hard and stiff. "Well, you finally got one thing right."

She forced another bite of pork chop, a forkful of mashed potatoes, three baby carrots, then laid her fork down and stared at him. "Ask about Ryan."

Maeve gave him a moment of reprieve as she served two specials and two glasses of chocolate milk, but then she left again. He sprinkled salt over his potatoes, buttered his roll, and started to cut into the pork chop.

"Ask . . . about . . . Ryan." It was her sternest voice, one guaranteed to make small children snap to attention—and grown men, too, for that matter. It made his fingers tighten around the fork until his knuckles turned white, and formed thin lines at the corners of his mouth.

He exhaled, put the utensils down, sat back, and looked at her head-on for the first time. "What about Ryan?"

"He's living with Danny and me, since we're the only people he knew in town when you dumped him here without so much as a 'So long.' He's making C's and D's in school, and he had a nightmare last night, even with the light on. He's lost weight; he's sullen and uncooperative; and he's headed for big trouble because of you. And you can't even be bothered to *ask* about him?"

For a moment, she thought she saw a flicker of something on his face—bleak regret? Sorrow? But it disappeared so quickly behind that impassive mask, that she feared she was kidding herself. His next words confirmed the fear.

"He's an adaptable kid. He'll get over it."

Leanne was stunned. How could he keep surprising her? He'd seduced her, made her fall in love with him, then ripped off the entire town. He'd played such a good father, then walked away and left his son behind. He was as dishonest as the day was long, self-absorbed, and superficial. He wasn't even worth the cost of the air that kept him alive . . . and yet he'd shocked her again.

This time when she moved to get up, she didn't let Eli stop her. If he hadn't scrambled out of the booth as quickly as he did, she would have knocked him to the floor and stepped in his middle on her way out. Clutching her purse so tightly she might just grind the leather to powder, she rushed out of the diner, darted across the street, and covered the block to her shop in record time. There she would have taken the stairs two at a time to her apartment, where she would have ranted, raved, and broken things, but a slender figure was waiting impatiently outside the shop door, arms folded, toe tapping.

A visit from her mother usually ranked somewhere between a root canal and a near-lethal case of food poisoning on Leanne's list of favorite things, but today she actually welcomed the distraction. Anger with an absent Cole would take a backseat to dealing with Phyllis in the flesh.

"Mom," she greeted her more warmly than she had in years, as she slid the key in the lock. "I'm glad you stopped by. Come in, please."

L OOKING AS IF HE'D SWALLOWED SOME DEVILISH little horror movie creature that was now killing him from the inside out, Cole left his lunch uneaten, muttered that he would be outside, then left the diner as quickly— and with as much attention—as Leanne had. Sophy watched as he stopped in front of Eli's old green truck, leaned against it, then bent his head as if he just couldn't hold it up anymore. Then she glared at Eli. "I told you it was a bad idea."

"We had to do something to get them together."

"Not like this. Not with half the town for an audience. But, no, you couldn't listen. You think you're so hot. Well, let me tell you—"

"Do *you* think I'm hot?"

She stared, mouth open, before remembering to shut it. He was the most arrogant guardian she'd ever known . . . and the handsomest, too, with black hair and dark eyes and a smile that could light up the heavens. Not that she was susceptible to a pretty face. She had a job to do here, and thanks to him, it had just gotten harder.

"You—you—" Frantically, she tried to recover the thread of the conversation before he'd interrupted and seized it with relief. "You can't just come in here and do things your own way. Gloria and I *know* these people. We know how to handle them."

He was absolutely unrepentant. "And I know how to handle Cole."

"You don't know squat about Leanne."

"She's a woman. What's to know?" He shrugged dismissively, then pointed to the pork chop on her plate. "Are you gonna finish that?"

Too numb to think of anything at all to say, she slid the plate toward him, and he speared the meat on his fork. He was obnoxious, arrogant, rude, chauvinistic, brash, egotistical, arrogant—

"You already said *arrogant*. Don't start repeating yourself." He ate a bite, then grinned. "Besides, those are awfully uncharitable thoughts for a guardian to be having. Face it, Soph. We have different styles. Yours is gentle, gradual, and subdued, and mine gets results. You'll see that soon."

Styles? Results? Soph?!

She couldn't speak for fear of sputtering. It was just as well, because he gulped the last few bites, then grabbed the ticket and got to his feet. "Gotta go. See you around."

Not if she could help it, she thought with a sniff. She would rather transfer to the North Pole than work with a guardian like him. He was too obnoxious, too smug, too arrogant—and, yes, she knew she was repeating herself, but something so dead-on accurate deserved repeating. She'd worked with many guardians over the years, some whom she'd liked better than others, but this one . . .

For heaven's sake, he'd called her *Soph!*

• • •

THE STREETLIGHTS WERE BUZZING SOFTLY WHEN Leanne locked up the store Wednesday evening. For a time she stood on the sidewalk, breathing deeply of the nippy air, letting it seep into her bones and chase away every last bit of heat from her body. She was tired—sleepless nights tended to have that effect on her—but the chill gave her a new burst of energy, enough to face the one-block walk to the grocery store without groaning inwardly.

She'd called upstairs on the intercom, to let Ryan know where she was going and to ask for meal suggestions. He hadn't offered any. She'd nagged him to finish his homework, and he said he already had. She really hoped he hadn't lied to her.

As the wind whipped down the street, she zipped the jacket to her chin, shoved her hands in the pockets, and started toward the store. Ryan had another appointment with J.D. on Thursday, and she had Halloween costumes to acquire, and she was on the decorations committee for the haunted house at the town's celebration, and there were pumpkins to carve and treats to bake, and she was suffering from the worst case of lack of concentration she'd ever experienced.

And she knew exactly who to blame.

She was scowling as she crossed the grocery store parking lot—had been scowling every time she thought of her run-in with Cole at Harry's the day before. She wasn't sure what bothered her more—that he was walking around free, that she still found him so damned handsome, that he'd pulled off his chameleon act so completely, or . . . no, no doubt about it. His uncaring attitude about Ryan won hands-down.

A close second was the act. She'd had to face that she knew virtually nothing about the man she'd fallen in—and out of—love with. He'd been playing a role with her, and he'd succeeded magnificently. She'd seen only what he wanted her to see, and none of it had been the real Cole Jackson. She doubted even he knew the real Cole anymore.

It was too bad for Ryan's sake. For herself, she didn't care anymore. Whatever tender feelings she'd had for him were gone. She might not be the quickest learner in the world—four broken hearts proved that—but eventually she *did* learn. But Ryan . . . it broke her heart all over again, to see him grieving for the father he'd believed loved him.

Inside the brightly lit store, she got a shopping cart and headed for the produce section. Cooking wasn't her strong suit. Before Danny's birth, all her meals had come from Bethlehem's limited choice of restaurants or the freezer case. Now she relied too much on sandwiches, hot dogs, and dishes such as spaghetti, chili, and stew. Maybe she should surprise the kids and cook a real dinner—roast beef with all the veggies or baked ham with wild rice and broccoli casserole. Maybe meat loaf and mashed potatoes or fried chicken, potato salad, and baked beans.

Or maybe one of her old fallbacks, such as chicken stew, she decided as she bagged carrots, potatoes, celery, and onions. It was a good thing her boys were easy to please. She added catsup and canned corn to the cart, then a box of cornstarch just in case she needed it for thickening the gravy, along with apples and caramel dip for dessert. She was browsing through the meat section, looking to be tempted on her way to the packages of boneless, skinless chicken breasts, when she bumped carts with another shopper and glanced up, an apology at the ready.

It died unspoken.

Cole didn't look any happier than she felt. His gaze narrowed, pulling the skin across his cheekbones taut, then slid into a wince. She noticed the nasty scratch across his left cheek and wondered whether one of his former *clients* had demanded a little interest on a failed investment. Not that she could imagine anyone in Bethlehem resorting to physical retribution, but he'd taught her plenty of things that had been unimaginable before.

She didn't want to speak, didn't want to even make eye contact, but he and his cart were blocking the chicken she needed. She tried easing her cart forward so he would have to retreat, but he just planted his feet and held his ground.

She unclenched her fingers from the cart's handle and made a show of looking around. "Where's your watchdog? Surely he's not foolish enough to let you out, unguarded."

A muscle in his jaw twitched. "Eli's getting dessert."

"And you haven't crept away like a thief in the night?" Then she smiled sarcastically. "Bad choice of words, huh? Since you really *are* a thief."

That muscle twitched again. "You all got your money back."

"And that somehow makes up for the fact that you stole it in the first place?"

"No one forced you to buy in."

"No. We did that because we trusted you. No one forced *you* to betray that trust and steal from us."

He shrugged, but without the cockiness she was coming to expect. Instead, he merely looked . . . weary. "It's what I do."

"And you don't regret it at all, do you? You're sorry you got caught, sorry they brought you back here, but you're not at all sorry for committing the crime in the first place, are you?"

He stared at her a long time, his expression unreadable, then abruptly took a few steps back so he could maneuver his cart around her.

Perversely, she swung her cart around, to block him. "What? No answer?"

"You wouldn't believe it if I gave it." He succeeded at the same technique she'd tried, pushing his cart forward until she had to either move or get run over. He walked a few yards, then turned back. "Hey . . . Ryan's birthday is next month—the thirteenth."

She should have known that, Leanne thought—should have asked him or found out from his social worker or the school or *someone*. What if it had passed unnoticed? How insignificant would that have made him feel? How badly would they all have felt?

All she could do in response was nod, and even that seemed more than he expected. With a curt nod of his own, he walked away.

Numbly she took a package of chicken breasts from the refrigerated case, then turned her cart toward the registers at the front of the store. That wasn't so bad, was it? Sure, she felt as if she'd been turned inside out and upside down, and there was a knot in her stomach that was taking its own sweet time at relaxing. But she'd seen him, talked to him, and hadn't cried, punched him, screamed at him, or anything else. That was a good sign.

Even if she'd *wanted* to do all those things and more.

She'd paid her bill and was on her way out the door, purse over her shoulder and a shopping bag in each hand, when someone called her name. She turned to see Eli, who'd spoken, and Cole, leaving the next register down. Eli was grinning as if seeing her had just made his day.

After lunch at Harry's yesterday, she could have happily gone a few years before seeing him again.

"How about a hand with that?" he offered, nodding toward her bags.

"I can manage."

"I didn't mean to imply that you couldn't. But it's not proper for a man to stand by with empty hands while a woman carries heavy bags."

"They're not so heavy, and I don't have far to go."

"And we're going in the same direction." With the grin brightening a hundred watts or so, he took the bags Cole was carrying, then gestured again with a nod. "Why don't you help her with those?"

Though Cole made no move toward her, she tightened her grip anyway. "It's not necessary."

"No, it isn't. That's what's nice about it."

Cole could refuse to take the bags. She could refuse to give them up. She could tell Eli to mind his own business and leave her alone. She could do a lot of things, and every one of them would be noticed, dissected, and passed on by the curious shoppers watching from nearby checkouts.

Grinding her teeth, she managed a semblance of a smile, let Cole have the bags, then spun around and walked out. He matched his pace to hers. Eli fell farther and farther behind—deliberately, she guessed. When they reached the sidewalk at the far edge of the parking lot, she glanced over her shoulder, to see the young man chatting pleasantly with Mrs. Franks—not an easy task, given the woman's sour disposition. "What's his problem?"

"He's very young."

"He can't be that much younger than you."

"I was never that young."

If that was true, it was very sad, but he seemed neither sad nor bitter. He was simply stating an opinion.

"He sets Sophy's teeth on edge," she remarked as they passed the courthouse. "I think she likes him."

"I don't know about that. *I* set your teeth on edge, and it doesn't have anything to do with liking, does it?"

In spite of the chill, her face flushed hotly. "No," she agreed, tight-lipped. "Nothing at all."

When they crossed the street that ran in front of her shop, she stopped, faced him, and held out her hands. When he didn't immediately give the bags to her, she took hold of the handles, but he didn't let go. "Ryan's smart enough to make straight A's with a little effort. He just doesn't see much reason to bother. He's not convinced that book-learning has much value in the real world."

Unwilling to acknowledge that he was actually demonstrating some concern for—to say nothing of understanding of—his son, she fell back on sarcasm. "Gee, where would he get that idea? From his father, the con artist? Or maybe his grandfather, who's also a con artist?"

Cole's forehead wrinkled in a frown. "His grand—oh. You mean Owen."

In J.D.'s office, it seemed as if Ryan hadn't made the connection that Owen was his grandfather, and even Cole had needed a moment to realize it. What kind of father had Owen Jackson been? He hadn't brought up a son, but a chip off the old cellblock, and the grandfather/grandson relationship had apparently been so tenuous that it had gone unrecognized by both Cole and Ryan. How much responsibility did the elder Jackson bear for Cole's choices in life?

She gave herself a sharp mental shake. She wasn't making excuses for him, remember? No matter how inadequate his father had been, the choices Cole had made were his. Certainly his father had influenced the boy, the teenager, and probably even the young man, but he was thirty years old. Old enough to make decisions for himself, and to suffer the consequences for them.

Too bad she and Ryan had to suffer with him.

She tugged until he released the bags, then took a few steps back. "Tell me something . . . is there anyone in your family who *isn't* a criminal?"

He pretended to think about it a moment, then gave a callous shrug. "No one I can think of at the moment. Besides Ryan."

"Why is that? Because you didn't have enough time with him, to teach him the tools of the family trade?"

His expression turned as hard and cold as the concrete beneath their feet. "Because that was the deal we made from the beginning. I'd take care of him, and he would stay out of the business."

"So even a little kid knew better than to make the choices you did." Thoroughly disgusted with him—and with herself for getting into the situation where they could even have this conversation—she shook her head disdainfully, turned her back on him, and headed toward her apartment. Just before she went inside, she surreptitiously glanced to the right. Cole was still standing there, shoulders slumped, hands at his sides. He looked about as defeated as a man could get while still standing.

But that wasn't her concern. Nothing about him was, except how to relegate him to the darkest corner of her mind.

And how to stop feeling that little shock every time she saw him.

And how to quit finding him so amazingly attractive.

And how—

"Oh, hell," she muttered as she reached the top of the stairs. Two small words that summed up her life quite well at the moment.

Oh, hell.

Chapter Five

ON THURSDAY THEY GOT A NEW RESIDENT at the house—an older man by the name of Murray, who would be with them only for a week or so, according to Eli. His age was difficult to guess—somewhere between fifty and seventy, Cole assumed. He carried an extra thirty pounds in his belly, his thinning hair was white, and he was either living someplace else in his mind or doing a damn good act of it. He would probably be completely harmless if not for his habit of driving after spending a few hours with his best friend, Jack Daniel.

He joined them before breakfast and went along afterward when they drove to City Park. He was no more familiar with a chain saw than Cole had been a few days earlier, but he followed directions well.

By Cole's count, they had cut down twenty-one trees, cleaned them up, and piled the discarded branches nearby. Today they were cutting the trunks into firewood, which they would deliver to elderly people who used it to keep their winter heating bills down. Later, the branches would be fed through a chipper, to make mulch. Then they would have the pleasure of mulching every tree planted along the sidewalks in the business district and every flower bed in the square. One more job he was going to hate.

Though, he had to admit, if not for the people, it hadn't been bad so far. He liked being outside, and he'd spent so much time behind a desk in his last couple of cons, that he could use the physical activity. Even getting scraped across the face by a falling branch yesterday hadn't amounted to anything more than a nuisance.

But he could live easier if he didn't see Leanne again. If she wasn't always looking at him as if she could barely contain her hatred. If he wasn't tempted to explain himself to her. It didn't matter if she knew the real reason he'd left Ryan behind, or if he told her details about his upbringing that he'd never shared with anyone else. It wouldn't change a thing if he tried to make her understand, other than costing him whatever pride he had left.

It would just all-around be easier not to see her.

Seeing Eli approach, Cole let the chain saw idle, then die. Even after he set it down, he still felt the vibrations in his hands and all the way up to his shoulders. He took the paper cup the kid offered and drank half of it in one swallow, then grimaced. The drinks offered under Eli's supervision were better suited to preschoolers than grown men—usually water and milk. This was the hard stuff—lemonade, made from a mix and tart enough to turn Little Mary Sunshine sour.

"Let's load up some of this wood and get it delivered," Eli said, bending to gather an armful of logs.

"I thought wood had to dry out before it could be used for firewood." Cole drained the last of his lemonade, tossed the cup in a nearby trash can, then picked up an armload himself.

"It does. Most of these trees have been dead so long they

could have been burned standing upright. The city just hadn't budgeted for removing them, until we came along."

Whoever would have thought that a baby-faced do-gooder and a convicted felon could be the solution to their problem?

While Cole had been cutting, Eli and Murray had unloaded the tools from the back of the truck. When they finished loading the wood, there was no room left for them. "What about that stuff?" Cole asked.

"We'll leave it here. No one will take it.".

Of course not, since the only bona-fide criminal in Bethlehem would be otherwise occupied. "It's a park, Eli," he pointed out impatiently. "Kids come here to play. You can't leave chain saws, gasoline, and an axe lying around."

"Oh." Eli glanced toward the playground equipment in one direction, the baseball fields in another, then shrugged. "Why don't you stay here and keep working, while Murray and I make this delivery?"

Stay here. Truly alone for the first time since Eli had gotten him out of jail. Free to disappear into the thick growth of woods that formed the back boundary of the park and never come back. The thought made Cole's chest tight, made his breaths shallow and unsteady. "You sure you trust me to be here when you get back?"

"No." Eli tossed the last logs into the truck bed, then slammed the tailgate shut. "But I guarantee, if you're not, I'll find you before sundown."

Not in those woods, Cole thought cynically.

"Even in those woods," Eli retorted.

After giving him a sharp look, Cole put on the ear protection and safety glasses, gave the chain saw a jerk, then revved the engine and went back to work. Though he was careful not to be obvious, he watched as Eli and Murray climbed into the truck, then drove across the dead grass.

The old pickup dipped and bounced over the curb into the nearest parking lot, then turned onto the street. Within moments it was out of sight.

And Cole was free to go.

But he didn't shut down the saw and make a run for it. He was almost finished cleaning up this trunk. It wouldn't take him ten minutes to get the job done, and another five to drag the branches to the side. Besides, as Owen always said, *A man needs a plan.* He'd already decided that the first chance he got, he was outta there, but that wasn't a plan.

Where would he go, and how would he get there? He needed money and transportation. Like an irresponsible kid, he wasn't allowed to have money in this program; what he'd had on him when he was arrested was in Eli's safekeeping. So he would have to find out where the kid had hidden it, or he would have to steal a stash.

As for transportation, he couldn't buy a bus ticket there in town, and he damn sure couldn't hitch a ride. That left his own two feet, stealing a car, or getting help. Crossing these mountains on foot when the nighttime lows were in the forties struck him as promising a low probability of success, and hot-wiring a car was one skill he'd never picked up in his checkered past.

But he could get help. All he had to do was get a message to the family, and someone would show up.

He was working on automatic pilot, caught up in his thoughts, when some sixth sense made him cut off the saw. An instant later, a small boy flung himself against his legs and climbed into his arms.

"Cole!" Danny Wilson squealed with delight, then threw his arms around his neck and gave him a sloppy kiss. "I didn't know you was home! Ryan's been stayin' with us and we're sorta brothers now, only we're gonna be real brothers someday and—hey! Know what I'm gonna be for Halloween?"

Cole couldn't think of an answer—couldn't think of anything but how good it was to see Danny, and how it felt even better to just once see someone who didn't hate him. He hugged the kid tightly, then became aware of an unholy screeching rapidly approaching. It was Phyllis Wilson, Leanne's banshee of a mother, and she was so furious she was shaking.

"Put him down! Danny, get away from that—that man right this instant! How dare you touch my grandson?" She snatched Danny away, careful not to touch Cole any more than necessary. He felt a sense of loss at the only friendly contact he'd had in a long time being pulled away.

She settled the boy on her hip, then shifted so he was away from Cole. "Don't you ever go near my grandson again. Do you understand? This is outrageous! What could they be thinking, letting a convicted criminal run around, armed and free, to terrorize the citizens of this town? I'm going home to complain to Chief Walker and Judge Monroe right this minute."

"I'm not armed—"

Spinning on her heel, she marched away, her back ramrod straight. Danny gave him a frantic look over her shoulder and wiggled to get down. "Grandma, I wanna talk to Cole. I wanna tell him what me and Ryan have been doin'! Grandma— Grandma—!"

As they disappeared into a brick house across the street, Cole leaned back shakily against the nearest tree. This was just what he needed—less than three days into his five-thousand-hour sentence, and already one of Bethlehem's law-abiding citizens was making a formal complaint against him. The best he could hope for was that the police chief and the judge knew Phyllis and would automatically discount her gripe. In her dealings with Leanne, at least, she was neither kind nor reasonable.

On the other hand, maybe her complaint would result in the cancellation of Eli's program and a quick transfer to the state pen. In the meantime, though, he was getting a letter out to his brothers immediately.

One way or another, he was getting out of this town. Before it killed him.

ALEX THOMAS WAS SITTING AT HIS DESK, THINKING about holidays and kids, Halloween costumes and Easter eggs and fireworks on a hot July night, when his secretary buzzed him. "Mitch just called—wanted to know if you could get over to the courthouse ASAP."

"Did he say what it was about?"

"No. There was a lot of loud talking in the background. Sounded like he had his hands full."

"Thanks, Eleanor." He loaded his briefcase, shrugged into his suit coat, tightened his tie, then left the inner office. "I'll head on home from there, so you can take off as soon as you're finished."

"Will do, boss," the older woman said with a salute. He knew better, though. Quitting time was five P.M., and while she might stay later, she never left earlier. She was worth every penny he paid her and then some, and he'd sworn he would do what he could to keep her happy, because no one else could possibly compete.

Passing his car, he half-wished he could ignore Mitch's call and go on home for a long, quiet evening with Melissa, but Mitch wouldn't have called unless it was important. Maybe Murray Walker—no relation to the chief—had gotten behind the wheel again, or the Smith boys had gotten caught, egging houses again. They were the only repeat offenders in his small criminal practice.

There was a lot of loud talking in the background, Eleanor had said, and Alex heard it for himself when he walked through the police department door. The desk sergeant, wearing a grimace, nodded toward a conference room halfway back, and Alex headed that way.

Judging by the sheer volume, he'd expected to find a roomful of people, but there weren't many—Mitch, Judge Monroe, the assistant DA, Eli, Danny, and Phyllis Wilson . . . which explained the noise. Smiling even though the mere sight of her made him grind his back teeth together, Alex closed the door. He stood next to the chair where Danny was sitting on the wooden arm and quietly asked, "What's up, Danny?"

The boy raised a teary gaze to him, with his lower lip stuck out. "Grandma's being mean."

She wasn't *being* mean, Alex thought uncharitably. She *was* mean. He wasn't sure what terrible wrongs life had done to justify her behavior, but she had more than most people—a family who tolerated her when they should have cut her off years ago, a grandson who loved her, a nice home, and no money worries.

"You watch your mouth, young man," Phyllis said sharply. "I am *not* being mean. I'm simply looking out for your welfare the way any reasonable person would."

"And what's threatening his welfare?" Alex asked, sliding his arm around Danny's middle and feeling the boy lean back comfortably against him.

"Your client," Phyllis declared.

"At one time or another I've done work for probably half the people in town, including you and your husband, your daughter, and your daughter-in-law. You have to be more specific."

"Cole Jackson."

Alex looked to Mitch, whose expression suggested he'd rather waste his time elsewhere. "When Mrs. Wilson took

Danny to the park to play this afternoon, Cole was over there working."

"Alone!" Phyllis added. "And he was armed!"

"He wasn't armed," Eli said.

"He had a chain saw and an axe."

Eli made an impatient gesture. "He was cutting down trees. Do you expect him to do it with his teeth?"

Phyllis flung her hand in his direction. "This person left that criminal alone with a weapon in City Park, where our children play. Not expecting such irresponsible behavior, I took my grandson there, and that man *grabbed* him!"

Before Alex had a chance to react to the accusation, Danny's small hands tightened on his. "He did not! I hugged him 'cause I missed him and he missed me, too. We was talkin', and *she* was mean and made me leave."

"Have you talked to Jackson?" Alex asked, and Mitch nodded.

"He tells the same story as Danny."

"Well, of course he does!" Phyllis's cheeks burned hotly. "He's a liar! Of course he's going to back up Danny's story!"

"Mrs. Wilson, he doesn't *know* what Danny said," the ADA said patiently. "He only saw the boy for those few minutes at the park, and they had no time to get their stories straight."

The facts had no effect on his grandmother. "That man should be in prison. He's a thief and a liar and a criminal. He has no right to be walking the streets of our town and making it unsafe for us to leave our houses in the middle of the day!"

"And what do you want us to do about it?" Mitch asked.

"Lock him up! Make him serve his sentence."

"He's serving his sentence," Eli retorted. "Five thousand hours of community service."

"That's a stupid sentence. Change it." She directed that to Judge Monroe, who shook her head.

"It's not my sentence to change. I'm not convinced it's the sentence *I* would have given, but I'm curious to see how this program of Eli's works out. It appears to have great potential."

"Potential for disaster, you mean." Phyllis sniffed haughtily. "I cannot believe you people see nothing wrong with what's happened. That man is a dangerous criminal who has caused nothing but trouble. You mark my words— you'll be sorry, every one of you. Come along, Danny."

Though he clearly didn't want to go, she gave him no choice, sweeping him up and stalking from the room.

The silence following her passage seemed to vibrate. Mitch broke it when he closed the door, then glanced around the room. "Any of you think Jackson is dangerous?"

Everyone shook their heads.

"Any of you besides Eli think it's a good idea to leave him out working on his own?"

The assistant DA shook his head, along with the judge. Alex chose not to answer.

"You've got to trust these people sometime," Eli said in his own defense. "Sure, he could have taken off . . . but he didn't. He could slit my throat and disappear in the middle of the night, but he hasn't. Cole's not violent. Even if he did escape, he wouldn't hurt anyone in the process."

"You sure of that?" the ADA asked.

"You wanna know if he is capable of violence? Yes, he is. So are you. So is everyone. But Cole's been a criminal practically from the cradle. He's not going to make that kind of abrupt change in his methods. Besides, if he takes off, I'll find him."

This time it was Judge Monroe who asked, "Are you sure of that?"

Eli flashed a cocky grin. "I haven't lost one yet."

"Yeah, like you've been doing it so long," the ADA muttered. "How old are you? Twenty?"

"Older than I look." Eli sprawled back in his chair. "So . . . you gonna let Mrs. Wilson scare you off the program?"

"Her? No." Then Mitch smiled grimly. "But be prepared. She recognizes Jackson as a troublemaker, because she's one herself. Don't take any chances for a while. Don't give her any ammunition to use against you. And *don't* leave Jackson alone in her part of town."

When Mitch signaled the end of the meeting by opening the door, Alex stepped aside and waited for Eli to approach. "Can we talk?"

"Sure." Once they were alone, Eli sat on the table, his feet propped on a chair seat, and asked, "What's up?"

"You said Cole has been a criminal practically from the cradle. What did you mean?"

"Just that. I imagine his father was using him in some sort of scam when he was still in diapers. The first time he got picked up by the police, he was six. Got caught shoplifting."

"A childish prank," Alex said tentatively, unable to imagine a six-year-old thief.

Eli shook his head. "Hungry brothers. He was stealing food because their parents weren't around. He was raised by the best con artists the great state of Texas ever produced, who occasionally went to jail and left the boys to fend for themselves. He and his brothers turned out just like them. I'm not sure they ever stood a chance at anything else."

How was your childhood? Alex had asked Cole last

week before his arraignment, and he'd given a careless answer. *Perfect. Two parents, five brothers, and a dog. We lived in a
great house, sat down to dinner together every night, and went to
church every Sunday.*

At the time, Alex had thought there was more—or
less—to the answer than it appeared, but he hadn't really
given it any thought since Cole entered his guilty plea.
"He told you all this? He didn't even want to give me his
date and place of birth."

"Nah. I don't think he would give a straight answer,
even if it was to his benefit. I've got friends all over the
place. Anything they don't know, isn't worth knowing."

Interesting. Apparently, there was a whole lot more to
Cole Jackson than anyone, with the possible exception of
Eli, was giving him credit for.

THE CLOSED SIGN HUNG ON SMALL WONDERS' unlocked door; Sophy was gone for the evening, and
Leanne was standing at the register, trying without much
success to balance the drawer. Ryan had had another un-
productive session with J.D., or so it seemed to her; her
mother had insisted on picking up Danny at day care that
afternoon, which meant Leanne would have to see her
twice in three days; she couldn't make the cash and checks
in the drawer add up to the total on the register tape; and
her head was pounding a rhythm that made her want to
crawl into a dark corner and stay.

And she still had dinner and a haunted-house-committee
meeting to face.

The door flew open, catching her off-guard, and Danny
stalked his way up the center aisle to the counter, his little
face like a storm cloud looking for a place to unleash its
fury. A few yards behind him was Phyllis, wearing pretty

much the same expression. Her stomach suddenly going queasy, Leanne managed a sickly smile. "Hi, guys. What's going on?"

Danny didn't slow his dogged steps until the counter was between him and his grandmother. He climbed onto the stool there, stood up, and folded his arms over his chest. "Grandma is mean and I don't like her no more."

"Whoa, honey—"

"This is all *your* fault," Phyllis said spitefully. "If you'd ever shown any taste whatsoever in choosing the men you sleep with—"

"Hey!" Leanne glared at her mother. "That topic isn't open for discussion, especially in present company."

Nostrils flaring and jaw muscles tensing, Phyllis averted her gaze to the ceiling, as if praying for patience, then looked at Leanne again. "You're right. We'll take that up later. Suffice it to say, though, that once again your abominable taste in men has come back to cause trouble."

Her abominable taste in men had *been* back nearly two weeks, and there was no doubt Phyllis had known before today. She wasn't much of a mother or a wife, but she was an exceptional gossip. Little things like the return of her daughter's ex-lover who stole a quarter of a million dollars registered big-time on her rumor radar.

Already fed up with Phyllis's interference, even though it had hardly begun, Leanne figured her best bet at getting a semi-accurate picture of events was Danny. Sliding her arm around his waist, she gave him a kiss. "I missed you today."

"I missed you, too, and I ain't ever goin' to Grandma's again."

"Why not, sweetie?"

" 'Cause she's mean and I don't like her."

Phyllis shook her finger warningly. "I warned you at the police station—"

The police— "What was my son doing at the police station?"

Too late, her mother realized what she'd said. She lifted her chin, straightened her shoulders, and pursed her mouth, while two spots burned in her cheeks. "I went to make a complaint with Mitch Walker and Judge Monroe. Naturally, I couldn't leave Danny waiting in the car, so I took him inside with me."

A chill of dread spreading through her, Leanne lifted Danny to the floor. "Why don't you run upstairs and see what Ryan's up to? You guys can figure out what you want for dinner, okay?"

"Okay." He chose a route that avoided his grandmother by a dozen feet on his way to the door. Of course, she couldn't take a hint.

"Come give Grandma a kiss."

"No!" he blurted, then dashed out the door, ran the few feet to the apartment door, and disappeared inside.

"That child is spoiled rotten," Phyllis declared when she turned back to Leanne. "One of these days you'll regret that you've let him get away with so much."

There was a part of Leanne that wanted to protest mightily. *She* didn't spoil Danny—she *loved* him. And if a four-year-old didn't deserve to be cut a little slack, who did? Besides, it was her mother who had bought him more toys than any three kids could play with, who took him out of day care on a whim, who let him get away with misbehaving.

But they'd had this argument before, and it wasn't worth the energy to repeat tonight. Phyllis believed what she wanted, and all the reality in the world wasn't going to sway her.

Instead, Leanne took a calming breath, wished for an

elephant-strength headache pill, and asked, "What were you complaining about to Mitch?"

With self-righteous indignation, Phyllis told her story. By the time she finished, Leanne was ready to skip the headache pill and go straight to a drug-induced coma. She pressed her fingertips hard against her temples, massaging for a moment, then dropped them. "Okay. So Cole was working in the park and Danny saw him."

"That criminal *grabbed* him. I had to take him away."

She didn't doubt the second part . . . any more than she believed the first. Cole wouldn't just grab a child, especially one whose shrew of a grandmother was yards away. Besides, Danny wouldn't have given him a chance—he would have leaped into his arms as soon as he saw him. He'd liked Cole from the beginning and had treated him to the same hero worship he lavished on Ryan. Like a lot of little boys, Danny wanted a father figure, and for a while, Cole had been it.

"Danny greeted this man whom he was very fond of, and you didn't like it, so you went to the police and filed a complaint?" In spite of her best efforts, Leanne's voice rose significantly by the end of her question.

"Of course I did. I told them I wanted him put in prison, and you know what they said? That he's serving his sentence, and that this program has great potential. Potential for disaster, I told them. I cannot believe the idiots we have working for us."

Leanne was appalled, but not for the reasons her mother expected. Phyllis didn't want Danny having any contact with Cole, so she'd tried to screw with his community service program? When she knew any problems with the program could result in his being sent to prison, after all? How mean-spirited could she be?

Of course, Leanne wanted him in prison, too, but that

was different. She had very good reasons for it. Her mother didn't even *know* the man.

And neither did she, whispered that sly voice she hated.

"All you had to do, Mother, was let them talk for a few minutes, then Danny would have gone off to play. There was no need to make such a huge incident of it."

"No need? *No need?*" Phyllis was close to sputtering. "So you're blaming *me*? You're saying it was *my* fault?"

Leanne's natural inclination was to say, *Of course not; no, you misunderstood*—anything to keep whatever little bit of peace they could manage. But she was flat-out of peace in every other part of her life. Why should her relationship with her mother be any different?

"Yes," she said calmly. "You overreacted. If you'd just stayed out of it, the whole thing would have been over in five minutes. Danny would have been happy, you could have spent the rest of the afternoon playing with him rather than at the police station, and you would have saved yourself some embarrassment."

Phyllis took a few steps back as if the impact of Leanne's words had been physical. Instead of a hot flush, her face was drained of color. Even the blue of her eyes was washed out and icy cold. "Embarrassment?" she echoed in a stiff voice. "I show concern for the safety of my grandchild and you think I embarrassed myself?"

"You didn't complain out of concern for Danny's safety. You wanted to cause trouble for Cole."

"You are so wrong." Tears welled in Phyllis's eyes, and she made a show of dashing them away before pressing her hand to her heart. "I don't understand how you can be this way, Leanne. Your father has never appreciated me, and your brother . . ." She made a dismissive gesture. "But *you*—you should see I've done the best I could for this family. I've sacrificed and struggled . . . and this is the thanks I get. You accuse me of being a troublemaker just because I'm trying to be the best grandmother my only grandchild could want."

Her mother should know better than to try to use her father and brother against her in an argument, Leanne thought dispassionately. Phyllis's life hadn't been any less happy than Earl's, and as for Chase . . . Leanne still hadn't forgiven her parents for the rift that had kept her brother away and out of contact for years.

Grimly she gathered the money spread on the counter into a bank bag, zipped it, and dropped it in her purse. She began flipping off lights, leaving her mother no choice but to move to the door or be left standing in the dark. There she opened the door and pointedly waited for Phyllis to walk through it. As soon as she did, Leanne locked up, then faced her. "You know, Mother, your poor-pitiful-me speech would go over a little better—with me, at least—if you would remember that Danny's *not* the only grandchild. You have a stepgranddaughter in Micahlyn and a foster grandson in Ryan."

Without a good-bye, she covered the distance to the apartment door in long strides, darted inside, and locked the door behind her, then gave a big sigh of relief.

The phone was ringing by the time she got to the top of the stairs. She heard Danny's voice—much closer to normal now, with no hint of the anger or the pout from earlier—then he bellowed. "Mom? Miss Maggie's on the phone!"

She mussed his hair as she took the phone from him, then dropped her purse on the kitchen counter. "Hey, Maggie May, I'm not already late for the meeting, am I?"

Maggie McKinney laughed. "No, you've still got an hour or so. But there's been a change in plans. Instead of my house, we're meeting at the Miller mansion. I hope that's okay."

Leanne inhaled deeply. "Oh, that's perfect." The perfect ending to the crappiest day she'd spent in a long time.

"I know it might be awkward, but Eli and his . . ."

"Convicts? Felons?"

"*Clients* are going to provide the labor for the haunted house, so it seems a good idea to get them involved right away. If you aren't up to this, I'm sure Miss Corinna can find something else for you to do, and we'll manage to get along without you."

It was an easy out, and Leanne wanted to grab it more than she could say. For reasons she couldn't even begin to put into words, she didn't. "Hey, my life has become a house of horrors lately. Let me share some of it with the rest of you."

"Are you sure?" Maggie's voice was rich with sympathy. She'd been through some tough times with her husband, Ross, a few years earlier. They'd grown so far apart that they'd forgotten why they had ever fallen in love, and had even reached the agreement that after the holidays, they would divorce and go their separate ways. But it had been Christmas, the season for miracles, and they had rediscovered their love and themselves instead.

Leanne didn't harbor such hope for herself. The first three men she'd fallen in love with had been happy to go their separate ways, and the fourth didn't even exist. It would take one heck of a miracle to turn Cole into the man he'd pretended to be.

"I'll be fine, Maggie. Don't worry. I'll see you in an hour."

After hanging up, she turned to greet the boys . . . and stared in surprise. They sat at the wicker table, set for three with paper plates, napkins, and soft drinks in cans. In the middle was a platter of sandwiches, along with two bowls of potato chips. To the left of each plate was a candy bar, sneaked from the Halloween stash she'd been collecting.

"You guys made dinner," she said, as pleased as she was surprised.

"And dessert," Danny said, holding up his candy bar.

"You said you had a meeting tonight." Ryan shrugged as if it was no big deal.

"Bless you both." She caught both of them in a hug, kissing first Danny, then Ryan. Whatever her feelings toward Greg, the rat who said so long when she told him she was pregnant, and Cole, the rat who'd sneaked out of her bed without so much as a so long, she was grateful to them both . . . for giving her a family.

Chapter Six

"WE'RE HAVING COMPANY THIS EVENING."
Cole glanced at Eli as he rinsed the last sinkful of dinner dishes and stacked each piece in the drainer. Since Eli didn't seem about to volunteer more and Murray was wiping down countertops in another dimension, Cole played the sucker. "Who?"

"I'm not sure. Maggie McKinney, for one. Holly Flynn, I think. It's the ladies in charge of the haunted house for the city's Halloween celebration. I told them we'd supply the labor, if they'd give us directions."

Was a haunted house the sort of thing Leanne would get involved with? Probably, he thought grimly, remembering the elaborate decorations in her shop windows. But surely having to deal with more than one Wilson woman a day qualified as cruel and unusual punishment. He would just spend the evening in his room.

"Maggie's bringing dessert," Eli went on. "I told her we would provide coffee and tea."

"Coffee? In this house? Hallelujah." Cole hung the dishtowel over the towel bar, then started toward the stairs.

"Where are you going?"

"To my room."

"But I just told you—"

"You didn't say I had to hang around."

"Yes, you do. And don't worry. It'll count toward your accumulated hours."

Cole scowled. If he had a reasonable sentence, like Murray, he might be eager to burn off another hour or three. But when he had approximately 4,968 hours left, it was tough to get excited about a few hours.

"Why don't you get the coffee started?" Eli suggested as the doorbell rang.

"With what?"

Eli pointed to a cabinet on his way out. When Cole opened the door, he found a coffeemaker, still in the box, and a one-pound can of coffee, along with a package of filters. As he washed the pot, he listened to the two new voices down the hall, both women, neither of them familiar.

He'd met a lot of people during his weeks in town, but he'd kept his distance from a specific few, including the two women Eli had mentioned. Their husbands, Ross McKinney and Tom Flynn, along with Lynda Foster, were the top dogs at McKinney Industries, were all richer than sin, and were, financially speaking, tougher than nails. Driven people like them didn't give up control of their money easily, and never would have let it walk away in his pocket.

"Smells good," Murray remarked as the aroma of brewing coffee filled the air. "I thought we would have to wait for Eli to reach legal age before we could have coffee again."

Cole glanced at him. That was only the second time he'd spoken since his morning arrival. If asked, Cole would have bet that he was totally unaware of everything going on around him, and he would have been wrong. That had happened before.

Murray breathed deeply again. "But don't you think it'd

taste better with a drop or two of Baileys Irish Cream? Or a dram of Irish whiskey, or maybe just a bit of Galliano." He closed his eyes and smiled dreamily as if he could taste it.

"Except for the occasional beer, I'm not much of a drinker."

The old man smiled at him. "That's okay. Except for the occasional DUI, I'm not much of a criminal."

He'd been called a criminal and much worse, but somehow the word had more of a bite to it when it came from a drunk. Everybody needed somebody to look down on, he guessed, and he was it for Murray. Didn't that feel great?

In the foyer, more voices joined the first two. He thought he recognized Kelsey Grayson's, and that was definitely Nolie Harper's, damn it, which just about guaranteed Leanne would be joining them. She and Nolie had been well on their way to becoming best friends even before Nolie had married her brother.

Despite Eli's decree, he considered disappearing upstairs. There wasn't a lock on his bedroom door, but there was plenty of heavy furniture that could be used to block it. What could the kid do?

Besides boot him out of the program and into the nearest penitentiary?

Wasn't that what he wanted? Wouldn't it beat the hell out of living in Bethlehem and seeing these people all the time? Besides, he'd been in prison before, once for ten months and another for sixteen. It wasn't so bad. Three meals a day, a place to sleep, and no expectations of a man beyond keeping his nose clean. He could handle that.

He couldn't handle *this*.

"Murray, Cole, come on in the dining room," Eli called.

Like a good obedient convict, Murray shuffled off. A knot growing in his gut, Cole stared at the coffeepot as the last drops splattered in with a gurgle. Sure, prison hadn't been so bad . . . not when he was nineteen or again when he was twenty-one. Not when he'd had the energy and optimism to carry him through.

He didn't have either anymore. He was tired of playing the games, of constantly moving, of always looking for the next mark. Most men his age were settled—had regular jobs, families or girlfriends or both. Their only thought when a cop pulled them over was, *Did I run that stop sign? Or, Was I speeding?* Winding up in jail wasn't even a possibility for most of them.

Neither was having to abandon their kids because the kids were better off without them.

"Cole?" Eli called.

Nah, he wasn't going to jeopardize his place in the program. Someday soon, one of his brothers was going to show up to rescue him. Escaping from this house would be a piece of cake. Escaping from the pen, he'd be lucky to survive, and tired or not, he was a survivor. All of the Jackson boys were.

He went down the hall and turned into the formal dining room as the doorbell rang. Eli glanced up. "Get that, will you?"

Thinking about that letter to his brothers he had yet to write, he pivoted, continued down the hall, and opened the door. He was wondering which brother would show up—Frank, maybe, since Cole's first stint in prison had been for saving his butt. Or Adam, who was the oldest and thought that put him in charge. Or maybe—

"Can I come in?"

Blinking, he cleared the thoughts from his head and stared at Leanne. She wore black pants, a rust-colored sweater that fell past her hips, black leather gloves, and the cold had turned her cheeks pink. Her lips were pink, too, a dark rosy shade, and her hair fell in straight lines to her shoulders. She looked incredible.

When he didn't move or speak, but just stood there like an idiot, she slipped through the half-open door, started down the hall, then turned back. For a moment she looked as if she thought better of her hesitation, then her mouth thinned. "I heard about your run-in with my mother today. I'm sorry."

A blast of cold rocketed through him, bringing him to his senses. He closed the door, then slid his hands in his hip pockets. "You can't apologize for her."

She made a gesture that might have been a rueful smile if it had fully formed. "Why not? This isn't the first time, and it won't be the last."

"She was concerned."

"No, she wasn't. She was . . . Phyllis being Phyllis." She gave a palms-up shrug that conveyed her frustration and helplessness fairly well. "Did she succeed in causing trouble?"

He shook his head, though it had certainly felt like trouble when a police officer had shown up at City Park, to invite him and Eli to a little sit-down with the chief. They'd put him in an empty room two doors down from the conference room and closed the door, but he'd still been able to hear Phyllis's side of the conversation. "I got the impression that her story didn't jibe with Danny's, while mine did. They did agree, though, that I'm too dangerous to let run loose among the decent folk in town."

He flooded the words with sarcasm, to hide the effort it took to say them. It was a sorry thing when average people found a man's mere presence offensive . . . and even sorrier when a man's character was so questionable that a hug from a little boy resulted in both of them being hauled in to the police station.

And he had no one to blame but himself.

He might as well have spoken that last thought aloud. She shrugged callously as she peeled off her gloves. "Hey, you steal people's life savings, you can't expect them to invite you into their homes."

He smiled. "I don't expect anything, sweetheart." It was better to expect nothing and be surprised, Owen said, than to hope and face certain disappointment.

Put off by his smile and/or answer, she turned on one booted heel and walked away.

Just as he'd expected.

He stood there a long time before following.

The dining room was second only to the living room in terms of size, and was the only one he and Ryan had never used during their residence. Seven-foot-tall china cabinets stood at each end, their shelves holding a small fortune in antique dishes, and the table stretched across the space between them. A large marble fireplace filled the third wall, with tall windows on the fourth. Two crystal chandeliers, small but worth a couple more small fortunes, illuminated the room. It was a great room for entertaining, Fred Miller had proudly pointed out.

The only entertaining Cole had done, was upstairs in his bedroom.

Leanne sat at the far end of the table, which left the near end for him. Eli sat on his left, Holly Flynn on the right. She gave him a look that was half-appreciative, half-disdainful—as if she despised him for ripping off her friends, but couldn't quite negate her feminine appreciation for his good looks. He gave her a cocky grin in return.

It wasn't conceit to say most women were attracted to him. Looks could be an important part of a con. If you've got 'em, use 'em, Owen had always advised. A man could empty a lonely widow's bank account with nothing more than a pretty face and a bit of charm. Cole was living proof of that.

He sat back, one ankle resting on the other knee, elbows braced on the carved wooden chair arms, hands folded across his belly, and listened to the discussion with half a mind. Name aside, the haunted house wasn't supposed to be scary to anyone over the age of two. It would serve Eli and his ladies' committee right if he covered himself with fake blood, attached a phony butcher knife to his chest, and staggered out of the dark corner to scare the bejeebers out of the kids. If he did, they'd think twice before making him work on their next Halloween project.

That thought stopped him cold. Serving his five thousand hours was likely to take two to two and a half years, Alex Thomas had said. He could be around for two more Halloweens. Jeez, he'd never stayed that long in one place in his life.

It was a scary thought . . . but he was leaving, remember? As soon as he wrote that damn letter, then it eventually caught up with one of the boys and they found time to come after him. Sooner or later—though a hell of a lot sooner than two and a half years—he was gonna blow this town.

And everyone in this room would go on with their lives as usual. Oh, they might pull the plug on Eli's program, but he was an ambitious kid, and Bethlehem took care of its own. He would find some other way to do good. No one would really notice Cole's leaving, except Leanne, and she would be happy to see the last of him.

And maybe her mother, who would also be overjoyed to see him disappear.

Ditto Ryan.

The women and Eli had been at the discussion for some time when Kelsey Grayson changed the subject. "Okay, you guys must be *way* stronger than me, but I can't sit here smelling that incredible aroma any longer. I need sugar, and I need it now."

Maggie McKinney lifted the lid of a pastry box and fanned the air toward Kelsey. "Are you hungry?" she asked innocently. "I'll warn you—it's a new recipe. A chocolate-cookie crust, cream-cheese filling, nuts, and whipped cream and cherries. The other is an Italian meringue with strawberries—from the freezer, I'm afraid, but still good."

Amid a chorus of groans, Eli spoke. "Cole—"

He stood up. "I'll get the plates." In less than a week, the kid had gotten damn good at ordering him around, and Cole had gotten pretty damn good at obeying.

He took plates and silverware into the dining room, then returned to the kitchen, to pour himself a cup of coffee. Standing at the sink, he gazed out the window into the dark yard while he drank it. When he heard footsteps, his fingers tightened around the mug, but he didn't turn to look—didn't even shift his gaze the few inches necessary to see the newcomer's reflection in the window.

The voice that broke the silence was soft, the accent not too different from the one he'd grown up with. "Wouldn't you like some dessert?" Nolie asked.

His glance was so brief that he caught just an impression of red hair, pale skin, and a green shirt. "Eli's got the sweet tooth around here."

"I noticed." She came closer and lifted one hand toward the cabinets. "Cups?"

He opened the door next to the sink, and she took one out, then poured herself some coffee. Instead of returning to the dining room, though, she leaned against the cabinet, partly facing him. "It hasn't been easy coming back, has it?"

The window reflected his mocking smile back at him. "It's punishment. It isn't supposed to be easy."

"At least now I have a better understanding of why you tried to talk me out of investing Micahlyn's money with you . . . sort of. I don't suppose you'd like to explain the finer details for me."

"What's left to know?"

"Why you warned me. You didn't do that with the others."

By the time she'd offered her thirty grand, he'd been feeling the first stirrings of a conscience—something Owen and Eloise had done their best to excise from their offspring. He hadn't known whether it was the town getting to him, or Leanne, or just life in general, but he hadn't wanted to rip off a twenty-something widow raising a kid by herself.

The attack of conscience hadn't lasted long. When he'd left town, her money had gone with him.

A few weeks later, he'd sent it back.

Since he didn't have an answer to offer, he shook his head instead and changed the subject. "I hear you and Chase got married."

Her smile was sweet and brightened her entire face. "Yeah. Hard to believe, isn't it?"

"Why do you say that?" As soon as the question was out, he remembered her insecurities last spring. Chase's ex-wife was beautiful and tiny and Nolie considered herself overweight and plain. Maybe she'd finally learned that smart men everywhere knew that curves were a lovely thing on a woman. "He's lucky to have you."

She blushed. "I'll tell him you said so."

Finally he faced her head-on. "No," he said quietly. "You probably shouldn't. He'll wonder why you were talking with the enemy."

"He doesn't—" She didn't complete the lie. Pushing

away from the counter, she started toward the hall, then returned. "Thank you."

"For what?"

"Returning the money."

Cole felt lower than scum. How could she thank him for giving back what he'd stolen? She should be damning him to hell . . . though she probably realized he was already there.

When he managed to respond, it was by breaking another Jackson rule. *Never apologize . . . unless it'll save your sorry ass.* "Nolie? I, uh . . . I'm sorry."

She nodded gravely, then walked away.

QUICKLY, QUIETLY, LEANNE DUCKED BACK INTO THE dining room as if she hadn't been on her way to the kitchen for a drink. Leaning against the paneled wall, she let Cole's last words repeat in her mind. *I'm sorry, I'm sorry, I'm sorry.*

Cole Jackson had apologized to one of his victims, and had even sounded as if he meant it. Would wonders never cease?

Of course, the key phrase there was *sounded as if.* Anyone could fake sincerity, and he was much better at it than most. His entire life was nothing but lies and manipulation, telling people what they wanted to hear, pretending to be what they wanted him to be. If he was truly sorry, if he had even one regret about everything he'd done, he would be making that apology to Ryan. He would be on his knees, begging his son's forgiveness. Instead, he hadn't even tried to see him.

A fact for which he didn't *deserve* forgiveness.

• • •

THE SMACK OF WOOD AGAINST WOOD ECHOED sharply through the cold night. Sophy directed a dry look toward Gloria, who was caressing the polished gavel she'd been toting around since last week's court session. Heavens, she'd been a judge for ten minutes. Just how long would they have to endure her judicial behavior?

"This meeting is now in session," Gloria announced. Her formal declaration was diminished, however, by her tinkling laugh. "The court recognizes Sophy."

She was about to bang the gavel again when Sophy caught hold of it. "Don't do that." As an afterthought, she added, "Please."

"But it has such a nice authoritarian sound to it." Even as she protested, Gloria released the gavel and Sophy laid it beside her on the railing.

They were gathered at the bandstand in the middle of the square. Sophy sat on one section of railing, Eli on another, and Gloria stood midway between them. A million stars twinkled overhead, and Sophy took her time gazing at each one. They were lovely and reassuring—a constant in a life that often didn't seem to have many.

Gloria's great sigh broke the stillness. "Louanne and Jack have a lot to overcome, you know. This is gonna be a tough one."

"You always say that," Sophy answered automatically.

"And I'm always right."

"Don't worry, Gloria." Eli smugly patted her shoulder. "You've got me to help."

Sophy didn't even try to restrain her delicate little snort. "Some help you've been—forcing Leanne and Cole together at Harry's."

"They've got to actually spend time together in order to resolve their problems."

His condescension grated on her nerves. "Of course they do . . . *when they're ready.* They weren't ready Tuesday."

There was nothing delicate or little about his snort. "By the time *you* pronounce them ready, they'll be too old to care."

Her fingers gripping the railing tightly enough to vaporize it, Sophy counted to ten, then added another ten. By the time she reached forty-seven, she acknowledged it wasn't working and gave up. Faking a sugary sweet tone, she asked, "If you're such an expert in these matters, why did they send you to Gloria and me for training?"

Eli jumped to the floor and spun around to face her. The outrage in his expression made her smile that much bigger. *"Training?"* His voice cracked, and he tried again, stronger this time. *"Training?!* They sent me here to *help,* because they didn't think you and Gloria could handle it this time!"

"In your dreams," she retorted. "We've been getting along just fine without your *help* for . . . well, forever."

"Yeah, right. When I showed up, you didn't even have a plan. *I* had to come up with the whole community service thing *and* give Mr. Miller the idea to let us use his mother's house."

Sophy couldn't argue with that. Of course, she and Gloria would have handled things just fine without his interference. Neither of them was really so big on plans. They liked to let things unfold more or less naturally, with a gentle nudge here, maybe the tiniest of pushes there. It had always worked before, and there was no reason to think this situation was any different.

"Anyone can come up with a good idea every millennium or so," she said airily. "The bottom line is . . . we don't need you."

He changed tacks then, the arrogance disappearing, the

smugness easing away, and smiled a most charming smile. If she didn't know better, she would think that even he, the most conceited guardian that ever existed, had a few redeeming qualities.

"You do that almost as well as Cole does," she remarked, and wondered if that was why they'd been cursed—er, graced with his presence. All guardians had the ability to transform themselves in one way or another. Noelle, who'd watched over Bethlehem before Sophy and Gloria, had once disguised herself as a geeky male clerk, complete with oiled hair, spectacles, and a bow tie, and no one had ever suspected a thing. That was before she'd fallen in love with Gabe Rawlins, one of her charges, and had traded her angel wings for womanhood.

But Eli seemed more skilled at it than most. Why, he could almost make himself appear likable.

Almost.

"Aw, you'd hurt my feelings . . . if I cared." He chucked her under the chin as if she were five years old. "Pay close attention on this one, Soph, and I'll show you how to do it *right.*"

Her temper surged, but before she could say anything, he disappeared. One instant he was there, the next he wasn't.

"Such a nice boy," Gloria said with a satisfied smile.

Because she suspected that *nice boy* was still around even though they couldn't see him, Sophy limited her response to another snort. "We'd best be going."

Gloria vanished, too, but Sophy took her time, fading out a little at a time. Just before she disappeared into nothingness, she saw the gavel rise from the railing, then smack down with a hard *cra-ack.*

"Court is adjourned," Gloria's disembodied voice intoned,

then her sweet laugh sounded like distant chimes. "Oh, I like doing that!"

SINCE SATURDAY WAS HER DAY OFF, LEANNE SLEPT IN late that morning, making it all the way to nine-fifteen before the creak of the bedroom door opening woke her. She kept her eyes closed and breathing steady, hoping whoever had wandered in would wander right back out. The ploy didn't work.

A shadow fell across her face just before a small finger-tip touched her eyelid. "I can see your eyes moving inside," Danny remarked, then he climbed onto the bed.

She lifted the sheet for him to scoot under, then cuddled him close. "Mornin', sweetie pie."

"Mornin', sleepyhead."

"What are you doing?"

"I'm bored."

She stifled a yawn. "What would make you un-bored?"

"I dunno. But I'm hungry, too. Can we go to Harry's for breakfast?"

"Sure. Why not?"

"But Ryan can't go. He'll have to have cold cereal, but without milk, 'cause I just drunk the last of it."

Ouch. That was a sure sign of trouble, since Danny would stick to Ryan like cockleburs to socks if he could, *and* since Ryan liked milk a lot and Danny drank it only under threat. Hey, hero worship only went so far.

She rolled onto her back, shoved her hair from her face, then stuffed an extra pillow under her head. "Leaving Ryan behind while we went out wouldn't be nice. How would you feel if we did that to you?"

"You go see Dr. J.D. without me."

Rather than try to explain, she tickled him. "Oh, so you want to go to the *doctor*? I thought you hated doctors."

"I do, but not Dr. J.D. I like playing with Gracie and Noah. They got cats, and their neighbor gots horses, and sometimes we go to the creek and wade."

"But the kids don't go to the office with him, and neither do the cats or the horses. It's just Dr. J.D. in a room with a desk and chairs."

"Oh." He rubbed his nose while considering that, then shrugged. "You know why Ryan can't go to breakfast with us? 'Cause I told him, let's go see your dad, and he said no, he ain't his dad and he don't want to see 'im. And I said *I* seen him the other day and he is, too, his dad, and I was gonna ask you if he could come spend the night like he used to, and Ryan said a bad word."

A curious sensation passed through Leanne at the mention of Cole spending the night. She ignored it and focused tightly on the conversation. "So he can't go because you're mad at him?"

"No, 'cause he's not here. He ran off and banged the door real hard after he said the bad word, and I thought he prob'ly waked you, so I come to see."

Throwing back the covers, Leanne disentangled herself from Danny and jumped to her feet. She grabbed jeans and a sweatshirt from the closet, scooped underwear and socks from the bureau, and hustled across the hall to the bathroom. "Did you look out the window to see which way he went?" she called through the barely-opened door.

"Nope."

Dressing in record time, she returned to the bedroom and sat down, to put on her shoes. "Get dressed, sweetie. We've got to look for him."

"After we go to Harry's?"

"Now." She lifted him to the floor, then swatted his

bottom when he dawdled. She brushed her teeth and combed her hair, then helped him with his shoes. He'd chosen black sweat pants and a pumpkin-orange Halloween sweatshirt with a glow-in-the-dark jack-o'-lantern.

As they clomped down the stairs, she said a silent prayer that they would step outside and the first thing they would see was Ryan walking down the sidewalk, sitting on a bench in the square, or holding up traffic in the middle of the street. But he wasn't among the people on the sidewalk, the benches in the square were empty, and traffic was moving along as it always did.

So where was he? Where would an angry kid go when he was mad at the world?

He wasn't throwing rocks at the Miller mansion. That was a good sign. And he hadn't hot-wired her SUV and gone for a joyride. Also a good sign.

They walked the block to Main Street, but saw no sign of him in either direction. He wasn't in Harry's, and no one there had seen him. He wasn't at the library, either, though the librarian promised to call Leanne's cell phone if he showed up. They returned to get her truck and set out to cover the entire town.

And if they didn't find him?

She would call the police. In the meantime, she was trying not to panic . . . yet. Bethlehem was a safe place. Bad things just didn't happen there.

But kids occasionally ran away. J.D.'s son, Caleb, had done it twice. Heaven knew, if anyone had a reason to run away and never stop, it was Ryan.

They had covered more than two-thirds of the town and were sitting at a STOP sign when Danny casually said, "There's Ryan," as if they hadn't spent the past hour searching for him.

"Where?" she demanded, and he pointed toward the

veterinary clinic across the street. Sure enough, in the yard at the back stood Ryan, holding a leash attached to a Great Dane doing his business.

She pulled into the vet's parking lot and ordered Danny to stay put. Just to be safe, she activated the child safety locks, then marched around to the back of the building. "Ryan Matthew Jackson, what are you doing running off like that?"

He startled when he heard her voice, but quickly hid it behind a resentful look. "Does it matter?"

"Oh, no. I *like* starting off my Saturdays by searching all over town for one of my kids." The Great Dane, practically big enough for her to ride, came over to sniff, starting at her feet and working his way up. When he'd gone far enough, she pushed his head away and scratched under his chin. "Be a nice brute," she admonished, then turned a stern look on Ryan again. "Whose dog is this?"

He shrugged.

"Where did you get him?"

This time the shrug was accompanied by a jerk of his head toward the clinic.

"I'm a little thickheaded before I've had my coffee. Clear things up for me. You got mad at Danny and you went out without permission and . . . ended up over here, taking a giant dog to the bathroom?"

Rolling his eyes as if she was too dense to believe, he hunched his skinny shoulders. "She was takin' the dogs out one at a time—"

"She who?"

"I don't know. Some lady. And I was lookin' at 'em, and we got to talkin' and she said I could help with 'em if I wanted."

Leanne studied him while she thought. Presumably, *she* was Dr. Collins, the vet, or one of her staff. Also presumably,

Dr. Collins had no clue that Ryan had sneaked out without permission or she would have made him phone home before turning any of her patients over to him. And—no presuming about it—Ryan liked animals.

"If you're done yelling, I need to take him in and get the next one."

"Oh, child, I haven't begun to yell," she warned him in a mild tone. "Go on. I'll wait." While he was gone, she stepped to the corner of the building, to check on Danny. On his knees in her seat, he was pretending to drive. He took his hand off the steering wheel long enough to wave at her, then immediately jerked the wheel as if he'd drifted into oncoming traffic.

Shaking her head, she returned to find Ryan coming down the steps with a smaller dog—though if his feet were anything to judge by, he wouldn't be that way long. The animal was so happy to be outside that he seemed to have forgotten what he'd come out for, sniffing everything and everywhere.

"Cute dog," she murmured.

"His name is Jerome. He's a 'found' dog. That means he's a stray. She's keeping 'im until she can find a home for 'im."

Leanne crouched to pet the dog. "Did you get lost, puppy, or did someone—" Abruptly she broke off, then stole a glance at Ryan. If he realized what she'd been about to say—*or did someone throw you away?*—he gave no sign of it.

Rising again, she leaned against the stoop. "I didn't know you liked dogs."

He shrugged as if it were inconsequential.

"Have you ever had one?"

"Nah. We never had the money or the space."

She looked from him to the puppy again, trying to stave off the idea forming in her mind, but failing miserably. They didn't really have the space, either, especially for this creature who looked like he might rival the Great Dane in size once he reached his full potential. And she didn't want to imagine what his feet would do to the wood floors she loved.

But, sheesh, every kid needed a dog. She'd had one when she was growing up—a dachshund named Barney who'd hated to see her leave, greeted her ecstatically every time she'd walked into the room, and slept with her at night. And she'd always planned to get Danny a dog. She'd just thought she would wait until he was old enough to be responsible for a pet . . . and she'd planned on something small and cuddly like Barney. Something that didn't already weigh as much as Danny.

After the dog finally remembered the purpose for his trip outside, Ryan sat down on the steps and the animal crawled into his lap, licking his face. Ryan scratched behind his ears and made the dog's entire body quiver so much he slid off his feet, which made Ryan laugh.

When was the last time she'd heard Ryan laugh?

Better question—*had* she ever heard Ryan laugh?

"Are there any more animals inside, waiting for you to give them a potty break?"

"A couple."

"Why don't you go ahead and do that? I want to talk to Dr. Collins for a moment."

He gave her a wary look, then stood up and carried the dog inside. She followed him, bypassing the kennels in search of the vet. A few minutes later, she and Dr. Collins joined him out back, with Jerome on a leash again.

"I already brought him out," Ryan said.

"I know." Dr. Collins bent to cup the dog's face in her hands. "You're a good boy, Jerome, and you be good for your new people, okay?" After pressing a kiss to the top of the dog's head, she straightened, then offered to trade leashes with Ryan.

He was confused. "You want me to take him back in?"

"I want you to take him home. Jerome is now officially a Wilson. Take good care of him."

As the doctor returned inside with the other dog, Ryan clutched Jerome's leash and stared at Leanne. "Really? You got Danny a dog?"

She slid her arm around his shoulders. "I got *us* a dog. He belongs to all of us—or, more likely, we now belong to him. Is that okay?"

"Yeah," he murmured. "That's okay."

Despite his subdued response, she knew it was better than okay when they reached the truck and he lifted the dog into the backseat. For a moment, he held the puppy close, and a single tear seeped from the corner of his eye.

Yep, it was way better than okay. In fact, Danny said it best in his most awed voice. "Wow, Mom, a dog! Woohoo!"

Chapter Seven

COLE WAS LYING ON HIS BACK, HANDS FOLDED under his head, when Eli rapped at the door. "You awake?"

"Yeah."

Opening the door, the kid stuck his head inside. "We're leaving for church in an hour. That'll give you time for a shower and breakfast."

"Uh, gee, you guys go without me."

"Uh, gee, that's not your call. Come on. Get moving."

Cole sent an unamused look his way, but Eli was already down the hall, knocking at Murray's door. Frowning, he rolled onto his side and stared out the window. It was dreary, gray, and threatening rain—a perfect day for doing nothing. Unfortunately, if Eli was insisting on church this morning, he probably had some kind of work lined up for the afternoon.

He wondered if this counted toward his time served.

He wasn't grousing because he really minded church. He had a fine appreciation for old gospel tunes—"How Great Thou Art," "In the Garden," "Will the Circle Be Unbroken"—and there was something appealing about the acceptance a person could find in a good church. He and Ryan had attended services in Bethlehem several times last spring, but that had been part of the job.

Now it was part of his punishment.

He showered and dressed in some of his investment-scam clothes—just about the only thing he'd been allowed to keep after his arrest. The things he'd stolen had been returned to their rightful owners, the laptop was probably tagged as evidence and in police custody, and his cash was locked up somewhere. After all, he needed clothes, but not the rest.

After eating breakfast, he climbed into the truck with Eli and Murray. The older man was humming a tune as Eli backed out of the driveway, and before they'd gone a block, the kid was singing it with him. He had a good voice: strong, clear, and rich.

Cole's brother, Bret, had a voice like that, but he wouldn't be caught dead singing "Amazing Grace," unless it was part of a con. Frank had pulled one of those a few years back, involving a tent revival and a handful of small towns in east Texas, and had made a pretty good haul. When he'd gotten caught, he had repented and asked for forgiveness . . . and gotten it. The folks he'd scammed, refused to prosecute.

Frank had always had an incredible streak of luck.

They arrived at the church a few minutes after the service had begun. Eli led the way into the last pew on the left, then decided for some reason to change places with Cole, then again with Murray. As he started to sit down, Cole saw the reason—the kid had wanted to be out of striking distance when Cole realized he would be sitting a mere two feet from Leanne.

He glowered at Eli as he slowly sat down, but the kid refused to look his way.

"I thought I felt the walls trembling," she whispered as the pastor instructed everyone to rise for a prayer.

As soon as that was over and they were seated again, he murmured, "I go to church."

"Casing the joint doesn't count. Remind me to tell the deacon to keep an eye on the offering plate."

"I've never stolen from a church," he retorted. That was another piece of advice from Owen. *Never steal from a church. That's what television evangelists are for.*

His gaze moved around the large room, scanning familiar faces, looking for the most familiar of all. He saw Leanne's mother—wasn't it wrong to give a man the evil eye in church?—and her father, with more distance between them than separated Cole from Leanne. He spotted Danny, sitting near the front with Miss Agatha and her husband, Bud Grayson. He saw a lot of people who had considered him a friend . . . but not Ryan.

Leanne leaned a few inches closer. "Ryan's helping out in the nursery this morning. All the older kids take turns."

"I wasn't looking for him." Inwardly he grimaced. If giving the evil eye in church was wrong, then lying certainly was. He'd be lucky if the walls didn't tremble, then fall on him.

The pastor's sermon was on forgiveness. Since that was something he neither wanted nor expected, he listened to little and thought about Leanne a lot. She wore a navy-blue dress that fitted as if it had been sewn onto her body. Her heels were black, and so was the jacket hanging over the back of the pew. Her hair was pulled back and tied with a black bow that didn't stop wispy strands from falling loose on her neck, tempting him to stroke them back into place. Of course, if he tried, if the Lord didn't strike him down, she would.

She looked lovely. Elegant. Like a doting mother and a

successful businesswoman. She looked strong and capable and soft and amazingly feminine. She looked . . .

Like the best time he'd ever had.

He hadn't meant to get involved with her when he'd come to Bethlehem. When he'd discovered that was easier said than done, he'd backed off on his restrictions enough to allow himself an affair with her, as long as an affair was all. That had been easier said than done, too. While he'd liked her from the beginning, at some point she'd become too important. No matter how he tried, he hadn't been able to walk away from her . . . until that last day.

At least he didn't have to worry about getting too involved this time. She wouldn't allow it, and even if she would, Eli was a pretty good guard dog. He didn't do nightly bed checks—yet—but he also didn't let Cole leave the house alone. Cole was pretty certain if he asked permission to go across the street and have wild, hot sex with Leanne, the kid would say no.

Thinking about sex in church was probably even worse than lying. He glanced over his shoulder to ensure that the stone walls were still straight and solid.

The minutes crawled past until, after one final prayer, the service was over. Cole's first impulse was to jump and run. Eli and Murray showed no inclination to do either.

"Gee, you survived," Leanne said, sliding forward on the bench and slipping into her jacket. "No bolts of lightning, no columns of fire and brimstone."

"Disappointed?"

She shrugged, an easy, fluid movement that made his breath catch. When the moment passed, he shrugged, too. "I told you—I'm not a total stranger to church."

"Too bad you never learned anything there."

He watched her pick up her Bible and a larger, brightly

colored kids' Bible, then find her keys in her bag. "Why are you talking to me?"

She seemed vaguely surprised by the question. "I've never refused to talk to you."

That was true, except for the times he'd seen her in the courtroom. Both times his actions had been designed to anger her into speechlessness, and both times there'd been little opportunity to see how well he'd succeeded.

She glanced at her watch, settled comfortably on the bench, and crossed her legs. Waiting for Ryan, he guessed, assuming that parents had to pick up their kids before the nursery workers could leave.

"Did you grow up in church?" Her tone was polite, a few shades too cool for friendly. Like someone just making conversation, but not really caring what was said.

"Oh, yeah, sure." The closest he'd gotten to church as a kid was when times were rough and the family was on the receiving end of a donation. He'd hated having people feeling sorry for them, hated being given food, clothes, and Christmas presents because Owen was in jail or Eloise had disappeared again. Given a choice between stealing and the pity and smug self-righteousness that accompanied most charity, he would choose stealing anytime.

"Oh, yeah, sure," Leanne repeated. "That's a lie, isn't it?"

He turned on his best used-car-salesman smile. "You wound me, sweetheart."

Her gaze darkened and the line of her jaw turned taut. "Knock it off. If you can't quit playing some part long enough to answer a simple question, then forget it." Chin raised, she got to her feet, stepped into the outside aisle, then headed for the door.

Cole stared hard at the wall. It was a sad day when a man couldn't smile at a woman without making her mad.

Hell, what did she expect? For him to sit there and agree face-to-face that he was a liar?

It probably would have been the first bit of honesty he'd given her.

The exchange hadn't gone unnoticed. Beside him, Murray leaned closer and said confidentially, "Women don't like phonies."

Cole grinned sardonically. "You're wrong, Murray. Women like me, and I am, first and foremost, a phony."

The old man studied him before slowly smiling. "They say you're the best at conning people. But you know who you've conned the best? Yourself. You don't have a clue who or what you are. Is it any wonder Leanne doesn't know, either?"

He was wrong, Cole thought, as Eli finally ended his conversation with a tall, white-haired woman and herded them toward the double doors at the back. He had no illusions about himself. He was a thief. A liar. A con artist. He was untrustworthy, undependable, and dishonest. He'd known wealth and extreme poverty, and he preferred wealth, any way he could get it. He'd done the best he could with Ryan, but it hadn't been good enough. Leaving him behind had been the hardest thing he'd ever done, and he was going to pay for it for the rest of his rotten life.

And that was okay, as long as Ryan didn't have to pay, too.

Getting out the church doors was only half the battle. They were stopped a half-dozen times on the way to Eli's truck to talk. Everyone greeted Eli and Murray, but few acknowledged Cole. Alex Thomas did, and Nathan Bishop and Maggie McKinney. Kelsey Grayson gave him a speculative look as she passed, and he wondered if the reason was personal or professional. She and her husband had invested money in his scheme, and, being the only social worker in town besides Eli, she was overseeing Ryan's foster care. Maybe she wanted to place the kid in a permanent home. Maybe she wanted to fix it so Cole could never see him again. It was no less than Ryan deserved.

And no more than Cole deserved.

Finally they reached the pickup, parked near the back of the church. He was waiting for Murray to climb in, then slide to the middle of the bench seat, when he became aware of a hard, unyielding gaze. He glanced up, then saw Ryan leaning against the building. He wore black pants and a white shirt, the sleeves rolled up to his elbows. He'd jammed his hands in his pockets, and was looking at Cole with pure disgust.

"Ryan."

He thought he'd spoken the name aloud, but it lacked sound. Numbly he took a few steps away from the truck and toward the church, then faltered to a stop when Ryan spun around and disappeared behind it.

The ache as he returned to the pickup was sharp and raw and, for a moment, it robbed him of breath. He climbed in beside Murray and slammed the door, then stared at the place where Ryan had stood, as if he could somehow bring him back. Of course, he couldn't.

And that, too, was no more than he deserved.

AFTER WORK TUESDAY, LEANNE CHANGED INTO JEANS and a sweatshirt, then found Ryan in his usual spot—stretched out on the sofa with a book. Jerome lay curled on his stomach as if he were normal puppy size, grunting softly as Ryan scratched behind his ears. "You two look comfortable."

Ryan glanced up. "He's just trying to escape all the noise from the video games in Danny's room."

She thought of the responses she should make—*It's your room, too* and *Jerome's lying with you because he likes you* and *You're part of this family whether you like it or not*—but instead took the easy way out as she sat on the coffee table. "Listen, I've got a committee meeting this evening. We're going to start decorating the haunted house over at the hospital. My dad's picking up Danny for dinner and a movie. You're welcome to go with me or with them, but I'll warn you— your father is working on this project, too."

Something flickered in his eyes at the mention of Cole, but was gone again too quickly for her to identify. "Can't I just stay here?"

"No."

"I'm *twelve* years old."

"I know. But them's your choices, partner—Dad and Danny or your father and me." Inside she winced. That sounded so . . . normal, as if she and Cole were a pair, which they'd never been, not for real. She'd been a fool, falling for his act, offering herself to be used. Who could blame him for taking her up on the offer?

"But what about Jerome? He's never been home alone at night."

"He'll go in his kennel and be just fine." On Dr. Collins's advice, one of her first purchases had been a jumbo-sized traveling kennel that occupied a quiet corner of the living room. When they were gone, that was where Jerome stayed—and her furniture stayed unsoiled and unchewed.

At least, he'd stayed there the few hours they were at church on Sunday. And for an hour or so Monday morn- ing before she'd decided to see how he liked the shop. And for an hour or so Tuesday morning before she'd decided she liked the shop better with him in it. Hey, she'd taken

Danny to work with her when he was a baby. Why not Jerome?

"The movie at the theater is for kids," Ryan announced in a superior tone.

"How convenient since"—she faked a huge surprised look—"*you're* a *kid.*"

For a long time he stared at the puppy, then asked in a low voice, "Doesn't it bother you—being around him?"

Oh, jeez. This was a discussion she didn't want to have, with him or herself. It demanded too close a look—too honest a look—at what she was feeling. Was she getting used to having Cole around? Getting over him? Getting to know him, albeit in some very small, minuscule, insignificant way? Was she still attracted to him? Letting lust overcome disgust? Still thinking, in that incredibly moronic part of herself, that *just maybe* he could be Mr. Right, after all?

She preferred to believe she was getting over him. When she'd first opened the shop more than eight years ago, Melissa Thomas had sent her flowers with an inspirational message—*If you can dream it, you can do it.* It had taken a lot of dreaming to get Small Wonders into the black and keep it there, but she'd succeeded. That first year or two had been on the lean side, but the shop had supported her, and later Danny, then Ryan, comfortably ever since.

So now she was dreaming of getting over Cole. She intended to be outrageously successful at it, too.

"You know, Ryan, we can't control the world around us. There are always going to be people we don't like or can't get along with, so it's up to us to learn how to manage in spite of them. Would I be happier if your father didn't live across the street? You bet. Am I going to let it make me crazy that he does live across the street? No way."

"But you have to see him. He's hangin' around town, workin' on the spook house, even showing up at church."

"How do you know he was at church?" The parents had been slow picking up their kids at the nursery Sunday. By the time Ryan had met her and Danny in the parking lot, Cole had been long gone—or so she'd thought. "Did you see him?"

He dropped his chin and mumbled something she took as a yes.

"Did he say anything?"

Ryan's shoulders lifted, then dropped. "He just looked at me like . . . like . . . I don't know. When he acted like he was gonna come over, I took off." Finally he met her gaze, his expression both defiant and vulnerable.

Leanne clasped his hand in hers. "It's all right to talk to him, Ryan."

His jaw jutted forward and he jerked his hand back, on the pretext of needing to scratch the dog. "I don't wanna."

"That's all right, too. But you know, sweetie, this is part of living in a small town. We're going to run into people all the time, and we just have to deal with it."

The doorbell rang—one long and two shorts—and she glanced toward the hall. "Danny, let your grandfather in!"

A moment later he zoomed past, then thundered down the stairs.

"So what's it gonna be? Dinner and a movie or work?"

"Dinner and a movie," Ryan said with a sigh, closing his book.

She ruffled his hair affectionately. "Good choice. Now make sure you don't enjoy that kids' movie *too* much. Run Jerome outside and let him pee, will you, then put him in the kennel."

As they both got up, her father followed Danny through the kitchen and into the living room. He greeted Ryan with the same affection he showed Danny and Micahlyn, then hugged Leanne. "Call your mother, princess."

"Call her what?"

He tweaked her nose with cold fingers. "She's been hell on wheels ever since your run-in with her last week."

"Ah, yes, her run-in with me, which was also part of her bigger run-in with Cole, Mitch Walker, Judge Monroe . . . Besides, Daddy, she's always hell on wheels."

Earl Wilson's only response was a shrug. His relationship with her mother was the great Wilson family mystery. She, Chase, and Nolie—in addition to a fair portion of the town—had spent hours speculating on why he stayed with Phyllis. There was certainly no affection between them, the kids were long grown, and it didn't seem possible they could ever have loved each other. He deserved better than he was getting, but he didn't seem to mind.

"How's Ryan?" he asked, dropping his voice even though both boys were outside with the dog.

She made a so-so gesture in the air. "He's seeing J.D. Grayson."

"Good. Has he seen his old man?"

"Just once. They didn't talk."

"Want me to have a talk with him?"

"Ryan?"

It was Earl's turn to shake his head. "Jackson. Explain to him that any man worthy of the name shouldn't lose touch with his own son."

Leanne's throat clogged. He was speaking from experience. The sixteen-year silence between him and Chase had finally ended a few months earlier. They still weren't best buddies, and there was a lot of wariness on both sides, but they were trying. If Cole would try . . .

"I'll keep that in mind," she said as the boys and Jerome raced up the stairs and into the room. "Right now you've got two hungry little goblins to feed. Thanks a bunch for helping me out." Rising onto her toes, she kissed his cheek.

"What's a grandpa for? Have fun, princess."

Once they were gone, she stood at the kitchen counter and ate a sandwich, washed it down with a Pepsi, then grabbed her coat and gloves and headed for the hospital grounds.

The building they were using for the haunted house was at the back edge of hospital property. More properly, she guessed, it was an equipment barn, though there was rarely any equipment inside. This was where they turned out every year to work on the hospital's float for the Christmas parade, a project she donated time to, since Small Wonders didn't have a float of its own. Besides, the float-decorating always turned into one great party.

She parked on the shoulder of the dirt road that circled behind the hospital to the barn. Nolie's station wagon was on one side, Kelsey's van on the other, along with a half-dozen other vehicles.

Including Eli's old green pickup.

She walked quickly to the barn, then stopped just outside the light spilling out the open doors. Rubbing her arms briskly, she took a few deep breaths and, for one wild moment, considered returning home and claiming illness. The sudden onset of an allergic reaction to convicted felons.

More likely, the sudden onset of a severe case of yellow-belly.

She forced herself through the broad double doors and into the brightly lit garage. "Why in the world are the doors open?" she asked as if every cell in her body wasn't aware of Cole on a ladder near the back of the room. "Haven't you realized it's *cold* outside?"

"Honey, it's cold in here, too," Holly Flynn replied. She was standing next to a second ladder with streams of orange and black crepe paper draped around her neck.

Cole looked Leanne's way—she could feel the impact of his gaze—but she refused to acknowledge him. Instead, she zipped her jacket, then shoved her hands in her pockets and looked around. Bales of hay, donated by Nolie's feed store, were stacked outside the doors, and a variety of lights, ranging from small spots to strings of tiny orange bulbs, was spread around. There was crepe paper, colored cellophane, yards of black fabric, fake cobwebs, and stuffed witches, goblins, and cats, along with one very realistic-looking skeleton. She sidled close to the skeleton, wearing a black top hat and bow tie, and asked, "Hey, big boy, you come here often?"

"I think I used to date that guy," Holly said.

That brought a laugh from Maggie. "You used to date every guy in town."

Holly had been Bethlehem's original party girl . . . until Tom Flynn had decided to take a wife. Their courtship had been more public than any other Leanne had ever seen, a fact which Holly had publicly bemoaned but secretly liked, Leanne thought. What woman wouldn't like having a man make it clear that he was crazy about her?

Unlike Cole, who'd rarely been seen in public with *her*.

Of course, he hadn't been crazy about her, either.

And she'd been just plain crazy.

Following Maggie's rough sketches, they blocked off a winding trail through the barn with the hay bales, then began setting up the scenes. Stuffed bats and a vampire would fly through the air from one side of the barn to the other, along with a witch on a broom, swirling in circles while a tape of creaking doors, screams, and witchly cackles played. The skeleton would be rigged to rise from its half-buried coffin and dance a merry jig and, her favorite, three grotesque witches—Holly, Maggie, and Emilie Bishop—would stoop around a giant cauldron while another skeleton "boiled" inside, courtesy of water and dry ice.

It was gonna be great, Leanne thought as she started her first job—using a chisel to turn a slab of old barn wood into an ancient tombstone. She'd completed about two-thirds of the inscription when a quiet voice spoke behind her.

"You people are weird."

She concentrated on keeping her hand steady and not looking at Cole. She knew he would be standing too close, and her traitorous mind would immediately leap to other times he'd been too close—so close she hadn't known where either of them stopped and the other began. So close she'd thought they would be that way forever. So close she'd fallen right into the dream trap.

If you can dream it, you can do it.

Wrong, Melissa, she thought flippantly. Some dreams were fulfilled. Others were shattered.

Just like some hearts.

"Why do you say that?" She was proud of the fact that her voice didn't quaver one bit.

"A town named Bethlehem, as in the Christmas song, getting all excited about witches and goblins and ghouls? That doesn't strike you as odd?"

She bent over, putting a bit of distance between them—necessary so she could get the R.I.P. just right. Not because the hairs on the back of her neck were standing on end and her skin was tingling. "It's all in fun."

"Some towns don't even allow Halloween celebrations."

"Some towns don't allow convicts to take up residence right in their midst."

Silence radiated from him for a moment. When he did speak, his voice was stiff, tinged with bitterness. "Yeah. I'll have to include that in my research before my next scam."

Finally she looked at him, and he *was* too close. She compensated by moving to the opposite side of the work-table that held her headstone. "I think part of the purpose of Eli's program is to ensure that there's not a next time."

"But there's always another fool waiting to part with his money. How am I supposed to resist such easy pickin's?"

"I don't know. By developing a conscience?"

"A conscience is a bad thing to have in my line of work. It'll just get you into trouble."

Gripping the chisel too tightly, she studied him. His blond hair was mussed, his faded jeans fitted snugly to his narrow hips and long legs, and his sweatshirt was too big. If she didn't know better, she would think he looked adorable. Handsome. Sexy. Dangerous to a woman's heart and virtue, but otherwise harmless.

But she did know better. If she needed proof that he was a coldhearted, self-serving crook, all she had to do was look around her. Virtually everyone in town had offered him friendship, and he'd thanked them by stealing their money. She had offered him both money and love, and he'd taken one but not the other, breaking her heart in the process. He had abandoned his own son with near-strangers. He would stoop to anything that suited his purposes, and she would do well to remember that.

The muscles in her jaw tightening, she returned to her work, making her words suitably scornful. "You talk about it as if it were a real job—your line of work, research."

"You think breaking the law without getting caught doesn't take effort? It's work, darlin'. Sometimes a lot of hours with very little payoff."

"Then why not get a real job?"

"Most real jobs are also a lot of hours with very little payoff."

"And very little chance of going to prison."

Abruptly he grinned, not that big phony grin that made her want to smack him, but just a regular everyday, amused grin. "Where's the challenge in that?"

"For most people, earning a living, taking care of their families, being happy, and being able to face themselves in the morning is challenge enough."

His gaze narrowed on her before he shifted and picked up one of the other headstones against the wall. It looked like stone, heavy and unwieldy, but in fact it weighed only a few pounds. The writing where the name and dates were carved was distorted by the inhuman figure emerging from the stone, hair streaming, mouth open in a silent wail. It was one of a set of four, with the figures in various stages of emergence. On her favorite, only the outline of the face and a pair of hands were visible, while on another only the legs and feet remained out of sight.

"Dean Elliott did those," she remarked. "You remember him. He was also one of your victims."

Grinding his back teeth, Cole carefully replaced the piece on the floor, then crouched there and studied the others. Elliott's work sold for a fortune—seventy-five grand wasn't unusual—yet he'd donated this stuff to the haunted house. Alone with a telephone and the pieces, Cole could probably unload them for twenty-five grand with minimal effort. A fraction of their worth, but not bad wages for an hour of his time.

He ran his finger across the face of the ghost that was just taking form. The texture was smooth, cool to the touch. "This one looks like you." Like when she first awoke in the morning, mind still hazy and lazy before she opened her eyes and faced the new day.

"Thank you. Most people don't notice the resemblance."

When he stood, she was smiling smugly. Suspiciously, he looked from her to the gravestone, then back again. "You modeled for Elliott?"

"Not exactly." She laid the chisel down, stepped back to study her work, then picked up a cloth and a pot of what looked like black shoe polish. "He did it from memory, I suppose."

Damn. And Cole didn't feel like laughing.

He hadn't known she'd been involved with Elliott, though it shouldn't come as a surprise. After all, when they'd met, she was thirty-two, had never been married, was mother to a four-year-old boy, and certainly wasn't a virgin. And, really, he wasn't surprised. He was . . .

Jealous? He wasn't sure. He'd never been jealous over any woman in his life.

"So you slept with him."

Her gaze narrowed at his accusing tone, reminding him once again of how unpredictable she'd been lately. She was like a hand grenade that may or may not be a dud, that might seem perfectly safe, then blow a man to bits without warning.

"I fail to see how that's any of your business," she replied, her voice as frosty as the night.

It wasn't. Logically, he knew that. But what did logic matter when the subject was a woman?

"Were you in love with him?" Before she could speak, he went on. "I know—that's none of my business, either. I was just wondering how often you fall in love. Is it something you do with every man you sleep with? Or did it actually mean something when you said it to me?"

A hot flush spread across her face and extended down her throat as she stared at him. Her mouth worked a time or two before she managed to form words. "You—you bastard."

He'd been called that all his life—by his mother when she was tired of messing with him, by most of the women he'd known. He wouldn't argue it with her, and damn sure wouldn't let on that, somehow, it hurt more coming from her. He just wanted to know . . .

He rested his hands on the tabletop next to the marker and kept his tone as casual and careless as he could. "They're simple questions. All they need is a yes or no. In fact, you can answer any one of them— Were you in love with Elliott? Do you fall in love with everyone you sleep with? Or did it mean anything with me?"

She was still staring at him as if he were a sight so horrible she couldn't look away. Finally, her breath catching with an audible gasp, she leaned toward him. "Go to hell."

When she would have spun around and stalked off, he caught her hand and leaned closer. "Honey, I'm already there."

Her gaze didn't waver, and neither did his. He just wanted to know—*needed* to know . . . but why? So he could feel worse than he already did? Whether she'd really loved him or not, she'd felt *something* for him and he'd hurt her. Running out on a woman who'd cared for him was bad enough. Running out on a woman who'd loved him was . . .

Well, hell. He didn't know what it was, because no woman had ever loved him. Oh, a couple of them had told him so, but they'd also loved everything else—chocolate, expensive wine, a new outfit, red sports cars, *Friends.*

Except Leanne. She'd said the words as if she'd meant them.

Judging by the anger in her eyes, she would certainly never say them again—at least, not to him. Maybe to someone like Elliott. He was more her type anyway. At least he had a real job and could face himself every morning.

She pulled steadily until her hand slipped free, then turned and walked away. He wanted to say something to stop her, to make her come back, but he was pretty sure she thought he'd said enough already.

When she joined a couple of her friends, drinking hot chocolate from a thermal carafe, Cole realized that she wasn't the only object of someone's scrutiny. Eli, going over the sketches with Maggie, was watching *him,* a grave look on his face. Great. Now he would probably get a lecture for being too chatty with one of the decent folk in town, for obviously making her uncomfortable, for daring to touch her. It didn't help any that she was Phyllis Wilson's daughter. That family very well might get him thrown in jail in spite of his best efforts.

He turned away, picked up a string of lights, then climbed the ladder to plug them into the last string he'd hung. They were like Christmas-tree lights, except the bulbs burned bright orange—too bizarre for his tastes, though they had nothing on the set of black-and-white lights in the shape of a giant spider. That one, Maggie had told him, couldn't go up until Halloween night, when it would hang in the corner of the doorway, right in the middle of an elaborate fake web.

He kept to himself the rest of the evening, taking instructions from Maggie and Eli, trying really hard not to even glance in Leanne's direction. By the time they called it quits, he was tired and about as stressed as he ever got. But good ol' Eli managed to ratchet it up another few notches as they approached the pickup.

Between them, Eli and Murray were carrying the skeleton, arms draped over their shoulders as if it were a drunk unable to stand. When they reached the truck, Eli glanced at the seat, then at each of them, then slid the skeleton onto the seat. "I hate to put this in back where it might get damaged. Leanne, would you mind giving Cole a ride home?"

Cole scowled and tried to resist the temptation to dangle the kid by his throat all the way home. "I'll ride in back."

"No, it's too cold for that. And Leanne's going to the same place, more or less." Eli flashed a grin at her over the bed of the truck. "You don't mind, do you?"

Her smile was tight and unwelcoming. "Of course not."

Cold or not, he could handle the short ride home in the back of the pickup. Come to think of it, it couldn't possibly be any colder back there than the chill he would get sitting next to Leanne.

But no matter how much more appealing freezing was, he didn't climb into the truck bed. No, like an idiot, he passed the truck, circled to the other side of the SUV, and slid into the front seat.

The dirt road curved along the edge of the woods to the far end of the hospital parking lot. If she'd just shifted into four-wheel drive and set off across the grass, she could have cut the trip time in half. But she didn't.

As they bounced over the rutted road at a crawl behind the other cars, he asked the one question that was with him every single day, the one that was hardest to keep in, and the hardest to let out. "How is Ryan?"

She glanced at him. "Do you care?"

"No. I just thought it would be an easy topic of conversation that couldn't possibly piss you off."

She pursed her lips the way her mother did when she was about to get *real* pissy, then quietly replied, "He's . . . okay. We got a dog Saturday—part lab, part who-knows-what-else. His name is Jerome, and he and Ryan have bonded."

"I didn't know he liked dogs."

"All kids like dogs or cats or both." She glanced his way. "Didn't you have a pet growing up?"

"Yeah . . . but they preferred to be called brothers."

Her smile was faint, unwilling, and faded quickly in the dim light. "How many?"

"Five. Too many to keep straight, according to Owen. He just called us all *son*. Said it was easier than remembering our names."

"What are their names?"

"Adam, Bret, David, Eddie, and Frank."

A soft sound came from her side of the vehicle that might have been a laugh if she hadn't stopped it. "They *alphabetized* you, and he still couldn't keep you straight?"

"Owen had a great mind for capers. Not so great for kids."

A minute or two passed in silence before she spoke again. Her voice was quiet and tentative, as if she couldn't believe she was chatting with him, or didn't want to upset the civility they'd managed. "Were you close to him?"

It wasn't as tough a question as she probably thought. He loved his father—loved his whole family with the exception of his mother. He would probably have to spend time on some shrink's couch to figure out exactly what he felt for Eloise. But Owen had been a good parent—nontraditional, but good. He'd done the best he could, had taught them everything he knew, and had never once left them because he didn't want to be bothered. When he had left—for a job or a stint in jail—they had always known he would come back.

"Yeah. I still am. I don't see him or the boys very often, but when we do get together, it's like no time at all has passed."

"But he taught you to steal." The civility teetered.

"Yeah."

"When other parents were teaching their children the difference between right and wrong, he was teaching you to lie, cheat, betray, and manipulate everything and everyone around you."

"Owen taught us the difference between right and wrong," he said defensively. Cole had just learned over the years not to let it matter. Until he'd come to Bethlehem last spring.

"What a wonderful parent he was."

The sarcasm in her voice rubbed him the wrong way. He matched it with his own. "I reckon he was better at being a father, even being crooked and all, than your mother was at being a mother."

"At least I didn't grow up to be just like her."

"Well, I was raised to be just like him. Sorry if that offends you."

She pulled into her usual parking space directly across the street from the Miller mansion, shut off the engine, and faced him. "You could have made a different choice."

Cole stared at the shop window ahead with its Halloween decorations and wished he'd ended this conversation before it had started. All he'd had to do was answer one question— Were you close to your father? A simple yes, no, or sort of would have done the trick.

But no, he'd had to tell her too much, and she'd had to expand on it.

"When was I supposed to make this different choice? When was I supposed to defy my family and my upbringing? How was I supposed to choose a different path when the path I was on was the only one anyone in the family knew? My brothers and I were raised to follow in our parents' footsteps, in our grandparents' footsteps. The possibility of *not* being a crook never even occurred to me until I was grown, and by then it was too late. I didn't know how to do anything else."

"That's a sad way to live."

Not sad. It had served him well for thirty years. But somehow, somewhere, it had lost its appeal. Maybe it was Ryan, or Leanne, or Bethlehem, or a combination of the three. Maybe he'd finally grown up. Maybe he *had* developed a conscience.

"When it's all you've got, you make the best of it," he said flatly.

"But it's not all. You've got a son."

"No." He jerked the seat belt loose, then opened the door. "I don't."

She got out, too, then met him at the back of the truck. "When Danny was born, I would have done *anything* for him. I don't understand how you can't feel the same way about Ryan."

It was easy to say she would do anything for her son when she hadn't been forced to prove it. *He* had. Walking away from Ryan had been the hardest thing he'd ever imagined, but he'd done it because the kid needed other things—stability, a home, a mother's love, a future—more than he'd needed Cole. Leaving Ryan behind had damn near killed him, but he'd done it . . . and she saw it as proof that he didn't care.

He waited until a car passed, then started across the street, grateful that she didn't follow. Once he reached the other side, he turned and found her still there, still watching him. "That's the difference between you and me," he said cockily. "You're one of the *decent folk*. I'm not."

And damned if he could ever forget it.

Chapter Eight

KELSEY GRAYSON'S OFFICE WAS ON THE THIRD floor of the courthouse, a small space that she'd gradually transformed from cramped to cozy. The first time Leanne had been there, between the desk, chairs, and file cabinets, there hadn't been enough air for two people to breathe. The file cabinets had since been moved into the receptionist's office, the institutional green walls painted yellow and the beige metal desk painted white, and the orange vinyl chairs had been replaced with old wooden chairs whose scars gave them character. With family photos on the walls, plus crayon renderings done by the younger members of said family, it was a much more pleasant place.

Not that Leanne's reason for being there was pleasant.

She sat in one of the wooden chairs, legs crossed, nervously bouncing her toes in the air. So far they'd exchanged plenty of small talk, but now it was time to get down to business, and even after thinking about nothing else since Tuesday night, she just wasn't sure she could do it.

After several moments of awkward silence, Kelsey came

around the desk to sit in the other chair. "I take it this visit has to do with Ryan."

Leanne nodded.

"Is everything okay?"

"We're getting along."

"That's an evasive answer."

"Ryan's been having a few problems since"—unable to bring herself to say Cole's name, she frowned—"since his father came back."

"That's understandable." Kelsey's gaze was steady on her. "J.D. told me he's been coming in."

Leanne nodded vaguely. They had another appointment that afternoon. It was a good thing she had Sophy, or the shop would be opening and closing like a revolving door.

"What's on your mind?"

Drawing a deep breath, Leanne plunged ahead. "It occurred to me yesterday that . . . Ryan doesn't seem to feel he belongs with us. He and Danny share a room, but he calls it *Danny's* room. He never says *my* anything. It's as if . . ."

"He's only there for a while?"

She nodded again.

"That's not unusual with foster kids, Leanne. He's very aware that Danny's your child and he isn't. He knows he's there until you get tired of him or we place him somewhere else or his father is able to take care of him. These kids, especially the older ones like Ryan, try not to get attached, to get that feeling of belonging, because they know how easily everything can change."

"I don't want things to change. I want to keep him forever. I want to adopt him," Leanne blurted out.

Kelsey studied her a moment. "Are you sure about that?"

She nodded.

"But—?"

"But I know either his father has to—to give up his rights to him or—or the state has to—to—"

"Terminate them," Kelsey supplied.

Leanne shuddered. She couldn't imagine how awful such a thing would be to most parents. Sure, there were some who obviously wouldn't mind, like Danny's father or Ryan's mother. But Cole, despite all he'd said and done, and all he *hadn't* said and done, would.

Or maybe she was just hoping he would. Maybe she needed to believe that the man she had fallen in love with last spring would be devastated at having his parental rights taken from him.

Yeah, like she apparently still needed to believe that the man she'd fallen in love with actually existed, her inner demon sarcastically pointed out.

"I'm really not comfortable with the idea of asking you to do this," she went on. "I know how I would feel if someone who wasn't even related to me tried to take Danny away from me. But . . . Ryan needs people who love him and can give him a stable home, people who will be there for him today and twenty years from now. He needs a family, and Danny and I want to be that family."

"You're already a single mother, Leanne. Adopting Ryan will more than double your responsibilities because of his experience with his parents. It may take him a long time to trust that you'll never send him away, or it may never happen at all. These problems he's having right now could resolve, or they could get worse as he gets older. You could be letting yourself in for a lot of frustration and heartache."

Leanne smiled dimly. "You know me, Kelsey. I'm an expert at frustration and heartache." Then the smile faded. "I know things could be difficult . . . but that's part of being a parent and a child. The bottom line is Ryan needs us, and we love him, and I really want to give him a real home. A permanent one."

After a moment's silence, Kelsey returned to her desk and jotted something on the pad there. "Mary Therese, my boss over in Howland, and I had discussed a petition to terminate Mr. Jackson's rights when he was arrested in Georgia. Since he didn't go to prison in spite of the guilty plea, we'd decided to hold off. Frankly, I didn't think you'd be interested in adoption and I didn't want to look at placing Ryan elsewhere so soon after he'd moved in with you. I think the child's been bounced around enough in his life."

That was an understatement. Even with J.D., Ryan wouldn't talk much about the years he'd lived with his mother, but in his three years with Cole, they'd lived in two dozen places in a half-dozen states. Ryan had casually explained that was because, in Cole's line of work, the risk of arrest increased proportionately to the time spent in one place.

"I'll have to interview both Ryan and his father. I can't guarantee I'll agree that terminating Mr. Jackson's rights is in the boy's best interests." Kelsey raised her hand to stall Leanne when she would have protested. "I do agree that Ryan needs stability and love and a family . . . but it's possible he needs his father more."

There was no doubt that Ryan loved Cole, Leanne admitted silently. If he didn't, he wouldn't be so angry and hurt. And despite his words to the contrary, if given the chance to take off with Cole tomorrow, to resume their life as it had been before Bethlehem, he would almost certainly go. He might object to the possibility of adoption far more vocally than his father.

But she really, truly wanted what was best for him, and in her heart, she believed that was her and Danny. They could give him everything Cole was unwilling or unable to give—love, acceptance, permanence.

"It's possible," Leanne acknowledged as she stood up. "It's also possible that the moon really is made of green cheese, that the end of the world is nigh, and that Cole's only crime is being misunderstood."

"Such cynicism in one so young." Sliding her arm around Leanne's shoulders, Kelsey walked through the reception area and into the corridor with her. "I'll be in touch about setting up the interview."

"Okay. But I won't hope too much."

"Oh, honey, there's *always* hope."

Not for everyone, Leanne thought as she started down the broad stairs. And certainly not for everything.

It was nearly noon Thursday when Cole unloaded the last logs of the last delivery of firewood from the City Park trees. He stacked them on the tiny back porch, dusted his hands, then stepped down into the yard and swiped his sleeve across his forehead. It had been cold when they'd left the house that morning, but the sun had finally cleared the clouds and heated the air about ten degrees more than he'd expected. It would be a great day for doing nothing, but was a little warm for physical labor.

"This is so sweet of you," the owner of the porch said as she offered him a glass of milk. She was about five feet tall, well past eighty, and so tiny a stiff breeze could probably knock her off her feet. Her white hair wound around in a bun, and her glasses hovered on the tip of her nose. She offered a plate filled with chocolate chip and oatmeal cookies. "Would you like one?"

"No, thank you." As an afterthought, he added, "Ma'am."

That was another of Owen's rules. *Be respectful to old folks and never mess with people on a fixed income.*

Hmm. Maybe he had a moral or two after all.

"You really should try one. The other boys said they were delicious."

Cole bit back a grin at the thought of anyone calling Murray a *boy*. The guy was old enough to be his father, and couldn't be much younger than the old lady herself. "If you insist," he said, and took a cookie from the plate, though he'd really rather have something more substantial. Breakfast seemed a long time ago.

She waited until he took a bite, then beamed and wandered across the yard to offer thirds to Eli. Cole sat down on the tailgate, a little tired but no longer sore. There was something to be said for real work—at least, when the weather was good and the job wasn't too tough. If Eli put them to work at the sewage treatment plant or mucking out kennels at the animal shelter, he would change his mind.

He was munching the last bite of the cookie when a small child, four or maybe five years old, rolled to a stop in front of him. He—or she; it was difficult to tell with the no-nonsense hair cut, T-shirt, and jeans—settled back on the tricycle, tilted his head back, and fixed a curious gaze on Cole. "Hi."

"Hi," he replied.

"Who are you?"

"Cole. Who are you?"

"Robbie."

That was no help in determining gender. He could ask for a middle name, but it would probably be something like Lou or Jo.

"What are you doing here?" Robbie asked.

"We delivered some firewood."

"Good. Now Gran won't get so cold." Robbie's gaze didn't waver. "I ain't seen you before."

"I ain't seen—I haven't seen you before, either," Cole replied. Then he added, "I'm kind of new to town."

"Huh." Unimpressed, the kid reversed, then pedaled around toward the front of the truck.

Alone once more, Cole glanced at the house. It was tiny, probably not more than six hundred square feet, and shabby. It wasn't the sort of neglect that stemmed from the owner just not caring, but rather from not having the ability to keep up with the regular maintenance. A few screens needed replacing, one of the porch railings was broken, as was a step, and the place hadn't seen fresh paint in at least a decade. Considering the old woman's age, the house really needed a ramp instead of steps, and considering the house's age, no doubt a little weatherstripping would go a long way toward making it more comfortable.

Someone who knew something about houses could probably find plenty of other things to fix, but he wasn't that person. He didn't know anything about anything except ripping people off—and, now, cutting down trees. And hurting people.

"We'd better get going," Eli said, coming toward the truck.

Cole slid to his feet, tossed back the rest of the milk in one gulp, then took the glass to the old lady. "Thank you, ma'am. See you, Robbie."

They returned to the park, where a chipper had been delivered while they were gone. Feeding branches into it would be a fairly mindless job, but once all those branches were mulched, they would head downtown with it.

He would rather cut down the rest of the trees in the park with a butter knife.

"I thought yesterday was your last day here," he remarked to Murray as they began gathering limbs.

"It was."

"So why are you still here?"

The old man smiled and shrugged.

Strange. He had a home—a tiny house similar to the one they'd just left. He'd pointed it out the day before when they were making another delivery of firewood. He didn't seem to have a regular job, though he must have some income to pay for his Jack Black and the car he kept driving while under the influence. He didn't seem to have any family, either, or any responsibilities.

Apparently, he was alone, sad, and lonely. It was a hell of a way to end up in life.

Cole should know, since it appeared he was on the same path.

The park was empty except for the three of them, and quiet except for the sound of the machine grinding up wood. All the school-age kids were in school, and the preschoolers . . . Phyllis Wilson had probably scared every mother in town with her tales about him. The old bat was probably in her house right that moment, watching him through closed blinds with the telephone in her hand, just waiting for him to give her a reason to call 911.

He glanced at the house from time to time. It was kind of stately-looking, built of brick with a big deep porch. It was the sort of house that looked as if it should provide shelter to the perfect family—respectable father, loving mother, typical son, spoiled daughter, obedient dog. It would always be homey and inviting, smelling of lemon oil and roast beef or fresh-baked bread, and everyone would love to visit there.

But the Wilsons hadn't been the perfect family, no more than the Jacksons had. Earl Wilson had run off Chase, and

Phyllis had alienated Leanne. She was a bona-fide witch, Leanne had once told him, and he'd seen the proof for himself.

But they hadn't encouraged her to become a crook, and that counted for a lot in her mind.

Frankly, he'd rather be a crook than have Phyllis Wilson for a mother.

Movement from the parking lot drew his attention that way, and he watched as Kelsey Grayson got out of a van. For a mother of six, she looked pretty damn good. Granted, she'd given birth to only one of them—one was J.D.'s from a previous marriage, and the other four were adopted. Still, he knew better than most what effort went into raising six kids, so he stood by the looking-damn-good observation.

She walked halfway to them, then gestured for him to join her. Cole glanced at Eli, who nodded, then went back to work.

When he reached her, she extended her hand. Looking at his own filthy hands, he shook his head.

"Mr. Jackson."

A knot started forming in his gut, twisting and tightening. It would be too much to hope that this was about the haunted house project, wouldn't it? Besides, Maggie McKinney was in charge of that. Kelsey was just one of the worker bees, like him.

But she *was* in charge of Ryan, more or less, being his caseworker.

He shoved his hands in his hip pockets to keep them steady. "Ms. Grayson."

"Can we talk?"

When he shrugged, she turned toward the nearest pic-nic table and took a seat on one bench. He straddled the other one. At first touch, the concrete seemed to hold the sun's warmth, but quickly the chill came through.

"You know I'm your son's social worker."

He nodded.

"I'm considering a request to file a petition to terminate your parental rights, which means you would no longer have any legal standing as Ryan's father."

He'd figured this was coming—had been expecting it ever since he'd left town last May, had thought he was prepared for it.

He'd been wrong.

His chest was tight, barely able to accommodate his shallow breaths, and the knots in his stomach turned to a cold, hard weight. He couldn't unclench his fists, hidden beneath the tabletop, or control the thudding of his heart. "I—I—"

He'd known things would never be the same between him and Ryan again. Had known the best thing he could do for the kid was to give him a chance at a better life, then get out of it. Had known Ryan would never understand, never forgive, but would be happier for it in the long run.

He hadn't begun to guess at how badly it would hurt.

"Let me stress that I'm only considering the request right now. Even if my department takes that action, the final decision is the judge's. You'll have a chance to present your side, and at his age, Ryan's wishes will be taken into consideration, too."

He smiled bitterly. "Ryan wishes I'd gone to prison and rotted there."

Kelsey smiled, too, sympathetically. "He's a child."

"A child who's old enough that the judge will consider his wishes."

After a moment's silence, she asked, "Why did you leave him?"

He could tell her the truth, and she might even believe him. Stranger things had happened. But it wouldn't make her decide against the petition. In fact, it would just strengthen her position. When *he* didn't believe he was fit to be a father, how could anyone else fail to agree? It would be a no-brainer for the judge. He could reach the right decision in his sleep.

"Mr. Jackson?"

He lifted his gaze to her face. She really did seem sympathetic. He wondered why. If he dealt with lousy parents all the time, he would despise every last one of them. He would take their kids away, then lock them up forever so they could never cause one more moment's harm to a child.

"You want me to relinquish my rights voluntarily?" he asked bleakly.

"Is that what you want?"

What he wanted had little to do with it. What was best for Ryan was all that mattered.

"I get the impression I'm supposed to believe the answer to my question is yes," she went on when he remained silent. "I also get the impression that's not what you want at all."

"You're wrong," he muttered.

"Which one's wrong?"

"Look, I move around a lot. This"—he spread his hands, indicating the park—"is the only honest work I've done in my life, and believe me, I'm not doing it by choice. I support myself and Ryan with money I've stolen or embezzled or scammed out of some poor sucker. I pay for his clothes and buy his food with that money. When I can't take him with me, I leave him with my father or one of my brothers, all of whom are in the same business. I teach him to look out for himself first, that the law doesn't matter, that no one else in the world matters. If I want something, I take it. If I don't want something, I leave it behind." He fell silent for a long, tense moment. "I left Ryan behind."

"So you're saying you don't want him."

Cole couldn't answer. Tried to, tried like hell to lie, but *couldn't*.

"How long has Ryan lived with you?"

"Three years."

"And what kind of trouble has he been in during those years?"

He scowled at the table. "He got caught shoplifting once."

"Though he'd done it other times, too, hadn't he?"

"Yeah."

"He stole some books, didn't he? And you made him work to pay for them." She smiled. "He told me about it. He said it was the first time he'd realized that most people worked regular jobs to pay for everything. How did his mother support him?"

The sudden tangent caught him off-guard. "I don't know."

"You didn't pay child support."

"I didn't know he existed until he was nine."

"She never told you she was pregnant."

He shrugged.

"He doesn't look anything like you."

He shrugged again. "Your little girl doesn't look like you, either." He'd met the whole Grayson family when he'd met with Kelsey and J.D. at their house one evening, from sixteen-year-old Trey all the way down to the baby, Faith, who was a softer, feminine replica of her father, without so much as a hint of her mother on her round little face.

"Where is Ryan's mother?"

He was positive she'd asked that question of Ryan at some point in the past four months. He gave the same answer he knew the boy would have given. "I don't know."

"So she just showed up on your doorstep one day, said, 'Here's your son,' and disappeared again?"

"Something like that." The evasion made him swallow hard. Truth was, it had been *nothing* like that. But if he told her the truth . . .

He didn't *tell* the truth, though, did he?

"Were you married to his mother?"

"No."

"Did you live with her?"

"No."

"Have a one-night stand?"

He relied on the shrug again.

"Then how did she know where to find you nine years later, to dump your son on you?"

Impatiently, he drummed his fingers on the table. "Look, this is all ancient history. Ryan's mother isn't around to take care of him. Neither . . . neither am I. What does any of it matter?"

"It's not unusual for us to have sketchy background information on children in our care, but Ryan's is even sketchier than most. I'm just trying to get a sense of what his life has been like—how you and his mother have provided for him, and how you've failed him."

"His life has been crappy. He's better off where he is now."

"You mean in foster care."

"I mean with Leanne. Just leave him there. He's got a good home for the first time in his life. Don't screw it up."

"We're not planning to screw it up, Mr. Jackson," she said politely. "In fact, Leanne would like to give your son a permanent home. She's the one who requested the petition severing your rights."

Cole felt a great sense of relief that Ryan wouldn't be uprooted again—almost as great as the shock that it was Leanne who wanted to take the kid away from him, for now and forever, in every way conceivable. It was Leanne who wanted him dragged into court and pronounced unfit to be a father. The woman who'd told him she loved him. The woman who had obviously lied.

God, how she must hate him.

Alex Thomas was finishing up a phone call when Melissa arrived for their lunch date. She wiggled her fingers as she moved to a chair, braced both hands on the wooden arms, then cautiously lowered her cumbersome body into it. She was going to the Halloween party dressed as a pumpkin with toothpicks for arms and legs, she had declared the night before. All it would take to pull it off was an orange outfit and a leafy stem curling out of the top of her head. No padding necessary.

He thought she looked beautiful, and had told her so.

On the phone, Melina was winding down. "I haven't heard anything back on Ryan or his mother, and my people are tracking down some stuff on the family. I'll keep you posted, though."

"Thanks, Melina." Hanging up, he smiled at his wife. "Hey, baby."

"Are you talking to me or Junior?"

"Both of you. Where do you want to go for lunch?"

"I would have said Harry's, but I saw Dr. Gregory going in as I was parking, so how about McBride Inn?"

Dr. Gregory was her OB doctor, who had told her last week to watch her calories and continue exercising. The exercise wasn't a problem—they took a long walk every evening—but when she was having cravings at odd hours of the day and night, watching the calories was.

"You afraid of getting caught with a mouthful of Harry's mashed potatoes and gravy?" he teased as he circled the desk and helped her to her feet.

"Sweetheart, when you've stepped on those scales in his office and watched the numbers rise month after month, *then* you can joke about it."

"There are things that happen in that office that scare me a whole lot more than a set of scales—such as anything involving stirrups."

After telling Eleanor where they would be, they started down the stairs at a leisurely pace. "How are things with Melina?" Melissa asked.

"Fine, I guess."

"Is she doing some work for you?"

"Yes."

"On?"

He gave her a dry look. "You don't really want to talk business, do you?"

"I would if you'd ever tell me anything juicy."

He could imagine her reaction if he told her that Cole Jackson had had a lousy childhood. *Now there's a news flash,* she would dryly remark, or *Tell me something the whole world doesn't already know.* Or, more to the point, *Duh.*

"What have you been doing this morning?" he asked as he pushed the heavy door open, then held it for her.

"I lazed around, watching game shows and soap operas, then went by the nursery to see how things are going."

Melissa's Garden was Bethlehem's best nursery—also the only one, though no less the best for that. She'd gotten into the business back when their early efforts to have a baby had failed. If she couldn't nurture a child, she could

damn well nurture plants. Last month, though, on her doctor's advice, she'd turned the daily operations over to Julie
Bujold. The girl was just out of high school, but she was as
responsible as someone twice her age, and she worked miracles with plants.

"And how were things going?"

"Smoothly, as usual. Julie has every—*oh!*" Steadying
herself with one hand on the hood of his car, she pressed
the other to her stomach and bent forward a bit, breathing
shallowly.

"Melissa?"

By the time he reached her, she'd straightened and was
smiling wanly. "I'm okay, really. That was one heck of a
kick. I felt it all the way down to my toes."

Holding her carefully by the shoulders, he helped her
into the car, leaned across to fasten the seat belt, then stared
into her face. The color was returning, and her smile was
growing broader and brighter. "Really, sweetheart, we're
fine. I think that was just Junior's way of telling me he's
hungry."

After another moment, he accepted the truth of what
she was saying, leaned close, and kissed her, then closed the
door and circled behind the car. Though she seemed to, indeed, be fine, he couldn't shake the sudden fear so quickly.
After they'd tried so hard, failed so often, then come so far,
if anything happened to this baby . . .

He uttered a silent prayer for forgiveness for even
thinking such a thing. It was going to happen this time. In
another six weeks or so, they would be holding their baby
in their arms. They would be parents.

Living proof that miracles did happen.

●　●　●

Bethlehem High School had an out-of-town football game Friday night. Though she usually attended all the home games—she was a good little civic booster—Leanne decided against driving an hour each way, to freeze in the stands while teenage boys played a game she really didn't care for. Danny and Ryan had gone, though, leaving with Earl and one of his fishing buddies, who happened to be the coach's father, right after school was out. They wouldn't be home until practically midnight, which gave her a long quiet evening to spend alone except for Jerome, snoozing on Danny's bed.

Not that she had to be alone. It was hot-dog night at Chase and Nolie's, and she had a standing invitation to that, with or without the kids. She could go to the Starlite and talk with Rourke for a while or find a handsome man to dance with or hook up with a few girlfriends for a night of giggles and gossip.

Instead, she wandered around the apartment, feeling lost and more than a little blue, and she didn't even know why.

Liar. It seemed she had at least one thing in common with Cole—a propensity to avoid the truth. She felt lousy because of her conversation on Wednesday with Kelsey. Because Leanne had set in motion an attempt to remove Cole permanently from Ryan's life, so *she* could have him. Forget that Ryan was *his son. She* wanted him, so Cole would have to give him up.

She wasn't being that selfish, she insisted as she turned into her bedroom. She truly believed adoption would be best for Ryan. If she didn't, she *never* would have said a word to Kelsey. Besides, it wasn't as if the termination of Cole's rights was up to her. If the judge agreed that Cole was a lousy parent, that Ryan would be better off with Leanne, then *he* would make the decision. The burden would be on *him*, not her.

Liar, liar . . .

She found herself at the side window, where family pictures sat along the sill. She picked up the most recent: a snapshot of Danny, Ryan, and her taken a few months ago. The light in the room was too dim to make out their faces, but rather than turn on the lamp, she reached for the rod that would tilt the slats on the blinds. She twisted it open just enough to get a glimpse of the Miller mansion, then abruptly stopped.

Cole was sitting on the porch steps.

Though he was in shadow, there was no mistaking him. Eli didn't have that thick sun-touched blond hair, and Murray lacked the long, lean lines of that body. It was definitely Cole, and he looked . . .

Lost. Blue.

Probably for the same reason she did.

She dropped the rod, then set the photograph down. It wobbled and fell back against the blinds, but she didn't straighten it. Instead, before she could think about what she was doing—before she could come to her senses—she stopped in the boys' door and snapped her fingers. "Jerome, wanna go for a walk?"

He sprang to the floor as if he hadn't been snoring two seconds earlier, then beat her to the stairs. She paused long enough to grab her jacket and gloves, plus his leash, from the coat tree, then ran down the stairs.

It didn't appear Cole had moved in the time it had taken them to get outside and across the street. She paused in front of the gate, then pushed it open with a creak, and walked to the steps.

"Too bad the barn doors don't creak like that," she remarked as she stood there, one hand clenching the leash, the other knotted in her pocket.

This close, she could see his face more clearly. She

searched for signs of anger, hostility, or bitterness toward her, but didn't find them. She didn't find anything at all besides an unnerving bleakness that made her feel sick inside.

After a moment, he took a deep breath and the bleakness disappeared, as if it had never existed. Leanne found it unsettling, but even his chameleon act was preferable to that unspoken sorrow. "Is this Jerome?"

"Yeah."

At the mention of his name, the puppy left the grass for the steps, climbing up to curiously sniff Cole. He raised one hand to scratch the dog, who immediately flopped over on his back and exposed his belly.

"Do you know how big he's gonna be?"

"Bigger than Danny and smaller than Ryan—I hope."

"You'd better." He scratched Jerome some more, then asked, "If he's the boys' dog, why aren't they walking him?"

"They've gone to a football game with my dad."

"Phyllis the Witch didn't go, too?"

"Heavens, no. The only football games she's ever been to were when Chase was on the team, and even then she complained the whole time. Dad was furious when Chase got himself kicked off, but she was glad, because then she didn't have to go anymore." She moved a cautious step forward, and he automatically shifted to his right, leaving two-thirds of the steps' width for her. Keeping Jerome between them, she sat down on the opposite side.

"Kelsey Grayson came to see me yesterday," he announced.

It was impossible to read anything in his voice or his expression. She swallowed hard and moistened her lips. "I—I'm sorry."

"You say that almost as if you mean it."

"I do mean it."

"Then why are you doing it?"

Another swallow did little to ease the lump in her throat. "Ryan needs a home—a family."

"I've given him a home *and* a family."

"But you can't give him either right now," she said softly. "And you can't give him security. You can't promise you'll always be there for him. What happens the next time you decide to clear out of town in a hurry? Who will you leave him with, and when will you go back for him, or *will* you go back for him? What happens the next time you get arrested and have to go to prison? Who will take care of him then?"

He tilted his head back to stare at the sky with a thoroughly unamused smile. "Thank you for being so certain those things will happen again."

"Have you left him before? Have you been arrested? Have you gone to prison?" Her gesture was impatient. "You know, when you make a habit of doing certain things, before long, people start to expect those things from you."

He didn't respond to that. How could he, without admitting she was right?

She loosely tied Jerome's leash to the railing, then drew her knees up and wrapped her arms around them. "I know it seems cruel, but . . . Ryan needs to believe he belongs somewhere, that he's *wanted* somewhere. On the outside he acts like nothing really matters, but inside there's still a little kid who needs love and security. I can give that to him. I already love him."

Cole tilted his head to skeptically study her. "The way you *loved* me?"

She stiffened. She *had* loved him, and still would—always would—if he hadn't deliberately destroyed it. That was his fault, not hers. "No," she said coolly. "The way I love Danny."

He had no response to that. He just looked at her a moment longer, then turned away, staring off into the distance.

"I just want what's best for Ryan," she said at last.

"You may find this hard to believe, but so do I."

She would give a lot to believe him. Before he'd left, she *had* believed him. He'd been twenty-seven when Ryan's mother had dropped off their nine-year-old son and never come back, and he'd accepted the responsibility with enough maturity that they'd gotten along better than many fathers and sons who grew up together. She had been impressed by their closeness, by their obvious affection for each other. It had been one of several things that helped her fall in love with him.

And yet, when he'd left town, he'd left Ryan, too—hardly the act of a loving father. *Why?*

"If you really mean that . . . will you avoid a court hearing, for Ryan's sake, and sign the papers? Give up your rights?"

That brought his gaze sharply back to her. For a long moment, his expression was harsh, his jaw taut, then everything went blank. "I can't."

Disappointment washed over her. She wanted to swear, to stomp her feet, to find the words to hurt him even half as much as he'd hurt her. But before she could think of anything scathing enough to say, he went on.

"I can't give up something I don't have." He took a breath, and something bleak flickered across his face before he resolutely finished.

"I'm not Ryan's father."

Chapter Nine

THIS TIME LEANNE TRULY WAS SPEECHLESS. SHE stared at Cole, her eyes wide, her mouth rounded in a silent *oh*. She felt so off-balance that if he poked her lightly on the shoulder, she would probably fall over backward, unable to lift so much as a finger to catch herself.

He *wasn't* Ryan's father? How could that be? Maybe he was lying—after all, he'd proven time and again that he was an expert liar. But deep inside she didn't think so. It didn't *feel* like a lie. Besides, paternity was too easy to prove . . . or disprove. And if he *were* Ryan's father and simply didn't want him anymore, he didn't have to lie about it. All he had to do was sign the papers, giving him up.

He *wasn't* Ryan's father. So how did he come to have custody of a child who wasn't his? Because he was related in some other way? Maybe, thanks to one of his many brothers, he was actually Ryan's uncle . . . but why lie about that? People would understand an uncle raising his nephew, especially in Bethlehem, where Nathan Bishop was helping to raise his wife's nephew and two nieces. Of course, Cole hadn't known that when he'd first come to town. Still . . .

She took a breath, the great shuddering kind that trembled through her, then asked in a soft, bewildered tone, "If you're not his father, who is?"

"I don't know."

"What about his mother?"

"I don't know her, either."

"Then how? . . ."

For a long time he didn't respond, but finally he turned so the post was at his back, settling in as if he needed whatever physical comfort he could find, to tell this story. "I was stuck in St. Louis one night, so I passed the time by hustling a few games of pool. When I left the pool hall, I ran into Ryan on the street—literally—and the kid tried to lift my wallet. Of course, I caught him. He wasn't very good at it, while I'd been picking pockets since I was tall enough to reach into them. He was looking for money for food, so I took him to McDonald's and fed him. He didn't have a place to sleep, so I took him back to the motel with me, and . . . we've been together ever since. At least, until . . ."

He'd left the boy with her.

She mimicked his position, then pressed one hand to her stomach, to rub the achy feeling there. "Where was his mother?"

He shrugged. "Three weeks before that, they were taking the bus from Arizona to Chicago and had a layover in St. Louis. He fell asleep on a bench in the bus terminal, and when he woke up, she was gone. Apparently, when they boarded the bus out of St. Louis, she didn't bother to wake him. She got on and rode out of his life. He'd stuck close to the bus station all that time, hoping she would come back, but she never did."

God, no wonder Ryan had nightmares. First his mother left him while he was asleep, then his fath—then Cole did the same. It was a wonder he could sleep at all.

The chill that made her shiver had nothing to do with the cool night. She hugged herself tightly. "You didn't turn him over to the police? You didn't let them try to find his mother so he could join her?"

"Me—call the police?" His expression said all that needed to be said on that matter. "His mother *didn't want* him. She left him without a dime in a bus station in a strange city. If the police had found her and given him back to her, she just would have done it again, only the next time he might not have been so lucky."

Lucky? What had been so lucky for Ryan the first time? That he'd tried to steal from the one person on the streets that night who would reward him for his efforts rather than turn him over to the cops?

Or that he'd tried to steal from the one person who knew what it was like to be abandoned by his mother? The one person who didn't balk at taking in and taking care of someone else's kid. The one person who would care about him.

Still more than a little dazed, she shook her head. "So you just took this child home with you as if he were a stray."

Cole's expression turned stony. "He *was* a stray. He needed a home, and I gave it to him. If I'd called the police, he would have wound up in foster care that much sooner."

Instead, he'd given Ryan a home for three years . . . before putting him through the whole nightmare all over again.

She watched as a car drove past—Georgia Blakely, a friend of her mother's, on her way home from her shift at the grocery store. The morning after Leanne's first night with Cole, the old gossip had seen her leaving his house bright and early, subjecting her to the third-degree from Phyllis. Thank heavens she hadn't been looking tonight, or Leanne would certainly have another visit from Phyllis, and she just wasn't up to it.

When the taillights disappeared down the street, she

looked back at Cole. "I've seen Ryan's birth certificate. It lists you as his father."

He made a dismissive gesture. "He had to have a birth certificate so he could go to school. His mother dragged him all over the country—"

"Like you did."

"—and she changed her name a lot." A grim smile touched his mouth. "Like I did. He didn't know what state he was born in or what name she was using at the time, so . . ."

"Let me guess," she said dryly. "One of your brothers specializes in forging documents."

"Eddie. Actually, it's just a hobby."

Between them, Jerome started to snore. She reached out to rub his belly at the same time Cole did. Even through her gloves, she felt a tingle when their fingers came into contact, and she hastily withdrew, then turned her head, to stare at the stars.

She didn't know whether to be appalled by his story . . . or impressed. On the one hand, a person just couldn't find a kid on the streets and take him home to keep. It was wrong. He should have called the police, no matter how contrary to his nature that was.

But on the other hand, he *had* taken Ryan in. He'd fed him, clothed him, given him a place to sleep, and some measure of security. Ryan's own mother had left him, helpless and defenseless on a bench in a bus station, and if she'd regretted it, it hadn't been enough to make her go back for him. But a complete stranger—a victim of the boy's clumsy attempt at stealing—had been willing to take responsibility for him.

And if Cole hadn't taken Ryan in, he never could have brought him here, and she and Danny would have missed out on a very important part of their lives.

"Okay," she said quietly. "You caught Ryan stealing. You

fed him because he was hungry. You gave him a place to sleep because he didn't have one. Against all logic, you took him home with you. You must have built a pretty good relationship with him, because he obviously loves you. *Why* did you leave him here?"

"Why does everyone keep asking that?"

She didn't know who else was asking. Kelsey, definitely. Maybe Eli. "If you answer, they'll stop."

"Why doesn't matter."

"Yes, it does. If you left him because someone was trying to kill you and would kill him, too, that would be entirely different from leaving him because you were tired of playing daddy and didn't want to bother with him anymore."

"No one's trying to kill me," he said scornfully. "I'm not that kind of crook."

"Were you tired of pretending to be his father?"

His only answer was a scowl.

"Did you want him out of your life?"

Still just the scowl.

"Did you resent having to take care of him, spend money on him, spend time with him?" She paused, but he said nothing. "Did he get in the way of your scams? Or did it worry you that he'd started stealing? Did you think you were a bad influence on him? Did you decide he would be better off without you?"

That last brought a flicker of something to his face. Guilt? Or was it shame?

Too restless to sit any longer, she stood up, walked to the end of the porch and leaned against the railing while she stared at the darkened store across the street. Could that really be it—he'd wanted Ryan to have a better life than he could give him? A more normal life? He'd thought a lying, cheating con artist wasn't the sort of father figure a twelve-year-old boy needed?

Leanne knew about Ryan's stealing. It had happened just a month before they'd come to Bethlehem. He hadn't needed the books, of course, but that hadn't stopped him from taking them. Cole had, in Ryan's words, gone ballistic. It was the only time he'd ever gotten mad at Ryan, the only time he'd yelled at him.

When Ryan had told her the story, she'd thought privately that it had been an overreaction from a man who stole for a living. Now she wondered . . . Was it because he'd seen proof of his influence on the boy? Because he hadn't wanted Ryan to grow up to be like him? Following in the family business was good enough for him, but not his son?

"What are you going to do now?"

Cole's question came from close behind her. How had he gotten to his feet and moved in on her without her hearing? He was there, close enough that she could feel the heat and the tension radiating from his body. "Do?" she asked, and grimaced when her voice managed to tremble even on that tiny word.

"About the petition."

"I'll have to tell Kelsey."

"What if they take Ryan away from you?"

She turned, leaning her hips against the railing. "And do what with him?"

"What if they find his mother and give him back?"

"To a woman who abandoned him?"

The faintest of mocking smiles appeared on his face. "Not ten minutes ago you thought I should have called the police so they could try to do just that."

She didn't try to understand her conflicting feelings. "If she didn't want him then, why would she want him now?"

"I left him in Bethlehem because I knew someone here would take care of him—would give him the kind of life I couldn't. I don't want him sent someplace else, and I don't want him going back to his mother."

"It's not your choice," she softly pointed out. "You have no claim to him."

"I l—" His jaw clenched as he bit off the word, then he muttered a curse and swung away.

I love him. She would bet this month's receipts at the shop that was what he'd been about to say. Had he stopped because the words were hard to say? Because he was unable to admit it even to himself? Or because they weren't true?

Did he even have a clue what it meant to love someone? Or was he so accustomed to deception and pretense that he'd lost touch with such basic, selfless emotions?

Maybe he thought it didn't matter, just as he thought his reasons for leaving didn't matter. But reasons always mattered, though not in the beginning, of course. When he'd first left Ryan, if she could have strung him up from the tallest tree, she would have, no matter what excuse he offered. But now . . . trying to give the kid a better life beat all hell out of trying to give himself a responsibility-free life.

"Will you see him?" she asked.

It was difficult to be sure, standing in the shadows as he was, but she thought she saw him shudder an instant before he said, "That's probably not a good idea."

"For him? Or for you?"

"He's made it clear he doesn't ever want to see me."

"He's twelve years old and hurting. I'm not sure he knows what he wants."

"He's twelve going on thirty. He knows."

She moved a few steps closer, but he didn't turn to look. That was all right. She had no problem with talking to his back. "Then let me ask a different question. Do you *want* to see him? Do you miss him? Do you want to try to explain yourself to him?"

"That's three questions."

Finally she moved around him, stopping a few feet in front of him. Light from inside the house shone through the windows on either side of the door, illuminating the right side of his face, deepening the shadows over the left. "They're simple questions. All they need is a yes or no. In fact, you can answer just one of them."

The sharpening of his gaze indicated he recognized his own words from the other night. But he didn't answer. *She* hadn't answered *his* questions the other night, either. But where he'd let her walk away, she had no intention of allowing him the same opportunity.

"For God's sake, Cole, you're a grown man. You're intelligent and capable. You can charm the rattles off a snake and you can face prison, but you can't say, 'Yes, I miss my son'?"

His mouth barely moved. "He's not—"

"For three years he was, in all the ways that count! What are you so damn afraid of?"

At their feet, Jerome lifted his head, alerted by the frustration in her voice, but Cole didn't react to it at all. Dully he said, "I've got to go in. I'll see you around." Then he disappeared inside, locking the door between them.

WHAT *WAS* HE AFRAID OF? Cole was up half the night thinking about Leanne's question, and it had occupied his mind all morning Saturday as they worked on the haunted house. She hadn't shown up that morning—he'd heard Maggie tell Kelsey that Leanne was bringing lunch and would stay for the afternoon, while Sophy ran the store. While trying to ignore the tightening in his chest on hearing that, he'd noticed that Eli's attention had perked up at the mention of Sophy. *He sets Sophy's teeth on edge,* Leanne had said one night. *I think she likes him.*

Maybe she'd been right. She was right about a lot of things, it seemed.

He and Eli were working on the system of wires and pulleys that would make the coffin lid open and the skeleton dance, when the gray skies opened up and rain started falling. The fresh scent replaced the mustiness inside the barn, and dropped the temperature a few uncomfortable degrees. A few minutes later Leanne arrived with lunch. She was a bit soggy from the walk from her SUV to the barn, but the food, stored in Danny's old wagon and covered with a plastic tarp, was fine.

"Yea, food's here," Holly Flynn called, and received a tart response from Leanne.

"And hello to you, too."

"Oh, Leanne, I didn't recognize you," Holly teased. "Leanne's here, everyone—and the food!"

Leanne pushed the hood of her navy-blue slicker off her head, then shrugged out of it and hung it on a hook near the door. She snagged a napkin from the wagon to wipe her face and hands, then another to dry as much water as possible from her sneakers. Finally, she looked up and right at him. His stomach knotted, and for the first time since they'd left the house after breakfast, he was warm inside and out.

And *that,* he realized, was what he was afraid of.

Someone who could make life seem better just by being around.

Someone who was that important to him.

Someone who had that kind of power over him.

Hell.

Lunch consisted of sandwiches, chips, cookies, and soft drinks. He took one of each and returned to the back of the barn to sit on a hay bale. The others mostly gathered at the front except Leanne. Her hands empty but for a Pepsi and a cookie, she came to stand in front of him. He slowly chewed the food in his mouth, swallowed, then took a drink of pop before asking, "Are you going to stand there and stare at me or have a seat?"

She moved to sit cross-legged on the next hay bale. If she noticed the frequent glances they were getting from everyone else, she gave no sign. "I talked to Alex this morning about . . ."

"And?"

"He said it will make adoption tougher. The state will try to find his parents. If they can't, the judge can terminate *their* rights the same as he could have terminated yours, if you had any. But it'll take time, and there's always the possibility that his mother's gotten herself straightened out and will want him back, and the judge could decide to give her another chance. Or the father might never have known about him and could be thrilled to have him. Or there could be grandparents or an aunt or uncle . . ."

"So don't tell Kelsey."

She stared at him. "I have to!"

"No, you don't. They think I'm his father. I'll sign the papers and you can have him."

"I can't do that, Cole." Her voice rose, drawing attention from the other women. Face flushing, she lowered it to a whisper. "I can't. It's wrong."

"What's wrong with giving a kid a home where he's wanted?"

"But Alex knows the truth."

"He's your lawyer, isn't he?"

"Yes, but—"

"Then attorney-client privilege would keep him from telling anyone."

"But—"

He watched her as he started on the second half of his sandwich, but he already knew what her final answer would be. She was too honest—maybe too honest for Ryan's own good. She wouldn't go through with an illegal adoption.

Of course, she was right. What if she did, and somewhere down the line the truth came out? What if Ryan's mother came looking for him? The fact that Leanne had known the truth before the adoption would certainly hurt whatever claim she had to the kid, and being taken away from what he thought would be his home and family forever, would seriously hurt Ryan.

While munching her cookie, she stared at the skeleton, sitting up in the coffin where he and Eli had propped him, but he doubted she actually saw it. Her mind was on more serious problems.

"I'm sorry."

She glanced at him. "For what?"

"Everything. I wish . . ."

He'd never believed in wishes—had never wished on a star or birthday candles or a wishbone. Wishes had no place in a con artist's life. Intelligence, planning, execution—that was what made the difference.

"What do you wish?" Leanne asked.

He shrugged. "Nothing."

She shifted on the hay, to look at the skeleton again. "If I were going to wish, I would wish for better instincts about men. This guy here"—she wiggled the skeleton's fingers with her toe—"he looks about my speed . . . unlike every living man I've gotten serious about. Hell, Danny's father left when I told him I was pregnant, because he didn't want to be a father. The next one really seemed to like being part of our little family, but then decided he didn't want to play father to another man's son. The one after him was already married. And then there was you. You not only left me, but you left your son with me." Suddenly, suspicion colored her voice. "You don't have a wife or two out there, do you?"

"No," he said with a scowl, then it faded. "However, I think my brother, Adam, did forget to divorce his first wife before he married the second one."

Her dark eyes widened, then slowly a knowing look came over her face. "You're teasing, aren't you?"

He shrugged. He wasn't, but if it made her feel better to think so, then she was welcome to it.

"Where do your brothers live?"

"When they're not in jail? Your guess is as good as mine." He polished off the chips, then crumpled the trash and stuffed it in the chips bag. "Owen has pretty much settled in Philadelphia, and everyone checks in with him. It's the easiest way to keep in touch."

"Why don't you all just get cell phones and trade numbers?"

"Uh, no. Cell phones mean records, which means a better chance of getting caught for one thing or another."

"It doesn't sound like a very pleasant way to live," she said, sounding a little sad. For him?

"As long as you don't know anything else, it's not bad. The problems start when you do get to know something else." He stood up, held out his hand for her empty can, then took it to the trash with his own. When he returned, he crouched next to the skeleton and began fiddling with the monofilament line attached to its left elbow.

"What problems?"

He barely glanced at her, just enough to see the faded denim of her jeans and the hem of her black sweater. "What do you mean?"

"You said the problems start when you get to know something else. What problems?"

He shortened the line so the arm would lift a few

inches higher, then measured a piece to attach to the left knee. For a moment she let him work in peace while he considered his answer. When her foot started tapping, though, he looked at her again. "Your mother does that."

"Does what?"

"Taps her foot when she's not getting what she wants fast enough."

Immediately her foot stilled, and he grinned. "You don't want to be accused of having anything in common with Phyllis, huh?"

She made a face at him and was about to prompt him for an answer, he was sure, so he saved her the trouble.

"If you've never lived a normal life, you tend to want one of two things—either to have that normal life or to never have it. People who have never had a real home usually either like moving around or they're desperate for a place to call their own. I've never lived in a town like Bethlehem. It's different from the rest of the world out there. It's the kind of place where people can . . . belong. Where everyone pretty much accepts everyone else, and you can fit in, and there's this whole *community* thing going on."

He gestured around them, to emphasize the last words. In Bethlehem, if a person got sick, someone was there to help him out. If there was a crisis, people pitched in to resolve it. People didn't just live there—they were neighbors, friends, and family to everyone else who lived there.

Fifty years ago places like this hadn't been at all uncommon. Even today such towns still existed, or so he'd heard, but Bethlehem was the first he'd experienced for himself. And it had made him want it for Ryan and for himself.

If they were lucky, Ryan could have it.

"So the town tempted you to go straight," Leanne remarked.

"The town." He looked up at her. "You."

Her jaw tightened and skepticism darkened her eyes. She didn't believe him. Now there was a big surprise, he thought as she responded, sarcasm coloring her voice.

"But you managed to resist."

"What could I have done, Leanne? I came here for the sole purpose of stealing from you people. Do you really think I could have said, 'Hey, I've changed my mind. Here's your money back. Can we still be friends?' " He muttered a disgusted curse. "They would have spit in my face while they were cuffing my hands behind my back."

"You don't know that," she challenged, "and now you'll never know, because you didn't have the courage to try."

He knew it was stupid, but when she stood up, so did he. They were so close he could feel her breath, could see the beat of her heart at the base of her throat. He could feel incredible heat—his, theirs—and incredible longing, his and his alone.

"I do know," he whispered, bending even closer. "I changed my mind, sweetheart. I gave the money back. But you still look at me as if . . . as if . . ." He couldn't find words to describe how low she could make him feel with one look. Instead, he trusted her to supply her own.

"As if you stole from me and my friends?" she whispered heatedly. "As if you betrayed us? As if you betrayed your son? You only came back because they *forced* you."

"Damn right they forced me! Do you think I wanted to face these people again after what I'd done? Do you think I wanted to face *you*? I never had much, but at least I had some pride. Until then."

She stared at him a long time before cynically answering. "Gee, sounds like you have a conscience after all, or facing up to what you'd done wouldn't have cost you your pride."

Before he could respond to that, she went on. "Bethlehem is full of generous, kindhearted people. You knew that from the beginning—it's part of what brought you here. You could have stopped at any time, right up to the moment you left Ryan, and they would have forgiven you everything. But you didn't want forgiveness. You wanted money."

Cole didn't bother to argue that point with her as she started to walk away. Instead, he caught her wrist and held her there. "What about you, Leanne? Would you have forgiven me? Will you ever forgive me?"

She looked at his hand, her gaze so sharp he could actually feel it, until he released her, then she took a step back. "I don't know, Cole. I honestly don't know."

He watched her leave, wanting to tell her that she was wrong about the money, wanting to plead with her about the forgiveness, wanting . . . oh, hell, just wanting.

"What was that about?" Murray asked as he came to the opposite side of the skeleton.

Cole wearily shook his head. "Damned if I know."

W ANT TO GO FOR A WALK?"
The look Nolie gave Leanne was chastising. "Gee, let's see. It's about fifty-five degrees, it's raining, it's almost suppertime, and we've been working all day. I don't think so."

Leanne shrugged into her slicker. "You don't have to be sarcastic about it."

"That wasn't sarcasm. That was just me. Want to come to dinner?"

"Not tonight. The boys and I still have costume decisions to make. Maybe we can get that done over dinner."

"It was easier when you were a kid, wasn't it? Chase says you went as a fairy-tale princess every Halloween."

"Until I was thirteen," Leanne admitted with a laugh. "He preferred to be things like blood-sucking ghouls."

"So *that's* why he became a lawyer."

They were standing in the doorway of the barn, watching the rain while they talked. Besides them, the only ones left were Maggie, Eli, Cole, and Murray. Though they hadn't spoken again after their talk about forgiveness, Leanne was way too aware of Cole for her own good.

Apparently, so was Nolie. With a glance over her shoulder, she lowered her voice and asked, "Is everything okay?"

Leanne pretended ignorance. "Sure. Why wouldn't it be?"

"You two seemed pretty cozy."

In spite of the cool temperature, heat seeped into Leanne's face. "You mean Cole and me?"

"No, actually I was talking about you and Mr. Bones."

"We were just talking about Ryan."

"You must have had a lot to say."

A sharp gust of wind blew rain through the open door, dampening their jeans. Nolie pulled her jacket tighter, then stepped back. "You're falling for him again, aren't you?"

If anyone else was asking, Leanne would have no qualms about lying or even telling them to mind their own business. But this was Nolie, family and best friend, who'd helped her pick up the pieces the last time, who offered her the same unconditional love and support she gave her husband and daughter. Leanne wouldn't lie to her, and she couldn't tell her to mind her own business, because family *was* her business.

"Again? I'm not sure I ever got over him the first time. I thought I had. Lord knows, I've had my heart broken enough times to know the drill. But ever since he came back, I've felt *so* . . ." She smiled ruefully. "I know—after everything he did, I'm nuts. Certifiable."

"No more so than any other woman who's involved with a man," Nolie said dryly.

"He's a crook. Trouble with a capital T. He broke my heart and, worse, he broke Ryan's. He can't be trusted. I *know* these things, Nolie. But . . ." Her mouth flattened with dismay as the words trailed off.

"You know them in your head. But your heart knows that you loved him."

"You know, our brains are in our heads for a reason— because our hearts can't be trusted."

Nolie slid her arm around Leanne's shoulders for a comforting hug. "Sometimes our hearts know what's really important . . . and sometimes I swear they're out to get us. Whatever you do, Leanne, be careful. Don't let him hurt you again." Then her voice lightened. "But if it happens anyway, I've got enough recipes for prize-winning cakes to feed your sorrow for a year or so, and two shoulders for crying on."

The smile her words summoned was exactly what Leanne needed. She returned the hug fiercely. "My brother was a smart man to marry you."

"I think so, too." Nolie released her and stepped back before imparting her last words of wisdom. "Think with your head . . . but listen to your heart a little, too."

Leanne tightened her grip on the handle of the wagon as she prepared to dash into the rain. "Give my brother my love, and give Mica a big kiss for me."

"I will."

"And come see us sometime."

"Hey, the road runs both ways."

Leanne stepped into the pouring rain and hustled to her truck. She was trying to manhandle the oversized wagon into the back, when an extra hand easily boosted it inside. She wasn't even surprised that she knew by seeing no more than the five fingers that it was Cole. Of course it was. Eli and Murray didn't make her heart catch.

Rain drenched him, flattening his hair against his head and turning it dark gold. It dripped from his nose and chin and soaked his clothes, but he didn't seem to notice. In fact, she thought with a nervous swallow, he didn't seem to notice anything but her.

She had to clear her throat to speak. "If I had an umbrella, I'd share it with you."

"And get that close?"

She ignored his jibe. "You're going to freeze out here."

In return, he ignored that. "I *don't* have a conscience."

It took her a moment to think back to her parting words to him earlier. *Sounds like you have a conscience, after all.* Had that been on his mind all afternoon? It was a silly thing to stew over . . . unless the jibe targeted the fundamental truths his life had been built on. Unless he felt the need to convince someone he was beyond redeeming. Unless that someone he needed to convince, was himself. "Is that an insult to someone coming from your background?"

"Damn right. It's a pesky thing that was bred out of the Jackson family generations ago."

"Right. So . . . wanting a better life for Ryan, leaving him in a place where he would get it, returning all the money you stole—none of that had to do with having a conscience."

He shook his head, sending raindrops flying.

He looked so serious, so intense, that she couldn't resist leaning closer and clearly, politely, using her father's favorite curse word. It made his eyes widen slightly and left him staring at her with surprise.

"You didn't take a dime from anyone who couldn't afford it. Nolie told me you wouldn't take her check until she told you she had other money set aside. You didn't go near any of the elderly people in town who live on social security."

"I don't target people on fixed incomes."

"Because your conscience tells you it's wrong," she retorted triumphantly.

His grin was faint and sardonic. "No, because Owen says it's wrong—and *he* wouldn't appreciate being accused of having a conscience, either."

Ignoring the cold and the dampness seeping through her jeans and shoes, she folded her arms over her chest. "What else does Owen say you shouldn't do?"

He ticked them off on his fingers. "Never steal from a church. Never admit guilt. Never tell the truth if a lie will suffice. Never bring attention to yourself. Never apologize. Never—"

"Okay. I get the picture." He'd been taught the finer points of living a life of crime, the same way she'd been taught to brush her teeth before going to bed, look both ways when crossing the street, and never play with fire. Obviously, she'd forgotten all about that last one.

"Your father should have been locked up."

The grin flashed again. "He has been. Many times."

"He should have been locked up once and for all, and you and your brothers should have been placed in a home where you could be raised properly."

"We *were* raised properly—for the lives we were going to live."

"The lives *he* decided you should live. He didn't raise sons. He raised six little partners in crime."

How different would Cole's life have been if he'd been removed from his father's influence when he was young enough for it to matter? There would have been no limit to what he could have accomplished. He was smart enough, diligent enough, clever enough, to have done anything, and done it exceedingly well.

But if he'd been a successful businessman, doctor, or lawyer, he never would have been hustling pool in St. Louis. He never would have caught Ryan picking his pocket, or taken him in, or come to Bethlehem. If he'd been raised differently, he would have become a different man, and he wouldn't have had the same empathy for Ryan, and chances were good Leanne never would have fallen in love with him.

And he wouldn't have broken her heart.

"I think it's interesting that you defend your father, yet you did with Ryan exactly what I think Owen should have done with you. You have no problem with being raised by a crook to be a crook yourself, but you don't want Ryan raised by a crook and you don't want him to become one himself."

"He deserves better."

"So the lifestyle is good enough for you, but not him. Why? Why don't *you* deserve better?"

"Because I *am* a crook, plain and simple."

A crook, yes. Plain and simple? No way.

As the rain increased in intensity, she glanced up into the swiftly darkening sky, got a face full of water, then wiped it away. "This is a hell of a place and time for a conversation. Why did you come out here?"

"I was on my way to Eli's pickup, and it looked like you needed a hand."

"I appreciate it, but you should probably—" She glanced to the other side of the road, where the old truck had been parked when she'd arrived. It was gone. So were Maggie's and Nolie's cars. A long look around showed that the barn was locked up, with only the outside light shining, and everyone was gone but them.

How had four people left in three vehicles without her noticing them? Granted, the rush and splash of the rain muted other sounds, but she still should have heard doors slamming and engines starting. For heaven's sake, had her attention been fixed so completely on Cole, that she'd gone deaf and blind to the rest of the world?

He glanced around, too, then finished her statement for her. "I should probably ask my neighbor for a ride home, though I couldn't get any wetter if I had to walk."

"No, you couldn't," she absently agreed, turning away from the rear of the truck.

As she settled in the driver's seat, he did the same in the passenger seat. The moment the engine was running, she flipped the heat to high and shivered uncontrollably for the moment or two it took to warm the air. Naturally, the temperature change caused all the windows to fog, but she absorbed the heat a moment longer, before switching the air to the defrosters.

Gazing idly at the rain-streaked windshield, she wondered what Nolie, Maggie, Eli, and Murray had thought when they'd hurried out into the rain and saw her and Cole standing there, talking as if it were the middle of a warm, dry day. She'd already fielded questions from Nolie and Holly about her conversation with Cole when she'd first arrived. No doubt the speculation about the two of them had already started, and this little incident tonight would just fuel it.

At the moment, she didn't even care. She was getting the feeling back in her toes and fingers and the discomfort of being cold and wet was easing. Besides, she was the only one living her life, so she was the only one who got a say in it.

Finally, when the inside of the truck was as toasty warm as the outside was cold, she switched the wipers on and followed the old road toward the parking lot. "Is Eli irresponsible or overly trusting?" she asked as the SUV bumped over the rough transition to the paved parking lot. "Leaving you behind like that, I mean."

"Probably a little of both. He's convinced he can find me in no time, if I decide to make a break for it."

"And you're convinced he can't?"

He shrugged, making her wonder if his shoulders were so broad or the space between the seats was really so narrow. "I've been running longer than he's been alive."

"So why haven't you taken off?"

"And leave all this behind? Getting dragged into the police station by your mother, for daring to show my face? Not being trusted to carry even a dime in my pocket, or to walk to Harry's for a cup of coffee, or to the grocery store for a newspaper? Getting bossed around by a kid half my age?"

Even though his tone was light and mocking, Leanne knew those things bothered him deeply. According to Ryan, he'd never had to stay around and face his victims before.

She settled for scoffing at the least important of his complaints. "Eli's not that young."

"No, but he looks it."

She pulled into her parking space and shut off the engine. A glance in her side-view mirror showed the green truck in the driveway across the street. "So why haven't you taken off?"

He was quiet a long time, long after the engine noises settled and the windows fogged over again. When he did finally speak, it wasn't to answer her seriously. "Wouldn't you miss me if I was gone?"

"I would survive," she answered tartly. Truthfully, she and Ryan would both be better off if Cole had never come back into their lives. Oh, sure, they would have hurt for a while, but time healed all wounds, her father was fond of saying. Someday in the not-too-distant future, they would have forgotten him and gone on with their own lives.

Unfortunately, foolishly, but also truthfully, yes, in some ways she would miss him. Even though seeing him hurt, even though it was a poor substitute for the future she'd once dreamed of, seeing him was better than not seeing him. Knowing why he'd left Ryan was better than not knowing. Knowing there were reasons—albeit, not always good ones—for the things he'd done, was better than wondering.

Once more she repeated her question. "Why haven't you taken off?"

"Because if I did, I'd miss the chance to do this." Leaning over, he slid his fingers underneath her hair to curve around her neck, and he kissed her. His touch was warm and made her hot. His mouth was gentle and made her hungry. He slid his tongue into her mouth, and she opened for him, no coaxing, no resisting, nothing but a faint whimper of pleasure. It had been so long, and she'd been so lonely, and his kisses were so sweet.

She touched him, just her fingertips to his cheek, and abruptly he pulled back. Before she could grasp that he'd ended the kiss, before she could wonder why, he had opened the door and slid to the ground. Giving her a brash, cocky grin—the phony one—he closed the door once again and dashed across the street.

And he'd never answered her question, she realized. Oh, sure, he'd offered that baloney—*if I did, then I'd miss the chance to do this*—but it hadn't been a real answer.

For the moment, though, it had to be enough.

Chapter Ten

HARRY'S WAS CLOSED FOR THE NIGHT, WITH only a few lights burning here and there. Sophy stood behind the counter, leaning one elbow on it, bracing her chin on her hand. Gloria occupied one of the barstools on the other side, which she occasionally spun in a circle with all the delight of a child. She was easily amused.

Not Sophy.

They'd been in the diner thirteen minutes, and only one car had passed in all that time. Virtually all of their charges were home, tucked in their beds, sleeping soundly and, for a lucky few, dreaming blissfully. Of course, where else would they be at three in the morning?

"Eli's late."

Sophy gave Gloria a dry look. "You do have a talent for stating the obvious."

"You shouldn't be so hard on the boy. I like him."

"Good. Then you work with him, you talk to him, and leave me out of it." Sophy gestured as if she planned to disappear, but Gloria's chastening look stopped her.

"He's just helping—"

Sophy restrained a snort.

"—and it's just temporary. Though I do wonder why."

"Gee, I don't know. Could it have something to do with the fact that you *poisoned* our last charge?"

A delicate pink flooded Gloria's face. "It seemed like a good idea at the time. Besides, Jolie was all right."

"Her name is Nolie—and trust me on this, Gloria. Guardians poisoning the humans they're watching over is *never* a good idea."

"We needed a way to get Chase out of hiding and into town, where he could see his sister. Having Nolie rushed to the hospital accomplished that." Now Gloria's lower lip eased out. "Besides, it was just a little case of food poisoning. Norie didn't suffer too greatly for it."

Sophy rolled her eyes heavenward. No, other than one terribly unpleasant evening, Nolie hadn't suffered greatly. But now Sophy was paying the price, and she hadn't even been involved.

The bell over the door tinkled, even though the door was securely locked, then Eli materialized on the stool in front of her. Caught off-guard, for one instant she was struck anew by how amazingly pretty he was. Not handsome or good-looking, but very definitely, very masculinely, pretty. Perfect blue eyes, perfect nose, perfect jaw, perfect cheekbones, perfect mouth, perfect silky black hair. The most talented sculptor that ever existed, couldn't have created anything to match.

What a shame he was perfectly smug and arrogant to match.

"You're late," she said flatly, straightening so she wasn't so close to him.

"Who made you keeper of the schedule?" he retorted.

"We don't actually have a keeper of the schedule," Gloria said. "In fact, we don't actually even have a schedule. But we could make one up, couldn't we? And then we could have a keeper— Oh. That was a joke, wasn't it?"

"Hardly." Sophy walked around the counter and took a seat at a table nearer Gloria than Eli. Just for fun, since they were meeting at Harry's, she'd dressed in a pink outfit similar to the one Maeve, the waitress, wore. The color went well with her natural blonde hair, but she preferred jeans, overalls, and T-shirts.

Not that it mattered. She wasn't here to think about how she looked. In fact, she couldn't remember a time in . . . well, all of time that she'd given her appearance a second thought. Why now? she wondered while deliberately keeping her gaze and her thoughts from straying as far as the counter.

"So, Soph . . . what's up?" Eli asked, turning to face her, resting his elbows on the counter behind him.

"No one said there was anything up." In spite of her gritted teeth, the words sounded fairly normal.

"Then why the meeting?"

"There doesn't have to be a problem for us to get together. It's something we do—Gloria and I. When we work together. Without interference."

He slid to the floor and came to stand in front of her. She had to tilt her head back, her gaze sliding over jeans and a snug-fitting black T-shirt before reaching his face. "Interference? Is that what you're calling me these days?"

She smiled sweetly. "If the shoe fits . . ."

He swung a chair around, straddled it, and leaned toward her. "You're afraid of being shown up, aren't you? Afraid you can't handle the big jobs."

"Before coming to Bethlehem, I worked in Buffalo," she said with a sniff. "I convinced Tom Flynn to marry Holly McBride. *That* was a big job."

"From what I hear, it was nowhere near as big as convincing Holly to marry Tom." He gave Gloria a wink and a grin in acknowledgment of her role before turning back to Sophy. "Maybe they could put you on nursery duty or something. I could put in a good word for you."

"*Nursery*—You are insufferable."

"Coming from you, I'll take that as a compliment."

"I wouldn't compliment you if you were the last guardian left in all the heavens." She took a few breaths to control her temper, then politely said, "You know, I've finally figured out why *we* got stuck with you."

"And why is that, Miss Know-it-all?"

"Because no one else would have you."

"Oh, right, Soph. Truth is, they sent me here because *you*—"

Before he could say anything more, she faded away, form first, uniform second, clunky thick-soled shoes last.

"Wow, I'm impressed," he said snidely. "Like every guardian can't do that. Is that the best you can manage?" When she didn't answer, he sprawled in the chair and faced Gloria. "She doesn't like me much, does she?"

"No, I'm afraid not," Gloria agreed gently.

"Huh. Wonder why."

Sophy was feeling some small sense of triumph when he shrugged and went on. "That's okay. I don't like her much, either."

Ohhh! She'd been right about him the first hundred times. He was arrogant. Smug. Conceited. Insufferable. Too hateful for words.

In her head, a tiny whisper added one more comment. *Too handsome for words, too.*

A BOUT THE TIME LEANNE WAS EXPECTING RYAN HOME from school on Monday, the phone rang, and it *was* the school—the vice principal to be exact. His name was Pete Harrington, and in her opinion, he was vastly underqualified for the job. Oh, he met the education requirements, but he was every bad teacher she'd ever met, all rolled into one. He took himself too seriously, lived for his rules and regulations, had little compassion, and didn't particularly like kids, so naturally when the position of vice principal had come open a year earlier, the school board had promoted him.

With a sinking feeling in her stomach, after exchanging greetings, she asked, "What can I do for you, Pete?"

"I'm calling about Ryan."

She bit her tongue to keep from tartly informing him she'd figured that out, since Ryan was the only child she had enrolled in the Bethlehem public school system. "What about him?"

"I wondered if you knew he hasn't been turning in his homework."

"In which class?"

"All of them. For a week now."

She sank onto the stool behind the counter. "But he's doing it. I've checked it every night."

"Well, he's not turning it in. He's also been misbehaving in class—talking back to the teachers, refusing to follow instructions—and he got into a shoving match with another student in the hall between classes today. Fortunately, a teacher broke it up." Pete hesitated. "I understand his father is back in town."

If you define "father" loosely. "Yes, he is."

"I presume that's a large part of the problem."

Some foolish place inside her resented a man who'd never even met Cole describing him as a problem, no matter how apt the description. "Yes," she admitted reluctantly.

"I told Ryan to have you call me last Friday. Did he pass on the message?"

She stared at the stack of Christmas sweaters she'd been folding for display, wishing she could cover for Ryan, knowing she couldn't. "No, he didn't. Is it standard procedure to ask a child who's having problems to pass on messages to his parents?"

"We have to show them trust until they prove they don't deserve it."

Or set them up to fail, you pompous jerk. "Well, I'll talk to Ryan the first chance I get."

"Maybe you can get some pointers from your mother. As I recall, your brother was a problem child, too, wasn't he? They used to say that one of the chairs in the principal's office had his name on it."

His remarks made her blood pressure shoot up about ten points, along with her temper. The last thing she needed from her mother was advice, and *no one* called her brother a problem child in that smugly superior voice. For damn sure, no one was going to imply the same about Ryan. She was opening her mouth to say so when the idiot went on.

"When can you come in? This afternoon would be good for me."

"Uh, no. I've got an appointment." This time they would have several new things to discuss with J.D.— Ryan's school problems and her almost uncontrollable need to tell Pete Harrington where he could shove his pomposity and smugness.

"My schedule's pretty full," Pete went on. "How about Friday around four?"

"That's Halloween. It'll be a really busy day for us."

"Perhaps it would be a good idea if Ryan missed Halloween this year."

She made a face at the phone. "I don't think so. Even if I did, I wouldn't extend his punishment to Danny, and I still have obligations for the town celebration that night."

Catching sight of Ryan crossing the street, she abruptly said, "I'll have to call you back about this, Pete. Thanks for letting me know."

She hung up, leaving him sputtering, then hurried to the front window, tapping on it just as Ryan unlocked the apartment door. When he looked up, she waved him inside.

He came two feet inside the door, dropped to his knees to greet Jerome, then finally stood and faced her. "What?"

"We have an appointment with J.D. in a little bit."

He glowered. "I remember."

"Good. I wasn't sure you would, since you didn't remember to tell me that Mr. Harrington wanted to talk to me, and you didn't remember to turn in all that homework you've been doing every night."

Beneath his dark skin, his face flushed a hot red. "So? Homework's stupid. School's stupid."

"And kids who never get an education grow up to be stupid."

"Cole never finished school. Are you saying he's stupid?"

"Not in the least. Cole got an entirely different kind of education." He apparently had an advanced degree from the School of Larceny and Hard Knocks—but what good was it doing him now? "You want to be like Cole when you grow up?"

"Hell, no," he blurted out. Grudgingly, though, he went on. "But there's worse people to be like."

That was certainly true, and she'd dated many of them. She'd kissed more frogs than any female in the gene pool. It was a wonder she didn't have warts.

Sliding her arm around Ryan's shoulders, she drew him to the sitting area at the back of the shop. Jerome followed on their heels and immediately jumped onto the wicker love seat, stretched out, filling it from end to end, and resumed his favorite pastime of snoozing.

"Do you like living with Danny and me?"

He shrugged, pulled away from her, and dropped down hard in the corner of the sofa. "It's okay."

She settled at the opposite end, turning to face him. "We love having you in our family, but, Ryan, they won't let you stay if you don't start behaving and doing better in school. If you fail and talk back and get into fights, they'll think I can't handle you, and they'll place you with someone else. I really don't want that to happen."

He stared at the piece of carpet fringe he was rubbing his shoe across. "It's not like school's a big deal."

"Yes, honey, it is. It's a very big deal. Cole said you're a smart kid. He said you could make A's if you wanted."

"I did it before," he mumbled.

"How about doing it again? Show your teachers and Mr. Harrington and anyone's who giving you a hard time just how smart you are."

"Mr. Harrington's an idiot."

Leanne was pretty sure that agreeing with him was a violation of some parenting rule somewhere, no matter how right he was, so she opted for diplomacy. "He's the vice principal. I think being disliked by the students is part of his job description."

Finally he looked at her, and for the first time—in a while, she realized—he grinned. "He'd be an idiot no matter what he did for a living. It's just the way he is, and you know it. You've got that look in your eyes like you think so, too."

Leaning forward, she grabbed hold of him and dragged him to her end of the sofa, then wrapped her arms around him. Though she was prepared for a struggle, he didn't try to pull away. He didn't lean against her, as Danny always did, or even soften the tiniest bit, but he didn't pull away, and that was something.

"Okay. Swear you'll forget I ever said this, but . . . yeah,

Pete Harrington's an idiot. So's his sister. So are his parents. It runs in their family. *But . . .* Pete isn't the one who matters here. You are. You can't go looking for trouble."

"Why not? That runs in *my* family."

"Is that what the shoving match today was about?"

Immediately he dropped his chin to his chest and stared at his hands. His nails were ragged, as if he'd been biting them, and a callus showed on his middle finger, from clenching a pencil tightly. "Nothing happened."

"So the teacher who separated you and the other boy just imagined the whole thing?"

After a long time, he lifted his feet to the coffee table with a *thud,* then sighed. "No . . . but it wasn't anything. This kid, Kenny, just said somethin' about Cole—they was workin' outside the school—and . . . that's all it was."

This kid, Kenny, in that context, *always* referred to Kenny Howard. He was the only child of the pastor of her church, and was hell-bent on proving that old saying about preachers' kids being the worst *everything.* First and foremost, he was Bethlehem's worst bully. Even J.D., one of the nation's top child psychiatrists before he'd come to Bethlehem, had been known to refer to Kenny as *The Bad Seed* on occasion.

Leanne mimicked his position, placing her feet on the table. "Let me tell you something. When Kenny speaks, *nobody* listens. The kid is a troublemaker with a capital T. I know it's really hard to ignore him when he starts picking on you, but that's what you've got to do with kids like him. If you don't respond, before long, they'll leave you alone."

"Or pick on you even more."

That was true. Years ago, when her brother had become the target of that generation's Kenny, he'd tried the ignoring route, but it hadn't worked. Beating the snot out of the kid, had.

But she couldn't advocate violence. She was *positive* that was against the good-parent rules.

Since she couldn't resolve his problem with Kenny for him, she shifted the subject to another problem she couldn't solve. "What kind of work was Cole doing at the school?"

"They were trimming some bushes and puttin' stuff around them and the trees. Stupid stuff."

"Hey, you helped Miss Agatha and Miss Corinna with their yard work quite a bit this summer. It's honest work." After a moment, she asked, "Did you see him?"

He shook his head.

"Would you like to?"

He opened his mouth to answer, then closed it again and settled for another negative shake.

Leanne pulled his head against her shoulder, then rested her cheek against his hair. "It's okay if you want to, Ryan. He *is* your father"—feeling him stiffen, she corrected herself—"the only father you've ever known, and he's living right across the street. No one would blame you if you wanted to spend a little time with him."

"I don't want to," he said defensively. "Besides, he's not gonna stick around too much longer."

"I don't know about that." She wanted to show a little faith in Cole, but what could she base it on? Gut instinct? Heaven knew, her instincts about the opposite sex were abysmal. Was it her head wanting to believe in Cole, or her traitorous heart?

Ryan showed no such ambivalence. He snorted. "Betcha he's just waitin' for one of his brothers to show up and take him away."

"Why would you think that?"

" 'Cause that's what they do. Whenever one of 'em gets in trouble he can't get out of by himself, he sends a letter to Owen in Pennsylvania, and the first one who checks in with Owen has to go get him."

"But he's been here almost three weeks. Don't you

think someone would have shown up by now if he'd written and asked for help?"

"Nah. Everyone's always busy. It takes a while."

They each checked in with their father, Cole had said. Maybe Ryan was right. Maybe Cole was just waiting for one of them to come around.

Was she a fool for still wanting to believe in him? Probably. But the worst that could happen was he could prove her wrong. And so what if he did?

It wouldn't be the first time, and it surely wouldn't be the last.

With a sigh, she hugged Ryan, then released him. "Why don't you run Jerome outside before we head off to see J.D.?"

He got to his feet, rubbed the dog's shoulder, then said, "Come on, boy, wanna go out?"

Jerome was already dancing in anxious circles at the door when Ryan turned back. He scuffed his foot back and forth before finally looking at her. "Did Cole really say I was smart?"

"Yes, he did."

Though he did his best to hide it, the answer pleased him. With a grunt, he hooked Jerome's leash on his collar and went outside.

AFTER DIMMING THE SPOOK-HOUSE LIGHTS, COLE joined the crowd gathered at the back of the barn Tuesday night to watch the trial run of the dancing skeleton. Dirt was piled around the coffin to make it look half-buried, with the tombstone Leanne had made tilted at a precarious angle at the head.

With a ghostly creak, the coffin lid lifted, then the skeleton rose as if by magic. Hidden between a black sheet and the wall, Murray and Eli worked the monofilament lines like puppeteers, bobbing the creature's head, lifting his arms and legs in a macabre parody of a dance, before slowly lowering him back into the casket, then closing the lid with another creak. It wasn't the least bit scary—though maybe a five-year-old would see it differently—but it was entertaining.

The women applauded before returning to their various jobs. Cole went back to work, too, making the web that would hold the giant lighted spider in the corner of the open doorway. They'd tried using the fake stringy webs that filled every corner of the barn, but the stuff tangled around the spider and even the slightest breeze made it dangle and spin.

Now he was building one out of wire. It would have more substance than a web should, but so what? It was make-believe, like the one-foot-diameter spider that would occupy it.

He was unrolling a length of narrow-gauge wire when the spool slipped from his hand and rolled a few feet away. Before he could secure the end he'd already started and bend over to get it, Leanne picked it up, gave it back, then sat opposite him.

"I told Kelsey the truth."

He carefully bent the wire around one of the spokes that made up the base of the web, then stretched it to the next spoke. "I figured you did, when she walked in here tonight, looking at me like some kind of insect."

"She did not."

"No, she didn't," honesty forced him to admit. Kelsey Grayson had an extraordinary talent for hiding her true feelings toward the scum she worked with. Either that, or she was the most understanding person he'd ever met.

"What did she say?"

"Wouldn't that be easier if the web was standing upright?"

"Yeah, but I only have two hands."

She stood it on end, balancing it in both hands. "They're going to try to find Ryan's parents."

"Don't let them take him away from you."

"How could I stop them? Throw him and Danny in the back of the truck and take off for parts unknown?"

"If that's what it takes, yeah." That was what he would have done if anyone had tried to remove Ryan from his custody. But then, he was used to breaking the law. Besides, in the end, he'd given him up voluntarily.

"She doesn't think they'll have much luck. They don't have much to go on."

"Chances are good his mother, at least, doesn't want to be found."

She nodded at that, then watched as he continued to weave the wire around the web, wrapping it securely around each spoke. When he asked her to steady a particular section, she did. When he asked for pliers or wire cutters, she handed them over. After a while, she finally spoke again. "You know, Ryan's been meeting with J.D. Grayson."

"Yeah. How's that going?"

She shrugged. "Slowly. There's an awful lot he doesn't want to talk about."

Given the kid's background, that was understandable. In his experience, the easiest way to deal with hurt was covering it up and pretending it wasn't there. Smiling when he felt like dying. Hiding behind phony charm. Lying.

But *easy* wasn't good enough for Ryan. He deserved the *best*.

Without giving himself the chance to think better of what he was about to do, he carelessly said, "There's a lot I don't know about Ryan, but if there's anything I can tell him . . ."

She stared at him as if he'd grown a second head. "You would do that?"

He wanted what was best for Ryan, and always had. Clearly she still didn't believe him. The knowledge settled heavily on his shoulders.

He came to the end of the wire, wrapped it off, and clipped it, then measured another length before meeting her gaze. "Yes, I would do that."

"You'll have to actually *answer* questions, you know."

"I answer questions all the time, darlin'."

She made a skeptical noise, then solemnly said, "I'll tell J.D. Thanks." After a moment, she changed the subject again. "Are you dressing up for the party Friday?"

"Oh, yeah, sure. I'll pull out my gray Armani and come as a stockbroker."

The joke didn't amuse her, but that was okay. He wasn't particularly amused by it, either.

"The only thing Halloween's good for is making mischief. I bet when you were a little girl, all you got were the treats."

"And all you did were the tricks."

He grinned. "Bet I had more fun."

"I bet you did. You probably had the biggest collection of masks around. Of course, you used them for professional reasons, too, didn't you?"

"Yes, ma'am. I never had to worry about getting caught with my hand in someone else's pocket when everyone on the street was wearing a mask."

"You still wear more masks than anyone I've known."

He leaned so close the web snagged on his shirt. "No, sweetheart, I don't. You just don't like the me you see."

She shook her head stubbornly. "Sometimes I think, 'Okay, this is the man I knew.' Then you smile, or stop smiling, or blink, or turn around, and you're like an entirely different person. Then I realize I don't know you at all."

Sitting back, he grimly studied her. He wasn't sure

exactly of the reason for it, but he recognized the discomfort in his chest as disappointment. He'd thought . . . he wanted . . .

Hell, hadn't he learned yet that nobody gave a good damn about what he wanted—including himself?

"Does your family know where you are?"

He pricked his thumb on the exposed end of a piece of wire, drawing blood. After watching it well for a moment, he wiped it away on his jeans, checked again, then pressed it hard against the denim to stop the bleeding. While he did that, he watched her.

She was holding the web in one hand, tracing the index finger of her other hand lightly over the wire. Her expression was benign, as if she'd just asked another of her ten million questions. Not as if the question might be significant.

Probably, for her, it wasn't. For him . . . after he'd kissed her Saturday night, he'd gone into the Miller mansion, changed into dry clothes, sat on his bed, and written a letter to his brothers. After bumming an envelope and stamp from Eli, he'd dropped it in the mail on the way to church the next morning. The letter had been short and to the point—*I need a ride. If any of you happen to be in the area, you can find me at the address below.*

They wouldn't bother to write back. That wasn't their way. One day one of them would show up in town, then disappear, and he would disappear with him.

When the bleeding had stopped, he went back to work and answered her question. "I told you, we don't keep in regular touch. Besides, I pleaded guilty, which is a major violation of Owen's rules. If they knew, they would disown me."

"So Owen's laws are more inviolate than the nation's."

He grinned. "In our family, yes, ma'am, they are."

"What about your mother? Does she have any rules regarding her sons?"

"Only one. Once she's birthed 'em, her job is done."

"You're exaggerating."

"Only a little."

"What is she like?"

"Eloise? She has blonde hair and blue eyes. She's a beautiful woman. Put her in a Halston or Chanel suit, with a bauble from Harry Winston around her neck, and you'd never guess she was born dirt-poor." Once more he grinned. "Of course, put me in an Armani suit with a Rolex and diamond cuff links, and you'd never guess I was born poor, either. Granted, I don't *have* the Rolex or the cuff links anymore, since someone saw fit to return them to their rightful owners before he sprang me from jail."

She glanced at Eli, then rotated the web to give him easier access to the section he was working on. "So your mother cleans up good. That doesn't answer my question. What is she *like*?"

It wasn't a subject he'd ever given much thought to. One good thing about the way Owen raised them was that they'd learned not to judge people. To accept most, at least, as they were. They'd always just accepted Eloise without thinking much about her.

"She's . . ." He shrugged. "She's got the face of an angel and lies like the devil. She could sell water to a man stranded in the middle of the ocean or charm a miser out of his last penny. She's the best actress I've ever seen. She can't spend more than a few weeks at a time with Owen, and can't stay away from him for more than a few months . . . barring incarceration. She's great at producing kids and lousy at mothering them. She's . . ." Again he shrugged.

"How long have she and Owen been married?"

"They've been together, more off than on, for about thirty-five years, but they were never married."

That made her look at him, her eyes wide. They were

brown, almost as dark as her hair, and glinted with surprise. Growing up surrounded by blue-eyed blonds, he'd developed a real fondness for brown eyes and brown hair during his short time in Bethlehem last spring.

"They've been together all that time and had six children and never married?"

"They never saw a reason to make it legal. If one of them found someone else, then they would have to go through the hassle of unmaking it." Reaching out, he tapped her chin to close her mouth. "Don't look so appalled. You never married your son's father, either."

"We had *one* son, not *six*. Besides, I would have married him if he'd asked."

That information didn't set well with Cole. She'd told him about Danny's father last spring—they'd dated for months; she'd gotten pregnant; he'd given her the big kiss-off and, for good measure, had moved away. End of story. Somehow she'd omitted the part about wanting to marry him, which suggested she had also loved him. Definitely something he didn't want to know.

So, perversely, he asked her. "Were you in love with him?"

"Yeah. And he broke my heart."

"Want me to beat him up for you?"

She gave him a wry look. "If you go around beating up everyone who's broken my heart, you're gonna be busy. Plus, you're on that list, too. You wanna beat yourself up?"

"I excel at it." He wrapped the last piece of wire around the last spoke, clipped it, then asked, "What do you think?"

His fingers brushed hers as he took it from her. Her gaze flickered and her jaw tightened, then she scooted back on the hay for a better look. "It looks good."

"Now we can stretch the fake stuff across it to give it more substance, then mount the spider right in the middle."

Smiling faintly, she got to her feet. "I'm all in favor of more substance," she murmured before she walked away.

Cole set the web down, then twisted to watch her. She spoke to Nolie, laughed at something Kelsey said, then gathered an armload of ghost-making materials and went to a quiet corner to work. He thought about following her—there was plenty of room for two—and asking what the reason was for her sudden melancholy.

He didn't, though. He still had this project to finish. He'd spent more than enough time alone with her in the past week. He was getting too involved with her—again, and look how badly it had ended last time.

And the most important reason—if he asked her why she'd gotten so blue, she just might tell him.

And he couldn't bear any more guilt.

A PUMPKIN WITH TOOTHPICKS FOR ARMS AND LEGS. That was how Melissa had threatened to dress up for the Halloween celebration. Alex had laughed and told her she was beautiful. As she studied herself in the mirror, rubbing the mild ache in her lower back, she smiled smugly. He would *really* laugh now.

She wore a shapeless orange outfit—she didn't even know what to call it. Sort of a dress with leg holes that hit about midthigh. Underneath it she had on a green turtleneck sweater and green tights, with brown suede Mary Janes on her feet and, on her head, the finishing piece—an orange cap with a brown stalk trailing a piece of leafy green vine in the center.

Alex, of course, wasn't dressing up for Halloween. Few of the men did, although they could always count on Harry, and in the last few years J.D. had gotten in the habit of donning a costume. It was probably easier than saying no to all his kids. In a few years, she fully intended to help Junior badger his father into the same surrender.

"Melissa? Are you read—" From the bedroom door came a great burst of laughter.

She turned to face him, still wearing that smug smile. "How do I look?"

"Wonderful." He gently poked at her stomach, pretended not to hear the rustling of the foam she'd used, and grinned. "And you don't even need padding."

She stuck her tongue out at him. "The prize for the best adult costume this year is a half-dozen of Miss Corinna's triple-dipped chocolate-and-caramel apples rolled in peanuts and pecans. Watch it, 'cause if I win, I might not want to share with anyone who insults me."

He immediately pulled a straight face. "Oh, honey, I'd wondered where every single pillow in the house had gone. Now I know." He nuzzled her neck, then stepped back so she could leave the room ahead of him. "Are you going to be warm enough in that?"

"I'm counting on you and the bonfire to keep me warm." Holding on to the railing, she made her way downstairs and started to turn toward the kitchen, but he stopped her. "I've already loaded the food into the car, along with a folding chair for you and a quilt in case you get cold. I just need to get the apples. Wait here."

As he went down the hall toward the kitchen, she went to the closet, reaching automatically for her very warm, slim-fitting black cashmere coat. With a regretful sigh, she took the very loose-fitting wool swing coat out instead. The cashmere didn't even come near covering her belly, and it wasn't fair to Junior to keep herself warm while letting him freeze, though he did have all that padding of both Mom and foam.

She was struggling into the coat when a sharp pain

sliced through her, making her breath catch. She clutched the closet door with one hand, while pressing the other to the side of her stomach, massaging firmly. Taking slow, measured breaths, she focused her whole being on easing the pain. *It's all right, it's all right.* That had become her mantra to get through these episodes in the past week. They'd been occurring at odd times, but they weren't severe and they never lasted long. When she'd called her doctor, he'd told her not to worry. Backaches and cramps weren't unusual in the last trimester. As long as there was no spotting or discharge, she shouldn't worry.

When she heard Alex's footsteps in the hallway, she gritted her teeth and straightened. She didn't want him to know she'd had another pain. *She* knew how to handle worry—God knew, she'd been through enough of it. *He* didn't handle it so well.

By the time he reached her, she was pretty sure she looked as if nothing more important than getting her other arm into her sleeve was going on. "I could use a little help here," she said, fumbling behind her.

With a chuckle, he held the sleeve, then guided her arm into it. She straightened the coat, then faced him. "Thank you, kind sir. How do I look?"

"With a little whipped cream and a sprinkling of cinnamon, good enough to eat."

"Do my shoes match?"

"Yes, ma'am."

She gazed down with a mock woeful expression. "Do you suppose I'll ever see my feet again?"

"One of these days, honey," he said, sliding his arm around her and ushering her out the door. "One day soon."

Chapter Eleven

EOPLE WERE STARTING TO ARRIVE FOR THE PARTY when Leanne made her last check of the grounds. All the tables were set up and covered with orange-and-black cloths. The galvanized tubs were filled with water and apples for bobbing, and the few other games were in place. A small stage had been erected for the costume contest that would take place later in the evening, and the wood was laid for the bonfire. Her parents were bringing Danny and Ryan with them, so all that was left for her, was to get dressed.

She got the garment bag from the back of her SUV and ducked inside the haunted house. It wasn't officially open yet, while the final touches were being made, and a corner of it had been turned into a dressing room for the humans who were part of the scenery. She waved at Nolie, dressed all in black, her red hair covered by a stringy black wig, her naturally pale skin turned deathly white, and her smile enhanced with the addition of fangs, before she ducked behind the curtain.

She'd gotten her costume from her cousin, Hailey, whose handmade costumes had become a profitable sideline to her quilting business. Leanne hadn't even had time to peek into the bag since she'd picked it up that afternoon. She'd asked for something beautiful—to be more accurate, for something that would make *her* beautiful. Hailey had assured her the costume was perfect, that the size wasn't a problem, since they wore the same size, and that she needed to wear her hair up and a pair of white tights.

She hung the garment bag on a nail in the wall, then unzipped it. Fabric spilled out, frothy layers of lace and satin and tulle. Her mouth forming an O, she pushed the garment bag behind the dress, then stared.

It was a princess-going-to-the-ball gown, with a pale blue fitted bodice, white sleeves that puffed on the upper arm, then fitted closely all the way to the wrist, and a skirt of sheer white, silver, and ice blue layered one atop the other. It was incredible.

Behind the dress was a cloak in the same colors, trimmed with fur, and in the bottom of the bag Hailey had included a pair of clear vinyl heels and—Leanne didn't know whether to laugh or clap her hands with delight— her very own tiara.

She stripped down to her tights, carefully stepped into the dress, then got the zipper halfway up before peeking through the curtains. "Hey, Vampira," she called. "Can you give me a hand?"

Baring her fangs, Nolie made her way through the maze, stepped behind the curtain, and gave a sharp whistle. "Oh, my gosh, you look beautiful!"

Leanne preened, wishing for a mirror to see for herself. "Can you believe this outfit? I just asked Hailey to pick out something pretty for me. I never dreamed . . ."

"Wait till Prince Charming gets a look at you. He'll be struck dumb." Nolie zipped her up, adjusted the puffy sleeves, then picked up the tiara, to position it on Leanne's hair. When she finished, she stepped back and sighed. "Oh, honey, you're beautiful. But I've got a suggestion. How about next year, *you* be the vampire and let *me* be the fairy-tale princess?"

"My brother already thinks you're the most beautiful princess of them all."

"Yeah, he does, doesn't he?" Nolie's smile was serene in spite of the fangs. "Put the cloak on. You don't want Cole to catch a glimpse of you when you're not ready to dazzle him."

Leanne let her sister-in-law help her with the cloak, grateful for its warmth, then faced her. "Nolie . . . do you think I'm crazy for wanting to dazzle him after everything he's done?"

Of course, she already knew the answer to that. She had passed crazy and was somewhere between reckless and lunacy, and until her sanity chose to return, there wasn't anything she could do about it. At that very moment, there wasn't anything she *wanted* to do about it. Later, though . . . that would be a different story. That would be the time for regrets.

Instead of answering right away, Nolie picked up the jeans Leanne had discarded, folded them, and draped them over the dress's hanger, then slid her sweater over it. "I think there's nothing particularly rational or sane about falling in love, for anyone. Look at Chase and me. What were the odds that a hotshot, big-city lawyer would ever fall for a plump, Arkansas farm girl? But it happened. We fell in love anyway."

"But did he break your heart along the way?" Leanne asked gloomily, thinking back to that awful May day when she'd discovered Cole hadn't just slipped out of bed early to get to work, but had slipped out of town—for good.

"Just once. But the important thing isn't what he did,

but what he does now, what he'll do in the future. The *really* important thing is having faith."

Leanne's voice dropped to a whisper. "I doubt anyone's ever had faith in Cole, not when it mattered." And she didn't know if she had the trust or fortitude to be the first.

Just as she doubted whether she had the sense or fortitude to not get involved with him again.

"Probably not."

She had trusted Cole—the whole town had—before he'd disappeared, but that had been easy. They hadn't known who he was or what he was capable of. The trick was trusting someone when you did know.

"Come on." Nolie swept back the curtain so Leanne could pass through. "They're about to light the bonfire. Let's go find our respective Prince Charmings and let them marvel over us."

Chase was right outside the barn with five-year-old Micahlyn, dressed as a ballerina, on his shoulders. He greeted his wife, kissed Leanne's cheek, and told her she looked beautiful, for a kid sister. She talked with them a few minutes, her gaze constantly scanning the crowd for one face in particular.

She didn't find him.

The fire department oversaw the lighting of the bonfire, officially kicking off the celebration. Holding her cloak together from the inside, Leanne strolled the grounds, greeting friends, searching unsuccessfully for Cole.

She did locate her parents. Her father was dressed in a Star Trek outfit, complete with pointy ears. Her mother, naturally, wore woolen pants, a sweater, a jacket, and gloves, and seemed embarrassed to stand next to Earl.

"Princess!" Her father embraced her, then straightened the tiara he'd knocked askew. "Haven't I always said my girl was a princess?" he asked of no one in particular. "This just proves it. You're by far the prettiest girl here."

"Thanks, Daddy. Where are the boys?"

"Ryan went off with his friends, and Danny's right over there."

She looked to the nearest booth, where her superhero-du-jour son was throwing darts at—and missing—a board full of balloons. Looking up, he grinned and waved, then caught his lower lip between his teeth and took careful aim again. No one looked more surprised than he when the balloon popped—probably because he had aimed for one at the opposite corner.

Finally Leanne couldn't avoid speaking to Phyllis any longer. Facing her, she opened the cloak wide. "Hello, Mother. Do you like my costume?"

Phyllis's gaze was, as usual, as cold as the night. "That's Hailey's work, isn't it? It's lovely. Of course, it's too . . . young for you."

"Too young?" Leanne repeated.

"You're a thirty-three-year-old single mother. Not a princess, no matter what anyone says."

Earl swore, making her mother cringe—the primary reason, Leanne had realized long ago, he did so. "Princesses stay princesses right up until they die—unless they become queens. So, honey, if you want to be a princess forever, you go right ahead and be one."

"Thanks, Daddy. I'll see you guys later." Raising her right hand, she formed a V with the two little fingers pressed together on one side, the other two fingers on the other. "Live long and prosper."

Her father's booming laughter followed her as she walked away. So did Phyllis's sharp, "Honestly, Earl!"

She covered the grounds, finding no sign of Cole, then wandered over to the bonfire. The flames leaped into the air, yellow and red, as the wood popped, crackled, and hissed. The heat it put out was incredible, warming her front to a feverish level, but leaving her backside chilled in spite of the cloak. She was in the process of turning her back to the flames, to even the temperatures, when her gaze fell on a lone figure, leaning against a tree and watching her from the edge of the woods near the back of the barn.

Cole.

Would he come to her if she stayed where she was? Probably not. Was she smart enough to keep her distance? The answer became painfully clear as she strolled across the ground to him, careful in the heels, coming to a stop a few yards in front of him. "You didn't dress up."

He wore snug jeans, faded and soft enough to cling, with a dark T-shirt and a black leather jacket. His boots were black, too, one of them planted in the dirt, the other resting against the tree trunk.

"Sure, I did."

"As what?"

"A thug? A punk?"

"A bad boy?" She smiled. "Women can't resist a bad boy, you know."

"The women around here seem to be doing a fine job of it," he responded dryly.

It seemed safer at the moment to not respond to his comment.

"You look beautiful." He reached out and hooked his finger in the fur at the neck of the cloak. "Are you wearing anything under that?"

As she'd done for her mother, she opened the cloak wide, then slipped it off her shoulders and did a slow twirl for him. When he saw the back of the gown—see-through from her shoulders to her hips—she thought she heard a faint choking sound, and when she faced him again, he looked almost as if he was in pain.

"You like?"

"Oh, yeah. Now put that thing back on before someone else sees you."

"I thought I'd leave it off for a bit—to cool down, you know."

He took the cloak from her arm, swung it around her shoulders, then gathered the edges together in front. "You cool down any more, and I'm gonna go up in flames."

She moved to stand beside him and looked out across the grounds. "Everything seems to be a big success."

"I imagine everything this town does is a big success."

She acknowledged that with a shrug. Folks in Bethlehem loved a party, so of course they were good at throwing one. "Why don't you come on out and join the fun?"

He glanced at all the people, with something in his eyes—wistfulness, perhaps—then shook his head. "I'm fine right where I am. But don't feel you have to keep me company."

Instead of taking him at his word and leaving, she hugged her cloak tighter. "Eli made you come, didn't he?"

"The word 'no' exists in his vocabulary only when *he's* the one saying it."

"Just because you're here against your will doesn't mean you can't have a good time. At least come out to the fire and get warm. You must be freezing." *She* certainly was.

His gaze skimmed over her, from head to toe and back again, and suddenly she wasn't the least bit cold anymore. "I'm wearing more clothes than you are. Though if you're really concerned about me freezing, you could raise my temperature by nothing more than coming a little closer."

Don't do it, don't do it, don't— The voice in her head was silenced by her first step toward him. How close would he let her come? After all, his back was against the tree, so he couldn't easily retreat.

She took another step, and another, and her full skirts brushed his legs. One more, and the fabric was crushed between them.

He swallowed convulsively. "This really isn't a good idea."

"What?"

"This."

"Sharing our warmth on a cold night?"

"Letting me kiss you."

"You haven't kissed me."

"But I'm going to if you don't . . ."

She gazed up at him. There was a look in his eyes she knew well—desire. Hunger. And a look she didn't know at all. Panic? Fear? Was he afraid of kissing her? Afraid of wanting her? Afraid she wouldn't want him? Or afraid she would?

"Leanne," he warned.

"I don't think you'll kiss me. Not here. Not now. Not—"

He proved her wrong. Cupping her face in his palms, he bent his head to hers, claimed her mouth with his. He thrust his tongue inside her mouth, stroking, tasting, then slid his hands lower, down her throat and inside the cloak, across her waist, to her hips, then her bottom. He lifted her to him, rubbing his erection hard against her, all the while stealing the breath and the logic and the reason right out of her.

There was nothing rational or sane about falling in love, Nolie had said, and Leanne was living, breathing, aching proof of it. If she was rational, she would run, screaming, the other way. If she was sane, she would put a stop, once and for all, to the kisses, the conversations, the temptation.

She couldn't say who ended the kiss. Her lungs were aching for breath, her body just aching. His eyes were huge, intense, and dazed. Her heart thudded loudly in her ears, and his breathing was raw and ragged.

Under the cloak, he still held her against him, and was still hard and hot, straining against her. In spite of that, he said, "I don't want this."

"The gospel according to Owen Jackson. *Lie like the devil,*" she murmured recklessly, as she deliberately rocked her hips.

He responded with a nerve-clenching shudder, then tried again. "*You* don't want this."

In the bigger sense—life, the future, the well-being of her heart—he was probably right. But it was hard to consider the bigger sense when he'd lifted his hand to her breast and was gently teasing her nipple through the dress fabric: tiny little pinches, tender caresses that ricocheted all the way through her before settling between her thighs. It was hard to think about life and the future when she'd been alone so long, when she'd missed him so much.

As for the well-being of her heart . . . if four broken hearts hadn't killed her, what were the odds number five would?

She was crazy. Flirting with danger. Her own worst enemy. Good sense had deserted her, and she proved it with her next words. "Come home with me."

"I—I can't."

"Then come behind the barn with me."

He looked scandalized . . . and tempted. "We could get caught."

"We could get caught right here, but that hasn't stopped you from playing with my breast. It won't stop me from . . ." Letting her voice trail off, she slid her hand down his front, over the waistband of his jeans, to the bulge that pulled the denim taut. Choking out a groan, he removed her hand and held it firmly at her side. When she reached out her other hand, he caught it in a similar fashion, then stared down at her.

"You don't know what you're doing."

"Of course I know. I may be dressed as a princess, but I'm the queen of bad choices and lousy decisions. Having sex with you wouldn't be my first mistake. It wouldn't even be my first mistake with you. But at least this time I *know* not to expect anything else."

As he stared at her, bleakness shadowed his eyes. He pushed her a few feet away, then let go and spun off. Startled, she grabbed his arm. "Hey! Where are you going?"

"What? You have more to say? Think of a few other insults? Let me save you the hassle. Liar, thief, cheat, scum, crook, embezzler, lowlife. How about bastard—literally and figuratively? That'll get you two insults in one."

"I wasn't insulting you!" she protested. "I just—"

"Lousy choices? Bad decisions? Having sex? Mistakes? You don't call those insults?"

"I was talking about *me*. I make lousy choices—"

He leaned close to her, barely whispering his reply. "And I *am* the lousy choice. The bad decision. The mistake."

Clutching the cloak tighter, she looked unhappily at him. "I didn't mean—"

"Yes. You did."

He pulled loose and backed away. When he would have turned into the darkness behind the barn, she hastily spoke. "What about my wanting to have sex with you, Cole? Do you consider that an insult, too?"

The cold stares her mother usually treated her to had nothing on the ice in his derisive gaze. "No. I consider that not likely to happen. Not in this lifetime."

With that, he left her.

• • •

HANDS SHOVED INTO HIS POCKETS, COLE CUT BE-
hind the barn to the road, clogged on both sides with
parked cars. He didn't know where he was going—to the
Miller house, probably, though if he didn't make the right
turns, who knew? He could be halfway to Howland before
this angry energy burned off.

Damn it, he didn't care what Leanne thought. He'd
never cared what *any* woman thought. From his mother
on, women had never been more than a temporary part of
his life. His father and his brothers—they stuck around, but
women didn't. They used and forgot the females they came
across, because it was easier than being the one used and
forgotten.

But hearing her say that he was a lousy choice, a bad decision, a mistake . . . if he didn't know better—and, by
God, he *did*—he would think her words had hurt. He
would think she had the sort of power over him no one
else had ever had—not his father, not his mother, not his
brothers.

But he did know better. He wasn't hurt. He was pissed
that she'd seen through the act he'd put on just for her. He
was pissed that she'd seen the real him when no one else
ever had.

Because truth was, he *was* a lousy choice for any woman
to make. Getting involved with him *had* been a bad decision, and having sex with him *had* been a mistake. But only
he was supposed to recognize that so clearly.

He was halfway to the parking lot, the sounds of the
party fading into the distance, when a closer noise slowed
his steps. It came from his left, soft, like a moan or a—

A whimper. Narrowing his gaze, he turned in that direction, looking between the cars parked there. It was

probably a couple of teenagers making out, or younger kids cooking up trouble. But when the sound came again, he recognized the pain in it. It was followed by a gasp, then sharp, heavy breathing and a whispered, "Oh, my God."

Finally he saw the person, standing between two cars, bent nearly double. Even in the dark, there was no mistaking her for a man. The legs extending beneath the costume were too shapely by far.

He took an uneasy step toward her. "Are you okay?"

She raised her head, but seemed unable to straighten. Reaching one pale hand toward him, she whimpered again. "Oh, God, please . . . help me."

It was Melissa Thomas, his lawyer's wife. He recognized her from their one meeting last spring, and from the courtroom when he'd been sentenced. Her face was ghostly pale, dotted with sweat, and even in the shadows, he could see her grass-green tights were stained with—

Jesus, she was pregnant.

And something was wrong.

He bolted to her side and helped her to the ground. Jerking his jacket off, he spread it over her, then said, "I'll get help. I'll be right back."

"Please . . . hurry," she panted.

The last time he'd run all-out, there had been a cop ten yards behind him, gun in hand. Luckily, Cole had been younger, lighter, and faster, and he'd lost the guy on a busy Atlanta street. He covered the distance between the cars and the party at that speed and then some, skidding to a stop in front of the barn and collaring J.D. Grayson. "You gotta come with me! She needs a doctor."

"Who needs—Wait—" Grayson handed his little girl to the teenage boy beside him before Cole dragged him away. "Who needs help?" he asked as they jogged back down the road.

"Melissa Thomas. I think she's having the baby."

"Oh, God, no."

She was easier to find this time. They could hear her weeping a half-dozen cars away. When they reached her, Grayson dug in the pocket of his pants, then tossed a set of keys to Cole. "That truck over there is mine. Back it down here, then lower the tailgate. Melissa, it's J.D. Talk to me, honey. Tell me what's happening."

Cole didn't hear her response as he trotted to the SUV, climbed in, and revved the engine. Having a baby wasn't that big a deal—if it were, Eloise never would have done it twice, much less six times. But Grayson's response—*Oh, God, no*—and the tone of his voice meant this was bad. Maybe the baby was premature, or there was some problem with her pregnancy. He'd heard something about her last spring, about not being able to have kids, but he couldn't remember. He'd never wanted to remember things that might make him sympathetic toward his marks.

He backed up to where Grayson and Melissa waited, then jumped out, opened the back window, lowered the tailgate, and shoved a bunch of gym bags and soccer balls aside. By the time he was finished, Grayson was standing there, Melissa in his arms. "Drive us around to the ER, then come back and find Alex," he directed as he gently lowered her into the cargo area, then climbed in beside her.

According to the truck's clock, it didn't take even two minutes to circle the hospital to the emergency-room entrance, but it seemed a damned long two minutes. Grayson snapped orders to a nurse taking a smoke break outside the door, and a minute later a whole group of staff descended on them with a gurney. After they were inside, Cole pulled away from the entrance, drove to the end of the parking lot, and stopped.

This was his chance. No waiting for his brothers to get his message, then come spring him. He could make a U-turn, head out of the parking lot and out of town. By the time anyone realized he was gone, he would have such a jump on them, that their chances of finding him would be somewhere between slim and none.

He wouldn't even have to worry about Grayson reporting the vehicle stolen for a while, since he had his hands full at the moment. He could drive to Howland, switch tags with a similar SUV, then head for Pennsylvania—or, better, Tennessee. Leanne and Ryan would expect him to go to his father's, but they would never think he would run to Eloise instead.

But when he moved his foot from the brake to the gas, he didn't cut the wheels in a sharp turn. He eased over the bump into the dirt road, drove to the end nearest the barn, and parked there. He found the boy who'd been with Grayson—his third son, Jacob—still in front of the barn, still holding the girl. "Here's your dad's keys. Have you seen Alex Thomas?"

"Yeah, he's right over—"

Seeing the man, Cole headed that way. Thomas was standing with a half-dozen other men, every damn one of them a victim of Cole's, and they were talking sports. He didn't wait to be acknowledged, but butted right in. "Grayson just took your wife to the ER. He wants you over there now."

Thomas's eyes widened, and he glanced in the direction where he'd apparently last seen Melissa. A lawn chair sat crookedly, with a quilt draped over it. The cup of hot cider he held, slipped from his hand, splattering to the ground, then, without a word, he raced off toward the hospital.

And without a word, Cole turned and walked away.

This time he made it home, not that he'd ever had a real home. He'd never belonged anywhere.

And Bethlehem wasn't going to change that.

I T WAS TWO HUNDRED EIGHTY-FOUR STEPS FROM THE labor and delivery waiting room to the door of Melissa's room. Alex knew because he'd paced them off about a hundred times while waiting to see her. Many of their friends had come to the waiting room after leaving the party, but he couldn't bear to sit at the moment—couldn't bear the sympathetic looks.

Couldn't bear knowing that after coming so far, he and Melissa might lose this baby, too.

The hospital had paged Dr. Gregory, who'd arrived at the ER, dressed in a clown suit, right behind Alex. Alex had seen him only once since then, when he'd stepped into the hall, to give him an update.

He hadn't seen his wife at all.

J.D. fell into step with him. "She's getting good care."

"I know."

"And everyone's praying for her."

He knew that, too, and he did believe in the power of prayer, in miracles and all those divine mysteries. How else to explain that they were *this* close to holding their baby in their arms? He'd been praying, too—formless, soundless prayers. *Please, God, please, please, please.* It was the best he could manage.

"What are they doing?" he asked as they reached Melissa's door, then turned and started back. Dr. Gregory had told him, but he hadn't heard the words. Alex had been too caught up in the grim expression the doctor wore and his inability to promise that Melissa and the baby would be perfectly fine.

"When she first came in, they started an IV and drew blood for some lab work," J.D. said quietly, his voice soothing as a psychiatrist's voice should be. "They put her on a fetal monitor, to check the baby's heart rate and to measure any contractions, and did a pelvic exam to determine whether the cervix is dilated and, if so, how much. When they took her out a while ago, they went to X ray for a pelvimetry study. That gives them the baby's position and also the size of Melissa's pelvis, to make sure she can deliver the baby."

Alex hadn't seen them taking her out of the room for the trip to X ray, and he'd been at the far end of the hall when they'd wheeled her out of the elevator and back into the room. By the time he'd raced down there, the door was already closed in his face. All he'd seen was hospital staff, and the faintest glimpse of Melissa's dark hair. "What now?"

"They're checking to see if the discharge she's having is amniotic fluid. If it is, they'll have to deliver the baby within twenty-four hours. If the sac is leaking and fluid can get out, then germs can get in, so it's safer for both Melissa and the baby."

"*Safer?* She's only seven and a half months pregnant! Having the baby six weeks early isn't safe for either of them!"

"I know. But it's safer than trying to delay, if the baby has been compromised." J.D. laid his hand on Alex's shoulder. "Is there someone I can call for you? Your Uncle Herb?"

"He's in Hawaii." After retiring and turning his law practice over to Alex, his uncle had thrown himself wholeheartedly into pursuing his other passion in life—flowers in general, orchids in particular. Wherever they grew profusely, he followed.

"What about your parents?"

Alex's smile felt like a fraud. His father was dead, and he got along well enough with his mother, when he saw her, which wasn't often since she'd remarried. Her new husband and his family came first with her now, and he understood that. His kids lived right there in the same town, and his grandkids called her grandma. They needed her more than Alex did, and she really needed to be needed. "I'll call my mother tomorrow, once we know . . ." *Something. Anything* would be better than knowing nothing.

But immediately he discounted that. If the news was bad, he could go on not knowing, indefinitely.

"What about Melissa's family?"

"I called her sister about an hour ago. Their parents will be down in the morning." Alex dragged his hand through his hair. "I *hate* this!"

"I know."

The sympathetic words tore at his raw nerves, making him scowl at J.D. "Stop saying that. You can't know unless you've been through it your—"

Abruptly remembering, he broke off and turned away. Maybe J.D. hadn't ever had to stand by helplessly while doctors fought to save his child's life . . . but he'd had to watch, knowing there was nothing they could do to save his first wife's life. Worse, though the accident that killed her hadn't been his fault, he *had* been driving drunk, and as a consequence, he'd lost custody of their only child. Trey was once more a part of his family, but for a long time they'd had no contact with each other, and Trey hadn't wanted any.

"I'm sorry," Alex murmured.

"Don't be. You're entitled."

As they reached the waiting-room door again, Alex sighed. "I just need to see her. I just need to know—"

"Alex."

He reeled to face Dr. Gregory. If the doctor's expression had been grim before, it was downright morbid now. "We're preparing Melissa for a C-section. The monitor's showing abnormal changes in the infant's heart rate with the uterine contractions. We can't wait to see what happens. I'm on my way to call a neonatologist at the University of Rochester Medical Center, to arrange for a medevac. You can see her for a few minutes before we take her to the OR."

Feeling a rush—of relief or panic?—Alex got halfway down the hall before turning back. "What do you mean—a medevac?"

But Dr. Gregory was already gone.

"J.D.?"

"At seven and a half months, his birth weight's going to be low, probably around three pounds. Plus, the respiratory system isn't as well developed as we'd like. He may be just fine, but if he's not, we don't have the equipment or the skills to take care of him. The Rochester Neonatal ICU can handle anything."

Wonderful. His wife would be in the hospital here in Bethlehem and their child would be hours away in Rochester.

As long as his wife and child *were,* he would be grateful.

He pushed open the door and went into Melissa's room. She looked so small in the bed, with an IV in her arm and wires connecting her to the monitor beside the bed. Her face was pale, her eyes red from crying. When she looked up and saw him, she didn't say a word, but burst into tears again.

Sitting on the edge of the bed, he gathered her close. "It's okay, honey. Everything's going to be okay."

"They're going to do a caesarian!"

"I know."

"I don't want my baby born on Halloween! I want to go home, Alex, please just take me home!"

He brushed her hair back and dredged up a grin from somewhere. "Junior's anxious to get out of there. You think if I take you home, he's just going to settle down and wait patiently until it's time?"

For a moment her lip trembled as if she might smile—or cry—then she clasped his hand. "I'm so sorry," she whispered. "I shouldn't have gone to the party tonight; I shouldn't have gone shopping and to lunch, I should have stayed home with my feet propped up!"

"Honey, going to the party or shopping or to lunch didn't cause this."

"But I bought baby things! I knew better, but I did it anyway, because I thought this time would be different! I thought this time surely—"

The tears started again, so he held her close. The first time she'd gotten pregnant, they'd celebrated by buying everything a baby could possibly need or want. Then, when she miscarried, she hadn't even been able to walk into the spare room they'd designated for a nursery, so it had been left to him to pack up all the baby things and get rid of them.

It was the hardest thing he'd ever done. Please, God, he couldn't do it again.

But this time *had* been different. So the baby was premature. Premature babies were born every day and survived, a lot of them much younger and tinier than Junior. Three pounds wasn't much, but if one-pound infants could make it, then a three-pounder's chances must be that much better.

"Hi, Melissa, Alex," a soft voice greeted. It was Betty Walker, Mitch Walker's sister-in-law and a nurse at the hospital. "Honey, we've got to take you downstairs to the OR now, okay? Alex, there's a waiting room down there on Two where you and the others can wait."

"Okay." He hugged Melissa one last time, then tenderly kissed her. "I love you."

"I love you, too."

Standing back, he watched forlornly as Betty and another nurse wheeled the bed, and his wife, out the door. The door swung shut, leaving him alone in the cold, empty room.

Forget the waiting room. There was a chapel on the second floor, too. That was where he needed to wait. Needed to pray.

Chapter Twelve

Poor Melissa and Alex," Sophy said with a heartfelt sigh as Dr. Gregory handed the baby to the waiting nurse.

Gloria turned an astonished look her way. "Why are you feeling sorry for them? They've waited forever for this baby, and now he's here."

"They waited forever for *a* baby. Not this one. They weren't counting on this one." Sophy gestured. "Look at the doctor's face. He knows."

The neonatologist who had come in on the helicopter from Rochester laid the baby tenderly in the transport incubator, and he and his nurse cleaned the infant, suctioned his lungs, and adjusted all the whistles and bells for the journey back to Rochester. There was concern on the doctor's face, and a growing sadness on the nurse's as they took note of what Sophy and Gloria already knew.

"Oh, but isn't he beautiful?" Gloria said with her own heartfelt sigh.

"You think all babies are beautiful."

"They are. Especially this one. Look at that sweet little face and that dusting of hair. It's going to be dark like his father's."

"And his mother's," Sophy felt obliged to point out on Melissa's behalf. The poor woman, fully anesthetized as soon as the baby was delivered, was being stitched back together, but even an excellent doctor like Dr. Gregory wouldn't be able to stitch her heart back together good as new.

Gloria was still marveling over the child. "Look how tiny he is, but so perfectly formed. Oh, babies are such precious gifts."

Usually that was true. Too often those precious gifts were given to someone who couldn't care less, but most babies were welcomed, treasured, and loved. Still, Sophy couldn't help thinking how unfair it was, after all their heartache, that Alex and Melissa were given *this* baby. They deserved perfection.

"He *is* perfect." Eli popped in beside her an instant after murmuring the words in her ear.

She looked sharply at him, then moved to put some distance between them. He didn't seem to notice, but lounged comfortably where she'd been standing.

"No one asked your opinion," she said bluntly.

"It's not my opinion. It's God's truth. What kind of guardian are you that you can look at that helpless, innocent child and find him unworthy of the parents he's been given?"

"I didn't say he was unworthy—"

"You said they deserved better."

"I said they deserved perfection."

"Implying that this child isn't."

Scowling, Sophy watched as the neonatologist and nurse prepared to leave. Within minutes, they would be back on the helicopter and in the air. Soon after, Alex would be off, too, hurrying through the night to his tiny newborn son, never guessing the heartbreak that awaited him.

"You really need to do something about that attitude," Eli said, giving her a sour look that made her face flame with heat.

Feeling a ridiculous urge to cry, she folded her arms over her chest. "I can't believe this—*you* giving me advice about attitude, when you have the worst attitude of any guardian I've ever known. You are so—"

"If you call me arrogant one more time, I'll clip your wings," he taunted, then added, "Metaphorically speaking."

"You—you—oh!" In an instant, she moved from the operating room to her most favorite place in all of Bethlehem, the very top of the First Church. Not on the roof—that wasn't high enough—but on the small steep roof covering the cupola that housed the church bell.

There, with the night all about her, the vast darkness like black velvet, pricked by millions of tiny stars, and the quiet seeping through her, she felt the peace she craved.

Pricked by guilt, shame, and especially disappointment.

Gloria was right—the Thomases' baby was beautiful. And—oh, how she hated admitting this!—but Eli was right, too. He was perfect, and he deserved the best parents any child could ask for. He'd gotten them, too.

She hoped.

But she'd had other hopes that were hard to let go. Hopes that every dream Alex and Melissa had ever dreamed would come true. That after so much trying, they would succeed beyond their wildest imaginings. That this child could be the fulfillment of every hope that lived within them.

That was impossible now.

"God doesn't give anyone more than they can handle."

With an extraordinarily loud groan, she rolled her eyes

heavenward. "Why me, Lord? *I* didn't poison Nolie. Why do *I* have to put up with him?"

"You may as well come down," Eli said from his spot on the roof. He wasn't sitting at the peak, as she and Gloria often did, but had stretched out on the slope, hands under his head, gazing into the heavens. He looked so relaxed.

She felt anything but.

"If you don't come down, I'll have to come up there, and it would be close quarters for the two of us."

She slid off the cupola roof onto the building roof, then grudgingly sat down. "There is no *two of us,*" she muttered.

"But you'd like there to be, wouldn't you?"

In an instant, she was ready to explode, but by sheer will she contained herself. He was like a bully, she counseled herself, and, as Leanne had told Ryan, the best way to deal with a bully was to ignore him. If she ignored Eli, soon he would get bored and go off elsewhere to seek attention. The sooner, the better.

He rolled onto his side, then sat up, facing her. He was wearing that insufferable grin again. "I'm not so easy to ignore, Soph."

She ground her teeth. Clenched her fists. Breathed deeply and counted stars.

"Soph?" He moved closer, so his pretty face blocked her field of vision, but she merely gritted her teeth even harder and turned her head the other way. There were millions of stars. Surely by the time she finished counting the first hundred thousand, he would be gone.

"So-oph?" he singsonged.

Still she ignored him.

"You know, I can't resist a challenge," he said as pleasantly as if they were carrying on a friendly conversation. "Let's see . . . what would make you pay attention to me? I could stand on my head. Or dance a little jig. Or . . . hey, how about? . . ."

Moving so swiftly she had no time to guess what he was up to, he leaned forward, brushed his mouth against hers, and murmured, "Try ignoring *this,* Soph."

Then he kissed her. *Kissed* her! Never in all of ever had anyone possessed such audacity. . . .

And never in all of ever had she imagined that it could feel so good.

He drew back, and after a moment, she opened her eyes, half-afraid he would be gone, more afraid he wouldn't. He wasn't. He sat there, still leaning toward her, and all the arrogance was gone from his face. His expression was soft, sort of surprised, and his gaze was intense. He'd kissed *her,* but he'd stunned *himself* into silence.

And she liked that a lot.

Even better, she decided, than the kiss.

Okay, so Halloween had been a bust. Oh, the town party had been great—at least, for most people—and Rourke's party at the Starlite had been fun—for most people—but all in all, to borrow a phrase from the boys, for Leanne the holiday had sucked. She'd been all dressed up like a fairy-tale princess, but there'd been no Prince Charming for her, and certainly no happily-ever-after.

It was for the best, she told herself as she moped around the shop Saturday afternoon. After all, Cole Jackson was no one's idea of a Prince Charming, and he sure wasn't the path to happily-ever-after.

She was in the middle of trading Halloween decorations for Thanksgiving when a customer came in. Grateful for the distraction, she summoned up a semblance of a smile, laid the soft-sculpture witch and the black cat aside, and approached the older woman. "Hi, can I help you?"

"I imagine so. That's what we're both in the business of doing, isn't it?"

"I suppose," Leanne replied, trying to remember where she'd seen the older woman before. The unruly hair was familiar, as well as the ugly but comfortable-looking shoes . . . shoes that she'd last seen peeking out of the hem of a long black robe. "You're the judge who sentenced Cole Jackson. Judge . . ."

"Gloria." The woman gave her a delighted-you-remembered smile. "And how is Jack?"

"Cole."

"Cole what?"

"Cole Jackson. That's his name. Not Jack."

Gloria waved one hand in the air. " 'What's in a name . . .' and all that. How is the boy?"

For starters, he was no boy and, from what Leanne could tell, never had been. Secondly, she was the wrong person to ask. He'd taken off the night before as if he couldn't get away from her fast enough, and when she'd run into him and Eli that morning after getting coffee and pastries at Harry's, he'd looked right through her.

"You'd have to ask Eli that," Leanne said, hoping she sounded warmer than she felt. "Can I help you find something?"

Gloria glanced around. "I'm looking for a gift for Melissa and Alex Thomas's new baby. You've heard the news, haven't you?"

Leanne nodded. Harry's had been all abuzz with it. Melissa was doing fine in Bethlehem Memorial, and the baby was listed in critical condition in the neonatal intensive care unit in Rochester. Melissa's mother and Alex were there, while Melissa's father and sister, Jenny, were keeping vigil in Bethlehem.

"A little boy. Two pounds and thirteen ounces, and born on Halloween night." Gloria's comforting smile came again. "Isn't that special?"

"Poor kid will get Halloween-themed birthday parties and cakes and cards for the rest of his life." *Please, God, let him have a life.* "I just hope he's all right."

"You and everyone else. There have been so many prayers going up for the wee one and his parents that I'm surprised you can't see them clogging the sky." As she talked, Gloria wandered to the side of the shop away from the clothes. She looked at blankets and quilts, gift baskets and toys, mobiles and tiny stuffed animals, then stopped at a display of small ceramic angels.

They'd come in just the day before, and Sophy had unpacked them while Leanne was busy with the party. The tallest was no more than four inches, the shortest only half that, and they came in all shapes, sizes, and colors. They were lovely little whimsical pieces.

"Aren't they sweet? The"—what had Gloria called him?—"the wee one could do with a guardian angel to watch over him, couldn't he?"

"Oh, he has plenty of them, believe me."

Leanne assumed she was referring to the hospital staff that was caring for him. *Angels* was, no doubt, an apt description. She could never work with preemies, could never handle the crises and the fears and the deaths . . . but thank God they could.

Gloria selected the only one of the statues that depicted more than one angel. "I believe I'll take this one."

Taking it from her, Leanne peeled the price sticker from the bottom as she walked to the cash register. It showed three angels, one male and two female, and they looked so . . . protective. She liked to believe that they all had such capable angels looking after them, though if they did, hers, Cole's, and Ryan's must be working overtime.

After she'd rung up the sale and made change, she wrapped the figure carefully in tissue paper, then slid it into a sturdy box. "Would you like this gift-wrapped?"

"No, thank you. I'm in a bit of a hurry. I plan to deliver it to him myself."

"All the way to Rochester?"

"Oh, it's not so far when you travel the way I do." With a cheery smile, Gloria tucked the box in her voluminous shoulder bag, waved, then turned toward the door.

Leanne returned to the side window display and began removing decorations again. After a time, she realized that she'd never heard the doorbell sound when Gloria left. A quick glance around the store showed the woman was, indeed, gone. Styrofoam cauldren clutched in her arms, she went to the door and opened it.

The bell dinged, but she hardly noticed, because a few feet to the right of the door stood Ryan, Jerome's leash grasped tightly in hand. He looked stricken, and a few feet to the left of the door was the reason—Cole. They stared at each other, ignoring the dog, ignoring her, both wearing stunned expressions.

Given a choice, Leanne would have furtively backed into the shop, closed the door, and taken refuge in the storeroom. Unwilling to be such a coward, she took a step forward, extending her hand to Ryan. "Come here, sweetie."

Ryan heard her, but it was Jerome who obeyed, as far as the leash allowed him to. Giving the dog a pat, she crossed to Ryan, slid her arm around his thin shoulders, and walked him to the door, then gave him a push inside. "Go back and sit down."

It was a sign of how dazed he was, that he obeyed without question.

The door slowly swung shut behind him and the dog, and she turned her attention to Cole. "You, too."

"No."

"Yes, damn it!" she gritted out. A passerby gave her a scolding look, and she lowered her voice. "Your son is in there, waiting. Now *go!*"

"He's not my son."

"He is in every way that matters. You took him in, you fed him, clothed him, taught him, raised him—"

"Deserted him."

"—and loved him. Now you're going to walk through that door and talk to him."

"He doesn't want to see me."

"He's twelve years old! He doesn't get to make that choice!" she exclaimed, then took a breath. "Not yet. Not without trying . . ."

He glanced through the glass door, and so did she, but they couldn't see Ryan. There were too many racks of pint-sized clothing in the way. Then he scowled back at her. "Eli told me to go to the hardware store and nowhere else."

"Eli didn't know you would run into Ryan. He won't mind."

For a long time Cole just looked at her, as if he were testing arguments in his mind. His expression was serious and edged with fear. He hadn't denied it when she'd said he loved Ryan, and her statement seemed borne out by the fact that he was afraid to face the kid.

She laid her hand on his forearm. "The worst he can do is reject you."

Abruptly he backed away, letting her hand fall. "Well, hell, I'm getting pretty good at that," he said with a bitter edge. He gazed inside the store again, straightened his shoulders, and pushed the door open. The bell rang just as it was supposed to.

Leanne was tempted to stay out there on the sidewalk, but she was in shirt-sleeves, and there was a cold wind blowing out of the northwest. She would turn blue in minutes, and it wasn't a good color for her.

Reluctantly, she returned inside and set the cauldron on the floor. Ryan and Jerome were sprawled together on the love seat, and Cole stood, hands at his sides, at the edge of the Oriental rug that marked the seating area. He appeared to be staring at nothing.

"Hey, kiddo." Leanne pressed a kiss to Ryan's head as she circled behind the love seat, then sat down on the sofa. "Where were you two off to?"

"We were gonna pick up Danny. I was gonna stop and see if it was okay."

Most Saturdays, Danny went to day care a few blocks away while she worked. Ryan had offered to baby-sit him instead, but she hadn't wanted him to feel as if he had to earn his keep. So she'd partially accepted his offer. Danny still went to day care in the morning, but if Ryan wanted to give up his afternoon to watch him, he could.

"Sure, it's okay." When he moved as if to get up, she added, "In a little bit. First, though . . . I think there are some things you two need to say."

Ryan's gaze never went near Cole, but the sarcastic tone of his voice made it clear who his words were intended for. "You got somethin' to say?" He waited half an instant, then said, "Yeah, I thought so. Me, neither."

"Sit down," she commanded before he got fully to his feet. "You, too," she said to Cole.

After a long stiff moment, he grudgingly obeyed.

"You"—that was directed to Cole—"need to tell him

why you left the way you did, and you"—this to Ryan—
"need to listen."

"It doesn't matter—"

She gave Ryan her sternest mother look. "Listen." Then
she got to her feet, returned to the side window, decided
they needed more privacy, and moved to the front windows. She was peeling fake webs from fake spiders and
tossing them in the cauldron when she finally heard the
low rumble of Cole's voice. She released a tiny sigh of relief, followed by another of regret.

Too bad she couldn't eavesdrop from up front.

S HE REMINDS ME OF ADAM," COLE SAID AT LAST.
"Kind of bossy."

"She's *not* bossy."

"Yeah, right." He rested one ankle over the other knee
and picked at a loose thread in the hem of his jeans. He'd
never been at a loss for words with Ryan, not since the
night they'd met, but at the moment he couldn't think of a
single thing to say.

Come to think of it, though, there *had* been another
time—the first time the kid had scared him out of a sound
sleep, screaming and thrashing in his bed. Cole had rushed
into the room, not knowing what the hell was going on,
and Ryan had thrown himself into his arms, sobbing. He
hadn't known what to do. Any comforting taking place in
the Jackson household usually involved a little friendly
punching, shoving, and teasing until the problem was forgotten. Hugs, patting, soft words—they hadn't been a part
of his life.

So he'd held Ryan. That was all—just held him, and patted his shoulder from time to time—and eventually the kid
had fallen asleep in his arms. Cole had eased him down

onto the bed, tucked him in, and headed straight to the kitchen for a stiff drink to calm *himself.*

Neither of them had ever mentioned that night again.

"You doing okay in school?"

Ryan shrugged.

"Did you have fun last night?" Cole hadn't been able to recognize Ryan at the party, but he'd seen a group of young boys with Earl Wilson, all bloodied and grotesque like something out of a horror movie, and guessed the one Earl hugged was Ryan.

Another damn shrug.

Cole rubbed his jaw, then forced a deep breath. "Look, about when I left—"

"It don't matter."

"I thought you needed a mother, a home—things I couldn't give you. I thought you'd be better off—"

"I am." For the first time since they'd come inside, the kid looked at him, his dark gaze derisive. "Livin' with Leanne is a hell of a lot better than livin' with you ever was."

The dull ache Cole had been vaguely aware of all night and all day sharpened and turned raw. He pressed his hand to his belly as if that would help, then leaned forward, bracing both arms on his knees. "Living the way I do . . . that's no way to raise a kid. You never finished a month at the same school where you started it. You never had a chance to make any real friends. Growing up like that, the only thing you were gonna be able to do as an adult was what I do, and I wanted something better for you."

Ryan's derision didn't ease. "Yeah, right," he scoffed. "That crap might help you with her"—he jerked his head toward Leanne—"but it don't mean nothin' to me. Your whole family's nothin' but a bunch of liars, and you're the worst of 'em all."

Shame heated Cole's face. "You think I'm proud of that? Because I'm not."

"Yeah, sure."

His movements jerky, Cole got to his feet and turned to face the back wall. He couldn't blame Ryan for being skeptical. He'd worked hard to become a master in the art of deception. He'd bragged that his parents were the best con artists Texas had ever produced, and that he was better than both of them. He *had* been proud.

But not anymore.

Finally, he turned back to the kid. "When I took you in, we had an agreement that you would never get involved in the business. Remember? You wouldn't help with any of the scams. You wouldn't lie, cheat, or steal. You would be a normal kid, living a normal life. And then you stole those books."

Ryan propped one large foot on the coffee table. "A normal kid living a normal life? Being raised by a bunch of thieves and cons and lowlifes? That's a joke."

Was that the anger speaking, or how he really thought of Cole and his family? *Thieves and cons and lowlifes.* Maybe they were, but every damn one of them had been good to him. Once Cole had brought him into the family, any one of his brothers would have done anything for him.

Cole leaned one shoulder against the storeroom doorjamb. "You're right. It was a joke." Though it had started out as very good intentions. But just as a mama dog couldn't raise her puppy to be a cat, a con man couldn't raise his kid to follow the straight and narrow. He'd tried, and look what he'd done. "That's why I left you here. Because anyone in Bethlehem could do a better job of raising you than I could. I'm sorry, but—"

His cheeks burning hot, Ryan swore. Cole's warning look only made him repeat the word, louder that time. "If you were so damn concerned about how I was turning out, why didn't you quit dragging me around? Why didn't you quit ripping off everybody you came across? Why didn't you just stop being a crook?"

"I don't know how to change the way I am."

"Don't wanna, you mean. It was just easier gettin' rid of me." Ryan jumped to his feet, and the dog jumped up, too, ready to go. "Well, you know what? I don't wanna see you. I don't wanna talk to you. I don't care what happens to you. So take off when one of your brothers gets here, and don't ever come back!"

Cole wouldn't have thought it possible, but Ryan beat the eager dog to the front door. Leanne stopped him there, talked quietly with him for a minute, then he and Jerome left.

He leaned his head back until it thunked against the wall, closed his eyes, and sighed. "Jesus."

The smell of Leanne's perfume, the awareness of her presence, reached him an instant before she spoke. "That wasn't too bad for the first time, was it? There's no bleeding, no bruises."

"Only on the inside." Opening his eyes, he watched her sit down on the love seat, crossing her legs. She wore a slim green dress that clung to her curves and flirted with her knees. Her hair was loose, the ends curling at her shoulders, and around her neck a gold heart dangled from a chain, just a thin outline with two tiny childlike figures swinging from it.

"The next time he says he's got nothing to say to me, trust him," he said wryly as he moved away from the door and sat at the end of the sofa.

"He had plenty to say, didn't he?"

"Yeah—and nothing I didn't already know."

"But he needed to say it anyway." She paused. "Did you explain to him why you left?"

"I tried."

"Did you apologize?"

"I tried. He wasn't impressed with either one."

"But he listened. He'll think about it. And the next time you talk, he won't be so angry."

"And you know this because? . . ."

"He wouldn't be so bitter unless he was hurting, and he wouldn't be hurting unless he loved you. It's easier to get over being angry than it is to stop loving someone. Trust me. I speak from experience."

He gave her a sidelong glance. "That's right. You're the queen of lousy choices and bad decisions."

"Don't—" Her mouth thinned, and for a moment it appeared that she would rise from the love seat and dismiss him from her presence. But the moment passed. The tension that held her stiff eased, and her mouth shifted into a sigh. "I'm sorry I said that, and sorry you took it so personally. I truly didn't mean it that way."

"I don't see any other way it *could* be taken." And he'd looked for one, too, while he'd spent a good part of the night staring out his bedroom window instead of sleeping.

"Maybe . . ." Her long fingers rubbed across the wicker of the love-seat arm. After a moment, she looked up. "You're right. Maybe Ryan's not the only one who's still got a lot of anger and bitterness toward you."

"You and Ryan don't have a monopoly on it, honey. I've got all sorts of enemies out there."

"We're not your enemies."

Sometimes it feels like it. But wisely he kept that to himself. Instead, he got to his feet. "I'd better get going before Eli figures I made a run for it."

He thought she was going to let him go without another word, but just as he stepped onto the tile that fronted the door, she spoke.

"Why didn't you do it last night? Make a run for it, I mean."

His fingers curled around the metal bar that stretched across the door as he breathed slowly. "When did I have the chance?"

The soft rustle of shoes on carpet alerted him to her approach. Reflected in the glass, he saw her stop at the nearest display and start rearranging little girls' sweaters. "After you took Melissa and J.D. to the emergency room. You were alone, you had his truck and a full tank of gas . . . why not get the hell out of Dodge?"

He was gripping the handle so tightly that his knuckles had turned white. He forced each finger to relax, then to let go, and he turned to face her. "The depth of your faith in me is underwhelming."

Her cheeks pinked a little. "I'm not saying I expected you to. I'm just asking why you let the perfect opportunity pass you by."

Slowly he exhaled. "I thought about it. I sat there in the parking lot and thought about just driving away. Nothing was stopping me. I could change my name, disappear. I've done it before. Someday I'll probably do it again. So your lack of faith in me is justified. Satisfied?"

"There's a big difference between thinking about doing something and actually doing it. I've *thought* about committing a lot of dastardly deeds over the years, but I haven't actually done them." She gave up fiddling with the sweaters and clasped her hands together on top of the pile. "Once again, you haven't answered the question. I didn't ask whether you considered running away. I asked why you didn't do it."

How about another dose of truth? he thought cynically. "It would have been wrong."

She didn't laugh or snort with derision, but simply nodded as if it were a logical answer. As if he could be trusted to care whether something was wrong.

"I—I'd better go."

Once more she nodded. "Thank you for talking with Ryan."

"You're welcome."

She smiled wryly. "And for not pointing out that I didn't leave you much choice."

"I'm used to not having many choices." He hesitated a moment, half-wishing he could stay longer, then forced himself to move. "See you."

So much for his stab at telling the truth, he thought as he walked out the door and turned toward Main Street. Not having many choices . . . that was just so much bull. Life was filled with choices. No one had forced him to break the law—at least, not after he was grown. He'd *chosen* to do it. Taking in Ryan—his choice. Dragging him around the country, with the law always one step behind—his choice. Coming to Bethlehem—no one to blame but him. Scamming these people—him again.

Getting involved with Leanne—done of his own free will.

Disappearing with a quarter million of the townsfolks' dollars—him and only him.

How many chances had he had every single day of his life to change? To make different choices? To make a different life for himself?

Why didn't you just stop being a crook? Ryan had asked.

It was a good question, and Cole had only one answer. Because he'd made the wrong choices.

Chapter Thirteen

J.D. GRAYSON TOOK COLE UP ON HIS OFFER TO DIS-
cuss Ryan with him. At his request, Eli delivered Cole
to the hospital Tuesday afternoon. Before closing the
door to the pickup, Cole bent to see the kid. "What do
you want me to do when I'm done?"

Eli glanced at his watch. "Murray and I will probably
knock off in another hour or so. Give me a call when
you're ready. If I'm not at the house, just keep trying."

With a grim nod, Cole closed the door, then faced the
hospital. He could save them both the hassle and just walk
to the Miller mansion after the meeting with Grayson.

For a moment he stood there on the curb and simply
observed. A young man with his right leg in a cast wheeled
himself out the automatic doors and lit up a cigarette, then
smiled at the young woman with him. A woman on her
way inside patiently matched her pace to that of her elderly companion. A pretty blonde girl pushed a cart filled
with flowers from the delivery van at the curb toward the
doors, and several women—mother and grown daughters,
by the looks of them—hurried past her.

Normal lives.

They were so far outside his experience that he felt as if he'd landed in an alien universe.

Squaring his shoulders, he went inside, got directions to Grayson's office, then located it down the hall. The waiting area was just a wide spot in the corridor, and the desk was empty, the door to Grayson's office ajar. He glanced at the clock—two minutes late. His chest tight, he rapped at the door, and it swung open.

Grayson was sitting at his desk, leaned back, with his little girl asleep on his chest. Cole glanced from the kid to the doctor. "I can come back later."

"No, come on in. My folks are baby-sitting this afternoon, but they left Faith with me while they check in on Melissa. They'll be back for her before long. Have a seat."

Cole chose the nearest chair and glanced around. If he'd ever thought about how a psychiatrist's office should look, he wouldn't have pictured this. There was no dark wood paneling, no comfortable couch, nothing elegant, homey, or austere at all. The furniture was past its prime, and he suspected the walls needed painting, though it was hard to tell with all the photos. The medical degree was all but lost in a jumble of family pictures.

"How is Melis—Mrs. Thomas?" he asked, the first thing he could think of to break the silence.

"She's recovering nicely. She's anxious to get out, so she can go to Rochester and see the baby. She got little more than a glimpse of him Friday night."

"Is he holding his own?"

"Even better. The NICU staff is impressed. He's a fighter."

Cole nodded, shifted in his chair, then gazed at his hands. He, Eli, and Murray had been making repairs on the concessions building at the soccer fields when Eli had gotten Grayson's call. His hands were dirty, and so were his clothes, a detail that bothered him far more in the psychiatrist's presence than it had with Eli and Murray.

He rested his hands on his thighs and fixed his gaze on Grayson. "You wanted to talk about Ryan?"

"Ryan . . . and you. I don't know if Leanne's told you, but Ryan's not thrilled at having to come see me. He spends most of our sessions angry or uncommunicative, or both. I thought maybe you could fill me in on some of the things he doesn't like to talk about."

"Did Leanne tell you that the father-son bit was just another scam?"

"Kelsey did. She's his caseworker," he explained unnecessarily.

"I don't know anything about his first nine years."

"But you raised him for the last three. You must have learned something about him during that time."

"What little I know I learned the hard way. I didn't know he had nightmares until he about gave me a heart attack in the middle of the night. I didn't know how much he liked books until he got caught stealing them." He looked away from Grayson's steady gaze and fixed his attention on the bookcase behind the desk instead. "I do know I was a lousy father."

He'd done his best . . . but when your best was nowhere near good enough, did it matter?

"I understand that you came to Bethlehem first last spring, then Ryan arrived a few days later."

"I left him in Philadelphia with my father, so he could finish the school year. He got Owen to buy him a bus ticket, and he showed up here one day."

"You were here almost two months. Did you routinely leave him with someone else for long periods like that?"

"No. He usually stayed with me. But he always wound up spending a lot of time alone, and he'd gotten to the age where he couldn't get caught up in school as easily as he used to."

"Why didn't you leave him with your father more often, where he could have a more stable home life?"

Cole would have given a lot for some glib answer that would satisfy the shrink without really telling him anything, but that would defeat the purpose of coming, wouldn't it? It was a sorry excuse for a man who couldn't be honest with a psychiatrist.

"I thought . . . *I* was the stability in Ryan's life. What town we were in, where we were sleeping at night, how long we would be there—I thought none of that mattered as long—as long as we were together."

He'd been a fool, living out this responsible-adult fantasy, casting himself as the dutiful father figure, while Ryan thought of him as a thief, a con, and a lowlife.

"What about the nightmares? Has he ever told you what they're about?"

Cole shook his head.

"How long has he had them?"

"As long as I've known him, but he refuses to talk about them. I just figured it has something to do with his mother, but he won't talk about her, either."

Grayson shifted the baby so she lay on her back in his arms. Her face screwed up as if she was going to cry, but she yawned instead and went on sleeping. "What do you know about her?"

He related the story of how she'd left Ryan in St. Louis and how *he'd* taken him in, then fell silent for a time. Ryan had plenty of memories, but few he'd been willing to discuss. Because they were too awful to remember? Or too precious to share?

"She moved around a lot, changed her name the way other people change clothes, and abandoned the kid to fend for himself." His muscles knotted. "She must have been a lot like me."

"Leaving a twelve-year-old boy with a woman who loves him isn't the same as leaving a nine-year-old all alone at a bus station in a strange city."

Maybe not, but it was still unforgivable.

"Did she sing songs to him? Read him fairy tales? Fix a special meal for him? Has he ever shared any memory of that sort?"

Cole shook his head.

"What about family? His father? Grandparents?"

Another shake. "He doesn't know anything about his father, and he's never mentioned anyone else. I got the impression his mother wasn't very maternal. He knew how to cook, to do laundry, and to handle money. He'd been taking care of himself a lot longer than a few weeks."

"Tell me about the nightmares."

"He doesn't like the dark. He wakes up screaming and shaking, then eventually goes back to sleep. He doesn't cry. He never cries, no matter what." It wasn't much to tell. The nightmares were awful for Cole, much more so for Ryan, and Leanne was a hell of a lot better at comforting him afterward. Cole had seen proof of that last spring, when Ryan had awakened them from a sound sleep. She'd taken him into her arms as if it was the most natural thing in the world, had patted and soothed and cradled him, and Cole had known then that Ryan needed a mother.

More than he needed a con-artist father.

"Have you ever asked him about the dreams?" Grayson asked.

"A couple times, but he didn't want to talk and I didn't push him." He should have—should have known how to get the kid to confide in him and then what to do to make everything all right.

Grayson smiled faintly. "We all know how to talk and we do it every day. But when it's really important, it can be the toughest thing to face." After a moment, he changed focus again. "How are things between you and Leanne?"

"Okay." Not that he knew what was between them, besides a lot of anger and bitterness on her part, but there was something. Something vital and intense, something neither one of them seemed able to walk away from. Something like what his parents had with each other.

The thought irritated him. While he was entirely too much like his father, Leanne was *nothing* like his mother. Eloise had never had an unselfish moment in her life. She'd never loved anyone half as much as she'd loved herself, while Leanne was generous and sweet. She loved Danny more than anything in the world, and probably loved Ryan almost as much. Hell, she had even loved *him,* though he hadn't deserved it. He'd been too damn stupid to suspect he might have loved her back.

He might have loved her . . .

Might still love her . . .

No. Loving people who weren't blood-related was just asking for trouble. He already had enough of that, and there was no shortage of it just waiting to find him.

Finally the weight of the silence in the room caught his attention, and he looked up to see Grayson watching him expectantly. Feeling like an idiot, he mumbled, "What?"

"I asked if you'd talked to Ryan yet."

"For a few minutes on Saturday." He related the gist of their conversation, but kept the lowlife comment to himself. Some things weren't meant to be shared.

"If you could have another chance to be Ryan's father again, would you take it?"

The question made Cole stiffen and straighten in his chair, and turned his voice cold. "Nothing's changed. All the reasons I left him in the first place are still there. I can't give him the kind of home he needs. I can't be the kind of parent he needs. If I got another chance, it would take away *his* only chance at ever living a normal life."

"Not necessarily. You could make changes in your own life. You could *become* the kind of parent he needs."

His laugh was short and sharp. "Go straight, you mean? Get an honest job? Stay in the same place? Give up the cons?"

"Does that seem so undesirable? Do you like your lifestyle so much you would choose it over Ryan?"

"It's not undesirable, doc. It's impossible. Being a con artist isn't just what I do—it's what I *am*. It's what I was born and bred for. I don't even have a clue how to settle down and go straight."

"You've been doing honest work in the past few weeks," Grayson pointed out.

"Because they're *making* me. If I hadn't tried to con the wrong woman in Georgia, I would still be doing the same old stuff. I never would have come back here, and I sure wouldn't have taken on an honest job."

"Anyone can change if they want to badly enough."

"Maybe in your world. Not in mine. I come from a long line of disreputable scammers. It's all I know."

"Anyone can change," Grayson stubbornly repeated. "A few years ago I was a drunk. If they'd ever done a blood-alcohol on me, they would have found more alcohol than blood. There were times, when I was quitting, when I would have crawled, groveled, even killed, for a drink . . . but I didn't. Because I wanted to be sober even more. If you find something you want more than you want to be a criminal, you'll find the strength within yourself to change."

Cole studied him. He'd known plenty of drunks—in

his line of work, he'd known all kinds of shady characters. It was hard to imagine Grayson, sitting there with his little girl, looking healthy, at peace, and self-satisfied, as one of them.

Just as it was hard to imagine himself going straight.

Though off and on for months, he'd been tormented by this image of settling down and making a family—him and Ryan, Leanne and Danny.

"You didn't answer my question," Grayson said quietly. "If you could have a chance to be Ryan's father again, would you take it? Even if it meant totally changing who and what you are?"

The three years he'd had with Ryan had been the best of his life. He'd felt like a responsible adult for the first time in his life. There had been times when he'd all but forgotten that Ryan *wasn't* his son . . . and times when he'd thought about retiring from the business for the kid's sake.

Ryan had needed him—to take care of him, to keep him safe, to love him. And *he'd* needed Ryan.

Finally he met Grayson's unwavering gaze. "Yeah, I would . . . but it's not gonna happen. Your wife's looking for his real parents. Even if she doesn't find them, they'll never give him back to me again, and he would never forgive me even if they did. So it doesn't much matter, does it?"

Grayson smiled faintly. "It matters more than you think, Cole."

*D*O YOU SUPPOSE I'LL EVER SEE MY FEET AGAIN? Less than a week earlier, Melissa had asked that question of Alex. Now she gazed at them without interest. It felt strange to look down without the swell of her belly blocking her view. When she stood up, she was continually caught off-guard by how light she felt—how empty—and when she sat down, she kept forgetting she didn't have to carefully support her own weight on the way down.

It was Wednesday, one of those bright, sunny, warm days that made autumn an even more special season. Dr. Gregory had discharged her from the hospital that morning, and she, her father, and her sister had immediately set out for Rochester. They were almost there, just minutes from her mother, Alex, and their baby.

Their baby. He was doing fine, Alex had assured her in this morning's call, but her fears wouldn't be quieted until she'd seen for herself. She wanted to cradle him to her breast and check his fingers and toes and gaze into his big eyes, and know deep inside herself that he would be all right.

From the front seat, Jenny reached around to pat her knee. "You okay back there?"

"I'm fine." Just chilled inside. Anxious. Afraid.

"You thought about names yet?"

Melissa caught the sharp look her father gave her sister, and so did Jenny, who ignored it. No one had come right out and told her not to choose a name yet—as if she might regret using a good name if the baby didn't . . . didn't . . .

Unable to finish the thought, she drew a breath. Everyone felt she should hold off until his condition was dramatically improved, but she'd named the child months ago in her heart, and that name would always be his, no matter what. "Alexander Maxwell," she announced as the hospital came into sight and her chest tightened. Somewhere inside there, Alexander Maxwell Thomas was waiting for his mother.

"Cool," Jenny said with a grin. "Isn't it, Mr. Maxwell?"

"Cool," their father agreed with a faint smile as he pulled up to the hospital entrance. "You girls go on in.

Mind your sister, Jen. I'll park the car and meet you up-stairs."

To the best of Melissa's knowledge, Jenny had never been in this hospital before, but she charged ahead as if she knew exactly where she was going. That was the way she went through life in general—never hesitating, never ex-periencing a moment's fear or doubt. Melissa didn't know whether to envy her four-years-younger sister or be eter-nally grateful for her.

She settled for both.

After an eternity and before she was ready, they'd reached the neonatal ICU. Alex and her mother met them, each of them hugging her tightly, then he slid his arm around her waist and walked with her to the nursing sta-tion. She was too numb, too nervous, to pay attention to introductions, sympathetic words, reassurances. Practically in a daze, she let him and a nurse lead her away, then help her don a mask, gown, a cap to gather her hair, and paper booties to cover her shoes. She followed Alex, who ap-peared far more comfortable in the same getup, into the NICU and to their son.

He was so beautiful, and so tiny! He lay on his back, naked except for a pale blue knitted cap covering his head, and it seemed there were tubes and lines everywhere—in his nose, his mouth, his arm, his neck. His color was splotchy, and his little face was screwed up as if he was con-centrating intensely on sleeping in spite of all the noise around him.

She bent to gaze at him, tears in her eyes, through the incubator's clear walls. "Hi, Max," she whispered. "You can't imagine how long I've waited to finally see you."

Alex stood beside her, his arm comforting around her waist. "Can she touch him?" he asked, and her pleading gaze shot to the nurse on the opposite side. Oh, yes, she needed to touch him, needed to feel that he was real and warm and alive.

"Sure. But you have to wear gloves."

It was a sorry substitute for skin to warm skin, but she would take anything she could get. She slid her hands into the gloves the nurse handed over, then tentatively reached through the ports in the incubator's side.

He *was* warm and real and very much alive. As she stroked his tiny arm, his fingers stretched, then relaxed. When she gently brushed his cheek, he turned his head her way and his mouth worked a time or two as if he were sucking on a bottle. He was so tiny, so fragile, and if she lost him . . . God help her, she couldn't bear even the thought.

She didn't know how long she stood there, rubbing him, whispering in a voice so low he couldn't possibly hear. Long enough for her back to ache, for the incision in her stomach to throb, for her legs to grow weak. By the time she realized how much she needed to sit, she was leaning heavily on Alex, but he held her without a word of complaint.

"Alex," a male voice greeted him. "How's the little one doing?"

"He's got a name now," the nurse said. "Dr. Bosquez, meet Max."

"Max . . . Maxwell? Your maiden name?" the doctor asked Melissa, then explained, "Your mother's spent almost as much time here in the past few days as your husband. You must be Melissa. How are you? You look like you could use a seat."

"I could," she admitted.

"Come over here and sit down and . . . we'll talk." He led the way to a desk pushed against the wall, held the chair for her, then took a seat on a stool with wheels. Alex leaned against the desk beside her, his hand on her shoulder.

"Max is doing really well," the doctor said. "He's gained three ounces since he got here, which puts him at three pounds even. Even though his respiratory system isn't fully developed, he's doing as well as can be expected there, too. There haven't been any crises, no infections, no problems at all, other than the fact that he got here six weeks early."

But . . . Melissa could feel in her bones that there was a *but* . . . at the end of that speech. Instead of confronting it, though, she asked, "When can he go home?"

"Barring any complications, probably in six to eight weeks. We want him to get up to at least five or six pounds, and we have to give his respiratory system the time it needs to handle breathing on his own."

"Do you expect complications?"

"We pray for the best, but we're always prepared for anything."

She looked up at Alex. He looked tired, as if he'd hardly slept since the last time she'd seen him. Most likely he'd spent every minute possible here at the hospital, doing his own praying.

But in addition to the fatigue and the worry, there was also a joy in his eyes she'd never seen there before. Always, when they'd gotten pregnant, they had celebrated together, and when she'd lost the babies, they had grieved together, but somehow *she* had been allowed to grieve more. She was the one who got the most sympathy from family and friends, while he was the one who'd had to deal with the details of the miscarriages—the one who'd had to pack away the baby things, to break the news to everyone. He had to be the strong one, when his heart had broken every bit as much as hers.

This time their dreams had come true. Max was tiny and fragile and breathing with the help of machines, but he was going to make it. They would never ache with such emptiness again. She wouldn't feel as if she was stealing the pleasure from her girlfriends when they got pregnant. He wouldn't have to watch fathers playing baseball with their kids, or taking them to see Santa Claus, or teaching them to ride bikes, with the bittersweet yearning to have those experiences with his own child.

This time there wasn't going to be any heartbreak.

But she feared she put the thought into words too soon when Dr. Bosquez finally got to that *but* . . .

Obviously uncomfortable with what he was about to say, he reached for her hand, sending chills through her. "There is something you need to know, Melissa, Alex."

Her heart started pounding in her chest, and she couldn't squeeze in enough oxygen to satisfy the ache there. She grasped his hand tighter, to hide the trembling in her fingers, and waited, wide-eyed, for him to go on, all the while wishing he wouldn't say another word.

She didn't get her wish. His eyes dark with sympathy, the doctor took a deep breath, then spoke.

"Max has Down syndrome."

IT SNOWED FRIDAY, THE FIRST SNOW OF THE SEASON. Fat white flakes blanketed the rooftops and covered the yellowed grass in the square with an icy blanket of white. It coated the cars and dusted the firs like Christmas trees.

Christmas, Leanne thought with a jolt. It was less than two months away. Where had the year gone? She'd spent last winter doing her usual nothing, the spring falling in love, the summer mothering the boys and getting over Cole, and the fall . . . she'd spent the fall falling for Cole again.

When would she ever learn?

Maybe after he'd broken her heart again . . . though

probably not. It had happened before, and she'd come back for more. Maybe she was hopeless. Or should that be hopeful?

She'd closed the shop and was working on the bank deposit when the door swung open and a red-haired tornado dashed down the aisle to the register. "Aunt Leanne, it's snowing!" Micahlyn said with delight. "Isn't it wonderful?"

"It's fabulous," Leanne agreed, lifting her niece onto the counter, removing her glasses to wipe away the snow, then replacing them. "If it keeps this up all night, tomorrow we'll be snowed in."

Micahlyn's eyes doubled in size. "I never been snowed in before."

"It's fun. You get to build snowmen and have snowball fights, and your mom can make snow ice cream. You freeze your little toes and your nose—oh, and you've got to make snow angels. You can't have snow without them."

"I never made snow angels before, either. I don't think I ever seen snow before."

"Well, my brother can show you how to do all of that, 'cause he's seen snow hundreds of times. By the way . . . who brought you here?"

Micahlyn looked around to her left, then her right, then giggled when the door opened. "Daddy! He's poky. Is Danny and Ryan upstairs? I wanna see their puppy."

"Yup, they're up there. Better watch out, though, or Jerome will give you a big sloppy kiss and try to stick his tongue in your mouth."

Chase stopped next to the counter as Micahlyn raced back to the door, and peeled off his gloves. "You should be used to males trying to stick their tongues in your mouth."

She stuck her own tongue out, then slid the money and deposit slips into the bank bag. "You guys get lost on your way home?"

"Nope. I'm here to invite you to dinner."

Hot dogs with lots of chili and onions . . . mmm. She'd missed having dinner with the family the Friday before, because of Halloween, and the week before that, because of Cole. Truth was, she didn't much feel like going tonight. It wasn't that she was down or anything. She just wanted . . . well, she didn't know exactly what.

"I . . . jeez, Chase, I don't think I'd be the best company tonight."

"Like you ever are? Someone's got a high opinion of herself," he teased.

"I just think I want to stay home." Maybe. Or maybe not.

He studied her a long time—debating whether to try to change her mind, she would bet. Even though he was no longer practicing law, once a lawyer, always a lawyer. Whatever he saw in her face, though, seemed to convince him that arguing wouldn't work this time. "Can the kids go?"

"Sure. But are you certain you want to take them? With this snow, you might be stuck with them until the spring thaw."

"They're welcome to spend the night. Besides, it's supposed to be in the forties tomorrow. All this is gonna be gone by Sunday."

She dropped the bank deposit into her bag, then shrugged into her jacket. "Come on. We'll go upstairs and you can see Jerome, too. Maybe he's got a brother over at the vet's that you can adopt for Micahlyn."

"Actually, I was thinking about getting her a pony."

She gave him a wry grin as she locked the door. "As I said, maybe he's got a brother over at the vet's. I noticed she called you *Daddy*."

"Yeah." He shrugged as if it was no big deal, but he couldn't hide the pleasure in his eyes. "She had a talk with her grandparents, and they said it was okay."

Micahlyn's paternal grandparents were the only family she had in the world besides her mother, and they hadn't been at all pleased when Nolie packed up their only grandchild and moved her to New York. The grandmother, in particular, had gone ballistic when she'd found out there was a man other than their deceased son in Nolie's life. They'd almost destroyed Nolie and Chase's relationship, but thankfully, everything had worked out for the best . . . more or less. Marlene Harper was still a spiteful witch, in Leanne's none-too-humble opinion, but she'd eventually accepted the changes in her daughter-in-law's and granddaughter's lives.

Not that Nolie, Chase, and Obie Harper had given her much choice.

They climbed the stairs to the apartment, then went into the living room, where Micahlyn and Danny were sprawled on the floor with Jerome. Grinning from ear to ear, she looked up at Chase. "Oh, Daddy, can I have one, too?"

He looked at the dog, then Leanne. "That's not a puppy."

"Sure he is, aren't you, Jerome? You're just a big baby."

At her cooing tone, he rolled onto his back, four long legs stuck up in the air, and waited for someone to scratch his belly.

"Guys, you want to spend the night at Micahlyn's house?"

Danny leaped to his feet, cheering, and so did Micahlyn. On the couch, Ryan shrugged. Spending the night with a four- and a five-year-old wasn't the most exciting thing a twelve-year-old could do, but it was a family thing and for that reason, Leanne suspected, he was willing.

After a whirl of activity, everyone had kissed Leanne good-bye, then trooped down the stairs. She stood in the living room, alone but for Jerome, and wondered again exactly what it was she wanted to do. As her gaze fell on the phone, the answer popped into her head.

Think with your head, Nolie had told her, but listen to your heart, and her heart was telling her she wanted to see Cole. To talk to him. Listen to him. Look at him. Spend time with him. It was foolish and risky, and overwhelming the warning in her head. She wanted to be with Cole.

She changed into gray wool trousers and a burgundy sweater, warm black boots, a coat, scarf, and gloves. After tucking her wallet into one pocket and her keys into the other, she left the apartment and crossed the street.

The Miller mansion looked like something out of a fairy tale, with its layers of snow. It was the sort of house that should be home to a loving, laughing family, with kids overflowing the bedrooms and parents who didn't mind. Instead, it had been home to one lonely old widow for years, to Cole and Ryan for a few weeks, and now to Eli and his charges.

She rang the doorbell, then brushed the snow from her hair and stomped it from her boots. When Eli opened the door, he looked surprised. "Leanne. What brings you out?"

For one moment her common sense whispered that she should rethink her plan. It wasn't smart. It could be disastrous.

Her irresponsible side snickered. As if she hadn't lived through dumb and disastrous before?

She ignored her common sense, told Eli what she wanted, and found herself waiting in the living room doorway while he went upstairs. Murray was sitting on the couch, watching the evening news. He gave her a smile that was part vague, part knowing, and all pleased, but didn't say a word, and before she could think of anything beyond hello, footsteps sounded on the stairs.

It was Cole, not long out of the shower, by the looks of him. Where his hair was still damp, it gleamed dark gold, and his feet were bare, though he carried work boots and socks in one hand. His jeans were clean and pressed, and his sweatshirt had that freshly-laundered smell when he got closer. "Hey," he said in greeting, stopping three steps from the bottom. "What's up?"

"I . . . I asked Eli if I could spring you for the evening. He said sure."

He looked puzzled. "For what?"

She shrugged. "A walk. Dinner. A talk."

The puzzled expression didn't go away as he studied her. She had the distinct feeling he wanted to turn her down, that he felt he *should* turn her down, just as she'd felt she shouldn't even ask. He didn't, though, but sat down on the step and tugged on one sock. "Where are the boys?"

"They went home with Chase."

"And you want to have dinner. With me."

She shrugged again. "If you don't want to—"

"No," he said quickly, then realized how it sounded and flushed. "I mean, I'd like that. I just can't figure why . . ."

"Why? . . ."

Now it was he who shrugged, his broad shoulders stretching the fabric of his shirt. "Why you would want to. Why Eli would agree."

"Judge Gloria said you should learn a few lessons with your punishment and emerge a better man for it. Maybe Eli agrees."

"So dinner with you . . . is that a lesson or punishment, or will it make me a better man?"

The question stung, but she gave no sign of it. Instead she smiled. "Interesting question. I guess you'll have to sit through the dinner to get the answer."

"Are you cooking?" He shoved his foot into his boot and laced it, then pulled on the other sock.

"Hardly. I've had a long week. I thought we could go to McCauley's."

"Go out. To a restaurant. What do you think the good citizens of Bethlehem would think, to see their convicted felon dining at the next table over with you and without his guard dog?"

"Most of them would think you have excellent taste both in food and dinner companions."

"It's not most of them I have to worry about."

She watched him lace the second boot, his fingers working quickly and efficiently. He'd had beautiful hands when he'd come to Bethlehem—long fingers, tanned, strong, and smooth, smooth skin. They were still long, tanned, and strong, but a month of hard work had taken care of the smooth part. There were nicks and scars and calluses now, but they could still take her breath away.

Finally he looked up and caught her staring. The hint of a smile quirked one corner of his mouth. "How about Harry's?"

"How about McBride Inn?"

"How about I cook?"

"In my apartment?" Heat began building inside her, so sudden and so hot that she half-expected to hear the snowmelt begin. She wanted to see him, wanted to sit down to a meal with him like any other man and woman who each found the other attractive. But him, her, her apartment . . . did she want to be that alone with him? With the boys gone for the night? With her bedroom just down the hall?

Yes.

She did.

"Okay," she replied, and her voice sounded breathy and hopeful.

"I'll be right back." He pulled himself to his feet and went down the hall to the kitchen. She could hear his voice and Eli's, but couldn't make out the words. When he returned a moment later, he got his jacket from the coat closet, zipped it up, then pulled on a pair of black gloves before opening the door.

The snow was coming down harder. When they reached the sidewalk, she gazed up at it, catching flakes in her hair, on her lashes and her cheeks. "I'll have to go to the grocery store. I don't keep much besides snacks and sandwich stuff in the house. You can come with me or wait at the apartment."

He gestured toward the store down the street, and she started in that direction. He walked beside her, hands in his pockets.

Because the silence was too comfortable, she wanted to break it, and latched onto the first thing to come to mind. "I thought Murray's sentence was only for a week or so."

"It was."

"Then why is he still there?"

"Damned if I know. When I asked him, he just shrugged. I asked Eli, and he said Murray would leave when the time was right."

"Which means?"

He shook his head, sending snowflakes scattering.

"Maybe he just likes living there—being a part of something. I know he's been alone a long time."

"No wife or kids?"

"His wife is dead, and his kids . . . I don't think they have much to do with him. I think . . ." She tried to recall the gossip she'd heard not long after Murray moved to town, but it had been years ago; she'd been younger and more self-centered, and the problems of a fifty-some-year-old stranger hadn't particularly interested her. "It seems they blamed him for his wife's death, but I'm not sure."

"Maybe he was responsible, and that's why he drinks."

"He certainly looks healthier than he did before this last arrest. Still, it's hard to imagine anyone staying in a program like this once his time is served, or a program that would let him stay."

"Eli is nothing if not unconventional," Cole responded in a dry tone. "Like your town."

She smiled brightly as they crossed the grocery store parking lot. "Thank you."

"I'm not sure that was a compliment."

"I'll take it as one anyway."

A blast of welcome heat greeted them as they walked into the store. Leanne pulled a cart from the corral, stuffed her coat, scarf, and gloves into the basket, then headed for the produce. There she indicated the fruits and vegetables with an open hand. "Your choice. What do you want to cook?"

He got mushrooms, onions, peppers, baking potatoes, bananas, brown sugar, butter, steaks, whipping cream, and a packaged pound cake. If he noticed the curious looks they got from other shoppers, he gave no hint of it, but concentrated on his choices instead.

When they reached the checkout and she dug her wallet out of her coat pocket, he shook his head. "I'll get it."

"But—"

He gave her a stern look. "I said I'll get it."

She'd thought he had gone looking for Eli to verify that it was okay for him to go out, and maybe he had. Apparently, though, he'd also talked the kid into giving him some of his own money, since not being trusted with so much as a dime had been one of his earlier complaints.

"I would have been more than happy to have you just do the cooking, but if you want to pay, too, go ahead," she said. "And if you want to play dish fairy afterward . . ."

"To quote Ryan, 'Dish fairy, my—' "

She smiled at the memory from last spring. She had invited him and Ryan, Nolie, Micahlyn, and Chase for dinner and, after the meal, had innocently wondered aloud if the dish fairies might visit. Danny and Micahlyn had been awed by the prospect of fairies, but Ryan hadn't been so easily fooled.

That was okay. Fairies or no, the kids had done the dishes anyway.

He paid for the food, then they split the bags between them and strolled back to her apartment. They left their shoes at the top of the stairs, then she drew a barstool to the dining room side of the counter and watched as he started dinner. He placed the steaks in a garlic, Worcestershire, and soy sauce marinade, cleaned and sliced the mushrooms, and scrubbed the potatoes.

"I can help," she offered as he rummaged through the island drawers before coming up with a grater.

"I don't think there's room for two in here."

She knew. That was why she'd offered.

"I can grate cheese, sitting here, out of the way."

In response, he set the cheese, grater, and a plate in front of her. She circled the counter to wash her hands, bumping against him as he put the potatoes in the oven, then she sat down again.

"I like the tile work," he remarked as he chopped onions.

"Thank you. I did it myself." Slowly she dragged the chunk of cheddar across the tiny holes in the grater while gazing at the backsplash. The tiles ranged in size from one inch square to twelve, in blues, whites, and yellows, and it had taken her more hours than any sane person would give up, to get them laid perfectly. And the first person who'd seen it besides Danny—her mother—had wrinkled her nose and moved on without a single comment.

How foolish she had been, expecting Phyllis's approval for anything she did.

How insulting and angry her mother would be if she knew Cole was in her daughter's kitchen at that very moment. And how sad that her mother's opinions meant nothing to her.

"You could open a restaurant." Her sudden pronouncement surprised Leanne as much as it did Cole. She'd been thinking about her mother and watching him place a mixing bowl and the beaters in the freezer, and without any thought on her part, the comment just popped out.

He smiled sarcastically. "Sure, and our slogan could be, 'Welcome to Cole's, where we fill your stomachs and empty your pockets.' "

"Actually, I think 'wallets' would sound better," she remarked. "But seriously, you like to cook and you're very good at it."

He was unwilling to even consider the idea. "The last thing Bethlehem needs is another restaurant."

Her breath caught, and a butterfly somersaulted in her stomach. Gripping the cheese tightly enough to crumble it, she tentatively asked, "You . . . you're thinking . . . about staying? In Bethlehem?"

He looked at her, realized what he'd said, then scowled. "I've still got about forty-eight hundred hours left on my sentence. There's no point in thinking about doing anything at the moment."

"There's always a point to thinking about the future," she disagreed.

"Why? So you can arrange it to death? Then there are no surprises, no point in living it."

"Life is full of surprises," she said reprovingly, "no matter how carefully you arrange it. When you went to work this morning and the sun was shining and you didn't need more than a light jacket, did you think we would have six inches of snow on the ground by dusk? Did you imagine for a minute that you would be cooking dinner for me tonight? When you walked away from me at the party last week, were you surprised to find Melissa Thomas alone and in labor? When you sneaked out of my bed five months ago, did you ever dream someday you'd be back?"

He gave her a long steady look, the knife still in his hands, the onions forgotten on the chopping board. "Is that what you *sprung* me for? So you could make another mistake?"

Heat flooded her face. "I didn't say that right. When you sneaked out of my bed and *out of town* five months ago, did you ever dream someday you would be back *in town*?"

Slowly he positioned the onion half-cut-side down, then sliced through it three times before chopping it. "You didn't answer my question. Is that how I'm supposed to thank you for the unexpected night out?"

Because sex hadn't been on her mind when she'd given the invitation—at least, not consciously—she didn't hesitate to pretend it wasn't on her mind at all. "I don't expect anything, Cole, except a good dinner."

He scraped the onions into a skillet on the stove, set the knife down, and came to lean on the counter in front of her. "Too bad," he murmured, his voice husky. "Because tonight . . . I wouldn't mind being your latest mistake at all."

Chapter Fourteen

NY FOOL COULD SEE SHE DIDN'T KNOW WHAT to say to that. Cole remained there, too close but not close enough, for a minute, or three or five, just to see what she would come up with. When she remained silent, he returned to the island and the green and red bell peppers waiting to be chopped. "How's Melissa Thomas and her baby?" he asked, sounding as normal as if he hadn't just raised the temperature between them by twenty degrees or so. As if he weren't disappointed that she'd had no response to his come-on.

As if he hadn't harbored some stupid hope that she would forget all about dinner and invite him into her bedroom.

"M–Melissa?" she echoed, her voice hoarse. "She's— she's fine . . . out of the hospital and . . . gone to Rochester. The baby . . . he's okay, too, as far as I know. I— I haven't heard anything in the last few days." Still speaking in that unfocused tone, she asked, "Is this enough cheese?"

"More than enough." He hadn't told her half the block would be plenty for the baked potatoes, so she'd grated all but a small piece.

Calling the dog over, she fed that chunk to him, then

covered the plate with plastic wrap and set it in the refrigerator. "What else can I do?"

Oh, he could think of a few dozen answers to that, and not one of them had to do with cooking . . . though he'd seen a few items in her refrigerator that could come into play if she was adventurous enough.

But he knew too well that wasn't what she meant, and there was no sense in pretending otherwise. Just being alone with her was torment enough. He didn't need to shovel it on.

"You can wash the mushrooms if you want. Other than that, everything's pretty much done."

She did as he suggested, then covered them with a damp paper towel. While he finished chopping the peppers, she took a bottle of wine from the refrigerator and filled two glasses. He wasn't much of a drinker, but he would take anything that might cool the heat in his blood a few degrees.

She leaned against the counter, ankles crossed, and sipped her wine. "When you came here, you said you were moving from California. Was that true?"

"Nope. I've lived just about everywhere *but* California."

"Why did you lie?"

"Because I've lived just about everywhere *but* California."

"Meaning you're probably wanted just about everywhere."

He shrugged and copied her position on the opposite side of the island. "Everywhere and nowhere."

"Ryan says you never finished school."

"I dropped out in tenth grade. I had more important things to do with my time."

"Like what?"

He shrugged again, and she frowned. "Stop doing that. Ryan does it all the time, and it drives me crazy. Say 'None of your business' or 'I don't want to talk about it,' but don't shrug again."

"Okay," he agreed slowly. "When I was sixteen, Owen went to prison for a while. Someone had to look out for the younger kids, so—" He started to shrug, then caught himself. "I did."

"What about social services? Why didn't they place all of you in a home?"

"They didn't know about us. Owen wasn't using his real name, and he didn't volunteer the information."

"Wasn't he worried about you?"

"He knew we would take care of one another."

"Taking Ryan when no one else wanted him . . . that was just natural for you, wasn't it? After spending all those years taking care of your brothers."

"I guess." He stood her steady, thoughtful gaze for as long as he could, then pushed away from the counter and took his wine into the living room, where Jerome lay on the sofa. He took a seat near the mutt's head, and she sat by his feet.

"Of all the places you've lived, which one did you like best?" she asked in a conversational, getting-to-know-you tone that they should have been hell and gone past, but weren't.

This one. "There are different reasons for liking a place," he hedged. "Winters are great in Palm Beach. Atlanta was great for things to do. If you like skiing, Denver's convenient. For a party town, you can't beat New Orleans. People are more trusting in small towns. My kind of scams rank lower on the cops' priorities in big cities. People tend to take paybacks more seriously, in my experience, out west."

"So you've never thought you might like to stay in any particular place."

Just this one. "I don't know *how* to stay in any one place. Even when I was a kid, growing up around Dallas, we never had the same address longer than a couple months."

She drew her feet onto the sofa and balanced her wineglass on one knee. "You've never stayed anywhere, and I've never left. Never wanted to. I've always loved Bethlehem— have always been happy right here. It's home."

Absently he scratched behind Jerome's ears. "I've never had a home. Just a long line of places I've settled for a few weeks or a few months. I've never had neighbors or roots or ties to the community." Or friends or connections or that warm sense of familiarity people like Leanne had for their hometowns.

"Have you ever wanted any of that?"

He glanced at her, but she was gazing off into the distance. Because the question was casual, unimportant? Or because it wasn't?

The smart answer would be the lie. *Never. Why settle in one place when you can wake up someplace new every day? Why be bored when there's a whole world of excitement out there?* "Sometimes," he replied quietly. "When I'd wake up and couldn't remember where I was. When it was time to move on and I didn't have the energy for it. When Ryan's new school would comment on all the schools he'd gone to in the past year. When I'd have to tell him it was time to quit and find another new school."

She gazed into her glass as she swirled the wine in lazy circles. "Did you ever want to stay in Bethlehem?"

A lot more often than was safe. She'd been a large part of it, Ryan another part. But it had been the town, too. The feeling that he'd found a place to belong, when he hadn't even known he was looking for one. The sense that he and Ryan could both have everything they needed right there.

He opened his mouth to lie, but sudden impatience

with the old habit made him change his answer. "For a while, I did . . . but I screwed that up."

Finally she looked at him with a hint of a shrug. "But you're here."

Yeah. He was there. Granted, coming back hadn't been his choice, but . . . staying had been. But staying because the judge had ordered him to and staying once he was free to leave were two different things. People had to put up with him now, because the court said so. Once his sentence had been served, they would be justified in running him out of town.

Before she could say anything else, the timer in the kitchen buzzed. He left his wine on the coffee table and went to shut it off. While butter melted in a saucepan, he sliced the mushrooms, then added them and brown sugar to the butter. He set the onions and peppers to cooking in olive oil over the back burner, put the steaks under the broiler, then cut the potatoes in half.

"I had a meeting with the vice principal at Ryan's school this week."

Leanne's voice came from behind him, much closer than she'd been two minutes ago. He didn't startle, though, because some internal radar had alerted him to her nearness an instant before. "Is he in trouble?"

"He thinks school is a waste of time. But what twelve-year-old boy doesn't?" Crossing to the refrigerator, she opened the door. "What would you like to drink with dinner? We have more wine, Kool-Aid, orange juice, Pepsi, and milk."

"Eli gives us milk with every meal. I realize he's still a growing boy, but I gave that stuff up when I was eight. How about more wine?" It had a nice bite to it, and if he drank enough of it, he might get the courage to go for what he wanted. Hell, he could even drink enough that

not getting it wouldn't hurt . . . at least, not enough to notice, with all the other hurts inside.

Taking the wine bottle with her, she set the table while
he finished up the dinner. As soon as she was seated at the
small wicker table, he served it.

"Steaks broiled to perfection, caramelized mushrooms,
sauteed onions and peppers, and cheese-stuffed baked potatoes," he announced. "And you can sit barefooted and cross-
legged to eat. Isn't that better than a noisy restaurant?"

"And a handsome waiter as well." She saluted him with
her wineglass. "Hope I have enough on me for a good tip."

It was a surprisingly comfortable meal. Anyone watching would never guess that he'd betrayed, hurt, and disappointed her, that she'd sworn to hate him forever. They
were like any man and woman, talking about nothing in
particular, even laughing a time or two.

Of course, if they were *any* man and woman, they
would be in a restaurant, one too elegant and expensive to
be noisy, instead of hiding out from disapproving eyes at
home. After dinner they would stroll through the snow to
the car, and he would take her home and walk her to the
door, where she would slide her arms around his neck,
brush her mouth against his, and ask in a sultry voice,
Would you like to come in?

And he *would* like. Very much. And would say so. And—

Leanne's long slender fingers waved in front of his face.
When he blinked and focused on her, she smiled. "Where
were you? On some warm Florida beach?"

"Uh . . . no." He shook his head to clear away the fantasy. "What did you say?"

"I asked if you wanted to go with us." She gestured to
Jerome, who was watching him intently from the other
side of the table. "The baby needs to go out."

"He looks like he'd prefer that *we* go out and let him clear away the food." The mutt was practically grinning, and he started drooling once he caught the whiff of the leftover steak on Leanne's plate.

"That would be his first choice, I'm sure, but it's not going to happen." Rising, she picked up both their plates and took them to the kitchen. Jerome was right on her heels.

There weren't many leftovers—the piece of steak, a few mushrooms, and a helping of onions and peppers. She filled a plate, covered it with foil, and put it in the refrigerator, then left the dishes in the sink. "Let me get my shoes, sweetie, and we'll go."

As she disappeared into the hall, Cole took the rest of the dishes in and found the dog, his front feet on the counter, his big tongue swiping the dinner plate on top in the sink. "Get down," he murmured, giving him a push. "Don't make me rat you out."

He got his boots, earning a glance but nothing more from Leanne, sitting on the steps, and took them back to the dining table to put on. He had never intended to stay in Bethlehem past June—or any other place that knew the meaning of winter. He was going to have to squeeze some more of his money out of Eli and buy a heavier coat if he wanted to survive.

A month ago survival had meant nothing if it had to be done in Bethlehem.

He wasn't sure, but he thought it came damn close to meaning everything now.

When he returned to the top of the stairs for his jacket, Leanne had put on the long wool coat that flapped around her legs, and wound a woolen scarf around her neck. She took another scarf, this one black and softer than anything he'd ever felt, and wrapped it around *his* neck. "Are you sure you won't freeze?" she asked as she clicked the snap on the leash and Jerome came flying.

"You have this real concern with me freezing. Do I look that delicate to you?"

She studied him as if seriously considering her answer. "You look like a surfer boy who rarely leaves the beaches."

He grinned. "Another reason I said I was from California. But I'm tougher than any sissy surfer boy."

Her only response was a soft grunt as she released the leash and let Jerome dash to the bottom of the stairs. There she looped it around her wrist, opened the door, and stepped outside into the cold.

The dog loved the snow, dashing here and there, diving headfirst into every drift they came to, then emerging all coated in white, to shake himself dry and shower them. They crossed the slush that covered the street and went into the square, where Jerome slowed his frenzied explorations long enough to do what he had to do, then immediately dove into another drift.

"I think that dog wakes up in a brand-new world every day," he commented.

"Are you implying unkind things about my baby's intelligence?"

"Not at all," he lied dryly. "Just making a statement."

"It might not be a bad way to live," she remarked as they followed the dog's lead toward Main Street. "He was dumped and left to die or survive on his own by people who didn't want him, but in spite of that, every day's a wonderful new day. I admire his resiliency."

Still following the dog, they turned onto Main Street and walked a block in silence before he stiffly said, "I didn't dump Ryan to survive on his own."

The look Leanne gave him was surprised. "I was talking about Jerome and his worthless owners, not you and

Ryan . . . though I admit to noticing a few similarities between Ryan's situation and Jerome's." Then she nudged
him with her elbow. "Feeling the sting of that conscience
you claim you don't have?"

Instead of admitting or denying it, he turned his gaze to
the storefronts. Harry's, back in the other direction, was the
only business still open. The others were locked up tight
and dimly lit, most with Thanksgiving messages or scenes
on their windows. "Eli told us today that we'll be handling
the Christmas decorations for the town."

"That'll keep you busy for a good long while. Christmas is our favorite holiday, and we do it up right. How
could we not, with a name like Bethlehem?"

"He's got us scheduled to work on floats for the Christmas parade, string lights, and put out tacky decorations."
He scowled. "I'd rather chop wood and pick cotton."

This time the elbow in his ribs was substantially more
than a nudge. "Our decorations aren't tacky! They're
beautiful. And the lights look incredible on the trees
and buildings when it snows, and the bandstand is always
gorgeous—like a scene from a Rockwell painting. And the
Christmas parade is the best time to be had in this part of
the state in cold weather."

"Funny. I thought that was you. In any kind of
weather."

She stopped abruptly and lifted her gaze to him. Her
dark eyes were wide and alive with emotions, most of
which he couldn't name. Wouldn't name. Slipping her
hand from her glove, she laid it, warm and soft, against his
cheek. "I'll take that as a compliment," she whispered as
she leaned closer. Before he could tell her he'd meant it as
one, she was kissing him.

It was a great kiss—sweet and warm, tasting of wine and
dark sugar, promising everything and doing a pretty good

job of delivering. It made him forget the snow, and the cold, and the discomfort in his toes, and stirred a hunger in his belly that all the steak dinners in the world couldn't touch. It made him want more than was wise, need more than was possible. It made him greedy, and grateful, and . . . sweet damnation.

It ended too soon—about the time he slid his hand into her hair and used the other to pull her against him. She drew back, gave him a few chaste little kisses, then pulled away, took his hand, and started walking again.

"Does the Jackson family have any Christmas traditions?" Her voice sounded almost normal, as if she hadn't just turned him on beyond bearing, as if the kiss had left her unaffected. But her voice was a shade breathier than usual, her tone a shade more satisfied than usual.

It took him half a block to get his brain functioning again. "You mean, like bail money in our stockings, stealing from the rich to give to ourselves, or ripping off the Salvation Army Santas?"

"I mean, like putting up a tree after Thanksgiving or making gifts for each other. Hanging mistletoe and drinking eggnog, getting together on Christmas Eve to go to church and having a big traditional dinner on Christmas Day."

"We didn't go to church the rest of the year. Why would Christmas Eve be different?"

She gave him a chiding look. "I'll let you in on a little secret. A great many of the people in church on Christmas Eve don't go the rest of the year."

He shoved his free hand in his pocket, then flexed his fingers around hers. It was a little thing, holding hands and walking the dog in the snow, but it didn't feel little. It felt like one of the best gifts he'd ever been given.

And because that sounded way too dopey even for him, he turned his attention to answering her question. "Yeah, we had a tree." Most years, at least. And most years it had even had presents under it. "We never bothered with mistletoe—the Jackson boys never needed an excuse to kiss their girls—and we didn't much care for eggnog, so we doctored it with rum. We still didn't care for it, so we quit adding the eggnog and just drank the rum. Usually Eloise would come back from wherever she was, and we would have the big traditional Christmas dinner in whatever restaurant Owen could afford that year. Sometimes it was the ritziest place in town. Usually it was more along the line of Harry's."

At the next intersection, they turned right onto a street just as deserted as and even more snow-covered than Main. The sidewalk stretched ahead of them, unmarked by footprints, smooth, clean, damn near pristine.

"Now that they're grown up, how do the Jackson boys celebrate?"

"Anyone who can make it to Owen's does. He still has a tree, still no mistletoe, and plenty of rum, and Christmas dinner is still eaten in a restaurant somewhere."

"You should invite them here."

This time he was the one who stopped and stared. She and Jerome walked ahead a few steps before his grip on her hand stopped her, then she came back and gently closed his mouth. Immediately he opened it again. "Invite my family *here*?"

Her head bobbed. "I'm telling you, Bethlehem does Christmas right. They would love it."

"*I'm* telling *you*, the last thing this town needs is the whole Jackson family here at the same time. They would carry off anything that wasn't nailed down and half the stuff that was."

She smiled blithely. "At Christmas? When they're being welcomed like long-lost members of the family?"

"That's what I did," he said bitterly. "You people welcomed me, and look how I repaid you."

She nodded as if his words didn't mean much, then tugged his hand, silently coaxing him into walking again. At the end of the block, they turned right again. A few blocks ahead, the Miller mansion was brightly lit against the night. Out of sight from their vantage point was Leanne's apartment: smaller, cozier, more dimly lit. After their stroll through the snow, he would walk her to her door. Would she slide her arms around his neck? Kiss him again? Invite him inside?

He hoped so. If the snow hadn't obliterated all sign of the stars, he would even wish for it.

Even at their lazy pace, they were at the door in just minutes. She unlocked it, climbed the first few steps, then looked back. "Aren't you coming in?"

"I wasn't sure . . ."

"Hey, we still have bananas, cake, and whipping cream, remember?"

Dessert. Of course. So much for hoping and even wishing.

Then, when they were about halfway up the stairs, she gave him a look too innocent by far for the gleam in her eyes. "Besides, I haven't yet tipped you for the excellent dinner."

HE SLICED THE BANANAS, CARAMELIZED THEM, THEN served them over slices of pound cake, with sweetened cream whipped to soft peaks. It was simple and incredible, and made Leanne want to purr with satisfaction. After indulging, they shared the dish-fairy chores, then stood on opposite sides of the island, each drying their hands while sizing up the other.

"About that tip," he said, his gaze dark and heated.

She hung the towel over the rack, then turned her pants pockets inside out. "We may have to negotiate that. My pockets have already been emptied."

"What would you be willing to offer?"

With an innocent shrug, she raised her brows. "Maybe a kiss?"

"Just one kiss?"

"Sweetheart, I could give you one kiss that would curl your toes and make your eyes pop."

"One kiss?" he asked skeptically.

"It's not the number of kisses that count. It's how—and where—they're done."

For a long moment the only sound in the apartment, besides her own nervous breathing, was Jerome snoring in his kennel. Then Cole broke her gaze, hung up the towel, then glanced at the clock. "When will the boys be back?"

"Sometime tomorrow, weather permitting."

"When is Eli expecting me back?"

"He didn't say." She smiled. "It's not as if he doesn't know where you are and who you're with and what you're doing."

"He's such a kid, I'm not sure he has the faintest idea what I'm doing." Slowly he circled the island, caught Leanne's hand in his, and started toward the bedroom.

The first time they'd had sex, it had been easy. She hadn't been in love with him yet. She had suspected he could break her heart, but hadn't expected it. She'd thought she could handle the attraction to him, spending all that time with him, and having sex with him without getting in over her head because, hey, she was the queen of bad relationships. She'd gone into that one with her eyes wide-open.

And she was going into this with her eyes open even

wider. Now she knew what it was like to love him. Knew how easily he could hurt her. Knew this was more than attraction, more than sex, and wanted it—wanted him—anyway.

A single lamp burned as a night-light in her bedroom, a silly little frilly thing with tinted glass and fringe sitting on the dresser. Along with the light filtering in around the edges of the blinds, it was all the illumination they needed.

He stopped next to the bed and drew her into his arms. It was the one place she'd longed to be. It was like coming home—warm, familiar, comforting.

For a time he just held her and kissed her and proved her right—that it wasn't the number of kisses that counted, but how and where they were done. Sweet kisses, lazy kisses, all-the-time-in-the-world kisses, accompanied by gentle, tormenting touches. Kisses that made her skin hot, her muscles quiver, her knees weak. Even one kiss that curled her toes. He removed her clothing as easily, as familiarly, as his own, then lowered her onto the bed, and he remembered the condoms in the nightstand drawer as if he'd put them there himself.

The room was warm, the night still, its usual sounds muffled by the heavy snow Every place they touched, her skin rippled, and every breath she took grew sharper, thinner, more ragged. When he suckled her nipple, she would have gasped if she'd been able. When he slid his strong, calloused hands beneath her and lifted her hips to meet his, the best she could manage was a groan.

The pleasure was intense, the need inside her growing more urgent with each thrust of his hips. It had been so long . . . felt so good . . . so necessary . . . so . . .

A cry wrenched from her as the long, shuddering waves of completion washed over her. With her vision reduced to starbursts of blinding brilliance, with her lungs struggling for the faintest breath, she clung to Cole as if she was never going to let go. As if she needed him to survive. As if she loved him, plain and simple.

And she did. No matter how crazy it was, how irrational and illogical and downright stupid. Knowing he could, and likely would, break her heart again. Knowing he couldn't stay, while she wouldn't leave. Knowing he couldn't fit into her life, while she wouldn't fit into his.

She loved him.

And she didn't know whether to laugh about it . . . or cry.

I SHOULD GO." Leanne took a deep breath, and the sensitive tips of her breasts brushed his arm. "What time is it?"

"Ten-thirty."

"Does Eli do a bed check?"

"So far it hasn't been necessary, since we weren't allowed to go anywhere without him." Instead of getting up, though, he turned onto his side and drew her nearer. For a long time he looked at her, his expression grave in the dim light.

What did he see? An enormously satisfied woman? A grateful lover? Or a woman who loved him in spite of everything?

She truly hoped not on that last. She'd said the words to him once last spring, early one morning when she'd awakened in his bed across the street. She had thought he was asleep, looking so sweet and . . . special, and she'd blurted the words out on a rush of emotion.

Only he hadn't been asleep. His eyes had popped open, and he'd look stricken. Appalled. Terrified.

Definitely *not* the response she was looking for.

Once he'd regained his equilibrium, he'd hustled her and Danny, then himself and Ryan, out the door. He'd canceled his lunch with her, and missed their dinner with Nolie and Chase. She'd thought she had seen the last of him, but he had come back that night, and every other night . . . for the next week.

Then he'd disappeared.

Most of that Saturday she'd thought he was working. She'd worried a little all day, but it wasn't until evening rolled around that she got really concerned. She'd gone to the Miller mansion, but no one was home—had called his office and gotten only the answering machine. Her next call had been to Fred Miller. Yes, he had an extra key to his mother's house, but no, he didn't feel right just letting himself in when Cole was in the process of buying the place.

She'd talked him into it, though, and around seven-thirty, he'd met her and the boys there and unlocked the door. The house had been too still, too empty. Immediately she had known in her gut that Cole was gone, and a check of his bedroom confirmed it. Ryan's belongings were all where he'd left them. Cole's . . . all gone.

All she had to do was close her eyes and she could feel that stillness, that emptiness, again. Back in the summer it hadn't taken long for her to realize that the feelings hadn't come from the house, but from herself. Some secret place inside her—the place that expected all men to leave her—had known he was gone. The stillness and emptiness had been her life without him.

And the hurt. The anger. The bitterness. The disappointment. The hostility.

And here she was, back again in the same place. Facing it all over again. And there was nothing she could do to stop it.

Nothing she *would* do.

It was better to have loved and lost than never to have loved at all, or something like that. Nonsense, she'd believed after her first broken heart. Pure and utter nonsense, spoken by one who had never loved and lost.

But every bad relationship had given her something. Sometimes it was just experience. With Greg and again with Cole, it had been a child. Whatever the gift, all those things had gone together to make her the woman she was today, and she loved that woman a lot.

Even if no man had ever loved her back.

She stroked her finger lightly across his mouth. "You look so serious."

"You look so beautiful."

"Oh, yes, my beauty is so great that it always makes men look as if they're in pain."

He bit the tip of her finger gently, then wrapped his hand around hers. "Actually, I was thinking about the fact that I'm thirty years old and I have to go home when the evening's hardly started, so some kid half my age won't get annoyed and come looking for me or, worse, call the cops. That's no way for a man to live."

His last words, quieter, grimmer, than the rest, stirred a faint hope to life inside her. He didn't know how to stay, he claimed. He was a crook, plain and simple. He looked out for himself first, and screw everyone else. But the first step to changing was to *want* to change, and before he could want it, he had to find dissatisfaction with the way things were. *That's no way for a man to live* . . . sure sounded like dissatisfaction to her.

But was it enough to overcome a lifetime of honing the finer skills of con artistry?

"It's not ideal," she agreed. "But life isn't, is it? We all make mistakes, and either we learn from them and become better people or we're doomed to repeat them."

"And you and I are repeat offenders," he said with a wry smile. "For most men my age, prison isn't an acceptable alternative, which makes breaking the law an unacceptable occupation, but here I am. . . . And you . . . hell, here you are naked. With me. Again."

"Being intimate with someone you"—she lowered her lashes so he couldn't possibly read anything in her gaze—"you connect with isn't automatically a mistake."

"Being intimate with an idiot who's already broken your heart once *is.*" Releasing her, he sat up on the edge of the bed, then reached for his clothes.

Leanne missed his warmth immediately. After settling both pillows behind her, she tucked the covers tightly around her. "Careful. You almost sound as if you regret it."

He stood up to pull his jeans to his waist, buttoned and zipped them, then sat down again, putting on his socks and boots as he faced her. "Don't you?"

"Do I regret getting my heart broken? Sure. I'm all in favor of suffering as little as possible. Do I regret having the affair? No. I would have wished for a different outcome, but I wouldn't undo it if I could."

He pulled his sweatshirt on and tugged it into place, leaving his hair standing on end, then leaned forward, placing one hand on each side of her. His blue gaze hard and intense, his jaw clenched, he asked, "Do you regret loving me?"

His voice was silky, soft and smooth slicked over steel. He wanted to be sarcastic, she suspected, but couldn't quite pull it off. Wanted to show how little he cared, or what a bastard he really was, but couldn't quite manage that, either.

She cupped her hand to his cheek, and he automatically turned, pressing a kiss to her palm. "No," she replied as she lifted her gaze to his. "I don't regret that at all."

Suddenly, frantically, he kissed her, a hard quick assault that left her short of breath and long on heat. Then he left her and the bed, left the room and, a moment later, the apartment.

She slid out of bed and into her robe, then went to the side window and raised the blinds. The snow had stopped and a few stars had finally broken through the cloud cover to gleam on all the white below. She watched as Cole crossed the street, then reached the Miller house with long, purposeful strides. He cleaned his boots on the porch, went inside, and closed the door, but still she watched. A moment later she was rewarded when a light came on in his bedroom and, seconds after that, he appeared at his own window.

For endless moments they just gazed at each other. Finally, with the cold creeping into her feet and along her legs, she waved her fingers lazily. He raised his own hand, though not in a wave. He just held it, fingers apart, palm pressed to the windowpane, in a gesture so forlorn it made her chest tighten around her heart.

Swallowing hard, she turned away, shut off the lamp, then snuggled back into the bed that retained the heat, the scent, and the memory of him.

As she did.

*B*E CAREFUL WHAT YOU WISH FOR. YOU JUST MIGHT *get it.*

As soon as they'd arrived at the hospital Saturday morning, Alex and Melissa had gone straight to the NICU to check on Max. She was still there, all gowned and gloved, touching the baby's tiny body through the incubator ports, talking and singing softly as if he were . . . as if nothing was wrong. As soon as he could leave, Alex had excused himself and come here to the chapel, to . . . what? Be alone? Feel bad? Stop pretending? Pray?

That last didn't much appeal to him at the moment. He'd prayed a lot of times for a baby, but they'd had to go through hell to get one and once they finally had, he'd come early. He'd prayed for Max to live, to be healthy, and then he'd prayed for the doctor's diagnosis to be wrong. Well, Max was still alive and his condition had been upgraded from critical to serious, but as for being healthy and the diagnosis . . . God apparently wasn't listening.

After dropping his bombshell on Wednesday, Dr. Bosquez had shown them the signs—Max's smaller-than-normal size, even for a preemie; the shape of his head; his ears and mouth, disproportionately small, and his nose, disproportionately wide; the epicanthic folds on his eyelids and the size and shape of his hands and fingers. Melissa had listened, all the while looking at the baby as if he were the most perfect baby in all the world, and Alex . . . all he could think of was that old cautionary saying and how true it had proven.

Be careful what you wish for. You just might get it.

He'd wanted a child—had prayed, begged, pleaded for one. He'd watched other men with their children and felt such a longing inside. He'd dreamed of coaching a five-year-old's soccer team, of being a scoutmaster, of being the proud-to-bursting father of a football player or honor student, a drama star or even a class clown. He'd dreamed of someday changing the name of his law practice to Thomas and Thomas.

So much for dreams.

"God must hate me."

A gasp sounded a few feet away. "Don't say such a thing! God doesn't hate!"

Startled, he glanced at the woman sitting farther down

on the pew. He would have sworn the chapel was empty when he'd come in, and he hadn't heard anyone else enter, but there she sat, a pretty blonde with curls, wearing the standard uniform of cotton top and pants. She didn't look old enough to be a nurse, though he knew well looks could be deceiving. After all, to the uninformed, Max looked like a very small but perfect baby, when he was anything but.

"You're Max Thomas's father. I've seen you around the NICU. I'm Sophy."

When she offered her hand, he grudgingly shook it, then swung his gaze back to the front of the chapel. On Sunday night he was returning home to Bethlehem for a few days, to get caught up on his work, while Jenny and her parents stayed with Melissa. Everyone would want to see pictures and hear updates and would be so excited for him and Melissa, and he would have to tell them . . .

He *always* had to be the one to break the bad news.

"You're disappointed, aren't you?" Sophy asked sympathetically. "I understand. So was I at first. You've waited so long to become a father, and you thought this time everything was going to be perfect, and then . . . *boom*!"

He didn't say anything—didn't even look at her. No one knew he was disappointed, not even Melissa, and he intended to keep it that way. It wasn't a reaction he was proud of—truth was, it shamed him all the way through his soul—but there wasn't much he could do about it. He felt the way he felt.

"He has tremendous potential."

This time he couldn't stop himself from looking at her. "To do what? To *be* what?"

"To be a healthy, happy, loving son. To make your life, and Melissa's, and the lives of everyone around him, better. To make a difference."

"He'll never be a lawyer, a doctor, a teacher, or a father."

"Neither will an awful lot of other people."

"He'll never make the high-school football team or play in the band or go to college. He'll never drive a car or go out on dates or live on his own. He'll never have the chance to travel without someone to take care of him. He'll never hold a job or be a productive member of society. He'll never be anything more than a child, no matter what his age."

The look she gave him was chastising. "You don't know many people with Down syndrome, do you?"

He'd known a few over the years, but not well. They were . . . different.

He wanted his son to be different in only one way—better. Smarter. More talented. More outgoing. More accomplished.

"*Every* child is different, Alex. Max's differences will just be more readily apparent. As for what he'll do or never do, no one will have a clue for several years, at least. He could be very high-functioning. He could go through school, hold a job, and live in a group home, if not on his own. He could even marry and have children of his own." She laid her hand on his arm. "Yes, there will be things he can't do, but there are things that every infant in this hospital, 'normal' or not, won't be able to do. Not every child can throw a football, learn the piano, or become fluent in multiple languages. Not every child can do math or pick up chemistry or interpret the finer points of the law. And not every child can be sweet and loving and generous and kind . . . but Max will be."

Maybe . . . but he wouldn't play soccer or baseball. He wouldn't memorize lines to act in a play, as his mother had been doing when Alex met her. He wouldn't fit in in a regular classroom, wouldn't advance with other kids his age, wouldn't have the wide-open future other kids faced.

"But he'll think you hung the moon and the stars," Sophy murmured, "and he'll love you without reservation for the rest of his long, happy life."

Alex looked at her, at the utter serenity of her expression, and the tightness in his gut eased a little. Loving and being loved—something else that not all kids could do. Something important. Something that mattered, that made a difference. And, after all, the world already had enough lawyers and doctors, didn't it?

Even so, he couldn't stop being disappointed. Couldn't stop thinking.

Couldn't stop wishing . . .

Chapter Fifteen

WHILE ELI AND MURRAY WATCHED A football game on TV Saturday afternoon, Cole stood at his bedroom window, staring out at the town and thinking—about Leanne, last night, Ryan, Owen and Eloise and his brothers, about mistakes and complications and screwed-up values.

He hadn't been kidding when he'd told Leanne that this was no way for a man to live. It was the only life he'd prepared for, the only one he'd ever known. For the first time in thirty years, he wanted to break with tradition.

He didn't have a clue what he would do, or how he would do it, or if he stood even the smallest chance of succeeding. He didn't even know if he would like whatever respectable life he might make for himself any more than, or even as much as, the disreputable life he lived now. He just knew he wanted something different.

Stability. A chance to fix things with Ryan. A chance to pursue things with Leanne. He wanted to know how it felt to face himself in the mirror each day and know he hadn't done anything to be ashamed of. He wanted an occupation and a lifestyle where prison wasn't one of the costs of doing business.

He wanted to reinvent himself.

And he wanted to believe he could do it.

The sun hadn't come out all day, but the temperature had warmed into the high thirties. Snow melted in a steady drip from the rooftops and trees—so steady that a few of the older women out running their Saturday errands carried umbrellas to keep them dry. A snowman built in the square that morning by Sebastian Knight and his little girl had shrunk into a featureless lump of snow, and the streets were filled with dirty slush that splashed onto the sidewalks when cars drove past.

By Monday there wouldn't be any sign of the snow left—a good thing, since they were scheduled to start work on the town's Christmas decorations that morning. There were miles of lights to check for burned-out bulbs and bad wiring, as well as painted decorations that would require touch-ups, and others needing a good cleaning.

Though he could think of a lot better ways to spend his time than decorating for a holiday he didn't care much about, Cole wished it was already Monday. The weekend was dragging out one endless moment after another, leaving too much time to think.

He was about to turn away from the window when movement across the street caught his attention. It was Ryan and Danny, both bundled against the cold, and heading toward Small Wonders from Danny's day care center a block or so away. Ryan was holding Danny's hand and listening as the kid chattered.

When they drew even with the Miller mansion, Ryan's gaze shifted across the street, and Cole automatically took a step back and to the right. He watched through the lace curtains as Ryan stared at the house.

Sometimes Cole was surprised at how much he missed the kid. There was an empty space inside him that had appeared last spring and wasn't going away. He missed the friendship, the teasing, the arguing, the affection, the responsibility. He missed the needing, and being needed.

If you could have a chance to be Ryan's father again, would you take it? J.D. Grayson had asked during their appointment.

He missed being Ryan's father.

When the boys turned the corner and moved out of his sight, Cole turned away from the window, his gaze falling on the nightstand. Next to the lamp was Kelsey Grayson's business card, complete with the state seal and her home phone number as well as the office number. Jacksons had always made a point of being unreachable except through Owen, but here in Bethlehem, *unreachable* was a foreign concept. Unlisted phone numbers were rare, and if you couldn't get a person on the phone, half the town would be happy to give you directions to his house.

He picked up the business card and tapped it against one palm. He didn't want to talk to Kelsey—didn't want to hear that she'd had any luck in locating Ryan's birth parents. He didn't want to even think about the fact that she was looking, that if she found them, they could take the kid away from the family who loved him.

But Kelsey's home phone number was also J.D.'s, and he had a question or two to ask the good doctor.

Folding his fingers over the card, he went downstairs to the kitchen phone and dialed the number. One of the Grayson brood answered the phone, then a moment later, J.D. came on. "What can I do for you, Cole?"

"Sorry to bother you at home, Doc, but . . . I want to see Ryan."

"Okay." Grayson sounded a little confused. "Shouldn't you be discussing that with Leanne instead of me?"

"I just . . . I want to be sure . . ." Cole clamped his jaw

shut. It was easy enough to put into words—*I want to know that my being around won't do him any harm*—but giving voice to those words was another matter. It was a shameful thing to admit that just spending time with him could hurt Ryan.

"You want to know that seeing you won't cause Ryan any further problems." Grayson paused. "What made you want to see him?"

I miss him didn't seem a good enough response. Neither did *I feel guilty* or *I need to feel needed*. He didn't know that any answer he might give could be good enough, but he tried. "He deserves to know that it wasn't his fault—that he didn't do anything wrong. I didn't get tired of him. I didn't think life would be easier without him. I *knew* it would be damned hard . . . but I left him anyway."

That was the bottom line, the one that was so hard for him to explain, and so hard for Ryan to understand. *I left him anyway.*

"One of the toughest concepts for kids to understand is doing something for their own good. You left him here so he could have a better life than you could give him, but all he sees is that you chose a life that didn't include him. You were right the other day, Cole—you *were* the stability in his life. Your leaving turned his whole world upside down, and it hasn't been right since. When he's older, your reasons for it will matter, but right now they don't. All that matters now is that he loved you and you left him. Now you're back, and he's got all this anger and hurt inside that he doesn't know what to do with."

"So he's acting up at school. But if I'm around, he can take it out on me."

"It would certainly be easier on him to vent all that emotion on the person responsible for it, though it might get kind of rough for you."

"You think it's not kind of rough anyway?" Seeing him, knowing how deeply he'd hurt him, unable to talk to him, to make him understand . . .

"He'll want to hurt you the way you hurt him, and to some extent you'll have to let him. You can't blow up at him or try a time or two, then write him off. That would just validate his belief that you didn't want to bother with him anymore."

"I understand."

"And this can't be a short-term thing, Cole. If you're not intending to be a part of his life for the rest of his life, don't even start. He doesn't need your pity or your guilt. He needs a father who will always be there for him. If you can't commit to that, then leave him alone. Let him work through things with Leanne and me."

Commit. Cole smiled thinly. He'd committed a life's worth of crimes, but he'd never truly committed himself to any sort of relationship.

Until now.

"I'm not going to hurt him again. I just want to make things right." He paused, closed his eyes, then quietly added, "Please."

Grayson was silent for a moment before exhaling. "Let me talk to Leanne, then I'll get back to you, okay?"

"Thanks." Cole hung up, his fingers wrapped tightly around the receiver for a long time before he finally let go. He'd asked. Pleaded. Now all he could do was wait.

The answer came nearly two hours later. He was back in his bedroom, studying the patterns in the pressed-tin ceiling, when Eli knocked at the door, then came inside. "Leanne Wilson called. She and Dr. Grayson agree that it would be a good idea for you to spend some time with Ryan."

Cole sat up, swung his feet to the floor, and took a deep

breath, but didn't get much air. His chest was too tight to let his lungs expand, leaving him feeling starved for oxygen and vaguely panicked. He had asked for a chance, and they were giving it to him. Now if he just knew what to do, what to say, how to make Ryan believe in him again. . . .

"She said to tell you that they'll be having dinner at Harry's at six-thirty. She thought meeting in public might keep things a little restrained this time."

Jacksons had never been particularly restrained about their emotions, no matter where they were. He'd seen some wild celebrations in public places, as well as knock-down-drag-out fights. Hell, he'd taken part in both.

But Ryan wasn't a Jackson.

Funny how easy it was to forget that.

Eli started to leave, then turned back. "I understand this was your idea."

Cole nodded.

"Good." With that, he left.

G OD, HE HOPED IT WAS A GOOD IDEA, COLE THOUGHT as he stood in the darkness across the street from Harry's and gazed inside. The café was brightly lit, and a couple dozen diners were spread around the room. Harry, as usual, was in the kitchen, visible only occasionally when he delivered food to the pass-through, and Maeve, as usual, was waiting tables.

Leanne, Ryan, and Danny sat in the corner booth, a round one big enough for twice their number. She was on one end, and Danny on the other, which left Ryan in the middle with no escape. Probably a smart move on her part. Danny was on his knees, chattering a mile a minute, using his facial expressions, his hands, and his entire body to tell his story. He looked so young and innocent, exactly the way a four-year-old should look.

Had Ryan ever been that young or that innocent? Probably not. He'd never had the security Danny took for granted—a permanent home, family who loved him, a parent who would die for him. Cole had given him what he could, but it hadn't been enough. The story of his life.

Maeve delivered drinks to the booth, then laughed at something Danny said. Her pen was poised over the order pad, but she was in no hurry to move on to the next customer.

Suddenly cold, Cole forced himself to step out of the square, to cross the sidewalk, then the street, and walk into the diner. The bell announced him, bringing everyone's attention his way. Some looked at him, then away, without interest. Some glances were speculative, some censuring. Still frozen on the inside, but now flushed hot on the outside, he pretended to ignore them all and went to the booth.

Maeve gave him a cool excuse for a smile, Leanne gave him the real thing, and Danny leaped into his arms. "Hey! Where've you been? I been wishin' you'd come and see us, but you never do. We've missed you, ain't we, Ryan?"

Ryan shot a pissed look at Leanne, then started to slide around the bench. She stopped him with her hand on his arm. "You're not going anywhere, sweetheart."

"I'm not eatin' with *him*!"

"Yes, you are." She tugged his arm until he had no real choice but to slide back toward her a few inches. Okay, so he could have twisted his arm, twisting hers, too, in the process, and jerked away, but he didn't. Cole knew he would never risk physically hurting her. He'd been taught better than that.

"Danny, sit down. Cole, you, too. Maeve, could we have one more menu?"

Looking as if she would much rather show him the door, Maeve left, then returned to slap a menu down in front of him. "I'll come back for your order," she said stiffly before walking away.

"This isn't fair," Ryan said hostilely. "You could have told me this was a setup."

"Then you wouldn't have come willingly, and you would have been embarrassed when I carried you in over my shoulder."

"I wouldn't have come *at all*." He slumped down in the seat, chin on his chest, arms folded.

Leanne brushed a strand of hair from his eyes and gently teased, "Sweetheart, don't make me remind you that I'm your boss. Until you're old enough to live on your own, you have to do what I say."

He snorted.

Resting his arms on the table, Danny leaned close to Ryan. "And even after you're all growed up, you still have to do what she wants, 'cause she's the mama, and you're the kid, and that's the way it is. Ain't it, Mama?"

Leanne rewarded him with a serene and loving smile. "It certainly is, sweet pea."

Ryan slumped lower and scowled harder. "I'm not your kid."

"Says who?" she challenged. "I say you're mine, and so does Danny, and there's no one around brave enough to argue with us."

That stumped him. He looked at her for a moment, and Cole could actually see him softening a bit. Then, as if he caught himself, he frowned again, clamped his jaw shut, and said nothing.

"You ready to order?" Maeve asked as she returned,

giving smiles all around except to Cole. He wondered if she would pour salt in his tea and sugar in his gravy. He wondered if he could possibly stick around long enough to earn a genuine smile from her, or to make people stop looking at him as if he were alien to their experience—long enough for Ryan to forgive him, or to die trying. That could be his epitaph, he thought grimly. *He died trying.*

Maybe just this once it could be enough.

I T WAS A SHAME THE PURPOSE OF THE EVENING'S dinner hadn't been to get Danny together with Cole, because Danny was having a ball. Ryan, on the other hand, was dealing with Cole by not dealing with him—not speaking to him, not acknowledging him at all.

But Leanne had to give him credit—at least he hadn't left. He could have, even though they'd blocked him in. He was an agile kid. He could have gone under or over the table if he'd been really determined to get away. Instead, he'd sat there, scowling, barely picking at his food, ignoring everyone.

It was a start. A pitiful one, but a start.

When they were finished, she slid to her feet, put her jacket on, then looped her arm firmly through Ryan's when he would have bolted. Keeping him at her side, she leisurely strolled to the cash register near the door, paid the tab, called goodnight to Harry and everyone else, then joined Cole and Danny outside on the sidewalk. "What now, guys?" she asked as cheerfully as if the meal hadn't been excruciatingly tense.

"Ice cream!" Danny shouted, jumping up and down.

"Ice cream? With all that food in your tummy, you couldn't possibly have room for ice cream," she teased.

"Uh-huh. See?" He pulled up his shirt, exposing his little round belly, then smiled sweetly. "Please?"

"What do you say, Ryan?" she asked. "You want some ice cream?"

The child might be able to turn up his nose at a hamburger and fries, but he liked ice cream every bit as much as Danny did. He obviously considered that before shrugging as if he didn't care either way.

"What about you, Cole? You like ice cream?"

"Sure." He sounded about as enthusiastic as Ryan had looked. She had to give him credit, too. He'd tried to talk to Ryan, to draw *some* response from him, and had kept trying—though without success—long after she would have given up.

They crossed the street and walked the short distance to the ice cream shop. With its wooden floors, little round tables, and curlicued chairs, it was one of Leanne's favorite places in town. It had been in the same spot for more than sixty years, with the same furnishings and the same employee. Mr. McCormack had been dishing up cones and banana splits ever since he was fifteen years old. Back then, his grandfather had owned the place, then his parents had taken it over, and now it was his. His children had no interest in following tradition, but his granddaughter had been helping out ever since *she* was fifteen.

Tradition could be such a wonderful thing, she thought as they waited in line. Alex Thomas came from a family of lawyers and little Max would probably become one, too. The McCormacks had brought smiles and wrecked diets with their ice cream shop through five generations.

And then there was Cole's family tradition.

Each armed with their own cones, they found a table near the door and squeezed in. She took a bite from her cappuccino-almond ice cream, then sighed. "The woman who invented ice cream should have been granted saint-hood."

"I think it was a man," Cole said. "Men made all the great discoveries."

"Did not—and the ones they did make were probably because of women."

"What? They nagged, so they get to share the credit?"

"Big talk coming from a man with so little imagination he orders plain vanilla." She sniffed superiorly. "That's only good for holding fudge sauce or fresh strawberries, or for serving with birthday cake."

Danny grinned. "Ryan and me like—what *is* this again?"

"Cherry pecan," Ryan mumbled.

"Yeah. It's our favorite."

"Remember the first time you had that?" Cole asked. "We were in Memphis—"

Ryan interrupted, his tone cold and snotty. "And you were stealing from that woman you were seeing."

Cole's features tightened and his mouth thinned.

"You left me then, too, remember? And Eloise had to come pick me up so we could meet you in Alabama." He made a derisive sound. "I should've known you'd do it again someday."

His fingers gripping the cone almost hard enough to break it, Cole leaned toward him. "I left you that time be-cause damn near every cop in the city was looking for me. It was too risky to go back for you. They would have taken us both into custody, and who knows if I ever would have gotten you back?"

Ryan leaned forward, too, until they were practically nose to nose. There was no physical resemblance between them at all—Cole was too blond, Ryan too dark—but their scowls were identically fierce. "Like that mattered? It would've just saved you the trouble of dumping me here."

"I didn't *dump* you."

"Oh, that's right. You thought I'd be *better off.* You thought if you left me here, I wouldn't turn out to be as big a loser as you are." The contempt in Ryan's voice made the words sound even uglier than they were, but only the twitch of a muscle in Cole's jaw showed that they'd hit their target.

"I always wanted you to be a better person than me. What's wrong with that?"

Ryan swore, making Danny's eyes open wide. "All you ever wanted was whatever was best for you. When it was okay for me to be around, you kept me. When it wasn't, you dumped me on someone else."

Leanne hated to interrupt when Ryan had finally started talking, even if he was just venting his anger, but they'd drawn attention from practically everyone in the shop. She laid one hand on Cole's arm and gripped Ryan's hand with the other. "Why don't we continue this conversation at home?"

"Why doesn't he just go to hell?" Ryan pulled free, tossed his ice cream in the trash, then stalked outside and across the street.

Leanne started to rise, but Cole grimly pushed her back. "Let me."

Danny watched him go, then looked fearfully at her. "Why's ever'one mad?"

She opened her arms, and he slid into her lap, resting his head on her shoulder while continuing to lick his ice cream. "Don't worry, babe. Everything's going to be all right." And that wasn't just words. She believed it with all her heart.

But it wasn't going to happen tonight.

• • •

B Y THE TIME COLE CAUGHT UP, RYAN HAD MADE IT
to the bandstand, where he leaned against the railing
and hung his head. Cole climbed to the top of the steps,
but didn't go any farther. He wanted to—wanted to wrap
his arms around the kid and hold him until everything was
all right.

But it might not ever be all right.

Instead he shoved his hands in his pockets. "I know how
bad it hurt when your mom left, Ryan. Eloise was always
leaving us. If she hadn't been so hung up on Owen, I doubt
any of us kids ever would have seen her again after we
were born. It hurt, knowing she didn't love or want us the
way a mother was supposed to. I can only imagine how
bad you were hurt, to have your mom take off the way she
did."

"You don't know anything about my mom," Ryan
muttered. "Besides, it don't matter. People don't matter."

"You're wrong. People are the only thing in life that
does matter." He wasn't sure, but he thought he heard another of those obnoxious snorts in disagreement. "Maybe I
didn't do a good job of teaching you that. I put too much
emphasis on the cons and not enough on the important
stuff, like family."

Ryan stared out at the street, his back to Cole. "I don't
have any family."

"Maybe not the regular kind. God knows, the Jacksons
don't qualify. But you've got some kind—Owen and the
boys and me, Leanne and Danny and Micahlyn and her
folks."

"Phyllis doesn't like me."

For the first time all evening, Cole felt a bit of relief.
"Son, Phyllis doesn't like anyone."

"Don't call me that."

"Okay. Sorry." He'd hated being called *son* himself, but unlike his father, he hadn't used the word because he couldn't be bothered remembering the kid's name. That made a difference—to him, at least.

He watched Leanne and Danny come out of the ice cream shop, then start on the long way home, bypassing the square. She wiggled her fingers in a wave, then tucked Danny's hand securely in hers. A car drove past, then the porch lights came on at Jillian Freeman's house. It was prime-time Saturday night, and the town already seemed to be half-asleep.

Five years ago the payoff on a score would have to have been significant to make him settle even temporarily in such a quiet little place. Even then, he would have taken off every chance he got to find some excitement elsewhere, and he would have celebrated getting *out* of town as much as the payoff.

Tonight it seemed peaceful. Full of promise. A place where a man could atone for his past, live with himself, and make a future worth living.

With the cold seeping into his joints, he went to lean against the railing across from Ryan, crossing one ankle over the other. "I'm sorry for leaving you the way I did. I can't tell you how many times I wanted to turn around, come back, and get you."

"But you didn't," Ryan said belligerently.

"No, I didn't. And if the cops hadn't picked me up, I probably never would have set foot in Bethlehem again." He watched the kid's thin shoulders stiffen before adding, "But I would have regretted it as long as I lived."

"Easy to say now."

"No, Ryan, it's not easy to say, and it damn sure wasn't easy to do. But I *know* what I am. I *know* what I have to offer, and it's not enough. You're a smart kid, and you have so many chances ahead of you. You can be anything you want. You can make a difference in people's lives. If you settle for being no better than me because that's the only choice I've given you . . . I couldn't live with that. My own life has been screwed up from the beginning. I can't screw up yours, too."

Finally the kid faced him. "I could be anything I wanted *with* you! I stayed out of the cons. I didn't lift wallets or pick pockets for fun. All I did was get caught stealing once—one freakin' time! And it was just the excuse you were lookin' for to get rid of me."

"Nobody made me take you in. Nobody made me drag you around for three years or tell people you were my son. Nobody made me love you—" Realizing what he'd said, Cole stopped abruptly, the words echoing through him.

Ryan didn't notice, though. "And nobody made you dump me, either! You did it because you wanted to—because you didn't want me anymore!"

"That's not true—" Weariness settled over Cole, cutting off his denial, weighting his shoulders, and stirring an ache behind his eyes. It's not gonna be easy, Eli had said. The damn kid had to be right, didn't he?

"What's it matter anyway?" Ryan asked. "You tryin' to impress Leanne? Tryin' to make her think you can be a good father? Why, when you're just gonna dump her again, too?"

"I'm not dumping anyone."

"Yeah, sure. One of these days Adam or Bret's gonna show up in town and you'll be outta here like that." He snapped his fingers. "By the time she even realizes you're gone, you'll already be in another state, running another scam."

His life in a nutshell—change his name, change his hair

color, add a pair of glasses, or grow a beard. Play up the inbred Texas twang, affect a Southern drawl, or maybe mimic a clipped Boston accent. Be somebody else, conning someone else, until either he took all he could get or the law got too close. He'd lived his entire life like that.

"I'm not going anywhere," he said flatly, but to his own ears, the words lacked conviction.

Ryan stared at him, long and hard, before shaking his head. "Yeah, sure. Guess we'll see about that." Turning, he walked away.

After a moment, Cole headed after him, catching up as he reached the apartment door. Ryan took the stairs two at a time and disappeared down the hall. The bedroom door slammed about the time Cole got to the top.

Leanne came out of the kitchen and slid her arms around him. After a moment, she sighed softly. "I appreciate your doing this. I know it's tough."

"For God's sake, Leanne, I'm not doing anyone a favor. I *owe* the kid."

Her body stiffened against his, making him regret the words and the tone. When she would have pulled back, he wrapped his arms around her. "Don't . . . I didn't mean . . ."

After a moment, she softened against him once more. She smelled of things too exotic to name, sweet and sexy and desirable, and he knew she would taste just as sweet, just as sexy. Before he could prove it, though, small footsteps interrupted.

"Hey, Cole, wanna see me and Ryan's room?" Danny asked. "It used to be just my room, but then Ryan came, so now it's his, too. Wanna see?"

The kid was like a monkey, climbing halfway up Cole's leg. He gave him a boost and settled him on his hip. "I think Ryan wants to be alone."

"That's okay. He don't mind if I come in," Danny said matter-of-factly. It had never occurred to him even once in his life that his presence could ever be unwanted. Lucky kid.

"Why don't we give Ryan a little time alone?" Leanne suggested, then scooped him away from Cole and to the floor. "You go take your bath, then Cole can see your room when you go to bed, okay?"

"Okay. He can read me a story, too." Danny clumped off, his boots echoing on the hardwood floor.

When he was gone, Leanne turned back to Cole. "Why don't you get comfortable and warm—"

Her face cupped in his palms, he kissed her, sliding his tongue inside her mouth to taste her. Yep, sweet as spun sugar, sexy and sinful as hell. Just that one kiss was enough to make him hard, to turn the chill inside him to feverish heat.

When he ended the kiss, she looked a little dazed. He felt it.

He brushed his thumb across her still-parted lips, then said softly, "All warm now." But uncomfortable as hell, in a pleasurable way. "Go take care of Danny. I'll wait."

L EANNE GOT DANNY'S BATH STARTED, CHECKED IN ON Ryan, then went into the living room. She knew better than to think she and Cole might have five minutes uninterrupted, and naturally she was right. On weeknights, Danny usually dawdled through his bath, but this time he was serious about it, in and out—and even clean—in no time. She knew why, too—he wanted Cole's attention again.

As soon as he was dressed in his pajamas, he showed Cole all around the bedroom, as if it had truly changed since the spring. The walls were still tomato-red, the shelves were still filled with toys and books, and the video games still spilled out onto the floor. The only real differences were that his twin bed had been traded for bunk beds and some of the books on the shelves were Ryan's.

He insisted that Cole lie down in bed with him and read his favorite book about dinosaurs. Though she could practically recite it from memory, Leanne remained in the doorway and listened, enjoying the sight of her sweet little boy curled up in Cole's arms. Though she'd never regretted Greg's disappearing act, she had always wished Danny could have a real father. It helped, having her dad around and now Chase, but the real deal would mean so much to him—and to her.

Ryan could practically recite the story from memory, too, but he lay motionless in the top bunk, listening to the words. Had anyone ever read bedtime stories to him, then tucked him in and kissed him and said *I love you?* It didn't seem likely that the mother who'd abandoned him had made a routine out of anything that didn't benefit her.

Not that Leanne really knew what kind of mother the woman had been. Yes, she'd abandoned him, but the reason for it could make all the difference. Maybe she'd been a good mother, but had suffered a breakdown and become unable to care for him any longer. Maybe she'd never meant to leave him in that bus terminal but something had happened to her.

Or maybe she'd just realized one day that she no longer wanted to be a mother.

That possibility boggled Leanne's mind.

As soon as Cole finished the book, Danny dragged another one from under his pillow and shoved it at him. "Now this one."

Looking at her, Cole raised one eyebrow, and she nodded that it was all right, then left the room. She was in the kitchen, making brown-sugar-and-cinnamon-flavored coffee when he eventually followed her. He came to stand behind her at the stove, where she stirred the coffee in a saucepan, sliding his arms around her and nuzzling her neck.

"Hmm, that smells good. And the coffee's not half-bad, either."

She smiled. "So Danny couldn't talk you into a third story."

"Just a very short one. You read to him every night?"

"Ever since he was a few months old. Now Ryan does it sometimes." She watched the muddy-looking brew boil, the coffee grounds bubbling up, then subsiding, only to do it again. The last thing she needed tonight was caffeine, but she figured the sugar and spices, along with the whipped cream that would go on top, would counteract it. If not, maybe Cole would.

When the timer went off, she reluctantly pulled out of his embrace and took a mesh strainer from a drawer. If she were a more proficient cook, she would have cheesecloth to go inside it. Instead, she lined it with a paper towel, then strained the coffee into a heat-proof carafe. She was spooning whipped cream into mugs when Cole chuckled.

"You planning to have a little coffee with your whipped cream?"

Making a face, she scooped one heaping spoonful from each mug back into the carton. For good measure, he took the spoon and removed that much more from his. Once she'd filled the mugs, they each took one, then went into the living room. She sat on the sofa, kicked her shoes off, and drew her feet onto the cushions. He walked to the nearest window.

"Eli says I should go to church with you guys tomorrow," he said after a while.

"It couldn't hurt."

"Are you sure? Ryan's friends will be there."

"They know who you are, and they know what you've done. Besides, most kids their age aren't too happy about the parents they've been stuck with."

He gave her a dry look. "Danny will adore you as much when he's sixteen as he does right now."

"Because I've trained him well," she replied with a smug smile.

"Why isn't his father around?"

She tried to remember if he'd ever asked about Greg before. It was something everyone eventually got to, but she couldn't recall him ever bringing it up. Because he hadn't cared?

"He wasted no time getting out once I told him I was pregnant. He'd thought we were having fun—dating, sleeping together. He hadn't signed on for anything as serious or long-term as fatherhood."

"Has Danny ever met him?"

"No. Greg not only got out of the relationship, he got out of *town*. He was afraid I would hit him up for child support or something. I never knew where he went and never cared."

"But you were in love with him."

"I was," she agreed slowly. "It's funny, though, how quickly you can fall *out* of love with a man when he tells you he wants nothing to do with his own child." She didn't realize the double meaning of her words until Cole's jaw clenched and he stared outside again.

"Like me, you mean."

Rising from the sofa, she set her coffee on the table, then went to wrap her arms around him. "No, that's not what I mean. You and Greg are nothing alike. His reasons for taking off were purely selfish. You wanted Ryan to have a better life. Greg wanted his own life to be better. He didn't want to give up his fun, marry me, run into me around town, or tell his new girlfriends that he had a son. He certainly didn't want to take on eighteen years of financial responsibility for a child he hadn't chosen to have. I doubt he even remembers Danny exists."

"What is it with parents?"

"It's not parents. It's just people. Some people are generous and loving, and some aren't. They're that way in all parts of their lives, not just with their kids."

"Some should never be parents."

Leanne rested her head on his shoulder while she considered that. "I don't know. I know more than my share of parents who have done an abominable job of parenting. My own mother wouldn't win any awards, and no matter how good my father was to me, he was lousy with Chase. But if they'd never become parents, Chase and I wouldn't be here. If bad parents were prohibited from procreating, none of us in this apartment would be here, and that would be a terrible shame. The four of us have a lot to offer."

"At least three of you do."

She elbowed him gently. "Ryan and Danny love you. That says a hell of a lot about you."

He gazed down at her, his blue eyes shadowed, his expression intent, and his mouth opened, then closed again. Ask, she silently urged. *Ask me if I love you.*

But the moment passed and the words didn't come. Instead, he set his coffee on the windowsill, pulled her hard against him, and grinned that phony grin. "Wanna make out while the kids are quiet?"

Deep inside she was disappointed. She didn't like the fake front he presented—didn't like that he felt it necessary, after all they'd been through, to present it to her. But there was nothing fake about his arousal, or about the heat building inside her. There was nothing fake at all about his need for her, or her love for him.

She managed a seductive smile and rose onto her toes to brush her mouth across his. "Oh, darlin', I wanna do a whole lot more than make out."

She gave him a hungry, greedy kiss, then grabbed a handful of his shirt and headed for her bedroom, dragging him behind.

I T WAS NEARLY ELEVEN O'CLOCK WHEN COLE WENT home. Leanne belted her robe around her waist and walked with him through the quiet, cool apartment to the top of the stairs. "See you tomorrow?"

"For church?" His look was wry. "After what we just did?"

"Some would say we need it more than ever after what we just did."

"Some would . . . but damned if I'm going to repent for it."

"See if Eli will let you skip just once. We could take the boys to the lake—go hiking, have a picnic or something."

"I'll ask." He kissed her, a sweet goodnight kiss that wasn't intended to stir her blood but did. "Either way, I'll see you in the morning."

Hugging herself, she watched as he took the steps two at a time, then let himself out. With a sigh, she turned off the lights they'd left burning, then quietly opened the door to the boys' room. The lamp on the nighttable showed Danny sprawled across the bed, his pillow on one side, his covers on the other, and snoring softly. Jerome lay on the fallen covers, also snoring softly, and Ryan was curled on his side, reading by flashlight.

She nudged the dog off the blankets, retucked her son, then leaned her arms on the edge of Ryan's bunk. "Let's go to the hardware store Monday and get one of those lamps that clamps onto the bed. You'll ruin your eyes using that flashlight."

With a faint smile, he nodded.

"Not sleepy yet?"

"Not really." He paused. "Is he gone?"

This time the faint smile and nod were hers.

"He says he's not goin' anywhere."

For a moment his words puzzled her. Of course Cole had to go home; it wasn't as if it was his choice. Then she realized he meant in the larger scheme of things. "Do you believe him?"

"He's a liar and a con artist. You can't trust him."

"Did he ever lie to you, Ryan? Did he ever con you?"

Because his answer was no, she suspected, he didn't say anything, but merely glowered.

"Come on, sweetie. You opened the subject—now you've got to answer. Did he ever lie to you?"

Grudgingly he muttered, "No."

"Did he ever con you?"

"He made me think I could stay with him, that he wanted me, and then he dumped me. That was a con."

"No, it wasn't. He thought he was doing what was best for you. That's what parents do, no matter how much it hurts them. If he was conning you, what did he get in return? What was the payoff?"

Again, Ryan chose not to answer.

"Why would he bother with you at all if he didn't want to? He wasn't the first person whose pocket you picked, was he? But no one else took you in. No one else offered you a home and food and clothes and security. Just Cole."

"Because he felt sorry for me."

"Probably, in the beginning. But if that was all he felt, don't you think it would have been easier for him to turn you over to the authorities? If he didn't care about you, he could have gotten rid of you so easily, without even a guilty conscience to bother him."

"Cole don't have a conscience," he mumbled.

"He has one. It's what made him take you in and look out for you and be a father to you, and it's what made him leave you here with us. He wanted what was best for you, just like I want what's best for Danny."

Ryan let his book fall shut, then clicked off the flashlight. "Yeah, but you didn't give him away."

"No. But if I *truly* believed he would be better off living with someone else, that living with me was hurting him in some way, I would find someone to take him. It would break my heart, but I would do it."

"But that'll never happen, 'cause you're a good mother. He's a lousy father."

"He's a pretty good father for someone who's never been one before, who was raised the way he was. You liked having him pretend to be your dad. You liked living with him, or you wouldn't be so unhappy without him."

"I'm not unhappy."

"So failing school and getting into fights is just a hobby with you."

He gave an elaborate shrug, then repeated, "I'm not unhappy. He did me a favor. I like it here with you and Danny. We don't need him."

I do. Wisely, she didn't say so out loud. Taking the book from the bed, she laid it on the nightstand, then brushed her fingers through his hair. "There's nothing wrong with needing someone," she said, then sang deliberately off-tune. " 'People . . . people who need people . . .' "

With a great groan, Ryan clutched his pillow to his ears. "No singing, please!"

Lifting her nose into the air, she sniffed. "Obviously, you have no appreciation for musical genius." Then she spoiled the effect by laughing. "You'd better get to sleep, kiddo. Me, too. I'm not as young as I used to be."

Stretching onto her toes, she tucked him in, pressed a kiss to his forehead, then said *I love you* and *Goodnight*. She was at the door when he spoke again.

"Hey, Leanne?"

She paused.

"He—he said that, too."

"He told you goodnight?"

"No. That—that he . . . loved me."

A lump formed in her throat and made her voice husky. "Well, of course he does, sweetheart. Didn't you know that?"

He shook his head.

She wondered whether to make a big deal over it—to explain how some people had trouble expressing their emotions verbally, but showed it through their actions, just as Cole had. Deciding that would be too much, she settled for a quiet reassurance. "Well, now you do. Goodnight, babe."

Chapter Sixteen

BY MONDAY MORNING, THE ONLY SIGN OF THE weekend's snowfall was the wet ground and layers of dirt deposited on all the cars around town. Though Cole had made a point of spending all his winters in warmer climes, he hadn't minded the snow as much as he'd expected. In fact, there was something to be said for a walk in the snow with a pretty woman . . . especially when it was followed by a roll in the sack with her.

Of course, the real test of his winter adaptability would come when Bethlehem got its first serious snowstorm, the kind that shut down the highways out of the valley and kept everyone close to home. Then he might be a good candidate for going stir-crazy.

He, Eli, and Murray had spent the morning at the city garage, where most of the town's Christmas decorations were stored. *Bethlehem did Christmas right,* Leanne had said, and their morning's work had proved her point. They'd unpacked literally miles of lights, giant velvet bows, jingle bells, acres of ribbon, and enough wreaths and garlands to create a forest of fake spruce. In a room off to the side were the nutcracker soldiers—five dozen of them, six feet tall, painted blue, red, or green, and wearing black hats with tall feathers curling overhead. When they went cross-eyed from checking wiring and bulbs on the strings of lights, Eli had said they could take a break by starting the touch-up painting on the soldiers or hauling in the bigger displays from the summer camp outside of town where they were stored.

Cole's eyes were *already* starting to cross from the work, and the mindlessness of it was making him antsy. Too bad they'd finished cutting all the trees. Getting outside and burning off a little energy was starting to sound really good.

Eli came to stand in front of him, stepping over boxes of bulbs. "You ready for lunch? I figured we could walk down to Harry's."

"Sure. Where's Murray?"

"Washing up."

"How long is he gonna stay here?"

Eli shrugged. "As long as he needs. He'll know when the time is right to leave."

"And you're just gonna let him hang around?"

"It's not like he's taking a bed that I need for someone else. We've got plenty of room, and as long as he's finding something he needs here, who am I to turn him away?"

What was Murray finding that he needed? It wasn't as if he was outgoing or even particularly friendly with either Cole or Eli. He did his share of the work, but pretty much kept his thoughts to himself. What was his life like, that he preferred living with them to being back on his own again?

The answer popped into Cole's head too quickly for comfort.

Lonely.

He wasn't thinking of himself a little there, was he?

"Why don't you wash up, too, then meet me outside," Eli suggested.

The bathroom was in the main part of the garage next door, the sturdy built-of-brick-to-stay-around-forever part. Their workspace was corrugated metal, a tacked-on afterthought devoted exclusively to housing the Christmas stuff. He ran into Murray on his way out. The old man smiled as he passed, and Cole realized that the gesture wasn't as vague as it had once been. His eyes were clearer, too, and his color better. Cole understood that staying sober could do that for a man.

Thank God he'd hadn't had to find that out for himself. Booze was one vice he hadn't embraced wholeheartedly. Other than the occasional eggnog-free rum at Christmas, he could go years without so much as a beer and never miss it.

He'd gone nearly six weeks without committing a crime, and he didn't miss that, either.

As soon as he'd washed away the grime, he grabbed his jacket and caught up with the others outside. It was only a few blocks to Main Street, then a few blocks more to Harry's. Eli and Murray walked ahead, with Cole bringing up the rear, hands in his pockets, gazing in the store windows they passed. He was thinking idly about showing up in church with Leanne and the boys the morning before— Eli had insisted they could go to the lake *after* the services—and the hike they'd taken around the lake's rocky shore. Danny and Leanne had both moved like mountain goats, and had laughed and called him "city boy" when he complained. Even Ryan had said it once, his tone not exactly friendly, but not dripping with disgust, either.

Later, when Cole had cooked dinner for them, Ryan had even grudgingly helped out in the kitchen. He wasn't giving in easily or gracefully, but he *was* giving in. A little. Very little.

Abruptly he came to a stop. He was in front of the bookstore, where a display of old books had caught his eye. The once-bright covers were faded, the pages were yellowed, and they showed signs of heavy wear, but that didn't matter. He'd read that series—a lot of them, at least—when he was a kid. Owen had teased that his interest had been professional—the series was about crime-solving kids, while he'd been a crime-*committing* kid, just looking for tips.

Truth was, he'd read them for the reason a lot of people read—to escape from his life through the pages of a book. Anything could happen in a book, while in real life, the possibilities were far more limited, though it didn't always feel that way in Bethlehem.

He didn't have a clue what had happened to his old books. They'd probably been left behind in one of their many midnight moves. When you had to take off at a moment's notice, you tended not to accumulate much in the way of possessions. The kind of things normal people kept—letters, photographs, baby clothes—had never been a part of his life.

"What are you doing?"

He glanced at Eli, then Murray, waiting ahead at the corner. "Ryan's birthday is Thursday."

"The kid likes to read, huh? You thinking about getting him those old books that you used to read?"

Cole gave him a curious look. "How do you know—"

"All boys used to read those books. Why don't you tell Betty to hold them for you, and you can come back tomorrow to pay for them. We're going on to Harry's. Want me to order for you?"

"Yeah, just a burger."

As Eli walked on, Cole went inside, his gut knotted. Betty was the full-time help at the store, working for Elena, the owner, and they'd both invested in his scam last spring. He wouldn't be surprised if they refused to do business with him now. Tired and discouraged, but not surprised.

Both women were working. After exchanging wary glances, Elena left the box she was unpacking and approached him. "Can I help you?" Her tone was neutral, polite enough under the circumstances, but nowhere near as polite as it had once been.

He asked about the books, and for a moment she looked as if she wanted to say they weren't for sale, at least, not to the likes of him. But she pasted on a grim smile, told him the books had just come in as part of a library she'd purchased at an estate sale, and gave him the price for the set.

"Can you hold them for me until tomorrow? I don't have any cash on me right now, but I can bring it by first thing in the morning."

Her gaze turned speculative as she considered it. Was she wondering who he would steal the money from, or whether, if she refused, he would come back after closing time and take them anyway? Whatever her thoughts, after a moment she shrugged. "Would you like them gift-wrapped?"

"Yeah, please."

"A special occasion?"

"A birthday. My son—" He caught himself, grimaced, then went on. "Ryan's birthday is Thursday."

"We'll have them ready."

He nodded, then headed for the door, eager to escape. Something stopped him there, though, and made him turn back, glancing from one woman to the other. "About what happened—what I did . . . I'm really sorry."

Elena offered that grim smile again. "So were we."

He nodded once more, walked through the door, and collided with someone on the sidewalk. "Sorry," he said again, catching his balance and extending a hand to steady the man. His gaze got only as high as the priest's collar. There was only one priest in town, and Cole had ripped him off, too. Facing three of his victims in less than a minute was more than he was prepared for, so he ducked his head and set off toward Harry's. He hadn't gone more than five feet before a familiar voice in an unfamiliar brogue stopped him.

" 'Tis too lovely a day to be rushin' about, laddie. You should slow down, take a look around you."

Cole spun around and stared, his eyes opened wide, his breath caught in his chest. *"Frank?"* he whispered, the best he could manage.

"That's Father Francis to you, son." Frank slid his finger between his neck and the collar, then reverted to his normal voice. "I guess it's true what they say—the clothes make the man."

"What the hell are you doing?"

"Answering your call. Well, your letter, to be more precise. You remember—*I need a ride. If any of you happen to be around Bethlehem* . . . I was closest, so here I am."

Cole rubbed the tension in the back of his neck, then looked around anxiously. The last thing he needed was for someone he knew to see him and Frank together. The resemblance between them wasn't so strong that seeing Frank alone would automatically make a person think of Cole, but standing side by side was too risky. They had the same blond hair, though Frank's was a few shades lighter, and the same blue eyes, though Frank's appeared guileless. He was masquerading as a priest, for God's sake, and managed to look innocent doing it.

"What did they get you for, bubba?"

"An investment scam."

"What was the haul?"

"Quarter mil."

Frank gave a low whistle. "Damn. So the town's as prosperous as it looks. Or, at least, it was. Is the money safe?"

Across the street, Leanne's father came out of the building that housed his insurance office and walked to the curb. Cole grabbed Frank's arm and hustled him back the way he'd come. As soon as they turned the corner, he released his brother. "Don't you know you'll burn in hell for pretending to be a priest?"

Frank laughed, his dimples showing. "Don't you know we're all gonna burn in hell anyway? Our fates were sealed by the time we turned ten. So . . . where's the take?"

Shoving his hands in his pockets, Cole leaned against the brick building and scowled at his brother. There was something wrong when a man felt a twinge of shame, not for stealing $250,000, but for giving it back. He *wouldn't* be ashamed if he was admitting it to anyone but family, and there was something damned wrong about that, too. "I returned it."

"You . . ." Frank made a big show of rubbing his knuckle into one ear, then cupping his hand behind it. "I didn't hear you right. Can you say that again?"

Cole started to cuff him on the shoulder, then wondered what any passerby would think about him punching a priest, and drew back. "I gave the money back."

Frank couldn't have looked more surprised if the Father, the Son, and the Holy Ghost had taken on physical form right in front of him. *"Why?"*

"Because it was the right thing to do."

"Right for *who*?" Dolefully Frank shook his head. "Jeez, Cole, remember the rules? *Admit to nothing, deny everything, lie like the devil, and always look out for number one. Never tell the truth if a lie will suffice. Never apolo—"*

"I remember," he said dryly. "I've heard them five years longer than you have."

"Damn! A man makes a score like that, he doesn't give it back. He goes to Tahiti or Australia or, hell, he blows it right here in the good ol' U.S.A. He lives it up until it's gone, and then he goes out and starts it all over again. Are you out of your freakin' mind?"

Maybe. But Cole didn't offer the answer out loud.

Frank leaned against the building, too, his gaze on the street, his brow drawn together. "Let me get this straight. You conned a quarter of a million dollars out of these people, they caught you, you gave it back, and they're letting you walk around free?"

Cole didn't bother to correct him on the order—that he'd given the money back long before he'd been caught—but focused on the last part. "I'm not walking around free. I'm part of an experimental work-release type program. My watchdog is waiting for me at Harry's." If he wasn't already on his way back, to find out what was holding Cole up.

"Okay, so what's the plan?"

"The plan?" Cole repeated stupidly.

"We gonna take off now? Do you need to get your stuff first? Is there a better time for getting out, when no one will be around to notice you're gone? *The plan,* bubba. A man needs a plan." Frank's tone turned impatient. "Jeez, you still want to split, don't you?"

Cole stared into the distance. He'd *wanted* to—when he'd written the letter, and for a time afterward. But now . . . well, hell, if he skipped out now, Eli would be short a man in getting the decorations up, and the cops and the judge would surely be pissed that he'd managed to lose his only real criminal. They would probably shut down his program, which wouldn't be a problem for him—he was young and energetic, and Bethlehem took care of its own—but Murray was neither young nor energetic nor, technically, one of Bethlehem's own.

If he skipped out now, he could kiss Leanne good-bye forever. She'd forgiven him once. She wasn't likely to do it a second time. That would be a greater loss than he was prepared to deal with.

And if he skipped out now, three days before Ryan's birthday, when he'd just told him Saturday night that he wasn't going anywhere . . . *Yeah. Sure. Guess we'll see about that,* Ryan had said. He hadn't managed to forgive Cole even once. He would damn sure never do it if Cole proved he didn't deserve it.

"Well, bubba?"

His gaze jerked back to Frank. "I can't just— There are things I have to—" He swore. "Your timing sucks."

"Oh, well, hell, pardon me for dropping everything to help you out, but doing it with lousy timing. I'll tell you what—I'll go back to Connecticut, where I've got a flock to fleece, and when you find time in your schedule to skip town, you can give me a call. Or better yet, you can get yourself the hell out of town."

Cole rubbed his forehead, then let his hand drop to his side. "Look, Frankie—" He broke off as a car pulled into the parking space in front of them and an elderly woman got out. He aimed for polite with his smile, but wasn't sure he managed anything more than a grimace as she stepped onto the sidewalk. "Miss Corinna."

"Cole." She smiled, gave Frank a curious look and a nod, then turned the corner onto Main.

Cole watched until she was out of sight, then became aware of Frank's gaze on him. Without looking, he could feel the censure, and confirmed it when he faced his brother again.

"They're doing it, aren't they? Setting you on the straight and narrow. Jeez, I don't believe this . . . unless . . . You have another con in mind, don't you? You ripped them off once, they forgave you, and now you're gonna do it again. What'll it be this time?"

"Nothing. There's no con."

"Yeah, right. I *know* you, bubba. No way you're gonna stick around a hick town like this, doing scut work for free, unless it's gonna pay off somehow."

Cole couldn't deny there could be a payoff if he was lucky, though not the kind Frank was envisioning. Like the rest of the Jacksons, Frank thought in terms of cold hard cash. But Cole wanted the big prize—Leanne, Ryan, Danny. A family, a home, a place to belong.

But hadn't he learned from the cradle that wishing was a waste of breath? He'd been born and bred for one kind of life, and what Bethlehem offered, wasn't it.

But people could change. Leanne believed it. So did Ryan and Eli and everybody else. If Leanne and Ryan could believe in him, wasn't believing in himself the least he could do?

"It ain't gonna happen, Cole," Frank said quietly. "Being a thief, a liar, and a cheat isn't what you do—it's who you *are*. It's in your blood. Like I said, our fates were sealed by the time we turned ten."

Cole walked to the corner, saw Eli going into the bookstore, then ducked back. "Look, I've got to go. There's a motel just outside town called Angels Lodge. Get a room there, and I'll be in touch."

"Don't take too long. You'd be surprised what a crimp this outfit puts in my social life." He fell into the phony brogue again. "When you call, laddie, ask for Father Murphy." When he reached his car, he turned back. "Hey, where's Ryan?"

"He's here. In a foster home."

"Good. We'll pick him up before we leave."

"No." Vehemence made Cole's voice sharp and heated his face. "He's staying here. He's not going to grow up like us."

"And that would be so bad?"

Rather than argue the point with him, Cole shrugged, then walked away. As soon as he turned the corner, he spotted Eli, heading his way. The kid's expression went blank before he mildly asked, "Take a wrong turn on your way to Harry's?"

"I was giving directions to this guy looking for the motel," he lied, gesturing as Frank, with a friendly wave, turned left onto Main.

Eli raised his brows. "New priest in town?"

"I think he's just passing through."

"Maybe he'll enjoy his visit so much he'll stay."

That was doubtful. Frank enjoyed a lot of things, but small-town honest living wasn't one of them. And since the Jackson boys were all alike, didn't that mean small-town, honest living wasn't for *him,* either?

WHEN ALEX LEFT HIS OFFICE MONDAY EVENING, HE was torn between going to church, where the doors were always open for those in need of spiritual solace, and the Five Pines Lounge, where the doors were almost always open for those in need of spirits of another sort. The desire for peace of some kind was strong, and he was leaning toward the oblivion offered by the Five Pines when he backed out of his parking space.

Instead, he found himself heading home. For a time he

sat in the driveway, looking at the dark house. In all the years of their marriage, he'd spent so very few nights in that house without Melissa that it seemed wrong somehow to walk through the door when she was hours away. He could delay it by going back downtown to Harry's or McCauley's for dinner, but that would mean facing people who now knew the truth.

All it had taken was one phone call Sunday morning to Miss Corinna. He'd asked her to tell their friends about Max, so he and Melissa wouldn't have to. He had thought that would be easier for him, but as he'd discovered when he'd gone to the office that morning, there was nothing easy about any of it. The expressions of sympathy he'd gotten, the sorrowful looks, the hugs and pats on the arm . . . it was almost as if someone had died.

In reality, part of him had.

When the cold shivered through him, he got his briefcase from the seat beside him and went inside the house. He didn't bother turning on lights, but climbed the stairs in the darkness and made his way, as he had hundreds of times before, to the nursery. There, finally, he flipped on the lights.

Once he and Melissa had allowed themselves to hope that this time there would be no miscarriage, he'd painted the room at her direction. There'd been no blue-for-boys or pink-for-girls discussion, no gender-nonspecific pastels. She had chosen a rich, dark green for the walls, with a wallpaper border of carousel horses about halfway up. The crib was made up with flannel sheets, a quilt, and a receiving blanket, and hanging above it was a colorful mobile.

There were shelves built into one wall, with figurines and baby books, stuffed animals, empty picture frames, and Alex's old baseball glove. Melissa had been optimistic when she'd put that there.

He picked up the glove, smelled the aged leather, and rubbed the signs of hard use. His father had given it to him when he was five or so, and on every warm day for months they'd played catch in the backyard. All that effort hadn't made him more than a passable catcher and a so-so pitcher, he recalled with a faint smile.

If Max wasn't much of a baseball player, he would just be following in his father's footsteps. If he didn't excel at riding a bike, he could thank his mother's bike-challenged genes for it. If he couldn't carry a tune . . . well, his grand-father *was* tone-deaf, and if he lacked the coordination to march in the high school band, he could blame his Aunt Jenny, who could trip in the middle of a perfectly clean floor, pick herself up, and do it again.

Every child was different, Sophy had pointed out in the hospital chapel. He knew that, of course. He'd gone to school with kids who couldn't behave to save their lives, as well as ones who couldn't misbehave to save *their* lives. There'd been the kids who had sailed through every class with effortless A's and the ones who'd struggled for C's. They'd had the actors who could become someone else in the blink of an eye and the kids who couldn't even be themselves without time to prepare. The graceful and the uncoordinated. The outgoing and the reserved. The kind, the cruel, and the indifferent.

Everyone *was* different. How boring life would be if that weren't true.

He and Melissa were different now. They weren't just husband and wife, lawyer and nursery owner, members of the community. They were parents. Mother and father to a beautiful little boy who would be sweet, loving, generous, and kind—who would think they'd hung the moon and the stars, and would love them dearly all his life.

Who deserved to be loved like that himself.

Alex had wanted a child, had pleaded and prayed for one. He hadn't specified a child who would become a lawyer or a teacher or an athlete—just a child who would be happy and healthy and loved.

He was a lucky man.

His prayers had been answered.

Y OU'VE BEEN A MILLION MILES AWAY ALL EVENING," Leanne remarked as she shifted on the sofa to face Cole. "Where are you, and what are you doing?"

He glanced at her, his gaze shadowed before he hid his moodiness behind a smile. "I'm right here, darlin'."

"In body only. Your mind is far, far away." It had taken about two seconds to realize that when he'd arrived for dinner. His kiss, quickly given and accepted in the hallway, had been about as sizzling as her brother's kiss might be, and she and the boys had found themselves repeating things to him all through the meal. For the past half hour he'd sat at the other end of the sofa, a cup of coffee growing cold in his hand, an air of melancholy surrounding him.

If he were anyone else, she might wonder if he was homesick, missing his family, or regretting the life he would be living if he wasn't in Bethlehem. But he'd never had a home to miss, and his contact with his family was sporadic. As for missing his guilt-free life of crime . . . she wanted to believe he didn't. Wanted to believe he never looked at an object he coveted and thought how easily he could acquire it. Wanted to believe he'd changed.

She just wasn't a hundred percent positive about it.

The television was tuned to her favorite Monday-night drama, and they were alone in the living room. Danny had been bathed, tucked in, and read to, and was now snoozing in his bed. Jerome was snoozing there, too, warming

Danny's feet, while Ryan read in the top bunk. The apartment was quiet except for the television, and she and Cole had been quiet, too—for too long.

Using the remote, she muted the TV. "Seriously, what's on your mind?"

"Nothing. I'm just tired."

That was a lie. He was distracted, distant, troubled. About what? The aspects of this life that agreed with him and the ones that didn't? The parts he wanted to change and the ones he couldn't change?

Which category did she fall into? The good? The bad? Or the convenient?

"Is work going okay?"

"Yeah."

"No more run-ins with my mother?"

"If there had been, you would have heard."

That was true, she acknowledged. The whole town would have heard, but as it was, Phyllis had been quiet lately.

Wishing for something to occupy her hands, she settled for hugging her knees to her chest. She couldn't force confidences that he didn't want to give, so she settled for the next best thing. "If you need to talk, you know I'm here."

His smile was faint and slid away as soon as it formed. "I know. But right now . . . I think I need to go."

"Okay." Her smile was no more successful than his. When he took his coffee cup into the kitchen, she followed as far as the bar that separated the kitchen and dining room and stood there awkwardly, arms hugging her chest, one foot balanced on top of the other.

After rinsing the cup, he faced her. "Before I go, can I use the phone?"

"Sure." She freed one hand to gesture to the phone a few feet away, but he gave it a wary look.

"In your bedroom?"

"Sure." Retucking her hand, she watched him leave the room, then listened to her bedroom door close. A private call. To whom? He didn't have any real friends in town. There was no reason to call Eli when he would be home sixty seconds after leaving the apartment, and no reason, as far as she knew, to call his lawyer.

So maybe it wasn't a local call. Maybe he was calling his father or one of his brothers. Granted, he and Ryan had both said they kept in touch through their father's post office box, but maybe he'd heard from one of them and gotten a temporary number to reach him.

Maybe one of them had shown up, as Ryan had predicted, to take him away. That's what they do, he'd said. *Whenever one of 'em gets in trouble, he sends a letter to Owen, and the first one who checks in has to go and get him.*

That was an awfully big assumption to make from one phone call, she chastised herself as she loaded the last few dishes into the dishwasher. Cole wasn't leaving. He'd told Ryan, and her, too. He intended to serve his time, and then . . . *then* he would be free to go wherever he wanted.

Please, God, let him want to stay right here.

She wasn't sure what alerted her to his presence—a quiet footstep registered subconsciously or the soft, steady sound of his breathing. More likely pure feminine instinct that tightened her nerves. Whatever it was, when she turned, he was standing in the doorway, his jacket in hand. "I'm leaving now."

Not trusting herself to speak without pleading, she nodded.

"I told Ryan goodnight."

She nodded again.

"I'll see you tomorrow."

She went to him, slid her arms around his neck, and

kissed him, long and deep and hungrily, and was rewarded with the first stirring of desire swelling against her belly. Breaking the kiss, she breathed softly of his scents. "Yeah. Tomorrow."

Now that he was leaving, he looked as if he would rather stay, but he walked out anyway. She stood where she was, a chill that came from the inside making her tremble. She could be so terribly insecure when it came to the men in her life. Maybe that was because they kept leaving her—first Greg, then Steve and Richard. Cole had been number four on the heartbreak list. Surely she could be forgiven for wondering if he might also be number five.

She picked up in the living room, started a load of laundry, and paid a few bills. Shortly after ten o'clock, Ryan came out to say goodnight. She hugged him and told him she loved him, and he mumbled, "Me, too," for the first time ever. For ten minutes the wonder of that kept her smiling and warm on the sofa.

Finally she got ready for bed, following through her nightly routine, changing into a T-shirt, folding back the covers, sitting on the bed to rub lotion into her hands. She was lying down and leaning on one elbow, about to turn out the lamp, when her gaze fell on the telephone next to it—or, to be more accurate, on the REDIAL button on the phone.

Who Cole had called was none of her business. She knew that, just as surely as she knew what she was about to do was wrong. That didn't stop her, though. She braced the receiver between her ear and shoulder, took a deep breath, and pushed REDIAL.

The call was answered on the second ring. "Angels Lodge. Can I help you?"

Cold emptiness spread through Leanne as she quietly hung up.

• • •

EEZ, COULDN'T WE HAVE MET AT A BAR?" FRANK grumbled. "This place must have a couple, and I could use something strong to drink."

"No, we couldn't," Cole replied shortly.

They were sitting in Frank's car in the darkest corner of the hospital parking lot. It was the only place Cole had been able to think of, where people sitting in a parked car this late in the evening could go unnoticed. He'd considered the town square, but decided it was too public, and its proximity to both the police and the sheriff's departments hadn't helped. He'd thought about City Park, too, but the proximity to Phyllis Wilson had persuaded him against that. He wouldn't put it past her to lurk at an upstairs window with binoculars, just waiting for the chance to get someone in trouble.

Leaning across the console, Frank rummaged in the glove compartment before coming up with a flask of booze. He offered it to Cole, who shook his head, then took a swig. "I take it we're not leaving tonight."

Cole stared across the lot to the emergency entrance. Less than two weeks ago, he'd driven Melissa Thomas right up to the door in Grayson's truck, then debated whether to keep on driving. His decision to stay that night hadn't been too difficult. Now the decision to go shouldn't be difficult, either.

"How is Owen?" he asked in a deliberate attempt to distract himself from the fact that it was.

"Same as ever. He's moved again, but he's still around Philadelphia."

"What name is he using now?"

Frank shrugged. "The only one I bother to remember is Delbert Collins."

That was the important one—the one to whom the post office box belonged. It was the only alias Owen had ever used that had never been tied to his real name or his criminal record. It was a safe name, one made up out of thin air and kept scrupulously clean.

"What about the others?"

Frank took another swallow of liquor. "Adam's doing six months down in Georgia. Bret's out in California, doing what, I don't know. David's gone to Jamaica with some lonely widow, and Eddie's got a sweet deal running down in Louisiana with a little rich girl whose family is big-time into all the Mardi Gras crap."

"And Eloise?"

"She's the reason Owen moved again. She came for a surprise visit and caught him entertaining the woman next door. She wasn't exactly pleased."

It was a hell of a way for two people to live—they couldn't stay together and couldn't stand to be apart. Watching them as he'd grown up, Cole had always sworn he would never get caught in a situation like that. So what had he done instead? Fallen in love with a woman he didn't deserve, in a town where he wasn't fit to live, where she was raising his son—because, damn it, legalities aside, Ryan *was* his—who wished he would rot in jail.

He shifted in the seat, listening to the vinyl creaking beneath him. "You ever think about going straight?"

"I considered it once," Frank replied, then slid into a fair impression of their father. " 'But I laid down and soon the temptation went away.' "

"Seriously."

Frank pretended to think about it before brashly answering, "Nope. Not for a minute. Hell, what would I do? Sell used cars? Unclog toilets? Mow yards? 'I can't do much—' "

Cole finished another of Owen's sayings with him. " 'But what I do, I'm damn good at.' Jeez, can't you carry on a conversation without quoting the old man every five minutes?"

"I don't know that I've ever tried. Besides, the old man gives good advice—the best for people like us." Frank gave him a sidelong look. "And you *are* like us, Cole. You always have been. You always will be. There's no changing that."

"People can change," Cole said quietly.

"Oh, sure. That's why you never see any repeat offenders in the joint," Frank retorted. "Maybe people like us *can* change, but they *don't,* not for long. Not for good. Remember when Adam married his first wife, and she made him promise to straighten up and fly right? He tried, he really did, but he just couldn't do it. He didn't even last four months before he was back to his old ways."

But he didn't try for the right reasons, Cole wanted to protest. He hadn't had any real desire to live an honest life. He'd been making the effort just for Beverly.

Cole didn't want to do it just for Leanne or just for Ryan, though they were both damned good incentives. He wanted it for himself, for his own pride and dignity, for his self-respect. *Those* were the right reasons.

But no matter what the reasons, Adam really *had* tried. And he'd failed. Why should Cole's luck be any different?

"You need to get out of this town, bubba. They're putting bad ideas in your head. You can't stay here. You stole a quarter of a mil from 'em. You think they're ever gonna forgive or forget that? Besides, what would you do? How would you support yourself and Ryan? You never even finished high school. You don't have a mechanical bone in your body. No one's gonna buy a used car from you after you already ripped 'em off, you don't know how to unclog toilets, and the yards up here won't need cutting for the next five months. What can you do, besides lie, cheat, and steal?"

He could cook, he could follow directions, and he could learn. He could get his GED and even go to college. People seemed to think that cheating and stealing came easily, but the sort of scams he'd run had required a solid grounding in a wide array of subjects. A man couldn't pretend to be an investment broker without having a firm understanding of investments and how they worked. Ditto for a pseudo-art appraiser, a phony lawyer, or a fake home security expert.

"I'm sure there's a woman involved," Frank went on, "you being a Jackson and all. But get real, bubba. There hasn't been a Jackson in four generations that ever held a legit job. What are you gonna do when you get bored with it? Start driving by convenience stores on your way home? Casing her friends' houses? Lifting the family valuables just to stay in shape?"

Cole couldn't even deny he'd wondered about that. This time in Bethlehem was the longest he'd ever gone without committing *some* crime—excluding the months he'd been incarcerated, of course. He wasn't at all tempted now, but who was to say that wouldn't change in six, twelve, or eighteen months? How could he *know* he could go straight when he'd never even considered it before?

But how could he know he couldn't, if he didn't try?

"Man, it's freakin' cold." Frank started the engine and turned the heater to high, then tossed the flask into the console. "These people around here . . . they're just messin' with your head, Cole. Making you think you can fit in, when you can't. Making you think you can be just like them, when you've *never* been like them. You weren't raised for this kind of life and you know it. The sooner you accept that, the sooner we can get out of here and life will get back to normal."

He didn't want to accept anything. He just wanted to go back to Leanne's apartment and spend the rest of the night making love with her.

He wanted to spend the rest of his life with her.

Frank didn't bother to cover his yawn. "I've gotta get some sleep. Why don't we plan on taking off tomorrow night, after your do-gooders think you're in for the night? We can be hell and gone before they even realize you've slipped out."

"I can't," Cole said to himself, then realized Frank was frowning at him. "Thursday is Ryan's birthday. I can't take off this close."

"Jeez. You're gonna make me masquerade as a priest three more freakin' days?"

"You could have taken the collar off when you left Connecticut."

Frank's smile showed the dimple that made him look oddly angelic. "I kind of like it. I feel a kinship with men of the cloth, what with so many of them being in the same business we are. Can I give you a ride home?"

"Nah. I'll walk. It's not far." Cole opened the door and was halfway out when Frank spoke again.

"Don't disappoint your family, bubba. We're the only ones who have accepted you the way you are, and we're the only ones who will."

With a grim nod, he slammed the door, shoved his hands in his pockets, and set off across the parking lot. It was true that they'd always known him for what he was and loved him anyway. That probably wouldn't change if he cleaned up his act . . . but things with Leanne and Ryan *would* change if he didn't. They deserved better than what he was.

They made him *want* to be better.

Chapter Seventeen

THE WEATHER TOOK A TURN FOR THE WORSE ON Tuesday, matching Leanne's mood. She sent the boys off to day care and to school under a sky the color of pewter, and the wind blew down the street with such force it actually whistled. The temperature, starting in the high thirties and dropping fast, left no doubt that for all practical purposes, winter had arrived. Oh, there would be a few more lovely days, some even warm, but the next several months promised to be downright chilly.

When the doorbell dinged shortly after noon, Jerome looked up from his snoozing spot on the floor, his ears pricked with interest. A person could be forgiven for thinking it was the noise that had disturbed him, or the blast of frigid air, but she knew it was the fragrant aromas of the food her visitor was carrying. He sprang to his feet and greeted Nolie with a nuzzle and some eager sniffs. Farm girl that she once was, she unconcernedly nudged him aside and approached Leanne at the counter.

"It's *cold* out there," Nolie said, and her cheeks were red to prove it. "I hope this is the worst it gets here."

"Oh, darlin', it'll get much, much colder," Leanne teased. She accepted one of the bags Nolie offered and headed toward the sitting area. "Doesn't it get cold in your part of Arkansas?"

"Not like this. At least, not very often."

Jerome beat them to the back and leaped onto the sofa. Nolie set her load down, removed her coat, scarf, hat, and gloves, then pointed to the floor. "Down," she said sternly, and Jerome hastily obeyed.

"How'd you do that?" Leanne asked. "I tell him to get down and he grins and wags his tail and gets more comfortable."

"You don't tell. You politely suggest, and when he refuses, you let him. You're lucky Danny's not a manipulative child, or he would obey like the mutt does."

As Leanne sat down on the love seat, she blew a kiss to Jerome, then began unpacking the bag. When Nolie had called to say she was bringing lunch, Leanne had been grateful—a visit with her sister-in-law was exactly the distraction she needed. The foil-covered plate giving off incredible aromas was a bonus, when she'd expected takeout from Harry's or the deli. "You cooked," she said, inhaling deeply.

"Jambalaya, left over from last night's dinner. But it's better the second day anyway." Nolie unpacked silverware, unwrapped a large foil packet of steaming cornbread, and tossed a plastic bag on the coffee table. "And for dessert, pralines. My dad had some Louisiana relatives somewhere way back who generously donated these recipes to the family cookbook."

Leanne peeled the foil from her plate, sat back, and took a heaping bite of sausage, shrimp, chicken, rice, and vegetables, then gave a great *mmm*. "Oh, Nolie, this is wonderful."

"Food like this is where I got these hips," her sister-in-law said matter-of-factly.

Though it was difficult with her mouth full, Leanne snickered. "My brother adores those hips."

"Yes." Nolie smiled as if pleasantly surprised. "He does." Without hesitation, she changed the subject. "How is Tall, Blond, and Handsome?"

Leanne used the food as an excuse to delay answering. Tall, Blond, and Handsome had been her nickname for Cole when he'd first come to town last spring. Then she'd looked at him the way all single women viewed single men—as a prospective date, a fling. How quickly she'd moved past that, to naming him Mr. Right, and how quickly she'd gone beyond that to heartbreak. Was she on her way there again?

Finally, her mouth empty and her nerves starting to prickle under Nolie's gaze, she shrugged. "Exactly as the name implies."

Nolie didn't verbally chide her for the evasive answer. The steady look in her blue eyes did it for her.

"He's, uh . . ." At a loss for words, Leanne shook her head. He'd stopped by earlier that morning. He, Eli, and Murray had been stringing lights over on Main Street, and he'd dropped in for a moment. His skin had been cold when he leaned close to kiss her, and even through his gloves, she had felt the chill in his hands. He would cook dinner for them, he'd said as soon as the kiss ended, and then he'd headed back out to work.

He'd been in and out so quickly that she hadn't had a chance—he hadn't *given* her a chance—to ask about his phone call to Angels Lodge. She'd spent every quiet moment since wondering what answers he might have given. Calling a friend? He had no friends. Making a date with another woman? She didn't want to believe it. Setting a new scam in motion? She really didn't want to believe that.

Making contact with one of his brothers, newly arrived in Bethlehem?

The possibility made her stomach hurt and tightened her chest so breathing became difficult. Even just wondering made her feel disloyal, but under the circumstances, how could she *not* wonder?

"You guys having problems?"

Blinking, Leanne focused her gaze on Nolie. "No," she murmured, and hoped it was true. "Nothing that you wouldn't expect."

"You're still in love with him, aren't you?"

Leanne scooped up a shrimp on her spoon and chewed it slowly before responding. "When Danny's father broke up with me, it was so easy to stop loving him. I was angry and hurt, and I was disappointed in myself for misjudging him, but the day he told me he wanted nothing to do with our baby, I stopped loving him. It was that simple. But with Cole . . . he lied to me. He betrayed my trust. He abandoned his own child. He broke my heart. But still . . . "

Before he'd come back, she'd been convinced she was over him. She'd been angry and hurt and she'd hated him, but that was it. She'd had no gentler feelings for him at all. No sweet memories. No forgiveness. Certainly no love.

And then he'd come back and . . . Had she been kidding herself all along? Had she ever really fallen out of love with him, or had it just been so easy to fall back into it?

Either way, what did it matter? She did love him. It was that simple. And that hard.

"I would guess that the way you loved Greg is different from the way you love Cole," Nolie said. "I loved Micahlyn's father with all my heart, and when he died, I thought I would never care for anyone that way again. Now I love Chase with all my heart, but it's not the same

as it was with Jeff. They're very different men, and I'm
different, too."

That made sense, Leanne thought as she polished off
the last of her food. She'd matured a lot since she'd found
herself pregnant and alone. Danny had taught her the
meaning of unconditional love. Life had taught her a few
lessons, too—hard lessons on what was important and
what wasn't.

Greg, ultimately, hadn't been important, but Cole was.

"How does he feel?"

Leanne scowled at her. "Oh, gee, there's the million-
dollar question. If I knew the answer to that, I'd be planning a wedding or crying my eyes out."

"You haven't discussed the future?"

" 'There's no point in thinking about the future,' " she
parroted. "Not when he's got some forty-eight-hundred
hours left on his sentence."

"That's forty-eight-hundred work hours. If you figure
he's putting in eight hours a day, then you've got about
double that to persuade him otherwise. For a woman of
your charms, that's not even a challenge."

"A woman of my charms," Leanne repeated dryly. "If I
were so charming, he wouldn't have left me in the first
place."

"His leaving had nothing to do with you and everything to do with our $250,000. Though I think his return-
ing the money had plenty to do with you."

Leanne took a break to wait on a customer, then sign
for a shipment of winter clothing. When she returned to
the sitting area, she caught Nolie slipping Jerome a chunk
of cornbread. "Ha! You talk so tough, but you're a sucker
for big brown eyes, too." Settling in, she took a praline
from the zippered bag. "You guys are coming Thursday
night, right?"

"We'll be here with bells on—and my blue-ribbon banana-split cake. Want me to provide candles?"

"I have some." She'd been tempted to get a regular birthday cake for Ryan—white with buttercream frosting—but Danny had insisted Ryan loved banana-split cake better than any other kind. Traditional or not, there would be candles and presents and birthday wishes. She intended it to be a birthday Ryan would never forget.

"How is the birthday boy getting along with Cole?"

"They talk. Some. Cautiously. It'll take time, but I'm hopeful."

Nolie studied her a long time, then nodded in agreement. "Yes, you are. Stay that way. It'll pay off in the long run."

After a few more minutes of conversation, Nolie gathered her dishes, bundled up again, and headed out into the cold. Leanne unpacked the new shipment of clothes, cleared space for them on various racks, and tagged them, then alternated the rest of the afternoon by waiting on customers and thinking about Nolie's advice. *Stay that way. It'll pay off in the long run.*

That was all she wanted—the grand prize. Love, marriage, happily-ever-after.

Sophy breezed in a few minutes late, wearing an overcoat that brushed her ankles and swallowed her hands. Her hair curled around the edges of her knitted black cap, and the scarf around her neck practically matched the color in her cheeks. She greeted Leanne cheerfully, then gave Jerome a vigorous belly rub before stripping down to her overalls and T-shirt.

"You're certainly in a cheery mood," Leanne observed.

"I usually am. Hey, did you hear that Melissa and Alex's baby's condition has been upgraded? He's gained nearly a pound, and he loves cuddling with his parents."

"That's wonderful." She'd heard the news that Max had Down syndrome from Emilie Bishop, and had felt so sorry for the Thomases. She couldn't imagine how it must feel, to want a baby so badly for so long, and to have to face a lifetime of difficulty once they got him. But if anyone could give him the love and care he needed, it was Melissa and Alex. "Any word yet on when he'll be able to come home?"

"Probably another four or five weeks, maybe a little longer."

At the front of the store, Jerome pressed his nose to the glass, then whined. Leanne checked the time. Ryan was due home from school within the next few minutes, and the first thing he usually did was take the dog to the square. But judging from the animal's next whine, louder and longer, he wasn't going to wait one second longer. "Watch things, will you?" she asked as she pulled on her coat and gloves, then grabbed the leash.

Jerome circled impatiently as she hooked the leash to his collar. As soon as she opened the door, he dived outside, dragging her with him, and made a beeline for his favorite bush in the square. Of course, it couldn't be a simple matter of taking care of business. No, he had to sniff first, to determine if anyone had strayed into his territory, then he had to mark it all over again just in case. She stood there, shivering and softly urging the dog to hurry. Her ears were going numb and her nose was slowly freezing solid, and—

Abruptly, Jerome lunged, pulling her off-balance before jerking his leash free. Catching herself on the wet, frozen ground was easier said than done. If not for a strong arm wrapping around her waist, she could have added *dirty* and *damp* to *frozen*. "Jerome!" she shouted, then looked up at her rescuer. "Thank you so—"

She wasn't sure which registered first—the priest's

collar or the familiar features. She'd never met the man be-fore—who would forget a sinfully sexy priest?—but she knew those eyes, that jaw, that nose . . .

Clutching Jerome's leash in one fist, Ryan stalked up to them and gave the man a vicious shove that sent him stum-bling back a few feet. "What the hell are you doing here?"

"Ryan!" she exclaimed, stunned by his display of vio-lence. "Stop that! You can't treat him like that!"

He spun to face her, tears in his eyes. "Do you know who that is? It's Frankie, Cole's brother! He's come to get him!" Unexpectedly, he punched the man, earning a grunt of pain for his effort. "I *knew* he wouldn't stay! I *knew* he would skip town the first chance he got! He's a liar, and I hate him! I *hate* him!"

Still holding tightly to Jerome, he ran toward the street. Leanne looked from him to the priest, trying to decide which one needed her attention more at the moment. When Ryan darted into the street in front of a car, caus-ing the driver to brake with a loud squeal, the decision was easy. Giving the guilty-looking man a glare, she spun around and ran after Ryan.

He was younger, faster, and had a good head start. By the time she jerked open the apartment door, *bangs* and *thuds* were coming from the living room. She took the stairs two at a time, then caught her breath at the top and tried to slow her racing heart. She'd been right—there was no friend, no other woman, no new scam. No, this was the worst possible truth. Frank Jackson had come to town.

Cole intended to leave.

She hung up her coat, then went through the kitchen, forcing shallow breaths into her lungs. Ryan's coat was on the floor, one glove on the dining table, the other dangling precariously from the television. His backpack rested on the coffee table, and its contents were scattered around the room, flung in anger and disillusionment. She sidestepped an airborne algebra book, hardly flinching as it crashed onto the hardwood floor, walked right up to him, and forcibly pulled him into her embrace. His thin body shook, and his breaths came in ragged gasps that punctuated his words.

"He said he would stay . . . he promised . . . he said he loved . . ."

"It's all right, babe," she murmured, stroking his hair with one hand, rubbing his back in soothing circles with the other. "It's okay."

His tears seeped through the fabric of her shirt, dampening her shoulder. "I hate him! I knew better than to believe him! I knew how good a liar he is! But he said . . . he promised . . . "

In the corner where his kennel resided, Jerome peered out, head resting on his front paws, his eyes huge and doleful. He stood and stretched, then wandered over and leaned against Ryan's leg. Finding the boy's hand hanging limply, he positioned his head underneath it, then rubbed it back and forth in a parody of a scratch.

Ryan's sob turned into a choked laugh. Shrugging away from Leanne, he knelt next to the dog and hugged and scratched him at the same time. "You always want attention, don't you?" He sounded stuffy and embarrassed. "You'd probably let me scratch you twenty-four hours a day if I could, wouldn't you?"

"He thinks it's no more than he deserves." Leanne sat down on the coffee table next to the backpack. "Hey . . . has it occurred to you that you might be jumping to conclusions?"

Ryan scowled. *"No."*

"Just because Frankie is here doesn't—doesn't mean that Cole's planning to run off."

Sitting back on his heels, Ryan gave her a look that made her feel naive in the face of his great understanding. "You think he just dropped by to say hello? They don't do that. They only show up when they've been asked for help. *He* asked them for help. He had to, or Frankie never would have come here."

"Maybe he was just in the area. Maybe he just wanted to see the brother he hasn't seen in months."

Now his look made her feel stupid as well as naive. "They *don't* do that," he repeated. "Ever. Frankie's here because Cole sent for him. Trust me."

She didn't want to. Didn't want to believe Cole had lied to them about leaving. Didn't want to think for a moment that he would work his way back into their lives and their hearts when he was planning all along to disappear again. Didn't want to know he could be so self-centered and uncaring.

She didn't want to know she could have been so terribly wrong about him.

She combed her fingers through Ryan's hair. "Honey, we can't just assume the worst. He deserves the benefit of the doubt."

He shook his head in the same disdainful way Cole did. "Cole says people like you are what makes life easy for people like him. He's already proven he can't be trusted, but you just keep on doing it over and over. Frank wouldn't be here if Cole hadn't written, asking for help gettin' out. He's gonna leave. I know he is."

What were the odds that Frankie Jackson's sudden appearance was as innocent as she hoped? Ryan was convinced otherwise, and he *knew* the family. All she knew was what Cole had told her—that he didn't see his brothers often. That he didn't even know what state they were in most of the time. That the only way he knew to get hold of

them was through a letter sent to their father. *Gee, I'm in
the area, so why not drop in and spend a few days with Cole*
didn't seem to be their style.

Besides, if Frankie's visit *was* innocent, why was he pretending to be someone else? And a *priest,* for God's sake.
She'd once thought Cole should worry about retribution
for simply walking through the church doors.

"You gonna call the cops?"

Startled by Ryan's hesitant question, she focused her
gaze on him. His eyes were red and filled with more emotions than she could name. A few were easy, though. Anger.
Betrayal. Bitterness. Hurt.

And fear. He was so sure he was right . . . and so afraid.

Was she going to call Mitch Walker? But what if she was
wrong? What if, by some quirk of fate, Frankie's visit *was*
innocent? Cole would be devastated by the proof of her
distrust.

And what if she wasn't wrong and she did nothing and
Cole did take off with his brother? She would bear some
of the responsibility for his escape. She'd never helped anyone break the law before, and she didn't want to start now.

But she also didn't want to cause trouble for him and
Eli's program, or to be the reason he wound up serving the
rest of his sentence in prison.

"Well?"

"I think we should talk to Cole, babe, and listen to what
he has to say."

He snorted. "He'll say what he wants you to believe, just
like he did before."

She couldn't deny that he'd played her for a fool before,
but she also couldn't deny him the chance to prove he deserved their trust.

"We have to talk to him," she repeated. "We have to believe in him until he gives us a reason not to."

Ryan gave a derisive shake of his head. "Cole says there's a fool born every minute."

"He stole that line from someone else."

He shrugged as if it didn't matter. "He steals everything."

A glance at her watch showed at least two hours, maybe three, before she could expect to see Cole walking through the door. She couldn't wait that long to talk to him. "Want to go with me to find him?"

"To *try* and find him, you mean. He's probably already gone."

"Do you want to go or not?"

He shook his head. "He's just gonna lie to you."

"You stay here in the apartment and do your homework, okay? Don't go out—and pick up your stuff, please." Leaning forward, she kissed him on the forehead, then stood up. "I'll be back."

He let her get to the kitchen doorway before grimly responding. "*You're* not the one who runs off."

THERE MUST HAVE BEEN WORSE JOBS THAN STRINGing Christmas lights all day when the wind chill was hovering in the single digits, but at the moment Cole couldn't think of any. He'd lost contact with his extremities hours ago. His eyes were watering and his nose was runny, and he was pretty sure he wouldn't thaw out until spring. But Eli and Murray didn't complain, and if they could stand it, so could he.

They were on the roof of the building that had once housed the office of Jackson Investments, stringing icicle lights along the top. Every single building in the business district would be outlined with the clear lights and, when the switch was flipped sometime around Thanksgiving, would put out enough wattage to persuade any nocturnal creature around that night had become day. Mere stars wouldn't be able to compete with the display, and airliners thirty thousand feet up would be able to see the town a thousand miles away.

It sounded like quite a sight.

The door that provided rooftop access creaked loudly enough to be heard over the traffic below and the sniffling closer at hand. He glanced over his shoulder, saw Leanne, and stopped breathing.

Would he ever reach the point where he could look at her without noticing how amazingly beautiful she was? He couldn't imagine it.

She stopped a few feet from the door, the wind whipping her black coat around her ankles. A red hooded scarf covered her hair and wrapped around her neck, and matching gloves provided a splash of color at her waist, where her hands were loosely clasped. Her face was pale except for the bright spots on her cheeks, and her breath formed white puffs before disappearing with the wind.

"Can I take a break?" he asked Eli. When the kid nodded, he moved away from the roof ledge and walked to her. "Hey."

She didn't smile, and there was something in her eyes that made his own smile fade. Wariness? Uncertainty? "Can we go inside?"

In response, he opened the door, then followed her into the stairwell. He expected her to head downstairs, but instead she gathered her coat close and sat on the top step. He joined her.

For a time she stared toward the landing below, as if she was putting her thoughts in order. The impatient part of him wanted to tell her to just spit it out. The fearful part wanted her to say nothing, not until that look was gone from her eyes, not until she could smile at him and mean it.

Finally she drew a breath. It sounded loud in the stairwell and made his gut clench almost as hard as her words did.

"Are you planning to leave town?"

It was his turn to draw a breath, but he couldn't. His chest was too tight, his throat closed off.

"I only ask because I met your brother this afternoon—well, sort of. Ryan punched him, then took off, and I went after him, and Frankie went . . ." She shrugged as if it wasn't important where Frank had gone. "Ryan's convinced that Frankie's here for only one reason. He insists you wrote to your father, asking for one of them to help you get out of town. He believes you lied to us when you said you weren't leaving. Did you?"

Aw, jeez, this was *not* a conversation he wanted to have, especially with her looking so pale and wary. He surged to his feet and took the stairs to the landing, his boots echoing loudly. There he stared at the wall, wishing he had never written the damn letter, or had sent Frankie away the day before, or had skipped the conversation with his brother on the sidewalk and jumped in his car with the order to—

No. He didn't wish he'd left. It may have been what he'd wanted in the beginning, and from time to time since then, when everything seemed impossible, but not anymore.

Not anymore.

Slowly he turned and climbed the stairs to crouch a few steps below her. "No. I didn't lie."

She studied him, the expression in her dark eyes intense, searching for a reason to believe him. He didn't flinch, but let her look all she wanted, let her see what she wanted, and hoped—prayed—it was enough. He barely breathed while he waited, just short little puffs that did nothing to ease the tightness in his chest or the knots in his gut. He needed her to believe him. It wasn't logical or reasonable, not when he'd given her two-hundred-fifty-thousand reasons not to, but he needed it more than he could say.

After what seemed like forever, she took a ragged breath, then nodded. "I didn't think so."

Relief washed through him, loosening his muscles in an instant. Too unsteady to stay as he was, he sank down on a step, the wall at his back, and exhaled loudly. She knew what he was and trusted him anyway. No one but Ryan had ever done that before. No one but Leanne might ever do it again.

"But you did write to your father, didn't you?" She leaned forward, arms resting on her knees, hands fisted against the chill, her chin dipped into the folds of the red scarf. "You did ask for your brothers' help."

He didn't want to admit it, didn't want her to reconsider her faith in him, but couldn't lie to her now. "Leaving Bethlehem last spring was the second hardest thing I've ever done. Coming back was the hardest. I *couldn't* come back—couldn't face you and Ryan after what I'd done. When the cops picked me up in Savannah and turned me over to Nathan Bishop, I figured getting shot would be better than that, but I never got the chance. I tried to escape on the way here, but Bishop was ready for it."

He gazed off at nothing, remembering the despair and dread that had eaten at him on the long drive from Georgia to New York. He would have gladly bypassed a trial and gone straight to prison if it had meant avoiding the people he'd betrayed.

"I didn't want to be here. Waking up every day in that

house, seeing your shop every time I looked out the window, seeing you and Ryan, and knowing you both hated me . . ." He grimly shook his head. "Yeah. I wrote Owen and asked for someone to come and get me."

But things had changed since then. *He'd* changed. Not as much as he could, nowhere near as much as he should, but he'd made a good start. It was the town, the people, and especially Leanne. She'd made him want to stay, to clean up his act, to be a part of her family. She'd made him want a normal life—going to bed and waking up in the same place, not just week after week, but year after year. Being a father to Ryan and Danny. Knowing what was really important. Living an honorable life.

For a time, silence settled around them. Not complete silence—the wind rattled around the building and carried faint snatches of Eli and Murray's conversation, a door opened and closed two flights down, a car horn sounded. But between him and Leanne, there was nothing but the ragged tempo of his breathing. She seemed lost somewhere inside herself, and he wondered bleakly if he could find his way to her.

After too long, she spoke, her voice low, her tone empty of emotion. "And now Frankie's come."

"Yeah. But I'm not going anywhere."

"Does Frankie know that?"

"He suspects it." For the first time since seeing her outside the rooftop door, he managed a faint grin. "The idea of me going straight scares him. He's afraid he might catch whatever I've got and have to settle down himself."

Her smile was pale but genuine. "He might even develop a conscience. That would surely throw the rest of the family into a panic."

"No kidding."

She unknotted her fingers, then slid her hand into his. It

was a simple gesture, but it formed a lump in his throat and made him forget the cold. When he tugged, she came to him willingly, letting him lift her onto his lap and hold her close. She smelled of cold and sweet, spicy flowers, and she felt . . . right. As if she belonged in his arms.

As if he belonged in hers.

"I'll tell Frank tonight. He's got a scam running back in Connecticut. He won't stick around."

She rested her head on his shoulder and slid one gloved hand inside his coat to press against his chest. "Why don't you invite him to dinner?"

"Are you sure you want him in your apartment and around the kids?"

Her soft laughter warmed him. "He's not going to corrupt them in one evening."

"Don't count on it. I've seen him corrupt plenty of young women in an evening or less. He might even corrupt you."

"I've already got the best Jackson of the bunch."

The best of the bunch. Considering who *the bunch* was, it wasn't saying a lot, but he'd take it.

Though his hands were still frozen, he pulled off one glove and raised his fingers to her cheek. She was so beautiful, her dark eyes so trusting. He wanted to kiss her, but there was something he needed to say first. With an odd, funny feeling in his chest and his throat dry as the desert, he said, "You know, darlin', I lo—"

The door above slammed open with the wind, hitting the wall and bouncing on its hinges. Frigid air blasted over them as Eli and Murray hustled in, then forced the door shut again. "It's colder than the North Pole out there," Eli said, stomping his feet to get the blood circulating again.

Leanne didn't startle or jerk away from Cole, but gracefully eased to her feet. "And you know that because? . . ."

"I've been there, of course. Just about everyone in my field goes there at least once, even if it's just on the way to somewhere else."

Why would a do-gooder social worker go to the North Pole, especially when it wasn't on the way to *anywhere* else? But Cole didn't waste much time pondering it. Instead, he was regretting the declaration he hadn't gotten to finish, and feeling a little relieved by the interruption, too. He'd never said *I love you* to any woman before, and it was damn near as scary as the prospect of becoming an upstanding, law-abiding citizen with roots. There would be another, better time, and when it came around, he would have built up enough courage to overcome the fear.

"We're knocking off for the day, Cole," Eli went on. "Let's get the stuff back to the garage, then head home to thaw out."

With a nod, he stood up, let the other two men pass, then followed them downstairs, Leanne's hand in his. When the others left the stairwell, he paused, pulled her closer, and kissed her. It wasn't the kind of kiss he wanted, certainly not the kind she deserved, but it would hold him for an hour or two.

"Want me to invite Frankie to dinner?" she asked as they entered the first-floor corridor, where the temperature was a good thirty degrees warmer.

He would really prefer that she tell Frank to get out of town and save him the arguments his brother was sure to offer, but that would be the coward's way out. Not that he was truly adverse to being a coward . . . "If you're sure you want him there. He's staying at the motel."

She paused at the main doors. Outside, Eli and Murray loaded two large boxes of lights into the back of the truck, then climbed in to wait for him.

"Who should I ask for?"

Cole's face flushed with regret that she knew enough about him and his family to ask the question. "Frank Murphy. Father Murphy."

With a rueful grin and a roll of her eyes, she nodded, pressed a kiss to his cheek, then pushed through the door. On the sidewalk, she glanced back to wiggle her fingers in a little wave, then set off toward the shop.

He was a lucky man.

God, please don't let me screw it up.

Chapter Eighteen

FRANK JACKSON WAS A CHARMER. Handsome, funny, and entertaining, he had a natural talent for storytelling, as well as a way with words that could turn any woman's head, to say nothing of a killer grin and dimples. Before they even sat down to dinner, Ryan had come around and was trading jokes with Frank as if he hadn't punched him just a few hours earlier, and even Leanne found herself enjoying his company.

Almost as much as she wished he would disappear and resurface a thousand miles away.

Cole didn't see his brothers often, he'd once told her, but when they did get together, it was as if no time at all had passed, and that certainly seemed to be the case. When she'd reunited with Chase last spring, it had taken a while for them to find the closeness they had once shared. Not so for Cole and Frank. There were times through the evening when they seemed to pick up conversations that had been dropped months before, no prompting, no reminding needed, and it took no more than a word or two to send them off on reminiscences about times past.

There was a lot of affection between them, she thought

as she watched them good-naturedly argue over something that had happened ten years earlier. Maybe Owen Jackson hadn't been the best father around, and no doubt about it, teaching his sons to follow in his footsteps had been wrong. But two of those sons, at least, obviously loved each other and weren't afraid to show it, which was more than she could say for a lot of people raised in more conventional ways.

So Owen wasn't the worst father around, either.

She was sitting in the armchair, her feet drawn into the seat, a glass of wine from the bottle Frank had brought clasped in both hands. Dinner was long over, dessert a sweet memory. Ryan and Danny had done the dish-fairy chores, then gone off to get Danny ready for bed. It was late, fiercely cold outside, and as fiercely comfortable inside. If not for the faint churning in her gut, she would be well and truly contented this evening.

But there was that churning.

"So . . . Leanne."

Frank's voice startled her out of her thoughts. She looked up to find him and Cole, sitting at opposite ends of the couch with Jerome between them, watching her.

"You gonna make an honest man out of my brother?"

The question was asked as if in jest, merely a play on words, but there was a sharp challenge underlying it that set off her internal warning bells. He believed that when he left town, Cole would be going with him—thought this evening was just another part of just another scam. Cole had said he would tell Frank he'd changed his mind and was staying in Bethlehem, at least for the duration of his sentence. Now seemed as good a time as any for that to happen.

"The only person who can make an honest man of Cole is Cole," she replied, her gaze on him. He was idly scratching Jerome and looking back at her with the faintest of smiles. He looked very much at home—on her couch, in her apartment, in her life—but she still had that queasy feeling. It wasn't going to go away until Frank did.

"Leanne knows why you're here," Cole said.

The look on Frank's face was comical—his jaw dropped, his eyes widened, his brows reaching for his hairline. "You trust her not to go to the cops?"

"About you?"

He snorted. "About *you*. How far do you think we'll get if she rats you out?"

"You'll get wherever you want to go. Me—I'm already there." He fell silent for a moment—not a hesitation that implied uncertainty, but more a pause to give weight to his next words. "I'm not leaving."

Leanne's gaze shifted from Cole to Frank, then back again. Sitting a few feet apart as they were, the family resemblance was unmistakable. So was the difference in demeanor. The younger brother didn't know whether to be dismayed or disbelieving, appalled or wheedling. The older was calm, relaxed, even relieved. The butterflies in her stomach started to settle one by one, and that contentment she'd been thinking about earlier began growing.

"You're kidding, right?" Frank said at last. "Come on, bubba, I *know* you. There's no way you're gonna make it in a nowhere little town like this. I admit, Leanne's pretty, but you don't go straight for a pretty woman."

Cole was still looking at her, still wearing that hint of a smile. "I'm not doing it for her. It's for me."

Frank muttered an obscenity. "You don't even know how to go straight."

"I've got a couple years left on my sentence, to figure it out."

Springing from the couch, Frank paced to the nearest window, then back again. "Why? Why are you doing this?"

Finally Cole looked away, focusing on his brother instead. "Because I'm tired, Frankie—of ripping people off. Of lying. Of pretending to be someone I'm not. I'm tired of dragging Ryan all over the place, of not having a place to call my own. Most of all, I'm tired of not—not liking who I am or what I do."

Frank dragged his fingers through his hair before planting both hands on his hips. "You think it's that easy to change who you are? You think you can just say, 'Okay, I'm one of the good guys now,' and that makes it true? 'Cause it's not gonna happen, bubba. What're you gonna do? You don't know how to do anything that doesn't involve breaking the law. You've never made a dime in your life that wasn't dirty. You've never stayed in one place more than a few months, or with one woman. You don't know how to live any life besides the one you were raised for."

Cole's reply was simple, his tone stubborn. "I can learn."

Frank's was even simpler, a snort of disgust.

For a long time silence hung in the air. Frank stared at Cole with something akin to horror, and Cole stared back, his expression resolute. He looked like a man who'd made up his mind and wasn't about to change it, Leanne thought. She hoped her own expression was as steady, but inside the butterflies had started turning cartwheels.

Abruptly, Frank shrugged, as if literally casting off his concerns. "You wanna stick around here? Fine. Give it your best shot. See how well you can fit in with these small-town, small-minded yokels. When you find out you can't . . . you know how to reach me."

"That won't be necessary."

Frank looked from him to her, then smiled an ugly smile. "Sure, it will. Maybe not tomorrow or next week or even next month, but you'll call. You're a Jackson, and no matter how hard you try, no matter how hard she wants you to try, you'll never change that."

Leanne spoke up at last. "I don't want to change who he is." She loved who he was. She just hated what he did.

The look he gave was pure cynicism. "Yeah. Right. Well . . . guess I'd better get back to the motel. If you're not going with me, bubba, I want to get an early start in the morning."

Cole didn't argue with him, a fact for which she was dearly grateful, but got to his feet. "Let me tell Ryan you're leaving."

Once he was out of earshot, Frank turned his attention to her. "You're dying to get up and do a little victory dance, aren't you?"

"Just a small one."

"You know you're both kidding yourselves."

"I don't know that at all."

"Cole's a con artist—the best I've ever seen. And right now he's running the best con I've ever seen—on you and himself."

"Why does it bother you so much that he wants a better life?"

He looked insulted. "Better? Stuck in one place? Working nine-to-five? Struggling to make ends meet? Doing the same drudge job day after day, living the same dreary life? How does that qualify as *better*?"

"Someday maybe you'll grow up and find out the answer to that for yourself."

"Not if I have anything to say about it." He let his scowl fade, then said, "I'll be back."

"Maybe." For a wedding or Christmas with the family. For a family reunion or to get acquainted with the newest member of the Jackson family. But *not* to take Cole away, her inner voice whispered delightedly. He wasn't going. Not tonight, not next week or next month, not *ever.*

Digging into his hip pocket, Frank removed his wallet, then withdrew a fifty-dollar bill. "Cole said Ryan's birthday is Thursday. Do me a favor and give this to him, will you?"

She looked at the money, then at him. Good sense told her to snatch the fifty, then hustle him to the coat tree in the hall. He could say good-bye to Cole and Ryan while putting on his coat, then she could push him down the stairs and out the door.

But her thoughts from a moment ago kept repeating in her head. *Christmas with the family, a family reunion, meeting the newest member of the family . . . see a pattern?* Frank was a part of Cole and Ryan's family and deserved to be treated as such, especially now that Cole had told him unequivocally that he wasn't leaving town or her. Instead of reaching for the money, she stood up, then folded his fingers over the bill. "Why don't you give it to him yourself, at his party? Whoever's waiting for Father Murphy to return can wait a few extra days, can't they?"

He grinned, showing the dimples. "You want me to stick around? Aren't you afraid I'll try to change Cole's mind?"

"To the contrary, I'm sure you will. *Try,* that is." But trying was a long way from succeeding. She didn't believe for an instant he would succeed. "Let's make a deal. You stay for Ryan's party, and I won't sic the police on you when you leave."

The grin broadened. "Blackmail, huh? Maybe I shouldn't worry about you corrupting Cole. Maybe next time I see you, you'll be working right alongside him in his newest scam." He returned the money to his wallet. "Okay.

It's a deal. I'll stay for Ryan's birthday, and then I'm outta here."

As Ryan's voice drifted in from the hallway, Frank headed that way, but turned back before he reached the kitchen. "But I'm not making any promises that I'll be leaving alone."

Leanne summoned her most serene smile. She didn't need promises from him. She had them from Cole, and that was all that mattered.

A SENSE OF ANTICIPATION SWEPT THROUGH LEANNE as she surveyed the living and dining room, though she couldn't honestly say whether it was because it was Ryan's birthday, she would be seeing Cole again very soon, or Frank would be leaving town in the morning. It wasn't that she was afraid Cole would change his mind and leave with him. He'd made up his mind. He'd chosen Bethlehem, Ryan, an honest life, and her over his lawless days.

It was just that resisting temptation was always easier when it wasn't staying a few miles away, sitting down to meals with you, and frequently reminding you of old times, good times, cons that had gone hilariously wrong and ones that had been textbook perfect. To hear Frank tell it, the Jacksons were damn near legendary in the right circles, Cole more so than the others. Leaving that life behind, in his opinion, was *not* the act of a sane man.

But hadn't Nolie said there was nothing sane about falling in love?

It was almost party time, and she was as ready as could be. Sophy was downstairs minding the shop, Danny was still at day care, and Ryan was over there with him, helping the teachers and staying out of the apartment until Leanne was ready for them at six.

As was their custom, he'd picked the menu—salad, spaghetti, and garlic bread. The salad was chilling in the refrigerator, the sauce simmering on the stove, and a huge pot of water simmered, too, ready to bring to a boil as soon as everyone arrived. The bread was sliced, buttered, and sprinkled with garlic and waiting in a cold oven, out of Jerome's reach.

The dining table and a card table were set with festive tablecloths and balloons tied to the kids' chairs, and a stack of presents waited on a table in the corner. She might have gone a little overboard—okay, so a present from Jerome was a bit much—but she wanted to overwhelm Ryan with the fact that he was absolutely part of the family.

The doorbell rang, bringing a lazy *woof* from Jerome. Figuring it was Cole, she ran down the stairs and opened it . . . to Eli. The young man looked uncharacteristically serious. "Hi. Is Cole here?"

"Of course not. I mean, he's supposed to be, later, but . . . he's been with you all day."

"No, actually, he hasn't. Not for the last couple hours. I thought maybe he came straight here when he got back, because of Ryan's birthday."

The chill that made her shiver came from the cold, nothing else. That was why her voice was the slightest bit unsteady when she asked, "Got back from where?"

"The town keeps some of their Christmas displays at the camp out on the lake. I sent him out with the truck, to pick up some of them around three this afternoon, and . . . we haven't seen him since."

The cold was making it difficult to breathe, too. Her lungs must have been rejecting the chilly air, because she couldn't fill them adequately. "Have you gone out there? Maybe he had a flat tire or—or ran out of gas or something."

"He took the truck. I don't have a way to go check."

The sound of a cheery, "Happy birthday, sweetie," drew her attention to the corner. Chase, Nolie, and Micahlyn had just gotten out of his truck, and Ryan and Danny had just come around the corner from the day care center. It was Nolie who had spoken and was giving a hug and a kiss to a bashful Ryan.

"Hi, Mama," Danny greeted, stretching onto his toes to give her a big hug. "Ryan comed to day care and stayed and teached us. It was *cool*."

"I bet it was." Absently she bent to kiss his forehead, then hugged Ryan. Micahlyn, cradling a prettily wrapped gift, lifted her cheek for a kiss but declined a hug on account of the present. Chase, carrying Nolie's famous banana-split cake, accepted a kiss on the cheek, too.

"You guys go on upstairs," she murmured. "I'll be up in a minute."

"Everything okay?" Chase asked, glancing curiously at Eli.

Acutely aware of the kids listening, she smiled. "Yeah. I'll be right up."

Once they were inside, she stepped out and let the door close behind her, hugging herself against the cold. She should have grabbed her coat when she passed the coat tree in the hall, but she'd been expecting one of Cole's hello kisses that curled her toes and heated her internal temperature to scorching.

"I'd better notify Chief Walker," Eli said before she could get her thoughts straightened.

"Do you have to? If Cole's run out of gas or gotten lost, it'll make him feel really lousy that you sent the cops after him."

"The truck had half a tank of gas, and I don't think it's humanly possible to get lost going to the camp and back."

She knew that. She'd spent weeks every summer at the camp when she was growing up. You took the street that ran past the hospital, followed it to its end after the pavement gave way to dirt, and you were there. There were no confusing directions, no intersecting roads for wrong turns, and only one house along the whole stretch. You just couldn't screw it up.

"Maybe . . ."The buzz of the street lamps distracted her. It was dark, cold, and sure to get colder. What if something had happened to Cole?

Like Frank, her been-fooled-before voice suggested. What if he'd sought out Cole today and resumed his efforts to persuade him to leave with him—and succeeded?

"I'd better talk to Chief Walker," Eli said again.

"He *didn't* leave. It's Ryan's birthday. He's expecting Cole at his party tonight. There's no way Cole would disappoint him."

"He disappointed him before," Eli quietly pointed out.

"But he wouldn't do it again." She was sure of it. Absolutely positive. Ninety-nine percent convinced.

Oh, God.

"Let me get my keys and we'll drive out to the camp—" Breaking off, she watched as Mitch Walker crossed the street from the Miller mansion. His expression was grim, and made her breath catch in her chest.

"Murray said I could find you over here," he said to Eli when he joined them. He gave her a curt nod. "We just got a call from Isaac Lester. He reported a pickup parked on the road up near his place—*your* pickup. Were you driving it?"

Eli shook his head.

"Was Jackson?"

He nodded.

"Where is he now?"

"Your guess is as good as mine."

"He *didn't* leave," Leanne insisted. "He promised me . . . he promised Ryan . . ."

Neither man looked convinced, and why should they? That lone house on the way to the summer camp was Isaac Lester's. Cole had last been seen in the truck, which had been abandoned on a rarely traveled country road. All they needed to convict him was to find out that Frank had unexpectedly checked out of the motel. . . .

Her stomach clenching, she abruptly spun around and raced up the stairs. She hardly noticed the heat or the fragrant aroma of the spaghetti sauce as she grabbed the phone book from its place in the junk drawer and thumbed through to the listing for Angels Lodge. Her hand trembled when she punched in the number. As it rang, she turned her back so she couldn't see Ryan, Nolie, and Chase watching her from the living room, or Eli and Mitch standing just inside the hall doorway.

Bree Aiken, the manager, answered with a friendly, "Can I help you?"

"F-Frank Jackson's room, p-please."

"I'm sorry. We don't have anyone registered under that name."

Of course not. *Never use your real name* was probably number sixteen on Owen's endless list of rules. "Murphy," she said breathlessly. "Frank Murphy."

"Oh, Father Murphy. Let's see . . . he checked out this afternoon."

Leanne's stomach dropped to her toes and her vision went blurry. "Can you tell me what time?"

"I'm sorry, ma'am—"

Pressing one hand to her eyes, Leanne interrupted. "Bree, it's me, Leanne Wilson. Please—it's very important. When did Frank leave?"

"Oh, hi, Leanne. I guess it's okay to tell you. He'd said earlier he was leaving tomorrow, but then he checked out about three-fifteen today."

Too shaken to even think, Leanne slowly hung up without another word. She felt as if everything had been drained from inside her—warmth, life, faith, hope. If she tried to speak, she would sob. If she tried to move, she would collapse in a heap.

A hot, sweaty hand covered hers where it rested on the counter. "He's gone, isn't he?" Ryan whispered. "Frankie's gone. Cole's gone."

She managed to turn on her unsteady legs and wrap her arms around him. "Frank's gone . . . but not Cole. He said he would stay. He said . . ."

"He lied."

"No." She couldn't offer any reasons for believing that, but she did believe. She knew in her heart he never would have voluntarily abandoned them again—*knew* it. She couldn't possibly love a man like that, the way she loved Cole.

But she'd loved him before . . . and he'd voluntarily abandoned them that time.

"Who is Frank Murphy?" Mitch asked.

Reluctantly she lifted her gaze to him, standing next to the refrigerator with his hands on his hips. "His real name is Frank Jackson. He . . . he's Cole's younger brother."

"And he's been here in town?"

She nodded.

"For how long?"

Feeling the censure in his gaze and his tone, Leanne straightened her shoulders, ignored her blush, and lifted her brows. "A few days. I'm not sure."

"And you've known that and didn't bother to tell anyone."

"We found out Tuesday," Ryan volunteered, hostility creeping into his voice. "But Cole promised he wasn't going anywhere. He *promised.*"

He hadn't promised, she thought dully—just spoken with great conviction. Lied with great conviction? her hated inner voice whispered.

"I'm sorry, Mitch," she said coolly. "I didn't know I was supposed to report back to you about anyone Cole spoke to."

"His brother is hardly *anyone*. He's also his frequent partner in crime, and if you didn't know that, Ryan certainly did."

The peal of the doorbell saved her from having to respond to that. Hope surged, but just as quickly faded. It wasn't Cole. Somehow she knew it all the way down to her toes.

"Want me to get that?" Eli offered, and she nodded.

"Where would they go, Ryan?" Mitch asked, coming to the island as Eli started for the door.

Ryan stared at him, his mouth clamped shut and his expression blank.

"I understand your grand—Cole's father lives in Philadelphia. Do you think they would go there?"

He got an answer this time, but not from Ryan. Chase came to stand next to him and rested one hand on the counter, the other on Ryan's shoulder. "Questioning a minor without permission from his guardian or his attorney?" he asked mildly. "I'm sure they taught you better than that in police chiefs' school."

Mitch scowled at him. "We all want the same thing—to find Jackson."

"Yeah, but they want to find him because they're worried about him. You want to lock him up."

"Look, guys, I'm not the enemy here. He's innocent

until proven guilty, right? But until we find him, it looks real likely that he's fled the jurisdiction, and if he has, he'll have to suffer the punishment. If he hasn't, he'll be real pleased to know you folks had faith in him."

"Have you sent—" Leanne broke off as Eli returned, carrying a large box. It was beautifully wrapped in red embossed paper with gold wired ribbon—the signature wrapping shared by several shops downtown.

"Elena, from the bookstore, brought this by. She said Cole was supposed to pick it up before closing time today. When he didn't show, she decided to deliver it. She didn't want to miss Ryan's birthday." Eli grinned. "Happy birthday, son."

Ryan stared at the package, an anguished look in his eyes. "Maybe he did leave," he whispered. "Maybe he thought sending a present would make up for it. Maybe—"

"Maybe nothing." Leanne gave him a shake. "He intended to pick it up and deliver it himself—that's all. He wasn't trying to make up for anything."

More determined than ever, she returned to the question Eli had interrupted. "Have you sent someone out to the camp to look around?"

Mitch nodded. "When Isaac called in about the truck, Sheriff Ingles sent a deputy to check it out. He drove all the way to the camp and saw no sign that anyone had gone beyond Isaac's place in weeks." As he finished speaking, his cell phone rang. He stepped into the hall to answer it.

"Something's happened," Leanne murmured.

"Yeah," Chase agreed just as softly. "Like maybe brother Frank met him on that dirt road because they knew it would take several hours for anyone to find the truck and realize Cole was gone."

She glared at him over Ryan's head. "No, not like that! I know you don't like Cole—"

"I don't like or dislike him. But I knew a hell of a lot of guys just like him in Massachusetts. I defended them, and I served time with them. I never trusted those guys, and I don't trust Cole." Chase's gaze shifted to Ryan. "I'm sorry."

"It's okay," he mumbled, still staring at the red gift Eli had placed on the island. "Only a fool trusts a Jackson. Cole says so himself."

And was she a fool? Leanne wondered, tears clogging her throat. When she'd asked him about Frank on Tuesday, had he told her the truth . . . or what she wanted to hear, as Ryan had predicted? And that whole scene with Frank Tuesday night . . . had that been an act for her benefit, to throw her off-guard? Was he well on his way to parts unknown to start his next scam? Had he betrayed them again?

Abruptly she released Ryan and pushed away from the counter. "Nolie, can you cook the spaghetti for me? The water's already heating. There's salad in the refrigerator and garlic bread in the oven. It just needs to be browned."

"Sure," her sister-in-law answered from the couch, where she'd been reading to Danny and Micahlyn, to keep them distracted from the adults' conversation.

"Where you going?" Chase asked.

"To look for Cole."

"Where?"

"In town. Outside town. Anywhere. Everywhere." She wouldn't accept that he'd left, until she'd proven to herself that he was nowhere around.

"Let the cops do that, Leanne. It's their job."

"Maybe. But it's my responsibility. I can't stay here knowing that he—" Could be hurt, lost, dead, or dying. "If

I'm not back when you leave, please take Danny and Ryan with you. Thanks a lot."

She didn't wait for further argument, but went into the hall, sidestepped Mitch, grabbed her coat, scarf, gloves, and purse, and headed down the stairs as she donned them. She was climbing into the SUV when the sound of running footsteps made her look up. Ryan and Jerome came flying toward her, the boy struggling into his jacket as he ran.

"Chase said we should come with you." He opened the rear door so Jerome could hop in, then jumped into the passenger seat.

She wanted to send them back, but he was worried, too—a good sign. As long as he believed looking for Cole was worthwhile, then he must believe they hadn't been abandoned again.

"Where are we gonna look?"

She shrugged as she started the engine. "Your guess is as good as mine, sweetie. The logical place, I guess, is the summer camp."

They'd driven a mile, maybe two, when Ryan turned his head her way. The dashboard lights made him look young and achingly vulnerable. "Do you think we'll find him?"

She had to try twice, but managed a smile. "I do."

She just wished she knew if she really did think so, or if she was lying to herself as well as to him.

OH, GLORIA . . . YOU REALLY SHOULD BE MORE careful."

The voice seemed to come from inside Cole's head, though it was hard to tell with the deafening rhythm already beating there. It was a soft voice, warm and sweet, and reminded him of Leanne, who was also soft, warm, and sweet, and waiting for him to show up for dinner. Too bad he lacked the energy to even open his eyes.

"*Me* be careful?" a second voice asked indignantly. "*I'm* not the one who stepped off into thin air!"

That was followed by a third voice—male, vaguely familiar. "No, you're the one who *appeared* out of thin air and startled him into falling."

Thin air . . . falling . . . was that what had happened to him? Why he was lying on the cold, damp ground? Why every shallow breath he took hurt like a son of a bitch?

"Do you think he's alive?" A female voice, not like Leanne's. Gloria again.

The man responded. "You don't see any death angels around, do you?"

Death angels? An involuntary snort of laughter slipped out, double-timing the pounding in his head and tripling his aches and pains. Was he laughing at the idea he could be dead, or the existence of angels? Oh, they probably did exist, but only for people who deserved them. Not for lowlifes like him.

It was a struggle, but he opened one eye, then the other. At some time while he was unconscious, darkness had fallen and the temperature had dropped. Stars twinkled overhead in the clear night, and a quarter moon shone brightly. He was in the forest and, judging by the silence, too far lost for anyone to find him. But how had he gotten there? The closest he'd ever gotten to the country was when he and Leanne had taken Danny and Ryan to the lake—

Ryan. Today was his birthday, and Cole was late for his party. He hadn't picked up the kid's present from the bookstore yet, and he needed a hot shower and a strong drink and— He tried to sit up, but the agonizing fire that shot through him made his vision go dark and his stomach heave. Sweet damnation, mainline painkillers, and a cast or two might be nice.

Lying still, he took inventory. He was freezing, of course. Knocking himself out in the forest on a frosty night could do that to a man. His head throbbed, his neck was bent at an awkward angle, and his left leg was bent at an impossible angle. His ribs hurt, and his chest, and he wasn't sure, but he thought his ankle was sending out occasional twinges to remind him it was still there. Gritting his teeth, he raised one hand to the knot on his forehead. His fingers came away sticky with congealed blood.

He was in trouble.

Bad.

"Look!" Gloria exclaimed. "He's awake! He's not dead!"

"Hey . . ." His voice was little more than a croak. "I could use a little help here."

When no answer came, he lifted his head, groaning, sweating, swearing, and took a look around. There was no one there. Nothing but trees, rocks, darkness, and cold. "Hello? Gloria? Somebody?"

No answer.

Weakly he laid his head down again, closed his eyes again. It had seemed such a simple job—take Eli's old truck to the end of the dirt road, load some super-sized plastic decorations in the back, and drive back to the city garage. Any moron could have done it without a problem.

But not Cole. First, he'd passed his brother on his way across town, and Frank had turned and followed him. When Frank passed him, then stopped, blocking the road, Cole had stopped, too, shut off the engine, and listened to his brother's arguments for leaving all over again. This time, though, he'd persuaded the kid he wasn't going, had said good-bye and watched him drive away . . . only to find out the truck wouldn't start.

He should have left it running. Shouldn't have gotten out to talk to Frank. Should have made it clear beyond a doubt that he wasn't leaving Leanne and Ryan, though in his own defense, he'd thought he'd done that Tuesday night.

Failing all that, when he realized he had to walk back into town, he should have stuck to the winding road. So what if it was three times farther than cutting through the woods? At least on the road he wouldn't have . . . what did Gloria say he'd done? Stepped off into thin air.

He remembered it vaguely. He'd been going down a steep hill, slipping and sliding but making better time than he would have on the road, and time had been important. He couldn't be late for Ryan's birthday dinner. Then she'd appeared. One second he'd been alone in the woods, and the next she'd been there ahead, hovering in midair, it had seemed, and shaking her head regretfully. "Should have stayed on the road, Jack," she'd said, and that was all he recalled.

Apparently he'd fallen, cracked his head and maybe some ribs, and broken his leg. The injuries weren't life-threatening, but the dropping temperatures were. Barring a miracle, he wasn't going to survive the night, and he wasn't exactly deserving of a miracle.

It was a hell of a way for a city boy to die. But at least it was peaceful. If Leanne was with him—and he wasn't banged up—it could be damn near perfect.

But Leanne wasn't with him . . . and he'd never told her he loved her . . . and things were still wrong between him and Ryan. So many regrets, and no time to fix them. He was worthless, Leanne had told him the day she'd come to see him in jail. Since then, he'd come to believe he could prove her wrong—sometimes believed he *had* proved her wrong—but in the end, he was the one who was wrong. He wished . . .

He wished . . .

I WISH WE COULD JUST TELL EVERYONE WHERE TO find him," Gloria said worriedly. "He doesn't look good."

"He could hear us talking when he wasn't supposed to," Eli responded. "Of course he doesn't look good."

Ignoring them both, Sophy gazed at Cole. He appeared unconscious, but she could hear his shallow, steady breaths, could feel his life force, however weak. Like Gloria, she wished they could take a proactive approach to getting him found, but that wasn't a guardian's job. All they could do was watch over him until he *was* found.

Sheriff Ingles's deputies and Chief Walker's officers were looking for him, but not actively. They considered him a fugitive and would be happy to take him into custody if they saw him, but they weren't out beating the bushes for him. No, Cole's best hope lay with Leanne and Ryan, who were just arriving at the summer camp. Did he know they believed in him when no one else did? Could he imagine the depth of their faith in him?

He would find out soon enough.

Sophy just wished they would hurry.

She knelt beside him. His eyes were closed again and he was shivering uncontrollably. His mouth moved, whispering pleas, prayers, mindless words that had no voice. She laid her hand against his forehead and found his skin cold on the outside, burning from inside. For a time she simply touched him like that, and gradually the shivers subsided, his lips stilled, and his breathing deepened as much as his injured ribs would allow. He looked as if he was merely taking a nap—comfortable, peaceful. Thankfully, it was a nap from which he would awaken.

Feeling a steady gaze on her, she looked up and into Eli's eyes. A blast of heat flamed through her. "Go away," she said quietly, as she hastily lowered her gaze to Cole again.

"No can do. He's my responsibility, too. Besides, if I leave you and Gloria alone with him, God only knows what will happen."

"Yes, He does, doesn't He? So beat it."

"What's the matter, Soph? Afraid to be this close to me? Afraid you can't keep your hands off me?"

She gave him her most disdainful look, when what she really wanted was to slap that smug arrogance from his— Good heavens, what was she thinking? She was a guardian, a protector. She'd never resorted to violence, not in all of forever. She'd never even *thought* about it.

But now that she had . . . "The only place I'd be likely to put my hands is around your throat," she said with a sugary smile.

"Yeah, right. When we finish up here, why don't we see about that?"

Her gaze caught on his mouth, as smug and arrogant as the rest of him, but also finely shaped and eminently kissable. "When we finish here, I've got better things to do," she replied. "Like watching the leaves rot or counting the dust particles in the atmosphere."

He leaned closer and grinned. "What is it you're afraid of, Soph? That I'll kiss you again? Or that I won't?"

Oh, yes, she thought as she gritted her teeth in a vain effort to ignore him. Physical violence was looking more appealing by the minute.

• • •

THE SUMMER CAMP WAS A COLLECTION OF RUSTIC buildings—a large kitchen and dining hall, a covered pavilion for rainy-day activities, and six cabins that slept fourteen each. Several docks extended into the lake for boating and swimming, blackened fire rings dotted the shore, and with a change of nets, a concrete slab converted from a basketball court to tennis.

A half-dozen flood lamps shone on the camp, and that many more were burned or broken out. Leanne kept her headlight beams on high as she followed the dirt lane that wove between the buildings. There was no sign of life, nothing to suggest that Cole had ever made it there. Which meant he was somewhere between the truck, three miles back down the road, and town.

Or a state or two away with Father Frankie.

The road looped around to go out the way it came in. Ryan sat in silence beside her, staring out the side window so she couldn't see his face. In the backseat, Jerome took in the view from one window, then the other. She tried to think of something reassuring to say, but her mind was too blank, numbed by fear and worry and more fear.

They passed Isaac Lester's house, a bright spot in the night, then soon left the glow behind for the quiet dark of the forest. If Cole had left them again, she would never forgive him. She'd let him go last time, but not again. She would track him down and make him damn sorry he'd ever heard of Bethlehem or her.

But if he'd left them again, he might already be sorry he'd ever heard of her. If he could walk away from her a second time, he certainly couldn't love her, not the way she loved him, or need her the way she needed—

A sob caught her off-guard, sounding choked and strangled and jerking Ryan around to look at her. Realizing it had come from her, she smiled unsteadily and gripped the steering wheel more tightly as they rounded the curve that would reveal Eli's old truck. She wondered why the sheriff hadn't had it towed yet, but was grateful he hadn't. It made the next step of her so-called plan easier.

When she parked nose to nose with the pickup, Ryan gave her another curious look. "What're we doin'?"

"Looking." She turned the key and climbed out, quickly zipping her coat to her throat, then pulling the collar around her ears. The pickup looked forlorn and abandoned in the moonlight, exactly the way she felt. She walked around to the driver's side, looked through the window, and saw nothing out of the ordinary. There were plenty of tire tracks in the soft ground—the deputy's, hers, some no doubt belonging to Mr. Lester. Maybe some to Frank?

There were footprints, too—the deputy's, hers, now Ryan's, and surely Cole's. He hadn't just been beamed out of the truck. He had climbed out and gone somewhere . . . but where?

Whining, Jerome strained at the leash. Leanne smiled faintly. "Why don't you take him into the grass? All the new smells are probably overloading his senses."

Ryan obeyed, letting the dog pull him around the truck and to the edge of the trees. Ryan stopped there, but Jerome didn't. Mulishly, he ducked his head and moved as far into the woods as he could, stretching the leash taut.

"Stop it, Jerome," Ryan admonished, pulling on the leash. It was a losing battle, though. Jerome tugged back and dragged his master a good three feet before Ryan caught himself. With a whine, the dog jerked again.

Curious, Leanne moved beside Ryan and called Jerome.

He glanced at her, whined, and pulled in the opposite direction.

Was it possible? . . .

He was a big overgrown baby, she reminded herself—not a tracker. Granted, labs were supposed to be very good trackers, but that required training or, at the very least, a strong bond between the dog and the person he was tracking. As far as Jerome was concerned, Ryan and Danny were the important people in his world. She and Cole were just the caretakers on the sidelines—the ones who took him out, scratched him when the kids weren't around, fed him . . . and Jerome did love his food and everyone who provided it. Maybe . . . *maybe* . . .

She looked at Ryan. Judging by his expression, he was wondering the same thing she was. She nodded into the trees. "Let's see where he wants to go."

"J EROME!" SOPHY CALLED SOFTLY, ONLY TO BE SHUSHED by Eli.

"That's cheating," he said in his most annoyingly superior manner, then he gave a sharp whistle, the kind dogs everywhere responded to. Jerome's bark was muffled by the distance.

"Oh, and that's not?"

"What? All I did was whistle," he said innocently.

"You two stop fussing," Gloria said testily. "Why, you're worse than any children I've ever dealt with. This is serious business here. We've put considerable effort into reaching this point with Jack and Louanne, so hush."

Chagrined, Sophy gazed into the woods. They were a fair distance from the dirt road up above. Even so, she could hear the crash of Jerome's oversized feet crunching over fallen leaves and rocks, nearly drowning out the softer footfalls of his master and mistress. It would take them a while, but they would reach Cole in time.

She lifted his hand into hers and briskly rubbed her heat into him. "You're going to be all right, Cole," she said so softly only he could hear. "Help is on the way."

He tried to move, groaned, and became still except for his fingers clenching hers. "Leanne?"

"She'll be here in just a minute. Just hold on, Cole. She's coming."

WHEN SHE STOPPED TO CATCH HER BREATH, Leanne had no clue how far they'd come from the road. Her lungs insisted a mile or more, but common sense suggested less than half that. It was rough going, making their way through the trees with only occasional flashes of moonlight to guide them. They'd slipped along the downward slope toward the valley, grabbing handholds where they could, sliding where they couldn't. She'd tripped over a fallen log and bruised her shin, and had lost her knitted cap on a leafless branch some distance back.

Jerome didn't seem to face any of the hazards she and Ryan did. Of course, his night vision was vastly better than theirs, and his four monster paws gave him a better grounding. Plus, he was on a mission. The excitement that made his whole body tremble made that clear.

Up ahead, Jerome barked. It wasn't his usual *feed me, walk me, I've gotta go* sort of bark, but an excited, urgent alert. As she headed in that direction, Ryan frantically called her name.

The boy was standing on an outcropping of rock at the edge of a bluff, staring wide-eyed and pale. Jerome's next bark came from down there, still urgent. She skidded to a stop next to Ryan and saw the dog fifteen feet below, crouched low to the ground and warily confronting the form lying motionless a few feet away.

Cole!

"Wait here." Spotting a break in the outcropping, Leanne headed down, sending showers of dirt and rocks to the forest floor below. Halfway down, her feet slid out from under her, making her land hard on her butt. She skittered the rest of the way down, then scrambled across the ground to Cole.

Except for the knot and the blood on his face, he looked as if he was merely sleeping. His eyes were closed, the corners of his mouth turned up in the beginnings of a smile. Heart pounding, she jerked off her glove and touched her shaking hand to his cheek. He was cold, dangerously so, but she felt the faintest movement, the slightest puff of breath against her skin.

Leaves and rocks rattled behind her, then Ryan appeared at her side. "Is he—is he dead?" he whispered, his voice choked and trembling.

In the moonlight, he appeared as pale as Cole, bringing the fear etched on his features into stark relief. She gave him a reassuring smile as she stripped off her coat to cover Cole. "No, babe, he's not. He's going to be all right."

Ryan scrambled to the other side, tugged off his own coat, and carefully laid it over hers. Almost immediately it seemed that Cole rested easier.

"Cole?" Ignoring her own chill, she bent over him. "Can you hear me?"

His lashes fluttered before he managed to open his eyes to slits. He smiled crookedly. "Didn't . . . leave . . ."

Tears stung her eyes. "Of course you didn't. We knew that, didn't we, Ryan?"

"You—you said you wouldn't," Ryan whispered.

With some effort, Cole shifted his gaze enough to see

the boy, and the faint smile came again. He lifted his hand a few inches, as if to touch one of them, then winced and let it fall again. "You . . . believed . . ."

That earned her warmest, brightest, most confident smile. "Of course we believed. Listen, I'm going to call for help, okay? We've got to get you to the hospital." She pulled her cell phone from her pocket, saw the signal strength was weak, and started to push to her feet.

"Wait." This time he touched her in spite of the pain, wrapping his fingers loosely around her wrist. "Have to . . . tell you . . ."

"Tell me at the hospital."

He shook his head. "Can't wait . . . I . . . love . . . you . . ."

Suddenly the night wasn't so cold or so dark, and the fear that had kept her going ever since Eli had appeared at her door disappeared. She looked at Ryan, whose lower lip was trembling as he swiped at his eyes, then she leaned close to Cole again and gazed into his glazed eyes. "I love you, too, Cole, forever and ever."

"Marry . . . me."

She'd always wanted to get married someday, but had never found the man worth it. What a hoot that the man seemingly the most unworthy of them all turned out to be the one and only man for her.

"Ask me again tomorrow when your brain's not addled from pain and the cold, because, sugar, once I say yes, you're stuck with a life sentence." She kissed him as gently as she could, then unwound his fingers from her wrist and lowered his hand into Ryan's. "Let me make that call, city boy."

She had to climb back up the hill to pick up a signal. After placing the call to 911, she stood on the outcropping of rock and watched the scene below. Ryan still held Cole's hand in his, and Jerome, not wanting to feel left out, had curled up against them both, sharing his warmth.

"I'm . . . sorry." Cole's voice drifted up on the chilly air, lacking substance but not conviction.

"For what?"

"Screwing up . . . your birthday . . . your life. Being a . . . lousy father."

Ryan shrugged. "Nothin's screwed up."

"I never meant to . . . to hurt you. Just wanted . . . you to have . . . good life."

"Yeah." It was Ryan's usual response, but this time it lacked the usual cynicism. "Well . . . don't let it happen again."

A chuckle escaped Cole before it faded into a grunt of pain. "I . . . love . . . you."

Leanne held her breath, and it seemed as if everything around her had gone utterly still as well. As the seconds dragged out, an ache started deep inside her, growing, knotting, and then—

"I love you, too," Ryan whispered.

Their little spot in the forest brightened and warmed a few degrees, or so it seemed to her. Truthfully, it was probably just the pure joy rushing through her. She returned the cell phone to her pocket, then started the journey back down the hill. As dirt and rocks slid beneath her feet, a slight breeze blew through the valley, and for an instant she would have sworn it formed words in an enormously satisfied voice.

And they'll live happily ever after.

I T HAD TAKEN A YEAR OR TWO FOR COLE TO GET warm again—quite a feat, considering that less than eighteen hours had passed since he'd foolishly decided cutting through the woods was a good idea. Some lessons took a while to sink in, but staying out of the woods without Leanne at his side was one he wouldn't forget. He was more grateful than he could say that he'd had a chance to live and learn it.

It had taken around thirty minutes for a deputy to reach them the night before, plus another ten minutes for him and the dispatcher to pinpoint their location and find a quicker, easier route for the paramedics. Cole hadn't minded the wait, though, not with Leanne on one side and Ryan on the other. They had both cried over *him*. The knowledge humbled him.

So did the understanding that when anyone else would have expected the worst, they had trusted him. Not one person had ever shown that kind of faith in him. On the contrary, people were usually quick to judge him, even his own family.

Rather, the Jackson family. Leanne, Ryan, and Danny—*they* were his own family now. They were where he belonged.

When the door to his hospital room swung open, he lowered his eyelids and looked through the lashes. If it was the nurse with another of her needles, he intended to fake sleep. Surely if the pain was manageable enough that he could sleep, she wouldn't wake him up to give him medication for it so he could sleep.

But it wasn't the nurse. Mitch Walker came into the room, hat in his hands. Stopping at the foot of the bed, he took off his uniform jacket, then fixed his gaze on Cole.

He knew he wasn't a pretty picture today. He'd been shaved where the laceration on his forehead extended beyond the hairline, and a row of black stitches stood out starkly against his skin. He was slumped against a stack of pillows, his broken ribs too sore to allow him to either sit up or lie down. His left leg was in a cast from hip to toe, and his right ankle was wrapped with an elastic bandage. He had bruises and scrapes elsewhere, but they couldn't begin to compete in the pain department with the other injuries, so he discounted them entirely.

"How are you feeling?" Walker asked.

"A hell of a lot better than I did last night."

Walker nodded, then glanced around the room. There weren't any flowers or cards—just sterile walls and furnishings designed for function rather than comfort. A TV bolted to the ceiling, a chair with little padding, another with none, a table to slide over the bed, a telephone on a night table he couldn't reach.

Finally the chief looked at him again. "I came by to apologize."

Cole blinked. "For what?"

"When the deputy found the truck and Eli said you'd been driving it and no one had seen you . . . I assumed you'd seen the chance to take off and grabbed it. I instructed my officers to keep an eye out for you, but . . . if you'd had to rely on our help last night, you wouldn't be here today. I'm sorry."

Cole started to shrug, but caught himself with the first sharp stab. "Under the circumstances, you made a logical assumption—you being a cop and me being a . . ." What was he exactly? Not a crook, not anymore. Not a thief, a liar, or a lowlife.

"You being a reformed con artist," Walker finished for him.

Reformed. Remade. Reborn. Cole smiled. He liked that.

"It was a logical assumption," he said again. "There were times when even I wasn't sure I was going to stick around. It's no big deal."

Walker looked as if he'd been let off too easily. He was

opening his mouth to say something when the door swung open again. This time it was Leanne, still wearing the same clothes as last night, looking tired and in need of a dozen hours' sleep, but beautiful just the same. She was carrying a cup of coffee in one hand, a sweet roll from the hospital cafeteria in the other, and she was . . . radiant. It was an extravagant word, but the only one that fit. There was an easiness about her, a peacefulness so pure that she practically glowed.

"Morning, Mitch." Balancing her breakfast, she raised onto her toes and kissed his cheek. "You haven't come to move the patient to the prison ward, have you?"

Walker scowled at her. "The hospital doesn't *have* a prison ward, and he's not in custody."

"Ha. He's in *my* custody." She set her breakfast on the bedside table, then grinned. "I found him. Now I get to keep him."

"The state might have something to say about that," Walker said dryly, then pulled on his coat. "You two take care."

"You, too." Leanne pulled the padded chair close to the bed, broke off a piece of the roll, and popped it into her mouth. Just watching her made Cole's mouth water, though it was debatable whether he was hungry for the roll or her. "How do you feel?"

He offered a shortened version of his answer to Chief Walker. "Better. Did you spend the night here?" He had vague memories, blunted by pain and dulled by medication, of gentle hands, a soft voice, her sweet fragrance. The attention from her had done him more good than the drugs the hospital staff had pumped into him, and he'd tried his best to stay awake and savor it, but he'd failed.

"Of course I was here. Do you think I could have gone home?"

She *could* have. She could do anything that was necessary—raise her son alone. Start and run a successful business. Take in Ryan and love him as if he were her own. Find *him*. Help him find himself.

Breaking off another piece of roll, she offered it to him. "Have you had breakfast?"

"If you can call it that," he said with an absent shake of his head. "Scrambled eggs, oatmeal, and applesauce, all with no salt, pepper, sugar, ketchup, hot sauce, raisins . . ."

"Already complaining about the food. You must be feeling better."

Gritting his teeth, he shifted on the bed so he could see her better, then for a long time just looked at her. She continued to eat her breakfast and let him look, a faint smile playing over her lips. It faded when he finally spoke. "You saved my life."

Her cheeks turned a pale pink and her gaze shifted away, then back. "We just did the logical thing—start where you had last been and go from there."

"I don't mean last night. From the beginning. When I first came here, when I was gone, when I came back . . . being friends with me and loving me and hating me and forgiving me and trusting me and loving me again. You saved my life."

She neatly wiped her hands on a napkin, stood up, and leaned over him, careful not to bump him. "Does that mean you belong to me from now on?"

"Whether you want me or not. Guess this means I do have a conscience," he said with a grin. He couldn't lift his arm to pull her closer or even raise his hand high enough to touch her face, so he settled for lacing his fingers through hers. "You never answered me last night."

"You never asked me anything."

"I tried." He stroked the palm of her hand, then slowly

lifted it to his mouth for a kiss. "I told you I love you, didn't I? I know, because you said it back. I didn't imagine it." Not something that important, that far outside his experience.

"No, you didn't imagine it."

"And I asked you . . . pleaded with you . . . to marry me. And you said—"

"Yes."

"No. You said, 'Ask me again tomorrow.' "

She smiled gently. "Guess your brain wasn't as addled as I thought. And now it's tomorrow."

"So? . . ."

"You still haven't asked."

He tried on words in his mind, wanting exactly the right ones, but the whole idea was so new to him, and she was so important, and if he screwed this up—

You can't *screw up, Jack,* a voice whispered in the distance. *She loves you, and you love her. It's meant to be.*

Meant to be. That was a hell of a notion. That his coming to Bethlehem, ripping off everyone, abandoning Ryan, leaving, returning the money, getting caught, and coming back again . . . all of that was *meant* to happen, just to get him and Leanne to where they were right now. All of it somehow fated, because *they* were fated.

Maybe it *was* fate, or luck, God, divine intervention. Whatever it was, it was also definitely one other thing.

It was right.

"I don't imagine this is the proposal you've always dreamed of," he said wryly. "I look like hell, I can't hold you, I can't even kiss you properly. But . . . I love you, Leanne, and I want to stay with you forever. Will you marry me?"

Her eyes were teary again even as she smiled at him. "The doctor tells me you have a mild concussion, and it really isn't fair to hold a man to anything he says in that condition, but I warned you last night, didn't I? Once I say yes, you're stuck with a life sentence. No appeals, no pardon or parole."

"So go ahead and say it."

She leaned closer, her lips brushing his. "Yes. Yes, I love you, I want you to stay forever, and I'll marry you."

Her kiss was cautious, her mouth barely touching his, her tongue sliding inside only tentatively, as if she was afraid of hurting him. It was sweet and full of promise, stirring aches that had nothing to do with last night's fall, and damned if he could do anything about them at the moment.

But that was all right. They had the rest of their lives to stir aches and satisfy them, then do it all over again.

A life sentence had never sounded so appealing.

Life had never sounded so appealing.

He was vaguely aware of the door opening, of footsteps coming into the room and a snicker or two, before Leanne finally ended the kiss with a soft sigh. When she stepped back, Ryan, Danny, and Eli came into view, standing just inside the door. Danny, at an age where his mother kissing a man was enough to send him into a fit of giggles, was grinning from ear to ear. Eli looked as if he hadn't expected anything else, and Ryan . . .

Ryan had told him he loved him last night. That alone had been worth breaking half a dozen bones and freezing half to death.

"You look better than the last time I saw you," Eli said.

"Thanks," Cole said dryly even as he frowned. As far as he could recall, the last time Eli had seen him, he'd been all in one piece, getting into the truck for the drive out to the camp. This morning was definitely not an improvement over that.

But lost somewhere among the pain and cold that had almost killed him last night was a faint memory—something about angels and thin air, a vaguely familiar voice. Eli's voice?

Impossible. Eli hadn't been in the forest when he'd fallen. If he had been, he would have called for help. The memory was so elusive because it wasn't a memory, just a trauma-induced hallucination.

Danny came to the bedside, wrapping his fingers around the side rail. "You got a lot of owies."

"Yeah, but I'm okay."

"That's what Ryan said." He bobbed his head with complete faith. "Everything's gonna be okay."

Cole shifted his gaze to Ryan, who'd made it as far as the foot of the bed and now stood, staring down at the covers. Was he embarrassed by his display of emotion the night before? Showing affection to anyone but a woman was something none of the Jacksons excelled at. His brothers did it with punches and insults. *Bubba* was the closest they ever got to an endearment. But crying, hugging, and saying *I love you* just didn't happen in their family.

That was one more way he intended to depart from family tradition, and there was no better time to start than the present.

He lifted his hand a few inches from the bed. "Come here, Ryan."

Dragging his feet, the kid circled around, hesitated, then offered his own hand.

Cole wrapped his fingers loosely around it. "I meant what I said last night."

Ryan's dark eyes widened.

"You thought maybe I forgot?"

He shrugged.

"I didn't. I love you, Ryan, and I'm sorry for everything

I did wrong. If you'll give me the chance, I'll do everything I can to make up for it."

Ryan's mouth worked a time or two before he finally muttered, "Yeah, well, don't let it happen again."

He'd said that the night before, Cole remembered, parroting the final warning Cole had given him months ago after the book-stealing incident. Smiling faintly, he offered the same words the kid had. "I won't." Ryan had made good on his promise. Cole fully intended to make good on his.

For a long time Ryan just looked at him, then he swallowed hard. "I know." Bending, he gave Cole an awkward hug, mumbled, "I love you," then abruptly turned away.

It was a better start than he had any right to hope for.

"Well," Eli said cheerfully. "I just wanted to check in on you. I've got to get back downtown. Those lights aren't going to finish hanging themselves."

As the door swung shut behind him, Danny scooted a chair close to the bed, then climbed up to stand on it. "Hey, Cole, when're you gonna get out of here? 'Cause Ryan won't open his birthday presents 'til you can be there, and I really wanna know what he got." Without waiting for an answer, he plunged ahead. "Hey, Ryan says my mom's gonna be his mom for real and you're gonna be my dad, and him and me's gonna be real brothers, so can I call you that? I never had . . ."

Tuning out Danny's words, Cole looked at Ryan, who was watching him with a hopeful sort of expression he'd never seen before, then at Leanne, who wore the same look. He figured he had it, too, for the first time in thirty years.

The promise of love.

The gift of a family.

And hope for the future.

About the Author

Known for her intensely emotional stories, Marilyn Pappano is the author of nearly fifty books with more than six million copies in print. She has made regular appearances on bestseller lists and has received recognition with numerous awards for her work. Though her husband's Navy career took them across the United States, they now live in Oklahoma, high on a hill that overlooks her home town. They have one son.

THE WESTERN WORLD.

VOL. I.

THE

WESTERN WORLD;

OR,

TRAVELS IN THE UNITED STATES
IN 1846-47:

EXHIBITING THEM IN THEIR LATEST DEVELOPMENT
SOCIAL, POLITICAL, AND INDUSTRIAL;

INCLUDING A CHAPTER ON

CALIFORNIA.

———

WITH A NEW MAP OF THE UNITED STATES,
SHOWING THEIR RECENT TERRITORIAL ACQUISITIONS, AND
A MAP OF CALIFORNIA.

———

BY ALEX. MACKAY, ESQ.

OF THE MIDDLE TEMPLE, BARRISTER AT LAW.

IN THREE VOLUMES.
VOL. I.

SECOND EDITION

NEGRO UNIVERSITIES PRESS
NEW YORK

Originally published in 1849 by Richard Bentley

Second Edition

Reprinted in 1968
by Negro Universities Press
A DIVISION OF GREENWOOD PUBLISHING CORP.
New York

Reprinted from a copy in the collections of
The New York Public Library
Astor, Lenox and Tilden Foundations;

Printed in the United States of America

TO

RICHARD COBDEN, ESQ. M.P.

𝕿𝖍𝖎𝖘 𝖂𝖔𝖗𝖐

IS RESPECTFULLY DEDICATED

BY

THE AUTHOR.

CONTENTS.

INTRODUCTION.

———◆———

It is now some time since a work has appeared professing to give to the English public a general account of the social, political and material condition of the United States. At the same time, so rapid is their development, and so great are the changes which, in every national point of view, they are constantly exhibiting, that the progress made by them each year would almost furnish sufficient material for a new work respecting them.

That which I now venture to offer to the reader is not, as too many such works have been, the result of a hurried visit to the American republic. Most of those who have written upon America have done so after a few months' sojourn in the country; but there is no country in the world less likely to be properly understood on so brief an acquaintance with it. Where populations are dense, and confined within limited areas, national life may be soon studied and appreciated. But when a country is almost continental in its dimensions, and its inhabitants are yet comparatively few, and in most cases separated widely from each other, it takes a much longer time, if not to understand national polity, at least to gain a thorough insight into national habits, pursuits, and peculiarities; in short, into everything which enters into the social life of a people. By travelling a man may thoroughly acquaint himself with the physical aspect of a country; but he must do more than travel over its surface to understand it aright, in that which constitutes its most interesting, its moral, aspect. A people, before they can be fairly portrayed, must be studied, not simply looked at. It is impossible thoroughly to study the Americans during a six months' tour in America. A man who professes to have traversed the Union in that time, must have been almost constantly on the highway, the railway, or the steamer. He has thus been brought in contact with American life but in one of its phases, and for reasons mentioned in the body of the work, is incompetent to form a correct judgment of society in America, in its proper acceptation. Besides, he is constantly viewing it from its least favourable side, a consideration which accounts for the many erroneous delineations of it which have, in some cases unwittingly, been palmed off upon the English public as correct moral portraits of our republican kindred. To comprehend the social life of America, the working of its political institutions, and the bearing of its polity upon its moral development, it is absolutely essential that a man should step aside from the hotel, the railway and the steamer, and live *with* the people, instead of living, as the mere traveller does, *beside* them. This I have done; having spent some years in the country before the journey described in the work was undertaken. During that period I had every opportunity of studying the American character in all its national, and most of its individual manifestations; of acquainting myself with the different phases of society, and with the manners and the domestic habits of the people; and of observing the working of their complicated political machine, from the administration of federal affairs, to the supervision of those of a township—from the election of a President to that of a Pound-keeper. My opportunities of observation I owe almost entirely to the courtesy and unreserve with which I was everywhere received and treated. Whether I have improved them or not the reader must judge for himself. The journey upon which the whole work is made to turn, was commenced in 1846, when I visited America for the second time, residing for several months at Washington, during a very critical period in our international affairs, and enjoying throughout the honour and advantage of a familiar intercourse with most of the chiefs of both Houses of Congress, and with many intimately connected with the executive government. So far as the work touches upon the political development and the material progress of the country, it deals with its subjects down to the latest period; whilst much of that part of it which treats of the social life of the Union, is the result of former observation, confirmed by subsequent inspection. I trust that this will suffice to show that I have had ample opportunity of studying the people whom I endeavour to delineate, and of observing the country which I attempt to describe. If I fail of doing either, it will not be from the want of materials, but from inability to turn them to account.

The great object of the work is more to instruct than to amuse. But as the press is now so prolific in matter claiming the reader's attention, it is essential—especially in the case of one hitherto but little known in the walks of literature—that he should endeavour to amuse in order to instruct. They are but few from whom the public will now accept that which is merely didactic. The judgment must now-a-days be reached, more or less, through the imagination. It is on this account that although my main object is to present the reader with a faithful account of the political system, the social life, and the material progress of the Union, I have thrown the whole into the form of a book of travels, mingling the instructive with that which is light, sketchy, and incidental.

The plan of the work is a simple one. I commence my journey at Boston, and after traversing the sea-board States, passing through those of the South and South-west, ascending the valley of the Mississippi, proceeding along that of the Ohio to Western Pennsylvania, passing thence through Western New York by the valley of the Genesee to the Great Lakes, descending the St. Lawrence by the rapids, and sailing up Lake Champlain, and down the Hudson to New York, make my way once more to Boston, terminating my tour, after having thus made the circuit of the Union, at the point at which it commenced. Had I confined myself simply to what I saw and encountered by the way, such a round, embracing such a variety of scenes, and so many latitudes and longitudes within its circumference, would have provided me with ample material for an interesting descriptive work. But I have not so confined myself, but make the description of my peregrinations through the country subservient to what I conceive to be a higher object than the mere painting of scenery and the relation of incidents by the way. My journey is but the frame in which I have as it were encased the more solid parts of the work. With these I never deal until circumstances either suggest them, or force them upon my attention. I identify each subject with some incident or locality, my connexion with, or sojourn in, which has necessarily brought me in contact with it.

The first four chapters are exclusively of a descriptive character, and so far the work in its plan exhibits no feature to distinguish it from the bulk of books of travels. In chapter IV. I describe the city of New York, but before proceeding further on my way, I take advantage of my stay at the commercial emporium of the continent to give some account, to which chapter V. is devoted, of the commerce and commercial policy of the United States. In this I not only describe the rapid development of American commerce, but also explain at length the relative positions of parties in America in reference to the great economical questions by which the Union is agitated. It will be seen that the locality naturally suggests the subject. The four chapters which follow, comprising my journey to Philadelphia, Baltimore and Washington, are also exclusively devoted to description and incident. Having arrived at Washington, and being then on the Federal stage, the best position from which to survey the Union in connexion with everything that concerns it in its aggregate, I take up general subjects, applicable not to a particular locality, but to the whole Confederacy. In this category, indeed, is that of commerce, but my reasons for dealing with it elsewhere than at Washington are obvious. My first object in treating of homogeneous subjects, is to portray the social life of America, as seen from a point which commands, more or less, a view of it in its aggregate manifestation. Before doing this, however, I devote a chapter to a description of the peculiar social development which Washington presents, the society of the capital itself differing in many of its essential features, for reasons explained, from society in its general and national aspect. Having depicted life at Washington, I take, in the chapter which follows, a general view of American society. That which will next engage the reader's attention is the political aspect of the United States, in describing which the character of the government is carefully considered, its complex machinery explained, and the line separating federal from local jurisdiction traced as broadly as possible. In this part of the work I also examine into the peculiarity of the Federal system as developed in America, the identification of the national system with it, and the strength which this gives to the political fabric—the cost of government in the United States, and the essential difference which exists between the British and American constitutions. After this follows a chapter descriptive of the Federal legislature, not only portraying both Houses in session, but also explaining their respective modes of conducting the public business. The next and concluding chapter of the first volume describes the judiciary system of the United States, in its federal and local capacities. The second volume opens with an account of party, its organization and its evolutions in America, after which follows a description of the artificial means by which the seaboard States and the States on the Mississippi have been bound together in bonds of indissoluble union

by the complete identification of their interests.
I then leave Washington for Virginia; and whilst in
the " Slave breeding State," take up the subject of
Slavery ; treating it both in its political, and in its
social, moral and economical aspects. Two chapters
follow of an exclusively descriptive character; which
bring me, on my way south, to the end of my jour-
neying by railway. It is whilst being jolted over an
American highway, in a lumbering and inconvenient
stage, that I take up the subject of railways in America, in their national light, and à-propos to railways,
also the telegraphic system of the Union. Two chapters of a descriptive nature again follow ; after which,
on reaching the State of Mississippi, while ascending
the Mississippi River, I enter at length into the whole
question of Repudiation. The next step in my progress brings me to St. Louis; and before leaving the
great valley, I take, as it were, a bird's-eye view of
the agriculture and agricultural interest of the United
States. Ascending the Ohio to Pittsburg in Western
Pennsylvania, I find myself in the midst of the mining
districts, which suggests to me the subject of the
minerals and mining interest of the Union. I then
pass through Western New York to Lake Ontario,
and by the Falls of Niagara to Buffalo. Before leaving Buffalo, which is at the western extremity of the
greatest of all the America canals, I take occasion to
glance at the artificial irrigation of the United States ;
in connexion with which I endeavour to explain the

rivalry which exists between Canada and New York, for the carrying trade of the North-west, and how far the Navigation Laws, in their operation upon the St. Lawrence, injuriously affect our own Province, in competing with its rival. My route then leads me through central and northern New York to the St. Lawrence, which I descend to Montreal; passing by the " Thousand Islands," and shooting the rapids on my way. I then ascend Lake Champlain, proceed overland to Saratoga and Albany, and descend the Hudson to West Point, the military academy of the United States; during my brief stay at which I take a rapid glance at the military spirit and the military establishments of America. Proceeding to New York, my next point is New Haven, the seat of the principal university in the Union, and, whilst visiting it, the subject of literature and education in the United States engages my attention. As kindred to, if not connected with that subject, the next chapter treats of religion in America. From New Haven I proceed to Lowell, the infant Manchester of the Union; and from it, as a favourable point of view, present the reader with a *coup-d'œil* of the manufactures and manufacturing interests of America. Then follow two chapters which conclude the work, the one taking a brief survey of American character, and the physical condition of society in America; and the other venturing upon a peep into the future. The reader will thus see that there are few subjects connected with either the national or the individual life of the people left untouched. Not only are the more solid portions of the work thus interspersed with sketchy and amusing matter, but they are prepared so as to popularize, as far as possible, the subjects of which they treat; my great object being, in dealing with the driest topics, not only to inform the judgment, but also to impress upon the imagination.

Having thus explained the nature and extent of the materials for it at my command, the object of the work, and the plan on which it is framed, I shall conclude this Introduction by briefly adverting to the spirit in which it is conceived. It has been too much the fashion of late to cheat the public with caricatures, under the false pretence of providing them with a correct portraiture of America. Where prejudice has not given a false colour to every thing which the tourist has observed, ignorance of the topics dealt with has frequently led him into error in attempting to sketch America life. My object is, divesting myself as far as possible of every thing like prejudice either one way or the other, so to make use of the materials at my command, as to present to the reader a faithful and unbiassed account of that great country which is, after all, the only rival that we have to fear. In so doing, I suppress nothing that seems to me to be really pertinent to my subject, merely because it may clash with an English prejudice, at the same time that I am not deterred from speaking what I conceive to be the truth, through fear of wounding the self-love of the American. But in treating of character, I have been careful throughout the work to distinguish between mere individual peculiarities and national characteristics. The incidents which I describe and the characters which I delineate by the way, must, unless they are particularly adverted to as illustrating some phase of national life, be taken as simple occurrences and personal sketches, having no necessary bearing upon anything beyond themselves. I take care that the intention shall be manifest, whenever they are designed to have a wider signification.

With these remarks upon the materials, object, scope, plan, and spirit of a work, designed as a correct account of a great country, and a faithful portraiture of a great people, I submit it, but not without diffidence, to the candid judgment of the public.

THE WESTERN WORLD;

OR,

TRAVELS IN THE UNITED STATES IN 1846-7.

———◆———

CHAPTER I.

A WINTER PASSAGE OF THE ATLANTIC.

Departure from Liverpool.—First Meal on Board, and its Revelations.
—Re-appearance of Passengers.—Congress of Nations.—Characters
on Board and their different Occupations. — A Specimen of
" Nature's Own."— Amusements.—The Smoking Room. — The
Log.—A Storm.—A Nor'-easter.—A New Impediment.—Arrival
at Halifax.—Question of Peace or War.—Arrival at Boston.

IT was not the brightest of mornings—that of the
4th of January, 1846—when I embarked for the New
World on board the royal mail steamship Hibernia.
The wind was in the west, and came cold and fitful.
The sky, though not wholly overcast, was loaded
with clouds, which came up in majestic procession
before the breeze; now piled one upon the other, in
gorgeous confusion—now broken into fragments,
ragged and straggling. It was not altogether what
might be called a stormy day, but was certainly not
such as a landsman would choose for taking to sea.

The moment of departure was an exciting one.
The captain, trumpet in hand, took his station on the
larboard paddle-box, and every man was ordered to
his post. Almost any species of occupation for the

mind is, at such a moment, a source of relief; and I sought it in watching for the first revolution of the wheels; but so smoothly and noiselessly did the ponderous engines apply themselves to their work, that it was not until I saw the water receding in foam from behind her, that I was aware that the stately ship had started on her voyage. About two hours afterwards the pilot left us. This was like snapping the last tie which bound us to home, and it was not until he waved us adieu that we *felt* our departure. The engines were stopped, to enable him to descend into his little boat, and when they resumed their work, it was not to stop again until they placed the noble ship that bore them safely alongside the quay at Halifax. Night was far advanced ere I went below. The last object ashore, on which my eye rested, was the light on Holyhead, which was then dipping into the channel astern of us. When I got on deck next morning, not a headland was visible on any side. Ireland lay on our right, but the line of our horizon was far above her loftiest peak; behind us was the spacious entrance to the Channel, and before us lay the broad Atlantic, foaming and turbulent.

I do not envy the man who could look, for the first time, on such a scene without emotion. It must be confessed, however, that to enjoy it, particularly on the first day after leaving port, a strong stomach is as essential a requisite as a well-constituted mind. In the former qualification, the majority of my fellow-passengers were deplorably deficient, nor were they long in developing their defects.

When it is tolerably rough, the first meal on board is the great test of the sea-going qualities of those who have the courage to sit down to it. When we first sat down to dinner, we made a snug little party of 107, of which number only two were ladies. The soup was scarcely on the table, when the gentleman on my right grasped his hat convulsively, and with livid visage hurried from the saloon, in which piece of significant pantomime he was soon imitated by several others. Some for a while struggled manfully against the agony; but at the sight of fish, paled and fled; others retained possession of their self-command, until sauces and condiments loomed upon their already half-jaundiced eyes. Despite the tortures which they suffered, it was ludicrous to see the half-fright with which some regarded what was placed before them, and the irresolution with which others set about disposing of what was handed them. Some, who would not have trembled at a shark, quailed before a piece of cod-fish; and others who, if necessary, would have manfully faced a mad bull, whitened at a sweetbread. The sea makes of some men what conscience is said to make of us all. Before the third course was over, scarcely one-third of the company remained at table. A lively sea had made speedy and sad havoc amongst the keenest appetites; and strong brave men were already stretched in dozens on their backs, puling like children.

Of those who braved out the dinner, scarcely one half ventured at tea-time to come to table; whilst next morning, at breakfast, I was one of nine only who sat down to coffee and hot rolls. The rest had disappeared I could not tell whither. And how deserted now the crowded quarter-deck of yesterday! It was scarcely possible to avoid the conviction that we had touched overnight at some port, and landed

most of our passengers. In the course of the afternoon a few stragglers made their appearance, emerging
from the penetralia of the vessel, with sunken
cheek, pallid countenance, wandering eye and uncertain step; some of whom ventured to climb to the
quarter-deck, whilst others looked wistfully, first at
the sky, which seemed reeling overhead, and then at
the water, which was leaping and tumbling around
them, the sight of which soon gave rise to unmistakeable spasms, which made them hurry back again
to their berths.

It was several days afterwards ere the original
company, with a few exceptions, re-assembled at
dinner. Every morning, during the first week, as
one after another was added to the convalescent list,
I encountered new faces on deck, as strange to me as
if their owners had been taken aboard overnight. It
was curious to witness how assiduous they were, as
soon as they regained their legs, in their devotions to
fresh air, shunning the very entrance to the saloon,
and, for some days, drinking weak tea and taking
highly spiced soups in an *al fresco* fashion on deck. No
sooner had all re-appeared of whom there was any hope,
than I found that we had on board the materials for a
very respectable congress of nations. We had Englishmen, Scotchmen, and Irishmen, on the passenger list;
Americans, Canadians and Mexicans, Frenchmen and
Germans, with a brace of Russians, and a solitary
Armenian. We had also a black cook on board. Shem,
Ham, and Japhet, were all represented. It was
pleasant to observe the peaceable demeanour of so
many "natural enemies" to each other. It almost
seemed as if such a thing as national antipathy had
never found even a ˉlurking place in any of their

bosoms. Amongst such an assemblage, it was but natural to look for a great variety of habit and character. But few read; the great majority walked about all day; some played at whist from morning till night, others at backgammon, and others again at chess. There was a young Englishman who passed amongst his fellow-passengers as chess mad. He constantly talked of the game when he was not playing it; was always playing it when he could beat up an antagonist; and dreamt of it, as he assured me, when he was neither talking of nor playing it. It was his boast, on reaching our journey's end, that he had played 157 games during the voyage, at the rate of eight a day. Most people on board ship disclose their peculiarities. One of my fellow-passengers was constantly indulging in the insane hope, that some homeward-bound ship would come alongside and take him back to Liverpool; being utterly unable, up to the last moment of the voyage, to explain to himself what could have induced him to leave England. Another soon became notorious for his unceasing complaints of cold in his ears, the cure for which lay in "another cap," which he had in his trunk, to which it was his declared intention every morning to resort, but which never made its appearance. Such as affected a knowledge of seamanship, were generally found in the neighbourhood of the compass. Some spent most of their time in all but bodily contact with the funnel, courting its warmth, and smoking nearly as much as it did. Some lived on soups, others entirely on vegetables; some ate next to nothing, and others were constantly eating. There was a good deal of wine consumed too, many blaming the "briny particles," which they were sure were

afloat in the air, for their oft-recurring thirst. I
must not overlook one very extraordinary character,
who soon became the lion of the company. He was
a young man from Alabama, about twenty years of
age, and was returning to America after a brief visit
to some of his relations in Scotland. He was one of
the most perfect specimens of "nature's own," that
it was ever my good fortune to witness. He had
escaped wild from the prairies to visit Scotland,
having never before seen any phase of life, but such
as it exhibits on a southern plantation. Nor had his
brief contact with civilized life effected any discernible transformation in his character. He used
to walk the deck with an "Arkansas toothpick" in
his hand, a frightful looking knife, with a pointed
blade seven inches long, with which he occasionally
whittled, then cleaned his nails, and then varied his
amusement by carving his teeth with it. One day he
approached the ladies who were on deck, shut his
knife with a tremendous click, and asked them why
the deck of the steamer was like a pan of new milk?
Being unable to discover any reason for this hypo-
thetical resemblance, he informed them, snorting at
the same time, in tones which would have done no
discredit to a hyena, that it was "because it strengthened our calves;" alluding to the muscular energy
required in order to keep one's feet when the ship is
tumbling about. One evening, after most of the
company had retired to their berths, a couple of
Frenchmen remained sipping wine at one of the
tables in the lower saloon. Our Alabama friend sat
opposite to them and listened to their conversation,
which was carried on in French, of which he understood enough to divine the drift of what they were

saying. They were consoling each other at the time for some imaginary evil by abusing England.

" Sir," said the exasperated Alabamian, after they had finished, to the more loquacious of the two, "why don't you speak English?"

" I can't," said the Frenchman, superciliously, and with a strong accent, "it sticks in my throat."

" It didn't stick in your throats though, at Waterloo, when you cried quarter, did it?" retorted the Alabamian, laughing derisively, until he aroused every sleeper in the ship. The Frenchman's " imperial " bristled with rage, but he deemed it prudent to make no reply, retiring soon afterwards with his companion.

Amongst those most delighted with the retort, was a Cornishman, who remained until nearly all had retired, and treated the fiery southerner to sundry potations of brandy and water. Thus occupied, they sat up till one o'clock, by which time they had exhausted the water, although some brandy still remained. The steward being in bed, an additional supply could only be had by the connivance of some of the watch. The Alabamian volunteered to procure it, the Cornishman handing him a shilling to give the man for his trouble. In a few minutes he returned, having replenished the empty jug, and laughing immoderately, as if he had perpetrated a good joke.

" 'Cute as he thought himself, I've done him slick," said he.

" What!" asked the Cornishman, " haven't you given the man the shilling?"

" No, to be sure," said he, laughing again, " but I showed it to him,"—and he tossed it towards his companion, as if he thought him quite at liberty to put it into his pocket again.

It was, in fact, a Yankee trick. On asking the man for the water, he had, without saying anything, shown him the shilling, the sight of which so quickened the energies of the poor tar, that he soon returned with the *quid pro quo*. No sooner, however, had the Alabamian got the water, than he coolly walked down to the cabin, repudiating his implied contract, and leaving the sailor in a state of stupor at his petty rascality and impudence. The Cornishman laughed at the trick, but obliged him nevertheless to seek the man out and give him his promised reward.

A sea voyage is, generally speaking, monotonous enough. Any incident, however trifling, goes some length to relieve its tedium. A ship in sight is an event which occasions an excitement that would appear ludicrous to people ashore. But on the dreary solitudes of the ocean, you hail such a sight as you would, after long absence, the appearance of a valued friend. It breaks in upon the sense of loneliness, which oppresses the voyager. From the moment of her appearance, until she slowly recedes from you, as the eternal circle of your horizon rises above her, she is an object of intense interest to all. You wonder what and whom she carries, where she has been, and whither she is going, and which of you will first touch the busy world again, from which you are now separated by the heaving billows. It was also a frequent amusement to us to watch the ludicrous gambollings of the porpoises, as they crossed our track in long and regular processions; and when they approached very near, how eagerly would we all crowd to the ship's side, to witness their pantomime in the water! A real whale was too important a

personage to cheapen his visits by their frequency.
But how we watched the monster, when he did
appear! and to what exclamations did he not give
rise from old and young, as he "blew his nose," as
the Alabamian termed blowing a column of water high
into the air. In the absence of other occupation, I
occasionally found amusement in watching the "multitudinous sea," as its restless billows leaped and
foamed around me ; and could sometimes fancy, as
they surged, and rolled, and curled before the blast,
that they were endowed with consciousness, and
nodded to me, as they passed, in token of recognition.

Day after day passed wearily on, each scarcely
marked by any distinctive feature from that which
preceded or followed it. There was little to vary the
routine of our duties or our pastimes. The breakfasts were all alike, as were also the dinners, with the
exception that, towards the end of the voyage, singing
was introduced, at the latter meal, with the dessert,
when there was something awful as well as romantic
in hearing the chorus of a hundred voices added to
the howling of the blast and the splashing of the
waves.

The smoking room was a temporary erection on the
main deck, a little in advance of the saloon, and so
built as to enclose the capstan. There, in bad weather,
the open deck being otherwise preferred, such as
chose to regale themselves with tobacco, assembled
shortly after dinner. It might have accommodated
five and twenty comfortably ; but when it was wet
and stormy, I have seen double that number crammed
into it, when the state of its atmosphere may well be
conceived from the simultaneous exhalation of fifty
cigars. Here the song was again raised, negro melo-

dies and political pasquinades, a great proportion of
the passengers being Americans, being most in favour,
and thus an hour or two were frequently cheerily spent.
The over-crowded enclosure sometimes presented
a very curious spectacle. As we were not always
vouchsafed the luxury of a lamp, but for the light of
the consuming tobacco we should sometimes have been
in total darkness. Familiar voices were heard, when
familiar faces were scarcely discernible — the fitful
ruddy glare of the cigars ever and anon bringing
them momentarily out, with Rembrandt effect, from
the darkness; the whole scene looking as wild and
unnatural as the phantasmagoria of a troubled dream.
And all this in the middle of the Atlantic, with the
stout ship that bore us tumbling about, like a reeling
drunkard, through the darkness; with the heavy wind,
laden with rain, beating against her in angry gusts,
and moaning through her shrunken rigging, and with
sea after sea sent in shivers over her deck, and falling
heavily around us. Yet the jest, the laugh, the song,
and the smoking went on within, apparently with as
much indifference on the part of those present, as if
waving corn fields and smiling meadows had surrounded them.

The turning point of each day, as to interest as
well as to time, was noon, when the observations
were taken. How anxiously did we all await the
moment when the result of the last twenty-four
hours' sailing would be posted up for general inspection in the cabin! Then would arise a series of daily
congratulations or murmurings, according to the result. No passenger can reconcile himself at sea to
anything short of two hundred miles a day; and on
our reckoning, one day, showing a run of only eighty

miles, a state of feeling pervaded the saloon, which, but for the opportune appearance of a good dinner, might have ripened into mutiny. Some, by a process of reasoning, intelligible only to themselves, came to the conclusion, that we might as well have been standing still; some blamed the ship, others the captain; but nobody thought of blaming the weather. There were a few who bitterly inveighed against their own luck; whilst our Yankee friends consoled themselves with predictions of what the American boats would do, should most of them burst in the attempt. But, after all, what weathercocks are men! Next day we had a splendid run—250 miles—and what ship was ever in such favour as the Hibernia then? The wind, which had scarcely veered a point since we left Liverpool, gradually increased, until, at length, on the ninth day out, we were driven about on the wings of a hurricane.

A storm at sea! It is a night witnessed never to be forgotten. The warring of the elements may be imposing upon land, but it is truly terrible at sea. Trees may be torn up by the roots, and stately mansions may be levelled by the blast; but the strong, solid earth is unmoved whilst the hurricane sweeps on in its path. But when the winds and waters meet, how different the result! It is on no impassive surface that the tempest then expends its fury, but on a sensitive element, which reflects its slightest frown, and trembles at its gentlest breath. When one sees the sky serene and peaceful above, and the ocean lying calm as a sleeping child below, it is difficult to realize the extent to which all this beautiful quiescence of nature may be disturbed. But convulsion is bred in the lap of tranquillity. Even in its calmest moods, the Atlantic is never wholly at rest; its surface may be as smooth as glass, but its mighty volume is ever heaving and undulating, as if disturbing forces were at work below. Thus it will sometimes continue for days, glancing in the sunlight like a waving mirror. A change from this state of rest is generally heralded by slight puffs of wind, which here and there darken the surface of the water, as the breath tarnishes the polished steel. As the wind becomes stronger and steadier, the whole scene undergoes a transformation: first the ripple, then the wave, and finally the raging tempest. I have known a few hours suffice to produce this change, obscuring the blue sky with drifting clouds, and lashing the quiet sea into billowy uproar.

About ten in the morning of the ninth day, it was blowing a half gale with us; the sea running very high, and the ship labouring heavily. By noon it had increased to a hurricane; and, as far as the eye could reach, the ocean presented but one mass of drifting foam. Sea and sky seemed literally to commingle; the sky poured down its deluge, and the waves shot up their spray. The aspect of the ocean, at such a time, is scarcely to be depicted. On all hands its surging waters leap in angry tumult around you. As they swell and curl and break, and the white foam rushes down their dark leaden sides, the waves roar and hiss, as do the breakers on the beach; and loaded as the air then is with vapour and rain, an indistinctness is thrown over the whole scene, which adds greatly to its terrors. The good ship stood her trial right well. Now she quivered on the top of a huge wave, from which she plunged, burying her prow deep in the trough, and beating back the resisting water in foam from her stalwart shoulders; she then recovered herself to meet the coming billow, up whose steep sides she would bravely climb, and plunge again to breast another. Thus she laboured for four-and-twenty hours, sometimes standing, as it were, on her prow, and at others lying almost on her beam-ends. Now and then, despite the most cautious steering, the baffled waves would strike her with a force, which made her quiver again from stem to stern; but she generally revenged herself by sending the assailant billows, in clouds of spray, high up amongst the rigging, whence they would descend in drenching showers over her whole length. All this time the engines kept steadily at their work, the tempest impeding, but not wholly interrupting her progress. About noon next day the wind greatly moderated, and by 6 P. M. had fallen below a half gale. The sea rapidly fell, and with this change came a period of inexpressible relief, the crew seeking repose after their exertions, and the very ship seeming to sleep after her heavy travail and fatigue.

As we crossed the eastern edge of the great bank, the sky cleared, and the temperature fell, but there came no change in the direction of the steady adverse wind, which now blew fresh, bearing the sharp frost upon its wings, from the icy coasts of Labrador and Newfoundland. For three days afterwards, it was intensely cold and intensely bright, the ocean glittering under the brilliant sunlight like a mass of moving diamonds. On approaching the coast of Nova Scotia, the temperature moderated, the wind veering round to the north-east. On Sunday morning, the 14th day out, we were within sixty miles of Halifax, and, of course, looked forward to making port that afternoon. But the horizon behind us rapidly thickened and darkened, and a few flakes of snow which eddied in the air gave unmistakeable token that a storm was in our wake. Half an hour afterwards, we were lying to, under bare poles, in the midst of a raging north-easter, which whirled the snow in blinding masses about the ship. There was no alternative left us but to keep her in deep water, which was effected by means of constant soundings, which sometimes showed a depth of forty fathoms, and, at other times, of three hundred—enough to convince us that we were in rather a dangerous neighbourhood. The wind continued to blow with unabated fury, and the snow to fall in undiminished quantities, for fifteen hours, during which it was impossible to see more than half a ship's length a-head. About midnight, there came a change, but only in the shape of a new impediment. The wind suddenly chopped round again to the north-west; the heavy clouds, flying from its icy breath, were speedily rolled away like a curtain; as if by magic, the whole heavens were at once displayed, and the bright stars twinkled cheerily down upon us from a sky of the deepest blue. We immediately resumed our course, but in half an hour's time were compelled once more to lie to. A dense vapour, which rose from the surface of the water like steam from a boiling cauldron, soon became so impervious to the sight, as to prevent us from seeing, even in daylight, beyond twenty yards from the ship's side. In addition to the detention caused us by the snow storm, this second impediment kept us, for thirty-six hours longer, to our soundings. The cold, all this time, was most intense. I once ventured on deck, just as the lead was heaved: and as

the men were drawing in the cord again, I made bold
to take hold of it with my naked hand—it was as if
I had grasped a bar of red-hot iron. The mist which
enveloped us congealed and fell in tiny flakes on the
deck; and this, added to the spray which, whenever
it broke over us, froze as soon as it touched the
ship, soon overlapped deck, paddle-boxes, rigging,
and every prominent object on board, except the hot
funnel, with a thick coating of ice, of which we must
have carried with us nearly a hundred tons into Halifax. On the morning of the sixteenth day, the mist
disappeared, and such as chose to face the cold were
on deck, eagerly looking out for land. I was in the
saloon about ten o'clock, when the cry of land was
shouted overhead. I rushed upon deck, and there,
directly a-head of us, lay the coast of Nova Scotia,
like a stranded iceberg. We hit it about twenty
miles above the entrance to the deep and well-shel-
tered bay of Halifax, long before entering which we
could discern the position of this town, by the thin
cloud of bluish looking smoke, which rose from its
wooden fires. The wharves were crowded, and we
were greeted with cheers on our arrival. Everything
around was such as to remind the Englishman that
he had passed to a new hemisphere. The deep snow,
the wooden wharves and houses, the furs in which the
people were clad, the enormous piles of cordwood upon
the shore, and the merry jingling of the sleigh-bells,
afforded undeniable proof, if such were wanting, that
we were far from home. We went ashore in parties,
and made merry for the evening. Our relations with
the United States, which were then rather critical, I
found to be the chief subject of interest, and the
chief topic of conversation.

"I hope we'll have war," said a young man, a native Nova Scotian, who stood near me at the bar of the principal hotel.

"Why so?" I inquired.

"Won't the prizes come in here if we have?" was the reply, given with an emphasis which showed that the speaker was in earnest and enjoyed the prospect. "'Tis an ill wind that blows nobody good," is a proverb of universal recognition. Let earth and ocean be deluged with blood, let continent be arrayed against continent, and peace and plenty give way to wholesale misery and crime, some would be sure to fatten on the general calamity; and there were few in Halifax who would not have welcomed war, with all its horrors, because it would have brought prizes into their harbour.

When we crossed the Bay of Fundy next day, it was as calm as a summer lake, although there are times when no sea on earth can assume an angrier mood. On the following morning, we had a stiff breeze off the land, which retarded our progress. Towards evening the wind fell, but was succeeded by another fog, which compelled us to lie to again for nearly twelve hours more, in sight of some of the lights which lead into the harbour of Boston. It was ten o'clock next day ere the steamer reached the dock; and glad enough were we all to land, after a tempestuous passage of nineteen days' duration.

CHAPTER II.

THE CAPITAL OF NEW ENGLAND.

COLD was the morning, crisp was the air, and bright was the sky, when we entered the harbour of Boston. There was scarcely a breath of wind stirring, but the waters of the spacious bay that fronts the town were slightly agitated by the uneasy swell which came rolling in from the Atlantic; the force of which was broken by the screen of islands protecting the entrance to the harbour. The sky was without a cloud; and the numerous masses of floating ice with which the deep blue water was speckled, looked like so many ornaments of frosted silver on a basis of steel. Some of the islands are fortified, one very strongly so, its sides being artificially sloped down to the water's edge, so as to remove every impediment to the free range of its guns. Numerous vessels, of all sizes and rigs, floated lazily on the bay, conspicuous amongst which was the frigate Cumberland, which has since played a not unimportant part in the Mexican war.

The deck was covered with a slight sprinkling of snow, which creaked beneath our feet, as we paced rapidly to and fro for warmth. It was an interesting moment, and I kept above notwithstanding the cold. Around me were the spots in which some of the most important episodes in the history of the New World were enacted; localities held classic by every American. Here was first planted the germ of the greatest colonial fabric that ever existed, and here was first struck the blow which revolutionized it into independent nationality. It was here that imperial Britain received her first and her rudest shock, which in its issues, wrested a continent from her grasp. Here first settled the stern and sturdy champions of that religious liberty, which they themselves so grossly outraged as soon as they had the power. I was afloat on the very waters into which was hurled the obnoxious, because taxed, tea, and in the midst of the very echoes which reverberated to the first cry of the revolution. No Englishman can look upon such a scene and escape, even if he would, the memories of the past. Its mementos are every where around him. Here are the memorials of a past race; there floats the emblem of a new power; whilst, side by side with the relics of colonial times, stand the issues and the trophies of independence. There is every thing to connect the past in mournful interest with the present and the future. English names are plentiful around you, and many objects within view have an English look about them. Yet, when the Englishman steps ashore, it is on a foreign, though a friendly land.

As seen from the bay, there is no city in the Union which has a more imposing appearance than Boston.

It seems to envelope, from its apex to its base, a conical hill, which rises from the water with a slight acclivity ; the successive terraces in which it mounts to the summit, being crowned by the spacious dome of the " State House," the seat of the legislature of Massachusetts. In addition to being thus ornamental to the city, this prominent object is highly useful to the mariner, the gilded cone at its top being discernible at sea long before any surrounding object becomes visible. At its base the town appears girdled with a frame-work of masts, sustaining a net-work of rigging. To give life to the scene, steamers are plying constantly to and fro, connecting the city with its different suburbs. That great shapeless mass, just seen a little to the right in the distance, looming up over every thing in its vicinity, is the obelisk erected on Bunker's Hill to commemorate a battle, which if not exactly won by the Americans, was the first irretrievable step taken by them in a long, eventful, and ultimately successful struggle. Hundreds of the " tall chimneys " in our manufacturing districts have quite as imposing an appearance as has Bunker's Hill monument. The small villages which are scattered about in every direction, glistening in the morning sunlight, are so many suburbs of the city, with which it is connected by long wooden bridges, with the exception of the insular suburb of East Boston, where we land, and with which, being separated from the town by a branch of the harbour, the communication is maintained by steam ferry-boats.

Landed at length—and if the reader will accompany me, we will take a stroll together through the town.

It is early, but the custom-house officers are at their posts. They do not look very promising, but we

pass without difficulty or delay; the examination
being more nominal than otherwise. I afterwards
found that civility and courtesy were uniformly extended by the federal officers, both to strangers and
natives landing in the country—a pleasing contrast
to the wanton and unmannerly conduct which is
sometimes pursued in our own ports, particularly in
Liverpool, where custom-house officials too frequently
conduct themselves as if vulgarity and insolence constituted the chief qualifications for office.

Carriages now convey us, baggage and all, to the
ferry-boat; which, in its turn, conveys us, carriages,
baggage and all, in less than five minutes, to the city.
Our first object is to search for an hotel, and refresh
ourselves with a thorough ablution and a comfortable meal on land. Passing the Tremont House,
which is full, we draw up at the United States Hotel,
an enormous pile of red brick, perforated by, I am
afraid to say, how many rows of windows having a
large wing on one side called Texas, and one in process of completion, on the other, to be called Oregon.
The next addition made will, doubtless, be California. We are ushered up a marble staircase into a
spacious hall, the floor of which looks like a gigantic
chequer-board, being composed of alternate squares
of black and white marble, looking exceedingly elegant, but, during this season of the year, being both
very cold and very slippery. We apply for rooms at
the bar, which, in the usual sense of the term, is no
bar, but the counting-house of the establishment, in
which a clerk, elaborately caparisoned, sits enthroned,
at a considerable elevation, before a desk, which in
point of cost and construction would be a piece of
extravagance in the Bank parlour. The walls around

him are literally covered with bells, each having beneath it the number of the room to which it corre-
sponds, and they count by hundreds. My flesh creeps
at the bare contemplation of the possibility of their
being all rung at once.

We dine comfortably in a private room, to gain
which we have to thread countless lobbies, lying at
all conceivable angles to each other. How a warm
meal finds its way such a distance from a fixed
kitchen, is a mystery to us. But notwithstanding
the appalling difficulties obviously in the way,—for it
is brought all the way from Texas to Oregon,—it is
as speedily as it is well served. So, now that we
have dined, for a stroll through the town,—and let us
first inspect its commercial quarter.

Although Boston is almost entirely surrounded by
water, you perceive that the real harbour is not very
extensive. Some of the wharves are built of wood,
others are securely faced with stone, the latter presenting a very substantial appearance. The depth of
the water enables vessels of all sizes, devices, and
rigging, to commingle, as it were, with the houses
and warehouses that line the shore, some of the slips
running short distances into the land, and being
flanked by piles of massive and durable buildings,
exclusively set apart for commercial purposes. Here
is a slip devoted apparently to the exclusive use and
occupation of European packets; large placards, attached to the shrouds, announcing their destinations
and times of sailing. Here we are now in front of
the coasting craft; and an extraordinary medley do
they present. What a variety of rig and build; and
how unfit some of the smaller ones appear for the
dangerous navigation of the American coast! Having

grown a little familiar with them, you can almost tell,
from their appearance, between what points they
trade. That substantial looking schooner which you see
scudding before a gentle land breeze, will be off Cape
Cod to-night, in her intricate and circuitous voyage
to New York. That prim looking brig, with her masts
so tall and tapering, her spars so trim, her rigging so
regular, her sham port-holes so very white, and her
hull of so shiny a black, will, as soon as she clears—
and she is already loaded—be off for the Delaware,
and be moored, in a few days, in front of the Quaker
city. The cluster of less elegant looking craft, which
lie a little beyond her, are, as their placards inform
us, "direct for Charleston," for "Mobile," or for
"New Orleans;" that is to say, as direct as baffling
winds and the gulf stream will admit of. But what
have we here? A whole slip full of small fry, packed
as closely together as herring boats at a fishing station,
and their slender masts standing as thick as bulrushes
in a swamp. There can be no mistake about them,
their rig and rakish contour bespeaking them for the
Chesapeake. They are, in fact, the far-famed Baltimore clippers; and "For Baltimore direct" say most
of them. You may well stare, but that extraordinary naval abortion, which you are now contemplating, is a veritable steamer. True, it seems to be
built of Bristol board; but, in these matters, such is
the taste here. It is for Newport, Rhode Island,
and has to ply along one of the stormiest of coasts.
The huge upper deck, stretched, from end to end, on
such slender posts, looks as if it would flutter before
the slightest breeze, like the canvass spread over a
peripatetic menagerie. It seems, in fact, to be
neither more nor less than a huge compound of

scantlings and white paint, with a touch of black at
some of the seams. Put a match to it, and off goes
the inflammable monster like gun-cotton. Its engines are good as compared with those on the Mississippi, though they would cut but a sorry figure on a
stormy night off the Isle of Man. As the steam
hisses through the escape-pipe, the whole mass tum-
bles like a very jelly. Yet, notwithstanding all this,
you have before you one of the strongest class of
American steamers. You have yet to witness those
constructed for the navigation of the inland waters.
But let me not anticipate your surprise.

Along the wharves there is every appearance of
great activity; and, thickly strewn around you, are
all the insignia of an extensive commerce. Raw
cotton in countless bales; piles of manufactured goods
for the South American and Chinese markets; whole
acres covered with parallel rows of clean white barrels, some of them well-nigh bursting with flour,
others full of salt; hogsheads of sugar, and others of
leaking molasses; stacks of leather, and pyramids of
marble blocks; bags of coffee, chests of tea, and
bulging orange boxes, are discernible on every hand.
By each pile is a clerk, busily noting all that may be
added to, or subtracted from it; dealers, wholesale
and retail, masters and men, consignors and con-
signees, and light and heavy porters, are bustling
about; the apparent confusion being heightened by
the drays, some of which are rattling empty, and
others crawling heavily laden, over the hard granite.

Leaving the water-side, you enter some short
crooked streets of warehouses, almost as dark and
dingy as Tooley-street, or Thames-street. Most of
them are fireproof, and seem to be mailed in iron

shutters. Passing them, we come to the Irish quarter, which, as usual, having no attractions, but the reverse, we may as well retrace our steps a little, and make for the heart of the town.

You are surprised to find, in a country like this, with so much spare land, and so many symmetrical towns built upon it, the streets of one of its finest capitals so straitened and devious. But this is easily accounted for. In the first place the foundations of Boston were laid ere the old irregular system of building had been departed from; and in the next, although there is land enough around it, the precise ground which the city occupies is of rather limited dimensions. It consists of an irregular peninsula, with a very uneven surface, the strip of ground called " the neck," joining it to the main land. This peninsula, to which the city proper is confined, is covered with houses, and the city now relieves itself from the pressure of population by means of the many small towns and villages, which are scattered like so many colonies over the mainland and islands around it.

" A fine town is this Baltimore !" said I, one day, to a new Englander with whom I was conversing in the capital of Maryland; " it is a pity that Boston is not as spacious in its accommodations and as regular in its plan."

" What we want in Boston," said he, " is *territory* to build on. If we were as flush of it as they are here, we would make them sing small in the city way, that's a fact."

It must be confessed, to the credit of the corporation of Boston, that they are doing all in their power to diminish the vocal performances of other communities in this respect, many of the more crowded thoroughfares having recently been both widened and straightened.

As might be expected, as you recede from the water-side, the business of the town assumes more of a retail character. As you advance towards the centre, you come in contact with its different markets and with its banking, civic, and other public establishments. Fanneuil Market is inferior in size, but superior in architecture and internal arrangements, to that of Liverpool. Immediately beyond is the very focus of the retail business of the town. The shops are large, having, in general, a wider frontage than with us. They are gorged with goods, so much so as literally to ooze out at doors and windows; and what a gaudy flaunting show they make! Piled in tempting masses on the hard brick pavement, you are ready to stumble over goods at every step you take, whilst from the upper windows stream whole pieces of flaring calicos and gaudy ribbons; the whole impressing one with the idea that business was making a holiday of it, and had donned, for the occasion, its most showy habiliments. A winding and irregular street now leads us up a rather steep ascent, in climbing which, we find ourselves in front of old Fanneuil Hall. There is no building in America held in such reverence as this. It is held sacred from the Atlantic to the Pacific, from the Lakes to the Gulf, as the " cradle of liberty," and the place in which the tocsin of the revolution was first sounded. It is large, but, in an architectural point of view, unworthy of notice, its historic associations constituting its chief attraction. We now advance up State-street, a fine business street, but neither so spacious nor imposing as Tremont Row into which it leads. Passing the

Tremont House, we emerge upon " the Common," a
large open space, about seventy acres in extent, in
the upper part of the town. For this miniature park
the Bostonians are indebted to the munificence of a
private individual, who devised it to the corporation, on condition of its being left perpetually open
for the health and recreation of the citizens. On a
commanding site on one side of this common, and
overlooking the whole town, the circumjacent suburbs,
and a vast stretch of sea and land beyond, stands the
State House, with its classic colonnade, surmounted by
the dome already alluded to. In the large hall, as
you enter it, is a statue of Washington, from the
chisel of Chantrey, the chief features of the interior
being the two chambers of the legislature. The House
of Representatives is a large square room, capable of
accommodating about 400 persons, scantily ornate,
and looking as cold and comfortless as a country
meeting-house. The Senate Chamber is a smaller
apartment, and somewhat more attractive in its appearance. Its chief ornament, and placed over the
door opposite the speaker's chair, is an old drum,
captured in one of the earlier battles of the Revolution. It is placed there as an incitement to American
youth, and as a terror to all British drummers. It is
not beaten, that I am aware of, in the senate, but it
by no means follows therefrom that hollow sounds
are alien to that body.

In the more immediate vicinity of the Common is
the fashionable quarter of Boston. The terraces,
which line it on either side, consist of spacious mansions built in the main of brick and granite : the
hall doors being approached by granite or marble
steps, and the window-sills and capping being fre-

quently composed of marble. Almost every house is garnished by Venetian blinds outside the windows, the green colour of which contrasts pleasingly with the red brick, sometimes painted of a deeper red, with white pencillings at the joinings, which impart to the whole a light, airy, and elegant appearance. Everything about these comfortable-looking dwellings is scrupulously clean; indeed, generally speaking, the credit of great cleanness is due to Boston as a whole, being admirably situated with respect to drainage, and its opportunities, in this respect, not having been neglected. But having glanced at their town, it is now time to take a passing peep at the Bostonians themselves. Let us then to Washington-street—the Regent-street of Boston—as it is now the hour for promenade. You had better, however, put up your cigar case, for smoking is not allowed in the streets. You may chew until you expectorate yourself away, and may poison your dwelling with smoke to your heart's content, but a whiff in the open air is a luxury not to be enjoyed in Boston under a penalty of five dollars.

This is Washington-street, as varying in width, and as irregular in its architecture, as the Strand. The shops on either side make a goodly display of rich, tempting, and ornamental wares; the pavement is spacious, and covered with pedestrians, who pass on, without looking to the right or to the left, or linger, as their fancy may dictate, by the " Dry Goods Store," the " Hardware Store," the " Book Store," the " Grocery Store," the " Hat Store," or the " Shoe Store,"—for they are all " Stores," without a single *shop* amongst them. Let no Englishman insinuate to any American that he keeps a shop—

that would be a grade too low for a free and enlight-
ened citizen to stoop to.   In all this flitting crowd,
you can scarcely point to a single individual who is
not well dressed.   The Americans cannot afford to
be niggard of broad-cloth, for there is no nation on
earth in which the coat goes so far to make the man.
Fustian (not moral) is little known in America.
Canvass-back ducks they have in abundance, but no
canvass-backed people.   The countenances of those
we pass bespeak a very general diffusion of intelligence, an intellectuality of expression being, as I afterwards discovered, more common to the Bostonians
than to the inhabitants of any other city in the Union.
The ladies form a very fair proportion of the throng.
They are generally of the middle height, well rounded,
of a good carriage, with features as pleasing as their
complexions are florid.   The bracing air of the sea-
board, however, is fatal to many of them, groups of
consumptive patients having annually to fly from
New England into the interior.   They are not shy,
and yet, at the same time, are not bold; discarding
in their promenades the affected prudery with which
they are so generally charged, and acting, as they
pass, as if they saw no reason why a daughter of
Adam should not look upon a son of Eve.

A view of Boston would be incomplete without an
allusion, however brief, to Mount Auburn, its chief
cemetery. Although not situated within the precincts
of the town, a more appropriate spot for the purposes
to which it is consecrated, can scarcely be conceived
than this.   It is very extensive, its surface being
beautifully varied by gentle undulations, the sides of
some of which are already clustered with tombs.
Well-kept walks and avenues are laid out through it in

every direction, skirted in the summer time with the richest foliage, the principal avenues taking their respective names from the trees which predominate on either side. Here and there, too, you come upon a small still pond, fringed with shrubbery, and reposing, as it were, in a state of funereal seclusion. If anything is calculated to deprive death of its terrors, it is thus preparing a sweet resting-place for the dead. How different from our foul, fetid, and over-crowded burying-places in the heart of London, which make the grave hideous to the imagination! But in Boston, as in Paris, they have taken these things under municipal control, not permitting the clergy, as with us, to turn to pecuniary account even the last debt of nature. The great objection to the *coup-d'œil* of Mount Auburn is, that there is too much sameness in its monuments. Many are exceedingly elegant, but there can be traced amongst them a similitude which soon palls upon one. In this respect it falls short of the Parisian cemeteries, but in none other, for, if it has not the artificial adornments, it is certainly not bedaubed with the frippery of Père-la-Chaise.

But the ramble becomes wearisome, and as I have to start soon by train for New York, it is time to return to our hotel.

CHAPTER III.

IN addition to the round-about journey by sea, the city of New York is approached from Boston by three different routes, each of which is a combination of railway and steamboat travelling. The Long Island railway being blocked up by snow, I selected the route by Norwich in preference to that by Stonington, the former curtailing the sea voyage by about thirty miles, a serious consideration, as the navigation of the Sound was then rather perilous, owing to the masses of ice with which it was obstructed.

As there was then only one train a day for the West, and as for the first forty miles two railways were blended into one, the bustle and confusion which occurred at the station before starting are perfectly indescribable. Everybody was getting into the wrong " car," and everybody's luggage into the wrong van. At length, after a hubbub, which would have been more amusing had it been less intense, the long heavy train started at four P. M. for Worcester. As it is my intention, in a future chapter, to present the reader with a general view of railways and railway travelling in America, I shall avoid, at present, all allusion to details connected with them, with the exception of a brief description of the carriage in which I found myself seated, and which was a specimen of a class very common in the United States. It consisted of one great compartment, constructed to accommodate sixty people. It was like a small church upon wheels. At either end was a door leading to a railed platform in the open air; from door to door stretched a narrow aisle, on either side of which was a row of seats, wanting only book-boards to make them look exactly like pews, each being capable of seating two reasonably sized persons. The car was so lofty that the tallest man present could promenade up and down the aisle with his hat on. In winter, two or three seats are removed from one side to make way for a small stove ; and, as I was rather late in taking my place, the only vacant seat I could find was one on the pew adjoining this portable fire-place. My immediate companion was a gentlemanly looking man under forty years of age, a loose drab coat enveloping his person, and a bushy fur cap covering his head. Directly opposite him sat a lady of about sixteen stone weight, who crushed up against the side of the car a gaunt lanky Vermonter, in such a manner as to render me apprehensive that she would occasion involuntary squirts of the tobacco juice which he was industriously distilling from his quid. Her travelling stock consisted of a carpet-bag, almost as plump and bulky as herself, which, as she was bringing herself to a comfortable bearing, she consigned to the safe keeping of the gentleman in the drab coat. The poor man had leisure afterwards to repent of the preference shown him, for having once hoisted it upon his knee, the owner, although she constantly kept her eye fixed upon it, never offered to remove it. He could not put it on the floor, which was moist with expectoration; nor could he put it on the stove, which was already getting red-hot. He had no alternative but to carry it the whole night upon his knee; but then the ladies are used to such attentions in America. I had no reason to complain so long as I was not the man in drab.

Finding, ere long, the heat of the stove rather uncomfortable, I repaired to one of the platforms attached to the car, where, for some time, I enjoyed myself in the open air, smoking a cigar and observing the country through which we passed. It was as level, and, in a scenic point of view, as uninteresting as marine deposits, of which it seems to be a specimen, generally are. The snow, with which it was then covered, gave it a dreary and monotonous aspect. Here and there were some slight undulations, swelling occasionally into small hillocks, crowned with stunted evergreens, the most luxuriant growth of the arid sandy soil. It is well cleared, and in the neighbourhood of Worcester affords considerable pasturage. Every now and then we came up with a neat little village, the houses of which, from their colour, were scarcely distinguishable from the snow; the churches, too, with their trim wooden spires, being painted white to their very weathercocks. If anything were wanting to prove the indomitable spirit of the pilgrim-band who, a little more than two centuries ago, laid the foundation of the Transatlantic empire, it would be found in the very character of the soil on which their first efforts were so successfully expended. Instead of seeking the rich alluvial tracts, which might yield them plenty without the previous penalty of toil, or the luxuriant savannahs of the south, where the gaudy magnolia perfumed the air and the wild vine intertrellised with the honeysuckle, they planted themselves in a high latitude, on a scanty soil, contented to labour, so long as their consciences were left free. Their landing-place was a rock, flanked on one side by the ocean, and on the other by a succession of sandy plains. What could be more cheerless than their prospects? Yet, by unceasing and patient toil, they soon converted their unpromising heritage into a garden, along the surface of which thriving communities sprung up, as if by magic; and, like a germ of indestructible vitality, from which emanates the future giant of the forest, soon expanded into that great social and political system, which, in its colossal strides, threatens ere long to monopolize the continent.

I had not been long engaged in such reflections, when from the next car, the platform of which adjoined that on which I was standing, emerged the " conductor," alias the check-taker — who is, in America, a peripatetic, instead of, as with us, a stationary functionary. Having received my ticket, he was about entering the car which I had just quitted, when he stopped short, and without speaking a word, eyed me for a moment, as if he took a great interest in me. At length, having permitted his quid to change sides in his mouth, he observed, in a tone which brooked not of contradiction, that it was "tarnation cold." To this I readily assented; when, finding me of a communicative disposition, he offered me his tobacco-box, and inquired if I preferred standing where I was to being seated within.

" 'Tis but a poor choice between being frozen and being roasted," I observed.—He looked at me again, as if he questioned my judgment, and then said—

"You're a stranger in these parts, I reckon." I replied that I was; and, to avoid questions, continued, that I had arrived that very day by the "Hibernia," after a very boisterous passage; that I was on my way to New York, whence I intended to proceed further south, and after seeing the country, to return to Europe before the close of the year. All this he received with great apathy, and then intimated that he was merely acting the part of a friend in telling me that I would be safer inside.

" Is there any danger?" inquired I.

" Supposing there was to be an accident," said he, " you wouldn't stand no chance here."

" Do they frequently occur with you?" I demanded somewhat hastily.

" We do sometimes run off the rail, that's all;" said he, without the slightest emotion; and then passed into the car without deigning to know how I received the announcement. There was but a pitiful choice, certainly, between an instantaneous crush to death, and a slow broil by the stove; but preferring the latter, I repaired to my place, and submitted to it until the train reached Worcester. The shades of night had, by this time, deepened around us; and the merry lights which twinkled from the windows, and gleamed upon the snow, told of comfort within, whatever might be the rigour of the season without.

The chief object of interest—a melancholy interest—in Worcester, is the Lunatic Asylum; a State Establishment, large, commodious, admirably regulated, and, alas! but too replete with inmates. So much, however, has already been written and circulated concerning them, that it is unnecessary for me here to dwell upon the nature and regulations of the different establishments to which the crimes and the misfortunes of society in America give rise.

For some minutes it appeared to me as if the Bedlam hard by had been let loose upon the station, or depôt, as it is universally called in America. To give a true picture of the confusion—the rushing to and fro—and the noise, with which all this was accompanied, is impossible. Some pounced upon the refreshment-room, as if they fancied it the up-train, and in danger of an immediate start; others flew about, frantically giving orders, which there was no one to obey; whilst by far the greater number were assuring themselves of the safety of their baggage. This was very necessary, inasmuch as the line here branched off into two; the one proceeding to Albany, and the other to Norwich, *en route* to New York. It is by no means an uncommon thing for a passenger to find, at his journey's end, that his luggage has, from this point, taken an independent course for itself, pursuing the shortest road to the far-west, whilst its owner is on his way south, or *vice versa*. This sometimes arises from the luggage being put into the wrong van, and at others from the vans themselves being put upon the wrong lines. Sometimes the separations are most heart-rending—husbands and wives, parents and children, being sent off in different directions. I found afterwards that this was the case with a lady in the carriage immediately behind that in which I sat. She had been torn both from her husband and her bandbox. She had no concern about the former, as she said he knew how to take care of himself; but her new velvet bonnet, oh !——She consoled herself by abusing the conductor, who bore it meekly for some time, but was at last goaded into telling her that that was not the way in which to treat a gentleman, and that she had no business to get into the wrong train; from which he derived but little satisfaction, as she insisted the whole way, that it was the train that was going wrong.

Detached from the Albany train, we were soon on our way to Norwich, led thither by an asthmatic locomotive, which went wheezing and puffing along at the rate of twelve miles an hour over the slippery rails. Although nearly threescore people were packed closely together, the utmost silence pervaded the car. Every one seemed as if he were brooding over some terrible secret, with which he would burst if he dared. The fat lady was already asleep, her unfortunate neighbour still patiently nursing her carpet-bag. One after another the company dropped into temporary forgetfulness, and before we had been an hour from Worcester two-thirds of them were asleep. The heads of some rested upon their hands, those of others fell upon their shoulders, whilst those of others again dropped upon their chests. A solitary lamp burned at one end of the car, and it was interesting to watch the revelations of character which it afforded, as its sickly light fell upon the faces of the sleepers. Some snored, others whistled through their noses, whilst others again breathed gently as does an infant in its cradle. Some were open-mouthed, others slumbered with knitted brow and compressed lip ; the features of some remained at rest, whilst those of others were occasionally distorted with pain, convulsed with passion, or agitated by some troublesome episode in a dream. Here a countenance bespoke grief, there disappointment; the faces of most, however, being lined with premature anxieties and care. Sometimes, as the train violently oscillated, the different heads would jerk about as if they were being thrown at each other, or were going right out through the windows. Every now and then a sleeper, half choked with his quid, would start up with convulsive cough, clench his teeth on the offending tobacco, and relapse into slumber. After a while the scene became oppressive to me ; I was then the only one awake, and felt, as I glanced at the different faces around me, as if I was taking an unfair advantage of their unconscious owners, and surreptitiously possessing myself of their secrets. Besides, the company of sleepers is a powerful opiate, nor was I long in feeling its influence, which, aided by the hot stifling air within the car, soon numbered me amongst them. I recollect dreaming that I had, through great interest, been appointed to the cookship in chief of the Reform Club ; and that my first business, as the successor of the immortal Soyer, was personally to turn the spit before the largest fire in his well-regulated Pandemonium. I awoke in an agony of perspiration, and found the stove, which was within three feet of me, red-hot. I could bear this species of torture no longer, and, determined to run all risks, immediately sought refuge in the fresh air.

It was a beautiful starlight night, the deep blue of the sky looking almost black in contrast with the

snow which lay thick upon the ground. The train
whisked over the face of the country like a huge over-
ponderous rocket, the wood-fire of the engine throwing up a shower of sparks which spread into a
broad golden wake behind us. On the platform of
the adjoining car I found a fellow-traveller, who, like
myself, had sought refuge from the heat. Our
mutual sympathy for fresh air soon led us into conversation, during which I inquired of him as to the
general character and social position of those who
journeyed along with us.

"Well," said he, "you see, as to position, they
are much of a muchness; but some do one thing,
and some another; some are farmers, who have been
to Bosting to sell shoes—some are merchants from
the west, who have also been to that ere city for
winter stock—some do nothin' that nobody knows on,
but manage to make a gentlemanly livin' on it: and
some are spekelators, who have been to the east to do
a stroke of business; I'm a spekelator myself, but
none of your dubitatious sort; I've lots for sale in
Milwaukie, and Chicago—if you do any thing in
that line, stranger, I'm your man."

Having assured him that I had no intention of
becoming a landed proprietor on Lake Michigan, or
elsewhere, I begged him to explain that portion of
his harangue which connected farmers with dealings
in shoes. I had heard much of the fertility of the
American soil, but was not aware that such articles
ranked amongst its products.

"Why, our people," said he, "can turn their
hand a'most to any thing, from whippin' the universe
to stuffin' a mosquito. These 'ere New England farmers, you see, farm it in the summer time, but their

poor sile givin' them nothin' to do in the winter, they take to it in-doors, and work for months at the last. They sell their shoes in Bosting for home consumption, and to send to Europe, Chainy, and South Ameriky."

I had scarcely received this piece of information, as to the winter occupation of New England farmers, when we suddenly came to a halt, under a sort of shed, which I was informed was the Norwich station. We were still eight miles from Alleyn's Point, where we were to take the steamer, and were soon informed by the conductor that we must stop at Norwich until news of her arrival should reach us. I could not exactly see the advantage of stopping for such a purpose—eight miles from the coast—but was obliged to swallow my disappointment. The truth was, that the Sound was so obstructed with ice, that, for the last two days, no steamer had ventured down from New York; and it was on the mere chance of finding one that night to take us up to town, that we were trundled off from Boston.

As we might be detained till morning, we all scrambled to the nearest hotels to secure sleeping quarters for the night. Alas! not only was every hotel full to overflowing, but there was not, in the whole town, a spare bed to be had for love or money. The passengers by the trains of the two previous days were still close prisoners in Norwich, as were also those who had arrived during the same period to proceed by the Long Island railway. Here, then, were upwards of a thousand persons suddenly added to the population of a small town, creating a demand for pillows and mattresses, for which the supply was anything but adequate.

After a patient but unsuccessful search for a bed, I returned to the hotel nearest the station, where I found most of my fellow-unfortunates in noisy assemblage convened, venting their imprecations against the railway company, whom they held responsible for all the annoyances of the journey. Everybody was sure that everybody had an action at law against the directors; and if everybody had been anybody else but himself, he would have had no hesitation in testing the point.

It was fortunate for us that the hotel was not unprovided with edibles. Whilst supper was being prepared, we were huddled into a small apartment, which did duty as an ante-chamber to a room behind it, fitted up as a bar-room, in which the more noisy of the company had congregated, discussing gin sling and politics, and the prospects more immediately before them. When supper was announced, the race for seats was appalling. Being near the door I was pushed in without any effort of my own, and was amongst the first to be accommodated with a seat. There was plenty enough for the most craving appetites, and sufficient variety to meet any conceivable eccentricity of taste. The bacon and ham were good; but ludicrous in the extreme were the attempts at chop, and the faint imitations of steak. There were several varieties of fish, including oysters, which latter were boiled into a sort of black broth; there were innumerable sweets and sweetmeats, fowl in every mode of preparation, very white bread and very black bread, Indian corn prepared in half-a-dozen different ways, with tea and coffee, beer, and every variety of spirituous liquor. We were all very hungry, and for some minutes forgot our annoyances in appeasing our appetites, the episode winding up by each man paying half a dollar to a sallow looking sentry in yellow shirt-sleeves, who stood at the door to receive it.

Such as were so inclined now disposed of themselves for sleep. The ponderous but very comfortable arm-chairs, which invariably form the chief feature in the garniture of an American tap-room, were immediately appropriated, as were also the chairs and tables in the adjoining rooms. Some laid themselves down upon the floor, with billets of wood for their pillows. I had luckily been able to seize upon a chair, and sat for some time musing upon the strangeness of my position. On my left sat a large burly man, about forty, in the attire of a farmer, and who, like myself, seemed indisposed to slumber. He chewed with unusual vehemence; and my attention was first attracted to him by the unerring certainty with which he expectorated over one of them, into a spittoon, which lay between two sleepers on the floor. He occasionally varied his amusement by directing his filthy distillations against the stove, from the hot side of which they sometimes glanced with the report of a pistol. By and bye we got into conversation, when I discovered that he was from the Granite State, as New Hampshire is called, and that he was on his way to Oregon, *via* New York and Cape Horn, a distance of 15,000 miles, but of which he seemed to make very light. His only trouble was, that he would be too late for the ship, which was to sail on the following day. I observed, that in that case his disappointment must be very great, inasmuch as many weeks must elapse ere a similar opportunity again presented itself to him. He assured me that it would be very trifling, for he had made up his mind, since he had supped, should he miss the ship, to "go west" to "Illinois State." I was astonished at the facility and apparent indifference with which he abandoned the one purpose for the other. But it is this flexibility of character that is at the very foundation of American enterprise. Let your genuine Yankee find one path impracticable, and he turns directly into another, in pursuing which he never permits his energies to be crippled by futile lamentations over past disappointments.

About five in the morning we were once more put in motion by the welcome intelligence that a steamer had arrived, and was in waiting for us at Alleyn's Point. We embarked about seven o'clock some miles above the mouth of the River Thames. The morning was bright and cold, and we had a keen cutting breeze in our faces as we dropped down towards the Sound. We stopped for some minutes to take in passengers at New London, one of the seaport towns of Connecticut, very prettily situated on the right bank of the river, close to its junction with the Sound. On the opposite bank is a tall obelisk, raised to the memory of some Americans, who are said to have been treacherously massacred, during the revolutionary war, by a troop of British soldiers. Whilst looking at this, two men, who were on deck, advanced and stopped within a pace or two of me. The elder, and spokesman of the two, was about forty-five years of age, and was dressed in a long overcoat, which was unbuttoned, and hung very slovenly down to his heels. He stooped, not at the shoulders, but from the stomach; whilst his sallow face was furrowed like a newly ploughed field. His lips were thin to a degree, his mouth being marked but by a sharp short line; and when he

looked at you, it was with nervous and uneasy glances,
furtively shot from beneath a pair of shaggy half-grey
eyebrows. His expression was malignant, his *tout
ensemble* repulsive. I instinctively turned away from
him, but it seems I was not to escape, for, having
brought me, as he thought, within hearing distance,
he muttered *to* his companion, but evidently *at* me—
" Yes, there's a moniment raised to the eternal shame
of the bloody Britishers; but we'll take the change
out of them for that yet, or Colonel Polk's not my
man, by G—d!" I looked at him, mechanically, as
he uttered these words. He stood between me and
his companion, as motionless as a statue, his eye,
which turned neither to the right nor to the left,
apparently fixed on the distant shore of Long Island,
but with ears erect, in evident expectation of some
rejoinder to this flattering harangue. Deeming it
more prudent to make none, I turned away and
paced the deck, which I had the satisfaction of per-
ceiving caused him no little disappointment. He
was one of the few in the seaboard and commercial
States, who had been seized with the Oregon mania;
and so powerfully did the poison operate upon him,
that it was with difficulty he could keep from biting.

On leaving New London, a few minutes sufficed to
bring us to the Sound, the shore of Long Island
being dimly visible to the southward. Its waters were
then smooth and glassy : but, sheltered and land-
locked though it be, the Sound is sometimes the
scene of the most terrific and disastrous tempests.
Our steamer was not one of the floating palaces
which usually ply on these waters; and, being neither more nor less than the ferry-boat connecting
Long Island with the mainland, presented us with

none of the accommodations generally found on this route. A more unshaven looking crew, therefore, than sat down to breakfast, can hardly be imagined. The majority of beards were of thirty-six hours' growth; and it was amusing to witness the degree to which each had taken advantage of its accidental immunity. Some merely peered through the skin, others were wildly luxuriant. Some were light, some dark, some utterly black, some red, some sandy, and some had a smack of blue in them. The ladies, who had come aboard at New London, kept as shy of us as if we had escaped from Worcester.

After breakfast I seated myself by the stove and commenced reading, but had been thus engaged only a few minutes, when I was accosted by a stout short elderly gentleman, dressed in snuff-coloured cloth from head to foot, who made me his confidant so far as to inform me, that we had been very lucky in getting a boat. Having nothing to object to so obvious a proposition, I categorically assented, in the hope of being able to resume my book. But in this I was disappointed, for he was soon joined by a middle-aged man, with a very self-sufficient expression, who asked me—

"Didn't our Prez'dent's message put the old Lion's back up?"

The steamer by which I had arrived being the first that had left Liverpool after the receipt in England of the President's warlike message, the most intense interest was manifested on all hands to know the effect which it had produced in Europe. I, therefore, replied—"Considerably."

"We expected it would rile him a bit—rayther—we did;" added he.

" Didn't it frighten him a leetle ?" asked the gentleman in snuff-colour.

" As an Englishman, I would fain be spared the
humiliating confession," replied I ; " particularly as
the whole will be published in the papers, in the
course of a few hours."

This, as I expected, only made them the more
curious. The first speaker returned to the charge,
urging me to let them know what had taken place,
and advising me, at the same time, that I might consider myself amongst friends; and that the Americans
were not a " crowin' people."

" Well, gentlemen," said I; " if you can sympathise
with a fallen enemy, I have no objection to speak
plainly with you." They shook their heads affirm-
atively, and showed, by drawing closer to, that they
really meant kindly towards, me.

" The publication of the Message," I continued,
" was all that was necessary to shake to its foundation the European settlement of 1815. Prince Met-
ternich immediately dismissed Reis Effendi across
the Balkan. M. Guizot notified Abd-el-Kader that
the triple alliance was at an end; whilst England, in
alarm, threw herself into the hands of Russia, enter
ing into an alliance offensive and defensive with that
power; and, as a guarantee of good faith, giving up
the temporary possession of Tilbury Fort to the
Autocrat, whose troops now garrison the key of the
Thames."

" Is that the way the British Lion took the lash
of ' Young Hickory ?' " asked the first speaker ;
" Well, I swan—"

" He needn't have been scared in such a hurry,
neither," said the gentleman in snuff-colour; " for
maybe we didn't mean it, after all."

"The Lion must have been considerably scared," added I, "thus to seek protection from the Bear."

Both gentlemen hereupon looked at each other, pressed their lips, shook their heads, and unbuttoned their coats, that they might breathe the more freely; and, after regarding me for some time with an air of evident compassion, turned suddenly round, and gr - ciously left me to my own reflections. They were soon the centre of a group of eager listeners, to whom they detailed the important news which they had just heard.

"Well, I declare!" I overheard the snuff-coloured gentleman say, "but we air a greater people than I thought for!"

"I know'd it," said a long Yankee from Maine; "we're born to whip universal nature. The Eurō-peans can't hold a candle to us already, e'en a'most "——

"We have certainly," continued the snuff-coloured gentleman, thoughtfully, "done what Napoleon himself couldn't do. We have introduced foreign troops into England. The mere wag of our President's tongue has garrisoned her greatest fort with Cossacks and Rooshians."

Such of my American fellow-voyagers by the "Hibernia" as overheard the convers tion enjoyed it greatly, as indeed did most of those who were within reach of our voice, who were amused at the gullibility of the two elderly gentlemen.

The truth is, that the more belligerent of the American people imagined that the President's message was sure to set the old world in a flame, and were mortified beyond measure on ascertaining the little impression which it had really produced.

As we approached the city, the Sound gradually

narrowed, and when near Herl Gate, a straitened passage through which the water rushes at some periods of the tide with a velocity which renders its navigation rather hazardous, we became fairly imbedded in ice, which, broken into masses of various sizes, completely covered the surface of the water, and through which it was with extreme difficulty that we made our way. Mass after mass grated along the sides of the boat, and then went—crunch—crunch —under the lusty paddle-wheels, coming up, broken in piecemeal, in our wake. It was long dark ere we reached the city. Light after light first appeared upon our right, then on our left, then before, and finally all around us, as we became gradually environed by the city and its insular suburbs. It was with difficulty we groped our way alongside one of the crowded wharves. The long terraces of shops and warehouses, which skirted the harbour, presented one continuous blaze of light; and from the multitude of figures which flitted rapidly to and fro, it would have been evident, had other tokens been wanting, that we were about to land in a great and bustling city. Eight o'clock was tolling from the nearest steeple as I stepped ashore; and immediately, from spire to spire, on all sides, the hour rang merrily through the keen night air. I jumped into a sleigh, and, in less than an hour's time, was oblivious of all my fatigues in a comfortable room in the second story of the Astor House.

CHAPTER IV.

NEW YORK, ITS SITUATION AND ENVIRONS.

BEFORE proceeding to describe the city itself, it may not be amiss first to give a brief sketch of its situation and environs.

Situated on the Atlantic, New York is completely sheltered from its turbulence by a group of intervening islands, which screen the ocean from its view. Its only water prospect is that afforded to it by the noble bay into which it projects. Nothing can surpass the security of its position, or the safety and practicability of its approaches. It stands, the insulated centre of a spacious and varied panorama; the objects which contribute, by their combination, to render its position exquisitely picturesque, also serving, in a double sense, as a security to it, inasmuch as they protect it from the turbulence of the ocean, and defend it from the attacks of a hostile power.

Thus, in beautifying and enriching its prospect, nature has sacrificed nothing essential to its position as a great maritime town.

The Hudson river, after running a lengthened course, due north and south, expands, about forty miles above its embouchure, into a spacious estuary, designated by the Dutch colonists the Tappan Zee. The western or New Jersey shore of this estuary, after running a considerable distance further to the south than the opposite bank, takes a long sweep to the eastward, terminating in the heights of Neversink, on the Atlantic. The east or New York bank runs parallel with the other, until it abruptly terminates at the Battery, which is the most southerly point of the city. Here the river and Atlantic would immediately unite, but for the intervention of the islands already alluded to, which, from their position, form a spacious bay, into which the estuary merges. This bay is formed partly by the coast of New Jersey on the west; partly by Staten Island, which lies between the city and that portion of the New Jersey coast already described as stretching to the eastward; and partly by the western extremity of Long Island, which is separated from the town by a ferry scarcely so wide as that between Liverpool and Birkenhead. Towards the south-east, and between Long Island and Staten Island, are the Narrows, the principal passage to and from the ocean; but the one island slightly overlapping the other, the Atlantic, which is from fifteen to twenty miles distant, is not seen from the city. New York stands upon a long projecting tongue of land, running southward into the bay, having the estuary of the Hudson, with the opposite coast of New Jersey, on the west; the narrow channel, called

the East River, separating it from Long Island, on
the east; and the spacious expanse of the bay, with
the undulating shore of Staten Island, on the south.
This tongue of land, which is of the average width
of about two miles, is, in reality, an island; a short
narrow strait, called the Harlaem river, uniting the
Hudson with the East River, and thus separating it
from the mainland about thirteen miles above its
most southerly point—the Battery. Independently
of the Harlaem river, which is of little or no advantage in a commercial point of view, the site on which
the city stands is washed on three sides by water,
deep and navigable to the very shore. The bulk of
the city occupies the southern extremity of the
island, where its foundations were first laid, that
being the point nearest to the Atlantic, and the
centre of the bay. It is now densely built from side
to side of the island, that is to say, from the Hudson
to the East River, extending northward for upwards
of three miles, for the greater portion of which distance it is almost as compact as London is between
Cheapside and the Thames, or Glasgow between the
Trongate and the Clyde. The whole island is comprised within the limits of the city, although but one-
fourth of it is yet built upon. It is already planned
and laid out, however, from the Battery to the Harlaem river. That it will cover this whole distance
one day, there can be no doubt. It can only expand
in one direction—northward. The rapidity of its
increase will be afterwards noticed. When the city
covers the island, it will have a coast of twenty-six
miles in length, which may be approached in all parts
to the water's edge by vessels of the largest burden.
Already the port extends around the city for a

distance of six miles. The foreign shipping, or that engaged in the foreign trade, as well as vessels of the largest class which make long voyages coastwise, are almost all accommodated at the quays on the East River side of the town; those which line the Hudson side being generally appropriated to inland and coasting steamers, as well as to other craft engaged in the inland and coasting trade.

The advantages of the commercial position of New York are not to be estimated in view only of the accommodation and safe harbourage which it can afford to every class of shipping. Its situation relatively to a large section of the continent is such as of necessity to constitute it one of the greatest commercial emporiums of America. By the Hudson River and the canal uniting it with Lake Champlain, it can hold a direct intercourse with Canada, and reach the great lakes in the upper country, though by a circuitous route. By the Hudson River and the Erie Canal, it is put in direct communication with the great lakes, and with the boundless and fertile grain-growing region which surrounds them, including Western New York, Canada West, and all of one and the greater portion of six other States of the Union. Once on the lakes, it is easy to descend into the valley of the Mississippi, the valley being connected in more places than one, by means of canals, both with the lakes and the Erie Canal. It has also a route to the Mississippi by the New Jersey and Pennsylvania Canals. With the exception of the great valley itself, the region which is and will continue to be chiefly, if not mainly, dependent upon New York for its supplies, will be, as it now is, the most populous in the Union; and, as will be after-

wards shown, it will yet share greatly with the other
Atlantic cities and New Orleans the trade of the vast
districts which border the Upper Mississippi and its
tributaries. With a harbour spacious, accessible, and
convenient, and fully equal, in every respect, to all
the exigencies, present and future, of so commanding
a commercial position, both as regards foreign and
inland trade, Boston, Philadelphia, and Baltimore,
although in themselves great trading communities,
must ever stand in the relation more of auxiliaries
than of rivals to it as maritime towns.

But to appreciate aright the position of the city,
together with its environs, continental and insular, it
is advisable to seek some commanding point of view,
from which the whole may be observed at a glance.
If the reader will accompany me, I shall lead him to
such a point.

Staten Island, as I have already observed, forms
the southern boundary of the bay, the portion of it
lying between the island and the city being from four
to five miles in width. Its outline, which is bold and
undulating, rises, at some points, to a considerable
elevation; its sheltered and well-wooded slopes, which
are generally deeply immersed in shade, from their
northern exposure, forming, during the fierce heats
of summer, a most refreshing feature in the prospect commanded from the town. Along the shore,
and nestled, as it were, at the feet of the uplands,
you can discern, on looking from the Battery, several
prettily-situated towns and hamlets, which seem almost to dip into the waters of the bay, whilst their
gay white walls present a pleasing contrast to the
dark-green foliage around and overhanging them.
There are isolated villas too, scattered along the

water-side, and embosomed, at different elevations, amid the luxuriant vegetation of the shady slopes which swell upward from the shore. The towns are watering places, to which families from the hot dusty city retreat, that they may enjoy the renovating luxuries of sea bathing; the villas are the country mansions of the wealthier of the citizens, who can afford to withdraw, during the summer season, from the sickening heats of the town. Far up above them all, on the topmost height visible to you, and embosomed amid the majestic remnants of the native forest, is the hospitable mansion of my warm, frank, and generous friend Mr. W——. Thither, therefore, let us hie; I promise you, first, a friendly reception, and, next, a magnificent prospect.

As it was summer when I first visited the spot, the reader must suppose that it is summer when he accompanies me.

We proceed by the Staten Island ferry-boat, which starts from Whitehall, near the Battery. Our landing place on the island is New Brighton, about six miles from town, and whither a sail of about half-an-hour will convey us. It is evening, and the steamboat is crowded with passengers, most of those on board being merchants and traders on their way home for the night. They are either standing or walking about in groups, on the promenade-deck and between decks, and talking eagerly upon matters connected with business or politics. Here and there, beneath the seats, you can see numbers of covered baskets, generally filled with such luxuries of the season as can be most readily procured in town. Some whole families have been in town for the day, and are now returning, in the cool of the evening, to their refreshing retreats, amid the trees, or by the water-side. Several children are gambolling upon deck, dressed in the coolest attire, and their whole bodies protected from the sun by broad straw hats, the rims of which sway up and down, like the wings of a large bird, with every movement which they make. Their youthful but languid-looking mothers are carefully watching them all the while, and snatch them nervously back, whenever, in their waywardness, they approach too near the slender cord taffrail, which is all that intervenes between them and the water. There is a fine fresh breeze on the bay, of which several outward-bound ships are taking advantage, to make a good offing for the night. Steamers are in sight, crossing and re-crossing all the ferries, whilst yachts and tiny craft of all kinds are skipping merrily over the lively waters. We land on a strong wooden pier, flanked by some straggling houses, mostly built of wood, and painted white as snow. We get into a hackney coach, which slowly jolts us up a steep and rugged ascent, whence we diverge into a pleasant winding road, cut but recently through the forest. Pursuing this for a short distance, a spacious and well-kept lawn, after the true English model, suddenly bursts upon us, at the top of which is our haven for the night. But, before we enter, let me draw your attention to that glorious sunset, lighting up the western heavens, as if by a mighty conflagration, and throwing a broad pathway of vermilion across the tremulous bay.

The house is large, and somewhat fantastic in its architecture, but otherwise well suited, in all respects, to the tranquil retreat in the midst of which it stands. The hall door is open to enable it to inhale the cool evening breeze. The hall itself is spacious, and so fashioned as to remind one of the description of a Roman villa. We are led by a servant to one of the many doors which open from it, and hear the ivory balls rattling as we approach. Mr. W—— is already at home, and in the billiard-room with some friends who have accompanied him from the city. Here he is, young and sprightly, his countenance beaming with intelligence and good humour. Let me introduce you.

As it is now too late to look at the prospect, we dine, and afterwards pass à most pleasant evening, our kind host being abundantly successful in his endeavours to entertain us, whilst his charming young wife and stately mother-in-law impart grace and vivacity to our circle. But, as we have to be up betimes in the morning, we separate with an early good-night.

Early morning, and here we are, after a refreshing sleep, in the observatory on the top of the house. The prospect below and around us is gorgeous beyond all that the imagination can conceive, and both the tongue and the pen fail in attempting to describe it.

On looking around, you find yourself on a commanding elevation, in the centre of a vast and varied panorama. But to comprehend the prospect in its magnificent aggregate, it is necessary that you should observe it in detail.

To the eastward, then, which we may select as a starting point, you have the broad and buoyant Atlantic, rolling in towards the land before a fresh sea-breeze. The sun has just risen above the restless horizon, and its oblique rays are tinging the wave tops with a golden lustre. Scores of vessels are in sight, some near enough to enable you to distinguish their rig, and others far distant, looking like so many specks upon the horizon. The approach to the bay is flanked far out to sea, on the south, by Sandyhook and the heights of Neversink in New Jersey; and on the north, by the wavy coast of Long Island, which comes sweeping in almost to your feet. Far down that coast you can distinguish, against the dark-green background, a cluster of white houses, on the windows of which the sunlight now glistens, as if it were reflected from so many topazes. This is Rock-away, a favourite watering-place, situated in the bight of a semicircular bay, which opens direct upon the Atlantic. Withdrawing your gaze from the distance, your eye rests, amongst the objects which seem to be more immediately beneath your feet, upon the channel called the Narrows, forming the main entrance to the harbour, and consisting of a narrow strait, between the confronting shores of Long Island and Staten Island. It is a few miles in length, whilst its prac-ticable channel for shipping is, at some points, very narrow. At the point at which the two islands ap-proach nearest to each other, you perceive it flanked by two strong forts, each mounting several tiers of guns, and so close to each other that either could apparently play with effect into the other. They might serve as a good defence against a sailing fleet, but their efficiency against a steam squadron, with line-of-battle ships in tow, would be very doubtful. On both sides of the strait you see villas and farm houses, with their white sides glittering in the morning sun-light, and the water in the channel now glowing beneath them like a tremulous mass of gold. Such is

the great gateway to New York from the " highway of
nations." As already seen, the city can also be approached by the Sound, which separates the northern
coast of Long Island from the State of Connecticut ;
as it also can by Raritan Bay, between Staten Island
and the main land to the south of it, and the long,
narrow, and devious channel known as Staten Island
Sound. All these approaches are fortified. From
the height, at which you now survey the Narrows,
the main entrance to the habour seems to lie at your
feet. You can look down upon the very decks of
the vessels that are now scudding gaily in before the
east wind, which, however, is becoming fainter and
fainter, as the sun mounts towards the zenith. What
huge floating object is that just opening the point
on which one of the forts is situated ? It is soon
evident that she is a steamer advancing at a rapid
pace towards the city. Her outline seems familiar
to me, and her dimensions suggest that she is a Transatlantic vessel. A look through the glass satisfies me
that she is the " Great Western," once the favourite
both of Europe and America. It is an exciting
moment for the passengers, all of whom appear to be
upon deck, some fondly recognising familiar objects,
and others gazing, for the first time, upon the landscapes of the New World. You can distinguish
these two classes of passengers by their looks and
gestures. Captain Matthews, one of the most affable, vigilant, and trustworthy sailors that ever commanded a ship, is on the look-out with the pilot, on
the larboard paddle-box.

But let us now, carrying the eye across a portion of Long Island, turn a little to the left, and
almost due north, we have the city and its principal

suburb, Brooklyn, before us. They lie about six
miles off; but in the clear crisp morning air, and
seen over the gleaming waters of the bay, they scarcely
seem to be half that distance. That small island
lying between us and the city is Governor's Island,
on which there is a circular fort of massive brickwork,
which, from the proximity of the island to the town,
almost merges, when viewed from this spot, into the
huge red mass of buildings behind it. This fort
seems much more capable of doing mischief than of
rendering any very great service to the town. Viewed
from this point, New York and Brooklyn stand out
in bold relief from every other feature in the scene.
The channel of the East River, separating the city
from its Long Island suburb, is so narrow and winding, that, seen from this distance, they appear to blend
into one, and indeed, but for the forest of masts and
rigging, which line for miles the eastern side of the
city, and which now seem to mingle with the houses,
you would not be aware that there was a strait between
them. The whole picture is striking in the extreme.
In the immediate foreground you have the wooded
slopes of Staten Island, darting precipitately down
from your very feet to the water's edge; next comes
the wide expanse of the noble bay, beyond which
rises in mid-distance, a huge mass of ruddy brickwork, which the eye can easily resolve into all the
outlines of a great city; whilst far beyond, and forming an appropriate back-ground to the whole, are the
uplands of Westchester, fading, to the eastward,
into the dim and distant coast of Connecticut. From
the dense mass of human habitations before you, rise
innumerable spires and cupolas, from the small,
white, trim, wooden steeple in the suburb, to the

beautiful and stately spire which towers, for some
hundreds of feet, over Trinity church. On the spot
on which your eye now rests, four hundred thousand
human beings are already awake and astir, as is
evident from the thin pale smoke which begins to
sully, but in that direction only, the clear blue sky.
Hark! the shrill tone of a bell comes ringing up to
us over the tree tops. A few minutes more, and the
first ferry-boat for the day leaves the island for
the city. On she speeds gallantly, lashing the
water into foam behind her; crowds of passengers
pacing her decks, most of whom have already breakfasted, and are ready for business. You perceive, too,
against the mass of houses in the city, columns of
white steam, shot up suddenly here and there from
escape pipes, their hissing sound by and by stealing
faintly to your ear across the waters of the bay.
These are from the boats plying upon the other
ferries, and from ocean and inland steamers preparing
for departure, north, east, and south. You have
scarcely noticed all this, when from the New Jersey
shore of the Hudson comes the shrill whistle of the
locomotive, indicating that the communication is
about to open for the day between New York and
Philadelphia. That is no echo to it, which immediately follows it from Long Island, on the opposite
flank of the city; for, if you listen, you can hear the
rapid panting of the engine as it drags the heavily laden
train over one of the lines of communication between
the city and New England. New York is now
beginning fairly to pour forth its daily life, and craft
of all kinds are emerging from beneath its shadow,
amongst which it is not difficult to distinguish the
adventurous and fast-sailing pilot-boat, making, almost

in the wind's eye, towards the Narrows, for the Atlantic.

It is when you direct your gaze a little to the left of the city that you become fully aware, in addition to its maritime superiority, of the excellence of its position, as regards inland trade. The view in that direction stretches far up the estuary of the Hudson, the broad highway to the far west, and is terminated by a faint line of blue hills, known as the highlands of the Hudson, and through which it forces its way, by a narrow and romantic channel, to the Tappan Zee. It is on this magnificent basin that the western side of the city reposes. On its eastern side, the trade of the East is concentrated ; on the other, the traffic of the West is poured. It thus immediately connects the foreign world with the vast and far interior. For a great *entrepôt* of trade, then, there is, perhaps, but one other position which excels it, and that will be afterwards considered. The produce of the world is accessible to it from the ocean ; whilst its facilities, natural and artificial, for communication with the interior, enable it to distribute that produce through a thousand different channels, at the same time that it is the point on which the productions of the interior are mainly accumulated for shipment.

Turning still to the left, you have, on the opposite side of the estuary, the undulating landscapes of New Jersey, with the pretty rural retreat of Hoboken in the foreground. About due west, is Jersey city, in reality another suburb of New York, and being the starting point for Philadelphia and the South. On the low projecting point on which it stands, it forms, with its modest and solitary spire, a not uninteresting feature in the scene. Almost in a line between you

and it, is another small island, crested with a fort.
The ferry-boats are now plying every ten minutes
between the two shores. A little to the south, and
far in the interior, is the city of Newark, in the same
State—a large and handsome town, but looking from
this distance like a cluster of white objects accidentally dropped upon the hill-side. On looking more
closely, you will observe that it stands not far from
the head of a large, shallow bay. Between us and
this bay is a cluster of beautifully wooded slopes,
separated from us by Staten Island Sound.

Carrying your sweep of vision still further to the
south, an extensive inland view of New Jersey opens
up to you, the foreground being occupied by the
islands just referred to, and between which and
Staten Island, you can here and there trace the romantic windings of the narrow sound, to which the
latter has given its name. I have approached the
city through this channel from Amboy, on the mainland, when there was not a breath of air to ruffle the
surface of the water, when the bay looked like a huge
mass of quiescent quicksilver, when town, hill, rock,
and wood, seemed afloat upon its surface, and when
all wore that luscious and dreamy look, which characterizes a fancy sketch from fairy-land. Small
villages are scattered in profusion along the course of
the Sound; and the rich greenery, in which the
islands are enveloped, is speckled, here and there,
with sturdy farm houses and inviting rural retreats.

In turning further to the left, till you look due
south, you see where the New Jersey shore takes the
sudden sweep to the eastward, which carries it, back
of Staten Island, to the Atlantic. The country here
is beautifully cultivated and uneven, and its outline

is marked by a succession of graceful undulations. This portion of the mainland is almost entirely screened by Staten Island from the city, the broad expanse of Raritan Bay intervening between the island and the mainland. Looking once more to the eastward, and out to seaward, the wavy land line becomes fainter and fainter, until at last, from the hazy heights of Neversink, the eye falls flagging upon the Atlantic, at the point where you commenced your survey.

You have now completed the circuit of a panorama, containing, within a diameter of from 60 to 100 miles, a greater variety and a more elaborate combination of all the elements essential to perfect landscape than, perhaps, any other prospect in the world. You have the ocean rolling almost at your feet,—you have a spacious bay, clustered with islands, and confined by a most irregular coast, two offshoots of which bay, the one a noble estuary, and the other a deep, narrow strait, encircle a great city, which they separate from its suburbs,—you have the mainland rising, near, into rich and swelling uplands, and, in the distance, into faint and hazy elevations; whilst the shore, all around you, is indented with beautiful creeks, and mantled in the richest verdure. The whole, taken together, presents a combination of land and water, hill and dale, town and shipping, island and woodland, corn-field and forest, of objects near and objects remote, of river and ocean, of bay and promontory, which for richness, variety, and imposing beauty, is not elsewhere to be seen.

But let us now descend to breakfast, for which a brief stroll through the grounds will serve as an excellent preparation. The lawn in front of the house commands a view of Raritan Bay and the Atlantic; whilst from the back of it may be seen the bay, New York, Long Island, and a large section of New Jersey. There is not a window in the house but commands a prospect as varied as it is extensive. It is but fit that a spot, around which nature has concentrated so many of her charms, should be decorated in part with the achievements of art; and on entering a smaller lawn, at the west end of the house, and screened from that in front by a belt of trees and shrubbery, we find it ornamented with elegant groups of statuary, and presenting a happy blending of art and nature in their most exquisite features.

After breakfast, we descend to New Brighton, and proceed by ferry-boat to town. Our landing-place is Whitehall, at the point from which we started on the preceding evening. As it is now my purpose to request the reader to accompany me in a short ramble through the town, we shall proceed at once to the Battery, than which a better starting point cannot be selected.

The long tongue of land on which the city is built, converges to a point at its southern extremity. On this point, and, as it were, at the foot of the town, is the Battery. Let not the reader be deceived by the formidable sound of its name, into picturing to himself a lofty mound, crested with massive walls, perforated with embrasures, and bristling with cannon. It derives its name from a purpose to which it was once applied, but to which it is unlikely that it will ever be applied again. It is a low spot of ground, almost level with high-water mark, and defended from the encroachments of the bay by a wall but a few feet in height, on a level with the top of which is a broad gravel walk, having along

its outward side a slight open railing, which is all
that protects the pedestrians, passing to and fro, from
the bay. Back of this walk are plots of grass of
various shapes and sizes, intersected by other walks,
broad and spacious, like that which skirts the water.
These promenades are all lined with magnificent
trees, which form shady avenues in all directions
through the grounds, which are a little more than
half the size of St. James's Park. When the
trees are in full leaf, the Battery has a fine effect
seen from the bay, as a foreground to the town. It
is a place much frequented in summer evenings by
the New Yorkers, who are attracted to it not only
by the shade which its foliage affords them, but also
by the fresh breezes which generally play along its
avenues from the bay. It is not now, however, a
place of fashionable resort, which is, perhaps, chiefly
to be attributed to its distance from the fashionable
quarters of the city, which lie to the northward. A
more delicious retreat can scarcely be imagined than
the Battery on a fine summer evening. In front
lies the vast body of the bay, bounded by the
amphitheatric sweep of the shores of Long Island,
Staten Island, and New Jersey, the whole of which,
with Governor's Island, and the other islets in the
bay, when seen from the level of the water, and
lighted up by the glow of an American sunset, presents a picture which may be more easily conceived
than described. When any exciting occasion calls
the New Yorkers in multitudes into it, the Battery
exhibits a most striking scene. The "Sirius" was the
first vessel that crossed from England to New York
by steam. Her arrival was unexpected; the "Great
Western," which followed her in the course of a few

hours, being that which was looked for as the real
harbinger of a new era in Transatlantic navigation.
As soon as it was rumoured that her smoke was
visible in the direction of the Narrows, the whole
population, as if animated by one impulse, seemed to
pour down to the Battery to welcome her. In an
hour afterwards she was abreast of the East River;
instead of immediately ascending which to dock, she
passed the Battery, turned and dashed past it again,
close to shore, when she was welcomed by the huzzas
of upwards of one hundred thousand people, crowded
upon the terrace walk that skirted the bay. I was
told by a passenger who had been an eye-witness of
the scene from on board, that it was one of the most
magnificent spectacles he had ever beheld.

I myself afterwards witnessed the Battery, when it
was densely crowded with people. It was on a 4th
of July, the great national gala-day of America.
The weather was fine, and every ship in harbour was
decorated with colours. The " North Carolina," a first-
class American ship, was lying in the harbour, where
she had been doing duty, for some time, as a guard
ship. At one o'clock she fired a salute in honour of
the day, and in commemoration of the important
event, of which, a little more than half a century
previously, it had been the witness. Lord Ashbur-
ton was then in America, engaged in negotiations
with Mr. Webster, American Secretary of State,
concerning the north-eastern boundary. The " Warspite" frigate, under the command of Lord John Hay,
which had conveyed his lordship to New York, and
was waiting to carry him back to England, was also
moored in the harbour. I observed that, whilst the
guns of the " North Carolina" were one after another

being discharged, speculation was rife amongst the crowd as to what the "Warspite" would do, which lay at some distance from the shore, with colours flying, but with no signs of life on board. The salute from the "North Carolina" being finished, a pause of a few minutes ensued, but the "Warspite" remained silent.

" The Britisher's out of gunpowder," said, at length, one near me in the crowd.

He had scarcely uttered the words, when a flash momentarily gleamed from the side of the frigate, followed by a wreathing cloud of smoke, and in a few seconds afterwards, the boom of a heavy gun struck with painful force upon the ear, reverberated through all the avenues of the Battery, and shook the windows in the houses which overlooked it. The contrast between the heavy metal which it indicated, and the guns on board the "North Carolina," was too striking not to be noticed by the crowd, who looked at each other with surprise, mingled with some mortification. As the "Warspite" continued to thunder forth her salute, she made popguns of the metal on board the " North Carolina." It is but just, however, to say, that the latter had not then her sailing armament on board; an American ship, in general, when fully equipped, carrying heavier metal than a British one. I could not help observing, however, that many were very causelessly annoyed, by one of their own first-class ships being outdone, on such an occasion, by a second-class ship in the British service. But, as time passes, let us leave the Battery for the town.

Passing through one of the iron gates which separate it from the streets, we find ourselves at once in Broadway. This is the great artery of New York,

commencing at the Battery, and passing in a straight
line along the whole length of the city, as far north
as it is yet built, and lying about midway between
the Hudson and the East River. It is a noble
thoroughfare, and serves at once as the Regent-
street and the Strand of New York; being a promenade for loungers, and a great highway for the
business of the city. Like most strangers, you are
disappointed at its width, which does not exceed that
of the Strand at the Golden Cross, whilst its name suggests very different proportions in this respect. You
have not proceeded many yards, ere you come to a
small open space, called the Bowling-green, there
being now but very little accord between its appearance and its name. Until within a few years, it consisted of a small circular patch of grass, surrounded
by a high iron railing, the tops of the different bars
of which were all broken off; it being with no little
satisfaction that a New Yorker informed you that they
were thrown by the revolutionary cannon against the
adherents of George the Third. It is now converted
into a tank, from the midst of which rises an artificial rock, made to look as natural as possible, and
from which, at different points, water is spouting in
abundance by a multitude of jets. The effect is
exceedingly good. Proceeding northward, Broadway rises from this point by a gentle ascent for
nearly half a mile. The terraces of houses on both
sides are both elegant and lofty, some being built of
red brick, and others of grey granite from Massachusetts. About half way up this ascent, a large
gap appears on the right, left by the devastating fire
of the previous year. A great portion of the area
over which the fire extended is already rebuilt, but

there is still enough left in ruin to indicate the extent of the catastrophe.   A year hence, however,
and the stranger would not know that it had ever
occurred.   The New Yorkers have been warned by
terrible experience of the necessity of constructing
their houses on a more fire-proof plan, nor have the lessons which they have received been altogether without
effect upon them.   They have now a better supply
of water than formerly for the extinction of fire.
During the great fire, which occurred about 1834,
and levelled from 500 to 1,000 houses, in the most
business quarter of the town, the firemen, who were
numerous and well-disciplined, were quite exhausted
by the time the fire was subdued; and had it not
been for the timely arrival of the Philadelphia firemen with their engines, who acted, on the occasion,
the part allotted to the Prussians at Waterloo, the
devouring element might again have made headway
and laid half the city in ashes.   Between the Battery
and the point where the last great fire occurred,
Broadway is generally occupied by private residences.
As you ascend, however, from this point, business
makes itself more and more manifest, until you are
at length as much in the midst of it as if standing in
Cheapside.

You do not proceed very far ere you pass Trinity
Church, of which more by-and-by.   Immediately
beyond this you come to the hotels, the chief of
which are situated in Broadway.   This one on the
left is the Franklin House; and that over the
way, and a little further up, is the Howard House,
an enormous establishment, generally the favourite of
Canadian travellers.   About one or two hundred yards
further on, is St. Paul's Church, on the left, with its

dark sombre portico, and its graceful spire. There is a burial-ground behind it, in which many of the revolutionary heroes are interred. By the time you reach this point you perceive that Broadway occupies the highest ground on the island, from the manner in which the streets incline, which lead from it, on either side, to the water. Those leading off on the left, towards the Hudson, are, generally speaking, straight and continuous to the water, not only the river, but the opposite shore of New Jersey, being visible, as you look along many of them. The streets leading, on the right, towards the East River, and into the chief seat of business in the town, are both narrow and crooked, the view along them being bounded, not by flood and field, but by piles of intervening brickwork. The descent of the land on either side from Broadway admirably adapts the site of the city to the purposes of sewerage.

Immediately on passing St. Paul's Church, you abut upon the Park, a triangular space, covered with grass, and ornamented with groups of trees. Its apex is towards you, as you approach it from the Battery, Broadway continuing its straight course along its left or western side, whilst another thoroughfare strikes off at an acute angle to the right, which after proceeding for some distance, merges into another great street, called the Bowery, which runs parallel to Broadway, and which has been aptly called by Mr. Buckingham the Holborn of New York. The Park, which is about the size of Kennington-common, is, as an open space, of the utmost value to New York. The island being narrow, the ground near its southern point was too valuable to be laid out into public pleasure-grounds.

The consequence is that, with the exception of
St. John's-square, a small open space about the size
of Burton-crescent, between it and the Hudson, the
Park is the only open ground within the more densely
built portion of the city.   In the newer parts of the
city to the northward, more attention is being paid to
public health and recreation; Washington-square,
which leads off Broadway to the left, and Union-
square, which will yet form part of its line, being
equal, and, indeed, the latter superior in size, to any
of our London squares.

Immediately on entering the Park you have the
Astor House on your left, on the line of Broadway.
To get a proper view of this enormous granite pile, you
must cross to the opposite side of the open space in
front of it.   Its chief elevation is on Broadway, its
two sides forming parts of two parallel streets, leading from the main thoroughfare towards the Hudson.
The basement story is low, and is occupied by a
series of superb shops, the whole of the upper portion of the building, which is on a gigantic and pala-
tial scale, being appropriated to the purposes of an
hotel.   A broad flight of granite steps leads to an
enormous recess in the wall, flanked by huge pillars,
and surmounted by a pediment, at the bottom of
which recess is the main entrance, approached by
another flight of steps.   Once within this, a double
flight of marble steps leads to an enormous hall, with
a tesselated marble pavement : this hall is surrounded
by sitting-rooms, and off one end of it is the great
dining-room, a noble saloon, in which hundreds of
guests daily sit down at the *table d'hôte*. The building
is a quadrangle, enclosing an inner court, with a fountain in the midst of it.   The number of bedrooms is

immense, and so complete is this mammoth establishment in all its parts, that it has its own printing
press to strike off its daily bills of fare. It seems, in
fact, to be a great self-subsisting establishment, doing
all but growing and grinding the corn, and feeding and
slaughtering the meat consumed by it. Nowhere in
the world is the hotel system carried to such an extent as it is in America. Travellers almost invariably
frequent the hotels, whilst many families, particularly
young couples beginning life, board and lodge in them.
Indeed, with the exception of Washington, where
every second house is a boarding-house, it is difficult
to find private lodgings in any of the American towns.
There are some in the greater cities, but one must
be positively directed to them to find them out.
There are many establishments too, of a private
character, where several families lodge together. The
influence of this, and of the habit of permanently
boarding at hotels, upon society, will be more fully
and more appropriately considered hereafter.

Immediately beyond the Astor House is the American Hotel, small in comparison with the monster
beside it, but not inferior to it in comfort. There
are many others in Broadway, but those already mentioned are the principal ones.

On the other side of the Park, and directly opposite
the Astor House, is the Park Theatre, the chief and the
most fashionable temple of the drama in New York.
The city is well supplied with theatres. Next in importance to the Park, is the Bowery Theatre, named,
like the other, from its locality. They are generally
well attended, but derive their chief support from
strangers visiting the town, either for business or
recreation.

A little beyond the Park Theatre is a building of a heavy and sombre cast, which, despite its unpromising exterior, has cut not a little figure in the world. It is Tammany Hall, the chosen rendezvous of the Loco Foco party, and where are, every now and then, celebrated the orgies of Democracy. It has recently been the scene of several tempestuous Irish demonstrations against this country. A little further up, but within the area of the Park, and about two-thirds of the way from its apex to its base, occupying a line parallel with the latter, stands the City Hall, a large and elegant building, approached by a noble flight of steps, and surmounted by a lofty cupola. Its front elevation, which is of white marble, looks down Broadway, in the direction of the Battery. —Ten chances to one that you are disturbed this very night by the bell in the cupola. From that elevation a view of the whole city is commanded, and day and night a man watches by the bell, with a hammer in his hand with which to strike it the moment he perceives any indication of fire. The number of strokes which he gives at a time indicates the ward whence the alarm proceeds. The city is divided into seventeen wards, and this arrangement directs the firemen at once to the spot where their exertions may be necessary. Numerous as are the fires in New York, the alarms of fire are still more so. I have been disturbed by as many as four in a night, and although they are sometimes groundless, they too often prove real. In front of the City Hall, and within the railings of the Park, is the finest fountain in New York. It gushes in all directions from the centre of the reservoir into which it falls, and with such force as to resolve itself into a large cloud of spray. The very music of it in summer falls with cooling influence upon the ear. It is supplied from the Croton, forty miles off, by means which will by-and-by be alluded to.

From the Park, where it seems to attain a considerable elevation, Broadway gradually descends for some distance, after which it gently rises again, until it reaches the northern suburbs. It presents less of a business appearance beyond the Park, than between it and the Battery, and you soon come to continuous terraces of private dwellings. The streets too, leading immediately from it, on either side, are here chiefly occupied by private houses. At its lowest level, after passing the Park, a street, which goes off from it on the right, leads to the district of the town unfavourably known as the Five Points. Though by no means attractive to the stranger, it is worth a visit. Both in its moral and physical aspect, it is not unlike the Seven Dials—the latter, however, being the better, and more regularly built of the two. The site which it occupies is low, and was once marshy ground, the cheapness of the land inducing the poorer class of the inhabitants to build upon it. It is now in the very heart of the city; and a filthier or more squalid place it would not be easy to conceive. It is the common haunt of the Irish, and the negro population of the city. But let us emerge again into Broadway.

Pursuing our way towards the north, there is but little now to attract us on either side. We soon cross Canal-street, the Farringdon-street of New York, both being very wide, crossing the line of the main thoroughfares, and covering a huge sewer, which runs below. The private dwellings with which the part of Broadway beyond this is lined, are

large and roomy, although not high, and are almost
all approached by a flight of steps. As we get near
the top, Washington-square is to the left, one side
of which is occupied by the University, a noble institution, accommodated in a noble marble pile. About
three miles from the Battery, Broadway first deviates
from the straight line, diverging a little to the left,
as Regent-street does into Portland-place; and
situated in the angle corresponding to that occupied
by All Souls' church, at the head of Regent-street,
is a new and beautiful Episcopal church, of the
purest gothic, and decidedly one of the most elegant
ecclesiastical structures in New York. A little beyond the turn, Broadway merges into Union-square,
from the other side of which it again pursues its
northerly course.

We have now fairly reached the northern limits of
the town, which already extends for three miles up
the island. From nine to ten miles of it are, therefore, as yet unbuilt upon, but its whole area, up to
the Harlaem River, is even now laid out into what is
destined to be future streets, avenues, and squares.
When the city covers the whole, Broadway, which
extends from one end of the island to the other, will
be thirteen miles long. The plan of the future city,
between Union-square and the Harlaem River, is one
of great regularity, streets running parallel to each
other, at regular distances, and extending across the
island from the Hudson to the East River, and being
intersected by other long streets, designated avenues,
which will run in the direction of its length, and
parallel to Broadway. The streets and avenues are
all numbered, instead of being named in the ordinary
way. This may not be very poetic, but it will be

vastly convenient. Washington, or Franklin-street may be anywhere in the town, the name not designating the position; but no one can be at a loss, understanding the plan of this part of the city, to know where Fifteenth-street, or Fourth-avenue is. These streets and avenues, of course, as yet, exist only on the chart; but those which are nearest to the town, are already partly built upon, some of the finest private residences being erected on either side of them.

It is not with the mere desire of following in the footsteps of others that, before quitting this part of the town, I direct attention to the number of vagrant pigs with which it is infested. I have seen specimens of this interesting race in Greenwich-street, not far from the Battery, but it is only when you gain the upper and more fashionable portions of the city, that they appear to be quite at home, and to have their acknowledged place on the public promenades. Sights to which we are daily accustomed, make but little impression upon us, and therefore it is that New Yorkers frequently express an honest surprise at the discoveries, in this respect, made by strangers. They are made simply because the attention of the latter is alive to everything; and if a New Yorker himself will only walk up Broadway, as far as Union-square, fancying himself, for the time being, a stranger, and ready to recognise every object that presents itself, he will find not only that noble thoroughfare, but also many of the streets that on either side lead into it, infested, to a considerable extent, by the quadrupeds in question. If, from its position, climate, or any other circumstance, it were a necessity imposed upon New York to submit to this infliction, it could not be too delicately alluded

to by a stranger; but when it is simply the result of a
defect in the police regulations of the town, it becomes
a legitimate subject of criticism.   There is surely
no constitutional maxim or principle enunciated in
the declaration of independence, that requires that
the freedom of the city should be indiscriminately
conferred upon these animals.   It would demand the
infusion of but very little stringency into its police
regulations, to rid a fine town of so unfavorable a
feature in a *tout ensemble*, which is otherwise both
attractive and imposing.   Every one must admit the
incongruity of the sight, such as I have seen, of a
huge filthy hog devouring a putrid cabbage on a
marble door-step.

But let us now hasten to the port of New York,
which we shall first explore on the East River side.
Turning off Broadway to the east, and descending one
of the streets which lead from it in that direction, we
very soon cross the broad thoroughfare of the Bowery,
after which we plunge into a labyrinth of narrow
and crooked streets, which by-and-by lead us to the
port.   The East River which, as already intimated,
is but a prolongation of the Sound, uniting it with
the estuary of the Hudson, and dividing Long Island
from New York, is deep but narrow, and flows, at
some states of the tide, with a heavy current.   Some
distance up from the point at which we have struck
it, is Blackwell's Island, forming one side of it, above
which the Sound gradually expands, and turns off in
a north-easterly direction, its surface being here
dotted with several other islands, by the narrow and
crooked channels between which vessels may find
their way to its more open portions, and through
them to the Atlantic.   At Williamsburg, on the

opposite side of the East River, and which you can
just discern some distance up, is a building yard
belonging to the general government. It is, in fact,
the Deptford of New York, but with this essential
difference, that it does not encroach upon the accommodation required in the port for the commercial
marine. The wharves which flank the city on the
east side, are numerous, and mostly built of wood,
projecting for a short distance into the water, not to
attain a sufficiency of depth, but to form between
them slips for the better accommodation of the craft
that are moored to them. Where we are now, high
up the port, these are of the smaller kind, consisting
chiefly of sloops and schooners engaged in the coasting
trade with Connecticut and the rest of New England,
and of numerous barges and lighters, which are almost
exclusively applied to purposes more immediately
connected with the port itself. Between the wharves
and the houses is a broad thoroughfare, as in Liverpool; and which, indeed, makes the circuit of the
town on its water sides. As we proceed southwards,
towards the Battery, it is some time ere the scene on
the left undergoes any change, the wharves being
all alike, and the craft in the slips differing but little
in character from each other. On the right, or land
side, we soon come to a succession of lime and coal
yards, in the latter of which, side by side with the
bituminous coal from Liverpool and Nova Scotia, may
be seen the anthracite product of the rich mines of
Pennsylvania. We next come to some private build-
ing-yards, with boats, barges, sloops, schooners, and
steamers, in different stages of completion. In the
one lowest down of all, you perceive a steamer on the
stocks, no further advanced than the setting of her

timbers. She is designed to ply upon the Hudson, and, from her proportions, reminds one less of that which she is destined to become, than of the skeleton of a huge boa constrictor.

Proceeding a little further in our course, we reach a point at which the island, trending suddenly to the south-west, gradually tapers off towards the Battery. The coast of Long Island here projects almost as much as that of Manhattan Island, as that on which New York is situated is sometimes called, recedes; so that the width of the East River lying between them undergoes but little change by that which is effected in the direction of the land. It is on gaining this point, that the port of New York exhibits itself in its most imposing aspect; the city side of the East River being covered, as far as the eye can reach, with a forest of masts and rigging, as dense and tangled in appearance as a cedar swamp, whilst numerous vessels of all sizes and rigs are also to be seen, on the opposite side, moored to the wharves of Brooklyn. The broad and deep canal, intervening between the two lines of vessels, is alive with every species of floating craft, from the tiny wherry to the enormous steamer, ploughing her way to the New England coast. Take your stand here, on the end of one of the wharves, and you will confess that, looking down towards the open bay beyond, as a marine view, that of New York, from this point, can scarcely be excelled.

Following the line of the quays, we soon come to the slip in which the Atlantic steamers lie. It is now occupied by the " Great Western," just arrived, as it was occupied by the " President," before she started on her last and ill-fated voyage.

The town on our right has now entirely divested itself of everything like a suburban appearance. Massive piles of warehouses line the shores ; their long and gloomy terraces, upon the one hand, confronting the shipping which becomes denser and more dense as we descend on the other. The broad quays are covered with the produce of every clime ; and barrels, sacks, boxes, hampers, bales, and hogsheads, are piled in continuous ridges along the streets, which lead at right angles from the port, and which are widened where they abut upon it, for the better accommodation of business. In these great reservoirs of trade, you see crowds gathered, here and there, around one who, standing on a pile of sacks or boxes, as the case may be, is vociferating so as to be heard over all the din, and gesticulating like one rehearsing his part in a melodrama. He is an auctioneer, and is busily disposing of the surrounding goods by auction. Some of those about him, who are cautiously outbidding each other, are merchants and traders from the neighbouring counties; some are from the interior of the State, and others, again, from the far west. Occasionally, too, you may discern a knot of manufacturers eagerly inspecting the bursting bales of cotton which lie around them. Some of these are from New England, others from Western New York, but the greater number are the agents of manufacturers in England.

As you proceed further and further towards the Battery, the town encroaches more and more upon the quays, leaving the whole way, however, a practicable thoroughfare between it and the shipping. The scene is now, in point of activity and animation, beyond all description, whilst the noise is incessant

and deafening : the sailors' busy song, and the dray-
men's impatient ejaculation, being occasionally distinguishable amid the confused and incessant din.
The vessels, which here occupy the slips, are almost
all either coasters of the larger class, or engaged in
the foreign trade. Passing under their bowsprits,
which overhang the footway, and threaten the walls
of the warehouses with invasion, you pass, one after
another, the slips, where lie the different lines of
packets which ply between New York and Liverpool,
London, and Havre, and the splendid vessels belonging to which formed the chief medium of communication between Europe and America, before the
adventurous Cunard started his unrivalled line of
steamers. The extensive connexion which New York
has formed with the domestic and foreign world, may
be appreciated by observing the different announce-
ments with which the quays are lined, intimating the
different destinations of the vessels that are moored to
them. In addition to those bound for the different
ports on the coast, are scores for England, dozens for
France, many for the Baltic, several for Spain and the
Mediterranean, a few for the coast of Africa, numbers for India, China, and South America, and some
for the South Seas, Valparaiso, and the Sandwich
Islands. Here they are, about to spread over the face
of the earth, to collapse again on the same spot ere
many months be past, to pour upon the city the produce of every clime.

We have now Brooklyn directly opposite to us on
the left, already alluded to as, in reality, a suburb of
New York ; if a city, with a corporation and municipal
government of its own, and a population of 60,000
souls, in other words, as large as Aberdeen or Dundee,

can brook the appellation. It has an imposing site
on the western extremity of Long Island, and so
near New York that you can reach it in two or three
minutes by any of the numerous ferries established
between them. The ground which it occupies slopes
gently up from the East River, making the great bulk
of the town visible from the New York side; whilst
in its immediate vicinity, and on a commanding position, may be seen terraces of stately and elegant
residences, chiefly inhabited by the merchants of New
York. It transacts a good deal of business, being the
chief source of supply for Long Island, which extends
for 150 miles behind it. The western terminus of
the Long Island railway, a link in one of the chains
of communication between New York and Boston,
is here. As on the New York side, the East River is
deep to the shore, and the slips, which resemble in all
respects those of the greater city, are well lined with
vessels from ports near at hand and afar off.

The densest part of New York now intervenes on
our right, between us and Broadway. It is a perfect
maze of narrow crooked streets, intersecting each
other at all angles, and running towards almost every
point of the compass. This was the spot where the
foundations of the city were first laid by the Dutch,
whose notions of convenience in the laying out of a
town,—and indeed the same may be said of those of
most other people at the same period,—were none of the
brightest. The streets were left to develop themselves
in the most irregular manner, the obstructive position
of a single house frequently diverting a thoroughfare
several degrees from the straight and convenient line,
which, otherwise, it seemed disposed to follow.
Pearl-street, the chief seat of the wholesale trade of

New York, was to me both a puzzle and an amusement. I seemed to meet it everywhere, in threading
my way through this mazy quarter of the town, and
never, for the life of me, could follow it for many
yards at a time. It always manages to elude one in
spite of oneself, turning off from him when he least
expects it, and crossing his path again when he has
begun to think it irrecoverable. The cause of all this
is explainable by its origin, which, it appears, was
neither more nor less than a cow-path amongst the
fields, which, in the days of the Dutch, lay behind the
small settlement on the water-side. It is nearly a
mile in length, commencing in the neighbourhood of
Whitehall, and deflecting from the line of Broadway
for some distance to the eastward, after which it pursues a circuitous course amongst the narrow lanes and
streets, which characterize this portion of the town,
until it loses itself in a labyrinth of them, not far
from the Park. It is a continuous thoroughfare,
although, from the way in which it here and there
turns up in portions across the stranger's path, it
seems as if it had been broken into fragments, which
had been severed from each other and had not yet
reunited.

We soon arrive at the spot where Wall-street, the
Lombard-street of New York, like so many others
leading down from Broadway, abuts upon the quays.
It is, in some respects, one of the most interesting
sights in New York; and as, by prolonging our walk
to the Battery, we shall encounter little that is different from that already seen, the quays extending
almost to the Battery, we cannot do better than here
diverge and take a stroll up Wall-street. For a few
hundred yards it is as broad and spacious as Oxford-

street, being flanked on either side with lofty warehouses, whilst piles of goods of all descriptions so
block up the thoroughfare and side walks, that it is
with difficulty you can thread your way through
them. Beyond this, and where it intersects the first
street running parallel to the quays, it contracts at
once to less than half its width in the part immediately in contact with the harbour; and it is between
this and Broadway, which you can yet scarcely see,
from a slight curve in the street, that it exhibits itself
in its more peculiar character. It is most irregular
in its architecture, almost every building being self-
contained, and of a different style, plan, size, and
shape, from everything around it. It presents a
greater number of stone fronts, some of them exceedingly chaste and elegant, than any other street in
town, brick being the chief material employed in New
York architecture. This building, with the pilastered
front, is a bank; that beyond is an insurance office;
beyond that again is a commission merchant's on a
large scale; whilst opposite you have a broker's
establishment, followed by two or three insurance
offices, which are again confronted by as many banks
across the way: and so on alternating in this way,
until you reach the Custom-house, about three-fourths
of the way up to Broadway. The buildings are all
provided with basement stories, which are generally
occupied by money-changers and solicitors. That
noble-looking pile, constructed of greyish blue granite,
on the left, which we are now approaching, is the
Merchants' Exchange, erected since the great fire
in 1834, when the old Exchange, with the Custom-
house, fell a prey to the flames. A finer effect can
scarcely be imagined than that produced by its deeply

recessed portico, formed by a lofty and massive colonnade, the shaft of each Ionic column, which is fluted, being composed of one immense block of granite. A low dome surmounts the edifice, which, however, is but partially seen, for the Exchange is so closely hemmed in on all sides by buildings, that no good view can be obtained of it from a distance. The great room is circular and of immense diameter, and is decorated with lofty Corinthian columns of marble, at least designed to be Corinthian, for they yet want their capitals. It belongs to a company of merchants, and is occupied along the basement and at the back, chiefly by brokers. It is made fire-proof, so as to avert from it the catastrophe which befel its predecessor.

A little further up, and on our right, we come to another edifice of a very different character, being entirely constructed of white marble in the form of a Greek temple of the Doric order. This is the property of the United States, being the Custom-house for the port of New York. It has two fronts, one on Wall-street, and the other on a street behind, running parallel to it, each of which is covered by a portico of eight massive columns. The Wall-street front is approached by a lofty flight of marble steps, as broad as the building is wide. The only side which it presents is deeply pilastered, something like the Cornhill side of our own Royal Exchange. It is fire-proof throughout, the roof being covered with immense slabs of marble. Its general effect is not so imposing as that of the Exchange. The ambitious marble looks less durable and massive than the sober granite; but, taking it all in all, it is decidedly one of the finest edifices in the country.

Between the Custom-house and Broadway, which is now full in view, Wall-street partakes more of the character of Fore, than of Lombard-street with us. Let us, therefore, turn sharp to the left, and make for the Battery, by plunging through the labyrinth of streets intervening between it and us. But before doing so, you ask, what noble florid Gothic pile is that, built of a dark brownish stone, which rises in such stately yet buoyant proportions at the head of Wall-street, and closes up the vista in that direction. It is Trinity Church, which we passed more than two hours ago in our walk up Broadway. It is but a few years since it was finished, and it stands in an enclosed space, on the western side of Broadway, directly opposite the junction of Wall-street with it. It is large, but it is not by its dimensions that it strikes you, particularly if you are conversant with the scale on which ecclesiastical edifices have been raised elsewhere. You are charmed by the purity and elegance of its design, as well as by the exquisite finish, which marks its every detail, without detracting, in the slightest degree, from its general effect. It is strongly and massively built, but the fret-work, with which it is profusely ornamented, gives it a light and airy appearance. Its beautiful spire, which rises for nearly 300 feet, resembles, in the elastic spring which it seems to take from the ground, that which surmounts the Hall of the General Assembly in Edinburgh. The spire of the latter, however, which is one of the most exquisite things extant of its kind, is much plainer and simpler, though not the less effective on that account, than that which forms the chief ornament of the former. There is not a city on earth to which Trinity Church would not be a first-rate architectural accession.

There is something both curious and suggestive in its position. It stands, pointing loftily to heaven, on a spot visible from almost every point of that street where Mammon is most eagerly and unaffectedly worshipped in America. There it is, as if perpetually to remind the busy throng that they cannot serve two masters. It actually seems as if, in a moment of serious reflection, they had, for their future benefit, taken that important text, and executed it in stone. But it is in vain that you look for any indication of the serious mood now. Amid the throng hurrying past you in all directions, and not one of whom seems to notice or care for you, you can discern the merchant's thoughtful look, the calculating brow of the money-changer, the quick keen glance of the attorney, the nervous twitching countenance of the speculator, and the quite business-like expression of the official; whilst, from the stream of faces gliding by you, you can pick out some flushed with hope, others clouded with apprehension, some radiant with satisfaction, and others shrivelled with disappointment; indicating, respectively, speculations that are promising or looking adverse, that have succeeded or failed. Trinity Church still looks down upon them, but how few of that anxious, quick-moving crowd seem conscious of its solemn rebuke! Take it and Wall-street together, and what a moral antithesis do they present! But its effect, if it ever had any, has been evanescent; and it is only when Sunday comes, and the places of business are closed, and when the bells toll and the churches are open, and multitudes flock into them in their holiday attire, that the world is—perhaps—for a time, forgotten.

Leaving Wall-street, the chosen seat of every species of speculation, and the great financial artery

of New York, we soon find ourselves, in threading
our way to the Battery, amongst the more sober-
looking, but not less imposing avenues of commerce.
Here we are in Pearl-street, which, before we proceed many hundred yards, we have lost again, for,
when we were least on our guard, it suddenly turned
a corner, and left us. We shall soon come to it
again, as the miner comes to a vein, which, for a
time, he has lost. Both it and the adjacent streets,
which are exceedingly narrow and very lofty, in the
latter respect more resembling Paris than London,
are replete with every variety of merchandise which
the overcrowded warehouses are disgorging upon the
streets. The narrow side-walk is covered with goods,
whilst the thoroughfare, not many feet wide, is also
here and there invaded, so that at some points you
have no alternative, in proceeding, but to jump over
boxes, or squeeze yourself, as you best can, between
bales of merchandize. Nor is mid-air even free from
the intrusion ; for from many lofty cranes, heavy and
bulky masses are dangling, in a way that makes you
feel nervous for your head, whilst you are busy taking
care of your feet. By-and-by we pass the Pearl-
street hotel, an immense brick pile, seven stories
high. It occupies the heart of what is yet known as
the burnt district, that which was devastated by the
conflagration of 1834. It is long since all traces of
this frightful visitation have vanished; the only
memorial of it now remaining being the evident new-
ness of the streets, which present on all hands long
narrow vistas of lofty red brick walls, perforated
with innumerable windows, which are generally protected at night by massive iron shutters.

Emerging at length from the wholesale quarter,

we cross Whitehall into the Battery, and passing the
lower end of Broadway, where we commenced our
walk, and of Greenwich-street, a long, wide, and
noble street running parallel to it, find ourselves,
after a few steps further, upon the broad and spacious
quays which line the estuary of the Hudson. The
whole aspect of things is somewhat changed from
that presented on the side of the city which we have
just left. Instead of the forest of masts which rises
over the East River, the Hudson, for some distance up
from the Battery, presents us chiefly with a crowd of
funnels. Instead of sailing vessels, we have steamers
in the slips, as varied in their classes and sizes as they
are in their destinations. Here are ferry-boats for
Jersey city and Hoboken opposite, their unsonorous
bells constantly belching forth harsh metallic sounds.
There, again, are larger boats for Alleyn's Point and
Stonington, rival lines to Boston, the remainder of
the way to which, from both points, is accomplished
by railway. Beyond is a splendid steam packet,
one of a line plying to Newport, Rhode Island, now
the most fashionable watering-places in America.
Still further up, we come upon steamers for Amboy,
about forty miles distant, on the New Jersey coast.
It is approached by Staten Island Sound, and is the
starting point for one of the railways to Philadelphia.
But here we are abreast of the slip in which lie the
Hudson River boats, plying between New York and
Albany, the latter being the political capital of the
State, and lying 160 miles up the river. One of these
boats, the "Knickerbocker," is getting up her steam
for a start. Her dimensions are enormous. In length
she exceeds by several feet the once-celebrated ocean
steamer, the "British Queen." Regarding merely her

upper works, her breadth is proportionate, her expanded wings and buoyant promenade decks giving
her great apparent width of beam. But look at her
hull, which is like a huge canoe, with a sharp wedge-
like prow, which seems as if it would split up any
floating log with which it might come in contact.
Her wheels, too, are of great breadth and gigantic
diameter, her paddle-boxes rising on either side like
the vertical sections of a huge dome, and almost competing in height with the ponderous funnels behind
them. She will be at Albany in nine hours after starting, including stoppages, for she can make her twenty
miles an hour in ascending, and has made twenty-two
in descending, the river. Where she is not as black as
jet, she is as white as snow, and as the steam hisses
from her escape pipe, she is as tremulous all over as
is the tiger before taking his spring. Still further up
we have a whole cluster of unshapely but business-
looking tugs, some of them intended to tow sea-going
vessels from and to the Atlantic, and others to tow
sloops, barges, and schooners up and down the river.
You can see two of the latter now making their way
from above into port, each with a group of barges
behind it, laden with barrels of flour and salt, which
found their way to Albany from the county of Onon-
daga and the far west by the Erie canal. The upper
slips are occupied by barges and the smaller sailing
craft engaged in the river trade. But we need not
further prolong our walk in this direction. The
quays, all the way up, are spacious and convenient,
as on the other side, and lined with rows of lofty and
massive warehouses. Towards the upper end of the
city, on the Hudson side, factories of the kind more
particularly appertaining to a port, make their appear-

ance, whose tall chimneys give some variety to this view of the town. Although business on this side does not wear that intensified aspect which it assumes along the East River, the Hudson side of the city is nevertheless replete with all the indications of great commercial activity. And when the trade of the city so increases, that it cannot find adequate accommodation on the East River side, the lower portion of the port on the Hudson will exhibit a similar scene to that now daily witnessed on the other flank of the town.

The citizen of London has ample opportunity of discovering that there are, within the precincts of the city, as many wonders beneath as above the surface of the ground. Whenever a shaft is sunk, no matter for what purpose, into Piccadilly, the Strand, Cheapside, or any of the other great thoroughfares, the number of parallel iron pipes, together with the apparatus for sewerage disclosed, is really astonishing. New York has also its underground marvels. Until recently, the iron tubes which permeated its site were solely those which were required to distribute over the city the gas with which it is lighted. New York was then but ill-supplied with water, the springs within it being but few, and the water procured from them being of an inferior description. It was to remedy this great defect that the city, some years ago, undertook one of the most gigantic works to be found either in the new world or in the old. That which it wanted was a copious supply of excellent water. On examination it was found, that the nearest source whence that could be procured, in the greatest abundance and attended with the greatest facilities for conducting it to the city, was about forty miles distant from it. About that distance above the town, the Croton River, a pure limpid stream, empties itself into the Hudson. The most feasible scheme that presented itself was to divert a portion of its current to New York. To accomplish this, a stupendous aqueduct has been constructed through the solid rock, over the valley, and across stream after stream, to the city. It commences five miles above the junction of the Croton with the Hudson, and I cannot do better than here transcribe the description of it given in the United States Gazetteer.

"The dam is 250 feet long, seventy wide at bottom and seven at top, and forty feet high, built of stone and cement. It elevates the water, so as to form a pond five miles long, covering 400 acres, and containing 500,000,000 gallons of water. From this dam, the aqueduct is continued, in some parts, by tunnelling through solid rocks, and crossing valleys by embankments, and brooks by ducts, to the Harlaem River, a distance of 33 miles. It is built of stone, brick, and cement, arched over and under, six feet nine inches wide at bottom, seven feet five inches at the top of the side walls, and eight feet five inches high. It has a descent of thirteen inches and a quarter per mile, and will discharge 60,000,000 gallons in twenty-four hours. It will cross the Harlaem River on a magnificent stone bridge, 1,450 feet long, with fourteen piers, eight of eighty feet span, and seven of fifty feet span, and 114 feet from tide-water to the top. This bridge will cost more than 900,000 dollars. It is in progress, and, for the present, the water is brought across the river in an iron pipe, laid as an inverted syphon. The receiving reservoir is at 86th Street, 38 miles from the Croton dam, covering thirty-five acres, and containing 150,000,000 of gallons. The water is thence conveyed to the distributing reservoir on Murray's hill, 40th Street, in iron pipes. This covers four acres, and is built of stone and cement, forty-three feet high above the street, and contains 20,000,000 of gallons. Thence the water is distributed over the city in iron pipes, laid so deep underground as to be secure from frost. The whole cost of the work will be about 12,000,000 of dollars. No city in the world is now more plentifully supplied with pure and wholesome water than the city of New York, and the supply would be abundant, if the population were five times its present number."

The Croton not only now circulates, as its life-blood, through the city, but is its chief protection from the ravages of fire.

New York is, after New Orleans, the gayest city in the United States. Public amusements are much in vogue ; and the town is amply supplied with the means of pandering to the taste for them. Balls, concerts, ballets, and operas, are well attended throughout the year; and the fashionable quarters, during winter, present one continued scene of gaiety. With all this, the New Yorkers combine a good deal of literary taste ; and if the theatre is nightly well frequented, so also is the library and the lecture-room. The city has several literary institutions, some originating with associations, and others the result of individual munificence.

As in Paris, a great deal of New York life is spent out of doors. During summer, the oppressive heat drives people into the open air, particularly in the cool of the evening ; and during winter they are tempted out to enjoy the pleasures of sleighing. At the close of a summer afternoon, Broadway, particularly between the Battery and the Park, is crowded with promenaders of both sexes, generally dressed in the newest cuts, and in the most showy manner; for the New Yorkers take their fashions direct from Paris, in which they come much nearer the Parisians than we do. It is impossible to meet with a more finished coxcomb than a Broadway exquisite, or a " Broadway swell," which is the designation attached to him on the spot. Whilst multitudes are promenading to and fro, there are generally groups of strangers, either seated in comfortable arm-chairs, disposed in dozens on the wide pavement, in front of the hotels, or standing upon the steps leading into them, picking their teeth, to indicate to the passers by that they have just risen from a champagne dinner.

New York abounds in churches, many of which, from their graceful proportions and neat façades, add much to the beauty of the town. Notwithstanding its gaiety, it is a great centre of religious action, the May meetings in New York exciting as much interest amongst a portion of the population as our Exeter Hall assemblages do about the same period of the year amongst a part of the population of London. What Baltimore is to the Catholic, New York is to the Episcopal denomination in America—its chief focus and stronghold; there being fewer churches in the world more wealthily endowed (not by the State) than the Episcopal Church of New York.

The city is also an important pivot of political action. Its influence is, however, in this respect almost exclusively confined to the State, in one corner of which it is situated. It exercises, for instance, but little influence upon the population of New Jersey, immediately across the Hudson. The ultra-democracy of New York are extremely excitable; but, although political excitement sometimes runs very high, it is seldom that it results in any outrage to either person or property. The great increase recently effected in the number of polling places at elections, has greatly conduced to the preservation of public order.

New York has upwards of thirty banks, whose combined capital exceeds thirty millions of dollars; and from thirty to forty insurance companies, possessing an aggregate capital of more than twelve millions. Its future destiny has been partly foreshadowed in its past progress. The aggregate tonnage of the arrivals in the port of New York, in 1810, amounted to 275,000 tons; in 1840, it had swelled to upwards of 618,000 tons. This is exclusive of steamboats, of which there are nearly a hundred, more or less, connected with the port, and of the smaller craft engaged in the coasting and inland trade. But its rapid growth is more correctly indicated by the increase of its population. In 1800, it contained 60,000 souls; in 1840, its population exceeded 312,000; in 1845, this latter number had risen to 371,000; so that, in the lifetime of a generation, the population had increased more than six-fold! In 1850, it is probable that it will exceed 430,000. When we consider the extent, resources, and capabilities of the immense region which it supplies, and that that region is yet but in the infancy of its progress, it is not easy to set limits to the growth of New York. The Americans are justly very proud of, and its residents passionately

attached to, it. On driving up to the Astor House,
after landing from Boston, a young New Yorker, who
had been in Europe for more than a year, was in
the same sleigh with me. "There goes the old
city!" said he in his enthusiasm, as we entered
Broadway; "I could almost jump out and hug a
lamp-post!"

CHAPTER V.

FROM no other point can the commercial condition
of America be so advantageously surveyed as from
the trading and commercial emporium of the continent. I propose, therefore, before leaving New York,
to compress within the compendious limits of a single
chapter, a succinct account of the commercial progress and policy of the Republic. My object is to
present, at a glance, to the reader, an adequate idea
of the extent to which American enterprise has, in
this respect, been pushed, and the variety of objects
which it embraces in its operations ; and to enable
him thoroughly to appreciate the exact position of
each of the great interests which, as with us, have

constantly struggled for supremacy, and the disputes between which have not even yet been finally adjusted.

The limits to which I have confined myself, will be an ample guarantee that the reader is not about to be overwhelmed by elaborate calculations, or overborne by a repulsive array of statistical tables. My wish is, so far as this humble effort goes, to popularize the subject, by combining interest with instruction, carefully avoiding figures, except when indicative of great results, or absolutely necessary to subserve the purposes of illustration.

It is with no desire to bespeak a surreptitious sympathy, that I here allude to the difficulty of the subject. Fertile and ramified as it is, it were easy to enlarge upon it, as compared with the task of abridging without crippling it. Despairing of complete success, I nevertheless proceed—in the hope of conveying at least some useful instruction—in the first place, to lay before the reader the general results of the application, to its abounding resources, of the diversified activity of America.

It must be borne in mind, that the whole fabric of American commerce is the product of but two centuries of human industry, acting, however, under the influence of extraordinary stimulants. Strictly speaking, its birth should not date beyond the peace of 1783, when the young Republic took it into her own hands, untrammelled by navigation laws or other imperial restrictions. But even tracing its era from the first epoch of western colonization, we find American commerce overtaking and gradually outstripping commercial systems which had flourished for fully two hundred years before its very germ was laid, until it now acknowledges no rival, save in its ancient parent, from whose thrall it broke loose when its freedom of action could no longer be controlled.

In estimating the progress of Transatlantic commerce, it is advisable to go no further back than the period from which commence the most regular, unbroken, and authentic accounts of its operations. In the year 1790, the condition of American commerce was such as may be readily appreciated from the following general statement of its results. The total value of the imports of that year did not exceed 5,000,000l. sterling, the value of the exports being about the same amount. If we descend a period of fifty-five years, its progress may be estimated from a glance at the results of the commercial operations of 1845. In that year the value of the imports exceeded 26,000,000l. ; in other words, they had quintupled in little more than half a century. The value of the exports was but a fraction below the same amount, exhibiting a corresponding increase. This rapid increase may be better illustrated by a glance at what the last quarter of a century has done. The aggregate value of exports for the year ending 30th June, 1821, was a little upwards of 14,000,000l. sterling ; whilst that of the year 1845 was, as already intimated, about 26,000,000l., showing an increase of nearly 100 per cent. The value of the imports of 1821 was also upwards of 14,000,000l., which, as compared with that of the imports of 1845, gives a similar result to that in the case of exports.* There is a feature in the export trade worth alluding to, as

* From official accounts recently published, it appears that the value of the exports and imports for the past year has, in either case, exceeded 32,000,000l. sterling. This shows an increase in both trades of about 23 per cent. in three years. So much for the free-trade tariff of 1846.

exhibiting still more strongly the rapid development of American wealth. Of the whole exports of 1821, nearly one-third consisted of foreign merchandize re-exported; whereas the re-exports of similar merchandize in 1845, scarcely amounted to one-seventh of the aggregate exports of that year. During the former year, only two-thirds of the aggregate exports were of domestic produce; during the latter, more than six-sevenths. This shows that the development of domestic industry has been at a ratio much more rapid than the mere aggregate commercial results would lead one to suppose.

It is unnecessary any further to pursue this branch of the subject, sufficient being laid before the reader to enable him to appreciate the rapid strides at which the commercial advances of America have been made. The objects embraced in the active and enterprising trade of the United States, both foreign and domestic, are as multifarious as may well be conceived. Its great staples, however, consist of cotton, tobacco, flour, sugar, and rice. Very nearly one-half of the aggregate exports of 1845 consisted of raw cotton alone, tobacco coming next in the scale, and then flour. The directions which this commerce has taken, are about as numerous as are the objects which it embraces, and are well indicated by the character of the shipping with which New York is all but begirt. There is not a sea upon earth but carries the enterprising flag of America; not a port, except such as they are absolutely prohibited, with which the Americans have not established a trading intercourse.

Nor is this all. The foreign trade alone is but an imperfect exponent of the progress of American industry. The expansion of that trade does not wholly rest with the Americans themselves : it is regulated by the measure of other people's wants as well as by that of their own. It is only when we look at the internal trade of the United States, which is receiving from the hourly development of their own wants such gigantic accessions, that we become fully aware of the rapidity with which the material interests of that country are unfolding themselves, and of the real extent of that impetuous activity, which is productive of results without parallel in the economic history of the world.

There is no other country which can boast of advantages superior to those of the United States, for the purposes either of foreign commerce, or internal trade. For the one, their geographical position is eminently favourable; for the other, the variety of their productions, and their physical conformation, admirably adapt them. Situated almost midway between its two extremes, they present a double front to the Old World, from one of which they can hold direct communication with Europe, and from the other, a communication, as direct, with Asia. The time, indeed, is not far distant, when Eastern Asia and Western Europe will find themselves most accessible to each other through the continent of America. The United States are thus not only well situated for the purposes of their own trade, but apparently destined to be the common ground on which the two great sections of the Old World will yet meet for the transaction of theirs. This advantage of position plays an important part in the development of the foreign trade of the United States; in further estimating their capacity for which, we cannot overlook the superabundance of their exchangeable commodities. As to their internal trade, Nature herself has thrown every facility in its way. With every variety of soil, climate, and production, America possesses in its vast rivers, estuaries, and lakes, those means of internal intercommunication, the want of which can only be supplied in other countries, even when physical obstacles are not insurmountable, by time, and by enormous outlays. Were the people apathetic, instead of being enterprising to a degree, the advantages which their country enjoys in this respect, would, of themselves, be provocative to industry and interchange. Such energies as the American people possess, acting on such resources, in the midst of such advantages, could be productive of but one result. Happily, too, they avoided a rock on which the bark of their prosperity, if not shattered to pieces, would have been greatly strained. That was not the country for artificial barriers, where nature had levelled almost all physical obstructions to trade.

The internal intercourse of America is as free as are the winds which sweep over its surface, and the waters which irrigate its valleys. The interchange of their commodities, too, is as free as the people are themselves in their personal intercommunication. For municipal purposes, the different States have their fixed known boundaries; but, in an economical light, they have no frontiers. It is when we take all this into account, that their progress appears less a miracle than a necessity. With unflinching energy, unbounded resources, and an unfettered internal trade, is it any wonder that they are so rapidly transforming the whole aspect of the country? How long could the wilderness withstand the persevering assaults of a civilization which brings such appliances to bear? If any one wants an illustration of the advantages of free trade, he has only to look at the internal aspect of American commerce, and at the advances which are being daily made under its auspices by the great Anglo-American Zollverein.

A circumstance which has a great deal to do with the progress of America in this respect, is the essentially commercial spirit of the people. This spirit, though not peculiar to them, is nowhere else so universally, or so unreservedly displayed. There is no class affecting to scorn the avocations of trade—no one compromises his position by being a trader. With every stimulus to exertion, idleness is not, in America, deemed an honourable pursuit. The inducements to occupation are great. A growing community has increasing wants, which will not go unsupplied if it has the means of supplying them. This is the case in the United States; the demand is with them in a state of as constant progression as is the supply. The basis for enterprise expands as the population increases; and if new actors come into the field, there are new objects for them to operate upon. The consequence is, that business never, for any length of time, assumes in America that overdone aspect, which is too often familiar to it in older and less-favoured communities. Besides, it is the rapid road to wealth; and wealth gives great, if not the greatest, consideration in America. The learned professions are not regarded as a whit more honourable, whilst they are but slenderly remunerative. The youth who wants speedily to make a figure, sees the shortest road to the attainment of his wishes through the avenues of business. It is thus that they flock in crowds from the rural districts into the towns, the farmers' sons preferring the yard stick, with its better prospects, to the plough. Some of those who have a more intellectual ambition, become lawyers and politicians; but the great majority get as soon as possible behind a counter, over which they soon jump, to become merchants on their own account. Children, too, very early discover the trading tendencies of a people who want many things, and have plenty of something or other to give in exchange for them. At school their bartering propensities soon manifest themselves, and before they leave it they become traders, both in habit and disposition. The bent of their lives is early taken, and seldom, if ever, lost. What a nation thus disposed can do, is illustrated by what a people thus habituated has done.

We frequently judge of a system from its monuments. American commerce need not shrink from being already tried by this test. Of the lordly cities which it has reared upon the sea-board there is no occasion to speak ; its rapid development is, perhaps, still more visible in the effects which it produces in the interior. Under its fostering influence communities start up, as it were by magic, in the wilderness : the spot which is to-day a desert, may, thirty years hence, be the site of a flourishing town, containing as many thousand souls. These inland towns are being constantly brought to the surface by the commercial fermentation, which never ceases. They arise under no other influence than that of commerce —they come forth at the bidding of no other voice. Crags and fastnesses are not sought in America as sites for towns. The harbour, or the river's bank, or the neighbourhood of the canal, is the place where they arise ; and what commerce does in this respect, no other power, unassisted by it, can do. Washington was designed for a great city; but there being no

commercial demand for it, the fostering care of the
federal government, from which so much was expected, has ludicrously failed in making it so. Imperial power may have reared a capital on the swamps
of the Neva; but it is commerce alone that could call
forth, and sustain, a vast emporium on the sedgy
delta of the Mississippi.

Occasional revulsions seem everywhere to rank
with the necessities of commercial existence. In
America they are not unfrequent, and are sometimes
most calamitous. In no other country is the credit
system carried to such an extent. Favourable as this
may be to enterprise, it sometimes leads to great
abuses. In the transactions of 1836 and 1837, we
have a memorable instance of this. The imports of
these years were enormous, far exceeding the amount
already noticed as constituting the value of those of
1845. The inflation of the currency, and the expansion of the credit system in every department of trade,
were then at their height. Previously to 1825, the
loans of the United States Bank scarcely varied in
their annual amount to the extent of three millions
of dollars. But shortly before the memorable years
in American commerce above alluded to, they had
expanded upwards of 60 per cent. in the brief space
of two years. The swarm of country banks followed
this example, and the train was thus laid for the
explosion which took place. Such was the glut of
merchandize in the hands of the importers, that they
laid aside the ordinary rules of caution in parting
with their stock. The transactions which ensued
were not more detrimental to the credit, than they were
perilous to the commercial morality of the country.
Capital was not felt to be a want—credit was, and did,

everything. Young men forsook their employment, fled to the sea-board, procured stock upon easy terms, returned, and set up for themselves; and the country swarmed with a new race of traders, in possession of no visible means. The consequences were not long in displaying themselves, and the disasters of the period are the best commentary upon the transactions which led to them. This, it is true, was an extraordinary crisis, but some of its accompaniments are permanent features in the American commercial system. Credit is too easily had, particularly by the young and in-experienced, and, consequently, frequently abused. Of the number of young men who set up for them-selves, the proportion who soon afterwards become bankrupt is great. I remember when it was a com-mon saying, that if a man wanted money, he had only to go and get stock, set up business, and fail when it was most expedient. But this evil in the system has a manifest tendency to cure itself.

Having thus glanced at the general features of American trade, it may be as well now briefly to direct the reader's attention to the commercial ques-tion, politically considered, in the United States. With a view to his better understanding the policy of the general government, the motives which have influenced that policy, and the effect which it has had, particularly upon the foreign commerce of the country—it is necessary to bring at once upon the stage the great interests which, almost since the date of its independence, have made a common battle-ground of the tariffs of the Union.

These are four in number—the manufacturing, the commercial, the cotton-growing, and the agricultural interests. In the commercial may be included the shipping interest; whilst with the manufacturers may be classed the sugar-growers, their interests being identical, although their occupations are dissimilar. Between these interests the great object of strife has been for high or low tariffs. Sometimes, in the struggles which have taken place, they have been equally divided; at other times, by adroit manœuvring, the preponderance in numbers has been secured for one side or the other. The commercial legislation of the country indicates the strength of parties in the different contests which took place.

It will be seen at once that the difficulty chiefly lay, as it still lies, between the manufacturers and the cotton growers. The commercial interest has almost invariably sided with the latter, although they have not always been unanimous amongst themselves. The agriculturists have acted a wavering part in the protracted struggle, until lately throwing their weight generally into the scale of the manufacturers; a circumstance which alone enabled the latter not only to maintain their ground, but generally to predominate in the national councils. Had the farmers been, from the first, true to their own interests, the contest would have been of short duration. The manufacturers unaided could not have kept the field, and a mere revenue tariff would, long ere this, have been engrafted as a permanent feature upon American policy. Hitherto, the brunt of the battle, on the free-trade side, has been borne by the cotton-growers, who, until lately, have been deserted by those upon whose co-operation they might naturally rely; whilst their allies in the commercial interest have been too apathetic to render them any very efficient assistance. But, notwithstanding the inequality of the battle

which they have had to wage, they have managed,
by the inherent justice of their cause, the excellence of their tactics, and the energy and talent of
their leaders, to preserve an unbroken front under
repeated discomfitures, until they have at length
apparently turned the tide in their favour so effectually, that it is not likely again to leave them
stranded. The history of the struggle is interesting,
and may be briefly sketched.

As already observed, the wavering of the agricultural body has constituted the strength of the one
party and the weakness of the other. The great
object of both, therefore, has been to secure the
farmers; and in this object the protective party have
heretofore generally succeeded. Their identity of
interest with the cotton-planters was obvious, but the
promises of the manufacturers were enticing and
specious.

In acting on the agricultural body, the manufacturers have appealed to their interest and their nationality. What the farmer wanted was a market for
his produce—the manufacturer promised to provide
him with one. He was reminded that New England,
which was the seat of domestic manufactures, was,
so far as regarded the chief articles of food, a
non-producing country. If he objected that his
market there was limited, it was replied, that the
industry which gave rise to it was as yet in its infancy ; that, judging from its past progress, it would
soon be able to meet all his wants ; and that it would
be steady in its requirements, and progressive in
their increase, instead of being characterized by the
constant fluctuations of a foreign demand, to which
the free-traders taught him chiefly to look. There was

something plausible in all this, and the agricultural mind, never very bright, was for a time carried away by it. A home-market, at one's own door, and steady and constant in its demands, seemed preferable to depending upon the wants of foreigners, whilst it appealed to a feeling of which the manufacturers were too adroit not to avail themselves.

It was upon this feeling that was based the celebrated " American System," of which Mr. Clay, if not the author, was the most eloquent champion. Independence in everything of the foreigner, was its motto ; and prohibition, where practicable, its policy. The national vanity was appealed to, to constitute the Republic a world within itself. Having the means of independence within their grasp, why not have the patriotism to use them ? Their capabilities were glowingly contrasted with their present condition. Why should they not clothe as well as feed themselves, when they had both equally in their power ? It was represented as degrading to a great people to be unnecessarily beholden to another people for anything. The mutuality of dependence was kept out of sight, as was the virtual independence to which such mutuality of dependence gave rise. It was no balm to the wounded feelings of the patriots, that, if England clothed America, America might feed England. Absolute independence was their aim, at whatever cost it might be purchased ; indeed, Nature herself had decided the question for them. They had the raw material in abundance ; and, as they were not deficient in skill and industry, why should they send it abroad to be spun ? The raw cotton was at their doors, inviting them, as it were, to convert it at home into the woven fabric. By so doing they would

greatly enhance the accumulations of domestic
wealth, whilst they would be, to all intents and purposes, a self-subsisting people. The influence which
this would confer upon them in peace, and the power
which it would give them in war, were dwelt upon
with befitting emphasis. All this, it was true, implied a preliminary struggle, but the probation would
be short—the result glorious.

Nor was it on the farmers only that this patriotic
policy was pressed. What would the cotton-growers
lose by it? The protectionists only meant to transfer
their market, having no intention to deprive them
of it. Let them only encourage New England industry, and it would soon absorb all their produce.
Not that it was supposed that the planters themselves
were likely to be deluded by this shallow argument;
its design being to follow up the impression made
upon the agricultural body by the appeal to their
own interests, by pretending that those of no section
of the community would be injured by the policy
proposed. This placed the planters in a position
doubly invidious. Even assuming that their interests
would be compromised, they were opposing those
interests to the general welfare and obvious policy
of the state; conduct which became much more
odius when it was taken for granted that they would
ultimately share with others in all the profits of
protection. But the planters were not to be hoodwinked. England was the great market for their
staple produce, and they were not to be driven from
it by any promises of what the northern capitalists
would yet do for them at home. Every effort was
used by the latter to show that these promises were
not groundless. The consumption of raw cotton in

England was compared to that in New England, to
show how much more rapid was the enlargement of
the latter than that of the former market.   A certain
period was taken from which to date the comparison,
such as the year 1816, when the home consumption
was about 11,000,000 lbs., while that of England was
about 80,000,000 lbs.   A later period was then
taken, comprising a few years, when it was shown
that New England had quadrupled her consumption,
whilst Old England had scarcely doubled hers—as if
doubling a consumption of eighty millions was not a
much greater feat than quadrupling a consumption of
eleven millions.   Proceeding with the comparison,
they at length reached the year 1845, when the home
consumption amounted to upwards of 170,000,000 lbs.
that of England to upwards of 600,000,000 lbs. ; in
other words, the one had increased sixteen-fold, whilst
the other had not increased eight-fold.   But so far as
the practical question before the planter was concerned, the English market was still the great field
for him, which had multiplied its demand in thirty
years by eight times eighty millions, whilst the home-
market had increased its demand by only sixteen
times eleven millions.   The one had increased its
consumption by upwards of 150 millions of pounds,
whilst the other had increased its demand by upwards
of 500 millions.   Which then, as to practical result,
had conferred the greatest benefit on the cotton-
growing interest ?   The planters well knew which,
and stuck fast to their creed.   So far as they were
concerned, the comparison was as fallacious as it
would be to say that a child of three years of age had
gained upon a man of twenty-one, because at the
end of six years it had trebled its age, whereas he

had added little more than a third to his. Taking small bases and large bases to calculate upon, the multiples may be very much in favour of the small, without affecting, in the least degree, the practical question at issue. That question is,—Has the English market, starting from 1816, kept its ground, as compared to the American ? Not only has it done this, but it has infinitely gained on its competitor. In 1816 it was in advance of the home-market in its consumption of raw cotton by only 69,000,000 of pounds ; in 1845 it was in advance by 430,000,000. It matters little, then, to the planter, by what multiple either England or America had in the meantime increased its consumption, for England has not only kept the vantage-ground on which she started, but greatly improved it.

The "American system" owed its temporary success more to a national weakness than to the soundness of its policy. A man might as reasonably strive to be independent of his shoemaker, as one nation endeavour to be independent of another, when their wants and aptitudes adapt them for mutual interchange. Yet such is the system which has made reputation for politicians, and fortunes for capitalists. Its advocacy is one of the distinguishing features of the Whig party ; its principal champions being Mr. Clay, Mr. Webster, and Mr. Abbot Laurence, himself a wealthy manufacturer. Mr. Webster's connexion with the question is not the most creditable passage in his political life, which he commenced by being an ardent free-trader.

It is now time to direct attention to the ground occupied by the free-traders. They take their stand upon the intrinsic merits of the question, and upon the federal constitution. They advise the farmers to look abroad for markets for their produce. The home-market is theirs already, and must remain theirs; whereas it is only by a concession of equivalents that they can secure the custom of the foreigner. Besides, the home-market can never expand in proportion to their wants, the consequence of being confined to which would be accumulated products and low prices. Yet it is for this that they are called upon to foster domestic fabrics, of an inferior description, at high prices. English goods of fine texture may be had for little wheat, but they must not take them, because they are English; American goods of a coarse texture will cost more wheat, but then they should be taken because they are American. Is this the principle on which, as a people, they should act? It is certainly not that on which individuals wish to act. Their true policy is to buy, not only where they can get the best article, but where what they have to give in exchange will go the longest way. In this policy the whole body of consumers, it is contended, have an interest; inasmuch as the farmer can virtually manufacture, by means of his plough, better and more cheaply than can the manufacturer with his loom. A free exchange, with England and other countries, of agricultural products for manufactured articles, would virtually transfer the seat of manufactures to the valley of the Mississippi. In every point of view the interest of the farmer is identified with free-trade; through its means alone can he dispose of his surplus produce, and fill the country with fabrics—foreign, it is true, but excellent and cheap. And as to the planters themselves, the home-market, which is secure to them, consumes but a fraction of their

yearly produce. Whilst any three of the grain-growing States can of themselves supply the home-
market with provisions, the State of Mississippi
alone can supply it with cotton. What then is to
become of the Carolinas, of Georgia, of Alabama, and
Louisiana, if the markets of Europe are to be ren-
dered inaccessible to them? So far from its being
their object to cripple the manufactures of England,
their policy is to stimulate them. The object of the
New England capitalist is twofold—to escape foreign
competition, and to glut the home-market with the
raw material, for the purpose of enabling him to
manufacture all the more cheaply, and sell all the
more dearly. And what is the effect of all this?
Simply, that twenty millions of people are mulcted
enormously to the benefit of a few thousand capitalists.
The revenue received from imports in 1845 exceeded
twenty-seven millions of dollars; but it would be
erroneous to suppose that this was the sum-total of
the tax paid for the benefit of the protected classes.
The virtual operation of the then existing tariff was,
by the enhanced value which it gave to domestic
fabrics, to burden the people with an additional tax
to double that amount for the benefit of the manufacturers. For every dollar, then, which that tariff
put into the federal treasury, it put two into the
pockets of the capitalists.

The constitutional ground taken by the free-traders
is—that a tariff bill is simply a *revenue* bill. Being
thus purely a bill for raising revenue, it should propose no other object beyond this, its constitutional
intendment. The moment that it is framed for the
purpose of embracing the profits of capital, it becomes a bill for something else than raising revenue,

and that something else is not included amongst the specified and enumerated powers of Congress. An unnecessarily high tariff is not only a means of raising revenue, but it is also in effect an enactment that capital, invested in particular channels, shall divide larger per-centages than that invested in other pursuits. The unconstitutionality of this is as obvious as are its injustice and inequality.

Such are the grounds taken by the free-traders on this great and engrossing subject, and such is the language which they hold to the farmers, whose support they are desirous of securing. It is to the ranks of the democrats as a party, that the advocacy of these doctrines is confined; the free-trade chiefs being Mr. Calhoun and Mr. M'Duffie in the Senate, and Mr. Mackay in the House of Representatives.

Anything like a detailed account of the protracted contest which has been waged by the parties, thus marshalled against each other, would be here manifestly out of place. Suffice it to say, that the commercial legislation of the Union has been frequently modified by their differences. The high protective tariff of 1828 seemed to bring matters to a crisis, resulting in that memorable struggle which threatened to dissever the Union, and which was only terminated by the compromise bill of 1832. This bill lasted till 1842, when a new tariff act was passed, more stringent than its predecessor in its enactments, during the Whig episode, which was marked by the accidental presidency of Mr. Tyler. During the interval which succeeded between that and the passing of the tariff-bill of 1846, free-trade principles made great progress throughout the valley of the Mississippi.

The farmers began to suspect that they had been hoodwinked by their New England allies; and the planters immediately profited by their suspicions. The result was a manifest change in the national sentiment, previously to the presidential nominations in 1844. A low tariff for revenue purposes alone was, for the first time, made one of the leading principles of the whole democratic party. The points which they assumed were these : that no more money should be levied on imports than was necessary for the purposes of government; that the maximum rate of duty upon any and every article should be the minimum duty compatible with the largest amount of revenue ; that the maximum duty, thus defined, should be imposed upon luxuries ; and that all arbitrary minimums and all specific duties should be abolished, and *ad valorem* duties substituted in their stead. Such were the commercial principles which figured amongst the more prominent objects of democratic policy in 1844, and to carry out which, amongst other things, Mr. Polk's government was installed into office in 1845. The result was the tariff-bill of 1846, which established, for the first time, the financial policy of the Union upon a purely revenue basis.

To the general reader, much of the foregoing may be very uninteresting. It will not seem misplaced, however, to such as desire to understand the commercial question as it exhibits itself in the United States. It is a question in which we, on this side of the Atlantic, have a deep interest. Nor is the struggle between parties yet over. The Union will yet ring with their strife; and it will not be uninteresting to the Englishman to be acquainted, when their future contests arise, with the parties in the field, the views which they entertain, and the interests which they have to subserve.

It cannot here fail to be remarked that, although the point at issue is the same as in this country, the parties in the two countries respectively are marshalled on very different sides. Here, the struggle of capital has been for freedom of trade; there, it has been for protection: here, the landed interest has contended for restriction; there, one section of it has ever fought for relaxation; and now all sections combined seem to struggle for the same end. In the New as in the Old World, the battle has been between the landlords and the cotton-lords, but they have changed colours in the fight. In both, protection is for the time prostrate; the cotton-lords having achieved in one country the triumph which has fallen to the landlords in the other.

In the sketch here given, I have confined myself strictly to the main features of the question—taking no notice of those minor interests which play their own parts in the contest, but subsidiary to the evolutions of the greater interests alluded to.

In a country in which the revolutions of party are so frequent and sudden as in the United States, it is not easy, from the past or present, to predicate anything with certainty of the future. But the signs of the times by no means favour the belief that the commercial question in America has yet attained its final adjustment. It is not likely that any very permanent deviation will again take place from the policy which triumphed in 1846; but there is some reason to fear that the commercial policy of the Union will occasionally be disturbed by being still made

to oscillate, more or less, between the views of the
protectionists and free-traders. The former are disappointed, but not discouraged by their late defeat;
and their strength and influence are yet such as to
require constant vigilance on the part of the friends
of free-trade. The late elections have given to the
Whig party a small majority in the Lower House ;
but so long as the Senate and the Executive Government remain in the hands of the democrats, no great
alteration of the existing tariff need be apprehended.
But who can tell how long this will continue so, or
how the whirlwind of the next presidential election
may affect the question ? There would be more hope
of the permanency of the settlement of 1846, if some
time were given it to show the advantages of its working. But the next election is already impending,
and the protectionists are busily at work, particularly
with Pennsylvania, whose weight in the federal legislature is great, and which was the greatest sufferer
by the late change in the tariff. Should she secede
from the democratic party and go over to the Whigs,
which there is every reason to believe she will do,
her defection, together with General Taylor's personal
popularity, will be almost sure to turn the scale at the
coming presidential contest in favour of the Whigs.
But even then, to affect the tariff, they must not only
have the President, but both houses of Congress in
their hands. They will have the Lower House, but
it is extremely doubtful if they can carry the Senate.
If not, the tariff is safe, for a few years more at
least : and every year's grace which it receives, will
increase the chances of its permanency ; for when
the West is once thoroughly alive to its advantages, so
far as it is concerned, both Whigs and Democrats from

that quarter, however they may differ on questions purely political, will be at one upon the commercial question.*

But a question here arises, perhaps more interesting still, which, without immediate regard to tariffs, concerns the commercial destinies of the Transatlantic Republic. This is a matter, in contemplating which, speculation finds itself utterly at fault. Taking the

---

* Since the above was written, the Presidential election for 1848 has transpired. Partly by the anticipated defection of Pennsylvania from the democrats, and the divisions existing in New York, and partly by the enthusiasm in his favour, occasioned by his successes in Mexico, General Taylor has triumphed over his fidgety and irascible competitor. This is an event over which, in the present state of the political affairs of the world, the friends of peace must everywhere rejoice. But it is the high-tariff party that has succeeded; and they have now the Executive Government and the House of Representatives in their hands. The Senate, however, is still democratic, by a considerable majority,—a circumstance which insures, for a year or two at least, the Bill of 1846. But it is by no means certain, considering the favourable experience that the Union has so far had of its working, that the victorious Whigs would have felt themselves authorized to meddle with it, at least to any serious extent, even had the Legislature been completely at their command. But, waiving all speculations as to what they would have done under such circumstances, it is sufficient, for the present, to know that the Senate remains democratic. A few years more, if it remains undisturbed, may give the tariff such a hold, that the policy which it symbolizes will become impregnable, no matter what may be the condition of parties. Pennsylvania, some of whose interests have suffered most severely by the change, has not shown herself to be implacable, after all. She has gone for the Whigs, but by so trifling a majority, that there is reason to hope for her return, very soon, to the democratic ranks. In truth, the people of Pennsylvania are becoming fully alive to the fact that they are interested in a low tariff, whilst it is only the iron and the coalmasters who are interested in a high one. If Pennsylvania finally throws herself into the free-trade scale, which she is likely to do, although for some time they may rejoice over temporary and partial successes, the game of the protectionists is virtually lost.

realisation of the past for our guide, the probabilities of the future seem to transcend the line of credibility. The Americans have it in their power to become all they dream of,—a self-subsisting, independent people, feeding and clothing themselves, and able to feed and clothe the world besides. To this, things ultimately, if left to take their course, will of themselves tend. But would it be worth the necessary cost to attempt to precipitate events ? The United States are greater in their prospects than in all they have yet achieved. What is there to prevent them doing all that we have done ? Have they not ingenuity equal to our own ? have they not industry and enterprise to a degree which does credit to their origin ? And if they want capital, are they not daily accumulating it ? Nay, more, what is to prevent them doing more than we have done ? Great as are our resources, they are trifling as compared to the undeveloped wealth of the North American continent. What we have done with capital, industry, and skill, they can achieve, and much more; for to these they add the raw material, for which our manufacturing interests are so largely dependent upon them. And in view of the rivalry at present existing, this is a dependence which cannot be contemplated with indifference. As regards the supply of cotton, we are as much at the mercy of America as if we were starving and to her alone we looked for food. She need not withhold her wheat: America could starve us by withholding her cotton. True, it is as much her interest as ours to act differently; and so long as it continues so, no difficulty will be experienced. But a combination of circumstances may be supposed, in which America, at little cost to herself, might strike us an irrecoverable blow :

a crisis might arise, when, by momentarily crippling
our industry, she might push in and deprive us of the
markets of the world. And who, should the opportunity arise, will guarantee her forbearance? Fill
England with provisions—let her harbours be choked
and her granaries bursting with their stores—what a
spectacle would she present on a stoppage of one
year's supply of cotton! It would do more to prostrate her in the dust, than all the armaments which
America and Europe combined could hurl against her.
What a tremendous power is this in the hands of a
rival! The day may come, even should inclination
be dead, when self-interest may drive her to the policy
of shutting up our English factories, and crushing our
English trade. She has, as it were, at her command,
the great dam, from which all our motive power is
derived, and has only to close the sluices, when she
wishes our machinery to stop. It is the consciousness
of this absolute dependence that induces many to
look anxiously elsewhere for the supply of that, for
which we are now wholly beholden to a rival. The
cultivation of cotton in India is no chimera; the time
may come when we may find it our safety.

Whatever may be our experiences, or the conduct
of America in this respect, it is yet destined to rear
up a fabric of commercial greatness, such as the
world has hitherto been a stranger to. On such a
theme it would be idle to speculate minutely; but
this much at least may be safely predicated of a people
with ingenuity equal to, and with resources ten times
as great as ours, and with an enterprise which drives
them with ardour into every channel of trade, from
ransacking the South Sea for whales, to trafficking
round the world with ice.

CHAPTER VI.

FROM NEW YORK TO PHILADELPHIA.

Cross the Hudson. — Scramble for Seats. — State of the Rail. — Device for obviating a Difficulty.—Aspect of the Country.— Triumph over Impediments. — A sudden Halt.— An awkward Plight.—An uncomfortable Night.—A dreary Morning.—Escape from a novel Confinement.— Arrival on the Delaware.— The Ferry-boat.—Arrival at Philadelphia.

MY destination, on leaving New York, was Philadelphia, about ninety miles distant from the former city. The journey may be said to be performed by railway, although it commences with one steam ferry and ends with another. We were conveyed across the Hudson, in about a quarter of an hour, to Jersey city, already noticed as forming a feature in the panoramic view of New York; on arriving at which the passengers jumped in crowds upon the floating slip where we landed, and fled with a precipitation, which might have led one to suppose that each and every of them had been pursued by a sheriff's officer, or as if they had been laying wagers with each other on the way across. I was still wondering at the cause of this spontaneous exhibition of agility, when it occurred to me that I might as well do as the rest did, in case there might be some danger which they were escaping. I accordingly took to my heels—I did not know why—and followed the breathless and panting crowd into a large unfinished-looking brick building, which, on entering, I found to be the railway station. Once within the station, the hurry-scurry, if possible, increased: men jostling each other, and rushing in at every available aperture into the cars, like so many maniacs—conduct which all the more surprised me, as it was still a quarter of an hour to the time of starting. Inside the cars, again, the scuffle was such, that I began to think the presence of the New Jersey police would be very opportune. I kept aloof until I found, from the quiet which succeeded, that the riot had, by some means or other, been quelled, and it was only on venturing inside one of the cars that I discovered the cause of the tumult. It appears that, in winter, there is a choice of seats, the preferable ones being such as are not too near, or too far from, the stove. The race then was for these seats; and, as I entered, those who occupied them regarded me with an expression, in which it was very easy to read—"Didn't you wish you might get it?" I consoled myself, however, for any loss that I might have sustained, by the reflection that I should be as wise as the rest of them, the next time.

The railway connecting the two capitals, lies entirely within the State of New Jersey, which is flanked on either side by the Hudson and the Delaware. For the right-of-way across the intervening State, the Company, which is principally composed of New Yorkers and Philadelphians, has to pay into the State treasury one dollar per head on the passengers conveyed by it—an arrangement which goes far to lighten the burdens of taxation in New Jersey. There is another, but less direct route, through the same State, connecting Philadelphia by railway, with Amboy on Raritan Bay, from which the rest of the way is performed by steamboat to New York, a very pleasant sail in the summer time, when one can enjoy the picturesque beauties of Staten Island Sound.

On the previous night there had been a severe storm, accompanied by a heavy fall of snow. The succeeding day had been bright, but the wind blew strongly from the west, carrying the snow in blinding whirlwinds on its wings. Towards the afternoon it had considerably abated, and there was every probability of our being able to proceed. As the line was buried in snow, three powerful engines were attached to the train. The first of these was preceded by an enormous snow plough, an indispensable feature in the winter appanages of an American railway. It was so contrived as, when impelled by the engine, to clear the line of snow to within a few inches of the rail, strong brooms attached to the frame of the engine immediately in front of the wheels completing the work, by brushing the rail bare and clean. We started at a slow and cautious pace, as befitted a train having no visible line to follow. For the first few miles we encountered no difficulty, the snow having lain lightly as it fell. We soon quickened our pace therefore, when the sturdy plough did its work nobly. It first bored into the snow, seeking for the buried line, like a ferret burrowing for a rabbit, and then tore up the white covering which concealed it, throwing it in fragments on either side, sometimes for a distance of twenty yards; and every now and then, when it encountered a slight drift, sending it in a shower over

the whole train, as a stout ship treats the billow that
would use her roughly.

Shortly after leaving Jersey city, we passed an
extensive cutting through the solid rock; a work in
every way more formidable than the celebrated cutting on the Birmingham line. From this we emerged
upon a vast flat sedgy country, as level as a bowling
green, covered with reeds in some places, and in
others with long rank grass, both of which, the latter
in brown tufts, peered here and there through the
snow. The whole of this level tract is one vast basin
surrounded by uplands, and bears every indication of
having been the bed of some shallow lake, which, by
degrees, drained itself off into the Hudson. It was
whilst crossing it, that the effect of the snow-plough
was most perceptible and curious. In front of us
nothing was to be seen but one widely extended
monotonous sheet of snow, whilst behind, as if summoned up by magic, lay the denuded rails as clean as
if nothing had ever enveloped them. It almost seemed
as if we were flying over the country and laying down
the line as we went along.

During the spring months a great proportion of
this tract is in a state of prolonged inundation; and
during the heats of summer, the still brimful streams,
which intersect it, seem as if in want of a compass
that they may know which way to run.

On quitting this dreary level, the country becomes
more interesting, its surface being broken into gentle
undulations, between which nestle warm and fertile
valleys. All around then wore the cheerless look of
winter, but a prettier piece of country can scarcely
be imagined than this in the months of July and
August, when the orchards are gleaming with their

golden crop, and the breath of summer rustles merrily through fields of waving Indian corn.

Our first stoppage was at Newark, the most considerable town in New Jersey, but not its capital.

" This is the great champagne manufactory of America," said a New Yorker, sitting by me.

"Champagne manufactory?" I repeated, not exactly comprehending him.

" The best cider in the country is made here," he added ; " and by far the greater portion of the best champagne, which we import, comes from Newark."

I frequently afterwards tasted this beverage in its real, and I have no doubt, in its assumed character, and found it excellent as a summer drink. Many is the American *connoisseur* of champagne, who has his taste cultivated on Newark cider.

Between this and the town of New Brunswick, nothing particularly occurred, with the exception that the difficulties, which the snow interposed to our progress, increased as we proceeded. It no longer lay softly on the ground, but was drifted in wreaths across the line. The imperviousness which it assumes in this state is almost incredible, being packed together by the wind, until it becomes nearly as hard as a board. Through some of these wreaths we made our way with difficulty, at one plunge, the whole train sustaining a shock in the operation, like that given to a ship struck by a heavy sea. Others were more formidable, and were not thus to be dealt with, bringing us to a sudden stop in our career, when the train would back, rush at them again like a huge battering ram, back again if necessary, and repeat the dose, until, by successive efforts, the obstacle was overcome. When more than usual force was required, in tender mercy to the passengers, who

were sometimes thrown "all of a heap" by these operations into the fore-part of their respective carriages,
the train would be detached, and the locomotives set
at it themselves, taking a good race, so as to strike
with the more effect. It was amusing to watch this
rough and novel species of tournament, the sturdy
engines sometimes nearly breaking a lance with the
enemy, and at others disappearing for a moment, amid
a cloud of snowy fragments, scattered about in all
directions, as if a mine had been sprung. The breach
at length made, back they would come for the train,
which they tugged along like so many camp followers,
until a fresh obstacle had to be stormed.

New as all this was to me, it was exciting and
amusing enough so long as it occasioned us no serious
detention ; but just as we were approaching the New
Brunswick station, we ran into a tremendous wreath
with such force, as to baffle all our efforts to get out
of it again. In vain did the engineers use every device which mortal engineer could hit upon. There
were the locomotives half-buried in the snow, and
there they would remain. The poor plough, which
bore the brunt of the battle, was completely invisible.
Our position was like that of a great sword-fish which
thrusts his formidable weapon into a ship's side with
such effect that he cannot extricate himself again.

" Snagged, I reckon," said a Mississippian to the
company in general.

" We're not aground, no how, that's clear,"
added a Missourian beside him.

" I should like to see the ground to put my foot
on," said a man from New Hampshire, who must
have stood about six feet six in his stockings.

" I am sure, stranger, you needn't want ground
where a seventy-four will float," ejaculated the

Mississippian, laughing and eyeing him from head to foot. The rest joined in the laugh against the New Hampshire Anak, who drew in his legs under his seat, as if he was shutting each of them up like a clasp knife.

We now anxiously watched the progress of every effort made for our relief, until at length the chilling intelligence was conveyed to us that the fires had all been extinguished, and that the water had become frozen in the boilers. He was a bold man who made this dismal report to about three hundred people, whose rage increased with the hopelessness of their position. We were in a pretty predicament certainly. With three locomotives but no fire, we were like a besieging army with plenty of artillery but no ammunition. There was nothing left for us but to seek the station the best way we could, which we did by making a detour of the wreath, and wading sometimes up to the middle in snow. On gaining it, we found it a large, comfortless room, leaving but little to choose between it and the carriages which we had left. We there learnt the impossibility of our proceeding, as the wreath, which had impeded us, extended for fully half a mile along the line. We also ascertained that the train from Philadelphia had also stuck fast at the other side of it.

Seeing how the case was, I made my way to the nearest hotel, in the hope of finding a bed. But there was no shelter extended to a forlorn British subject by this house of Brunswick, the beds being pre-engaged, as at Norwich. So back again, it being now dark, I scrambled through the snow to the station, where I found many loading themselves with billets of wood, others provided with kettles full of hot water, and others again with bottles of spirits, with glasses and sugar. These were signs not to be mistaken, and I inquired of a fellow-passenger where the orgie was to take place. He informed me that they had just made up their minds to make a comfortable night of it in the beleaguered carriages. I abdicated all independent action, and followed the crowd. We were soon once more seated in our respective cars, with a brisk fire in their respective stoves; and as a constant intercourse was kept up between us and the bar-room at the station, we were not wanting in some of the creature comforts. We had a newly married couple in our carriage, and they alone had my sympathy. The ceremony had been performed that very day in New York, and they were now on their way to Philadelphia on their marriage trip. They were both young, the bridegroom apparently not exceeding twenty, and the bride looking about sixteen. There she sat, in her ribbons and orange blossoms, looking shy, confused, disappointed, and half sorrowful. Poor thing! I pitied her.

I slept fitfully during the night, as did most of my fellow-sufferers, some of them dreaming of express trains, and waking to a dismal reality. The wind still blew fiercely from the north-west, the fine snow beating like steel filings against the windows of the cars. When morning broke, we found ourselves completely imbedded to windward, in a fresh accumulation, which had risen against us, in that quarter, overnight. We emerged with difficulty from our prisons, and again sought the hotel, where we breakfasted, and remained till nearly evening. In the mean time, every appliance was brought to bear to clear the line. A small army of men with shovels prepared the way for the snow-plough, which kept constantly at their heels; at one time, in a mere freak, pushing these men, shovels and all, deep into the wreath, from which they were extricated, more frightened than hurt. These operations had scarcely been continued for a quarter of a mile, when those at work encountered another party, similarly employed, coming in the opposite direction. They met with a shout, in which we all joined, and the passengers of the two trains solaced each other, for some time, with a mutual recital of their sufferings. We found that we had fared the better of the two; for, the Philadelphia train having been interrupted half a mile from any succour, the passengers by it had to weather the night, as they best could, without fire, or any of the other comforts, which were at our command.

It was seven o'clock ere we finally quitted New Brunswick, and, in three hours more, we were on the left bank of the Delaware. The picture was gloomy enough, which loomed upon my sight, in the imperfect light of a star-lit sky, as I stood upon the deck of the ferry-boat. In the foreground was the broad expanse of the Delaware, literally covered with broken masses of ice, which floated up and down with the tide; whilst on the opposite shore gleamed the lights of the city, as few and far between as are those of London on the Thames. It was some time ere we got under weigh, and we took fully twenty minutes to cross, the ice sometimes defying the efforts of the lusty, thick-headed ferry-boat. To save time, our luggage was distributed to us on board. It was bitter cold, and I was heartily glad when, at length, after a somewhat chequered journey, performed, under ordinary circumstances, in from four to five hours, I stepped ashore in the " Quaker city."

CHAPTER VII.

PHILADELPHIA.

ON landing, I found all as still as if we had entered
the precincts of a churchyard. The ferry-boat slip
was deserted, not a soul appearing to welcome us, or
give us succour. On inquiry of the captain, as to
the means of getting my luggage transported to
Jones's Hotel, to which I was recommended by a
friend in New York, that functionary informed me
that outside were plenty of porters to execute our
orders. "Outside" had reference to a high and close
wooden paling, which railed off the slip from the
adjacent street, in which paling was a door, which, in
due course of time, was thrown open. The gush
which follows the displacing of the plug from a water
cask, is not more spontaneous or impetuous than
was then the crush of the grinning, jabbering, and

officious negroes, who sprung upon us from their ambuscade, and overpowered us before we had time to recover from our surprise. I found myself in a moment between two of them, who leered at me most hideously, their white teeth, and the whites of their eyes, shining ghastlily in the feeble light of the solitary lamp, which did its best to illuminate the slip.

"Porter, Sa," said one of them, thrusting, at the same time, into my hand a card, with 23 upon it, in large characters, as black as himself.

"I'm in de cheap line, massa," said the other,— "no 'nop'ly's my word."

"Cheap!—neber mind him, Sa; he's only a nigga from Baltimore, just come to Philadelphy," retorted the first speaker, regarding his competitor with scowling eyes and pouting lips. He then continued: "I'se born here, Sa, and know de town like a book. Dat ere nigga not seen good society yet—knows nuffin—habn't got de polish on.—Git out, nigga, and clean you self;" and he turned upon his heel, and laughed heartily—yhaw—yhaw—yhaw.

It was not his familiar contact with good society, or any superior grace which I perceived in him, but the circumstance of his nativity, which induced me to give the preference to 23, judging myself safer in the hands of a native citizen, who had a reputation to sustain, than in those of a mere bird of passage. I accordingly commissioned him to carry my luggage to Jones's.

"De best house in Philadelphy, Sa," said he, as he transferred my portmanteau to his truck.

"Is it far off?" I inquired.

"Good bit from de water," said he, "but not fur when you get dere."

Having delivered himself of this incontrovertible proposition, he disappeared in the crowd, from which he soon emerged, bearing upon his shoulders a huge leather trunk, formidably studded with what appeared to be the heads of large brass bolts.

" Where to, Sa?" he demanded of the owner, as he suffered it to drop heavily beside my portmanteau.

" Congress Hall," was the reply.

" De best house in town, Sa," he added, in a tone which displayed an utter unconsciousness of having contradicted himself.

" You told me Jones's was the best," I remarked.

" Well, so I did," he replied, coolly ; " some say one de best, some toder,—I tink both best,—dat's all."

There was no rebutting this view of the case, so off we started.

Philadelphia goes early to bed, and the streets were lonely and silent, but much better lighted than the portion of the town abutting upon the Delaware. Our course lay up Chestnut-street, the lofty and regular terraces of which frowned gloomily, at that hour, over the narrow thoroughfare.

" Holloa, 23, where are you going?" asked I, as he turned his truck into a street, which led to the right.

" Only up dis turnin' a bit, to Congress Hall," said that sable numeral: "but you needn't wait—dis child follow with de luggage—he knows de way to Jones's by husself, by dis time, I s'pose."

"Yes, but I don't know the way," added I.

" Straight ahead, Sa, and that's Jones's," said he ; and he left me to act as I pleased. I made the best use I could of this very definite direction, and dis-

covered the hotel, some distance further up Chestnut-
street. It was fully half an hour, however, ere
Blackey made his appearance; and, on my remon-
strating with him for his delay, he assured me that it
was all right, as he had only stopped to converse in
the street with a "coloured gen'leman, a friend of
his, in the shaving line," who was a "great genias,"
and "knowed all about de foreign relations." I
asked him how he would like to wait half an hour for
his pay, to which he replied that he had "no objections, if I would pay de discount for de use of de
money."

The city of Philadelphia, perhaps more than any
other upon the continent, is marked by characteristics peculiarly American. A European, suddenly
transferred to Boston, might mistake his whereabouts,
from its crowded, crooked, and intricate appearance.
New York, too, is distinguished by but a partial
regularity, which is the case with all the growing
towns of the Old World. But everywhere in Philadelphia are discernible the same symmetry of outline
and regularity of plan. Long, straight streets, each
of which is the counterpart of all the rest, and intersecting each other at right angles, with a few small
and well wooded squares, will enable the reader to
form a tolerably accurate estimate of the town.
There is but one short cut that I could discover in all
Philadelphia, and that is in the neighbourhood of the
Exchange. So unlooked-for an oddity in such a
place put me on inquiry; but nobody could tell me
how it got there. It is found so useful, however,
that many wish it multiplied to an indefinite extent.
Distances within the town are measured by blocks,—
a block being the square space enclosed between four

streets. The same flaring red brick, which enters into
the composition of New York, stares you everywhere
in the face, relieved here and there by a marble
building, or a terrace, stuccoed and painted to resemble marble. Most of the streets are lined on
either side with trees, the boughs of which frequently intermingle above the thoroughfare, and, in
the summer time, conceal, by the luxuriance of their
foliage, as you look along the vista of the streets, the
houses on both sides from your view. This is chiefly
confined to the private streets, although some of the
busiest thoroughfares are marked by the same arbo-
rescent feature. At every intersection of two streets,
the country is visible in four different directions,
seen as through the diminishing end of a telescope.
In one respect it differs from most other American
towns ; for, with plenty of room to spread in, the
streets are equally narrow. With the exception
of Market-street, which is very wide, the other
streets of Philadelphia scarcely exceed the width of
Ludgate-hill. In nothing did the prudent Penn
show his foresight more than in this. To make a
street wider than is absolutely necessary is a great
mistake,—a very wide street, whilst the expense of
keeping it in repair is great, being but ill adapted
for business purposes,—a fact, in discovering which,
Penn seems to have been a couple of centuries in
advance of his countrymen. Besides, whether de-
servedly or not, Philadelphia enjoys the reputation
of being the hottest city in the Union, the feature in
question greatly contributing, during summer, to the
comfort of its inhabitants, the streets lying in one
direction, being constantly in shade, which, with the
exception of a short period, at noon, may also be said

of those intersecting them. The value of this may
be appreciated, when it is understood that, in
summer the thermometer sometimes rises to above
100° of Fahrenheit in the shade. It rose to 104°
one Sunday that I afterwards spent there, when, if a
breath of air swept by, it gave little relief, feeling
more like a hot blast than otherwise. On the following day the thermometer ranged at about the same
point, when nearly thirty deaths occurred in Philadelphia from strokes of the sun, almost all the victims
being labourers, and such as were exposed to its fierce
mid-day heat. Horses too, everywhere, dropped dead
in the streets; a similar mortality, though to less
extent, visiting on the same day the cities of Boston,
New York, and Baltimore. It is as a resource against
this intense heat that the windows of all the private
residences are flanked outside by Venetian blinds, and
many of them by solid shutters. Curious enough is
the spectacle which a fashionable street in Philadelphia presents from about ten in the morning till five
in the evening of a broiling summer's day. It looks
quite deserted, the shutters being all closed, so as not
only to exclude every particle of light, but also
every breath of air; the families melting, in the meantime, in some secluded back room in the more sheltered part of their respective habitations. About
the latter mentioned hour, they begin to migrate to
the front, when the street presents a new aspect,
shutters, windows, doors, and all being now thrown
open to catch every breath of the cool evening
air. Without this strategy against sun and heat,
there would be no living in Philadelphia during the
months of July and August. Such of the residents
as can add to this the luxury of summer furniture,

exchanging the carpet for a light grass matting, and substituting slim cane-bottomed chairs for those of a heavier calibre, manage, during the period referred to, to eke out a tolerable existence. The same plan, as far as the means of parties will permit, is adopted during the hotter months, throughout the Union; the only mode of keeping a house then comfortable being to close it up for the day, and to open it at night.

Philadelphia abounds in public buildings, some of which, architecturally speaking, are of considerable pretensions. The most striking within the precincts of the town, both as regards appearance, and the associations connected with it, is the old United States Bank. It assumes the form of a Greek temple, with a fine massive portico turned upon Chestnut-street. The whole edifice, which is large, is constructed of marble, and is approached in front by a broad and magnificent flight of marble steps, by which you ascend to the lofty platform, on which it appears to be elevated from the street. It has now a deserted and gloomy look, as if ashamed of the transactions of which it was formerly the scene. The marble steps, once so crowded with busy and scheming multitudes, now echo but to the occasional footsteps of the stranger who is curious enough to ascend them. The carcass is still there, in all its pristine beauty, but the restless, scheming, and unscrupulous soul which once animated it, has fled. I looked upon it and thought of Sidney Smith; and then crowded to my mind recollections of the misery which had been wrought, both in Europe and America, by the injudicious transactions and criminal speculation of the fallen monster. The vaunted "regulator," which was so beneficially to influence the financial movements of a continent, could not properly control its own; and the institution which was to consolidate business by moderating speculation, became itself the most audacious and the most unfortunate speculator of the time. The Exchange, in which is included the post-office, is a showy building, but merits no very particular attention.

To me the most interesting building of all was the " State House." It is a long pile of red brick, having stone facings, with an open archway through the centre, passing into a small square behind, and surmounted by a quaint-looking cupola, which rises to a considerable elevation. It is situated in Chestnut-street, a little back from the line of the street, having a broad, open, brick pavement in front. Its architectural pretensions are of a very slender order, but its historic recollections are stirring and suggestive. It is one of the few remnants now left in Philadelphia of colonial times. And to what events in the history of humanity did it give birth! Within its walls took place the earliest meetings of the Continental Congress; and, in a small room on the ground floor on your left, as you enter the centre archway, was discussed and adopted the declaration of American independence—the great deed of separation between the mother-country and her tributary continent—a document which, in view of the influence, whether for weal or for woe, which it is yet destined to wield over the fortunes of the human race, is entitled to be regarded as the most remarkable ever penned. It is painful to contrast with the noble race of men which the trying circumstances of their country then called forth, the many degenerate successors who

have since represented them at Washington. The pile
which witnessed their steady resolution and anxious
deliberations is already more a monument of the past
than a thing of present utility, the transference of
the state government to Harrisburg having deprived it
of its legislative character. But it is not for what it is,
but for what it has been, that the Philadelphians
justly prize their old " State House."

The principal edifice in the outskirts of the town,
and indeed the finest in the whole city, is Girard
College, a marble structure, built after the fashion,
and of about the same dimensions, as the Madelina
in Paris. It is the result of a magnificent bequest
made by a wealthy banker of the city, whose name
it bears, for the education of poor orphan children,
the trustees being strictly enjoined by the will, to
erect a plain edifice, and thus economise the funds
for the principal object in view; and to prohibit the
entrance into the institution, in an official capacity,
of any clergyman of any denomination. I believe
that in the latter particular they have been faithful
to their trust, although as to the former, they contrived to overstep the terms of the will, and, in
building a marble palace, have so crippled their
resources, that the chief purpose of the testator has
been well nigh frustrated. The city and its neighbourhood abound in charitable institutions, some of
them established on the most extensive scale, one of
which forms, as it were, a small town by itself, on the
right bank of the Schuylkill, on the road from
Philadelphia to Baltimore.

The street architecture of Philadelphia is of a high
order, being much more regular and pleasing in its
effect than that of either Boston or New York. The

private residences in the fashionable quarters are large and exceedingly commodious ; but such is the sameness in their internal arrangements, that when you have seen one, you have virtually seen all.

For most purposes connected with a great city, the situation of Philadelphia was admirably chosen. Occupying a site more than a hundred miles above the mouth of the Delaware, but yet not beyond the reach of tide-water, and being accessible to ships of the deepest draught and the largest burden, the real capital of Pennsylvania combines all the advantages of a seaport with the safety of an interior town. About four miles below the city, the Schuylkill, after running parallel with it for several miles of its course, turns suddenly to the left, and empties itself into the Delaware. Where the city stands, the distance between the main stream and its tributary is about two miles. One set of streets runs parallel to each other, from stream to stream ; the others intersecting them at regular distances, and running parallel to the rivers which flank them. The spot chosen was such as almost necessarily to have suggested this arrangement for the future city. Its greatest length is now in the direction from river to river, the space between them being almost entirely filled up ; the town, at the same time, resting on a broad basis on the Delaware, where it is most densely built and its chief business is carried on. Front-street, which looks upon the river, with a broad quay before it, has, in some places, a rather dilapidated look; but in it, as in the two streets immediately behind it, is conducted the chief wholesale business of the town. The streets parallel to the river are named, 1st, 2nd, 3rd, and so on ; whilst those which stretch from stream to stream are called after the different kinds of trees abounding in the neighbourhood, such as Chestnut, Pine, Walnut, &c. and by other names, to distinguish them from the numbered streets. In receding from the Delaware, Third-street seems to be the dividing line between the wholesale and the retail business of the town; partaking itself largely of both, and with the exception of Market-street, which is the great retail mart, being the most bustling of any in the city, comprising, as it does, the Exchange, some of the banks, and many of the newspaper offices.

It is to the Schuylkill that Philadelphia is indebted for that superabundant supply of fresh water which ministers so much to the comfort of its inhabitants. Close to the town, a dam is thrown across the river, and by the power thus attained, the Schuylkill is made to pump itself into an enormous reservoir, constructed on the top of a contiguous mound, which goes by the name of Fairmount. It is from this elevation, perhaps, that the best bird's-eye view of Philadelphia is obtained, lying, as it does on a hot July day, like a great flat overbaked brick-field below you. The supply of water, distributed from this reservoir, is inexhaustible; at least, the Philadelphians use it as if it were so. You meet it everywhere, lavished on every purpose, municipal, domestic, and personal. Philadelphia seems to begin each day with a general ablution. On arriving one morning early from the south, I found the streets deluged with water, some recondite plug seeming to have been extracted in front of every house, and the water so squirting and gushing about in all directions, that it was no easy matter to avoid it. Not only were windows, doors, and doorsteps being cleaned, but the

brick pavements themselves came in for their share
of scrubbing; and, shortly afterwards, when the sun
had dried them, they looked as clean and fresh as if
they had just been laid down.   In winter, of course,
the general bath is less frequently repeated.   Nowhere
is the utility of this superfluity so perceptible as in
the market, so widely and justly celebrated for its
cleanliness.   And no thanks to it.   St. Giles's would
itself be clean, if subjected to such an ordeal.   The
market consists of a long succession of narrow sheds,
running down the centre of Market-street, which
sheds, at the close of each day's operations, are, one
and all of them, copiously visited by the purifying
influences of Fairmount.

Nowhere does Philadelphia present the same impetuous activity as New York.   It has an orderly
and decorous look about it, very much at variance
with the turbulent scenes of which it has recently
been the witness. It is nevertheless a lively town in its
external aspect, and, under a prim surface, conceals
a good deal of gaiety.   But of society in Philadelphia
I shall have occasion hereafter to speak.   A mannerism
pervades the streets different from any thing witnessed elsewhere.   In Chestnut-street, the principal
promenade, there is far less jauntiness than in Broadway.   Philadelphians, both in dress and manner,
are subdued, as compared with their more showy
neighbours.   But their manner combines grace with
quietness; their dress, elegance with simplicity.   Catch
your Philadelphia belle dress in anything but the
richest stuff, but yet she wears it as if the severer
attire of her ancestors was constantly before her eyes.
They do not discard the fashions, but then they do
not worship them with the devotion characteristic of

their sisters on the Hudson. I was seated, one Sunday evening, with a crowd of loungers, on the balcony of the hotel overlooking Chestnut-street, watching the streams of people that passed to and fro, on their way to their respective churches. Not far from me was seated an officer of the army, in conversation with a friend.

"Who, think you," said the former, "was the most flashily dressed man I met to-day?"

"Can't tell," said his friend.

"Why, a corporal in my own company, to be sure," added the officer. "He looked like a blue jay amongst fan-tails."

"Is he a Philadelphian?" inquired the other.

"No," replied the officer, "he's from the 'land of steady habits.'"

"Ah, from Connecticut," said his friend; "he must have passed through Broadway on his way here then."

With this exception, external life in Philadelphia is pretty much what life in New York is. Indeed, so constant and regular is the intercourse now between the two, that it could not be otherwise. Amusements are as varied in the former as in the latter, but the passion for them is not so great. The number of theatres is small in proportion to the population, and it is seldom that they are all open together. The Philadelphians are fond of music, and when a good operatic company make their appearance, they receive them well. They do not dislike the ballet, but they have no enthusiasm for its extravagances. The city abounds with libraries and literary institutions, and to the credit of its inhabitants, most of them are well sustained. There are also many pleasant excursions in the neighbourhood, to which they resort in the summer time. Steam ferry-boats connect the city every ten minutes with the New Jersey shore of the Delaware. On a summer afternoon, hundreds crowd these boats on their way to the gardens in Camden, a small but scattered town on the other side, and which may be, in fact, regarded as one of the suburbs of the city. Many of those whose business is in Philadelphia reside here, escaping in New Jersey the heavy taxation of overburdened Pennsylvania. In the tea gardens there is a touch of Parisian life; crowds regaling themselves in the open air, beneath the trees, with the multiform drinks of the country.

The Delaware presents a curious contrast in the character of its opposite shore. The Pennsylvanian bank is composed of a heavy impassive clay, which disappears altogether on the New Jersey side, where you encounter a deep fine sand. This contrast is observable from Cape Ann, to the northernmost point of New Jersey upon the river, and is so complete, as to elicit the astonishment of all who witness it. Indeed, nearly the whole state of New Jersey is one great bank of sand, intervening between the Delaware and the Hudson, and the difference alluded to may be accounted for on the supposition of its being a later formation thrown up by the joint action of the sea, and the two great rivers which flank it.

The city is seen to great advantage, when viewed from Camden, on a bright summer day. And with such a view I shall take leave of it for the present. The river is about a mile in width, and the town seems to rise from the water on its opposite shore as abruptly as a sea-wall. Its outline is almost unbroken by a single spire or turret. Down the river its limit seems to be marked by the navy yard, the sheds of which loom over every object in the level district which surrounds them. Out of these sheds have issued some of the largest ships in the world, and some of the finest in the American service. The district contiguous to them is Southwark, chiefly inhabited by working people. Carrying your eye over the body of the city, you have to your right, some distance up the river, the suburban district of Kensington, of which it is enough to say that it is the Irish quarter of Philadelphia. Farther up still, and terminating the city in that direction, is the port of Richmond, called into existence by the rapid increase of the coal trade. It is easy to distinguish it by the cluster of coasters which are constantly at its wharves. The city too, is in front well lined with shipping, which come close to the shore, as at New York; but as compared with which, Philadelphia as a sea-port is insignificant. It is destined to be more of a manufacturing than a maritime town. Below the town, the river swells into a noble basin, which is frequently studded with shipping. A sail upon the Delaware is a treat; and prominent amongst my most pleasant recollections of America, is my approach by steamer from below to Philadelphia at an early hour on a July morning, when the mists of daybreak, succeeding a dewy night, were rolled away by the rising sun, displaying the river so full and lively, and its banks and islets so fresh and green, and the distant city, yet scarce awake, reposing under a sky without a cloud or a speck to tarnish its deep and lustrous blue.

CHAPTER VIII.

A JOURNEY FROM PHILADELPHIA TO BALTIMORE AND WASHINGTON.

Dangerous Customers.—Delaware.—Wilmington.—Tobacco chewing.
—A painful Incident.—The Susquehanna.—Canvass-back Ducks.
—The Suburb of Canton.—Baltimore.—Position and Trade.—
Baltimore Beauties.—Departure for Washington.—A slight Acci-
dent.—Arrival in the Capital.—Fellow-Travellers.

ABOUT a hundred miles of railway connect Baltimore
with Philadelphia, the petty State of Delaware being
crossed by the road uniting the capital of Maryland
with that of Pennsylvania. In its application to both
places, I use the word " capital" in its virtual signification, not in its political sense; Harrisburg being, as
already mentioned, in the latter point of view, the
capital of Pennsylvania, whilst that of Maryland is
an insignificant town on the Chesapeake, called Anna-
polis.

For two miles out of Philadelphia you are drawn,
at an exciting trot, by a number of horses. Emerging from a small cramped station in Market-street
you proceed along a number of streets, the carriages
being so constructed as to enable them, without
diminishing speed, to be whipped round the rectan-
gular corners formed by the intersections of the
streets with perfect safety. In quitting Philadelphia,

you leave it quite as suddenly as you enter it. It is
not, like most large towns, surrounded, on its land
sides, by long straggling suburbs. It seems everywhere to begin and to end all at once. At one
moment you seem to be in the midst of a densely
built district, at the next you are as completely in
the country, as if the neighbourhood of the town
was all an illusion. A curious effect has this abrupt
transition, being something like that which would
be produced upon a cockney, if he were lifted from
Cheapside and let down instantly on Wimbledon-
common. One likes to see the straggling adjuncts of
a town accompany him some way into the country.
Philadelphia may have a good deal of the *rus in urbe*,
but it has none of the *urbs in rure;* and in quitting it,
you feel as if you had taken leave of a friend, without being shown to the door.

You have to cross the Schuylkill by a long covered bridge, ere you succeed in your search for a
locomotive. This civic proscription of railway engines may appear very unreasonable to us, but it is
a very necessary piece of municipal policy in America, where every town ranks amongst its more prominent qualities a very high degree of inflammability.
With us, locomotives are fed on nothing but coke; in
America they devour nothing but wood; and, like a
horse kept exclusively upon oats, the latter are difficult to manage, from the nature of their diet. They
are constantly attended by a formidable train of obdurate sparks, and sometimes amuse themselves on
the way by setting fire to a barn, a hayrick, and the
like, and, when they have nothing else to do, burning down a fence. Such customers would soon make
Philadelphia too hot for them, and therefore their

exclusion ; the corporation having a sufficient number of turbulent spirits already to deal with, without the admission of those who would be sure to excite a flame.

Shortly after passing Chester, the last station in Pennsylvania, you enter the State of Delaware, somewhat larger in area than Middlesex, and with a population in number a little more than half that of the parish of Marylebone. Estimating its resources in 1776 from their present development, it did a bold thing to rebel in that memorable year, and may have been bullied into the act by its bigger brothers and sisters. I amused myself for some time trying to calculate the infinitesimally small chance it would have of subsisting for a single lustrum, as an independent constitutional entity on the continent of Europe. Providence has luckily placed it where it can hold its head as high as any of its neighbours, and it sometimes holds very saucy language to the "great powers" around it. Comparatively weak as it is, it has contrived to secure, in one branch of the federal legislature at least, as good a footing and as potent a voice as New York, which is twenty times its size, with nearly thirty times its population. This microscopic State, however, has managed to do that which more puissant sovereignties have ever been unequal to—it has kept clear of debt. Side by side with Pennsylvania, it affords a notable instance of prudence in juxtaposition with prodigality ; the one being in a state of chronic struggle to sustain its reputation, the other scarcely knowing what to do with its revenue, although it makes a very large hole in its annual receipts for such laudable purposes as education. Delaware had, at one time, a geographical importance, of which the construction of the Philadelphia and Baltimore Railway has gone far to deprive it. Situated between the estuary of the Delaware and the head of Chesapeake Bay, it interposes, at one point, a breadth of only sixteen miles between them. This made it an important link in the then direct communication with the South. A canal, of sufficient dimensions to admit of the passage of steamers, was constructed from Newcastle to the Chesapeake, by means of which an unbroken steamboat communication was opened between Philadelphia and Baltimore. A railway has since been laid down parallel to this canal, many persons preferring this route between the two cities in the summer time, the sail from Baltimore to Frenchtown, along the head of Chesapeake Bay, being only equalled in beauty by that, after crossing the neck of land by railway, from Newcastle to Philadelphia, by the Delaware.

Though few in number, the people of Delaware are not wanting in spirit and enterprise. They boast of a foreign trade, and do " a good stroke of business" with their immediate neighbours. They manufacture also to a small extent, and have in Newcastle a large locomotive establishment, where many of the engines used throughout the Union are fabricated. On the Brandywine, or the Brandy and Water, as it is sometimes called, are some of the largest "flouring mills" in the United States. But one has scarcely time to reflect upon the manifold elements which enter into the sum-total of the importance of Delaware, when he finds himself alongside of Wilmington, its capital. There is a refreshment-room here in connexion with the station, which is the open street;

and on my asking for a cup of coffee, I was presented
with a decoction of parched peas, to which, being
amongst the acquired tastes, I had not sufficient time
to reconcile myself. Here, however, was afforded
one undeniable proof, that political excitements do
not always depend, for their extent, upon the importance of the interests at stake. A political meeting had been held that day in town, connected with
some local election, and the refreshment-room was
then the scene of a species of adjourned meeting of
some of those who had attended. The noise and
uproar were tremendous, and the warmth with which
the merits of this, that, and the other candidate were
canvassed, made me think for a moment that the interests of the Union, if not those of foreign states,
were involved. I soon discovered that there were
two sorts of candidates, the " winning horses" and
the " gone geese," the majority backing the former,
but a few exhibiting an obdurate sympathy for the
more questionable form of animal, and that too when
it was obvious from the epithet applied to them, that
they had taken their departure from the field. Politics in America exhibit everywhere the same agitated aspect. I have seen New York convulsed with
an electoral contest, and Delaware shaken to its little
centre with the same, and could not but think of the
story of the fly and the bull, when in their public
assemblies I have heard the people of the latter
emphatically assured by their orators, that the eyes
of the world were upon them.

A journey by railway south of Philadelphia, and,
indeed, south of the Hudson, has many things about
it that are disagreeable to the stranger. It is then
that he is brought in close contact with tobacco-

chewing, to an extent that is positively disgusting. If previously unaware of the existence of this depravity of taste, he might fancy, seeing a number of men with their respective jaws constantly in motion, that they belonged to the race of animals chewing the cud—with the expectoral accompaniment as a slight modification of the practice. Nowhere is this disgusting habit so essentially annoying, as in a railway carriage. In the open street it is possible to avoid the nuisance, as it is in a public room, such as a bar-room, by giving a wide berth to the spittoons; but in a railway carriage there is no escaping it. Think of being cooped up in a small compartment, with no vacant space but the narrow aisle in the centre, with nine-and-fifty distillers of tobacco-juice around you! The constant spitting which takes place from the moment that the passengers take their seats, is carried on to so formidable an extent, that scarcely five minutes elapse before the floor is absolutely moist with it. I once ventured to walk from one end of the carriage to the other, and got such a fright, from the many perils I encountered, that I never afterwards subjected myself to a similar risk. On leaving Wilmington I found myself seated beside a man who carried on his knee what appeared to be, from the care he took of it, a large picture, framed and glazed, and which was enveloped for protection in some stout canvass; it not only covered his own knees, but partially mine also. I observed him cram his mouth full of tobacco when I took my seat, and we had been but a few minutes together, when he turned round to me and said—

"Stranger, will you let me spit?"

I told him that I could have no objection to

his so indulging himself, so long as he did not spit
on me.

" That's just," said he, "what I didn't ambition
to do; but you see, with this 'ere thing that I'm a
carryin', unless you spread out your feet a bit, I
have no place to do it in."

" If that's all," I replied, "I'll exceed your wishes
by giving you the whole place to yourself;" whereupon
I left him, and sought the platform, preferring the
cold, but fresh air, to the deleterious fumes within
the car, and to having my neighbour coolly deposit
his filthy expectorations between my knees.

Both in New England and in New York tobacco-
chewing is a habit by far too prevalent; but to the
stranger, this plague in American life only begins
to show itself in its detestable universality after he
has crossed the Hudson, on his way to the South. A
New York railway carriage is a clean affair, as compared with one on the line between Philadelphia and
Baltimore, or, more particularly, between the latter
and the termination of railway travelling in North
Carolina. The floor is regularly incrusted with its
daily succession of abominable deposits; so much so,
that one might almost smoke a pipe from its scrap-
ings. It too frequently happens, also, that the seats,
the sides of the car, the window hangings, where
there are any, and sometimes the windows themselves,
are stained with this pestiferous decoction. I was
once on my way from Baltimore to Washington, when
two men got in at the half-way station, somewhat the
worse for liquor, and the first thing that one of them
did on seating himself, was to take out his quid, and
trace his initials with it upon the window, surrounding them afterwards with a framework of flourishes;

conduct which seemed to excite but little disgust, many near him laughing, but only regarding it as one of the stupid things that men "a little sprung" would sometimes do.

Let it not be said that this is only joining in a hacknied cry, or falling readily in with a common prejudice. I confidently appeal to every candid American who has ever travelled southward, for a corroboration of my assertion, that it is scarcely possible to exaggerate the extent to which this disgusting habit is carried in the southern and middle States, but particularly the former. Many travellers however have, unwittingly I dare say, conveyed a false impression, when they have left their readers to suppose that it is a habit indiscriminately practised under all circumstances. It has not been permitted to invade the sanctuary of private society. Men may chew in the streets, in bar-rooms, on board steamboats, in railway cars, in short, in all public places, not even excepting the halls of legislation, but I never yet saw any one, in the presence of ladies, violate with the practice the decorum of a drawing-room. But little do the ladies know the agony to which their admirers sometimes subject themselves by this bit of gallant self-denial. "Oh! for a chew;" whispered on one occasion, under these circumstances, into my ear, a young man, in tones indicative of the deepest distress. I advised him, if he were in any pain, to step into the next room, and take one; but he shook his head despondingly, saying that " they (the ladies) would smell it on my breath." About an hour afterwards I left with him, and his first exclamation on gaining the street was, "Thank God! I can now use my box." To say that gentlemen chew in society in America, is

quite as great a calumny as to say that the ladies
smoke; but that, with this exception, America is
grinding at tobacco from morning till night, is what
no American will dispute; and there are many in
the United States in whom the habit excites as much
disgust as it can do in any European.

It was between Philadelphia and Baltimore that
I first witnessed for myself the extent to which
the Anglo-Americans carry their antipathy to the
coloured race. At one end of the car in which I was
seated sat a young man, very respectably dressed,
but who bore in his countenance those traces, almost
indelible, which, long after every symptom of the
colour has vanished, bespeak the presence of African
blood in the veins. The quantity which he possessed, could not have been more than $12\frac{1}{2}$ per cent.
of his whole blood, tinging his skin with a shade,
just visible, and no more. If his face was not as
white, it was, at all events, cleaner than those of
many around him. I observed that he became very
uneasy every time the conductor came into the car,
eyeing him with timid glances, as if in fear of him.
Divining the cause of this conduct, I determined to
watch the issue, which was not long delayed. By-
and-by, the conductor entered the car again, and, as if
he had come for the purpose, walked straight up to
the poor wretch in question, and, without deigning to
speak to him, ordered him out with a wave of his
finger. The blood in a moment mounted to his
temples, and suffused his whole face; but resistance
was vain; and with a hanging head, and broken-
hearted look, he left the carriage. He was not a
slave; but not a soul remonstrated, not a whisper was
heard in his behalf. The silence of all indicated their

approval of this petty manifestation of the tyranny of blood. These bold defenders of "life, liberty, and the pursuit of happiness," these chivalrous assertors of the Declaration of Independence, looked with utter indifference on this practical violation of the " rights of man."

" Sarved the d—d nigger right," said a youngster scarcely twenty, at the other end of the car, and those immediately around him laughed at the re-mark.

" He'll know his place better the next time, the b——y mongrel !" said another; and the laugh was repeated.

Curious to know what had been done with him, I sought the conductor, whom I found returning from the front part of the train.

" Blow me," said he, " if you can't reg'late a thousand of your out-and-out onpretendin' niggers much more easier than one of these composition gentry : they think because they have got a little whitewash on their ugly mugs, that they're the real china, and no mistake."

" But where have you put him? " I asked; " he surely can't ride on the engine?"

" Put him ?—in the nigger crib, to be sure, where he should be," said he.

" Can I see it ?" I inquired.

" You can, if you have a taste that way," he replied; "keep on ahead, straight through the baggage van, and you'll see them all alive."

I did as directed, until at length I passed through the van in which the luggage was stowed, and between which and the tender was a cold, comfortless-looking box, with a few hard, uncovered seats, which were occupied by about a dozen negroes. There they were by themselves, of both sexes, and of almost all ages, some of them silent and sullen, others jabbering like so many monkeys, and laughing immoderately —but all looking equally stolid when their features were at rest. One of them, a woman, had a child in her arms, which she pressed close to her breast to keep it warm; for though the day was bitter cold, there was no stove in the comfortless " crib." Here I found the poor outcast who had so excited my sympathies; he was seated by himself in a corner, with a gloomy and vengeful expression, and regarded me with a scowl, as if I had been a willing party to his humiliation. His entrance had afforded considerable merriment to the negroes, who rather rejoiced, than otherwise, at the treatment he had received. Nothing can be more deplorable than the position, or rather the un-position, of the mixed race in America. Between the negro and the white man there is an impassable gulf, each having his determinate place; but the mulatto, or rather the mixed race beyond the mulatto in the quantity of white blood, are buffeted between the two; for whilst they are not good enough company for the white man, they elicit no sympathy from the black, who charges them with affecting to be too good company for him. It is but justice, however, here to say, that I afterwards traversed the whole State of New York in a railway carriage, in which were seated a respectable negro and his wife, neither of whom was molested, although the carriage was crowded, during the journey.

This feeling the Americans, and more particularly the southerners, carry with them on their travels. It is but a short time ago since the captain of a British steamboat, plying on Lake Ontario, unwarrantably lent himself to this prejudice in favour of a party of Virginians, who had taken passage with him from Toronto to Kingston. There was a young coloured man on board, highly educated, and well known to the white as to the negro population of the province, who had taken a cabin berth, paid his fare, and received a receipt for the money. At dinner, he appeared near the foot of the table, the party in question being seated at the top. Seeing him, they rose and were about to leave the cabin, when the captain stopped them. They informed him that they could not sit at table with a black man; to which the captain most improperly replied, that they need not leave, as he would order him away. But he was not to be ordered away—maintaining his right to sit there with the best of them—whereupon the captain took hold of him by the collar, and threatened force. Against this conduct the rest of the passengers loudly remonstrated; but the young man, finding himself actually assaulted, rose, and left the table. The Virginians, thereupon, dined in peace. But, on arriving at Kingston, the captain was apprehended on a warrant for the assault, and had to pay a heavy fine for his officiousness,—the press of the province being unanimous in its condemnation of his conduct, and his command being only continued to him on condition of his not offending in a similar manner in future.

But whilst I have been thus digressing, the train has been speeding at the rate of twenty miles an hour, over a very fertile and slightly undulating country, and has, at length, arrived at the left bank of the Susquehanna. Here the river, before entering

the Chesapeake, expands into a broad and imposing
estuary, across which the passengers are conveyed by
steamboat, the upper deck of which is so contrived,
that the baggage vans can be wheeled upon it, and
wheeled off again, to join the train at the other side,
without disturbing their contents. The landing-place,
on the southern bank, is at the town of Havre de
Grace, which was a witness to some of the naval
evolutions of the late war. It is very prettily situated
on a high sloping bank, and commands a noble prospect, both of land and water. During the proper
season, this estuary is visited by myriads of canvass-
back ducks, compared to which, for flavour and delicacy, the wild duck of Europe is not worth a thought.
I have seen the Susquehanna blackened with them
for miles, as also the Gunpowder Creek, the estuary
of which is a little further on, and, being shallow, is
crossed by a long low bridge, built upon piles, of
sufficient width to receive a single line of rails.

There are few towns in America but present some
monuments of gigantic but unfortunate speculation.
Baltimore is no exception, for, on entering it from
the north, you pass through the suburb of Canton, a
melancholy instance of misguided enterprise. The
streets are all nicely laid out, paved, and macadam-
ized; you have everything there to make a fine town
but the houses. A few have been built, apparently
as decoy ducks to others, but to no purpose. An
American Canton would not rise on the banks of
the Patapsco, and " Canton lots " rapidly sunk in
the market.

It had never been my lot to encounter such a hubbub as saluted us on entering the station in Baltimore : it was like Pandemonium let loose. There

was not an hotel in town but was represented by one
or two negroes, who did the touting for it, each
having the name of his boniface displayed on a band
which surrounded his hat.

" Barnum's, gen'lemen—Barnum's—now for Barnum's—only house in town—rest all sham—skin but
no 'possum—yhaw, yhaw—Barnum's, Barnum's ! "

" Cause Eagle eaten all de 'possum up, and left
nuffin but de skin—de Eagle's de house, gen'lemen—
hurra for de Eagle ! "   This was said by another.

" Get out, you brack man," said the representative
of Barnum's, himself the blacker of the two ; " tell
your massa to send a gen'leman next time, will you—
it's lowerin' to de profession to hab you here—get
out.—Barnum's, gen'lemen—Barnum's ! "

Having been recommended to Barnum's, I consigned
myself to his lieutenant, who told me that I had some
" 'scrimination " in listening to him, instead of to that
" onmannerly and dispectful nigger," his rival of the
Eagle. I found the hotel all that it had been described to be, being in fact one of the most admirably
managed establishments of the kind on the continent.

Baltimore is most advantageously situated, a few
miles above the entrance of the Patapsco into Chesapeake Bay. It has an excellent harbour, which is
constantly crowded with shipping, the Baltimore
clipper, " built to beat everything that carries rags,"
being conspicuous amongst the rest. The foreign
trade of Baltimore is large, and its communication
with the interior great and daily increasing,—the
Baltimore and Ohio railway opening up a direct and
rapid communication between it and the great West.
The portion of the town which adjoins the harbour
is dirty and unattractive enough, but as you recede

from the wharves, and gain more elevated ground, its
aspect improves very much, the streets being spacious,
and regularly laid out—well-paved, and tastefully
built. Baltimore-street, its principal thoroughfare,
is one of the finest streets in the Union.

In one respect, Baltimore enjoys a very enviable,
in another a very invidious, reputation. It is said to
be full of pretty women, a "Baltimore beauty" being
a sort of proverbial expression. I can say, from per
sonal observation, that, in so large a population, I
never saw so small a proportion of unattractive faces.
Indeed, this characteristic of Baltimore extends more
or less to the whole State of Maryland. The women
excel in figure as well as in face, the former being
more rounded than in other parts of the Union, New
England excepted; but it has a springiness and flexibility about it, to which that of the beauty of the
north-east is a stranger. If it contains a greater
number of beauties, it also gets credit for containing
a greater number of blackguards, for its population,
than any other city in the Union. The Mexican war
has cleared many of them off, since the breaking out
of which, I understand that the police force of the
town has been materially reduced.

Baltimore is the chief seat of Catholicism in the
United States. It contains a large cathedral, built at
great cost, plain enough externally, but very sumptu-
ously adorned in the interior. The State has, to some
extent, retained the Catholic character which marked
its early settlement. The original settlers were Ca-
tholics, and were amongst the first of the colonists to
promulgate the principle of religious toleration; for
which liberality they were afterwards nobly repaid by
disabilities imposed upon them by their Protestant
brethren, as soon as they obtained the ascendancy.

Baltimore is affectedly called the "monumental city." Its monuments consist of a pillar, raised to General Washington, of a piece with Nelson's column in Trafalgar Square; and a small erection, the body of which, resting upon a low pedestal, represents the "bundle of sticks," typical of union in the fable, raised to the memory of some local patriots, who did good service to their country in the late war.

It was here that, like most European travellers on the same route, I found myself, for the first time, waited upon by slaves. It is no mawkish sentiment, but a genuine feeling of repugnance, with which an Englishman submits, for the first time, to the good offices of unrewarded service. A friend from Canada was travelling with me, who felt in unison with myself. The poor creatures themselves seemed to suspect our sympathy, and waited upon us with an alacrity which they did not show in attending to our fellow-passengers. On leaving, we gave each a small gratuity, which they received with a mixture of wonder and timidity. It may be to my shame that I confess it, but the truth is, that I soon became accustomed to this order of things, and received the services of a slave with the same indifference as if they had been those of a hired servant. Custom is, generally speaking, more than a match for the finest sensibilities.

I mentioned this circumstance once to a Virginian lady, resident in Washington. Brought up as she was, from the very cradle, in the midst of slaves, it was, she said, with an awkward feeling that she received, for the first time, the services of a white waiting-woman—yielding sometimes to an impulse which led her to apologize for troubling her; and every now and then detecting herself calling her

" Miss." How much, after all, are we, even in our best feelings, the creatures of circumstance!

I left Baltimore by the late night-train for Washington. For two-thirds of the way, we went on smoothly enough; but when within about ten miles of Washington, a violent jerk to the whole train apprised us that we had run against something, not, however, sufficiently formidable to bring us to a sudden halt, or to dislodge us from the line. The engine-driver gradually slackened speed, and on stopping the train, we discovered that we had run against a cow, which had been lying on the line.

" Sure on't," said the driver, as soon as he had satisfied his curiosity.

" You seem familiar with such accidents," I observed; " are they frequent?"

" Now and then of a night," said he, " we do run agin somethin' of the kind, but they gin'rally manage to get the worst on't."

" But do they never throw you off the rail?" I inquired.

" They seem to take a pleasure in doin' it, when they find us without the ' cow-ketcher,' " he replied.

On walking to the front of the engine, I discovered what the " cow-ketcher" was. Utterly unprotected, as American railways are, either by fences or police, the presence of this device is a very necessary precaution in the case of all night-trains. It is appended to the front of the locomotive, and consists of a strong iron grating, turned up a little at the projecting points, which is made to trail along the line a few inches from the rails. It is by no means uncommon, on arriving at a station, to find a sheep or a hog dead or dying in it. A cow or a horse is too formidable an obstacle to be run against without being observed. On this occasion, the unfortunate cow was lifted off the rail, on which it had been lying, but its body was frightfully lacerated by the process.

" I can stand a hog, but them 'ere cows are the devil to pay," said the stoker, as he proceeded, with the help of some others, to drag the carcass off the machine, and deposit it by the side of the line.

"Might they not as well take it into Washington now?" I observed to one of the bystanders.

" I suppose they would," said he, " but that they want to leave room for the next;" a remark which enabled me certainly to resume my place, with a very comfortable feeling of security.

It was two in the morning ere we reached Washington. The night was cloudy and dark, and as we approached the town, the outline of the Capitol was barely discernible, on our left, looming up against the dull heavy sky. A more miserable station than we were ushered into can scarcely be conceived. We were but few passengers, and there we stood shivering by the light of one wretched lamp, upon the cold moist platform, whilst our baggage was being distributed. I turned and looked at two of my fellow-unfortunates who stood by me. Their faces were familiar to me, but seen then under circumstances how different from those in which I had last witnessed them, when, amid the glare of footlights and all the scenic trickery of the stage, Mr. and Mrs. Charles Kean acted their parts with *éclat* before a brilliant London audience! They were now in America, on their way south, in fulfilment of an engagement.

There was but one hotel in which room was to be had, and that was at the other end of the town. I was conveyed to it in a carriage, which seemed to traverse a dark avenue, in which neither a light nor a house was visible. Thinking that he had taken a circuitous way by the outskirts, I was surprised when the driver told me that we had " come right through the town," his course having been "straight down Pennsylvania-avenue," from the station. I conceived a gloomy idea of Washington from the nocturnal aspect, or rather want of aspect, of its main thorough-fare. In the darkness I could see no trace whatever of a town, the hotel, in which I was to take up my quarters, having more the appearance of a road-side inn than anything else. The cold wintry wind whistled through the high leafless trees, with which it was flanked, and the solitary lamp which burned over the door, only made darkness visible, there being no trace of another habitation to be seen on any side.

I got a fire lighted in my room, and went imme-diately to bed. I slept uncomfortably, and awoke about ten next morning, feverish and unrefreshed. Before recovering complete consciousness, I lay for some time in a state of semi-stupor, with my eyes half open, and rivetted upon what appeared to me to be some huge glowing object, which pained them, but which, at the same time, had such a fascination about it as kept my look fixed upon it. I involun-tarily connected it with the uneasy state in which I felt my whole frame to be. It seemed as if the whole of the sun's light was being concentrated by a gigantic lens, and thrown thus intensified upon my brain. On my becoming fairly awake, it turned out to be neither more nor less than the anthracite fire, which burnt smokeless and flameless in my grate, and which looked like one mass of iron glowing at a white heat. For

seven hours it had been thus steadily burning, apparently without diminution. The heat which it
threw out was so intense and so dry, that my skin,
under its influence, seemed to crackle like parchment.
This I afterwards found to be the great objection
to anthracite coal in its application to domestic purposes. Admirably adapted for smelting, it throws
but an unwholesome heat into a room, drying up all
the juices in the body, warping every piece of furniture within its reach, and finding some moisture to
extract even from the best seasoned timber. It
requires a peculiar construction of grate to burn well
in; and unless provided in this way to its taste, will
soon eat up the bars of an ordinary one. It has a
slaty uninflammable appearance, but is nevertheless
highly combustible, soon lighting, and burning for a
long time. Its want of flame and smoke would send
gladness to the heart of Mr. Mackinnon.

CHAPTER IX.

THE CAPITAL AND THE CAPITOL.

Bird's-eye View of Washington.—The Plan and the Execution.—
Stroll through the Town.—Public Buildings.—The City Hall.—
The Post-Office.—The Treasury.—The Executive Mansion and its
adjuncts.—The Capitol.—A strong Contrast.

To convey to the mind of the reader anything like
an adequate idea of Washington, is no easy task. It
so violates one's preconceived notions of a capital,
and is, in its general features, so much at variance
with the estimate which one forms of the metropolitan
proprieties, that it is difficult, in dealing with it as a
capital, to avoid caricaturing a respectable country
town. It is as unique in its physical character as it
is in its political position, answering all its purposes,
yet at the same time falling far short of its expectations.

Washington presents itself in two distinct aspects,
one comprising that which it is, and the other that
which it was to be. The difference between the intention and the reality is great indeed, and can only
be appreciated by viewing the city from some point,
from which both design and execution can be estimated together. The point in every way most favour-

able in this respect, is the dome of the Capitol; and, with the reader's consent, we will ascend it together, and take a bird's-eye view of Washington.

The view from this elevated point is extensive, and in some respects pleasantly varied. The whole of the district of Columbia is within the range of your vision, with a considerable expanse of the circumjacent States of Maryland and Virginia. You have water, town, and field at your feet, with long stretches of forest beyond, and hazy wooded slopes in the distance.

Both the site and the plan of Washington are beneath you, as if delineated on a gigantic map. The ground upon which the city is laid out is on the north bank of the Potomac, at the head of tide-water, and about 120 miles from Chesapeake Bay. On the noble estuary of that river the southern side of the city rests, being flanked on the eastern side by a broad and deep creek, called the East Branch. In a northern or western direction, there are no particular marks to designate its limits. If the design of its founders was too grand for realization, it was because of its being incommensurate with the wants of the locality. In a commercial point of view it is a superfluity, and politically and socially speaking, it is not that powerful magnet which, like the centralizing capitals of the old world, can draw to itself the wealth and fashion of the country. In that on which they chiefly relied for its future greatness, its projectors committed a capital blunder. There are too many social and political centres in the United States for the presence of the federal government to command at Washington a monopoly of the wealth, the talent, and the fashion of the country; too many foci of commercial action around it, to admit of the forced growth of a large community, in a country where such communities can only as it were spontaneously arise.

The Capitol was very appropriately selected as the centre of the whole plan. From it was to radiate magnificent avenues, of indefinite length in some directions, and of an almost fabulous width in all. Having secured this great frame-work, it was easy to fill up the rest of the diagram. In these avenues all the side streets were to begin and terminate; the whole being conceived pretty much on the plan of an out-door spider's web, with its beautiful radiations and intervening parallels. Some of these avenues are laid out and can be traced, from a variety of marks, by the eye, others having, as yet, no definite existence but in the intellect of the surveyor. The avenues, being designed as the great thoroughfares, were to be called after the different States of the Union,—a very appropriate starting point for the nomenclature of the capital,—the same idea being carried out in the navy, the different States giving their names to the ships of the line. From the direction of the East Branch to Georgetown, one avenue was laid out, extending for about three miles, broken only in two places by the grounds of the Capitol and those of the President's house. This is in the main line of the town, and nearly one-half of it is covered with grass.

Such being the plan of Washington, what has been the execution? The main body of the town lies to the west of the Capitol, on low ground, completely overlooked by the elevated plateau, on the slope of which that pile is built. The basis of this part of the town is Pennsylvania-avenue, running almost from your feet, a broad straight course for a full mile, until it terminates in the grounds of the President's house, built upon a similar though a less elevation than the Capitol. On the north this avenue is flanked by a low ridge, which the city completely covers, streets running along it parallel to the avenue, and others intersecting them at right angles. In this direction, and in this only, has the city anything like a town look about it. In every other direction, you have nothing but incipient country villages, with here and there a few scattered houses of wood or brick, as the case may be, and ever and anon a street just begun and then stopped, as if it were afraid to proceed any further into the wilderness. Taking a rapid glance at the whole, plan and execution considered, it reminds one of an unfinished piece of lady's needlework, with a patch here and there resting upon the canvass, the whole enabling one to form an idea, and no more, of the general design. Let us now descend, and take a short stroll through the town.

We emerge from the grounds of the Capitol upon Pennsylvania-avenue, which originally consisted of two rows of houses and four rows of trees. The latter are now reduced to two, which, when the trees have attained their growth, will throw a grateful shade upon the thoroughfare. The first feature about the avenue that strikes you, is its amazing width. The houses visible on the opposite side, are three hundred feet distant from you, enough to destroy all community of interest and feeling between them, if houses had either one or the other. There seems, in fact, to be little or no bond of union between them; and instead of looking like the two sides of one and the same street, they seem as if they were each a side of two different streets. The mistake of this prodigality of surface was discovered too late to be remedied. In the first place, it destroys the symmetry of the street; for, to be well-proportioned, the houses on either side should rise to a height of twenty stories at least, whereas they are, generally speaking, only three. In the next place, the cost of keeping it in order is ruinous; and as Pennsylvania-avenue is the Broadway of Washington, all the other streets are beggared for the sake of the pet. To pave it was like attempting to pave a field—a circumstance to which is attributable the fact, that the rest of the streets, with the exception of their broad ample brick footways, are left unpaved. In wet weather, to cross any of them, even Pennsylvania-avenue, is a hazardous matter. Nobody ever crosses them for pleasure. It requires serious business to drag you from one side to the other.

Turning from the Avenue to the right, we have at the top of the street, which we thus enter, a large unfinished brick building, with the holes occasioned by the scaffolding yet in the walls, and with a liberty pole rising to the very clouds in front of it. This is the City Hall, the funds for building which were raised by a lottery; but some one decamping with a portion of them, the building, which was founded in chance, runs a chance of never being completed. Continuing almost in the same line to the westward, we come to the General Post Office, the choicest architectural *bijou* in Washington, being a neat classic structure built of white marble, and about the size of the Trinity House. Its beauties are, however, almost lost from defect of site, the fate of so many of our own finest public edifices. Immediately to the north of the Post Office is the Patent Office, an imposing pile, with a massive Doric portico in the centre, approached by a broad and lofty flight of steps. But one quarter of it is, as yet, built; the design consisting of four similar fronts, which will enclose a hollow square. Farther west, and at the end of the nearest parallel street to Pennsylvania-avenue, is the Treasury, a handsome building, the front of which presents one of the finest, as it is certainly one of the longest, colonnades in the world. But this brings us to the Executive mansion and its adjuncts.

In the midst of a large open square, on a piece of high ground overlooking the Potomac, though about a quarter of a mile back from it, is the President's House, or the " White House," as it is more gene-rally called. It is a spacious and elegant mansion, surrounded by soft sloping lawns, shaded by lofty trees and dotted with shrubbery. Within this square, and forming, as it were, its four angles, are the four departments of State, those of the Treasury, of State, of War, and of the Navy, each of which is approached by the public from one of the four streets which encompass the Executive grounds. To each a private path also leads from the President's house, the chief magistrate sitting, as it were, like a spider, in the centre of his web, from which he constantly overlooks the occurrences at its extremities. With the excep-tion of the Treasury, which is new, the departments are plain brick buildings, painted in singular taste, of a sort of diluted sky-blue colour.

With the exception of the Capitol, to which I shall presently advert, this list comprises the only architec-tural features worthy of notice in the general view of

Washington. Separated, as they are, at great distances from each other, their effect is entirely lost. On my once suggesting to a resident, that it would have been much better had they all been placed together, so as to have formed a noble square, which, viewed as a centre, would have imparted a unity to one's idea of the town ; he told me that they all now deeply regretted that this had not been the case, the only reason assigned for scattering them being to prevent the different heads of departments from being constantly disturbed by the intrusion of members of Congress. As they are, Washington has no visible centre—no one point upon which converge the ideas of its inhabitants. But let us back again to the Capitol.

It is a thousand pities that its front is not turned upon Pennsylvania-avenue. The city being intended to grow the other way, the front of the Capitol was turned to the east; but the town having taken the contrary direction, the legislative palace has the appearance of turning its back upon it. But notwithstanding this, it has a most imposing effect, rising, as it does, in classic elegance from its lofty site, over the greensward and rich embowering foliage of the low grounds at its base. As seen at one end of the Avenue, from the grounds of the President's house at the other, there are few buildings in the world that can look to better advantage. I have seen it when its milk-white walls were swathed in moonlight, and when, as viewed from amid the fountains and shrubbery which encircle it, it looked more like a creation of fairy-land than a substantial reality. Passing to the high ground, on its eastern side, we have its principal front, the chief feature of which is a deep Corinthian portico, approached by a double flight of steps, and from which seems to spring the lofty dome, which crowns the building, and gives solidity to the whole, by uniting it, as it were, in one compact mass. This elevation is well seen from the spacious esplanade in front, and from the ornamental grounds immediately beyond. The stairs leading to the portico are flanked by pedestals, designed for groups of statuary, one of which only is as yet occupied by a marble group, representing Columbus holding a globe in his extended right hand, with an aboriginal native of the new world, a female figure, crouching beside him in mingled fear and admiration. The execution of this group is much better than its design, which is ridiculously theatric. Ascending the steps, you have, beneath the portico, in a niche on either side of the door leading into the body of the building, a marble figure of Peace and War. Passing through this door, you are ushered at once into the rotunda, surmounted by, and lighted from the dome. It extends the whole width of the main building, the perpendicular part of its walls being divided into large panels, designed for the reception of historic paintings. Most of these are already filled, chiefly with incidents in the revolutionary struggle; whilst those still empty will, no doubt, soon be occupied by representations of some of the more prominent events of the Mexican war. Turning to the left, on entering the rotunda, you pass through a door which leads to the House of Representatives, an enormous semicircular chamber, with a lofty vaulted roof resembling, on the whole, the bisection of a dome. A row of massive and lofty pillars, composed of a kind of "pudding stone," which takes a polish equal to that of marble, spring from the floor, and form an inner arc to the outer one formed by the circular wall of the chamber. Between the pillars and this wall is the strangers' gallery. The speaker's chair occupies, as it were, the centre of the chord of the arc, being immediately in front of a screen of smaller pillars, supporting another gallery, occupying a deep recess in the wall, and which is set apart for such private friends as members choose to introduce into it. The seats of members radiate from the chair back to the great pillars, leaving an open semicircular space immediately in front of the clerk's table. The hall looks well, but is ill-adapted for its purpose, it being far too large to speak in with comfort, in addition to which, its acoustic arrangements are anything but perfect.

To get to the senate chamber you have to cross the rotunda. Its general outline is, in most respects, similar to that of the House of Representatives, differing from it in this, that it is not above one-third the size. It is lighter, neater, and much better in its effect than its rival chamber in the other wing of the Capitol; and is, in every way, admirably adapted for public speaking. It is also provided with galleries for the public, seats being raised around the body of the chamber for the diplomatic corps, the judges, and such members of the government as choose to be witnesses of the deliberations of the Senate.

Ascending one day to the gallery, I witnessed a sight which brought into painful contrast some of the lights and shadows of American life. Crouched at the top of the dark staircase was an object, the precise form and character of which I did not at first comprehend; nor was it until my eye had adjusted itself

to the imperfect light, that I discovered it to be an
aged negro, his hair partially whitened with years,
and his fingers crooked with toil.   Near him was the
door leading into the gallery.   It was slightly ajar.
The ceiling of the chamber was visible to him, and
the voices of the speakers came audibly from within.
Some one was then addressing the house.   I listened
and recognised the tones of one of the representatives
of Virginia, the great breeder of slaves, dogmatizing
upon abstract rights and constitutional privileges.
What a commentary was that poor wretch upon his
language !   To think that such words should fall
upon such ears ; the freeman speaking, the slave
listening, and all within the very sanctuary of the constitution.   I entered the chamber, and could not help,
during all the time that I remained there, seeing in
fancy that decrepit old slave kneeling at the foot of
the chair in impotent supplication for justice.

Immediately after the house had risen, I perceived
him busy with others cleaning out the chamber.
Indeed, during the session, the whole Capitol is
daily swept by negroes ; the black man cleaning what
the white man defiles.   Who will erase the moral
stain that casts such a shadow over the republic ?
Will the white man have the magnanimity to do it ;
or will the black man have to purify the constitution
for himself, as he now sweeps the dust of his op-
pressor from the steps of the Capitol ?

p. 145 - 174

CHAPTER X.

LIFE IN WASHINGTON.

Peculiar Social Development in Washington.—Causes of this.—
Heterogeneous Elements of which Society in the Capital is com-
posed.—Exceptions to Washington Life, in its exterior aspect.—
Refined Circles in Washington.—The Rotunda and the Library.—
American Statesmen.—John C. Calhoun.

FROM the district of Columbia, as from an elevated
point of sight, there are some respects in which the
whole confederation may be advantageously viewed.
To the federal capital, whilst Congress is in session,
converge as to a focus the diversified peculiarities
and conflicting interests of the Union. Elsewhere
you come in contact with but its *disjecta membra ;*
whilst here, although some features may be but
faintly traced, the republic is to be seen in its entire
outline. Here the east and the west, the north and the
south; the free interest and the slave interest; the commerce, the manufactures, and the agriculture of America, meet face to face, discern their relative positions,
and measure each other's strength. This is the arena
common to all parties; the spot where great material
interests clash and are reconciled again; where
national policies are built up and overthrown ; where
faction developes its strategy, and moral forces exhaust themselves in periodic conflict with each other.
Here also is to be seen in constant whirl the balance-

wheel, such as it is, of the most complicated political machine on earth ; and here may be best appreciated the working and the value of the constitution.

Contemplated from th e capital, however, the republic is better understood in its political than in its social character. It is quite true that the different phases of American society are to be met with in Washington. But to form a correct estimate of social life in America, it must be carefully considered beyond the bounds of the capital. Its development in Washington is peculiar, owing to the heterogeneous elements which are there thrown together, and considered alone would afford but an inadequate idea of the social system of the continent. In the singular moral agglomeration which Washington presents, whatever may be disagreeable in American society comes strongly out. A more extended survey leaves a better impression. But before taking this survey, it may be as well to initiate the reader into some of the peculiarities of Washington life.

The first thing that strikes the stranger is the unsettled aspect which society there presents. Long before he has analysed it, and searched into its peculiarities, he discerns the traces of instability which are deeply imprinted upon it. He scarcely perceives a feature about it that is permanent—a characteristic that is durable. It affords no tokens to him of constant and undeviating progression ; but, on the contrary, all the evidences of froward and fitful life. It seems to have had no past, whilst it is difficult to divine what its future will be—to have been formed to-day, and not designed to last beyond to-morrow. It appears, in short, to be a mere temporary arrangement, to give time for the organization of something better.

Nor is all this difficult to account for. It is the natural consequence of the fluctuating materials of which it is composed, and of the frequently irreconcilable qualities of its component parts. It is like a fabric of coarse texture, hastily woven of ill-assorted materials, speedily dissolved only to be woven again anew. No sooner does it assume a shape than its outlines disappear again, to be once more brought into form, which it is destined again to lose. It is this succession of semi-formation and semi-dissolution—this periodicity in its construction and disintegration—that makes the chronic condition of society in Washington present the same phenomena to the stranger, as other social systems have exhibited when in a state of violent transition.

The better to understand this, let me here present the reader with a general idea of the capital. At best, Washington is but a small town, a fourth-rate community as to extent, even in America. When Congress is not sitting, it is dull and insipid to a degree, its periodical excitements disappearing with the bulk of its population. It is, in fact, a town of boarding-houses and hotels; the principal occupation of those left behind, after the rising of Congress, appearing to be, to keep the empty town well aired for the next legislative session and the next influx of population. During the recess, the population consists of the *corps diplomatique,* the chief and subordinate officials of the government and their families, idle shopkeepers, boarding-house keepers, and slaves. Sometimes the diplomatic body and the higher civil functionaries of the republic, withdraw altogether for the sickly months of August and September. A more forlorn and lifeless appearance can scarcely be

conceived than is then worn by the American capital.
It is like a body without animation, a social *cadavre*,
a moral Dead Sea.

From this state of torpidity it is annually roused
about the beginning of December, the first Monday
of which is the day fixed by the constitution for the
assemblage of Congress. For some weeks previously
to this, the note of preparation is sounded ; the hotels
are re-opened, whole ̄streets of boarding-houses are
put in order for the winter, shopkeepers replenish
their stocks, and the deserted village once more
assumes the aspect of a tolerably bustling town. But
it is not till about the beginning of the year that the
tide of population may be regarded as at its full.
And what a motley heterogeneous assemblage does
Washington then contain ! Within a narrow compass
you have the semi-savage " Far Westerner," the
burly backwoodsman, the enterprizing New-Eng-
lander, the genuine Sam Slick, the polished Bosto-
nian, the adventurous New Yorker, the staid and
prim Philadelphian, the princely merchant from the
sea-board, the wealthy manufacturer, the energetic
farmer, and the languid but uncertain planter. Were
Washington a large town, with a permanent and
settled society, this influx of incongruous elements
might periodically merge in without sensibly affecting
it. But this is not the case, and it is from the different pursuits, the diversified habits, the opposite
views, the conflicting sentiments, the unadjusted sympathies and incompatible tastes of this motley concurrence of legislators, placemen, place-hunters, partizans
and idlers, that the characteristics of Washington
society annually arise. It is impossible for such materials to combine into a structure, either harmonious

or ornamental. Let me not be understood, however, to say that there are no exceptions to this unflattering picture: for amongst the permanent, as well as the occasional residents of Washington, are many who would do honour to any society; but they are not sufficiently numerous to impart a character to Washington life. They have, generally, their own coteries, to which they confine themselves. They withdraw from that which is foreign to their tastes, and thus the better features of Washington life are concealed beneath the surface. They can neither resist the tide, nor guide the current; so they modestly dip their heads, and let it pass over them. It is the rough incongruous crowd that gives society its tone and colouring: and what renders the thing all the more hopeless is, that whilst the general characteristics of the crowd remain, the individuals are constantly changing. Those present to-day are gone to-morrow, their places being occupied by others of the same stamp with themselves. You might as well attempt to construct a city of the ever-shifting sands of the desert, as to organize anything like a permanent social fabric out of the incoherent and evanescent materials which are to be found in Washington.

To reduce the moral chaos, thus annually presented, to something like shape and order, the most powerful influences are required, and some of the best of these are wanting. In no part of the republic is the social sway of woman so limited as it is in the capital. This does not arise from any inferiority in the Washington ladies, but from the absolute paucity of their numbers. The great majority of those who crowd into the city during the session, either leave their families behind them or have none to accompany them. It is quite true, that most of the members of the Senate, and several of the Lower House, are accompanied by their wives and children; but these, with the flying visitors, male and female, who constantly come and go, are exceptions to the rule. To the great bulk of the merely sessional residents, the stay of a few months in Washington is regarded more in the light of a protracted "spree" than as anything else. They may, to be sure, have their legislative and other duties to attend to, but these merely constitute a part of the round of excitements to which they give themselves up. A walk in the streets, a visit to one of the hotels, the very complexion of the boarding-houses, will suffice to show the dearth in Washington society of the more softening influences. When neither House of Congress is sitting, groups of male idlers are constantly to be seen loitering in the streets, or smoking and chewing in crowds in front of the hotels, where they ogle with little delicacy the few women that pass; or noisily congregated in the bar-room, treating themselves liberally to gin slings, sherry cobblers, and mint juleps. The more quietly disposed of the members of Congress take up their quarters in the boarding-houses more convenient to the capital, where they are accommodated in messes, sometimes twenty of them living together under the same roof, and daily meeting at the same table. These "Congress messes" are imitated elsewhere, and for one boarding-house with mixed company, there are ten in which no female but the landlady is to be met with. It is obvious that such a development of social life can give rise to but little variety of mental occupation. Parties, generally speaking, with no very extensive range of intellectual acquire-

ment, thus kept constantly together, under almost the
same circumstances, have but few topics of conversation, but these unfortunately are prolific of wrangling
and excitement. Politics and party questions occupy
nine-tenths of their time, in discussing which their
minds are kept, as it were, in a continual state of
fever heat. The habit of disputation which this
engenders, and the state of normal antagonism into
which it casts their minds, are by no means favourable to the cultivation of the social amenities. Their
constant intercourse with each other is as that of
partizans or political opponents. The tie of friendship is subservient to considerations of party and self-
interest, and it is seldom that they find those amelio-
rating influences intervening between them, which, in
other portions of the world, partly separate only to
keep men in kindlier contact with each other. The
Sabine women interfered between their kinsmen and
their husbands, and made friends of those who had
been mortal enemies. It is a thousand pities that
the genial presence of similar arbitrators does not
interfere to soothe the asperities of political disputation in the American capital.

From all this may be readily conceived how coarse
and unattractive a surface Washington society presents to the world. On most persons who come in
contact with it is its effect speedily discernible. In
the case of some it tarnishes the lustre of pre-con-
tracted refinements; in that of others, as colours are
fixed by fire, it aggravates the rougher and more
repulsive features of their character. Many sink to
the condition of moral bears—demeaning themselves as
if they had never known a social restraint, and as if
the more graceful conventionalities of civilization were

essentially alien to their nature. In their mutual intercourse, but little courtesy of manner or suavity of disposition is displayed. They are manly without being gentlemanly. When they do approach a lady, their demeanour is more that of elaborate awkwardness than of ease and self-possession. Their politeness partakes largely of the characteristics of their daily life; it is bustling, obtrusive, and sometimes offensive. Time and again have I seen ladies blush at the awkward ambiguity of their compliments. But how can it be otherwise with those, who generally exchange the duties of the day only for the grosser amusements? In the way of the higher amusements, Washington is very ill provided. Were music cultivated, or did the drama flourish in it, or were there other sources of intellectual pastime to which the jaded politician could resort, the aspect of things might be changed. But as it is, the approach of a third-rate vocalist, of a peripatetic juggler, or a strolling equestrian company, creates a sensation in Washington equal to that of an English village under the same lofty excitements. I once witnessed the performance of an equestrian company there, when the whole population seemed to have gathered under the tent, including the diplomatic corps, and the functionaries of government, with the exception of the President. This want of intellectual amusement, combined with the inadequacy of female society, throws many into a course of habitual, but still temperate dissipation. From morning till night the bar-rooms of the hotels are full; the bar, indeed, being the chief source of the hotel-keepers' revenue. Amongst those who frequent them is generally to be found a large sprinkling of members of Congress.

Some of these gentlemen, for want of other occupation, raised a subscription two or three years ago, for the purpose of presenting a testimonial to one of the bar-keepers of the National Hotel, whose fame as a compounder of gin sling and mint julep was almost co-extensive with the bounds of the republic. Amongst the ornaments of the bar was a portrait of this functionary, exhibiting his adroit manipulations in the more critical operations of his calling. The testimonial consisted of two silver cups, similar to those used by him in compounding his mixtures, the inscription on one of them testifying that they were a token of the admiration of the donors, for his " eminent services at the Washington bar." I do not mean to say that this was a national tribute to the worthy in question, but it speaks volumes, that its principal promoters were members of the federal legislature.

Few as are the virtues of social life which sparkle on the surface of Washington society, it was some time ere I was made aware of the extent to which its vices were covertly practised. Walking home one morning, about two o'clock, with a friend, he asked me, whilst passing down Pennsylvania-avenue, to accompany him to a place where he would show me a feature of Washington life to which I was yet a stranger. We thereupon entered an open lobby, and passed up stairs, when, on opening the first door we came to, I beheld, as thick and as busy as bees in a hive, a set of men in crowds around several tables, engaged in the hazards, and plunged in all the excitements of gambling—the game being faro, and the stakes by no means contemptible.

I remained for some time contemplating a scene, singularly diversified, as respects character and the

display of passion.   The company was of a very
mixed character, comprising artizans, tradesmen, shopkeepers, a few professional men, and many idlers.
Noisiest and busiest of all, was one of the members
for Alabama; and it was not long ere I heard exclamations, alternating between satisfaction and disappointment, breaking from lips which I had heard
discourse most eloquently in the Capitol on the aris-
tocratic vices of England.   The night was hot, the
atmosphere of the room was stifling, and most of
those present were in their shirt-sleeves.   In a back
room, the door of which stood invitingly open, was a
table amply set out with a gratuitous provision of
edibles, and every species of alcoholic beverage.   On
entering we were invited to partake, but declined.
The less experienced hands vainly endeavoured to
drown their excitements by frequent potations—the
more knowing kept aloof from the bottle.

On quitting this scene, we entered three other
houses close by, only to witness, in each, a similar
exhibition.

" I am surprised," said I to my friend, on our
finally emerging into the open air, " to find so small
a community as that of Washington so largely
impregnated with some of the worst vices of the
wealthier and more luxurious capitals of Europe."

" Many of those whom you have just seen," said
he, " are driven to the gambling-table merely to while
away their time."

" But could they not," inquired I, " accomplish the
same object by seeking other occupations ?"

" The worst of it is," rejoined he, " that their
opportunities in that respect are limited.   Such of
them as have a taste for society soon exhaust the

round of their acquaintances, and having no other sources of legitimate pastime within reach, must elect between *ennui* and questionable devices to avoid it. Such, on the other hand, as have no taste for social intercourse, resort, perhaps naturally enough, to equivocal practices. Add to this, that some of the members, who receive eight dollars a-day and live perhaps upon three, have spare cash in hand, which they look upon as so much money found, and which they are willing to risk, on the ground that, if they lose it, they will be none the poorer. This calls annually to Washington a number of professional gamblers, who generally manage to fleece a few of the people's representatives, although they sometimes get plucked themselves."

As already intimated, the foregoing description is not universally applicable to Washington society. It is its portraiture, as it strikes the stranger who stands aside an impartial observer of its general development. Such as I have shown it to be, is it in the main,—the ungainly product of unsympathetic elements,—the rough fabric, woven of intractable materials. Its softer and more attractive features have to be sought to be observed : they do not, however, enter into the general picture, being more like ornaments upon the frame. Notwithstanding its general roughness, there are pleasant byways in Washington life. Its turbulent current is flanked by many quiet eddies, where refinement prevails, and whence the social graces are not banished.

The better portion of Washington society is confined to a very narrow circle. It has a fixed and, at the same time, a flitting aspect, a nucleus and a coma. Its permanent centre is composed of the

families of the resident officials; its varying adjuncts
consist of such families as are only sessionally resident, and such flying visitors as are eligible to its
circle. Amongst the members of the resident families is to be found a degree of refinement and elegance, which would do no discredit to the best society
in the most fashionable capitals. Their mutual intercourse is easy and graceful, and pleasantly contrasts
with the general boorishness which surrounds them.
Nor are they deficient in spirit, humour, vivacity, or
intellectual acquirements—the young ladies being
well disciplined both in the essentials and the accom-
plishments of education, and well trained to all the
conventional elegancies of life. Amongst the resident
families may be comprised the different members of
the diplomatic corps, embracing the representatives
of all the great powers, with the single exception of
Austria. Forming a large proportion of the circle in
which they move, their influence upon its general
character is permanent as it is obvious. Superadded
to these are the families of such members of Congress
as choose to come thus accompanied to the capital
during the legislative session. These again comprise
two classes; such as fuse into the more select society
of the town, and such as combine to form a circle of
their own. The latter generally consists of New
Englanders, who are more staid of habit, more sedate
in their social deportment, and more severe in their
moral and intellectual discipline, than the more mer-
curial Southerner, with whom they are placed in
temporary juxtaposition. It was my good fortune to
know several families from Massachusetts and the
neighbouring States, who were thus banded together,
having monopolized several contiguous boarding-

houses, and holding but little intercourse with any beyond the pale of their own circle. But the great majority of these temporary residents merge at once into the society of the capital. Composed, as it thus is, of different but not unharmonious materials, the better order of society in Washington exhibits a mixed but very pleasing aspect, presenting a happy combination of European urbanity and American accessibility. It is thus characterised by a politeness which disowns frigidity, and a cordiality which discards affectation.

It is unnecessary here to enter into further particulars concerning it, partaking, as it largely does, of the characteristic features of American society ; of which a general view will be taken in the following chapter. It may be as well, however, to make a passing allusion to its accessible quality—not that it throws its doors open to every stranger who knocks for admittance, but that it is readily satisfied with a good recommendation and a gentlemanly deportment. The following may serve as an illustration of the ease which marks its general intercourse, and the perfect confidence which its different members have in each other. The first time I went to the President's house was without any formal invitation. I was visiting one evening a family which honoured me with its friendship and intimacy, when an invitation came from Mrs. Polk, inviting its members to the Executive mansion, which was hard by. The attendance of a professional vocalist had suddenly been procured, and the invitation was to a private concert, in one of the family drawing-rooms. The young ladies declined, on the ground of having visitors ; an answer was immediately returned, inviting them to bring their friends. We accordingly went ; and thus my first

presentation to the President and his Lady was of a
more agreeable character than had it been attended
with all the formalities of a state occasion. It is very
common for the families of such members as live in
the hotels, to give weekly " hops," as they are called,
which are neither more nor less than dancing parties,
divested of some of the usual ceremonies of such
assemblages. To one of these, occurring on the
same evening at the National hotel, my friends were
invited, as was I, to come under their auspices. The
amusements of the evening were thus pleasantly
varied between music and the dance ; the demeanour
of all whom I met at both places being such as bespoke a refinement at once easy and unexceptionable.
The true source of this rather attractive feature of
American life will be subsequently considered.

The life of such of the residents as move in this
circle is one of constant excitement during the
session, and of comparative repose during the recess.
I once remarked to a lady, that Washington must
be very dull when Congress was not sitting. She
assured me that it was quiet, but not dull. It was
true, she said, that, for the sickly months, it was
deserted by all who could afford to leave it ; but it
appears that, for some time after the rising of congress, the resident society enjoys many a pleasant
réunion, without the presence of strangers, or of the
excitements which mark the period of the year when
they are drawn to the town. The *élite* of Washington then meet each other almost as friends who had
been separated for some time ; when their intercourse is of the most easy, friendly, and informal
description.

During the season, the time of the fashionables
is pretty well occupied with balls, public and private,

soirées, concerts, and other entertainments. In addition to the part which they take in the "west-end" doings of Washington, the *corps diplomatique* keep up a distinctive circle of their own; forming, as it were, a less world within a very little one. Prominent in that circle is the sexagenarian envoy of Russia, with his young and lovely American wife; between whom and the bachelor plenipotentiary of England a friendly emulation seems to exist, as to who can give the best dinner-party. In the summer time, when the grounds around the White House are clothed in verdure, and the still more beautiful precincts of the capital are shrouded in foliage, and enamelled with flowers, a military band performs for some hours twice a week, in each alternately, when Washington presents a scene as gay as Kensington Gardens sometimes exhibit, under similar circumstances; the population turning out in their best attire, and promenading in groups to the sound of music, over the soft grass, amongst trees, shrubs, and flowers, and amid refreshing fountains, whose marble basins are filled with gold and silver fish.

The Rotunda of the Capitol and the Library of Congress are two favourite places of lounging during the day, at least between twelve and three, whilst both Houses are sitting. The latter particularly seems to have been consecrated to the purposes of flirtation. It is a large and handsome room, occupying the whole breadth of the back wing of the Capitol, well filled with books, which are seldom read, however, during these hours. It is flanked by a spacious colonnade balcony, which commands a noble prospect, comprising the basin of the Potomac, and a considerable portion of the State of Virginia, the principal part of the town, and long successive sweeps of the fertile plains of Maryland. On this balcony, in the room, and in the different "chapters" or recesses into which it is divided on either side, may daily be encountered during the session a fair representation of the beauty and accomplishment of America. Here are to be found the exquisitely formed and vivacious creole from New Orleans; the languid but interesting daughters of Georgia and the Carolinas; the high-spirited Virginia belle, gushing with life, and light of heart; the elegant and springy forms of he Maryland and Philadelphian maidens, and the clear and high-complexioned beauties of New England. They are surrounded by their male friends, aged and young, the *attachés* of the different embassies enjoying a mustachioed conspicuity in the scene, and pass the hours in frivolous chit-chat, laughing and merry all the while. Now and then a busy politician enters from either House, with bustling gait and pensive brow, refers to some political volume, and disappears, leaving the room once more in the possession of the idler, the flirt, and the coxcomb.

The conversation of one of the groups of idlers chanced one day to take a literary turn, when a discussion arose as to the authorship of the passage, "Music hath charms, &c." Being unable to solve the difficulty, two or three of the ladies bounded towards a sofa, on which reclined the veteran ex-President, John Quincy Adams,* jaded with political warfare and panting with the heat, which was excessive. He had just come from the House of Representatives, where he had been listening to a fierce debate, involving the character of one of the first statesmen of the Union, and one of the greatest ornaments of his country. Without ceremony, they

---

* Since dead.

presented their difficulty to him, and begged him to solve it ; but the "best read man in America," as he was styled, was discomfited, and had to own himself so, after being convinced of his error in hinting that the passage might be found in the " Merchant of Venice." The incident is trifling in itself, but it is nevertheless characteristic.

But one of the most interesting of all the features of Washington life is the society of its leading politicians. The ability and grasp of thought of some of these men are only equalled by their suavity and courtesy. It must be confessed, however, that this description applies to but few in number—the real statesmen of the country—not the crowd of brawling and obstreperous political adventurers who unfortunately play too conspicuous a part in the social drama of the capital. Foremost of those who do honour to their country by the pre-eminence of their talents, the purity of their intentions, and the lustre of their social qualities, is John C. Calhoun, one of the senators for South Carolina. It was my privilege frequently to enjoy the society of this gifted and distinguished personage, who, by the charms of his conversation, as well as by his affable demeanour, excites the admiration of all who approach him, whether old or young, friend or adversary.

The foregoing sketch may suffice as an outline of social life in the American capital. If, in its main features, it is not as attractive as are the conventional phenomena of more polished communities, it will be seen that it is not deficient in traits, which relieve the rudeness of its general character, or in veins of sterling ore beneath, which, to some extent, atone for its superficial asperities.

CHAPTER XI.

GENERAL VIEW OF AMERICAN SOCIETY.

IF there is much in the social development of
America that strikes an European as different from
that to which he has been accustomed, he should
recollect that society, in the two hemispheres, rests
upon very different bases. In the old world, where
the feudal relations are still permitted so largely to
influence the arrangement of the social system, society

presents an agglomeration of distinct parts, each having its determinate relation to the rest, and the members of each having the range of their sympathies confined to their own particular sphere. European society, in its different manifestations, is constituted, as it were, of a series of different layers, which, though in close contact, only partially fuse into each other. The consequence is, that, although a common tie of mutual dependence unites the whole, there is no common feeling pervading it, each class looking chiefly within itself for its sources of enjoyment and intellectual gratification, and recognising the others more as political necessities than as social adjuncts. The sympathies of one order touch, but do not intertwine with, those of another, each living within itself, as if it had no interest in common with the others, and holding little intercourse with them. This distinctiveness of class is also accompanied with an inequality of position, which exaggerates the prevailing exclusiveness, and fetters the general relations of society with a constraint and formalism, which renders one class, by turns, arrogant and awkward, and the other supercilious and condescending. Within each the social graces are more or less cultivated, and the refinements of life more or less displayed; the constraint is visible at their line of contact, as mutual dislike is often found to pervade the borders of two civilized and amicable states. In its general aspect, therefore, the internal intercourse of European society is less marked by kindness than by formality, less regulated by sympathy than by rule.

Very different from this are both the basis and the manifestation of society in America. There social inequality has never been a recognised principle, moulding the social fabric into arbitrary forms, and tyrannically influencing each person's position in the general scheme. Society in America started from the point to which society in Europe is only yet tending. The equality of man is, to this moment, its corner-stone. As often as it has exhibited any tendency to aberration, has it been brought back again to this intelligible and essential principle. American society, therefore, exhibits itself as an indivisible whole, its general characteristics being such as mark each of the different classes into which European society is divided. That which developes itself with us as the sympathy of class, becomes in America the general sentiment of society. There is no man there whose position every other man does not understand; each has in himself the key to the feelings of his neighbour, and he measures his sympathies by his own. The absence of arbitrary inequalities banishes restraint from their mutual intercourse, whilst their mutual appreciation of each other's sentiments imparts a kindness and cordiality to that intercourse, which in Europe are only to be found, and not always there, within the circle of class.

The ease, and sincerity of manner, which spring from this social manifestation, are so marked, as immediately to strike even the most apathetic observer. There is very little in America of what we understand by acquaintanceship. Intercourse leads to friendship, or it leads to nothing, it being contrary to an American's nature to feel indifferent, and yet look cordial. Having none of the sympathies, he has none of the antipathies of class; his circle is his country; and in that circle, admitting of no superiors, he sees none but equals. Not but that there are in America many who are superior, in the share which they possess of all the conventional ingredients of a gentleman, to the great bulk of their country-men, and to whom cultivated society is more grate-ful than that which is rude and undisciplined. The distinction of polish and refinement is all the differ-ence that is discernible on the surface of American society, there being no exclusiveness of feeling, or isolation of sympathy concealed beneath a polished exterior. The American is first and essentially an American, and then a gentleman: with him refinement is not the enamel which conceals what is beneath, but the polish which brings out the real grain, ex-hibiting him in a better light, but ever in the same character. I have often been struck with the readi-ness with which the ease and frankness characteristic of American intercourse, have led parties to an unre-served interchange of views and sentiments, although they might have come from the most remote parts of the country, and had never seen each other before. How can it be otherwise, when the Georgian can put himself at once into the position of the Missou-rian, and the resident of Louisiana finds in himself the counterpart of the inhabitant of Maine? It is this ease of manner which so frequently offends the stranger, who does not comprehend its origin : that which is the natural result of the universality of feel-ing and sympathy in America, is regarded as an im-pudent liberty with us, when a member of one class dares to address one of another, in those terms of familiarity, which nothing but a community of inter-est and sentiment can render tolerable. An American can be as reserved as anybody else, when he comes in contact with one whom he does not understand, or who will not understand him—and this is the reason why so many travellers in America, who forget to leave their European notions of exclusiveness at home, and traverse the republic wrapped in the cloak of European formalism, find the Americans so cold in their demeanour, and erroneously regard their particular behaviour to themselves as the result of a general moodiness and reserve.

It is obvious, however, that to retain this ease and accessibility of manner, it is very necessary to guard the equality of condition which is at their very foundation. Americans are all equal, not only in the eye of the law, but in social position, there being no rank to which one man is born and from which another is excluded, any more than there is political status, which, instead of being gained by personal effort, is a mere matter of inheritance. In European society, the superior ranks have every advantage in the cultivation of manner, for when not with equals, they are with inferiors, and thus learn ease and acquire self-possession. So it is with all Americans, who have no superiors to put, by their presence, an awkward, constrained, and artificial cast upon their actions. But let this equality of condition be invaded, and let a distinct class arise in America, with distinct interests and views of its own, and let that class take form and obtain an organized footing in the community, and the natural and unaffected manner, which marks the intercourse of society in that country, will give place to the artificial traits which indicate its European manifestations; and against this danger American society has constantly to struggle. It is difficult, where there are vast accumu-

lations of wealth, to adhere to a horizontal scale in
social conditions. In America wealth has great influence, and the circle of its possessors is daily being
enlarged, a state of things which would bode no good
to the social equilibrium, were it not for the presence of other and counteracting influences. If there is
a very wealthy class in America, there is not a very
poor class, by whose co-operation the wealthy class
might act with effect upon the mass intervening between the two extremes. Indeed, so far as competence involves the absence of poverty, there is in
America no class which can strictly be denominated
poor; that is to say, there is no class whose condition is incompatible with their independence. It is
evident, therefore, that although wealth has un-
doubtedly its influence, and invests its possessor with
a certain share of adventitious consideration ; it has,
as yet, no power in America to alter the essential
characteristic of society — that universal equality
which is based on universal independence. In the
political equality of the people is also to be found
another of the counteracting influences which check
the social tendencies of wealth. In the great political lottery which is constantly being drawn in
America, no man, however rich, can tell how greatly
he may be benefitted by another man, however indifferent may be his circumstances: and, indeed, it is
not the rich who have there the greatest political
influence ; it is the busy bustling politician, who
plunges into the thick of the fight, and works his
way to the influence which he covets, at the expense
of his time, his convenience, and often his better
feelings. With so many, and frequently such rough
competitors, to deal with in the political race, the

wealthy, to whom life has other attractions, retire from the scramble, leaving the ring in the possession of the energetic, the needy, and the adventurous. Thus it is, that if the rich man has a political object of his own to subserve, he cannot afford to lose the aid of his less wealthy neighbour, but frequently more influential politician. The consequence is, that between the political footing of the one and the wealth of the other, they meet on neutral ground, where they find themselves restored to that equality which, but for the circumstances in which they are placed, might have been permanently disturbed. If, on the other hand, the rich man has no selfish object in view, he knows not how soon his poorer neighbour, in the constant fermentation which is going on around him, may be suddenly thrown into a political position, which gives him in the eye of wealth fully as much consideration as it can draw to itself; and this process is of daily occurrence in America. The political arena is filled with those who plunge into it from the very depths of society, as affording them a shorter road to consideration than that which they would have to pursue in the accumulation of property. Daily accessions being made to the wealthy class itself, whilst there is no definite section of society from which it is known that they will spring; and daily transmutations going on from obscurity to political importance, whilst political aspirations are limited to no class, and political aid may be received from an individual, emanating from the humblest sphere,—render it impossible, without the presence of a poor and absolutely dependent class, for wealth, at least in its present development, to over-ride the social order of things

established in America. Keeping this in view, it
need surprise no one to find a free and unreserved
intercourse subsisting externally amongst all the
members of the community. The man of leisure,
the professional man, and the merchant, the me-
chanic, the artizan, and the tradesman, meet each
other on equal terms, the only obstacle that can
arise between them being, on the part of any of them,
impropriety of behaviour or infamy of character.
So long as the ballot-box is in the hands of those
with whom the suffrage is universal, so long will the
poorer classes have it in their power to check any
social aberrations in the more wealthy, should the
latter be inclined to substitute for the general easy
intercourse which prevails, an exclusive social and
political regime.

The reader will scarcely have to be told that all
this is applicable only to society in its grander and
more comprehensive sense. It has nothing to do with
the arrangements of the parlour, or the etiquette of
the drawing-room. It is not society in its purely
domestic or *in-door* character, to which his attention
has been drawn; but to society in its general and *out-
door* sense, to the great social life of the people considered as a people. When we leave the national
survey for the comparatively insignificant arena of
fashionable life, we find much that will appear exceptional to what has been here said; but the exceptions
are mere grafts upon the great social trunk which we
have been considering, drawing their life and nourish-
ment from it, and partaking of many of its characteristics, instead of being growths emanating from the
root, and typical of the very nature of the tree. The
picture just considered, if it possesses no very strong

lights, is devoid of deep shadows; but that which I am now about to sketch, in connexion with the social habits of the people, in a more limited sense, is more marked with differences, if not replete with contrasts.

It may as well here be premised that, in America, the ladies exercise an undisputed sway over the domestic hearth. Home is their sphere, and to them all the arrangements of home are exclusively left. In many respects, this is the case in every civilized society; but in Europe the family is, in some points, as much under the control of external influences, as the individual, denying to those who manage the household that perfect freedom of action which they enjoy in America. Let no querulous lady, who thinks that she has not enough of her own way, imagine that this implies, on the part of her more fortunate American sister, an absolute immunity from marital control. Wives in America know their place, and keep it, as generally as they do here, although how far that may be, might be difficult to tell. But, whilst in their social relations they are less fettered by existing institutions than European women, there is a more general abdication in their favour, on the part of husbands, in all that concerns the domestic arrangements and external relations of the family, than is, perhaps, to be found any where else.

The consequence of this is curious enough. The social position of the husband is not carried, in all its extent, into the social relations of his family. His sphere of action is without, where all are on an equal footing; but in the position of his family, and in their intercourse with those of his neighbours, he finds no such principle very generally recognised. Equality without—exclusiveness within—such seem to be the

contrasts of American life. The professional man
may be on the very best of terms with the blacksmith, but ten chances to one if the daughters of the
professional man know the blacksmith's daughters,
or if they would acknowledge it if they did. In-door
life in America is fenced round by as many lines as
social life in Europe. There is not a community
there, any more than here, but has its fashionable
quarter and its fashionable circle. This may be all
very natural, but it is not in conformity with the
general aspect of their national social life, that they
carry with them into these coteries all the exclusiveness of feeling which forms so marked a feature
in the social fabrics of the old world. In a widely
extended country, like the transatlantic republic, and
a widely scattered community, like that which peoples
it, it is to be expected that these feelings would
manifest themselves, in different places, in very different degrees. In some, however, they assume a
form quite as inveterate as they do with ourselves ;
and young ladies will turn up their delicate but
saucy noses at the bare idea of an acquaintanceship
with those, with whose fathers or brothers their own
fathers or brothers may be on terms of the most perfect familiarity. The circle once drawn, it is not
very easy for those without to transcend it. The
family that introduces a new member, is held responsible for his or her good behaviour and respectability ;
and it is not always that the countenance of a particular family will suffice to give a party the free
range of the favoured circle.

In great communities, where the circle of society
is large, and the lines have been long drawn, one
need not be surprised at this, the fashionables finding

within their own circle sufficient sources of amusement and gratification. But it is singular to witness
the speedy development of the feeling in a new community, where inequality of circumstances is scarcely
yet known; where all are, side by side, though in
different ways, perhaps, equally engaged in the pursuit
of the same end. Indeed, it is in these communities
that the feeling is generally carried to its most ludicrous extent; society in the older and larger cities
having assumed a fixed form, in which each family
has its appropriate place; but in the new towns, the
prize of social pre-eminence being yet to be striven
for, those who are uppermost for the time being,
assume a very supercilious attitude to those below
them. It is in these matters that the men in America
take very little part. Whilst they are engaged providing the means, the mother and the daughters are
using them in working the family into its true position as regards society.

The exclusive feature of American society is no
where brought so broadly out as it is in the city of
Philadelphia. It is, of course, readily discernible in
Boston, New York, and Baltimore; but the line
drawn in these places is not so distinctive or so difficult to transcend as it is in Philadelphia. The
fashionables there are more particular in their in-
quiries, than are their neighbours, before they give
admittance to the stranger knocking at their gates.
As a general rule, an unexceptionable recommendation is all that is necessary in America to secure the
stranger a ready acceptance by those to whom he is
presented. The presumptions are all in favour of his
fitness for the sphere which he aspires to adorn. To
this, however, society in Philadelphia forms the most

notable exception; a recommendation there only operating to put the new comer on his probation, and if found wanting, his recommendation goes for no more than it is worth; being estimated more from the proved qualities of the party receiving, than from the standing or authority of the party giving it. Once admitted, however, society in Philadelphia will be found amply to compensate for any delays and uncertainties with which the preliminary ordeal may have been accompanied. It is intellectual without being pedantic, and sprightly without being boisterous. It seems to be a happy blending of the chief characteristics of Boston and New York society. In both society is more accessible than in Philadelphia. In Boston the nucleus on which it turns is the literary circle of the place, which, comprising individuals and families of all grades of wealth, gives to society there a more democratic cast than it possesses either in New York or Philadelphia. It must be confessed, however, that there is a literary affectation about it, which is easier to be accounted for than endured, Bostonians always appearing to best advantage when they are farthest from home. In New York, again, the commercial spirit predominates over every other, and largely infuses itself into the society of the city. There is a permanent class of wealthy residents, who form the centre of it; its great bulk being composed of those who, by themselves or friends, are still actively engaged in the pursuits of commerce. With a few exceptions it is, therefore, in a state of constant fluctuation, in accordance with the fluctuating fortunes of commercial life. Its doors are guarded, but they seem never to be closed, and you have a constant stream flowing in and out. The consequence

is, that there is much more heart than refinement
about it. It is gay to a degree, sprightly and cordial,
but far less conventional than the corresponding circle
in Philadelphia. Society in the latter has all the
advantages incident to a large community, in which
the commercial spirit does not overbear every thing
else, and in which literature is cultivated as an ornament, more than pursued as a business. In their
habitual intercourse with each other the Philadelphians have an ease of manner which is perfectly
charming. They are familiar without being coarse.
It is not until the stranger gets upon the footing of
being thus treated by them, that he begins to appreciate the real pleasures of Philadelphia life. It is
only after he has surmounted the barrier of formalism
which encounters him on his first entrance, that he
becomes aware of the genial and kindly spirit that
pervades the circle to which he is introduced. In
many respects, Philadelphia life is the best counterpart which America affords to the social refinements
of Europe, whilst it has at bottom a warmth and
cordiality, the manifestation of which is not always
compatible with the exigencies of European etiquette.

In a social point of view, there is this difference in
America between the north and the south; that in
the former, society, in its narrower sense, takes its
chief development in towns, whereas, in the latter, it
is more generally confined to the rural districts. This
difference is chiefly attributable to the different systems which obtain in the distribution of property,
and to other causes, social and political, which will be
presently adverted to. As a general rule, in the north
and west there is no such thing as a country society,

in the ordinary acceptation of the term. The land is divided into small lots, each man, generally speaking, occupying only as much as he can cultivate. The whole country is thus divided into farms; there are few or no estates. The rural population is almost, without exception, a working population, with little leisure, if they had otherwise the means, to cultivate the graces of life. As you travel through the country you see multitudes of comfortable houses and good farming establishments, but no mansions. There is not, in fact, such a class in existence there as is here known as the country gentry. A more unpromising set of materials from which to construct an elegant social fabric, can scarcely be conceived than these northern and western farmers. The following incident will illustrate the whole class. I was acquainted with a farmer in Western New York, who was lucky enough to stumble upon a piece of land with a good "water privilege," which he soon turned to account, and became the "jolly miller" of the surrounding district. By means of his mill, he amassed what, for one in his condition, was a considerable fortune; and, at the instigation of his wife, who was fonder of show than her husband was, turned some of it to account in building a handsome two-story stone house, in contact with the unpretending wooden one, which they had inhabited for years. It was not, however, until the house had been built that they discovered that they had no use for it. When I knew them, and it had then been built five years, but two rooms in the whole house were furnished,—a parlour for great occasions, and a "spare bed-room;" the family continuing to eat, drink, and sleep in the old wooden building, to which they had been

accustomed, and which still remained as a wing to the
new house, which was seldom or ever made any
use of. And so it is with most of them. Their
habits are those of industry and frugality, predisposing
them neither for fine houses, fine clothes, nor fine
equipages. It is quite true that many of them do
move into their "new houses," but they bring all the
tastes and habits of the old house with them, and
alter their condition but little by the change. Such
is the phase which rural life presents in the north
and west, with a few slight exceptions, such as are to
be found in the upper portion of the Genesee Valley,
along that of the Mohawk, and by the shores of the
Hudson in New York, where some families have
accumulated in their hands large properties, and live
in a style which presents a marked contrast to the
rural life around them.

In the south, on the other hand, things assume a
very different aspect. In the States of Maryland,
Virginia, the two Carolinas, Georgia, and Florida, as
indeed in all the Southern States, land is possessed,
as with us, in larger quantities; the owners, as in
England, generally living on their estates. It is thus
that, although Baltimore has its social circle, the
chief society of Maryland is to be found in the counties; whilst, in the same way, the capital of Virginia
affords but a faint type of the society of the State. In
the rural life of these two States, and in that of South
Carolina, are to be found many of the habits and predilections of colonial times, and a nearer approach to
English country life than is discernible in any other
portion of the republic. The country is divided into
large plantations, containing, in many instances,
many thousands of acres; on which reside the dif-

ferent families, in large and commodious mansion-
houses, surrounded by multitudes of slaves and by
all the appliances of rural luxury. It is thus that,
removed as they are from the necessity of labour, and
being interrupted in their retirement only by the
occasional visits of their friends and neighbours,
the opportunity is afforded them of cultivating all
those social qualities which enter into our estimate of
a country gentry. In the society of the Southern Atlantic States, but particularly in that of the three last
mentioned, there is a purity of tone and an elevation
of sentiment, together with an ease of manner and a
general social applomb, which are only to be found
united in a truly leisure class. Any general picture
of American society would be very incomplete, into
which was not prominently introduced the phase
which it exhibits in the rural life of the South.

In some instances, American society is broken into
subsidiary divisions through the influence of religion.
I do not here allude to the effect which sect has in
this respect, and which is in some places so powerful
as virtually to establish a system of mutual non-inter-
course. The division referred to is more into con-
gregations than sects; the frequenters of particular
places of worship having frequently little or no social
intercommunication with those of others, even when
they belong to the same denomination. The *odium
theologicum* has nothing to do with this, nor would,
probably, any such social division exist, especially
between members of the same denomination, but for
the frequency with which their religious duties bring
the members of each church together. Between
Prayer meetings, and Bible Society meetings, and
Dorcas Society meetings, and Sunday School

Teachers' meetings, nearly every night in the week, in addition to Sunday, sees them brought together,— a constancy of association, which soon induces them to regard all beyond their own number with a feeling of indifference. The Dorcas Societies, in particular, are great favourites with the ladies more religiously inclined; seasoning, as they do, a bit of this world's enjoyment with the simultaneous performance of the obligations of charity. The ladies of a congregation, married and expectant, the latter generally predominating, meet in rotation at their respective houses at an early hour in the afternoon; sew away industriously by themselves until evening, when the young gentlemen are introduced with the tea and coffee; whereupon work is suspended, and a snug little party is the hebdomadal consequence, characterised by a good deal of flirtation, and closed by prayer: the young men afterwards escorting the young ladies home, and taking leave of them, to meet them again next week unde· the same happy circumstances.

Bitter as party feeling frequently is in the United States, it is seldom permitted very materially to influence the relations of socie⁺ᵛ. Not that the ladies eschew politics, but they ⅃o not refuse to commingle on that account; nor will they permit the political disputes of their male r⁻ ₁tions to disturb the arrangements which they have made for themselves. Fathers, brothers, and husbands, may tear each other's eyes out at their political tournaments; but wives, sisters, and daughters meet each other in friendly intercourse as before—gathered under the same roof, singing the same songs, and giggling at the same nonsense. Sensible, this, as compared with the ridiculous extent to which party hostility has been carried in the neighbouring province of Canada, where those on opposite sides, and all connected with them, have not only refused to associate but actually even to deal with each other.

There is no feature common to all the departments of American society, which will so soon impress itself upon the stranger as the prominent position occupied in it by the young ladies. In Europe, if they are not kept there, they at least remain somewhat in the background. In America, on the other hand, they are in the foremost rank, and in fact constitute the all in all. Cards of invitation are frequently issued in their names—it being often " The Misses So-and-so" who invite, instead of " Mr. and Mrs. So-and-so." The mother is invariably eclipsed by her daughters. Indeed, I have known instances in which parties were given, at which she never made her appearance; the whole being done with her concurrence and assistance, but she keeping back from a participation in the prevailing gaiety—just because she has no inclination to join in it, prudently judging —wise woman!—that her time for such frivolities is past. The young ladies take the whole burden of the matter upon themselves—receive the guests, and do all the honours of the house. The absent mamma has her health frequently inquired for, but nobody ever thinks of wondering that she is not present. She is perhaps all the time in an adjoining room, superintending the arrangement of the comestibles. She regards the whole as the young ladies' doing, and leaves them to work their way out of it the best way they can. And very well they generally manage to do so—the opportunity which it affords them of cultivating the virtue of self-reliance being by no means thrown away. The young gentlemen, in making visits too, *may* ask at the door for the lady of the house, but such considerateness is a piece of pure supererogation, the young ladies being the parties generally called on, and frequently the only parties seen, if not the only parties asked for. Nor is a long acquaintanceship necessary to establish this footing of pleasant familiarity. You are introduced at a party to a young lady, dance with her, talk a little, and, if she is at all pleased with you, the chances are all in favour of your being invited to call upon her—but by the somewhat guarded phraseology that "we" and not "she" will be very happy to see you. It is your own fault if, from that moment, you are not on intimate and friendly terms with her.

Agreeable as all this may be in some respects, it has very serious disadvantages in others. It imparts to society a general air of frivolity with which it could favourably dispense. When pert young misses of sixteen take it all into their own hands, what else could be expected? Not that all young ladies in America remain at sixteen, either in conduct or in years; but the younger portion of them just admitted into society make themselves more or less the pivot on which it turns. A young girl lives a life of great seclusion until she does come out, but, having an occasional peep at the conduct of her elder sisters or friends, her mind is made up as to the part she is to act before she is formally ushered into the arena. With the exception of some of the more refined and intellectual circles of the large towns, it is sometimes painful to witness the frivolous character of an American social assembly. There is no repose, nothing of a subdued tone about it. The few whose refinements and tastes would favourably influence it, if permitted to do so, are overborne by the numbers as well as by the forwardness of those who impress it with their own immaturities. Society in America is thus like a young hoyden that wants taming—like an inexperienced romp, as yet impatient of the fetters of conventional propriety. The difficulty is, that the remedy for this does not seem very near at hand, for the young blood which influences society to-day will be superseded by that of to-morrow. American society is thus deprived of the best of all teachers—experience; for, by the time that a lady learns how to act an easy and more subdued part, there is no prominent place for her in the social circle.

The consequence of this is, that both men and women of intellectual tastes and quiet habits withdraw more or less from society altogether. It is seldom, therefore, that conversation in a social assembly takes a sober, rational turn. Dreary commonplaces, jokes and vapid compliments, form the staple of conversation, all which is attended by a never-ceasing accompaniment of laughter, which is frequently too boisterous for all tastes. Such being its prominent characteristics on the female side, the picture does not improve when we examine the part borne in it by the men. It is seldom that one ever sees the generality of men rise above the level of their female acquaintances, either in intellectual culture or social refinement. In all civilized communities, women have, in this respect, much in their power. It is for them to select their own associates; and such as aspire to their intimacy will be careful to possess themselves of all those qualifications which are made indispensable to its enjoyment. In American society, the really intellectual man holds a position of comparative isolation. To take his part with the rest, or to be tolerable in their sight, he must be-little himself to the social standard adhered to by those around him. The great proportion of the young men who frequent the social circle, if any thing fall within than exceed this standard. Indeed, it could scarcely be qtherwise, when we consider how alien are their common pursuits to the acquisition of those higher qualities which shine so prominently in the social arena elsewhere, and how little is really required of them to come up to the mark in the estimation of those with whom they associate. A good command of common-places, with a large stock of the "small change" of conversation, will do far more for a man in American society, generally considered, than the possession of higher qualifications will accomplish for him. The Americans certainly worship talent, and hold in high esteem the man of great intellectual acquirement; but they generally prefer reverencing him at a distance to coming in close contact with him; at all events, if he takes any share in their *réunions*, he is more acceptable when he leaves his distinctive qualities behind him. I have seen grave senators, who understood this well, cut the most ludicrous figures, in attempting to render themselves agreeable to giggling young misses, who made very little ceremony with them. Some of them succeed well in the process of intellectual descent, particularly those who have no very great distance to descend. But others find their attempts mere caricatures on frivolity, and, after a few awkward endeavours to accord with circumstances, very frequently withdraw altogether from circles, to the requirements of which they cannot conform themselves.

There is no other country within the pale of civilization, where women might effect so much by elevating the social standard. As a general rule, the men in America fall far short of the women in intellectual culture and moral refinement. Most of them enter upon the walks of business at an early age, before the character is formed or the tastes are well disciplined. The unremitting attention which they pay to business ever afterwards precludes them from, if it does not indispose them to, making any effort at improvement; and society, exacting no very high standard of excellence from them, wears a rough garb, and what is worse, exhibits an unprogressive aspect. If the better educated and the more intellectual class of women in America would play a more prominent part than they do in the social circles of their country, the happiest results would accrue. But they shrink from the task, deeming it hopeless on a comparison of the means with the end, and content themselves with vainly regretting the unintellectual mould in which society around them is cast. I have heard many women of superior acquirement deplore this state of things, when they contrasted the dreary monotony of society in their own country with the happy combination of features which distinguishes many of the social circles of Europe. In confining themselves to these vain regrets, they under-estimate their own power. They could do much to improve the aspect of things around them, by united and persevering effort. But before anything can be effected in this desirable direction, they must put some check upon the absolute social sway of young ladies in their teens. They must cripple the now unbounded influence of youth, inexperience, and thoughtlessness; and make discipline, settled character, and knowledge of the world, the pivots on which society should turn. The matron must, at least, divide the sway with the giddy-headed girl, or it will be vain to expect that society in America will be speedily rescued from the tyranny of frivolity to which it is at present subjected.

Another feature in American society, which soon excites the surprise of the stranger, but which is, in fact, a mere illustration of the foregoing, is the little attention which is paid in the social circle to married women. She may be young, beautiful, and accomplished to a degree, and may, indeed, but yesterday, have been the reigning belle, but, despite of all this, from the moment that she submits to the matrimonial tie, the American woman is, socially speaking, as the common phrase is, " laid on the shelf." From habit and old associations she may for a while make her appearance in company, but at longer and longer intervals, until, after a very short time, in the great majority of cases, she disappears altogether, only again to cross the threshold of society when her taste for its enjoyments is blunted, when her cheek is faded and her youth gone, and when she has daughters of her own to introduce. Whilst the young ladies engross all attention to themselves, the married ones sit neglected in the corners, despite the superiority which they may sometimes possess, both in personal charms and mental accomplishment.

Many of the peculiarities of American society can be directly traced to the education of young women in the United States—by which I do not mean the

system of teaching adopted in schools, so much as
the moral and social discipline which they undergo.
A freedom of manner, and a liberty of action, are
extended to them, very different from the strict and
vigilant guard which is kept over young women in
the older hemisphere; and which seems to be but a
necessary corollary from the political order of things
in America. In a country where there are so few
conventional restraints, and where the very institutions of society give rise to great latitude of action
and freedom of intercourse, more depends upon
individual character, than in communities where the
conduct of parties is more regulated by the rules and
the machinery of class. A young girl in America is
in every way a freer agent than her European sister:
the whole course of her education is one habitual
lesson of self-reliance—the world is not kept a sealed
book to her until she is tolerably advanced in years,
then to be suddenly thrown open to her in all its
diversity of aspects. From the earliest age she begins to understand her position, and to test her own
strength—she soon knows how to appreciate the
world, both as to its proprieties and its dangers—
she knows how far she can go in any direction with
safety, and how far she can let others proceed—she
soon acquires a strength of character, to which the
young woman of Europe is a stranger, and acts for
herself whilst the latter is yet in leading-strings.
All this would tend, were her entrance into society
a little longer delayed, or were the sway which she
acquires over it somewhat postponed, to impart a
much more sedate and serious character to American
social intercourse than it possesses. It is this very
freedom of action that precipitates her into an

influential social position, at a time when she is neither fitted for it nor able fully to appreciate its responsibilities. Her course of education tells unfavourably upon society, before it has fully succeeded in telling favourably upon the individual—by which time, as already intimated, in nine cases out of ten, her influence over the social regime is gone. The order of things around her exposes her to more dangers than the young girl in Europe has to encounter, but she acquires strength of character to meet them. The whole tendency of her education, whilst it is attended with some risks, is to unveil these dangers to her, and to arm her against their approaches. How far this may strengthen the character at the expense of the affections—how far it may fortify the judgment, but weaken the heart—it is not necessary here to inquire.

The latitude of action here referred to, necessarily involves a free and habitual intercourse between the sexes. This is permitted from the very earliest ages, and never ceases until the young girl has left her father's house for that of her husband. The freedom thus extended is one which is seldom abused in America, and is more an essential feature than an accidental circumstance in a young woman's education. The young man invites her to walk or ride with him, and her compliance with the invitation is a matter solely dependent upon her own humour; he escorts her to the concert, or home from the party, the rest of the family finding their way thither or returning home as they may: indeed, I have known the young ladies of the same family escorted by their male acquaintances in different vehicles to the same party, where they would make their appearance, perhaps, at different times. Nor is this confined to cases in which the young men are recognised admirers of the young ladies, a friendly intimacy being all that is required to justify invitation on the one side, and compliance on the other. A young woman here would regard such conduct as a disregard of the proprieties of her sex; if it were looked upon as such in America, it would not be followed. The difference arises from the different views taken in the two hemispheres, by young women, of their actual position. In America it neither impairs the virtue, nor compromises the dignity of the sex. It may be somewhat inimical to that warmth of imagination, and delicacy of character, which, in Europe, is so much admired in the young woman, but it is productive of impurity neither in thought nor conduct.

That such is the case, no stronger proof can be given than the almost Quixotic devotion which the Americans pay to the sex. The attention which they receive at home and abroad, in the drawing-room, in the railway-carriage, or on board the steamer, instead of resulting from familiarity, is dictated by the highest respect; for whilst the young woman in America is learning the realities of her own position, she acquires a knowledge of that of her companions, and knows how to keep them in it.

This will not seem to accord with the impression, which is so general here, of the overdone prudery of the American women. They are as ready as any of their sex to resent a real indignity; but nothing could be more erroneous than to suppose that they carry their regard for delicacy so far as to bespeak a real impurity of imagination. That in some parts of the country an over sensitiveness in this repect exists, is not to be denied; but it is confined to certain localities, where it is directly attributable to circumstances, which have had no existence in others. It may yet be traced, to a certain extent, amongst the descendants of the Puritans; but even amongst them, not in that degree in which some writers have improperly left it to be inferred that it is a general characteristic. If there is any difference between American and European women in this respect, the latter, as a general rule, are the more liable to the charge; the former often conversing upon subjects on which the latter would be backward in touching, with an unreserve which bespeaks the absence of all improper thought or motive.

For several years past, the town of Newport in Rhode Island has been the most fashionable sea-bathing place in the country. I once spent a fortnight there during the season. The very first day I was there, whilst strolling with a friend on the beach, we met a party of ladies and gentlemen with whom he was acquainted, and to whom he immediately introduced me. After conversing for a short time, I was surprised at a proposition made to us by one of the young ladies to go and bathe with them. I afterwards found that this was no uncommon occurrence at Newport—the ladies and gentlemen having different accommodations, in which they provided themselves with suitable bathing dresses, habited in which, they dash out, hand in hand, sometimes forty of them together, into the surf upon the beach. I confess I thought this more in accordance with the social habits of Paris and Vienna than with those of the United States. There was in it a latitude which was no more typical of the general habits of the people than is the prudery which is, in some instances, carried to an excess. Indeed these may be regarded as the two extremes, between which are to be found the real sentiments and true habits of the people. The error lies in that summary process of generalization, which extends, without inquiry, to all, the peculiarities which are observable in a few.

The precocious age at which marriages frequently take place in America, has also occasionally its visible effect upon society. It appears ridiculous to those accustomed to the order of things on this side of the Atlantic, to see the boy and the girl, as yet apparently unfitted for final emancipation from the boarding-school, assume with the utmost nonchalance the conjugal responsibilities. In a new country, where every one has plenty of room, and where energy and industry are sure at once to command a competence, early marriages are not only allowable, but in some cases desirable. The relationship, which, in a crowded community like this, may weigh like a millstone about a young man's neck, is found in America to be frequently the spur to enterprise, when enterprise is all that is necessary to ensure success. But this does not justify marriages at ages at which even the precocity of America does not ensure maturity of judgment or character. Were the infant couples, which one everywhere meets with, to settle down into domestic habits, beyond occasionally finding out that they had made a mutual mistake, the mischief might not extend. But in a great many such cases, marriage does not result in immediate domesticity. The connexion is formed before either party can become at once reconciled to the cares and troubles of housekeeping. Hence it often happens that these never enter into the calculations of a young couple contemplating matrimony. It is to the hotel they look, not to the domestic hearth, as their immediate home, after the ceremony is performed. The American towns, the larger ones particularly, are studded with hotels, half the support of which is derived from permanent boarders, who generally consist of newly-married parties, who are anxious as long as possible to postpone the disagreeable duty of keeping a house for themselves. There is something exciting about this hotel life, which is pleasant to the young woman, inasmuch as it leaves her much of the freedom which she possessed before she came under the nuptial obligations. It gives her no trouble, and causes her no anxiety; there being an abundance of servants always about her to do her bidding, and the table to which she daily sits down being both elegant and sumptuous. All this is very different from the comparatively tranquil and secluded life which an American wife leads in her husband's home—a life, the contemplation of which is disagreeable to her who has become the wife ere she was yet fairly the young woman. She breakfasts with her husband in the "ladies' ordinary," at which a large and mixed company assemble; after which, she is left alone till dinner time, when her husband, who has been at his business, returns and dines with her in the same company as before. He then leaves her again, and does not return till evening, and sometimes not till a late hour. During his absence she is left to her own resources, and inexperienced as she often is, must be thus exposed to many risks. A stranger or traveller, in passing to or from his own room, along the lobbies of his hotel, if he chances to look in at any of the open doors which he passes, may see a neat little parlour, with a young woman alone in it, perhaps,. for want of other occupation, listlessly thrumming the piano. Returning again, he may observe the same party, varying her occupation by leisurely strolling along the lobby, either alone or in company with some others similarly circumstanced, on whom she has called, perhaps, at some of the adjoining rooms. This mode of life, in addition to its many exposures, has other evils attendant upon it; a couple cannot always thus live, and it is but a poor preparation for the domestic life, to which they must sooner or later betake themselves. It frequently begets a carelessness and want of forethought, that are discernible in their effects long after it is abandoned. Nor are the evils of the system confined to those who submit themselves to it. Its influence extends, more or less, to their friends and acquaintances whom they visit, and who are in the habit of calling upon them. This mode of life is not confined to hotels, but it is in connexion with hotels that its evils are most apparent. To be sure, it is but a small proportion of the American people who resort to it; but the domestic life of America would, on the whole, be improved, if parties did not marry until they could reconcile themselves to the quiet and the duties of home.

The taste for music is universal with the American ladies, in which a very large proportion of them become great proficients. Many of them are also excessively fond of dancing; although there are others by whom this harmless amusement is looked upon as a heinous sin. By none is it more denounced than by the Presbyterians of the north, the terrors of

Church censure hanging over those who might be inclined to offend. I have seen all the Presbyterians at a party withdraw as soon as dancing commenced. So long as there was nothing but gossiping and promenading, arm in arm, about the rooms and lobbies, there was no harm done; but the moment that it was proposed to continue the chit-chat in a *vis-à-vis*, and to move the feet to the sound of music, instead of doing so at random, in the sight of these well-meaning people, some recondite line of the moral law was about to be transcended, to which they would not be parties themselves, nor would they stop to witness the sin of others.

There is another point, in reference to which the impression prevalent in this country is somewhat erroneous, — that involved in the relation between master and servant in America. It is quite true that the gulf which separates these two classes of society in England is greater and more impassable than it is in America; the master in the former occupying higher, and the servant lower ground, than in the latter. But it is equally true, that in America there is a broad and distinct line drawn between the two conditions of master and servant. If the servant is not as obedient as he is in Europe, or the master as exacting, it is not because the servant puts himself on a footing of equality with the master whilst the relation subsists between them, but because both parties look to the time when that relation will be dissolved, by the servant becoming himself a master. There is in America, with the exception of the Slave States, no permanent class of servants as in other countries; but to suppose that, so long as any individual acts in the relation of a servant, he puts himself, in all respects,

on an equality with his master, is to be in error ; and
much more so to think that, should such equality be
asserted, it would be conceded by the master. In
America, as elsewhere, the servant, so long as he
remains a servant, is in subordination to the master,
although the tie is more easily and more frequently
broken, because the servant is not in the same position
of absolute dependence as elsewhere. He may become unmanageable from the readiness with which he
can find employment; but the moment he trenches
upon the master's prerogatives he is dismissed, instead of being permitted to share them. It is quite
true, that in many of the rural districts, particularly
in the newer settlements, masters and servants live
upon the same footing. But this occurs in a state of
society in which the drawing a line of distinction
would be as impossible as it would be ridiculous.
The farmer who works side by side with his servant,
tilling the same field with him, and coping with him
constantly at the same work, could scarcely sit in one
end of the house at his meals whilst the servant sat
at his in the other. The farmer, his sons and servants,
work together and eat together, living as nearly in a
state of equality with each other as can be. This, however, is the case in the rural districts of Canada as well
as in those of the United States. But to think that
the same practice in its totality, or even in a modified
form, enters into all grades of society, is erroneous.
In American society, in the ordinary sense of the
term, the servant is the servant, as in Europe. In
America they may be more impertinent, and less
easily kept in their places; but this results not from
the master's giving way to any unreasonable claims,
but from the fact that servants there can more easily
find other places than with us.

Amongst a people so widely scattered, and living under such different circumstances, one may naturally expect to meet with every variety of character, and every stage of social development. It is almost impossible for one at a distance, in contemplating a moral picture so diversified as is that presented in America,—from the life of the backwoods-man on the Miami or the Wabash, to that exhibited by the polished commercial community on the coast, and from the indolence and impetuosity of the Southerner, to the plodding enterprise and the equanimity of the New Englander,—to distinguish at all times between a local peculiarity and a general characteristic. Hence it is, that amongst the mistakes fallen into, the whole American people are too readily blamed by the European, for the savage character which duelling assumes in some parts of the country. It would be equally just to comprehend the abolitionists in the blame of slavery; or to say, that because steamers are constantly being blown up on the Mississippi, they are necessarily being so upon the Hudson also. Nowhere is the duelling spirit prevalent in the South so severely reprehended as in the Northern States. It is seldom that a duel occurs in the latter, but far more seldom that it is attended by any of the savage accompaniments which so often characterise the duels of the South. Even in the South itself there are differences in this respect, there being some districts in which the propensity to duelling assumes the type of an ineradicable chronic distemper. In places thus afflicted, society displays a degree of over-sensitiveness, which is quite unnecessary for the conservation of honour. In no place, perhaps, is this over-sensitiveness so much exhibited as in the capital of Virginia. But a high degree of physical sensibility, whilst it may result from a fine nervous organization, may also be the consequence of an inflammatory disorder : and so with this over-sensitiveness of feeling; it by no means proves a healthy moral state, or a clear perception of the real nature of honour. It is curious to witness the extent to which, in such places as those alluded to, all parties are equally infected. When a quarrel arises and a duel is the consequence, the whole community take sides, ladies and all, and the merits of the quarrel are discussed with the utmost coolness ; one set coming to the conclusion that the challenger under the circumstances could not but challenge, and the other that the challenged could not but fight. But I allude to this merely to remove the impression that the duel is a practice which universally obtains in America, or that it is countenanced by the tastes, the habits, and the views of society at large. So far is this from being the case, that some, even of the Western States, have lately adopted the most stringent provisions for its suppression.

It is scarcely necessary, in here concluding this survey, again to remind the reader, that society, in the larger communities already named, has reached a point of development, which renders much of the foregoing nearly as inapplicable to it, in connexion with these communities, as it would be to the social condition of London or Paris.

I cannot do better than close this chapter with a brief reference to the style and characteristics of American beauty. There are two points in which it is seldom equalled, never excelled—the classic chasteness and delicacy of the features, and the smallness and exquisite symmetry of the extremities. In the latter respect, particularly, the American ladies are singularly fortunate. I have seldom seen one, delicately brought up, who had not a fine hand. The feet are also generally very small and exquisitely moulded, particularly those of a Maryland girl; who, well aware of their attractiveness, has a thousand little coquettish ways of her own of temptingly exhibiting them. That in which the American women are most deficient is roundness of figure. But it is a mistake to suppose that well-rounded forms are not to be found in America. Whilst this is the characteristic of English beauty, it is not so prominent a feature in America. In New England, in the mountainous districts of Pennsylvania and Maryland, and in the central valley of Virginia, the female form is, generally speaking, as well rounded and developed as it is here; whilst a New England complexion is, in nine cases out of ten, a match for an English one. This, however, cannot be said of the American ladies as a class. They are, in the majority of cases, over delicate and languid; a defect chiefly superinduced by their want of exercise. An English girl will go through as much exercise in a forenoon, without dreaming of fatigue, as an American will in a day, and be overcome by the exertion. It is also true, that American is more evanescent than English beauty, particularly in the south, where it seems to fade ere it has well bloomed. But it is much more lasting in the north and north-east: a remark which will apply to the whole region north of the Potomac, and east of the Lakes; and 1 have known instances of Philadelphia beauty as lovely and enduring as any that our own hardy climate can produce.

CHAPTER XII.

POLITICAL ASPECT OF THE UNITED STATES.

Complexity of the American System.—Its Double Aspect, central
and local.—The Constitutional System in its Federal capacity.—
The Executive Power—Its Authority, Responsibility, and Means
of Government.—The Legislative Power—Its Constitution, Func-
tions, and Modes of Action.— Single and Double Chambers.—
The Veto Power.—Mode and Terms of Election to the Two
Houses of Congress.—Basis of the Representation.—The Ballot.—
Peculiar Position of the Senate.—Its Executive Functions.—The
Doctrine of Instructions, as applied to it.— The Presidential
Election.—Mode of conducting it. — Manner of Election, when
no Choice by the People.—Single and Double Terms.—Views
entertained by many, of the President's Position and Power.—
Anomalous Position of the Vice-President.—Territorial Govern-
ment.—The American System, in its relation to the different
States.—Their Sovereignty, Independence, and Separate action.—
Conflict of Jurisdictions.—Prospects of the Union—Its Weak-
ness—Its Strength.—Combination of the National and Federal
Principles.—Nullification.—Cost of Government in England and
America.—Contrast between the Political Systems of the two
Countries.—Note.

BY those who have not closely examined into its
constitution and working, it is very generally, but
very erroneously, believed that the political scheme
of America is one of the most simple arrangements,
and that the machinery of its government is free from
the complications observable in the institutions of
other countries. The only thing in which the American system is simple is the principle upon which it is
based—the political equality of man ; the govern-
mental superstructure which is raised on this foun-

dation presenting to the eye of the careful observer one of the most elaborate political devices on earth. The complicity which characterizes the American system is not, however, that which arises from confusion, being solely attributable to the number of its parts, and the necessary intricacy of their collocation. Whatever may be thought of its absolute excellence, or of its adaptation to its purposes, every one who comprehends it must admit that the American constitution is one of the most ingenious pieces of political mechanism that ever resulted from the deliberations of man. Let not the reader shrink from the brief sketch of it which follows, under the idea that it is to assume the character of a minute analysis, or a learned and technical commentary ; my object being to present such a picture of it to him as may not only inform the mind, but also leave an impression upon the imagination.

The federal character of the republic was the chief difficulty in the way of the organization of the general government. When there are but one people and one set of interests to provide for, it may be a comparatively easy matter, if the people are understood and their interests appreciated, to devise a constitutional framework for their political life. But in America the case was widely different. In framing a constitution for the whole body, the social and political peculiarities and conflicting interests of thirteen different and independent communities had to be studied ; and the task of framing such a system as would reconcile all, whilst it offended none, was one, the magnitude of which is only understood when it is considered that, previously to the Revolution, they had but little in common with each other, either as to tastes, sympathies, or habits; that great event uniting them, for the first time, in the pursuit of a common object, and for the avoidance of a common danger. And not only had the necessities of the times to be consulted, in devising the constitution; the exigencies of the future had also to be provided for. The fabric to be reared must be such as to afford accommodation for future as well as for present applicants; sufficiently compact to meet the wants of existing communities, and sufficiently elastic to embrace future sovereignties, without distorting its outline or impairing its strength. How far its framers succeeded in their object may be inferred from the fact, that the constitution devised for the thirteen original States, has, without any essential change in its character, expanded its dimensions, until at present no less than thirty different and mutually independent communities are embraced within its pale. The American confederation now exhibits no less than thirty-one different political systems in contemporaneous operation; the federal government which, for certain purposes, extends over the whole Union, and the thirty different constitutional schemes, which the thirty different States have adopted for themselves, for the management of such matters as do not fall within the purview of the powers of the general government. One of the grand difficulties originally in the way was to draw the line between general and local jurisdiction. In most instances it is broadly traced, but in some points so lightly defined as to give rise to frequent struggles between the Federal and State authorities.

The republic then presents two aspects, one in its confederate, the other in its separate capacity. And first, for a brief glance at its confederate side.

In taking this glance, it may be as well at once to refer to the broad and simple basis on which rests the whole structure of the American government. At the foundation of all, and permeating the entire system, is the principle of the absolute sovereignty of the people. The presence of this fundamental idea is discernible in the whole constitutional arrangement, as its influence is perceptible in its every modification. It is the grand rule to which power, in all its delegated forms, is the exception. There is no authority possessed either by the general government, or by the State governments, which has not emanated from a voluntary abdication *pro tanto*, on the part of the people. Government is not in America a self-subsistent power, coercing the people into subjection; but the instrument of their authority and the exponent of their will. The assertion of this popular sovereignty necessarily implies the subjection to the strictest accountability of all the departments of the government. With but few exceptions, the elective principle is applied to every office in the State, whilst the tenure of office is of but brief duration. Authority proceeds from the people only to merge again in the fountain whence it flowed. It thus never becomes independent of its source, periodically lapsing into it, as the vapours which exhale from the earth fall again upon its surface in showers. By the time that power can acquire any independent interests of its own, it sinks again into the body of the constituency, the ruler being retransformed into the citizen ere he forgets the rights and privileges of the citizen. It is obvious that this constant creation and surrender of authority is necessary to the maintenance of that rigid responsibility, which is a corollary to the principle on which the government is founded. In considering the structure of the federal and state governments, it will be seen that throughout, the people appear as the great depositories and dispensers of power, that those clothed with authority are made as directly as they are frequently responsible to them, and that revolution is averted from the system itself, by the constant changes which are taking place in the *personnel* of its administration.

The original articles of confederation having been found inadequate to their purpose, the present Constitution was adopted a few years after the close of the revolutionary struggle. One of the greatest alterations then effected in the federal system, was the establishment of a single Executive. By the Constitution, the whole executive power of the government, with some checks, to be hereafter noticed, is vested in the President of the United States. To arm this department of the government with sufficient authority to give it that efficiency which would secure the due administration of the laws, and command respect both at home and abroad, and at the same time so to regulate the exercise of its authority as to prevent it from trenching upon the other elements of the system, was the great problem, to which were directed the most anxious deliberations of the convention which formed the Constitution. And in no other part, perhaps, has the Constitution proved so faulty as it has in this, when we consider, in illustration of it, the manner in which Mr. Polk contrived with impunity to override it, in taking those steps in the conduct of his government, which were the proximate cause of the Mexican war. Although the power of declaring war and of making peace is

expressly vested in Congress, the Executive managed,
without nominally usurping the prerogatives of Congress, to get the two republics into a "state of war,"
which necessarily devolved upon Congress the necessity of providing the means for carrying on hostilities,
a course by which the legislative body virtually took
upon itself the responsibility of the contest. It was
in vain that many voices were raised against the gross
invasion of the Constitution of which the Executive
had been guilty, and that many warnings were given
of the danger of appearing even to sanction it. The
passions of the democracy were roused for the time
being; they were seized with a lust for war, and
cared not what came of the Constitution so long as
the predominant appetite of the moment was gratified.
But the whole transaction is pregnant with serious
lessons to the American people, affording, as it does,
a proof of the ease with which an unscrupulous
government may violate their charter; and the ready
indemnity which it may receive for so doing, at
the hands of a misdirected populace. This should
be a serious reflection to a people who regard the
Constitution as the basis of their whole political system. In view of recent events, can they any longer
repose in the full confidence that it is a foundation of
rock for the Union?

To the President is entrusted the management of
the foreign relations, together with the administration of the internal affairs of the Union. As regards
the former, however, he is not, as is the case with
the executive department in constitutional monarchies,
invested with unfettered discretion, subject only to a
general responsibility to public opinion; the Senate
so far participating in executive authority as to have

a direct and immediate control over the foreign relations of the republic. For instance, no treaty can
be concluded with any power without the assent of
two-thirds of the Senate; nor can an ambassador or a
secretary of legation be appointed to a foreign government without the confirmation of his appointment by
a majority of that body. To a certain extent, the
President is still left the power of independent action; it being his duty to initiate, that of the Senate
to ratify or disapprove. Both Houses of Congress
may urge him by resolution to adopt a particular
course, with regard to a foreign power, but he is not
compellable to listen to them. Sometimes, again, in
matters in regard to which an absolutely independent
action is left him, he prefers taking the advice of the
legislative bodies; which they may tender by joint or
separate resolution, or which they may refuse, leaving
the executive to act upon its own responsibility.
Such was the conduct pursued by Mr. Polk on the
Oregon question. It was quite competent for him
to have given notice to the British government of the
expiration of the then existing treaty, at the end of
a year from the time of giving the notice. But he
shrank from the responsibility of the tremendous
issues apparently contingent upon such a step, and
wisely sought, in taking it, to shelter himself under
the previous sanction of Congress. This participation by one branch of the legislature in the treaty-
making power, as well as in some other executive
functions, whilst it is a peculiar feature in the
American political system, affords an instance of the
vigilant and jealous spirit in which the executive
department was conceived.

The President governs through the medium of a

Cabinet of his own choosing, to whose shoulders, however, is not transferred, as with us, the whole responsibility of the acts of the government. The Americans do not recognise the principle that the President can do no wrong. On the contrary, they acted, in determining his position and duties, upon the supposition that it was in his power, if it was not his inclination, to do every mischief, and therefore fettered his actions. The ability to do wrong involves responsibility for doing it; and although the policy of the government may frequently be the result of evil counsels, no one ever thinks of screening the President behind his Cabinet. The constitution of the Cabinet is itself a pretty good indication of the range of Presidential authority. It is composed of the heads of the five principal departments of State—those of the Treasury—of State—of War—of the Navy, and of the Post Office. The Attorney-general of the United States is also frequently a member of it. In this list the reader will miss the Home department—that of State having no concern with any matters but such as appertain to the foreign policy of the country. The Home business is attended to by each State for itself. The internal administration of the federal government is exceedingly limited, being principally confined to the management of the Post Office—the raising of the revenue—enforcing the observance of treaties—the control of the Indian tribes—and the municipal government of the district of Columbia, and of the territory comprised within the limits of such forts and dockyards as are in the possession of the United States. The President is also Commander-in-Chief of the army and navy—the executive government having the exclusive control of the movements of the existing land and naval forces of the confederation. He is also Commander-in-Chief of the militia, when actually in the service of the United States, until which time they remain under the exclusive direction of the authorities of their respective States. So far reference has been had to him in his executive capacity. His legislative functions will be considered in treating of the legislature.

No one connected with the executive government is permitted to occupy a seat in either House of Congress. This is very different from the rule which obtains with us, of requiring the presence of the heads of departments at least in one or the other House of Parliament, and is considered by many in America a disadvantageous feature in their political scheme. The result of it is, that with the exception of such messages as are from time to time transmitted to Congress by the President, all direct communication is cut off between the legislative bodies and the executive government. The former are consequently very frequently in painful uncertainty as to the views and policy of the latter, which, in such cases, can only be removed by such revelations as the private friends of the executive may make, authorizedly or otherwise, either in or out of Congress. The inconvenience of this was frequently felt both in the Senate and in the House of Representatives, during the progress of the Oregon discussions; he whole country being tossed about between alternations of hope and fear, as the President's friends affected to give utterance to his sentiments in either House of Congress. I well remember the depressing influence produced, particularly on the commercial

States, by the oft-repeated insinuations, by Mr. Allen
of Ohio, in the Senate, of his knowledge of the sentiments of the President—whom he represented as
not having swerved a hair's breadth from his ex-
pressed determination to adhere to the line of 54° 40'.
Nor do I forget the consternation which seized the
ranks of the war party, when Mr. Haywood, of
North Carolina, who was known to be a personal
favourite at the White House, laboured for two
whole days to show that there was nothing in the
Presidential message which necessarily precluded the
executive government from accepting the 49th
parallel of latitude as the boundary on the Pacific,
should Great Britain choose to make the offer. I do
not say that if any members of the Cabinet had been
present on these occasions, it would have been advisable for them to have disclosed to the whole world
the views of the executive government; but their
presence would have at least prevented others from
speaking in their behalf, and from occasioning the
unseemly spectacle of having a grave body like the
Senate alternately elevated and depressed by the
volunteer declarations of some of its members, who
either knew, or only affected to know, what they
pretended to reveal. Besides, the government is
often placed at this disadvantage by being wholly
unrepresented in Congress—that it is frequently un-
defended, when its policy is impugned; for, whilst
it is easy to attack it, they only may be competent to
defend it who are in possession of all the motives of
its conduct.

The legislative power of the United States is
vested in the federal congress, consisting of a Senate
and House of Representatives. The American

people were well trained in the school of popular institutions, long before they were called upon to institute an independent popular government. The consequence was, that when they set about the task of framing a constitution, they proceeded to their work, not like dreamers or theorists, but like practical men, who well understand the business in which they are engaged. When the question before them related to the distribution of the legislative power, there were certainly not wanting those who counselled the propriety of having only a single Chamber. But this was a peril which America was by the prudence of her statesmen enabled to avoid. There are many who cannot dissociate the idea of a double Chamber from monarchy, with which it is most frequently found in juxtaposition. They thus contract an aversion to the principle from one of its manifestations. They fancy that they cannot have the benefits without the drawbacks of a double Chamber; whereas a very little reflection might teach them that all that is valuable in the principle might be secured, whilst all that was objectionable was avoided. It by no means follows that, because in most instances in which a double Chamber exists or has existed, one only has, even theoretically, represented the people, whilst the other has, confessedly and notoriously, represented but a class or section of the people, or been entirely constituted of that class, two Chambers could not exist, each of which represented the whole people, though in different modes and degrees.

In countries where there are distinctions of class, the double Chamber has a double object to fulfil; for not only are two legislative bodies, co-ordinate and independent of each other, deemed necessary as a check upon mischievous and precipitate legislation, but one of the two is designed to keep up the power and privileges of a certain class. But where no such distinction exists there can be no such object as the latter to fulfil; when, if the purpose first named be deemed a desirable one, the sole object of a double Chamber would be to secure it. How far a double Chamber is capable of securing it has been abundantly proved by the legislative experiences both of this country and America. But when the Americans adopted the double Chamber, they had only the experience of England to guide them. They adopted it simply to check reckless legislation; and having once established a dual legislature, they invested one branch of it, with a view to other objects, with peculiar powers. But both Chambers, as will be immediately seen, were made elective, so that both might represent the whole nation. They differ only as to the mode in which, and the terms for which, they are elected. Thus all the benefits of the double Chamber have been secured tc them, without their having any cause to be jealous of either of them; at the same time, as will be afterwards shown in treating more particularly of the federal legislature, both Chambers can act a co-ordinate part, really as well as nominally, from being both based upon the suffrages of the people. America has been saved from many a precipice by her double Chamber.

As the legislative body is itself a creation of the Constitution, so its powers are strictly defined by that document. It is a common saying with us, that the powers of Parliament are transcendent and omnipotent; but it is otherwise with the American Congress.

It is only within certain limits that it can constitutionally act; beyond these limits it is as impotent as a child. It is not a body concentrating in itself all legislative powers except such as may be expressly denied it, but a body possessing no legislative power whatever, except such as is expressly conferred upon it. If it transcends the circle of its authority, the Supreme Court of the United States stands by to annul its acts, a relation between the judiciary and the legislature, which will be hereafter more fully explained. Its powers, which are specifically enumerated in eighteen consecutive clauses of the Constitution, have all, more or less, reference to the common interests and general welfare of the Union. Indeed, it can only legislate in matters exclusively federal. Its chief powers are to levy and collect taxes for the purposes of revenue, to regulate foreign and domestic commerce, to coin money, to declare war, and to provide for the common defence by raising and equipping armies, and by maintaining a navy; and, when necessary, by organizing and equipping the militia.

With the exception of money bills, which must originate in the House of Representatives, any legislative measure within the power of Congress to enact, may be initiated in either House. In respect to the introduction of bills, a practice prevails which might be very usefully imitated in this country. At the commencement of each session, both Houses appoint standing committees upon different subjects, within the province of one or other of which such legislative acts as they may be called upon to consider must necessarily fall. Each House, for instance, has its standing committee on Foreign Relations, on Ways and Means, on Military Affairs, on the Judiciary, &c. When it is found necessary to legislate on any of these subjects, the matter is generally referred to the appropriate committee, which is instructed to report a bill in reference to it, should it see fit so to do. Should it refuse to do so, the power of the House over the subject is not gone, inasmuch as a bill may be introduced independently of such adverse report; and every bill which is introduced, not emanating directly from a committee, may be referred to the appropriate committee, according to the nature of its subject-matter. The consequence is, that bills are in general much more carefully prepared than they are with us; so that the statute-book is prevented from being overloaded, as ours is, with acts to amend acts, and to amend again the amending acts themselves. A bill having passed one House, is sent into the other, where, if it is rejected, it is dropped, as with us, for the session. When both Houses concur, it is transmitted to the President for his approval, and, on receiving his signature, becomes law. If he retains it for ten days after it is sent up to him, without signifying his approval thereof, or dissent therefrom, it then also becomes law. If, however, he dissent within the ten days, the bill is vetoed, when, in order to enable it to become law, it must afterwards receive the assent of two-thirds of the members of each House. If it do so, it becomes law without any further reference to the President.

It is this veto power which, although the first clause of the Constitution declares that all legislative power shall be vested in Congress, defining Congress to consist of a Senate and House of Representatives, makes the executive virtually a co-ordinate branch of the legislature. It is extremely rare to find parties so unequally matched in the United States as to render it likely that a bill vetoed by the President will be afterwards assented to by so large a majority as two-thirds of either House. The consequence is, that the veto of the President is tantamount to the rejection of the bill by either of the two Houses themselves; and scarcely a session passes in which the power thus vested in him is not frequently exercised. Thus, although, as compared with the constitutional sovereign of this country, he may be fettered and restricted in his executive capacity, his legislative power, although theoretically not greater, is, practically speaking, much more so, being by far more frequently and more boldly exercised, in opposition to the two other branches of the legislature, than it has been in this country for nearly two centuries past.

Such being the constitution of the different departments of the federal government, and such the scope respectively of their authority, it may not now be amiss to inquire how, and how often parties are elected to fill them. With the exception of the judicial office, and the different departments of the executive government, immediately within the control of the President, as well as the more subordinate amongst offices purely ministerial, every post in America must be filled by election. Indeed, in some of the States the elective principle has been carried so far as to include the judiciary itself within its range.

Both Houses of Congress, as already observed, are elective bodies, although in different modes and degrees—the Lower House springing directly, the

Upper only mediately from the people.   No one can
be returned to this or to the other House of Congress, unless, if he seeks to be a senator, he resides
within the State which he wishes to represent; or, if
he confine his views to the House of Representatives,
he be a resident of the county or electoral district within the State for which he is desirous of
becoming member.   It is not difficult to discover
some propriety in this rule as regards the Senate; but
in its extension to the other House, the services of
many eminent men are lost to the nation; for, if they
are repudiated by the successful machinations of
faction in their own localities, they can represent no
other constituency in the country.   This, however, is
all the mischief which the rule works in America.
A similar rule adopted in this country would operate
in a similar manner, at the same time that it would
be liable to the additional objection, that it would
enable the government, from the power which the
still rotten state of the representation gives it of controlling many constituencies, to get rid of a troublesome member of the House, by simply taking care to
have him defeated in his own locality.   But now the
defeated candidate may be returned by another constituency, over which the government may not have
the same power.   For some time the rule was with
us as it now is in America, but it was soon changed.
The House of Representatives is entirely renewed
every second year, from the whole body of the people.
It consists at present of about 230 members—to prevent it from greatly exceeding which number, the
basis of representation is enlarged every ten years,
after each successive census.   At present there is a
representative in Congress for every 70,000 people;

at the adoption of the constitution there was one for every 30,000.

Whilst population is thus made the sole basis of representation, the suffrage is, for all purposes,—municipal, state, or federal,—universal. In a country like America, the whole of whose political fabric rests upon the recognised equality of man, it is difficult to see how any other basis for the representation could have been assumed. In America too, where the people are all, more or less, industrious, population and property are pretty equally distributed throughout the country. Thus, whilst the only basis is assumed which conforms to the spirit of the whole system, the representation, in effect, rests upon the double basis of population and property. The Americans thus aimed at a single intelligible basis, and secured a double one. How different is it with us! It defies the ingenuity of man to state the basis on which representation in Great Britain rests. Indeed it has none, at least none that is intelligible.

It is scarcely necessary here to add, that, with one or two exceptions, the vote in America is universally taken by ballot. One of the objections offered to the adoption of the ballot in England is, that in America, where it prevails, there is no concealment in voting. Generally speaking, this is perfectly true; but they are driven to desperate shifts for argument, who make use of this as one against the power of secret voting. Even if the objection to open voting were simply that it is open, the want of concealment in America would be no argument against the ballot, seeing that, although secret voting is within the reach of every elector, it is not compulsory there. The objection to open voting in a country like this rests

upon the power which it gives to parties, exercising
an undue influence, to control the elections. The
vote by ballot, without concealment, would be no
cure for this evil; but it does not follow that the
vote by ballot must necessarily be without concealment. Let it be made compulsorily secret as regards
all, and what becomes of the argument founded on
the want of concealment? In this country, were it
adopted, it would be necessary that, for some time at
least, it should be made compulsorily secret; else he
who voted secretly would be marked by those who
sought to influence him, as much as he who voted
openly against them. If, in America, the vote by
ballot is given in ninety-nine cases out of a hundred
without concealment, it is because the constituencies
are so numerous as to be independent—the electors
are at liberty to consult their own wishes, and there
is nobody to call them to account for the mode in
which they have voted. Still, any elector has it in
his power, if he so chooses, to vote secretly, and
some invariably do so. No argument, therefore, in
regard to the adoption of the ballot here, can be
drawn from the practice of a country, whose electoral
system presents so many points at variance with our
own. Here we have numerous small constituencies
amenable to local influences. There, all the constituencies are large, the terms for which parties are
elected are short, fortunes are not sufficiently great
to permit of money being squandered at elections, and
the emoluments of office are too small to tempt any
one to throw away much money in the hope of
attaining place.

It is obvious, that the more populous States will
have a larger share in the representative body than

their less populous neighbours. The basis of representation will soon extend to 100,000 persons for each member, when a small State like Delaware, with a population below that number, would be precluded from all share in the representation, but for a provision in the constitution, to the effect, that each State must have at least one member in the House of Representatives. The population of Delaware is, at present, above the mark; but it will not long continue so, when it will owe its possession of a voice in the Lower House to the constitutional provision referred to. Whilst that State has but one member, New York has about thirty-four—the disparities between the rest of the States ranging between these two extremes. This, it is evident, would, in a time of great excitement, result in the virtual political extinction of the smaller States, but for the conservative character of the Senate.

This branch of the federal legislature does not, like the other, spring directly from popular election. Its members are appointed by the legislatures of the different States, each State having two representatives in the Senate. In this body, therefore, the smaller States are on an equal footing with the larger, Delaware and Rhode Island having each as potent a voice in it as New York or Pennsylvania. Thus it will be perceived that whilst it is the people, in their aggregate character, that are represented in the House of Representatives, it is by States that they are represented in the Senate; an arrangement which was adopted to meet the views of all parties. The people of the weaker States justly feared that, if the basis of the representation were alike in the case of the two Houses, their influence in the confederacy would be contingent on sufferance; whilst those of the larger and more powerful States naturally objected to the principle of equality of representation being extended to both Houses, which would totally deprive them of that share in the general administration of affairs, to which their superior wealth and population fairly entitled them. The arrangement, therefore, is such, that the three millions of people who inhabit the State of New York, have that legitimate influence in the government, which, from their numbers, and the important interests which they have at stake, they can justly claim over the eighty thousand who inhabit Delaware; whilst these eighty thousand, again, are protected in the Senate from being utterly overwhelmed by the three millions. The result of this difference is that, in the Senate, there is no change in the strength or the relative position towards each other, of the different States; whereas, in the House of Representatives, every census introduces a material alteration into the relative positions in the Lower House of the different members of the confederation. By nothing have the successive changes, in this respect, which have already taken place, been so strongly marked, as by the indication which they have afforded of the growing power of the West. In no part of the country is population increasing with such unexampled rapidity as it is in the Valley of the Mississippi; and as every 70,000 added to its numbers during the current decade will entitle it to an additional member in the Lower House, the increased influence which it will thus acquire from the new apportionment of the representation which will be consequent upon the census of 1850, may be readily conceived. The time is within the recollection of the present generation when the voice of the West in Congress was utterly insignificant; but even already it almost divides the representation with the Atlantic States, and, in 1850, will in all probability outnumber them in the House of Representatives. In less than twenty years it will have the decided preponderance ; for whilst population increases in the West, it diminishes in some of the sea-board States. By the last apportionment, not only was the representation of Indiana, Illinois, and Ohio greatly increased, but that of Virginia and other States was actually diminished; the western States thus doubly gaining ground by their own progression and the recession of some of their neighbours. This growing influence of the West is regarded with uneasiness and jealousy by the sea-board communities; and nothing but the peculiar constitution of the Senate will by-and-by interpose as a breakwater between them and its overwhelming force. The arrangement, therefore, originally entered into as a protection of the smaller against the larger States, will soon be found of the last importance in shielding one great section of the confederacy against any abuse of the growing power of another, in preserving an equipoise between the commercial interests of the sea-board, and the great agricultural interest of the interior. So rapid is the progress of this political transformation, that, but for an arrangement adopted with other objects, a monopoly of the whole power of the Republic would soon be achieved by an interest, which, when the Constitution was framed, had scarcely an existence; and the whole influence of the country be centred in a section of it, which was, at that time, an almost unbroken wilderness.

The only change incident to the Senate, is the

increase of its members consequent upon the introduction of new States into the Union. Comprising
originally only twenty-six members, it now numbers
sixty, each new State adding two members to the
body of the Senate.

One of the chief sources of the conservative tendencies of the Senate is to be found in this, that its
members, holding as they do their seats for six years,
are not so immediately amenable to popular caprice
as are those of the other House of Congress, which
returns every second year to the people. But lest so
long a lease of power should place the Senate for
several years together in antagonism with public
opinion, the framers of the Constitution were careful
to subject it to a wholesome popular influence without rendering it subservient to popular caprice.
They consequently determined that, as the House of
Representatives was to be renewed throughout every
two years, the Senate should also, to the extent of
one-third of its whole number, be renewed every
second year. Thus, whilst it is entirely changed
every six years, it is never wholly changed at once;
an arrangement which renders it a more faithful
reflex than it would otherwise be of public opinion,
in a country where public opinion undergoes such
frequent and violent mutations; and, at the same
time, enables it to bring to its deliberations a large
share of legislative experience, which generally gives
to them quite a different cast from that of the discussions which are carried on in the other wing of the
Capitol.

If, in its executive capacity, the Senate differs
from the corresponding branch of the legislature in
this country; it also further differs from it in this,

that, with the exception of the trial of impeachments, the Lower House having the sole power to impeach, it has no judicial functions, no appeal lying to it from any of the ordinary tribunals of the country, local or federal. In this respect its powers also vary from those of many of the State Senates, which present themselves in the triple character of legislative, executive, and judicial bodies, an appeal in most cases lying to them in the last resort from the local tribunals. When in executive session, the proceedings of the Senate are conducted with closed doors. None but a citizen of the United States, of the age of thirty years, can be a member of the Senate, twenty-five being majority, so far as eligibility to the House of Representatives is concerned.

It is in connexion with the Senate as a legislative body, that the doctrine of instructions has been more particularly contended for in America. Representing, as they do, the different States in their collective capacity, many parties hold that the vote of each member, irrespectively of his private opinions, should accord with the political views prevailing, for the time being, in the State which he represents. For instance, one of the senators for New York may be appointed during the ascendancy of the Whig party in the legislature of that State. Should the Democrats turn the tables on their opponents before his term expires, the consequence is, that a democratic Legislature and a democratic State are, it is contended, misrepresented in the Senate, if the senator in question regulates his vote by his own private views. It sometimes happens, that a democratic State and Legislature are represented by two Whig senators, and *vice versa*. To obviate this inconvenience and injustice, as it is considered in some quarters, the principle of instructions has been resorted to ; which, if generally carried out, would draw a line of separation between the action and the judgment of each member of the Senate, and convert him into a mere machine for recording the ever-changing opinions of others at a distance. The general recognition of such a principle would destroy the conservative character of the Senate, by rendering it as subject to all the caprices of the popular will, as is the House of Representatives. It is a principle, however, but partially acted upon, being as fiercely contested as it is contended for. Instances have come within my own personal observation of senators speaking on one side of a question, and, in obedience to instructions, voting on the other.

The legislative body, as thus constituted, is compelled by law to assemble once in each year, the first Monday of December being the day appointed for its meeting. The President may, however, convoke an extraordinary session, whenever the exigencies of the public service may appear to him to require it. Once assembled, the power of adjournment or prorogation is in the hands of the two Houses exclusively; with this exception, that every second year, the Congress, which lasts for two years, being measured by the duration of the House of Representatives, expires by law on the 4th day of March. But it is now time to consider the mode in which parties are elected to the chief executive offices in the republic.

None but a native-born citizen of the United States is eligible to the office of President. When elected he retains his post for four years, at the end of which period he may be re-elected for another term of equal duration. There is nothing in the Constitution to prevent an eligible candidate from being elected a dozen different times to the Presidency, although custom has limited the longest presidential career to two terms, or eight years.

The Presidential election, like most elections in America, occurs in the month of November, but only once every four years. The nomination of candidates takes place, generally speaking, during the previous May or June. The mode of nomination is this. Each of the great parties appoints delegates to meet at a given place, on a given day, in a national party convention, for the purpose of selecting, from the party ranks, the most available candidate for the coming contest. Party discipline is sufficiently strong to guarantee for the person nominated on either side, the general support of the respective parties. Each party has its own central national committee, which manages everything up to the nomination; after which the issue is generally left to the local efforts, throughout the country, of the political friends of the candidate.

Although elected by the people, in contradistinction to an election by States, the President is not immediately elected by the popular vote at the ballot-box. It is not directly for either of the candidates nominated that the adherents of either party vote, but for the electoral colleges, by whose votes the issue is afterwards to be decided. Each State has its own electoral college, consisting of as many members as the State has representatives in both Houses of Congress. Thus, if New York has thirty-four members in the Lower House and two in the Upper, her electoral college will consist of thirty-six; whereas

that of Delaware will consist but of three, that
State having but one member in the House of Representatives, and two in the Senate.   The two parties
in each State have each their own electoral " ticket;"
and according as the Whig or Democratic ticket
carries the day, will be the vote of the State for the
presidential candidate.   The electoral ticket being a
general one in each State, the triumphant party
carries with it the whole electoral vote of the State.
Thus New York, in the case supposed, would give,
in the event of the Whigs succeeding, the whole of
her thirty-six votes for the Whig candidate.   The
successful candidate is he who has got a clear majority,
not of all the electoral colleges, but of the aggregate
number of members composing all the electoral colleges.   If it were otherwise, the decision would be
by States, not by the people at large.   Taking the
House of Representatives to consist of 230 members,
we have, with the sixty composing the Senate, an
aggregate of 290, which would be the aggregate
number of all the electors in all the electoral colleges throughout the Union.   It would in that case
require the vote of 146 at least for a choice.   This
mode, by giving New York, say thirty-six voices, and
Delaware three, gives certainly to the different States
very different degrees of influence over the presidential contest; but as the President is to spring from,
and to represent the whole people, no other arrangement would be compatible with his so doing; for it
is clear that a candidate might have a majority of the
States, but not a majority of the people.

But when no clear majority of the aggregate number of all the electoral colleges appears, from there
being more than two candidates in the field, or from

any other cause, in favour of any one candidate, and
when there is consequently no election by the people,
instead of a new election being resorted to, the Constitution has provided for the choice then devolving
upon a different quarter. The electoral colleges
having failed to do that for which alone they were
elected, are, *ipso facto*, dissolved, and the choice of
President falls upon the House of Representatives for
the time being. But the vote is not then *per capite*,
but by States, in which case the one member for
Delaware in that House has as great a voice in
the matter as the whole thirty-four from New York.
The contest is then decided by the majority of States,
it being, now that there are thirty States, necessary
that sixteen of them should in such case vote for one
or other of the candidates. The House is limited in
its choice to the candidates, not exceeding three who
received the greatest number of votes from the
people. Should there be no choice at first by the
House, successive ballotings are resorted to, until an
election takes place. On two separate occasions
already has the election thus devolved upon the
House of Representatives, and it was not, on the
first of these, until upwards of thirty ballots had been
taken, that Mr. Jefferson was elected by a bare majority. Formerly, he who had the next greatest
number of votes for the presidency became Vice-
President. So long as this remained the rule, it is
very obvious that the President and Vice-President
must generally, when elected, have belonged to different parties; for who so likely to have the next highest
number of votes to that given for the successful candidate, as his opponent? The inconvenience of such
an arrangement was felt by all parties, inasmuch as

its tendency was to put in jeopardy all party triumphs; for if any casualty happened to the President, the nominee of the defeated party became President in his stead. To remedy this the alteration was made in the Constitution by which the party successful for the time being fill both offices with their own nominees; it being now the rule for each party to nominate a candidate for the vice-presidency, when one is nominated for the presidency, and to vote for the one as vice-president, as the other is voted for as president. They are thus nominated together, voted for together, and elected together. Both the President and Vice-President may be inhabitants of the same State; but the people of each State, in voting for the candidates, must vote for one at least who is not an inhabitant of their own State. Thus the Whig or Democratic nominees for the two offices may both be from the State of Virginia. In that case, the people of all the other States may vote for them, but the people of Virginia in voting would be required to substitute an inhabitant of some other State for one of them. But the candidates are generally inhabitants of different States. As the Vice-President may be called upon to act as President, he too must be a native-born citizen of the United States.

Such is the mode in which a great people proceed in the choice of their own first magistrate. It argues much in favour of the permanency of the political institutions of America, that nearly sixty years have gone by without their having been shaken to their foundations by the successive and periodic contests for such a prize. To keep the office one of purely popular origin, and at the same time to counteract the excitement naturally attendant upon an election to fill it, was the great object of the authors of the Constitution; and it was with this view that they interposed the electoral bodies between parties and their candidates, and devolved the whole matter upon the House of Representatives, in the event of there being no popular choice. Many in America regard the presidential election as the great test of the soundness of the Constitution; and some great authorities, such as Chancellor Kent,* are ready to pin their faith to its permanency, provided it withstand the shocks of a few more contests of the kind. Much, however, in the way of the maintenance of tranquillity on those occasions, is attributable to the short term for which the President is elected. Were he, when once chosen, to hold office for life, or for a much longer period than he now does, without re-election, the stake would be all the more important, and the struggle all the more desperate. There are many objections to a double presidential term, the chief of which is, that the first term is generally treated as mere electioneering ground for securing the second. To make the term extend to eight years would be hazardous; and to confine the President to a single term of four years, would be to restrict the office by limits unnecessarily contracted. To get rid of the evils of double terms, and at the same time to avoid the dangers of too greatly extending a single term, some propose that the President should, in future, be eligible for only one term, extending over six years. How far this would avoid difficulty, on the one hand, and prevent abuse on the other, it is not necessary here to inquire. The difficulty might be overcome by the adoption of the rule forming part of the new

* This eminent jurist has died since the above was written.

French constitution, which requires that a term should intervene before any one holding the office of President can be re-elected for a second term. This, it is supposed, will effectually prevent the first term from being made use of to influence the elections for the second. By the adoption of a similar rule the Americans would remove the evil of which they now complain, without lengthening the duration of the presidential term, a step which would be attended with no little peril.

The power and position of the President do not constitute those features in the federal system, which give to all parties the greatest satisfaction. His position is, in many respects, more analogous to that of the prime minister, than to that of the sovereign of this country. In this, however, it differs materially from the position of the head of the Cabinet here, that for a given time the President's tenure of power is certain, without reference to the state of public opinion. So long as the executive and legislative departments are in accord, this is of little consequence—but the evil is felt in all its magnitude when the executive is at war with public opinion, and with Congress as its representative. With us such a state of things would lead to a speedy dissolution of the Cabinet; but not so in America, where the head of the Cabinet has a fixed tenure of office. A President may be for three-fourths of his administration at loggerheads with all parties around him, public opinion being impotent to displace him, until it can next constitutionally apply itself to the ballot-box. This, considering the legislative influence which the President wields through the veto power, occasionally impedes for a time the course of legislation, the President having it in his power to foil all the efforts of Congress, except in the very rare case of a majority of two-thirds being opposed to him in either House. This temporary independence on the part of the executive, of public opinion, which may sometimes occur, is not only a blunder in the theory of the Constitution, but it is also one, the practical evils of which have been gravely felt, on more occasions than one; and it is the actual occurrence of these evils, more than their theoretical possibility, which has led many to regard this as the weak point of the system. Few, however, who do so, are ready even to hazard a conjecture as to the mode of applying a remedy, the object being to bring the executive office into more thorough subordination to public opinion, but the mode of securing it being extremely difficult to devise. The patronage of the President is great, and sometimes very unscrupulously exercised.

In contemplating the general polity of the American Union, one cannot fail being struck with the anomalous position occupied in the constitutional system by the Vice-President. This functionary, although the death, disability, or absence of the President, may devolve upon him at any moment the chief responsibilities of the executive government, has no seat in the Cabinet, being as much a stranger to its deliberations and its policy as the humblest of his constituents. As both the President and Vice-President invariably belong to the same political party, one would think that it would be insisted upon as subservient to party interests, that the man who may be on any day called upon to administer the government, should be fully cognizant of the policy pursued by the President and his Cabinet. But the views of the govern-

ment, and the motives which influence them, are as a
sealed book to him, except so far as he may guess at,
as others may do, or surreptitiously acquire a knowledge of, them. Politically speaking, he is a complete
nonentity, his only duty being to preside *ex officio* over
the deliberations of the Senate. And yet this is the
man whom the accident of a moment may place at
the head of affairs, and to whom his party look for
carrying out its policy, should the President be by
any cause removed. He is sometimes treated with the
most singular indifference by the President, and by
the various heads of departments; a species of treatment but ill calculated to secure a cordial cooperation
between him and the President's Cabinet, should he
be called upon to take the President's place. This
cordiality was far from existing in the only instance
in which the presidential office has as yet devolved
upon a Vice-President. The Cabinet of General
Harrison treated Mr. Tyler with the utmost contempt, and felt rather uncomfortable when, by the
death of the President, about a month after the
installation of the Whig regime at Washington, the
man to whom they had unreservedly given the cold
shoulder, suddenly appeared amongst them as their
head and master. The result was but natural. One
by one, Mr. Tyler got rid of the members of the
Cabinet which his predecessor had formed, and
afterwards wrecked his own reputation and ruined
his party, by attempting to play a slippery game
between the two great parties in the country. Had
Mr. Tyler been a member of the Cabinet before he
was called to the head of affairs, he might have fallen
in with the views and objects of his party, instead of
being alienated from them, as he was by the super-

cilious conduct of its chiefs. The very party that elected him lost its golden opportunity by the accession of Mr. Tyler to the Presidency ; but whether the Union lost or gained by his administration, is quite another question. The darling Whig policy of the day was the re-establishment of the National Bank. A bill which passed both Houses of Congress for that purpose, was vetoed by, to use a seeming paradox, the accidental President of a Whig choice.

The territorial government of the United States is partly vested in the federal executive, and partly in the people of the different territories themselves. The territories are such portions of the public domain as are being rapidly settled, and have had limits assigned to them, with a view to their eventually becoming members of the Confederacy as States. This they become on their attaining a population of 80,000 souls. Until they are admitted as States, their affairs are respectively administered by a Governor appointed by the President, who co-operates with a legislature chosen by the people of the territory. They send representatives to Congress, who can speak, but have no vote. All the States, with the exception of Vermont, which have been admitted since the original thirteen established their independence, were territories before becoming States.

So far the political system of America has been glanced at only in its connexion with the Confederation in its collective capacity. The federal constitution is but a component part of the entire system— the most prominent to us, because it is through its means that the Republic is brought into connexion with the exterior world. But it is far from being the great feature, or the most imposing ingredient in the constitution of the whole body politic. The portion of their constitutional scheme most worthy of study, and most replete with hope or apprehension for mankind, is that by which their internal affairs are regulated; by which the relations between man and man, amongst them, are defined and enforced; by which their industry is stimulated, their enterprise fostered, and life, property, and reputation are protected. If we would understand the working of the principle of self-government, which lies at the foundation of all their institutions, we must look beyond the machinery chiefly contrived for the maintenance of their external relations, and view the system to which this is a mere incident, in its broader, deeper, and more important character, as affecting the great, scheming, enterprising, speculating, and industrious hive at home.

It will be gathered from what has already been said, that the federal government and legislature have but little concern with the internal affairs of the country. Such powers as are not expressly conferred upon the general government by the Constitution, are, by implication, reserved to the different States. No control over matters of a purely local character having been conceded to it, it follows that such matters remain under the exclusive management of the States themselves. On all questions of a nature purely domestic, and affecting its own interests, each State is entitled to act a sovereign and independent part for itself. Thus, over all matters connected with the material improvement of the State, such as the construction of roads, railways, and canals—with the regulation of its financial system—with its criminal and its penal legislation—with its judicial and ministerial arrangements, or with taxation, whether for State or local purposes, the people of each State have reserved to themselves exclusive jurisdiction. They have, of course, as States, no power over taxes or imposts, which, being designed solely for the support of the general government, can only be imposed by it. Each, for the common benefit of all, has parted with some of its inherent powers, and vested them in the federal government; but, beyond these exceptions, its jurisdiction within its own limits is as supreme as if no confederation existed. Thus no State can, by itself, enter into any treaty whatever with a foreign power. It can contract no alliance with a foreign government, or with any other State or States. It can neither declare war nor make peace by itself; nor can it coin money, support an army or navy, or pass any particular laws of naturalization for itself. But it possesses every power which a State can wield, beyond these and some others conceded to the general government. Thus, although it cannot coin money, it can borrow it; and, as it seems, even when it cannot always repay it. And in borrowing money, it has no power to pledge any other credit but its own; a fact which should be borne in mind by such capitalists as are apt to delude themselves with the idea that they can look, in case of default, for payment, to the sister States, or to the general government.

It will be seen, then, that the Union consists of thirty different communities, having no political concern or connexion with each other, beyond that which exists on the common ground on which they all meet at Washington. Thus New York has no connexion whatever with Pennsylvania, except that

which is traced through the medium of the federal
Constitution. This remark does not apply to the
powerful tie of material interests which unites them
all, or at least sections of them, together in bonds,
stronger than any which mere political systems could
create. But in mutually prosecuting their material
interests, their legislation is separate and independent, although a common interest frequently dictates
a common policy.

Not only are the different States independent
communities in fact, but they exhibit all the outward
forms and manifestations of such. Each embodies
its separate political existence in a separate institutional system; the basis of which is, in all cases, a
State Constitution, which generally opens with an
assertion of the sovereignty of the people of the
State. They have their own governors, their own
legislatures, their own judicial and municipal systems,
their own militia for self-defence, their own political
organization for every exigency, in short, which does
not come within the supervision and control of the
United States. This will suffice to give the reader a
general idea, which is all that can be here attempted,
of the mutual relations between the States and the
federal government, and their respective positions in
the general system of the Union.

It is this division and distribution of authority
that give to the political machine so complicated
a character in America. It is true that there is but
one line drawn, that which separates general from
local jurisdiction; but it is not always easy to determine on which side of the line certain questions
should fall. A struggle is thus, more or less, constantly waged between the federal and local autho-

rities, the States being extremely jealous of anything
that savours of encroachment by the general government on their rights. The great object is to confine the
action of the general government within the smallest
compass compatible with the due discharge of its
functions. Whilst certain powers are conferred upon it
by the Constitution, that document also concedes to it
in general terms the right of adopting all such measures
as are necessary for carrying its specified powers into
effect ; and it is in acting on this general power,
more than in anything else, perhaps, that the local
and federal authorities are brought most frequently
into conflict. One party, for instance, denies the
constitutional power of Congress to create a National
Bank ; the other party contends for it, under the
general clause alluded to, as being the best means of
enabling the government properly to manage the
fiscal affairs of the Union. Some, again, contend for
the power of Congress to construct roads throughout
the Union without the consent of the States through
which they might pass, as being one of the means
best calculated to carry out the power specifically
conferred upon them of providing for the common
defence. Others dissent, on the ground, that if such
a principle were admitted, the general government
might, upon the same plea, construct railways and
canals through any State or number of States. The
consequence is, that a great national road, intended to
unite, with a view to military amongst other purposes, the city of Baltimore, on the Chesapeake,
with that of St. Louis, on the Mississippi, has been
suspended until this dispute is settled, although
nearly two hundred miles of it have been already
completed. So far, however, as questions of this

nature go, involving, as they do, the disbursement of the common revenue, the real source of the objection may be found in the mutual jealousy of the States; Maine, for instance, being unwilling that the common fund, to which she contributes, should be applied for the more immediate benefit of other sections of the Union. I must confess that there are good grounds for this jealousy, considering the propensity to jobbing discovered by the federal authorities. Indeed, in this respect, I have heard several Americans declare, that they believed their own government to be the most corrupt on earth. But it is not only on legislative points that the general government now and then finds itself at loggerheads with the States, the federal judiciary being frequently in conflict with the local tribunals. But more of this in its proper place. Enough has here been said to indicate how frequently local and federal jurisdiction so closely approximate that it is difficult to distinguish the line of their separation—and to show how easy it is for the Union to come in collision with its different parts; whilst it will appear from the rapid *coup-d'œil* which has thus been taken of the constitutional system in its twofold aspect, that the political organization of America, so far from being the simple thing which many suppose it to be, is a machine complicated in its structure, and delicate in its working.

It is not uncommon, in the annual messages through which the President communicates, at its opening, the condition of the country to Congress, to find it asserted that the experience of the Republic has already sufficed to demonstrate the efficiency of the principle of self-government. So far as it is applicable to the American people themselves, the assertion, perhaps, cannot be impugned; but the proof which they have given of their aptitude for self-government cannot be taken as evidence of the stability of their present system. The dissolution of the Union would not necessarily imply the annihilation of the principle of self-government in America. That principle might, in new forms and under other manifestations, long survive the wreck of the confederacy. The question in which we are most interested, and that which is involved in the greatest doubt, has less to do with the maintenance of democratic institutions in America, than with the stability of the Federal Union. We fear that, in this respect, the experiences of the past are more pregnant with warning than suggestive of security. The Americans must bear in mind that their system, although it has withstood many, and some very rude, shocks, has not yet encountered danger in some of the most terrible forms in which it is competent to assail it. The ship that has withstood many a rough sea, and is capable of weathering many more, may perish in a moderate gale if her cargo shifts, or her ballast is disturbed. There is but little fear of the American system sustaining any very serious injury from external violence. The danger is that, whilst all is calm and serene without, the elements of disorder may be accumulating within. And this is not a danger which the Americans can afford to despise. Their constant exhortations to each other to regard the Union as paramount to all other political considerations, show that they appreciate the danger, and that they look upon the very greatness of the Confederation as, in itself, an element of peril, comprising, as it does, geographical distinctions which may be incompatible with permanent union, and a

diversity of interests which may yet prove an overmatch for patriotism. And should a serious shock come
from within—should a mine be sprung beneath the
capital itself—to what quarter could the general government resort with confidence for aid. A common
object, or a common danger, may arm it with power
for external action; but the Union has as yet afforded
no evidence that, in the presence of internal convulsion,
it would not prove itself a house of cards. Some years
ago a mob assailed the State legislature in the capital
of Pennsylvania, and the members had to fly for
their lives. To quell the tumult the governor had
to send to Philadelphia for detachments of militia,
for he could place no reliance on the militia of Harrisburg and its vicinity, a moiety of whom were at
least fellow-partizans with the rioters. Nor was the
succour which he received from Philadelphia of the
most reliable kind; a large proportion of the militia,
in fact of the whole State, having party sympathies
with the disturbers of the public peace, and being,
therefore, not very likely to act with much energy
against them. Luckily the commotion subsided
before the cohesive powers of the commonwealth
were put to the threatened test. And in what predicament would the federal executive find itself in
the presence of a similar but more extended disaster.
The United States army, even if faithful to the
government, would have no more effect in quelling a
popular outbreak, than the words of Canute had in
checking the approaches of the sea. Would the
government not find itself deserted on all hands, considering that at such a time political objects are, in a
popular state, most readily subserved, by unscrupulous politicians, by siding with the people against

power in any shape? That this is not a mere fan-
ciful danger is proved by historical events of a very
recent period. In 1832, when South Carolina
threatened to dissever the Union, her troops were
exposed in daily parade in the streets of Charleston,
side by side with those of the government, with
whom the exciting events of each day might have
brought them in collision. What a lesson is conveyed by this open, undisguised, and defiant preparation for resistance to the constituted authorities
of the country! It is true that, in this instance,
the central government was strong, because the turbulent State stood alone, the principles which she
advocated being distasteful to the great mass of the
people. Nullification, of which South Carolina was
and still is the champion, was a doctrine odious to
the vast majority of the American people; and the
probability is, that had South Carolina ventured to
carry it out by an insurrectionary movement, she
would have been crushed in the attempt. But this
no one can with certainty affirm, for, in a country
like the United States, the consequences of a blow
once struck, no matter from what cause or with
what success at first, would be utterly unforeseen.
It was the conviction of this which caused every
friend of the Union to rejoice that the squabble,
which convulsed the petty State of Rhode Island in
1842, was terminated without the intervention of
United States troops. I do not say, that the constitution would not be proof against domestic convulsion, but with recent events still fresh in their
recollection, even Americans can hardly assure themselves that it would be equal to such an emergency.
They should remember, that although there may be

much in America to favour the growth and stability
of the principle of self-government, the confederation, at least, is surrounded by many perils; and
that, although democracy with them may be indestructible, there may, nevertheless, be quicksands at
the foundations of the Union.

It was with a view to making adequate provision
to meet all the dangers to which the federal system
might be exposed, both from without and from within,
that, in the early days of the republic, a party arose,
who have since become so odious, under the designation of Federalists. Their object was to form a
strong central government at Washington, not such
as would swamp the legitimate authority of the States
within their respective limits, but such as would consolidate the political system, by forming it into a
more compact unity, with all its parts in proper subordination; and as would enable the general government to act with promptitude and vigour for its own
protection, whenever its existence might be endan-
gered by a revolutionary movement. It was in
opposition to this party that was immediately organized that of the democratic republicans, headed by
Mr. Jefferson, the " Apostle of Democracy," and
basing itself upon the principle of State Rights, in
contradistinction to that of centralization. In the
eyes of those composing this party, the federal
government was only a necessary evil, which must be
endured, but which should not be strengthened. Their
policy was, therefore, to reduce its authority to the
lowest practicable point, and to prevent it from
becoming dangerous by keeping it, as it were, in a
state of constant political inanition. Besides, it would
be alien, they contended, to the whole spirit in which

their institutions were conceived, to place any portion of the system beyond the reach of revolutionary action. The people's right to revolutionize their government at pleasure lies at the foundation of the whole system, and federalism, in its more odious sense, would be but a practical denial of that right. Thus were the parties originally, and thus have they ever since continued at issue, the one simply contending for so strengthening an indispensable feature in the political scheme, as to enable it, under all circumstances, to answer the purposes of its creation; the other resisting with the popular cry of State Rights, which the federalists never dreamt of invading, and which could only be compromised by pushing their doctrines to an extreme. They both equally professed a reverence for the Union, differing only in the price which they were willing to pay for what was admittedly so great a blessing. Their foresight has yet to be proved, and it will be well for the Union, when the day of trial arrives, if the apprehensions of now extinguished federalism are found to have been utterly groundless. These parties, in their more modern manifestation, are found amongst the Whigs and Democrats of the present day, the latter having no more spiteful epithet to hurl against the former than that of Federalist. It is true that a modern Whig as emphatically repudiates the charge of federalism, as a cavalier may be supposed to have denied the accusation of being a round-head. But there is little doubt, considering their more conservative character, of the Whigs, as a party, being the legitimate representatives of the Federalists.

Such being the perils which environ the Union, it is but right that we should now briefly inquire into the nature of its guarantees. It must be confessed that these, when properly understood, are such as greatly diminish the dangers to which it would otherwise be inevitably exposed. Like the solar system, the Union is regulated in its complex and delicate working by the combined action of centripetal and centrifugal forces. But for the presence of the one it would not long withstand the disintegrating tendencies of the other. The federal system, in its simple form, unmixed with any other element of political existence, must ever be extremely difficult to sustain. The mutual jealousies and conflicting interests of its component parts, exercise a repelling influence, which it has not always sufficient cohesive power to resist. When States are bound together by no tie but the federal one, it is seldom that they remain long together without disturbing causes manifesting themselves to unsettle the foundations of their union. There is no national sentiment, embracing the entire confederation, to rally the people around it in a moment of danger, particularly when it is menaced not from without but from within. The inhabitants of each State give their first thoughts to their own State, and only such as they have then to spare to the confederation.

In framing the American constitution, the great object was to secure the benefits of a federal union, which would not be constantly liable to disintegration from the mutual jealousies, the conflicting interests, and the independent action of the several States. To effect this, the framers of the constitution most wisely intertwined the national with the federal principle, so that the people might exist at once in the double capacity of a united people, and of a confederation of States. In its preamble, that instrument sets forth, not that the States of the Union, but that " We, the people of the United States," do establish and ordain, &c. Here the national principle is recognised and affirmed as lying at the foundation of the federal superstructure. It is as a federal body that the United States chiefly manifest themselves to the external world, but it is mainly as one people that their action is regulated. Were the Union purely federal, its legislative body would assume the federal type, representing, not the whole people, but the different States which they comprised. The executive too would be provided for by a totally different arrangement from that now prevailing. But the American executive is the representative of the entire American people in their collective national capacity. It is not this State that is this year entrusted with executive control, and that State the next, the executive government being constantly wielded by the whole people, without reference to their divisions into States, by their own representatives, springing, every four years, from their common suffrages. And precisely so with one of the branches of the legislature. The House of Representatives is not a body representing the different political communities of which the Union is composed, but the whole people of the Union, as if no such distinction existed between them. It is in the Senate, and in it alone, that we find the Union represented in its federal capacity, that body being composed of the delegates, not of the people, but of the States. But even in the Senate they do not vote as States, but *per capite,* as in the House of Representatives. The number of States being thirty, the Senate consists of

sixty members, there being two from each State.
A vote may thus be carried by the senators from
twenty-nine States dividing against each other, when
both, or one of those representing the thirtieth, might
turn the scale. Thus, even in the Senate, although
they represent the States, they do not act by States.
We see then that the executive, and one branch of
the legislative power, are purely of national origin;
whilst the other branch of the latter, which assumes
a federal type, never carries it into action. The only
occasion on which there is a purely federal action at
Washington is, when the people having failed to
elect a President, his election devolves upon the
House of Representatives. The course of procedure
in such a case has already been explained. The national principle is thus made to underlie the federal,
in America, so that the different States, which appear
to be merely set together in federal juxtaposition,
like type bound together from without, are in reality
amalgamated below, like stereotype.

There are thus two political states of existence in
America, the national and the federal. It is the
national principle which almost exclusively manifests
itself in Washington, the federal being exhibited in
the independent local action of the different States.
This is the very reverse of what is generally the case
with federal States. It is generally in their federal
capacity that they act externally, leaving the national
principle to erect itself at home. The consequence
is, that there are generally displayed great weakness
and indecision, when promptness and vigour are required—conflicting nationalities frequently interfer-
ing with general action. In America, the national
feeling, particularly so far as external action is con-

cerned, is all with the Union, which is so embodied
as to enable it to act, not as a number of States
working in concert, but as one great power. This is
that which renders it almost impregnable to all
external assaults. The chief danger to it, as already
intimated, is from within. The two principles cannot
co-exist in active development, without the most perfect system of checks to keep them from encroaching
on each other. The national principle could only
predominate at the expense of State sovereignty and
independence; whilst the federal principle, if pushed
to an extreme, would tend to cripple all national
action. It was evidently for an extension of the one
that the Federalists contended, whilst the States'
Rights party rallied in maintenance of the other.
These parties being now, properly speaking, extinct,
none daring to avow himself favourable to any further extension of the national principle, the chief
source of peril is in the conflicting material interests
of the different sections of the confederacy. But
storms from within would be much more potent for
mischief, were it not for the extent to which the
national principle obtains. The Americans divide
themselves into States only for local purposes; for all
other objects, they regard themselves, and feel, as one
united people. Their first affections, therefore, are
for the Union, their next, for their respective localities. They are less like different States uniting for a
common object than like one people dividing into
States for particular local objects. To tear them
asunder, therefore, will require a greater force than
generally suffices to dissolve the flimsy connexion
which binds together different States, having but few
sympathies in common, or perhaps cherishing mutual

antipathies, but which enter into a federal tie as a mere political expedient. No force can do it short of that which can rend a nation asunder. In the case of America, that force can only come from within, and nothing but the conflict of material interests is likely to set it in motion. Should a really serious demonstration from this quarter be once made, how far the central government is capable of resisting it has been already briefly considered. There is no question but that the national sentiment cherished by the American people serves to postpone the crisis, or but that, should it ever arise, that sentiment would form the only source of strength to the executive government.

Nullification having been incidentally alluded to, a brief explanation of its nature and objects will not here be out of place. When the dispute between South Carolina and the central government was pending, the whole question of general and local powers was opened up and discussed. Two parties sprung up in the South, particularly in the State just mentioned, entertaining strong views of the powers and rights of the different States. The one party were known as the Nullifiers, the other as the Seceders. The Nullifiers maintained that when an act of the general legislature was in manifest violation of the constitution, each State being for itself the judge as to whether it was so or not, and directly inimical to the interests of a State, that State had the power, *quoad* itself, to annul the act, and to prevent it from being carried into execution within its limits. Thus South Carolina contended that she had the power and the right, whenever the circumstances seemed to her to warrant it, to prevent the United

States tariff from being in force in the port of Charleston. The chief answer to this was, that all acts of Congress were valid, unless unconstitutional, and that the Supreme Court of the United States was the sole judge as to whether they were unconstitutional or not. It followed that, until they were pronounced to be unconstitutional by the only competent tribunal, no State could resist their execution. If this were so, the interests of a State might be trampled in the dust by acts which came within the letter of the constitution, when, unless it had some means of defending itself, it would be utterly remediless. This consideration gave rise to the Secession party, who contended that, when the federal connexion became manifestly injurious to the interests of any section of the American people inhabiting a State, they might withdraw entirely from the Union of their own accord. To this it was replied that, although the constitution was ratified by the States, as States, it could not be rescinded by one without the consent of all. Others again contended that, although the constitution, which is the symbol of the Union, was ratified by the States, that form of ratification did not alter its essential character as a document emanating, not from the States, but from the whole people as one people, and binding them together as one, without necessary reference to their division into States. From this it would follow, that it could not be rescinded by the States, as States, but by the people of all the States, as one people.

Before concluding this chapter a brief inquiry into the expenses of the American government, with a view to contrasting them with those of the government of this country, may be neither uninteresting nor uninstructive. For the four years ending June

30, 1846, the average annual expenditure of the United States, exclusive of payments on account of the public debt, was twenty-two millions of dollars, or 4,950,000*l.* say, 5,000,000*l.* sterling. For the same period, our average annual expenditure, exclusive of payments on account of the public debt, was 22,000,000*l.* sterling. The American people being now about twenty millions, their expenditure for army, navy, ordnance, pensions, civil contingencies, and foreign intercourse, in short, for everything but the debt, amounts to about 5*s.* sterling per head. We, being about thirty millions of people, have to pay 14*s.* 8*d.* sterling per head, to defray the expenses of the State, exclusive of the debt; that is to say, for the mere expenses of government, we pay absolutely between four and five times as much as the American; and, individually, nearly three times as much. When the debt of both countries is thrown into the scale, this difference is, of course, greatly increased; inasmuch as we pay yearly, as interest upon our debt, more than the whole principal of the debt of America, even after the war, amounts to.

But it may be urged that this comparison is not fair, inasmuch as in the case of America, no account is taken of the expense of the State governments. It is quite true that the yearly expenditure for the support of the general government is not the sum-total which the Americans have to pay as the expenses of government. It is but proper, therefore, that, in comparing the expenditure of the two countries, the expense of the State government in America should be superadded to that of the general government.

There being no less than thirty different States,

with thirty local political systems to support; that is to say, thirty executives, thirty legislatures, thirty judiciary systems, and thirty different groups of miscellaneous *et ceteras*, connected with thirty different governments to provide for, one might naturally suppose that the aggregate expense of all this would greatly exceed that incurred to support the general government. But the expense of all the State governments taken together does not exceed five millions and a half of dollars, which is but a trifle over a million and a quarter sterling. This added to the 5,000,000*l.* for the support of the general government, gives 6,125,000*l.* as the aggregate cost of government, both general and local in America. This makes the cost per head of government in America, exclusive of the debt, 6*s.* 3*d.* sterling, to contrast with 14*s.* 8*d.*, the cost per head of the government of England, exclusive of her debt. The Mexican war has materially enhanced the American debt, but even with this addition, it does not exceed 20,000,000*l.* The annual interest upon this will be, even at the rate paid by America, little more than 1,000,000*l.** So that, taking into view the taxation imposed for the payment of the interest of the debt, the tax per head will not exceed 7*s.* 6*d.* sterling. More than this may be raised for some years to come to pay off the principal of the debt, but it is not necessary to take any extra efforts of this kind into the calculation. If we add, in the case of England, the taxation necessary for the pay-

---

* The State debts are not included, because the sums borrowed have been invested in works, which are already in some cases wholly, and in others partly, paying, and will soon in all cases wholly pay the interest upon them.

ment of the annual interest upon the debt to that raised for the ordinary expenses of government, it gives us no less than 1*l.* 14*s.* as the proportion paid per head. That is to say, taking every thing into account, on both sides, we pay more than four and a half times per head as much as the Americans pay in the way of taxation.

But some may urge that we have not only an imperial government, but also from thirty to forty colonial governments to sustain. But if, in addition to the general government we have the governments of thirty or forty colonies to support, let it be remembered that the Americans have also their general government, with thirty local, certainly, not colonial, governments to sustain. They may differ in name from our colonies, but they occupy an analogous position to that occupied by the colonies, so far as this question is concerned. The Englishman pays for his imperial and his colonial governments, the American for his imperial and state governments. Englishmen pay four millions sterling for the government of from thirty to forty Colonies, Americans pay about a million and a quarter sterling for the local government of thirty States. The Colonies contain an aggregate population of five millions—the States, one of twenty millions. But the four millions paid by the imperial government is only half what it takes to support the government of the Colonies, the other half being defrayed by the colonists themselves. It thus takes eight millions sterling to govern five millions of colonists; and as England pays one-half of this sum, she may be said to pay four millions sterling for governing two millions and a half of colonists. She thus pays at the rate of 1*l.* 12*s.*

for the government of each colonist—more than double what it costs her to govern a subject at home; for we have already seen that 14*s*. 8*d*. was the cost per head of government to Englishmen, exclusive of the interest on the debt, and, indeed, including the four millions expended upon the Colonies. Whilst the cost of governing an English colonist is 1*l*. 12*s*. that of governing an American citizen in his own State is, on an average, 1*s*. 3*d*. per head per annum. Thus the cost to the American citizen of administering the local affairs of his State, is about one twenty-fifth part that which it costs for the administration of the affairs of an English colonist. There is, therefore, but little that tells in favour of our system, when we take its colonial element into account.

But the proportion borne by what is paid per head by the Americans, as the expenses of government, to that which is paid per head by us in the same way, is annually diminishing: inasmuch as, whilst the American people are rapidly increasing in numbers, their expenditure exhibits but little tendency to increase at all. It is quite true that their yearly expenditure is now much greater than it was in the earlier days of the Confederation, but it is not materially increased now beyond what it was fifteen years ago. During the four years ending 1836, the average annual expenditure of the United States' government was a little above twenty-one millions of dollars. During the four ending 1846, it was, as we have already seen, about twenty-two millions. In 1835 the population of America did not exceed fifteen millions—it now exceeds twenty. We thus see that twenty millions of people pay little, if any, more for

their government than fifteen millions did about thirteen years ago. Thus, although the expenditure, if
it does not remain stationary, is but slightly increased,
the burden of taxation upon the individual is rapidly
diminishing; and there is no reason why, when the
population of America is thirty millions, which it
will be fifteen years hence, the expenses of its government should increase beyond its present figure. If
it does not, the burden of taxation on each individual
in 1863, will be only half what it was in 1835. What
prospect have we of any such relief as this, considering how much it is the tendency of the times with us
to increase instead of diminishing our expenditure?
Since 1835 it has increased by about ten millions; and
although, in deference to the universal clamour now
raised for reduction, some trifling diminution may be
effected, yet even that relief, trifling though it will
be, will be but temporary, it being the interest of the
tax-spending class to have as much of the public
money pass through their fingers as possible. We
delude ourselves in expecting any permanent improvement in this respect, until the tax-paying class exercise
a more direct control over the spending of the taxes.

But why should this improvement not take place ?
Is it necessary that England should have a government inordinately expensive, to have a government
sufficiently good ?   The American government is
cheaply administered, and in what particular is it
wanting ?   No one can charge the general government with any want of efficiency in the administration
of the foreign affairs of the Confederation. Its internal government is adequately provided for by its
State, or local authorities.   Life and property are as
secure there as here.   If there is less security in the

South than in the North, so is there in Ireland than in Great Britain, although we have in Ireland, in aid of the military, a civil force greater than the whole military force of America. View them which way you will, the contrast of the American system with our own is, as regards its expenditure at least, eminently unfavorable to us. This should not be ; for there is no reason why England should not have as good a government as any other country, at as cheap a rate.

Having thus hurriedly glanced at the leading features of the political system of America ; having shown the basis on which it rests, and the principles which regulate the action and the distribution of its powers ; having drawn attention to what are considered by some to be its weaker points, and exhibited the party distinctions which have originated in the contradictory construction of some of its provisions, the reader has probably anticipated me in noticing the grand difference which exists between the British and American Constitutions. At the basis of the former is power, from the spoils of which the superincumbent fabric of popular liberty has been reared ; power still retaining all the franchises and prerogatives not conceded by it;—at the foundation of the latter, is popular liberty, the necessities of which have called power into existence ; power in this case, however, wielding no more authority than has been conceded to it. Liberty in England has been wrung from power—power in America has arisen out of liberty. In the one case, power has been fettered that freedom might expand ; in the other, freedom has been restricted that power might exist. Without his charters, the Englishman would have no freedom of action—without his constitutions, the American would have no restraint upon his.   It is by deeds of concession that the people in England vindicate their liberty—it is by deeds of concession that power in America vindicates its authority.*

---

* Since the foregoing was written, I perceive that Mr. M'Gregor, in a letter addressed to the people of Glasgow, has stated, *inter alia*, that, taking into account the total taxation, general and local, to which they are subjected, the Americans are far from being a moderately-taxed people.   He cannot, by this, have intended to convey the idea that there was anything like an equality of taxation between them and ourselves.   In case, however, some should draw such an inference from a statement of this kind, proceeding from so distinguished a source, I shall present the reader with a comparison of the total taxation of one of the most highly-taxed States in the Union, with the total taxation of Great Britain and Ireland.   For the sake of comparison, the population of New York may be taken at 3,000,000, and that of the United Kingdom at 30,000,000.   The population of New York is about a seventh that of the whole Union. Taking 29,000,000 of dollars as the expenditure of the General Government in 1846, including the interest of the debt and other charges, New York would contribute the seventh, or say 4,130,000 dollars.   The total taxation of the State, for the same year, for state, county, and town purposes, fell under 4,000,000.   But, taking the round sum, this gives 8,130,000 dollars as the total taxation, paid during that year, by the 3,000,000 of people inhabiting New York.   Reduced to sterling money, this sum amounts to about 1,690,000*l.*, or 11*s.* per head.   The New Yorkers thus pay actually less per head for the support of the General Government, the interest of the general debt, the support of the State Government, and for all local and municipal purposes, than we were last year called upon to pay for the support of our military establishments alone !   The gross revenue of this country for last year exceeded 60,000,000*l.* If to this be added, the local taxation of the three kingdoms, their total taxation, for all purposes, general and local, is not over-estimated at 80,000,000*l.*   This, distributed over 30,000,000 of people, gives 2*l.* 13*s.* as the taxation per head in this country, which is nearly five times as great as the taxation per head, for all purposes, in New York.

It is quite possible that the Americans are not moderately taxed, and that there is room, with them as with us, for financial reform ; but it is, at the same time, very evident that, taking the whole of their taxation into account, they are, as compared with us, a *very moderately-taxed people.*

CHAPTER XIII.

THE FEDERAL LEGISLATURE.

My stay in Washington afforded me frequent opportunities of attending the deliberations of Congress. The debates and resolutions of this body have now obtained a world-wide importance, whilst its attitude and demeanour excite interest and attract attention. Like everything else in America, much that is fabulous has been written about it, as well as much that is true; and by the majority on this side of the Atlantic, the picture is too apt to be viewed on its unfavourable side. I have regularly attended the discussions of Congress for months, during which time questions of the highest interest, both of a foreign and domestic character, were debated within its walls, and may, therefore, without egotism, consider myself competent to convey an honest, if not a very vivid impression of it, to the mind of the reader. It is said that there is nothing so solemn but has its ludicrous side ; and if I wanted to find subjects for caricature, with which to amuse, there is little doubt but that the Capitol might furnish me with material. My object is to present a truthful picture, amusing peradventure, in parts, but as instructive as the truth can render it throughout. In dealing with America, the reader has been long enough amused by different writers, at the expense of his confidence. It is high time that portraiture superseded caricature.

The constitution and functions of the two Houses of Congress having been considered in the previous chapter, the object now is to present them in their very action and aspect; and if the reader will again accompany me, we will first proceed together into the House of Representatives.

In addition to the public gallery, which takes the semicircular sweep of the chamber, and that set apart for the private friends of members, the floor of the House is frequently thrown open for the accommodation of strangers. Being admitted to the privilege of the floor, we shall take our station in the vicinity of the chair, as being the best position, perhaps, both for seeing and hearing what is going on.

The hall, as already described, has a dark and dingy appearance even on the brightest day. It is but ill lighted for so vast a space, and its sombreness is increased by the darkened colouring of its appointments and decorations.

From the point you occupy you have a good *coup-d'œil* of the whole House. Face to face with you are the representatives of the Union, the aggregate result of the last electoral fermentation.

It is true, they are a motley assembly ; but how
could they be otherwise, when you consider whence
they are drawn ? There is a representative from
Maine, his fresh complexion and hardy frame bespeaking him from the North, where his constituents
are now clothed in furs ; there again is one, from
whose body the hot suns of Alabama have nearly
dissipated all the juices, except that of tobacco, with
which he is at this moment overflowing ; behind him
sits a member from beyond the Alleganies, aye even
from beyond the Mississippi, in whose keen eye,
wrinkled face, and general quickness of movement,
you can read whole stories of adventurous life in the
Far West; while close beside you is the languid
Carolinian, accustomed to have everything done for
him at his nod. And what pages in the history of the
Union may be read in the varied physiognomy of the
House ! In the assembly before you, of two hundred
men or thereabouts, you can readily trace the dark
hair and eye, and the high cheek-bone of the Celt, the
sleek and rotund contour of the Saxon, the ponderous
outline of the Dutchman, the phlegmatic temperament of the German, the olive hue of the Spaniard,
and the nimble figure of the Frank. It is a true reflex
of the great busy mass without, scattered far and wide
for thousands of miles from where you stand. It is
at once a type of the past and the future of America.
In the representatives of the American people, you
have an epitome of the story of their ancestry, and a
clue to that of their posterity. In one respect the
scene rises to the dignity of a moral phenomenon.
You have different races, with all their diversified
habits, predilections, histories, creeds, and traditions ;
you have the representatives of almost every country

in Europe living together, not a paralytic life, but a
life of constant industry and active competition, and
regulating their political existence by the machinery
of a constitutional and democratic regime. In one
sense, truly, you have a congress of nations in this
Congress of the United States.

The House is certainly, on a general view, wanting
in that polish which characterizes the corresponding
chamber in St. Stephen's. But one would be disappointed to find it otherwise, when he considers that
those who compose it vary as much in their occupations and positions in life as they do in their lineage
and physiognomy. There are but few men of independent fortune, or of any scholastic attainments
amongst them. You have the merchant and the
manufacturer, who have come from their mills and
counting-houses to the work of legislation. You
have the lawyer; you have the cotton-grower and the
sugar-grower; the owner of labour, and the man who
hires it, and who even labours for himself. There is a
large sprinkling, too, of farmers, whose rough hands
have just relinquished the plough, that their un-
polished tongues might have a swing in Congress.
It is not necessary to be an independent man to be
a representative, where men are paid for the labour of
legislation; or to be over-refined, to be a delegate
from a section of the country where refinement would
be as much an offence as it is a rarity. But for the
principle of paying men to legislate, it would be impossible for many of those before you to undertake a
Washington campaign. To some of them the eight
dollars a day, given in consideration of Congressional
duties, is positive wealth. But many of these men
are burly fellows, who make up in dogged honesty

what they may want in refinement and manners. Nor is the House entirely composed of this unhewn material. There are classic columns, with noble Corinthian capitals, in the moral, as in the physical structure of the Capitol. A close inspection of the mass before you will show that there are many glittering veins, not mere tinsel, but of genuine metal, which permeate its different stratifications. True, that hon. member from one of the Southern counties of Ohio, would be none the worse of another button on his coat ; it would be no impeachment of the republican simplicity of his neighbour from Indiana, if the other side of his shirt-collar were visible ; nor would it transform that restless-looking being from Arkansas into an enemy of the Constitution, if his hat were brushed with what remains of the fur, instead of against it, as it appears to have been. But the picture has its lights as well as its shadows. Intermingled with the rest, are men both of dress and address, and such as would in every way pass muster very creditably in any assembly on earth. Amongst those on the Speaker's left, it is easy to distinguish, from his elevated manner and gentlemanly bearing, Mr. Winthrop (since elected Speaker), the member for Boston ; from his ease and dignity of deportment, Mr. Grinnell from New Bedford ; and on the right of the chair, from his calm and student-like attitude, Mr. Seddon, from the capital of Virginia. These are but specimens of dozens around them, who bring to the House minds as cultivated as they are polished in exterior, and who may well bear comparison with the many foreigners who, in common with yourself, occupy the floor ; amongst whom are several members of the *corps diplomatique,* and secretaries and attachés

to the different legations.   Nor is *bonhommie* wanting
in the picture.   There are many with "lean and
hungry" looks, many of atrabilious temperaments,
impassive souls, and gloomy dispositions; but there
are others with jolly faces and rotund proportions,
which remind one very much of some of the characteristics of John Bull.

Not far from Mr. Ingresoll, of Pennsylvania, who
has scarcely yet recovered from the excitement consequent on his libellous attack on Mr. Webster,
sits Mr. King from St. Lawrence county, New York,
his sides at this moment shaking with laughter,
although it is difficult to perceive that anything very
jocose is transpiring around him.   A little to his
left, and turned up to the skylight, is the good-
humoured face of Mr. Pendleton, familiarly known
as the "Lone Star," being the only Whig in the whole
delegation of Virginia; whilst standing on the floor,
near the central entrance, very short of stature, and
very boyish in appearance, but both kind and communicative, is Judge Douglas from Illinois, apparently incapable of disturbing the dust beneath his
feet, but sometimes raising quite a hubbub with that
tongue of his, which occasionally emits very fiery
material.   The assembly then, like all other assemblies of the kind, is a mixed one—not being one of
perfect gentlemen, in the conventional sense, because there are many gentlemen in it; nor one
entirely composed of boors, because many of those
present remind you of trees with the bark on.   The
picture is as varied as such pictures generally are,
although it may want the exquisite finish of a line
engraving.   Overhanging the members, and peering
in mid-air in groups, from between the massive

pillars, are the sovereign people, with a wakeful eye
upon the conduct of their delegates. With us, hon.
members keep their hats on, and strangers are obliged
to uncover; but in Washington, strangers in the
public gallery keep their hats on, whilst hon. members
sit uncovered below. Like the "gods" at either of
the "Nationals," the occupants of the gallery present
a perfect cloud of downward looking faces, most of
which are shrouded to the eyebrows in hats, in all
forms and styles, and in all stages of decomposition.
From the opposite gallery, behind the chair, and
directly overhead from where you stand, bright eyes,
set in sweet smiling faces, are watching with a sort
of bewildered interest all that is going on below.

The House is not, as with us, divided into two distinct and opposite sides. Whigs and Democrats
manage to sit very friendlily together, without having
the table and the whole width of the floor between
them. There is no ministerial bench, simply because
ministers have no more right to be there than you
have; nor is there an opposition bench, to be occupied by a heterogeneous phalanx of fault-finders, like
the medley of protectionists, conservatives, chartists,
confederationists, and repealers, who now flank the
table on the Speaker's left in the House of Commons.
You can never estimate the strength of parties by
looking at the House. Friends and enemies, they sit
all together; and it is only when a member gets upon
his legs that a stranger can discover his political bias.
As a general rule, the floor on the right of the
Speaker is chiefly occupied by those who support the
administration, but it is a very ordinary thing to see
Whigs in the very heart of the enemy's camp, and
Democrats wandering from their sphere, and getting
lost amid the Whig constellations.

As we enter the Hall there is some one speaking, but, from the multitude of points against which the sound is broken, the reverberations are so confused that it is some time ere you can exactly fix upon the spot from which the speaker is addressing the House. This is all the more difficult from the confusion which prevails upon the floor, and the noises which are constantly breaking out all over the House. The orator is straining every nerve to be heard, but in vain. Sometimes his voice lapses into a perfect screech, but to no purpose ; he might as well try to be heard on the raging beach, as to get audible utterance in the midst of that unceasing hubbub and concatenation of all conceivable sounds, which rise and swell from the body of the House, and break into petty, but multitudinous echoes against the galleries, pillars, capitals, and cornices which decorate it. The Speaker's efforts to command silence are praiseworthy, but useless. The ring of his bell, or the knock of his hammer, may cause a lull for an instant, like the momentary cessation of the roar in Cheapside, but the hubbub rises and swells again immediately as before. Such as are desirous of hearing what the gentleman has to say, who is in pursuit of oratory under such difficulties, gather round him in a group, leaving the rest to pursue their different avocations in the distance. And a rather unruly set the rest are on such occasions—some of them walking about and talking in groups on the floor, others taking it comfortably in their arm-chairs, and holding an animated conversation, sometimes over three or four rows of desks with each other. In the midst of all this confusion I could distinguish one noise which at first puzzled me exceedingly. It differed from every other ingredient in the acoustic medley, and gave me at first the idea that many of the members were amusing themselves by constantly firing small pistols in the House. I had heard and read much that made me think that they might thus be practising with blank cartridge in case of need, and had scarcely given myself credit for this brilliant conclusion when I was undeceived by an apparent explosion close to my ear. The truth is, that each member has his own desk, to which is appended his own proper name— being found in all sorts of stationary and Sheffield penknives *à discrétion*, at the public expense. Here then he transacts much of his private business, and writes all his private letters; thus judiciously blending together his public and private duties in a manner which makes both agreeable to him. The members have a post-office of their own contiguous to the Hall; and whenever one of them has a letter to send to the post-office, or a motion or an amendment to submit to the Chair, he strikes the flat surface of the paper with all his force upon the polished mahogany before him, which produces the noise alluded to, and which fifty echoes seem to stand waiting on tiptoe to catch up and scatter all over the house. Nor is this done from mere mischief, for it at once summons one of several boys to his side, whose business it is to carry the documents to the Chair, or to the post-office, according to their destination.

As nearly all the members are sometimes writing, and all want the boys at once, and as the boys cannot be everywhere at one and the same moment, the choruses of summonses with which they are saluted resemble platoon firing, with the small instruments of offence already alluded to. These boys are quite a feature in the *coup-d'œil* of the house.   When they have a moment's rest they frequently meet on the vacant space on the floor in front of the table ; where they sometimes amuse themselves with pantomimic gesticulations, not altogether compatible with the dignity of the House.   More than once, when something had occurred to disturb their equanimity, have I seen two of them meet and shake their heads at each other, accompanying the action with a by-play, which unmistakably indicated a mutual castigation as soon as the forms of the House would permit.   I mention this merely as illustrative of the confusion which sometimes prevails, and of which the urchins in question manage to take advantage.   In short, the House generally looks like an assembly about to be called to order, with somebody in the chair having no legitimate right to be there, but merely occupying it for the moment to try how it feels.

There are many to whom it will at once suggest itself, that this departure from the decorum of a deliberative assembly is not peculiar to Washington. The House of Commons, if not as systematically so, is frequently quite as unruly.   And there is this difference in favour of the House of Representatives, —that, however indifferent they may be to an orator, they never try to put him down.   They may not listen to his eloquence, but they never attempt to smother it.

Disorderly as it generally is, I have been in the Hall, when, though crowded, it was as still as death, when a pin might almost be heard drop upon the carpet, and when order reigned along all its benches. Never, in my experience, was this transformation from its usual character so complete or so impressive, as when, from the table of the House, was read the correspondence between Mr. Pakenham and Mr. Buchannan, in which the former offered, in the name of his government, and the latter refused, on behalf of his, to submit the Oregon question to friendly arbitration. It was then that even the most sanguine began to relinquish their hopes of peace, and the dispute looked really serious. The House was crowded in every part, and not a sound disturbed the death-like silence which pervaded the Chamber, save the voice of the clerk, as he read the documents in their order; which, in reply to a resolution, had just been communicated to the House. There was then but one speaker, whilst all were listeners; whereas, generally, none are listening whilst all are speaking.

Nor does it always require so impressive an occasion to command this change for the better. As with us, there are some men who never speak but they are listened to. These are generally men of influence in the national councils and men of eloquence in debate. It is refreshing in the midst of so much inane and wearisome talk, to listen to a speech that is at once temperate and eloquent. But it must be confessed that these are like angels' visits, nine-tenths of the speeches delivered being as illogical in their structure as they are inflated in their style.

Were the House of Representatives as numerous as is the House of Commons, it would be impossible ever to get through with any work at all. Every member of the former feels that it is his bounden duty to speak. Such appears to him to be the first and the last object for which he is sent to Washington, the Alpha and the Omega of his representative responsibilities on the federal stage. A silent

member is a luxury which the House may know in time.
No matter how punctual he may be in his daily
attendance in the Capitol; no matter how earnestly he
watches the progress of the debate, or how invariably
his name is found in the division lists; if he does not
open his mouth, his constituents fancy that they have
got a *cadavre* to represent them, and he may find his
silence inimical to his prospects. Each member is
thus compelled, as it were, to expose what is in him,
and selects as many opportunities of doing so as he
can. A regular talking member is a catch for a constituency. His prowess, in this respect, in the House,
magnifies them in their own eyes; for, looking on
from a distance, they take it for granted that he influences the House, which, by logical consequence,
gives them great influence over the legislation of the
country. So long as constituents will thus exact
speeches, and members find speechification the
readiest way of retaining favour, there will be no lack
of it in the legislative halls. Almost every member
manages, once during a session, to make what he
designs as his culminating effort, which being duly
reported, is read by his constituents and by them
alone. Indeed, it is spoken for them, and it is his
consolation that they will canvass it, if the House
does not listen to it. He generally reports it at
length for the papers himself, and it answers his purpose if it appear even months after it has been delivered. It is the great proof that he has been faithful
to his trust; and it is sometimes printed in pamphlet
form, and sent down by the bushel to the country, as
a solace to his friends and confusion to his enemies.
It is singular, too, to watch the adroitness with which
each manages to connect his own locality, by some
peculiar tie, with every great question which excites

the attention of the House; thus endearing himself all the more with his constituents, by giving them the most affecting proof that their interests will not be lost sight of, whatever may be the excess of his patriotism. When constituencies begin to feel that there are other modes in which their interests may be subserved than by seeking for their representative a mere talking machine, there will be more work and less speaking done in the House, and the style of oratory will improve in proportion. Little else can be expected but rant, where speaking is done to order.

Not only have members a desire to be thus frequently upon their legs, but, having once got upon them, they would forget to sit down but for the "gag law," which limits each member to an hour. It was to prevent speeches of a week in length that this very salutary rule was applied. It was at one time thought advisable to extend it to the Senate, but on Mr. Benton letting it be understood that he would hold any man personally responsible who would attempt to gag him, the design was not persevered in. In the Lower House the evil thus provided against had grown to be so enormous, that, for their mutual comfort, members at length submitted to be generally plugged. Some affect to regard the process as a degrading one; but as the stream of words would flow on, what alternative was left? Often have I seen a syllogism fairly winged by a word from the Speaker, announcing that the hour was up; and many a fine trope and metaphor have been crushed and mangled by the fall of his hammer, preparatory to his making the fatal announcement.

In its style, American oratory is totally different from anything ever listened to in our legislative assemblies.　The debates of the House of Commons are dry, business-like, and practical, even to a fault; the speeches delivered there not being cast in scholastic models, with lengthy exordiums and elaborate perorations.　Here members grapple with their subject at once, dispose of it, and resume their seats.　It is not so in Washington.　There a speech is delivered, not so much with a view to elucidate the subject, as to making a speech, and it is as ingeniously contrived, and elaborately prepared, as if it were destined, beyond all doubt, to take a prominent part in the political literature of the country.　In St. Stephen's, tropes and metaphors are only tolerated from a few, and by these they are but sparingly used; in the Capitol, speeches are made gaudy with excess of imagery, and their point and strength are sacrificed to the frippery of words.　No matter what may be the point at issue, their range is generally as illimitable as the speaker's fancy.　The bill before the House may be for the better regulation of the Post-office, but that does not deter a member speaking upon it from commencing with the discoveries of Columbus, and ending with the political exigencies of his own township.　This discursive tendency is the worst feature in American oratory; it renders the debates wearisome and pointless, sometimes producing a good essay, but never a good speech.　The defect would not be so hopeless, were the inflation of the language used, or the quantity of imagery resorted to, at all proportioned to the subject in dispute.　But I have often been amazed at the utter prodigality of bombast, the absolute extravagance of metaphor, with which the treatment of a very petty point was overloaded.　When once let loose upon

this discursive field, the American orator seems to
lose all self-control; his fancy is then like a wild
horse scampering over an illimitable prairie. The
Americans themselves are keenly alive to this defect
in their public speaking, but it is much easier to
deplore than it is to eradicate it.

The figures which are most fondly resorted to, are
those in which the American Eagle acts a very prominent part. This poor bird has a very hard life of
it, and it is high time that his case were taken in
hand by the "Animals' Friend Society." Not that
they mean him any harm, poor bird! but that they
never give him any rest, keeping him in the constant
performance of the most extraordinary gyrations,
putting him in the most unenviable positions, and
sometimes making him act the most incompatible
parts at one and the same time. How often have I
heard an excited orator conjure him up in all his
inflated dimensions, and with expanded wing send
him sweeping over the length and breadth of the
continent which he proudly claimed as his own! On
how many lofty rocks is he not daily made to perch!
What imperial panoramas are not constantly stretched
beneath his feet! How he is made to soar above all
other eagles, with one head or with two; and how the
poor earth-bound British Lion is made to tremble at
the very shadow of his flight! The poor o'erlaboured
bird! He is painted in so many different colours,
and put in so many unaccountable positions, that it
is a miracle if he preserves his identity and continues to know himself. Nor is he always sent on the
most unexceptionable of missions. Frequently have I
heard him commissioned to gobble up the "whole of
Oregon," without asking any questions for conscience

sake; and often is he confidentially informed, that
he will one day be let fly at Canada, as the hawk
used to be let slip at the pigeon. He is at this
moment gorging himself with Mexico, having Cuba
and the other West India islands in prospect as a
dessert. It is no wonder that an hon. senator
should express his fear in the Senate that they were
rapidly transforming him into an obscene bird of
prey. His case is a very pitiable one, and I have
often wondered that some of his more considerate
admirers have not interposed between him and the
oratorical martyrdom with which he is threatened.
Is compassion dead in New England? or is benevolence
effete in Philadelphia?

How fallen in its general character is American
oratory from its pristine grandeur! The days were
when Philadelphia was the forum, and humanity the
audience—when patriots spoke in periods of scathing
eloquence, and the world, with breath retained and
ear erect, stood listening to their words. But these
were times when great principles were in dispute;
when topics were discussed which concerned man in
his universal capacity, and in which man, therefore,
universally took an interest. Now, however, these
principles are admitted—these topics are disposed of
—the rights of humanity are no longer problematic;
they are acknowleged axioms in America. The platform has become contracted; questions of a minor
character and of mere local importance have superseded the grand, broad and universal theses, which
distinguished the debates of the first " Continental
Congress." The orators of that time could be eloquent without being ornate; they brandished the
flaming words of truth, instead of wandering as their

successors do in mazes of overwrought metaphor and inane imagery. The exciting questions of the revolutionary era have passed away, leaving nothing behind them for consideration but points of ordinary humdrum legislation. And the orator of the present day should suit himself to his circumstances. It has not fallen to his lot to discuss abstract propositions, the depth and breadth of which were such as to enable the speakers on them in former times to command the ear of humanity ; but to apply his mind to matters of routine, and to questions which affect only his countrymen. His is a practical mission, and his should be a practical style. Appropriateness is the perfection of speech-making. To get poetical over a bank bill is evidently a mistake ; to jumble imagery and statistics together, a want of judgment and a defect in taste.

In the list of American statesmen, several are to be found whose style of speaking is an exception to that of the great bulk of American orators, and who sometimes, when addressing themselves to constitutional questions, carry their hearers back in imagination to the days of Randolph and Patrick Henry. And in summing up this digression on American oratory, let me add, that in the House of Commons we should be none the worse for a slight infusion of American fancy into our dry discussions; whilst in the Capitol they would be all the better for a liberal adaptation to their debates of the practical style which characterizes ours.

It is to the inexpressible relief of those in the habit of frequenting the House of Commons, that anything arises, during the course of the evening, savouring of a " scene." How drowsy members wake

up from their semi-torpid state, and how their languid countenances light up with interest, when some
incautious word, or ill-advised expression, gives rise
to a personal episode in the dull, dull debate! Talk
of the excitement of the cockpit! that dignified arena
never presented anything half so stirring and amusing
as the intellectual fisticuffs in St. Stephen's. Fancy,
reader, the assembled representatives of England
looking on, whilst Roebuck and Disraeli were bespat-
tering each other with as much filth as they could
command! When is the House so full as when a
" scene" is expected? When was it that members
used to come rushing in scores from the Clubs, or
that Bellamy's poured forth its throngs, unmindful
of half-consumed steaks, and regardless of unfinished
pints of port? It was when Disraeli, in his intellectual jaundice, was vomiting forth bile at Peel.
Why, even the great orator from Edinburgh himself
could not command such a house as did, on these
occasions, the hon. member for Shrewsbury. But
when Peel was expelled from office, Disraeli was
driven out of his element. Peel in power used to
rouse him to the sublime in personality—Peel in
opposition does not tempt him to the effort. Not
that the hon. gentleman is not, in his intellectual
temperament, quite as bilious as ever, but there is
little at present to excite his bile. The rattle-snake
must have something to bite, ere the poison will
distil from its fangs. And Roebuck is no longer
present to lash, with his scorpion whip, the Irish
landlords into fury. For some time, at least, the
House must trust for occasional amusement to Henry
Grattan and Sir Benjamin Hall.

In this particular, our cousins in the Capitol

exhibit the weaknesses of their European kinsmen. They have their scenes, and they love them too. They are sometimes, perhaps, of a more boisterous character than we would like to see imitated at home; but they are frequently of the harmless and amusing kind. Tradition speaks of some which have resulted in personal *rencontres* on the floor of the House; one of which, described to me by an eyewitness, ended in the discharge of a pistol, which missed its aim, but lodged its contents in the doorkeeper. I never witnessed a tragedy in the House of Representatives, but have seen many a farce there. To the credit of the House, scenes of the serious character alluded to are now almost entirely traditional. Hard words, very hard, are sometimes passed from member to member; but they generally reserve any breaches of the peace, which they may meditate, for Bladensburg, or some other point out of the jurisdiction of Congress. Of those which I witnessed, the scene which made the greatest impression upon me, was rather of the melancholy type. The occasion was the memorable one on which the octogenarian ex-President, John Q. Adams, quoted Genesis in support of his country's claim to the whole of Oregon. He was in the habit of styling Mr. Greenhow's work the "Gospel of our title," but, not contented with a gospel, he must have a Pentateuch for it too. His voice was feeble, and he was hemmed in by a crowd of members, eagerly listening to what he said. His quotation of Scripture elicited from those around him a mingled expression of amazement and regret. At that moment, and as it were in pity for the poor old man, a solitary bar of sunlight struggled into the chamber, and played for a second or two amongst the few grey hairs that still skirted the base of his brain, as if to remind the lookers-on that, in the traces of advancing age without, there was sufficient apology for the strides of imbecility within.

The scenes with which members are sometimes favoured, arise quite as unexpectedly and incidentally as they do with ourselves. I have known the most insipid debates suddenly enlivened with them; whilst I have seen questions of the most stirring party interest disposed of without their occurrence. Indeed I generally found that, when the House had any very serious work before it, its decorum was marked and exemplary. Never was this more impressed upon me than when the last tariff bill passed through its later stages in the House. The question was one of intense interest. It was a party question, as well as an issue pending between monopoly and free trade. The House was so equally divided upon it, that it was impossible to foresee the ultimate fate of the bill. Excitement was at its height, and I repaired to the House in the full expectation of witnessing a scene. But although the battle was keenly contested by both parties, and although, on more than one occasion, fortune seemed to waver between them, everything passed off with the utmost quiet and decorum; the decisive vote in committee, of the day, being only carried by a majority of one. It is a mistake to think that great party questions cannot be decided without confusion and violence, or that the House cannot be thoroughly excited without coming to blows. Scenes have their origin there as here in the idiosyncracies of some and the ill-regulated passions of others, but they are promptly suppressed the moment they transcend the rules of parliamentary propriety.

The funniest feature in the proceedings of the

House is a division. There are three ways of taking
the sense of the House in Washington. The Speaker
may call for the Ayes and Noes, and decide at once, as
with us. Any member dissatisfied with this may call
for a division, whereupon the Speaker names two
members, who take their stand on the middle of the
floor, the pros and cons passing successively between
and being counted by them. To the looker-on the
confusion on the floor when the division is taking
place seems inextricable, the whole House appearing
to twirl round in two great eddies, in the midst of
which it is no easy matter to keep one's eye on the
tellers. How they manage to count everybody, and
how they refrain from counting some six times over,
were problems beyond my comprehension. It is not
always that a division, when once commenced, is persevered in, the minority "giving it up" when it is
evidently hopeless. To make things still surer, a
member may demand the "yeas and nays," whereupon each member's name is called from the table in
alphabetical order, and his vote duly recorded. A
great deal of time is thus lost, especially when members, for the purposes of obstruction, choose to "avail
themselves of the forms of the House." And whilst
the yeas and nays are being taken in the House of
Representatives, we may pass into the Senate.

Crossing the Rotunda, we get into a series of passages which lead to the ante-room of the Senate.
But let us to the gallery above the Chair, as affording
the best view of the House.

As already intimated, the Senate Chamb r is, in
form, similar to the Hall of Representatives, but
much smaller in all its dimensions. It is much better
lighted, more cheerful, and better adapted in all

respects than the other House for the purposes to
which it is applied.   Indeed, it is now being found as
inconveniently small as the other Chamber is unnecessarily large ; for, as the introduction of each new
State into the Union adds two new members to the
Senate, it will be difficult by-and-by to make room
for the representatives of yet unborn States.   Let us
see who are present.

In the back row, to the President's right, that tall
thin man, with pale face and restless eye, is Mr.
Allen, of Ohio, the chairman of the Senate Committee on Foreign Relations, a rabid "whole of
Oregon" man, and one of the noisiest of the leaders
of the war faction.   As he speaks he makes his arms
swing about as do those of a windmill, and sometimes
causes the blood to spirt from his knuckles, from the
force with which he brings them in contact with his
desk.   Next to him, and on his right, sits one of
rather rotund proportions, with light hair and a face
not unlike that given to Louis Philippe, by Horace
Verney, in some of his late pictures.   He is generally
writing or reading, being apparently indifferent to all
that is going on around him, but with a watchful eye
on everybody and on everything all the while.   If he
sleeps it is with his eyes open.   He seems never to
attend, and yet he is never taken by surprise.   Watch
how, if anything interesting is said, he quietly shuts
his book, keeping his finger at the page, listens until
he is satisfied, and then resumes his reading; or how,
when any personal squabble arises, he leans upon his
elbow and enjoys it.   This is Mr. Benton, of Missouri,
the genius of the West, the foe to national banks, the
champion of a metallic currency.   He was at one
time a very Sempronius, but is now more peaceably

disposed. He is still, and has ever been, one of the giants of the Senate. In the same line, and near the centre of the room, is the "war hawk," Mr. Hannegan, with squat figure, low brow, and square head and face. There he sits, chewing tobacco all day long, except when he is speaking, or doing the agreeable to the ladies in the ante-room. Mr. Hannegan is an honest man, of Irish extraction, and therefore harbouring a becoming hatred of England, entertaining the sincere conviction that she is a political ogress or ghoul, or something worse, if possible. He is one of the most energetic chiefs of the "now or sooner" party. Directly in front of him, with very red neck and face, sits General Cass, whilom minister in France, and now looking like a moral soda-water bottle, ready to burst or fly the cork. He cherishes enmity to England as one of the cardinal virtues, and can hardly think or speak of her without verging on apoplexy. A little to his left, and almost in front of Mr. Benton, sitting calm and erect and attentive to all that is going on, is the shrewd, clear, persuasive, nervous, and impressive Mr. Calhoun, the leader of the South, the advocate of free-trade, the friend of peace, and the champion of slavery. Beside him is his colleague Mr. M'Duffie, who first startled the ear of the Senate by threatening on its very floor the disseverance of the Union. But the fire of his eye is gone, his tongue has lost its eloquence, and he is now paralytic and effete. That physical phenomenon near him, looking like a man seen through a glass which only magnifies latitudinally, is Mr. Lewis, from Alabama. His arm-chair seems to be drawn out sideways, until it resembles a small couch, so as to give him admittance. He looks like a "prize man," like

three veritable Alderman Humphreys rolled into one.
And yet this man has but one vote, having a colleague in one of the back rows, whom he could
almost put into his pocket. Turning now to the
Speaker's left, sitting close to the clerk's table, (for
he is amongst the last of the new comers,) is " Sam.
Houston," the conqueror of Texas,—for it is absurd
to call him its liberator, as he can only be said to have
delivered it in the sense of having delivered it into
his own hands. He is very tall, very loose about the
joints, and, on the whole, rather greasy looking, with
a very high narrow head, and a small cunning-looking
eye. He is dressed from head to foot in homespun
grey (court-dress perchance in Texas), and passes
most of his time lolling back in his chair, with one
leg overhanging his desk, in which position he whit-
tles away at wooden cigar-lights, which he has brought
with him from the hotel, occasionally pointing them
that he may pick his teeth. In default of these, he
cuts up every pen within his reach. Even now you
may see the debris of his day's labours lying in heaps
at his feet. And yet this is the man who has added
a territory to his country, out of which a whole con-
stellation of States will yet arise. He would be truly
lordly in his manner, and succeeds in being awkwardly
polite. Beside him sits his colleague, the quondam
Secretary of State to the now defunct republic of the
" Lone Star." Immediately behind them you come
upon a whole galaxy of Whigs, the first of whom to demand attention is Daniel Webster, one of the greatest
statesmen, as he is certainly the most profound constitutional lawyer of the Union. Like Mr. Benton,
he is generally busy with books or papers, neither of
them speaking but on great occasions. Is that a

cheque-book that he is just signing? No; but a
lady's album, which the little boy beside him, for
a *douceur*, has smuggled into the Senate, with the
intention of procuring for the owner of the said
album the autographs of the "remarkable men" in
the body. It is next handed to Mr. Crittenden from
Kentucky, who signs it as if he were used to it,
without asking any questions. Take him all in all,
he is perhaps the most accomplished orator in the
Senate, having a classic diction, with a vein of sarcasm, which sometimes gives great piquancy to his
speeches. He was Attorney-general during the
brief administration of General Harrison, and is set
down amongst those who are " on the track," on
the Whig side, for the Presidency. In front of
him is Mr. Clayton, of Delaware, a man of strong
practical mind, although not possessed to any great
degree of the " gift of tongues." A little to his
left is the " other Clayton," from the same State, a
man who is supposed to have lost his articulation
since taking the oath, on his admission to the body,
as he has never since been heard to speak—a marvel-
lous forbearance, all things considered. He chews
and votes, and votes and chews. He appears to be
thoroughly stained with tobacco, his complexion
being that of a well-coloured meerschaum. Yet a
most worthy man is the " other Clayton." In this
part of the House there is an *hiatus*, which you
would fain have filled up. You would like to see
Henry Clay in his accustomed place;—the eloquent,
the imperious, aye, even the tyrannical, the ugly, the
gentlemanly Henry Clay. He gave up his seat in
the Senate to gain the Presidency, and lost both.
Like the man between two stools, he stumbled be-

tween the Capitol and the White House. He is now a scientific farmer in Kentucky, and dreams now and then of another race for the executive chair, which, if it ever take place, will certainly be his last, for he is verging on seventy; and since General Harrison's sudden death, parties have become chary of selecting "very old men" as their candidates. It is, now-a-days, the most contemptuous way of speaking of a candidate, to say that he is "too old for President."

The *coup-d'œil* of the Senate is striking. In all that enters into our conceptions of a deliberative assembly, it is as far before the House of Lords, as the House of Commons is before the House of Representatives. The mode in which business is occasionally transacted in the House of Lords is a perfect farce. Sometimes the most important questions are disposed of by less than half a dozen peers. I remember one occasion, on which the Duke of Buccleugh, in moving the second reading of some Scotch bill with which the Duke of Wellington had entrusted him, was about to enter into an elaborate statement of its nature and objects, so as to meet all objections to it at once, when he was stopped by Lord Lyndhurst, then Chancellor, who was standing by the woolsack impatient to get to dinner, and who asked him very drily, if he was addressing himself to noble lords opposite? pointing to the opposition benches. The noble duke at once saw the absurdity of his position, for there was not a single opposition peer present—himself, the Duke of Wellington, the Chancellor, and Lord Stanley, constituting the entire House. There are no such legislative burlettas in the Senate of the United States. Every member, unless detained by illness or urgent business, is daily at his post. They are, generally speaking, an intellectual body of men—gentlemanly in their mutual intercourse, and courteous in their deportment towards each other. They will tolerate no sleight-of-hand tricks by which to secure a vote one way or the other; and I have frequently known a division postponed, at the instigation of one member, on account of the unavoidable absence of another. The Senate takes a just pride in its own good character, and the Americans are justly proud of the Senate. It is very careful too of its reputation, reproof being frequently administered to the few fiery spirits who have latterly got into it, by a reminder, when they are guilty of any indecorum, that they are not in the other wing of the Capitol.

The Senate is the truly conservative feature of the Constitution. It is the balance-wheel, by whose action the whole federal system is kept from resolving itself into its original atoms. It is to it that the country looks for salvation, when, for a season, the democracy may have run mad. It has more than once preserved the integrity of the Union, by its calm and resolute intervention between the country and destruction. On every occasion of this kind, it has called down upon itself a storm of obloquy, which has more than once threatened its extinction. Such was the case when it steadily placed itself between the other House of Congress and the precipice to which it was rushing, when, by an overwhelming majority, that House adopted the warlike Oregon resolutions. Calm and dignified, regardless of menace, and unmindful of every thing but its duty, it rejected them at its leisure, and so modified them, that their adoption, in their altered form, became as necessary to the maintenance of peace, as, in their original shape, they would have been the certain prelude to war. It was adroitly as it was patriotically done. The resolutions, which originated with the war party, became at last the most potent weapons in the hands of the peace party. The latter thus took from the former its own weapons, and turned them against itself. After some difficulty, and with many contortions of countenance, the House was obliged to swallow the modified resolutions of the Senate. A bellicose House, and a warlike administration, were thus bearded and successfully defied by the conservative Chamber; and the United Kingdom and the United States, and indeed the whole world, remained at peace. As soon as it was suspected that the Senate would reject the resolutions of the House, the cry of " Look to the Senate !" was raised throughout the land, with a view, if possible, to create such a pressure from without as would compel it to accede to them. " Look to the Senate !" was written on every wall in Washington ; and as you walked the streets the menace stared you, from the brick pavements, in the face. But instead of a threat, " Look to the Senate !" at last became a cry of hope,—the friends of peace taking it up as a cry ominous of good. It was well for all parties that they did not look to the Senate in vain. It was well for the United States—for the next greatest calamity to an unsuccessful war with England, that could befall them, would be a successful one.

To one in the habit of regarding the distribution of power between the different branches of the legislature in this country, the great influence of the Senate in the American system is a matter of some surprise. We are accustomed to look upon a resolute

House of Commons as an overmatch for its colleagues in legislation. It is not often that the House of Lords resists its voice; it never ultimately succeeds when it does so. But the Senate feels itself to be, in all respects, the coequal of the other House of Congress, and frequently beards it so as to defeat its all but unanimous purposes. The solution of this difference is to be found in the different constitution of the two bodies. The strength of the House of Commons is without; its foundations lie broad and deep in public opinion; it represents the people, and is irresistible. The Lords, on the other hand, represent but their own order, whose interests are always supposed to be in antagonism with those of the masses. It is enough that they resist the House of Commons in a favourite measure, to raise a cry and direct the whole force of public opinion against them. Occupying but a narrow basis, they cannot long resist, and the House of Commons is omnipotent.

Not so the House of Representatives. It has its match in the Senate, which springs from the same source, and has a footing as broad and as deep as itself. When the two Houses at Washington disagree, the people only see the two classes of their own representatives in conflict. A victory by the one or the other is a triumph neither for nor against the people; it is only the success of the one set of delegates against the other. The contest does not, as too often with us, assume the odious form of class against class, when the peers are coerced into acquiescence that the people may not be roused to frenzy by defeat. The Senate is as strong out of doors as its rival. It is otherwise with the House of Lords.

There is something poetically suggestive of the

territorial vastness of the Confederacy, in the mode in which the President of the Senate recognises its different members as they rise to address him. It is not " Mr. Calhoun," or " Mr. Benton," for instance; but " The Senator from South Carolina," or " The Senator from Missouri," as the case may be. During the hour set apart for ordinary routine business, when they succeed each other rapidly on the floor, the effect of this style of recognition upon the mind of the stranger is singular and impressive. Just now, it may be, a senator from the St. Lawrence, anon one from the banks of the Mississippi. You have senators from the Great Lakes, and senators from the Gulf; senators from the Atlantic, and senators from the spurs of the Rocky Mountains ; senators from the sources, and senators from the mouths of the Mississippi ; senators from the neighbourhood of the West Indies, and senators from the vicinity of Newfoundland. It is difficult for the mind thus to follow them about over the range of an entire continent. The very names of the different States give rise to curious reflections. In New York, Louisiana, Florida, and Texas, what have we but the accumulated spoils of England, France, Spain, and Mexico? Here they are now represented one and all under the same roof, united in the same bonds, and revolving in the same political system. How long thus to continue? is the question, considering the distances at which they lie, the interests which they possess, and the different skies under which they spread. Will their delegates still be sitting together as they do now, when the senators from Oregon and California are ready to come in ?

The habitually calm and dignified attitude of the Senate presents a striking contrast to the fierce ex-

citements which occasionally carry the House of
Representatives beyond the bounds of prudence and
the limits of self-respect. Never was this contrast,
in my experience, so complete, as on the first meeting
of the two Houses after news had arrived in the
capital of the actual commencement of hostilities on
the Rio Grande. The intelligence reached Washington on Saturday night; and such was the impatience of many members of the Lower House to act
upon it, that they would have abolished the intervening Sabbath for that occasion if they could. On
Monday morning, there was a universal rush to the
Capitol. A message from the President was communicated to both Houses, and before the close of
that day's sitting, the House of Representatives, in
the midst of an excitement which it was almost
appalling to witness, passed, through all its stages, a
bill for the appropriation of ten millions of dollars,
and for raising a volunteer force of fifty thousand
men to prosecute the war. They did not then foresee
how small a proportion this sum would be to the
ultimate cost of the adventure; nor would they listen
to the prediction, since truly verified, that instead of
volunteers, they would require many thousands of
regulars to prosecute the war with effect. The Senate
took the matter much more coolly. True, there were
in it a few excitable gentlemen, such as Mr. Hannegan
and Mr. Allen, who found themselves in a "scrim-
mage" at last, and Mr. Sevier of Arkansas, who seems
more fitted to charge at the head of a dragoon regiment than to act as a legislator, and who was for making
every man a brigadier-general on the spot, and trusting
to Providence for recruits. But the majority were
calm and collected, and smothered, if they did not

quench, the fires of their more excitable colleagues. On the message being read from the table, Mr. Calhoun immediately rose, and counselled the Senate to remember its own dignity—to be carried away by no mere impulses, but to act with the deliberation and calmness which generally characterized its proceedings. His words fell, in the main, upon willing ears; and the business of the day, stirring and important as it was, passed off with the utmost quietness and decorum.

To account for the difference thus existing between the two Chambers, for the quiet orderly bearing of the one, and the occasionally intemperate conduct of the other, is no difficult task. The Senate is, generally speaking, composed of men advanced in years, and of great political experience. Most of its members have been governors of, or held high posts in, their respective States; and most of them, by their translation to the federal Senate, have gained the summit of their ambition. They can, therefore, sit down calmly to the work of legislation, bringing the tempering counsels of age to bear upon the teachings of experience. A few of them may aspire to the Presidency, and may intrigue and manoeuvre to obtain it; but the majority have realised all their political aspirations, and can therefore give their whole thoughts to their country's good. Very different, however, is it with the more fiery material on the other side of the Rotunda. In the House of Representatives a grey head is the rare exception. Composed chiefly of young blood, the great majority of its members bring inexperience and personal ambition to the work of legislation. They have no past on which to repose—the future is all before them.

They have merely commenced to mount the ladder, and the strife is who will mount it the quickest and the highest. Notoriety is what they want; and if a fiery speech or eccentric conduct will secure it, they deliver the one as readily as they pursue the other. Most of them too are but *débutants* on the only really respectable political arena of the country, and have not yet thoroughly divested themselves of the contracted views, contentious habits, and miscellaneous vices of the petty spheres in which they have hitherto revolved. By the time their minds become expanded, their deportment sedate, or their views really and disinterestedly patriotic, they are either transferred to the Senate, or altogether disappear from the political field. Thus differently constituted, it is no wonder that the two Chambers are frequently so differently conducted.

But we must now leave, as the Senate is about to resolve itself into executive session. It is nearly three in the afternoon, and we have scarcely gained Pennsylvania-avenue, when the " star-spangled banner," which waves over the Capitol during their sittings, is run down from its flagstaff, to announce that both Houses are up for the day.

CHAPTER XIV.

THE JUDICIARY SYSTEM OF THE UNITED STATES.

WANDERING one day in the basement story of the Capitol, which resembles, in some respects, the crypt of one of our cathedrals, I got lost amongst the numerous and stunted pillars which support the dome of the edifice. On extricating myself from these, I strayed into some tolerably lighted passages, in one of which was a door, to which my attention was directed by familiar sounds which proceeded from within. I entered, and found myself in what appeared to be a large vault, newly whitewashed. It was full of people, the first whom I recognised being Mr. Webster, who was on his legs speaking in a very dry and leisurely style, upon patents, and the law of patents. He did not seem to be addressing anybody in particular, but before him were seated four or five very shrewd-looking and very attentive gentlemen, all in a row, and habited in black gowns—a rather curious spectacle in the republican hemisphere. There were also many ladies and gentlemen present, evidently in the character of amateurs. I had scarcely recovered from the first surprise occasioned by my accidentally stumbling on such a scene, when the conviction flashed upon my mind that I was in the Supreme Court of the United States.

As the subject which engaged the attention of the Court was very crotchety, and the argument of the "constitutional lawyer" exceedingly dry, my mind soon took counsel of its free will, and wandered to topics more relevant to the place than to the case. I was astonished to find the first tribunal in the land so very wretchedly lodged. The chamber resembled a small section, but pretty well lighted, of the London Dock vaults, its space being broken by the short massive pillars, which supported its low half-arched looking roof. It is in fact neither more nor less than a sort of cellar to the Senate Chamber, the floor of which is partly supported by the pillars in question. It may be more convenient than becoming, thus to have the laws, which are made above, sent down stairs to be executed. And yet, as we shall see by-and-by, there are cases in which the gentlemen in the area are the constitutional superiors of the occupants of the first-floor.

I seated myself on one of the back benches, and, taking no interest in the immediate question, inasmuch as I was not a patentee, amused myself with jotting down some memoranda, by the help of which

I now proceed to lay before the reader a succinct account of the judiciary system of the Union. In doing so it is not my intention to confine myself to a consideration of the federal judiciary only, and the mode in which its functions are exercised, in contradistinction to the means whereby justice is administered in and by the different States of the Union—my design being to take a general survey of the distribution of judicial power between the States and the United States, and of the different systems by which justice is nationally and locally administered. Nor would this be the place, in which to enter into a minute analysis of the nature and limits of all the powers conferred upon, and exercised by, the different courts of the Union, or into an examination of all the instances in which their jurisdictions conflicted or were co-ordinate with each other. There are certain broad lines, connected with the outline of the subject, which arrest the attention of every one on the spot to observe for himself, and it is simply these which it is at present my object to trace.

The want of a national, in contradistinction to a local judiciary, was one of the greatest defects of the federative system which preceded the adoption of the present constitution. That document confers upon the United States, in addition to their legislative and executive powers, a judicial authority, which the articles of confederation did not extend to them. The authority, so granted, is strictly limited by the terms by which it is created; the Union, which is, in all its parts and manifestations, the mere creature of the Constitution, having no judicial power whatever beyond the range of the enumerated cases in which such power has been conceded to it. The principle that all powers not specifically granted are reserved to the people of the different States, is as applicable to the judicial, as to the executive and legislative departments of the federal government. The clause of the Constitution creating the judicial power of the Union, confined it to the eleven following cases :— 1st, To cases, in law and equity, arising under the Constitution itself. 2nd, To similar cases arising under the laws of the United States. 3rd, To similar cases arising under treaties made, or which should thereafter be made, under the authority of the United States. 4th, To all cases affecting ambassadors, other public ministers, and consuls. 5th, To all cases of admiralty and maritime jurisdiction. 6th, To controversies in which the United States should be a party. 7th, To controversies between two or more States. 8th, To those between a State and the citizens of another State. 9th, To those between citizens of different States. 10th, To controversies between citizens of the same State, claiming lands under grants of different States; and 11th, To such as might arise between a State, or the citizens thereof, and foreign States, citizens or subjects. This limitation embraces a wide range, it is true ; but, in the far more extended field which lies beyond, the administration of justice between man and man is confined to the constituted tribunals of the separate States. The United States courts can no more issue their process into Pennsylvania, in ordinary cases, between citizen and citizen, than the United States can construct a canal from Philadelphia to Pottsville, and tax the Pennsylvanians for its cost.

But the framers of the Constitution were not satisfied with specifying the limits to which the judicial power of the Union was to extend. They also prescribed the mode in which that power was to be

exercised, by designating the channels through which
the administration of justice was to flow. The judicial power of the United States is declared by the
Constitution to be vested " in one supreme court,
and in such inferior courts as the Congress may,
from time to time, ordain and establish." From this
it appears that, in constructing the machinery whereby justice is, in its national sense, to be administered,
Congress, with one exception, is entrusted with a
species of unfettered discretion. The Constitution
itself provides for the establishment of the Supreme
Court. So far as that tribunal was concerned, Congress
had no option, having the power neither to prevent its
erection, nor to abolish it when constituted, nor to
curtail or enlarge its jurisdiction. But the important matter of the creation of inferior courts was left
entirely to its discretion; and the greatness and responsibility of the power thus conferred upon it will be
better understood, when the jurisdiction of the
supreme court and that of the inferior courts are
considered.

The Supreme Court of the United States is a court
of original and of appellate jurisdiction. Its original
authority, however, extends to only two of the cases
already enumerated, its jurisdiction in all the others
being exclusively of an appellate character. The cases
in which it has original jurisdiction are such as affect
ambassadors, other public ministers and consuls, and
such as a State may be a party to. With regard to
the former, the Constitution remains in this respect
unaltered; but with reference to the latter, a very
important amendment was afterwards proposed and
adopted. It would certainly appear that, when the
citizens of another State, or of a foreign State, had
claims to prosecute against any one State, the impar-

tial administration of justice would require that the party thus proceeded against should not be the party having the sole power to adjudicate in the matter. It was to provide against this, that the article of the Constitution creating the judicial power not only extended the authority of the federal courts to cases in which a State should be a party, either plaintiff or defendant; but also, by giving these courts original jurisdiction in such cases, impowered the States, or the parties proceeding against a State or States, to resort to them at once, without initiating their proceedings elsewhere. In cases in which a State was plaintiff, no objections were ever raised to the arrangement made by the Constitution; as it was obviously more proper that the plaintiff should, in such cases, resort to the national tribunals, than appeal to the courts of a sister State, of which the defendant or defendants might be members. But the most serious objections were very speedily raised to the liability of the States to be sued in certain cases before the federal courts. The number of the claims presented against them in these courts, and the decisions in which some of them resulted, particularly that in a case in which the State of Georgia was the defendant, when the Supreme Court solemnly decided that its jurisdiction equally extended to cases in which States were defendants as to those in which they were plaintiffs, so alarmed the different States for the consequences, that in 1798, only nine years after the adoption of the Constitution, an amendment to it was ratified to the effect, that " the judicial power of the United States " should not extend to cases " commenced or prosecuted against one of the United States by citizens of another State, or by citizens or

subjects of a foreign State." The result of this is
that, in such cases, a State can no longer be made a
party defendant to an action in any of the federal
courts; although it is still liable to be made a defendant, or to be sued in these courts, when another
State or a foreign State, instead of the citizens of
another State or the subjects of a foreign State, is
plaintiff. But as this amendment has reference only
to one of the two instances in which the jurisdiction
of the Supreme Court is declared to be original, the
question has since arisen whether the Supreme Court
has been divested by it of any more than its original
jurisdiction in the cases contemplated by the amendment. Thus, although the citizens of one State can
no longer sue another State, or the citizens of a
foreign State any of the United States, except in the
tribunals of the State proceeded against, it does not
necessarily follow that the Supreme Federal Court
has not appellate jurisdiction in the matter, so as to
enable either party, dissatisfied with the decision of
the State Court, to apply for its reversal in the national tribunal. If the Supreme Court has not been
divested of this appellate jurisdiction by the amendment, in the cases specified, it follows that, in these
cases, a State may still be summoned before it, when
it is called upon to defend a writ of error. It has
been decided that the appellate jurisdiction of the
court has not been taken away; and the whole
question affords an excellent illustration of what was
said in a former chapter of the intricacy of the American system, as seen in the lines of distinction, sometimes so nice as to be almost impalpable, which intervene between federal and local authority.

Explicit as the terms of the Constitution would

appear to be in all that relates to the organization
and authority of the national tribunals, the point just
alluded to is not the only one which has given rise
to perplexing questions between American jurists.
Much argument has been lavished, for instance, upon
the question, whether the affirmation of certain
powers, in specified cases, in the Supreme Court,
does not preclude it from exercising in these cases
those other powers which are exclusively conferred
upon it in other cases. It is perfectly obvious that
the Supreme Court has no original jurisdiction, except in the two cases in which such jurisdiction has
been granted it; nor is it in the power of Congress,
by any act, to enlarge or curtail that jurisdiction. In
all but these its jurisdiction is exclusively appellate.
Thus, for instance, in all admiralty and maritime
cases, and in such as arise under the Constitution, the
laws, or the treaties of the United States, the Supreme
Court has appellate but no original authority, unless
the character of the parties vest it with such. So
far all is plain enough. But the question is, Has
appellate jurisdiction been denied it in cases in which
original jurisdiction has been conferred upon it?
Thus, in a controversy in which a State may be
plaintiff, its powers are original; but does an appeal
lie, in such case, from an inferior national tribunal to
the Supreme Court of the United States? The current
of authority seems to be in favour of the affirmative of
the question; but there still exists some diversity of
opinion upon it. If the negative were to prevail, it
is very obvious that one clause of the Constitution
would directly countervail another. For instance,
the Supreme Court has appellate jurisdiction in all
cases arising under the laws, treaties, and constitu-

tion of the Union. But it has original jurisdiction in a case where a State may be plaintiff, or where two States may be the litigant parties. If the case pending between two States in one of the inferior tribunals, say a Circuit Court, should be one arising under the laws, constitution, or treaties of the Union—to deny the power of appeal in such case to the Supreme Court, because it had original jurisdiction of the matter, would be to decide that the Supreme Court had not appellate jurisdiction in all such cases; whereas, in all such cases, that jurisdiction has been expressly conferred upon it. The true interpretation of the Constitution appears to be, that although in cases in which original jurisdiction has been granted to the Supreme Court, parties may resort in the first instance to that court, they are not compelled to do so; nor is the court divested of its appellate jurisdiction, should they initiate proceedings in an inferior tribunal competent to entertain them. From this it will be obvious that there are two principles which regulate the jurisdiction of the court—the nature of the case, and the nature of the parties. Thus, whatever may be the nature of the case, although it should arise, for instance, under the laws or treaties of the Union, whenever a State is a party, with the exception provided for in the amendment alluded to, the court is clothed with original jurisdiction, of which the parties may avail themselves if they please. And again, whatever may be the nature of the parties, if they do not avail themselves of the original jurisdiction of the court when it is in their power to do so, and the case is one in which the court is invested with appellate power, there seems to be but little reason why the nature of the parties should, in such case, operate to divest it of that appellate power.

This question is closely identified with another, which has likewise given rise to considerable discussion. Some have contended for the exclusive character of the original jurisdiction conferred upon the Supreme Court; whilst others have insisted that the inferior courts may be invested with concurrent jurisdiction in all cases in which that of the Supreme Court is made original. On this point there seems, as yet, to have been no authoritative ruling, although the weight of opinion is in favour of the view, that it is quite competent for Congress to vest, in such cases, a concurrent jurisdiction in the inferior courts. There are some cases also in which the appellate power of the Supreme Court of the United States extends to the revision of the judgments of the State courts. But more of this when the State courts are adverted to.

Congress, in execution of the powers conferred upon it in reference to inferior tribunals, proceeded immediately to the erection of such tribunals all over the country. And here let me observe, that these tribunals must not be confounded with the State courts, with which they are co-existent. In some respects they may be regarded as a mere amplification of the Supreme Court, for the more prompt and efficient administration of justice; whilst in others, such as the nature of their powers, they very materially differ from it. But they are essentially federal in all their ramifications, having, like the Supreme court, cognizance only of such matters as involve considerations in which all the States are equally interested. The whole country is first divided into circuits, each having its circuit court; and each circuit then subdivided into districts, each of which has its district court. Each circuit may comprise a State, or several States ; each district, a State or a fraction of a State. The judges of the Supreme Court are the circuit judges, each judge having his own fixed circuit. The judges of the district courts are local and subordinate functionaries, each resident within his own district. The federal government has also throughout the country its own justices of the peace, and in every district a district attorney, subordinate to the federal Attorney-general, and whose duty it is to watch over its interests, and to prosecute or defend in its name, and a ministerial officer to execute its process, known as the marshal of the district. The federal courts compose a system, the parts of which are in regular subordination—an appeal lying from the district courts to the circuit court of the circuit in which they lie, and from the circuit courts to the Supreme Court of the United States.

The inferior courts can of course exercise no jurisdiction, even with the sanction of Congress, beyond the circle of the judicial powers vested by the Constitution in the United States. But although that document has specified the character of the jurisdiction which the Supreme Court is to assume in the different cases within that circle, it has left that of the powers and authority of the inferior courts, as well as their creation and organization, to the discretion of Congress. The United States are invested with a certain amount of judicial authority. With the exception of creating the Supreme Court, and declaring in what cases its jurisdiction is to be original, and in what only appellate, the Constitution leaves to the United States the power to devise the mode in which the whole of their judicial authority shall be exercised, and the machinery by which it is to be kept in operation. Thus it is equally silent upon the powers of the inferior courts, with the exception of the limitation placed upon the judicial powers of the Union, as it is upon their precise number and character. The distribution of the powers of the Supreme Court by the Constitution, was no rule for Congress in the distribution of jurisdiction amongst the inferior tribunals. It was, for instance, not prevented from conferring upon the inferior courts original, when the Supreme Court had only appellate, jurisdiction. Nor was it prevented, although some have contended otherwise, from conferring concurrent jurisdiction on the inferior courts in cases in which original jurisdiction had been vested in the Supreme Court; or from giving them, each in their order, appellate jurisdiction over courts immediately inferior to them, in all cases in which the Supreme Court was entrusted with a similar jurisdiction. With the exception of the distribution made by the Constitution, Congress was left at liberty to distribute the judicial powers as it pleased. Original jurisdiction in one tribunal or another, or in several sharing it in allotted proportions, should be co-extensive with the judicial power. As the original jurisdiction of the Supreme Court was limited to a mere fraction of the judicial power, unless Congress had been authorized to vest original jurisdiction in the tribunals of its own creation, to the full extent of its judicial authority, that authority, except so far as the Supreme Court had original jurisdiction, would be a mere nullity. The circuit and district courts of the United States were, therefore, constituted courts of original jurisdiction, to the full extent of the judicial power of the United States; unless the opinion of some, that they cannot lawfully exercise such jurisdiction in cases in which that of the Supreme Court is original as well as appellate, be the correct one. The district courts are courts of admiralty, both in civil and criminal cases, and both as instance and as prize courts.

In every well-regulated government the judicial is necessarily co-extensive with the legislative power. Unless a government has the power of administering its laws to the extent to which it can make them, its legislative functions are a mockery, so far as they are not sustained by judicial authority. If the American system furnishes us with any exception to this indispensable condition to a well-balanced government, it is not by the judicial power falling short of the legislative, but by its apparently transcending it. Not only in the federal system, but in that of the different States, is the legislature in some cases in seemng subordination to the supreme judicial tribunal. But it is only seeming. Within the pale of their respective powers, the general and State governments are uncontrolled, and the courts are compellable to administer their enactments. But beyond the pale of their powers they are checked in the exercise of legislative authority by the terms and by the spirit of the several Constitutions. It is as the interpreter and guardian of the Constitution, therefore, that the Supreme Court of the United States may be called upon to annul an act of Congress. The Constitution is the supreme and fundamental law, which all, the legislature included, are bound to obey; and it is when any act of the legislature in the opinion of the

Supreme Court violates this, the fundamental law of the land, that that Court sustains the fundamental law, in opposition to the unconstitutional act, and thereby renders the latter a nullity. In all this it will be seen that the judicial power confines itself strictly to its own proper functions, without arrogating to itself any legislative prerogatives. It is bound to sustain the Constitution against all innovators; and when a statute is at variance with the Constitution, the statute must fall, for the Court has no alternative but to give effect to the Constitution. In controlling the legislative power, therefore, it is only vindicating the supreme law. In the same way the Court is bound to sustain, against all invaders, the treaties of the Union.

No matter how unconstitutional an act of Congress may be, the Court cannot of itself initiate proceedings to lay it aside. It must wait until a case is brought before it involving the legality of the act, ere it can arrest its operation. A law may be notoriously unconstitutional, but the Supreme Court has nothing to do with it until the question involved in it is judicially raised. When that is done, the Supreme Court has power to declare it repugnant to the Constitution, and to refuse to give it effect; whereupon it becomes a dead letter, there being no appeal from the decision of the Supreme Court on any constitutional or other question.

There are cases, too, in which this transcendant power extends to the acts of the different State legislatures. This branch of the judicial authority arises from the very necessity of the case; for in a political system like that of the United States, the terms and spirit of the Federal Constitution are as liable to be violated by a State as by the federal legislature. In all such cases, the integrity of the Constitution could obviously be only safely entrusted to the guardianship of the Supreme Federal Court. Thus, the Constitution prohibits any State from passing a law impairing the obligation of contracts. Should any State pass a law violating this clause, on its being brought before the Supreme Court of the United States, in the regular course of judicial proceedings, the law would be set aside as repugnant to the Constitution. Perhaps the most notable case in which this power has been exercised as regards a State, was one in which a law of the State of New Hampshire was annulled as violating the clause in question. But the Supreme Court of the United States can only exercise this power when the State law infringes the Constitution of the United States. We shall presently see to whom the power of annulling its acts is entrusted, when a State legislature infringes the State Constitution.

Such is a general view of the powers and organization of the federal judiciary. Let us now glance briefly at the judicial system as it relates to the several States.

With the exception of the State of Louisiana, the common law of England is the basis of the jurisprudence of all the States of the Union. The common law is coeval in America with our colonial dominion. Long before the Revolution, it had of course undergone many statutory modifications, to render it more conformable in some points to the circumstances and wants of the colonies. The Revolution produced but little change in the jurisprudence of the continent, the system remaining in all essential parts the same

– the alterations which ensued being chiefly confined
to the machinery by which justice was administered.
The common law, therefore, remains to this day, with
the exception alluded to, at the foundation of the
American juridical system. The alterations which
have been effected in it since the period of independence, are perhaps not greater than the changes which
have been engrafted upon it at home during the last
seventy years. The civil law is the basis of the jurisprudence of Louisiana, which, until 1803, when it
was purchased by the United States, was a colony of
France. In the States in which the common law prevails, the decisions of English courts of justice, down
to the separation of the colonies from the mother country, are authorities in the American courts. Since that
period the decisions of the different State courts are
the only authorities cited in their respective States.
English decisions down to the present day, although
they have no absolute authority, still carry great
weight with them. It would only require the addition of their own reports, and of a few American
text-books, to make the library of an English lawyer
complete for all the purposes of an American practitioner.

Like their political systems, the principle which is
at the basis of the jurisprudence of the different
States is the same; it is the machinery for its administration that is diversified. To enter into any
details concerning the judiciary of each State would
be as uncalled for as it would be tedious. My object
is to show the bearing of the State and Federal
systems upon each other, which will be sufficiently
answered by a rapid sketch of the provisions made
for the administration of justice in any one State—
say New York.

In the State of New York, the judicial power is as ample as the State Constitution, and the State legisture acting within the limits of the Constitution, have made or may make it, with a reservation in favour of the powers exclusively conceded to the Federal tribunals. It is co-extensive with the legislative authority of the State, and with the common law, except so far as it has been modified by State legislation.

In civil questions, arising between citizen and citizen, or in matters which involve the criminal law of the State, the State courts alone have jurisdiction; the federal courts having no greater share of concurrent or appellate jurisdiction in these cases, than have those of a foreign country. Each State, in the exercise of its sovereignty, administers justice for itself, except in cases affecting the United States, the cognizance of which has been expressly conceded to the courts of the Union. In addition to other instances, in which an appeal lies from the decision of the highest State tribunal to the Federal courts, these courts are permitted to exercise the same supervisory control in cases pending before a State court, in which any of the laws of the Union are incidentally brought in question, and the decision of the court is against the law or laws so involved. But in all other cases the two jurisdictions are, in their respective spheres, as separate from and independent of each other, as the political system of the State is independent in its own sphere of that of the United States. Thus, when M'Leod was arrested, it was by the authorities of the State of New York that he was brought to trial before the supreme court of the State at Utica; the courts of the United States having nothing to do with the case, his imputed crime, murder, being a violation of the law of the State, not of the United States. But, on the other hand, when M'Kenzie, the Canadian rebel, was tried for levying war within the territory of the United States against a power with which they were at amity, his trial took place before the district court of the United States, sitting at Canandaigua, in the State of New York; his crime being a violation of the laws, not of the State, but of the United States. These instances serve to show the basis on which the two jurisdictions rest, and to designate the line which separates them.

The State of New York had, until very lately, when, on the revision of the Constitution, the Court of Chancery was abolished, two sets of tribunals, one having an equitable, and the other a common-law jurisdiction. In Pennsylvania the two jurisdictions have long been blended in one set of courts, the common-law tribunals having an equity side. New York, in following her example, has got rid of a court which has long been an ornament to her jurisprudence, and over which some of the ablest of her jurists have presided. As the change has as yet been but a year or so in operation, it is impossible to say definitely with what result it has been attended. The Court of Chancery, whilst it existed, was presided over by a Chancellor, assisted by eight Vice-chancellors, there being one in each of the eight judicial subdivisions of the State.

The highest common-law court having original as well as appellate jurisdiction, is the Supreme Court of the State. In many points its position and powers are analogous to those of the Court of Queen's Bench in this country; in others, the two tribunals are very dissimilar. At one time its sittings were chiefly held in Albany, the capital of the State; but it is now peripatetic—its four terms, viz. January, May, July, and October terms, being held respectively in Albany, in New York, in Utica in the centre, and in Rochester in the western portion of the State. It sits to adjudicate upon appeals and matters of law, but a trial at bar may be had before it, on proper cause shown, as in this country.

Like the analogous court in the federal system, the Supreme court of the State is the guardian and interpreter of the Constitution of the State, as it has the power of virtually annulling, by defending the Constitution from invasion, any act of the legislature which it may regard as unconstitutional. This feature of the judicial system runs through the whole polity of America, both state and federal. It was necessary to interpose some power between the legislature and the Constitution; for had the legislature been the sole interpreter of the Constitution, it is evident that the latter would have been only what the former chose at any time to make it. But here the analogy between the Supreme Court of the United States and the Supreme court of the State ends. The original jurisdiction of the latter is almost co-extensive with the judicial power, whilst it is unlike the former in this also, that it is only in constitutional questions that it is a court of final appeal; in all other cases its decisions may be carried by writ of error to the Court of Errors, or rather, as it is officially styled, the Court for the Correction of Errors, composed of the Senate of the State.* The Senate is strictly a court of appeal, with the single exception of cases of impeachment, of which it has exclusive jurisdiction.

* A distinct Court of Appeal has since been created.

For the trial of issues of fact, Circuit courts have been established throughout the State, which is divided for this purpose into eight circuits, corresponding with its eight senatorial districts. To each circuit is appointed a local judge called the circuit judge, who holds his court for the trial of all issues of fact, and of criminals, although their alleged crimes may be of the highest penal description, twice a year, in each county comprised within his district. The circuit judge, before the abolition of the Court of Chancery, was also the vice-chancellor of his circuit; but in some of the circuits, such as the eighth, or that comprising the western portion of the State, the amount of business, both of an equity and common-law cast, at length became so large as to require a division of the duties, and the appointment of a separate vice-chancellor. All cases pending in the Circuit courts, are supposed to originate, as with us at Nisi Prius—in bank, that is to say, in the Supreme court, by whose authority, appearing on the record, they are sent down for trial, and to which they are returned after verdict for judgment. All points of law arising during the trial from the decision of the circuit judge on which either of the parties may choose to appeal, are transferred to the Supreme court for argument and adjudication. So a demurrer may, as with us, take the case entirely out of the Circuit court, and transfer its decision to the Court in bank. In short, the relation between the two courts is in almost all points the same as that subsisting between the courts at Westminster and those of Nisi Prius in this country.

Subordinate to the Circuit courts in power and position, though without any very direct relationship between them, are the County courts. These courts, of which there is one in each county, whilst they have appellate jurisdiction over tribunals inferior to themselves, have also, to a certain extent, both in civil and criminal cases, a concurrent original jurisdiction with the Supreme court; for the Circuit courts may be regarded as mere amplifications of the Supreme court for the trial of issues of fact. The County court has cognizance only of such matters as, being otherwise within its jurisdiction, arise within the limits of the county. It formerly consisted of five judges, one of whom was styled First Judge, whose duration of office was five years, and whose appointment lay with the Governor and Senate of the State. As it was not necessary to be a lawyer to be a county judge, the decisions of the County courts were frequently very wide of the legal mark; nor did they attach to themselves that respect and confidence which, under a different regulation, they might have inspired. I have known instances in which all the five judges were farmers—not a single professional man being on the bench. The consequence was, that most suitors, when their cases were important, preferred resorting to the Supreme court; when, had the County bench been properly constituted, justice might have been administered to them much more cheaply and more speedily than by the superior tribunal. I have frequently heard bitter complaints made of this radical defect in a court which had cognizance, concurrently with the Supreme court, of civil cases, involving property to a large amount; and of all criminal cases, which were not capital in their nature, or punishable with imprisonment for life in either of the State's prisons of Auburn or Sing

Sing. Appeals lie to the County court from the decisions of the different justices of the peace throughout the county, and from those of the civic tribunals, which may be erected for the local administration of justice, in such towns as may lie within its jurisdiction.

The State, like the United States, has not only a chief law officer in its Attorney-general, but it has also in each county its district attorney, whose duty it is to institute an inquiry into all offences committed within the county, and to follow up such inquiry with a prosecution of the offenders, when necessary. Sometimes this duty, both as regards the State and the United States, is vested in one and the same person. There are also coroners appointed for each county, with duties analogous to those of the coroner in this country, both as to investigating into the causes of fatal accidents, and the service of process when the sheriff is party to a suit. Each county has also its sheriff, who nominates his subordinate functionaries, but who is himself elected to his post every two years, if I mistake not, by the people of the county. The county clerk is also an elective officer, who has charge of the county office, which, although having but little to do with the judicial system of the State, is nevertheless so important a feature in its general polity, that I cannot here avoid alluding to it. The county office is not only the place where copies of all process in cases pending in the County court are filed, but it is also part and parcel of the general registry system, which prevails throughout the State. In New York, all transactions concerning land, to be valid and binding upon future parties claiming an interest, must be registered in the county office of the county in which this land is situated. The result of this general system of registration is, that no more obscurity hangs over transactions in real, than in personal property—the books being open for the inspection of all, on the payment of a small fee—so that the state of any landed property can be at once ascertained, as regards the true ownership of, and the liens and encumbrances which may be upon, it. In a country where land is a commodity as marketable as any personalty, claims to it, but for this system, would become inextricably entangled, whilst the ease and advantage with which it works recommend it to more general adoption amongst ourselves. The whole system of conveyancing too is exceedingly simple, fee simples and leaseholds being almost the only species of tenures existing in the State.

The bar of New York is, in the main, exceedingly respectable. Proof of competency, by examination, after a probation of seven years in an attorney's office, is necessary to admittance as an attorney of the Supreme court. A certain scholastic career, previously to its commencement, may curtail this long probationary term to three years. After practising for two years in the inferior capacity, the attorney, on satisfactorily passing another examination, is admitted to the degree of counsellor, equivalent to that of barrister with us. All branches of the profession are united in America in one and the same person —the counsellor being his own attorney and special pleader, an arrangement which obtains in our own provinces as well as in the United States. The practitioner of one State cannot practise in another, without regular admittance to the courts of that other

State. The terms upon which admittance is given in these cases vary in the different States. To become a member of the bar in Massachussetts, no regular course of study whatever is required; from which, however, it does not follow that no knowledge of the law is requisite—admission being only had on passing a pretty rigorous examination. It is no matter where or how the necessary knowledge is acquired, if it is possessed. The simple proof of qualification is all that is demanded, no questions being asked as to the antecedents of the applicant. Nor can the practitioner of any State, even though he should have been admitted to practise in every State, plead in the Supreme court of the United States, without express admission to its bar.

Such is a very cursory sketch of the machinery adopted for the administration of justice in the State of New York. I have not selected that State because I think that its judicial system is better than that of any other, or because I wished very particularly to acquaint the reader with its precise scope and character, but because some such selection was necessary in order to illustrate the distinct and independent systems which enter into the juridical polity of the Republic. It will be seen that the line of demarcation separating the two great departments of the judiciary system is coincident, or nearly so, with that which intervenes between the two grand primary subdivisions of the civil polity of the nation—the United States both legislating and administering justice in matters affecting the entire confederation, whilst each State reserves to itself all the judicial and legislative attributes of sovereignty in matters purely affecting its own welfare and internal management. In cases involving the interests of the whole Republic, the States have abdicated their sovereign functions; in those which simply affect themselves, they admit of no control, either from one another or from all combined. In the one case, they are as if they had no separate existence; in the other, they are as independent as if they were fettered by no federal obligations.

END OF VOL. I.